FORT LAKHISH

IN THE DAYS OF LEHI

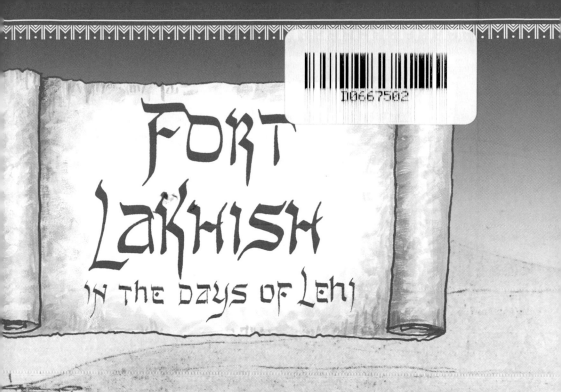

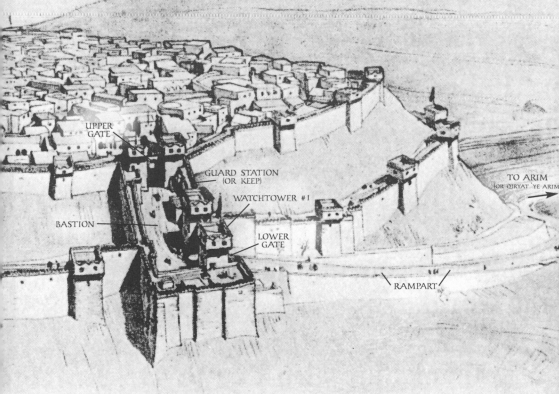

UPPER
GATE

GUARD STATION
(OR KEEP)

WATCHTOWER #1

BASTION

LOWER
GATE

TO ARIM
(OR QIRYAT YE ARIM)

RAMPART

POWER *of*
DELIVERANCE

OTHER BOOKS AND BOOKS ON CASSETTE
BY DAVID G. WOOLLEY:

The Promised Land Series Vol. 1:

Pillar of Fire

VOLUME 2
THE PROMISED LAND

POWER *of* DELIVERANCE

A NOVEL

DAVID G. WOOLLEY

Covenant Communications, Inc.

Cover illustration by Dave McLelland

Cover design copyrighted 2002 by Covenant Communications, Inc.

Published by Covenant Communications, Inc.
American Fork, Utah

Printed in Canada
First Printing: October 2002

09 08 07 06 05 04 03 02   10 9 8 7 6 5 4 3 2 1

ISBN 1-57734-941-5

Library of Congress Cataloging-in-Publication Data

Woolley, David G., 1960-
   The power of deliverance : a novel / David G. Woolley.
     p. cm. -- (The promised land ; v. 2)
   ISBN 1-57734-941-5 (alk. paper)
   1. Bible O.T.--History of Biblical events--Fiction. 2. Jews--History--To 70 A.D.--Fiction. I. Title
PS3573.O674 P69 2002
813'.6--dc21

                    2002073867

Author's Note

The second volume in the *Promised Land* series is the story of divergent families thrust together by circumstance and forced by their faith to seek the tender mercies of the Lord to make them mighty, even unto the *Power of Deliverance*. The stories of their lives are a fulfillment of the opening verses of the prophetic allegory of the olive tree. They were some of the young and tender branches cut from the tree of the House of Israel, some deported from their lands, others compelled to flee Jerusalem and all of them hidden away in the vineyards of the earth—grafted into non-Israelite societies—while the loftier branches of Judah's ruling noble class remained in the Holy City until its destruction. *Power of Deliverance* is the story of a time when the Lord of the vineyard began hiding these young and tender families across the face of the whole earth before Jerusalem was leveled to the ground. Notes exploring the historical and fictional details of this book appear at the end.

Amidst the financial and political turmoil leading up to the Second World War, British archaeologist John L. Starkey was not deterred from gathering support for his work: unearthing proof that a hillside archaeological dig named Tel Ed Duweir, twenty-five miles south of Jerusalem, was indeed the site of the ancient Fort Lakhish. On January 29, 1935, he found the first of eighteen Lakhish letters, the only recorded eyewitness account outside the Book of Mormon and the Old Testament to the volatile turn of the sixth century B.C. in Jerusalem. The Lakhish letters stand in memorial to Dr. Starkey's diligence in providing another voice from the dust, reaffirming the Book of Mormon account of Lehi and his family.

A project of this scale requires the efforts of many. I offer my sincere thanks to Bonnie Arbon. She has been the first hearer and reader of *Power of Deliverance* as she was for the first book in the series, *Pillar of Fire*, and she has been instrumental in preparing this work for submission to the publisher.

My dear father, Dr. Don G. Woolley, has assisted me in gathering research for this volume and his help is reflected in the historical notes in support of some of the plot lines portrayed in this novel.

The expertise of the editorial staff and management team at the publishing house, Covenant Communications, has raised the standard of this work to a level worthy of the sacred accounts this book portrays. The Covenant Team has been extraordinarily patient with my slow, methodical writing habits, as have readers who have unwearyingly waited for me to research the details of this volume and piece them together into the stories portrayed in *Power of Deliverance*. I recently received a note from a reader telling me that it was time I moved on with the next volume. With the publication of this work, I humbly submit that we are moving once again, documenting through fictional eyes the lives and times of men and women recorded in ancient writings we hold sacred.

Preserved within the pages of the Book of Mormon is the prophetic knowledge that Jesus Christ is our Savior and Redeemer. I have felt His presence, inspiration, and sustaining power throughout the writing of this book and I pray it is acceptable to Him. The immense task of producing *Power of Deliverance* has drawn me to reflect daily on the eternal truths taught in the holy scriptures. May God bless your life as you study them.

David G. Woolley

Provo, Utah

October 2002

The tender mercies of the Lord are over all those whom he hath chosen, because of their faith, to make them mighty even unto the power of deliverance.

1 NEPHI 1:20

LIST OF CHARACTERS

While this is a work of fiction, and all of the characters have been fictionalized, many are based on what we know of the historical figures of the time period. In cases where the names of historical characters are not known, the author has created names. These are marked with an asterisk (*).

FICTIONAL CHARACTERS

The Family of Jonathan the Blacksmith
Jonathan, *Blacksmith*
Ruth, *Wife & Weaver*
Elizabeth, *Eldest Daughter*
Aaron, *Eldest Son & Firemaster*
Daniel, *Son & Forgingmaster*
Sarah, *Youngest Daughter*
Joshua, *Youngest Son*

The House of Josiah the Potter
Josiah, *Second Elder of the Jews*
Rebekah, *Josiah's Only Child*
Mima, *Rebekah's Ethiopian Handservant*

Others
Moriah, *Apprentice Scribe of Lakhish*
Jebus, *Chief Scribe of Lakhish*
Beuntahyu, *Aaron's Horse*
Pella, *Jawbone Innkeeper*
Beulah, *Regiment Commander's Daughter*
Nathan, *Friend to Setti & Nightwatchman*
at Lakhish

Historically Based Characters

The Family of Lehi the Olive Oil Merchant
Lehi, *Olive Oil Merchant*
Sariah, *Lehi's Wife*
Rachel*, *Eldest Daughter*
Leah*, *Daughter*
Laman, *Eldest Son & Pressmaster*
Lemuel, *Son & Stablemaster*
Sam, *Son & Caravanmaster*
Nephi, *Youngest Son & Keeper of the Oil*

The Royal Family of Judah
Zedekiah, *King of Judah*
Miriam*, *Queen of Judah*
Mulek, *Prince and Heir Apparent of Judah*
Dan*, *Prince of Judah*
Benjamin*, *Prince of Judah*

The Family of Lord Yaush, Governor of Southern Judah
Lord Yaush, *Commander of Fort Lakhish*
Sophia*, *Wife*
Setti*, *Son & Captain of the Night Watch*

The Family of the Prophet Uriah
Uriah, *Prophet of God*
Deborah*, *Uriah's Wife*
Shemayahu*, *Uriah's Father*
Benuriah*, *Eldest Son*
David*, *Son*
Unnamed*, *Infant Daughter*

The Family of Ishmael the Vineyard Master
Ishmael, *Vineyard Master*
Isabel*, *Ishmael's Wife*
Nathan*, *Eldest Son & Master of Olive Culture*
Seth*, *Son & Watermaster*
Nora*, *Eldest Daughter*
Abigail*, *Daughter*
Hannah*, *Daughter*
Mary*, *Youngest Daughter*

The Family of the Prophet Jeremiah
Jeremiah, *Prophet of God*
Eliza*, *Jeremiah's wife*
Zoram, *Keeper of the Keys; Jeremiah's son*

Other Major Characters
Ezekiel, *Chief Accountant & Lawyer of Jerusalem*
Laban, *Captain of the Guard*
Zadock, *Chief Elder of the Jews at Jerusalem*
Shechem, *King of Robbers*
Hannaniah, *False prophet*

FORT LAKHISH

*Six hundred years before
the birth of the Anointed One*

CHAPTER 1

Setti warmed his hands over the torch flames and coughed on the smoke swirling from the oil-soaked rags. Black wisps hung about the high walls of the bastion like mist over a marsh, but this was no river walk. It was a catwalk above the main gates of Lakhish, and there hadn't been a river flowing past the fort in a very long time. Setti wiped the drizzling rain off his brow and marched down the catwalk toward watchtower number one. There was a stone roof to keep the winter rains from spitting cold into his face, though there was nothing he could do to keep the winter night's air from drafting through the arched windows that opened onto the surrounding valleys. Foot soldiering and cavaliering may be more dangerous assignments, but those men got a good night's rest, something Setti hadn't had in six months.

All was well along this side of the bastion—the light rain hadn't put out any of the torches. The gatekeepers at the upper and lower entrances were in good spirits since they hadn't been forced from their dry stoops to open for anyone, and none of the watchmen were sleeping on duty, at least none at watchtowers two and three. Setti peered across the bastion to the east wall. The watchman at tower number six above the upper gate was at his post, and the watchman at tower five was just finishing his rounds of the east wall, his wet cape dragging on the stone catwalk behind him. And then there was Nathan's post, tower number four. Where had he gone? Nathan wasn't sequestered beneath his tower keeping out of the drizzle, and there was not a sign of his red-plumed brass helmet climbing any of the stairwells leading up from the cobblestone entrance to the city.

Setti leaned over the railing and called to tower number four. The cold, February night air forced the torch smoke to linger longer over the bastion than it ever did in the hot summer months, obscuring Setti's view of the adjacent wall before quietly dying on the night. But it wasn't so thick he couldn't see Nathan's head shoot up from below the level of the stone railing, his thin frame snapping to attention like an olive branch in a stiff wind, and he cleared his throat not less than four times before returning the call that all was well. His thinly pitched voice was rougher than usual; his helmet hung from the end of his hand like a milk pail and his straight black hair was matted against his ear. He was a nineteen-year-old man who looked no older than a boy headed to milk goats from his father's pens before daybreak.

Setti returned the all well, but everything wasn't all right, not really. Nathan had been dozing again; and no matter that they were close friends, Setti would have to discipline him. And this time he wouldn't let Nathan reminisce about the time he taught Setti to fly off the rocky outcrops along the north face of Lakhish when they were seven. Why did he ever believe Nathan could get him airborne with nothing more than two palm branches tied to his arms? They were eleven when Nathan lowered Setti into the fort's well on a rope and when it broke he left him there, wet and cold, till morning when he could get another rope from his father's shop without telling anyone what he'd done. And it was Nathan's arrow that missed the target and flew through the open windows of the commissary, swishing past the head of the lieutenant of regiment five and lodging in a leather satchel hanging from a hook on the wall. They were fourteen then and he still hadn't paid Nathan back for telling everyone it was Setti's arrow.

Setti was captain of the night watch and Nathan would learn to stay awake or they'd never get assigned to the day watch, to say nothing of another post away from the duties of watchman, no matter how many times Nathan insisted they didn't have to worry about a promotion—Setti's father would see to that. Setti may be the son of Lord Yaush, commander of the southern legions of Judah's army, but Papa promised Setti the day he joined the rank and file that he'd receive no favors. It was impossible to explain that to Nathan after Setti received three promotions in as many months—first from apprentice watchman, then to tower number two, and now captain of the night watch. His quick advancement had nothing to do with his father's command of Lakhish. He'd earned his post and it was his duty to hail the gatekeeper to open for anyone wanting to enter the bastion and come into the city. From sundown to sunup Setti was charged with the safety of five thousand men and their families who slept within the walls. He removed his helmet, scratched the side of his head, and replaced the head covering. There was nothing Nathan loathed more than cleaning away rubbish from the kitchens, except maybe clearing the sewer channel that emptied out the east wall of the city. He'd let Nathan choose—two days with the commissary cooks or dig out the sewer line. That was a much better punishment than making a report, and it would keep Nathan from getting into trouble again. No, it wouldn't keep him from trouble; there was no punishment that could keep him from making mischief, but maybe—just maybe—it would keep him from falling asleep at his post. And it would even the score. It wasn't Setti's arrow!

The stomping of horse hooves and the churning of chariot wheels storming up the approach turned Setti toward the lower gate and he leaned over the west-facing lookout. Who could that be? There were no patrols scheduled for tonight, and the soldiers on a tour of duty along the Egyptian-Sinai border weren't expected back for two weeks. Setti checked the entry log, quickly unscrolling the papyrus. Not a single entry was listed for this watch, and if there were any changes in the patrol schedule, he was the first one Papa would inform.

Setti angled his torch over the outside wall, and the light fell on seven horsemen riding mighty Arabians, the animals arching their manes against the pull of the reins. What sort of riders would come to Lakhish at this late hour, or was it an early hour? Setti scanned the night sky. The North Star was where it always was, but the constellation below it, the one that wise men called the great square of heaven but which looked more like a ladle dipping water, had sneaked farther to the east without his seeing.

An odd-looking chariot reined in behind the Arabians, driven by two coachmen and drawn by three steeds, high-stepping against the drag of the cart. It was a high-bearing rig, with four wheels like a mule cart instead of the customary pair and there had never been one with a canopy in the two years Setti apprenticed as a watchman. But this was no chariot; it couldn't be with the canopy sewn of tanned leather, two hides thick, and nailed to a frame of cedar. The lone rider sat sequestered beneath it and Setti had no way of knowing who came to Lakhish unannounced. He had to be Hebrew; his escorts were dressed in tunics from the king's army, the sideboard was inscribed with the shield of the royal house, and the ensign flag of Judah streamed out behind the cart. But what sort of royalty would come without warning, or at least a bit of fanfare: a trumpeter, a drummer, anything to distinguish the man from a commoner? He preferred the protection from the sun that plagued travelers in this part of the kingdom. But it was winter at Lakhish. The sun wouldn't rise for hours and there was no need to ride obscured in the seat of this four-wheeled carriage except to hide from the view of others.

The lead rider pulled up beside the lower gate, steam snorting from the horse's nostrils. Setti judged him to be a lieutenant by the blue dress tunic he wore and the silver buttons strapping his long cape over his shoulders, the hem of it rising on the horse's sudden movement and flapping about its haunches. He circled around in front of the chariot and reared the animal's front legs, calling for the gate to open.

Setti stuffed the entry log under his arm. He wasn't about to hail the gatekeeper and welcome these men into the bastion, not until he knew whom he was greeting. He started down the eighty narrow steps chiseled into the wall of the bastion, the torch throwing its light ahead of his stride, the wooden dowel of his entry log poking out like an arrow planted in his chest, and the thin papyrus scratching against his gray tunic. He reached the cobblestone floor on a dead march, and on his command the gatekeeper reeled in just enough rope on the wooden draw wheel to let Setti slip between the thick center timbers of the lower gate. He pulled the entry log from under his arm and unrolled it. He said, "I don't show any record of your coming."

The lieutenant said, "You won't find one."

"Does Lord Yaush know about this?"

"Of course he knows." The lieutenant sidled his mount in next to the opening. "Do you think we'd drive all the way from Jerusalem without sending word?"

Setti marched the torch over next to the lieutenant. "Yaush didn't mention anything to me."

The lieutenant stuck his head around the gate to see into the bastion and when he came back he said, "Your commander was to keep this to himself."

"That isn't the usual protocol for arrivals, and never for any after sundown."

"This isn't the usual arrival, boy." The lieutenant leaned over the saddle, snatched the torch from Setti, and held it to the sideboard of the carriage. The flickering flame cast an unsteady light over the royal seal, and the order written beneath the emblem was unmistakable: *Hail to the King of Judah. Bow low and let him pass.*

Setti found the next empty line on the ledger with his finger, the one right below the entry of a shipment of dates delivered by the farmer from Debir, six miles south of Lakhish. "What name am I to enter?"

"There's to be no record of this." The lieutenant leaned forward in the saddle, gripped the reins with both hands, and slowed his speech. "We never came to Lakhish."

No record? Setti stuffed the log under his arm, the dowel pointing back at the lieutenant, at what he had just said. Where did he get his authority to order a breach in procedure? Setti was duty bound to record everyone who passed into the city, and he'd lose his post if he were to disobey, no matter that his father was commander or not. He said, "Wait here while I wake Lord Yaush."

The lieutenant handed back the torch. "Go and fetch him if you must, but hurry." He slowly worked his hand over his thighs, massaging them. "My legs tire of this animal."

Setti stepped to the gate, but before entering the bastion, he said, "It shouldn't take more than a— "

"Stop!"

The flap on the canopied carriage raised, and the passenger leaned out, his head hovering over the sideboard. He was dressed in a flowing black robe with a matching turban and a white shawl falling from under the brim to his shoulders. He clutched the end of it with long fingers, draped it across his face and it was impossible to see anything but his eyes peering over the cloth. The brittle sound of his voice echoed off the high walls of Lakhish like the shrill cry of a child.

But this was no child; it was the king of Judah and his command was certain. He did not want Yaush to be disturbed. The king said, "Let him sleep. I'll be the one to inform him of my arrival; you're not to say a word to him. Is that understood?"

"Of course, sire." Setti removed his helmet and stepped back, his shoulders pinned against the cedar wood of the gate. He was trapped there by the monarch's penetrating voice. He never remembered the king of Judah having such a shrieking tongue, but he'd only heard him speak once at the coronation from across the temple courtyard. "I didn't mean to go against your— "

"I don't care about your intentions. Just do as I say." The king pulled the leather flap down and he was gone as quickly as he had appeared, hidden behind the thick cover shrouding his carriage.

Setti stuck his head around the center timbers, his helmet tucked under one arm and the entry log poking out from under the other. He hailed the gatekeeper to open for the king, steam shooting from his mouth and mixing with the drizzle. The heavy double doors obeyed his cry, and the carriage whisked inside, kicking up water from a puddle and showering Setti with muddy water. He should be pleased to welcome a royal visitor to Lakhish, no matter how late the hour or how odd his arrival. No king had ever come to the fort since he was captain of the watch, but there was something about the monarch that wasn't right. The king didn't appear to be as tall or as thin as he remembered, but then he was sitting down inside the carriage and most of his stature was concealed behind the leather canopy. But why did he cover his face? Zedekiah was a friendly man who mixed with commoners and princes alike—not the sort to hide behind a veil.

Setti returned inside the bastion with the timbers thundering into place against the gate stop, but the sound wasn't enough to turn him back toward it. He stood in the middle of the bastion, staring up the incline toward the upper gate. It closed behind the last horsemen and sealed off his view of the royal carriage. The king of Judah had come to Lakhish, but if the arrival wasn't Zedekiah, and Setti had no way to be certain, then he could be court-martialed for compromising the fort's security. Even worse, he would lose his honor as captain of the watch if he'd risked the safety of Lord Yaush. Setti fitted his brass helmet back over his brow, but kept his gaze on the upper gate where the king disappeared into the city proper.

What had Setti just done to his father?

A draft filtered through the shuttered windows, down along the stone walls and about the bedroom like a sea wind swirling off the Gulf of Aqabah—a welcome respite after a border patrol, but this was not a ride through the Empty Quarter of the Arabian Peninsula. It was Lord Yaush's sleeping quarters and the draft left him shivering in his bed. He reached over and reclaimed his portion of the lambskin his wife, Sophia, had stolen during the night. He quickly covered his feet and stuffed what was left under his large frame to keep her from stealing it back. It was a battle Yaush fought every winter night, and he did it without reinforcements. He was commander of five thousand, but still managed to lose the blanket war to Sophia despite his large, four-and-a-half-cubit frame that should have kept the bed covering pinned beneath him till sunrise.

Lord Yaush was a pillar of a man, like the stone columns supporting the entrance to the palace-fort—tall, stout, and quarried from the finest pedigree of southern Judah, though last evening at dinner Sophia said he was beginning to look like a fatted lamb. What did she know about livestock? Sophia was the daughter of a perfume merchant and she'd never shorn wool, shepherded a flock, or birthed a lamb in her forty-three years, though she did have a fine sense of smell—a talent she sprinkled liberally on her husband. He allowed her to scent his bath water and military dress, but drew the line when she daubed his leather sheath with frankincense. A sweet-smelling sword was not a fitting weapon for the commander of Lakhish.

Twenty years of perfumed bliss had trained Yaush to smell a dishonest merchant at twenty paces. Last week, during his inspection of the tax collection at the fort's duty import office, the monkeys trained to sniff out concealed shipments of frankincense missed a large sack of the perfume wrapped in sheep fat to cover the scent. The poor creatures didn't understand that a caravaneer traveling from the Southern Arabian Peninsula should smell like camel hair, not mutton.

Sophia settled into a steady breathing and Yaush turned onto his side to envy her. She could sleep in a stable with a torrent raging outside and never feel the water sieving through the wood slats. She claimed it was her conscience—innocent and as untroubled as a little child—though the only thing "little" about the woman was her girth. She did not have much of what kept stout women warm in winter, and blessedly the month of February here wasn't as fierce nor as long-lived as it was in Jerusalem. Yaush pulled the hem of the lambskin blanket up under Sophia's neck. Her chest rose and fell with each breath, her lips were open slightly, and Yaush leaned over and kissed her cheek. If only he could fall under the same spell and grow deathly ill with slumber. But sleep was not an enchantment she could cast on him. The duties of commander invaded his rest like an unwelcome guest and today he was to host an emissary from Jerusalem. Captain Laban's letter didn't say whom he was sending, only that he was to speak to no one about the visit and that he should make ready the guest room on the main floor of the west wing and not require the man to climb the stairs for any reason. The cook was to prepare a meal of the fat of a lamb, dipped in olive oil and served with lemon rinds and onion. What sort of officer requested such an odd meal?

The visitor would have stayed at Hebron last evening with his escorts before riding the last leg of the journey through the hill country tomorrow. Or maybe it was today? Yaush stuffed his hands under his head, but there was no pillow supple enough to soften his worries. He didn't even know how long he'd lain awake listening to Sophia sleeping beside him, but, heaven willing, there still remained the promise of a long night's rest.

Sophia's hair was pulled back off her ears and braided into a sleeping tail tied with a sash and tucked beneath the collar of her robe. Her cheeks were flush with fine olive oils and her stillness reminded Yaush he hadn't slept, not even long enough for his lids to rub like sand across his eyes or his hand to find its way beneath his body and go numb under his weight. He hadn't yet startled himself with his snoring; he hadn't even so much as nodded off, not with the mystery he kept hidden in his personal vault, away from the eyes and minds of any who might discover the secret before he could decipher it for himself.

Protocol required he archive all correspondence from Laban with the scribes in the fort's treasury. But these letters begged the rule's pardon. He couldn't let the scribes read them, not until he found the reason for the stir they caused. He'd caught his most trusted courier, Hosha Yahu, along with the prophet Uriah, intercepting them. Hosha was dead and Uriah sat in prison, but they were good boys, born in Arim just up the road from Lakhish. He'd known them since their youth and if there was anything he could do to help their cause he would. Uriah awaited execution and unless Yaush could find something in the Lakhish Letters—any information hidden among the writings in the eighteen leather parchments written in Captain Laban's hand—Uriah would join Hosha Yahu in an unmarked grave on the outskirts of Arim and be forgotten by everyone but his—

What was he thinking? Yaush turned onto his side and pulled the lambskin over his shoulder. Captain Laban was chief among captains, the commander of the king's armies in every city and region of the kingdom and there could be no curse more damning than to help Uriah against the wishes of his superior. Yaush took a deep breath and rubbed his hand over his brow, but he couldn't push the letters from his mind, no matter how hard he rubbed. They haunted the furthest retreats of his thoughts. There could be something in the letters that would liberate Uriah, but in freeing the man would he incriminate Laban? Court-martials were for foot soldiers, not the captain of the guard, and if the letters shed any evidence against Laban, he could never reveal it, not if he hoped to retain his title as Lord Yaush, commander of Fort Lakhish, governor of southern Judah.

Yaush turned onto his back. He'd read the letters more times than there were mortared bricks spanning the arched ceiling over his bed, but he'd found nothing that could help Uriah. Was he missing something hidden between Captain Laban's pen strokes—an idle phrase or a solitary word that explained why Uriah would intercept the letters before sending them on to the fort? Yaush turned onto his side and adjusted the collar on his robe before rolling over onto his belly. The pillow had lost its form, and he fluffed it with fury, pressing his face into the soft, silken middle. The answer had to be hidden somewhere in Laban's words.

"It's those letters, isn't it?" The soft voice came from Sophia's side of the bed. She reached her hand onto his shoulder.

"Sophia?" Yaush rolled over, his elbow pushing the pillow off the bed. "I thought you were asleep."

She rearranged the lambskin blanket over her legs. "Not with a wild boar sleeping next to me."

"I wasn't sleeping." Yaush swung his legs out and sat on the edge of the bed, his feet coming to rest on the cold stones. If he stayed in bed any longer, his tossing and turning would give Sophia a case of seasickness. He said, "I'll go to my office and let you sleep."

"What is it in those letters that bothers you so?" Sophia sat up, her head missing the headboard by less than a finger's width. "You haven't slept well for two weeks and you hardly eat anymore. Only last evening the cook cleaned away your meal without your taking a single bite."

"It's nothing in the letters."

"Don't play me for the fool." Sophia folded her arms. "I married you because you were a smart man."

"And I agreed to the marriage because I'd found the finest woman in all of Judah." Yaush leaned over the bed and kissed her on the cheek.

"You know what I'm talking about." Sophia pushed him away. "We've had no peace since—"

"Since the day we got word Uriah was imprisoned."

"There's nothing you can do for the boy."

"He's not a boy; he's a prophet."

"It's out of your hands." Sophia pulled her knees up to her chest, the ends of the lambskin blanket gathering at her feet. "Uriah was caught stealing your mail."

Yaush gripped the bedpost. "Must we hide our faith from everyone?"

"Only from some." Sophia twisted the ends of the blanket with her fingers. "If it weren't for Captain Laban and his vengeance against the . . ."

Yaush held his finger to her lips and immediately Sophia fell silent. He crossed to the finely crafted hardwood door and put his ear over the crack between the planks. The timbers were cut square and sanded to a smooth finish, without any slivers or knots to prick his ear. However, through a flawed spot in the timbers, the quiet fall of footsteps penetrated through and allowed him to hear the careful placing of sandals immediately outside the bedroom. It couldn't be the palace watch. They'd come and gone four times during the night and finished their last rounds long before Yaush wrestled the blanket from Sophia.

She sat up in bed. "What are you doing?"

Yaush pulled back from the door, raising his hands to keep her from speaking more. Whoever was in the hall came quietly for a reason, the sound of his quick breathing pulsing through the seam in the wood. The brass latch turned, the bolt clicked, and the door pushed open.

Yaush reached around and grabbed the arm of the intruder. He jerked him forward into the door planks, the man's head banging into the wood hard enough to startle the most thickheaded trespasser. Yaush stepped around the half-opened door, spun the man around and held him by the neck, his arm taught as a cord.

"Papa?" Setti struggled to speak, his voice strangled by the hold on his throat.

"Son?" Yaush released him. "What are you doing sneaking about like this?"

"I didn't want to wake you, but . . ."

"But what?"

"Are you and Mama all right?"

"What's wrong, Setti?" Sophia threw off the lambskin blanket and let it fall to the floor as she hurried to his side, untying the sleeping tail from under her robe and letting her dark brown hair cascade over her shoulders. "Shouldn't you be at the gates?" She glanced toward the window. "It's well before first light."

"I was worried."

Setti's eyes were wide and his voice frail. It was unlike him to be timid about his speech. He had his father's bravado that resonated from deep in his chest, and he possessed his mother's eloquent choice of words. There was not another soldier at Lakhish who didn't turn an ear when he spoke. Not because Setti was the son of Lord Yaush, but because his words commanded their attention. And though he had the men's respect, he never undermined the authority of his superiors—a difficult chore since commander Yaush was also his father. But there he stood, hesitating on each word.

Sophia said, "Worried about what?"

"Well, I . . ."

"Come now, son," Yaush said. "It isn't like you to be short on words."

Setti removed his brass helmet and his straight, black hair fell into his eyes, half hiding the concern that furrowed his brow. His narrow lips were drawn together and when he spoke they disappeared into his white teeth that were as straight and true as was his loyalty to his father. Setti's hair fell over his brow, and his penetrating blue eyes peered out from behind the thatches of black. He was searching the hall, his gaze stopping on the flickering light of the last stubborn lamp that danced from the sconce opposite the door. They were alone, except for the smell of burned-out wicks lingering in the hall.

Setti gripped Yaush by the arm. It was a powerful grip, stronger than the usual greeting he'd gotten from his son. He said, "I wanted to be sure."

Sophia said, "Sure of what?"

"The letters."

Yaush turned the full force of his gaze onto Sophia. "You told him about them?"

Sophia said, "Only that they caused you sleepless nights."

"You shouldn't say such things, neither of you." Yaush took both of them by the hand. "Idle talk begets rumor and once that beast escapes there's no caging it."

Sophia said, "We've not mentioned the letters to anyone."

"There's nothing in the letters to mention, not a single thing that should cause such a stir."

"But they trouble you." Sophia ran her hand across Yaush's brow. "More than you're saying."

"I'm not troubled by them." Yaush turned away, his gaze resting on the table in the hall. The maidservants hadn't set out the usual steaming pot of wither-root tea, waiting for the commander and his wife to wake. It was still too early for them to be about their duties, but not too early for a shot of anything that would calm his mind. Wine, tea, why he'd drink a tankard of salt water from the Dead Sea if it had power to rid him of the concern over the eighteen letters hidden in his personal vault. They were evidence, and though there was not to be a trial, what they contained could have power to damn him an accomplice. If only Uriah wasn't in the dungeons, Yaush could forget the letters. But the man needed a lawyer and the only evidence that could help his cause could be in the letters. Cursed things! Yaush leaned against the doorpost. He said, "I'm not troubled at all, do you understand that?"

Sophia lifted the hem of her robe and stepped to his side. "You most certainly are."

"You, my good lady, should go back to bed and get some sleep." Yaush adjusted Sophia's robe over her shoulders. "The sun won't be rising for hours."

Setti said, "You've spent weeks studying the letters."

"Look at both of you." Yaush rubbed his hands together and forced a weak smile. "You've created a stir over nothing."

"I'm sorry, Papa, it's just that . . ."

"No more about the letters." Yaush patted Setti on the shoulder. "You should get back to your watchtower and forget this senseless worrying."

"I just, well . . ." Setti combed his fingers through his hair. "I thought the letters could be the reason Zedekiah came to Lakhish this morning."

"What?" Yaush stepped to his son and the collar of his sleeping robe slipped down over his shoulder on his sudden movement. He pulled it back in place and tied the sash tight around his waist. "The king of Judah is here?"

"He arrived by chariot not an hour ago." Setti scratched the side of his head. "If you could call it a chariot."

"Why didn't you tell me sooner?"

Setti pressed his arm against his side, the wooden dowels of the watchtower log pointing back at Yaush as he spoke. He said, "I thought you knew."

Yaush began playing with the gold band on his ring finger, twisting it over the knuckle and rubbing the skin red. It was something he did whenever he was under pressure and there was reason to worry about . . . *What was he doing?* He forced his hand down at his side. He would not let them see his anxiety, no matter how much reason he had to be concerned that the King of Judah was in the palace. Yaush glanced about the hall. There was not a maidservant dusting tables, freshening oil lamps, or burning frankincense to sweeten the musty smell that lodged in the mortar between the giant stones rising up the corridor and spanning the high ceiling. The winter rains were never kind to stonework, to say nothing of the wood beams in the roof, and the smell wouldn't be gone till summer. Why didn't Captain Laban send word his guest was to be Zedekiah? A military visitor wouldn't bother with the unmilitary details of mildew, but the king? There was hardly time to get things in order before first light, and with a bit of luck His Majesty would sleep well past a proper waking hour and allow Yaush to marshal the palace help and make another review of the letters before . . .

No, that couldn't be the reason Zedekiah came to Lakhish. Yaush turned his gaze down the dimly lit hall toward his study where he kept the letters hidden. The king couldn't have come about the letters. What did he care about a few harmless writings from Captain Laban? Yaush said, "I was expecting someone else."

Setti held out the ledger. "I have yet to make a record of it."

"Don't. We're not to follow protocol with this arrival."

"But Papa . . . ?"

"I have my orders too, son." Yaush spoke with a quick, precise rhythm, cutting off the ends of his words and clicking his tongue on the rigid letters of his speech. There was to be no mistake; Setti, as captain of the night watch, was to obey him in this matter—not as his son, no matter how much his heart told him otherwise. Yaush said, "This matter is to be left unrecorded, is that clear?"

"Yes, sir." Setti refitted his helmet over his brow and stood straight, the heels of his boots clicking together.

Yaush started down the hall with Sophia trailing behind him. He straightened his robe as he went, picking his way over the cold stones of the hallway. He should have at least put on a pair of sandals before heading to the study. But if the king had come to Lakhish about the letters, this could be his last chance to review them. He paused long enough to see Sophia pass before the stone etching of Fort Lakhish chiseled into the west wing wall. She seemed to be part of the sculptor's vision, the parapets and towers rising above her head like the points on a crown, and the impregnable double walls surrounding her with the protecting graces of Judah's finest fortress. If only he could call for the artist to come and chisel her into this portrait, encased in stone, safe and out of harm's way until this was over and he could bring her back from a stony sleep. But he could no more protect her than he could turn back the Jordan.

Sophia stopped in front of the etching, her brown head of hair nestled directly below the towers of the main gate. She said, "What are you looking at, dear?"

Yaush took her hand. It was cool and soft, and he would have stayed and shared his warmth with her if it weren't for the letters pressing on him like a grinding stone in an olive press. He said, "Everything is going to be fine." He left her standing there, beneath the stone portrait; but she wasn't safe, not as long as he pursued his investigation and, God willing, it would come to a quick and peaceful end.

"Yaush?" Sophia said, "Where are you going dressed like that?"

He didn't stop to answer; he couldn't, not if he didn't want to lie. He turned beyond the high-backed benches and under the archway leading to the main hall. He'd never lied to Sophia, never told her anything but the truth—he'd never had reason to do otherwise until now, and telling her any more than what she already knew about the letters would only trouble her sleep. Yaush rubbed his eyes and yawned. Sophia didn't need to lose any sleep over the letters. He was losing enough for both of them.

Sophia gathered the hem of her robe and leaned up on her toes. "Yaush, did you hear me?"

He turned the corner and left her in the company of Setti. It was better neither of them knew the details of his studies and he prayed the letters wouldn't put them at risk. Whatever he discovered in them could lead to his ruin and he would not lead his family down that path. If he were implicated in a scheme against Captain Laban, he could lose more than his rank of twenty years.

He was risking his life.

Yaush found the door to his study ajar. Odd. He always locked the chamber before he left and only the maidservants had a key to the room. It creaked open in his hand and the light from the hall spread across the marbled floor, lighting a narrow path to his desk that stood beneath the window. He turned past the large floor lamps beside his chair, leaving them unlit. He didn't need their light until he got the letters from the vault.

In the corner of the study, opposite the window, stood a small door, recessed into the thick limestone of the inside wall. It was crafted of hardwood, four hands thick, and the planks were nailed together with iron crosspieces and inlaid into the wood to keep a chisel from prying them free. The lock required two keys, one above the latch and another below the hand piece. Yaush fitted the keys into place, unbolted the door and pulled it open, unleashing a rush of musty air that had the smell of aged dust—if it were possible for dust to rot with time.

The only valuables inside were a gift for Sophia's birthday—a gold chain necklace with five sapphire stones—and a stash of money not even Jebus, Yaush's personal accountant, knew about. He let the man tally his fortunes and secure them in the main vault of the palace treasury, but kept aside this pittance. It was money Jebus couldn't note in his ledger, and Yaush didn't have to suffer his advice about its disposal. It was his money to do with as he pleased, and it pleased him to hoard it here in remembrance of simpler days. There were fourteen stacks of coins, accumulated over the years since he started playing pitch and toss with the soldiers in the street outside the fort's commissary, each stack measuring more than a fist tall. The ones near the back had collected more dust than a camel running the trade route, and Yaush ran his fingers lightly over the silver coins, removing the dust of time and returning some of the luster of the past. What had it been, three years since his last game, or was it four? How the duties of Lakhish deprived him of the simple pleasures he once enjoyed with his men. It was five years since he retired from playing without a loss to his name, guarding his winnings like a trophy. It reminded Yaush of better, less disturbing times; back when he could toss a silver coin as true as a hawk eyes its prey, and when there were no worries about his superiors to trouble his steady throwing arm. Yaush braced himself against the coin shelf. That was in the days before Laban was captain of the guard.

The Lakhish Letters sat on the third shelf from the top, the only valuables among the land ownership records, military maps, and water-right documents that didn't have a thick covering of brown dust over them. There was no time for anything to collect on the letters with Yaush reading them once each day, though Sophia insisted it was not less than three. What did she know about his doings in the study? These were his private chambers and yet somehow she always knew, down to the flavor of tea he took at midmorning and how long he napped behind the closed door. How did she ever come by her information? It was not he who told her about the necklace he was guarding in here until her birthday, but she informed him yesterday that it would go very nicely with a blue silk robe from Tanis. Sophia always knew.

The Lakhish Letters were stored in an open container the size of a firebox. But these documents lacked the power to warm his soul and he quickly walked them out of the vault, pulling the door shut behind him with his foot and marching them to his desk.

He removed the first scroll and held it up to the dim light filtering through the window. The sunrise was a good while away, but the sky had brightened enough that he could read without lighting the lamp. This was the letter he'd received seven months ago, immediately after Laban's appointment as captain of the guard last August, and what a blistering hot month it had been, to say nothing of the weather.

There was nothing in the first letter to give him reason to pause except the instructions for an inspection. Yaush was to have the signal station rebuilt, a new well dug inside the walls, and all the soldiers called home from patrols to meet with Laban, the new captain of the guard. Yaush closed the scroll, the dowels slapping together and splintering the wood. He'd done exactly that. The fort was ready for inspection last August when Laban came and Yaush should have left it at that. Yaush rubbed the tightness from his neck—reading was usually an enjoyable exercise, though these letters were not the stuff of psalms. He couldn't have known that buying wines from Uriah would be the beginning of his troubles. He never should have purchased the new wines to serve during Laban's inspection tour. Uriah delivered them at the same hour Laban arrived, the two of them meeting at the gate outside the fort, and what an unfortunate meeting that was.

Yaush tapped his fingers against the side of his head. Uriah had said something to Captain Laban that riled his anger, but what was it? He lowered the scroll from in front of the window. It had something to do with a family secret. No, that wasn't it. Uriah quoted a scripture. That's what it was—a proverb about treasures of wickedness profiting a man nothing while righteousness delivered from death. That's exactly what Uriah said to Laban or was that something he read from another scroll last month? Or maybe he'd heard the proverb in the sermon of the high priest when he was at Jerusalem two months back. Yaush scratched his fingers through his matted hair, raising it off the back of his head. Why did he have such an insufferable memory? It was fading more, but then he couldn't recall how much it was fading, and he had no way of knowing what state his mind was really in. It wouldn't be long before he ordered the scribes in the fort's treasury to follow him about and record every word that fell from his lips and every thought that flashed through his mind.

Yaush curled his toes under his bare feet to chase away the chill that seeped from the stone floor and unscrolled the next fifteen letters, laying them side-by-side on his desk, the soft leather edge of one pushing against the edge of another. He smoothed them flat with his palm and squinted through the morning shadows. Uriah was mentioned in all of them. He was a traitor in one, guilty of delivering Judah into the hands of the Babylonians in another; a saboteur in the next; his preaching of peace with Babylon weakening the resolve of Laban's military men in yet another. Accomplice, liar, turncoat—profiteering on the blood of his own people and the list of Uriah's transgressions went on. But there was something odd among all of Laban's accusations. Each one made reference to Uriah's damaging influence on the Babylonian war. Yaush leaned over the mass of letters laying before him, his fists planted on the desk and his gaze turned into the reading. How could Uriah be guilty of such crimes? The war was over long before any of these were written. Yaush raised his gaze from the letters. In fact it wasn't until the men met face-to-face during Laban's inspection that the captain began his tirades against Uriah. Why would Laban accuse Uriah of crimes that he could not have committed, not unless he could travel back in time? Laban had lodged a mountain of accusations that Uriah could not have possibly climbed.

Yaush cleaned away the layer of scrolls from his desk and took out the second-to-last one. It was the one Shechem, king of robbers, had delivered to the fort. Why did Laban ever trust the man to spy for the military in these parts? Shechem and his men knew the southern hill country better than any of the military scouts, but that was no reason to trust him—there was never a reason to trust an outlaw. Yaush nodded slowly. At least that alliance was no more, not after Shechem tried to steal the captain's sword during King Zedekiah's coronation. He had a penchant for symbols of kingship and it was a fortunate thing he hadn't wrestled the blade away from Laban's servant or it would be hanging on the wall of Shechem's hideout somewhere in the caves of southern Judah. Shechem was a criminal of the worst kind and Yaush still chafed at having accompanied him to Uriah's inn. That was the beginning of Uriah's troubles. If only the boy hadn't bothered with his mail, then he wouldn't be sitting in the dungeons awaiting his execution, and the courier, Hosha Yahu, would still be alive and maybe, just maybe, Hosha could shed some light on the letters. But Hosha was gone and there was no way Yaush could raise him from the dead, not even to save the living.

Yaush returned the letter to the box and neatly stacked all of them in order except for the last one, the one he'd received immediately after the coronation, informing Yaush that Uriah had been captured and awaited execution in Jerusalem. He opened the scroll, the leather draped between both hands. It was the oddest of all the letters. There was mention of the unfortunate appearance of robbers at the coronation, but nothing that Laban and his men were not able to thwart. That wasn't the odd portion of the letter. Yaush scrolled to the bottom of the soft leather. It was the phrase about Zedekiah and his sons, a veiled curse against the monarch. No, it wasn't a veiled curse, it was outright slander against the king. It was scratched into the parchment with a different color of ink, as if it were an afterthought or possibly a note Laban made to himself, but it was there and Yaush had no way of knowing if it was intended for his eyes. The first portion of the phrase was lost along the fringe of the leather scroll, but it continued in flowing script across the bottom of the letter . . . *to see the princes of Judah cursed, and their father with them.*

Yaush turned to the window, the scroll open in front of him, the brightness of predawn falling on the windowsill. But it did not have the power to break the chill that descended over his heart. Yaush had to be misreading the scroll, and he angled the parchment to the glow of morning. If he could only know the first part of the phrase, the part before Laban wrote the curse against the royal sons and their father, then he could be sure that Laban didn't mean these words, not literally. A curse like this, if it was a curse at all, was a wish of death and there was no way Laban intended such a thing. It was most certainly a slip of the pen in a moment of anger, or maybe he was writing of their narrow escape during the coronation. That was it. Laban was writing about the threat Shechem posed to the royal family, and there was not a Jew in the kingdom who didn't understand that the aim of every robber since the day Cain slew Abel, was to murder the king and rule over his kingdom. But even then, Laban shouldn't write such an oath, not against the royal family, even if he was referring to Shechem and his band of robbers. The captain should distance himself from even the appearance of such slander. He was charged with protecting the royal family, not cursing them to the grave.

Yaush raised his gaze from the letter and scanned the skyline of Fort Lakhish. The deep blue light silhouetted the watchtowers sprouting along the east walls, each with an orange flame dancing between the columned enclosures. This was Yaush's fort. He hadn't built it, but until he was appointed commander there was only one wall surrounding Lakhish where now there were two protecting the hilltop. He added the second wall against the advice of officers at other forts, but the new wall set halfway down the hill deterred the most determined enemies from attempting to take the fort. The Babylonians never bothered with Lakhish, passing by in the dark of night to besiege the capital. And despite the fire Yaush lit atop the signal station, the warning did not keep Jerusalem from falling. Yaush turned his gaze down toward the bastion, the long corridor connecting the outer gate with the inner gate. It was an ingenious deterrent engineered by the commander himself, his most daring fortification.

Yaush gripped the windowsill with his free hand. The square roof and open balconies of this palace, rising above the dwellings of five thousand soldiers and their families would not have a single foundation stone laid if he hadn't seen to its building. The wide corridors and cavernous halls rivaled the grandeur of those in the palace in Jerusalem, except that they weren't decorated with gold or carpentered with hardwoods imported from the north. Yaush laid the scroll on the sill in front of him. Before he came, Fort Lakhish was nothing more than a military outpost on the trade route, fit for stabling a few mules and housing a small garrison of men. But now it was the pride of the Jewish army, and he could lose all of it if he wasn't careful with his handling of these letters.

"Do you always read in the dark?"

The voice came from behind Yaush. It was a thinly pitched whistle that rasped across the chamber like an arrow piercing his hearing. If a man's voice had power to chill, then this man's shrillness could call down a winter storm and freeze the very depths of hell. Yaush spun from the window and peered across the chamber. The reason the door to the study was left ajar was seated on a solitary chair in the shadows. A man had been there all this time, watching Yaush read the letters, not making a sound, not bothering to introduce himself, simply sitting there carefully studying Yaush.

The unannounced guest wore a black, pointed turban with white and black head shawls covering his brow and flowing from beneath the headpiece down past his shoulders. His pleated robe fell over his thin frame, which he pushed back into the angle of the chair like a soldier seated at attention, though this was no soldier. He had wide, rather large eyes, with a nose that sprouted on his face like a finger. When he stood, the light from the hall found its way over the white, almost powdery complexion of Zadock, Chief Elder of the Jews.

"Sir, I didn't know that you . . ." Yaush pulled the open collar of his sleeping robe tight around his neck. "I should go and dress before we— "

"Stay! I want to be on the road back to Jerusalem before the sun rises." Zadock's lips barely moved as he spoke. "I have to make a man a prophet."

Make a man a prophet? Yaush peered at the Chief Elder through the shadows. It was an odd thing to say, though there was little the Chief Elder said that wasn't somewhat odd, and he did it with a grating voice and a twisted smile without the slightest hint of piety. But whatever he intended by his words remained hidden behind dark, unreadable eyes. He couldn't want more prophets in Jerusalem, not after seeing to the banishment of Jeremiah and the capture of Uriah. And with talk of a prophet named Lehi appearing at the execution grounds to save Uriah, he couldn't possibly mean what he said. Maybe he'd misunderstood the Chief Elder, or maybe Zadock had misspoken. That was it, the man had slipped on his speech, and he didn't really mean to say that he was going back to Jerusalem to make a man a prophet. It was God who called men to prophethood, not the Chief Elder, and for Zadock to see to the calling of a prophet, well that was the business of soothsayers and magicians, and the Chief Elder of the Jews would never keep company with men of such ill repute.

Yaush loosened his hold on his collar and said, "The captain of the night watch said the King had come to Lakhish."

"Your son told you that, did he?"

"How did you know he was my son?"

"Setti." Zadock stroked his chin with the tip of his finger. "He seems a lively lad."

"You've met?"

"I make it my business to know everything about the men who have power to condemn traitors in this kingdom."

"Setti doesn't know anything about Uriah."

Zadock stepped down along the desk, the hem of his robe falling just above the floor, the sole of his sandal sneaking from under the cloth. "I didn't mention Uriah's name; you did."

"I'm sorry, sir." Yaush pulled the last letter from the windowsill and quickly scrolled it back into the box with the others. "I shouldn't assume anything."

"About Uriah you should. He's the reason I— "

"Oh that lad; he's not caused us any trouble here."

"You caught him stealing your mail, didn't you?"

"Well, yes, but . . ." Yaush folded his arms and leaned against the side of the table. "That's hardly a crime worthy of treason, wouldn't you agree?"

"Do you have any evidence against him?"

"I thought Uriah was already found guilty."

"He was, but there's been a . . ." Zadock passed his tongue over his lips. ". . . there's been a delay in carrying out his sentence."

"You mean his execution."

"Exactly."

Yaush came around the desk, his face turned away from Zadock's omniscient gaze. Praise be to heaven! There was still time to save Uriah without raising suspicions. Yaush asked, "What sort of delay, sir?"

Zadock approached the desk with an inaudible stride. There was not even the brush of leather over the ground or the creak of the straps about his ankles. It was as if he walked without a sole. It must be the Chief Elder's cobbler; the princes and nobles of the city could afford to hire the finest artisans. Zadock stopped before the desk, his hands hidden beneath the folds of his robe. He said, "There's to be another trial." He drew his hands out from under his robe and pointed his long fingers at himself. "And the king has appointed me chief prosecutor."

"I could think of no better lawyer, sir." Yaush kept his gaze turned to the floor.

"Save your breath; I don't need your good wishes." Zadock cleared his throat, but it did little to alter his rasping voice. "What I need is evidence." He scanned the room, his gaze resting on the box of letters set atop the table. He said, "Have you any?"

"Nothing but a few wine bottles from his inn, but that only proves him an innkeeper. Beyond that I really can't think of— "

"What about the letters?"

Yaush turned his gaze up quickly, his head snapping to attention at the end of a stiffening neck. "What letters, sir?" He reached for the wooden box of scrolls. He said, "We get so many."

"The ones Uriah intercepted with the help of the courier."

"There's really nothing in them of any value, nothing that could be used as evidence against him."

"You do have them, don't you?"

"It's military protocol to keep all of Captain Laban's letters in the archives." Yaush pushed the box of scrolls across the desk, away from Zadock. "Do you want me to have the scribes look for them?"

"No!" Zadock raised his voice, filling the dark room with the shrillness of his speech, and there was no doubting his resolve. He did not want the letters to come to trial. He pointed his finger at Yaush and said, "They're not to come to Jerusalem."

Yaush said, "Don't you need them as evidence?"

Zadock leaned over the desk. He said, "Guard them in your vault and see that no one reads them. They're safer here away from the eyes of any in Jerusalem who might stand in our way." His gaze didn't move from Yaush and he didn't blink, not even when a draft filtered in through the window. He said, "See that you're in Jerusalem for the trial."

"Me, sir?"

"I'll notify you as soon as Zedekiah sets the date for hearing testimony." Zadock turned toward the door.

Yaush asked, "Is there a reason you want me at the trial?"

Zadock stopped in the doorway before going out, the light from the hall silhouetting his robed frame. He said, "You're my lead witness."

CHAPTER 2

The prophet Uriah reached out in the darkness and rubbed the blood back into his cold legs, but the ropes dug into the sores on his chest and he pulled back until the pain passed. He was bound by cords with enough slack to lean his head against the moss-covered brick of his prison cell and listen to the endless drip, drip, dripping of water seeping into this well.

No sunlight reached this place, no window showed the glow of day or the dark of night, and Uriah measured time by meals—lemon rinds in the morning, weevil-infested bread at lunch, and scraps of putrid vegetables for dinner. It was hardly enough to keep him alive and his mind was blurred by want of food—or was it the gash in his brow that dimmed his wit? He ran his fingers over the scab. He'd not dressed the wound properly and spent the first weeks in prison suffering from infections and fevers that made counting his meals difficult, but he would not lose count. Keeping track of days was the only thing that kept him sane; if he lost his mind it wouldn't be long before death was his cellmate and he did not want that companionship, not until he held his children one last time and felt the touch of his wife's hand in his.

Tonight's meal would be thirty-seven—if you could call the moldy scraps the prison guards threw him a meal. Uriah glanced up the narrow shaft and waited for them to throw down the food. He was certain it had been thirty-seven days since he was saved from the execution block and the prison guards brought him here, stripped him of his clothes, wrapped a loincloth around his waist, and tied him into a harness of ropes, lowering him into the well of the prison like a puppet on a string. His bare legs were covered with rashes from living in dampness for so long, and though the knee-high waters from the rains two days back had receded, the sores on the undersides of his feet hadn't, not with the puddles that covered the floor and folded his hands and feet into a furrowed mass of sloughed skin.

The faint glow of an oil lamp filtered down the shaft from above, and he slowly raised his head to the light, water seeping down over his uncombed black hair and dripping off the end of his nose. The jailer leaned over the edge and spoke through holes in his teeth, his speech cluttered with whistles. He cursed the day Uriah was brought here, cursed the work it caused him, and cursed Uriah to die and make room for another prisoner before throwing him his dinner—the skins of rotten potatoes tonight. Uriah scrambled to them, pressed them to his tongue and drew whatever strength the molded food had to share with him. It was the only thing he would enjoy tonight with the rains gone and the flooding ended. Rainy nights were the best for sleeping, with water seeping through the foundation wall and flooding his cell, but tonight was a dry one and no matter how many times he begged heaven to send more rain he would have to fight the rats alone. There was no high water to keep them away and he huddled against the wall, made fists with his hands and waited in the darkness for the sound of their feet scratching over the brick and the cut of their sharp teeth through the skin of his cold limbs. But they weren't going to bite him tonight; he wouldn't let them. He was going to fight them off with the fury of a . . .

Uriah's arms began to shake and he dropped his hands into his lap. He was a fool for making fists that tight. He didn't have the strength and he waited like a helpless child for the creatures to come out of hiding. He lowered his head, his chin pressed into the cords tied about his chest, and before nodding off, he mumbled the same prayer he offered every night.

"Dear God, deliver me from this place."

There were no soldiers standing guard at the west-wing doors leading down to the palace prison, but there was no need. No prisoner ever escaped from the catacombs below. Laban peered at his reflection in the door mount—the snarling brass head of a lion that hung from the center plank of the palace prison door—and parted his hair along the left side of his head. Foolish barber. He'd paid the man four shekels for his work and he didn't have the sense to comb in any perfumed oils to keep the part in place. Laban's sideburns were shaved short, without any of the locks and curls that dangled about the ears of zealots. At least the barber got that right. There was nothing worse than going about Jerusalem with the grooming of a religious fanatic. And if Laban had his way, he'd outlaw the style. It was embarrassment enough that any Jews at Jerusalem still followed the laws of Moses; they didn't have to wear their superstitions curling about their ears in locks of uncombed hair.

Laban turned his head to the side and examined his short-shaven sideburns in the brass reflection. The hair blended perfectly into the thin line of beard gracing his jawline. Moses taught thou shalt not shave the corners of thy beards, but what did that dead prophet know about fashion? He lived a thousand years ago before Phoenician styles became more fashionable than the unshaven locks of Hebrew law. Laban rubbed the brass head of the lion for good luck. Prophets! What a plague they were. At least Moses was dead and Laban didn't have to suffer the man's fetish for foolish barbering. He straightened his collar and pulled the thick cloak off his shoulders to keep from raising a sweat on his brow. As soon as Uriah was dead he'd be rid of yet one more fetish. Starvation was a subtler death than dying by the sword and though it was a slow means to silence the man who knew his secret, he had more than enough patience as long as it worked its miracle before the trial began.

Zadock turned into the hall and slowly approached the prison door, the freshly pressed pleats on his black robe lifting and falling with his stride. His shrill voice echoed off the stone walls of the west wing. He said, "How is he?"

"Nothing's changed." Laban combed through his hair with his fingers. "But it shouldn't be much longer."

"We can't wait. We have to act now." Zadock draped a cloth over his mouth to filter the stench from poisoning his breathing. He spoke through the linen. "Open the door."

Laban placed the key in the latch. "If we wait this out, there will be no need to try the man in a court of— "

"The door, Captain."

Laban ground the thick prison door open on its hinges and the smell of rotting flesh drafted past him in a rush of diseased air. A rat skittered across the landing and Laban chased it into the shadows with the tip of his boot. He led the Chief Elder down the circular steps into the catacombs below. This was his domain, the only place in the palace where the king and queen never ventured. He rattled the metal gate at the bottom of the stairs with both hands. "Open up in there!"

The jailer emerged from a small room at the far end of the dungeon and lumbered over. His beard was an unkempt wiry mass at the end of his chin and his dark-eyed gaze studied them like a snake inspecting intruders to its territory. He carried a small clay lamp, its glow lighting the floor ahead of his stride and guiding him around the prisoners that lay chained to the walls. The men stirred from their sleep as he passed, trapped between their nightmares and the ugliness of their life in this prison. Only eleven men had ever escaped these haunts—each one dressed in burial clothes and laid to rest in pauper's graves on the flats south of Jerusalem.

"I wasn't expecting a visit tonight, Captain." The jailer held the lamp level with his face and the light cast black shadows in the gaps between his teeth.

Laban pressed his face to the iron bars. He said, "Did you hear him say anything?"

"Nothing new, just the usual gibberish, but it's hard to know if it's the food or the gash in his brow that's turned him daft. I've starved a lot of men before, but none of them carried on like Uriah, something about treasures of wickedness profiting a man nothing, while treasures of— "

Laban pulled on the iron bars with both hands. "Are you sure he said treasures?"

The jailer picked at the wax in his ear and flicked it off the end of his finger. "I hear everything."

"When was the last time you spoke with him?"

"I don't speak to anyone down here, sir." The jailer scratched the side of his head. "Come to think of it, it's been three days since Uriah said anything."

Zadock spoke through the cloth of his sleeve. "Is he still alive?"

"That he is, sir. I heard him stirring at the bottom of the well not an hour ago."

"Curse him!" Laban rapped his fist against the metal bar and the jailer jumped back from the clanging. "How much longer can he live?"

The jailer said, "If your soldier hadn't hit him so hard before he brought him here, I'd have a better idea."

Laban said, "Have you been keeping back his food?"

The jailer said, "He gets nothing but rotten scraps."

"Stop feeding him altogether. We have to starve him before—"

"Take us to him." Zadock stepped in front of Laban, the jailer's lamplight streaming through the metal bars and striping his face with shadows. "I want to see him, now."

The jailer let them through the gate, guided them around the legs of the chained prisoners and told them to crouch beneath the low-lying beams that cramped the life out of these chambers. He recruited three of his strongest guards to follow them down a long corridor that ended at a thick wood post sprouting out of the floor like the trunk of a felled tree. Three ropes were lashed about the stump and the ends trailed off through a hole in the floor.

The guards steadied themselves around the edge of the well and slowly pulled up the ropes, their shoulders thrown back to counter the dead weight of Uriah's body and the coil of cords growing at their feet until Uriah appeared, his head reeling to the rhythm of their heaving. He was naked from head to toe except for a cloth about his loins and a harness of ropes that wrapped around his bony ribs, across his chest, and under his arms. His shoulders were rubbed red with rope rashes and his limbs and face had gone pale as the whitest moon. The dried blood from the gash in his brow hadn't been cleaned away since the day he arrived here. His dark black hair was stuck against his brow, clumped together with dried blood. His gaunt cheeks sunk into his mouth, and his beardless chin sagged.

The soldiers dragged him from the edge of the well and laid his thin body against the post, his wet legs collecting the dirt and hay from the floor like a mop. His head fell against the wood and his mouth hung open like a dead fish, and when the guards tied him to the post Laban ordered them to stand down—he wasn't afraid of Uriah or his God. Laban would kill Uriah straight out, but he couldn't raise the suspicions of a king who sat on a throne that should be his. They could do nothing that would draw Zedekiah's suspicion. If Uriah didn't die on his own they couldn't help the man into his grave.

Laban slapped Uriah across the cheeks and his eyes opened. They were filled with a faraway look, his gaze drifting past Laban to the ceiling beams above him. The corners of his mouth turned into the slightest of smiles and Laban glanced up to see what he was looking at. Thick foundation stones supported the palace with cedar cross beams holding them in place. It was nothing that should cause Uriah to smile, but there he sat as if he were seeing into heaven. What a fool! Uriah was going to die in this prison without a single flute-playing, sword-bearing, wing-backed cherub to come and carry him away to eternal rest. There was nothing but unending darkness waiting to receive his soul, and if he hadn't already found some celestial light in this life, there certainly wasn't any in the night that was about to engulf his mind when he died. Though Uriah's delusions eased his pain and allowed him to forget his plight, his days of preaching the superstitions of his fathers were over. Laban slapped him again, but he didn't flinch; he didn't even blink. He sat silent and listless with only the traces of a smile giving life to his lifeless face.

Zadock said, "How much longer will this take?"

"His mind's gone, that's certain." The jailer lifted Uriah's head by the hair. "I don't know how long he can hold on. He's stronger than other men I've kept in the well."

Laban stabbed the toe of his boot into the ground. He said, "Where does he get his strength?"

"He keeps babbling about deliverance, that God will deliver him once he's completed his mission."

Laban said, "What mission?"

The jailer tapped his forefinger against his temple. "The man isn't right in the head."

A metal ball on the end of a chain hung from a hook on the wall next to a row of spikes, three whips, and a branding iron. They were instruments of torture and Zadock picked a rod from among the metal tools, set the end of it beneath Uriah's chin and lifted his head until he could see into the man's brown-eyed gaze, like a doctor examining a patient before the surgery. "Clean him up."

Laban said, "What?"

"You heard me." Zadock walked a circle about Uriah, the hem of his robe brushing over the prophet's long legs. He removed the cloth from his mouth. He said, "See that he's fed three good meals a day. Have him washed, perfumed, dressed in a clean robe. And move him to the upper prison."

Uriah lifted his head from against the post. He gazed up at Zadock and his voice was a whisper, hardly audible from deep in his throat. He said, "By the grace of God I will be delivered."

Laban tapped the tip of his boot in a nervous rhythm. "There's no power that can deliver him."

Uriah leaned over and between gasps for breath he said, "The tender mercies of the Lord are over all those whom he hath chosen."

"Jailer!" Laban pointed at Uriah. "Shut him up!"

"I can't do that, sir." The jailer stepped back and shook his head. "There's an odd feeling about him."

"The only thing odd about the man is that he's still alive." Laban pushed the jailer aside and kicked Uriah in the stomach, bending him over at the waist and drawing a groan from deep in his throat. He took Uriah by the hair, jerked his head back against the post and raised his fist to strike him across the brow and put him out of his misery when Zadock said, "No more, Captain."

Zadock dismissed the jailer and his guards and told them he'd call for them when he needed them. He waited until their footsteps fell silent, then said, "If you want my help in these matters, you'll do this my way."

Laban tightened his grip on Uriah's hair. "We're almost rid of him."

"We have a trial to think about."

Laban said, "There will be no trial if he's dead."

"We haven't time to wait for that."

He was wrong. There was plenty of time, there had to be. Laban let go of Uriah's hair and let the man's head fall back against the post. If Uriah died in this prison he could avoid the fickleness of a public trial. Laban worked the short stubble of his beard between his thumb and forefinger. He had two secrets—his pedigree and his conspiracy—but Uriah only knew about the less damning one and though it was not a crime for Laban to have a cousin, he had to keep secret his blood ties to the prophet Lehi if he ever hoped to gain the throne. And it was his conspiracy that complicated matters. He and Zadock had to be vigilant. They had to silence anyone who found out their plot to see the princes of Judah cursed, and their father with them.

Laban said, "What if Uriah tells his lawyers about Zedekiah's coronation?"

"Uriah won't have any lawyers."

"He has family. And once his father is notified, he'll hire someone to defend his son."

Zadock said, "You haven't notified anyone, have you?"

Laban said, "Not yet, but the law requires Shemayahu be informed."

"Curse the law, Captain, we have a trial to win."

"If word gets to Shemayahu about his son and . . ." Laban tapped his finger against his upper lip. "And he hires a lawyer who finds a witness . . ." He mumbled through his fingers. "And the witness knows what happened at the coronation, we'll be the ones facing trial for the crime of— "

"Stop that. You're talking like a fool." Zadock pulled Laban's fingers from his mouth. "I'll take care of this."

Laban straightened the tails of his tunic beneath the belt of his kilt and pulled his cloak over his thick shoulders, hiding the brass buttons that decorated his strength. A trial could be their undoing. He said, "This is too large a risk."

Zadock turned away from the edge of the well. "I'll arrange for the trial to begin as soon as Uriah's presentable. See that he's groomed, dressed in fine robes, and fed three meals a day. And don't forget to let him out in the afternoon sun. I want his skin bronzed like a healthy working man."

Uriah reached for Zadock's feet. "God has heard my prayers."

"Let go of him." Laban kicked at Uriah's hands.

Zadock leaned over Uriah. "See that he's nursed back to health and do it quickly."

Uriah raised his gaze to Laban, but he was really looking past him toward the ceiling, his face brighter than the yellow glow of the lamp. He said, "I go like a lamb to the altar, but I do not fear the power of God's deliverance!"

CHAPTER 3

Aaron climbed the narrow street past his home at twice his father's pace. His father, Jonathan, usually led out, but not this morning. He slowly scaled the incline with his head down and his hands behind his back. It wasn't like Jonathan to walk like that. He never went anywhere without a confident stride and his head held high. But this morning was different. It had something to do with their early-morning meeting at the shop, and Papa said he was going to stay back and collect his thoughts on the way. When did Papa ever take time to collect his thoughts? He never bothered to gather anything but more work for their blacksmithing business and though the customer they were to meet at the shop had something for them to smelt out of steel, it wasn't the sort of business Papa preferred.

Ishmael the vineyard master of Beit Zayit left word of a visit first thing this morning. If only the word had been left with someone other than Papa, there wouldn't be any problem, but Papa didn't trust anyone associated with the prophets. He was an Elder and he was expected to behave like one.

Aaron stopped beside the gate to the cobbler's home and waited until Jonathan caught up. He passed without raising his gaze from the cobblestones. He pulled the collar of his tunic up around his neck and plodded up High Street, lost in his thoughts. And since the only thing he'd talked about since rousting Aaron out of bed was their meeting at the shop, Papa was lost somewhere between not saying anything about his concerns and telling Ishmael straight out that they didn't smith for prophets or anyone that had anything to do with them, especially the new prophet from Beit Zayit. The account of Lehi's call to prophethood did not sit well with Jonathan. It festered in him like an infection that would not heal. Not a day went by that he didn't bring it up and no matter how carefully Aaron explained, Papa would have nothing to do with heavenly visions and prophetic dreams. If Jonathan wanted to speak with God he could do it on his own; he didn't need a mediator prophet to do it for him. And he usually ended any discussion of the matter with a stiff rebuke—if God could speak to an olive oil merchant he could speak to a blacksmith just as well. Aaron raised the collar of his tunic to match Papa's—pulled high around his neck—and stepped into stride behind Jonathan. Papa didn't understand that God didn't speak to men who would not hear. Jonathan never bothered to ask God anything, never offered a family prayer, never knelt in private prayer—said he never had need to.

Aaron followed close enough behind Jonathan to be his shadow, and though they wore matching brown toques to cap their heads and the same woolen mittens over their hands, Aaron looked nothing like his father. He was tall and thin, Jonathan stout and strong. Aaron's sandy-brown bangs lifted and fell across his brow with each eager step, while Jonathan's thick black locks were steady as his stride. Aaron was really his mother's shadow. He had her blue eyes, thin nose, and long jaw instead of Papa's brown eyes, pointed nose, and square chin that made him a strong-looking figure. The same silent, powerful man Aaron had known since he was a boy. And though Aaron had lost most of his childhood fancies, Papa was still the most powerful man in the world, at least in his world. And they did share one trait—common sense—though Jonathan would never admit Aaron had any left. Not since his feet were healed. Aaron told Papa it was a miracle done in the name of the Anointed One, and Jonathan, well . . . they didn't speak about it much anymore. It only made working together uncomfortable. Aaron shortened his stride to match Jonathan's. Why didn't Papa see that it was the power of Yeshua that had breathed life back into his feet? The last time they spoke about Aaron's healing, Jonathan said miracles were for Rekhabites and no one in his family had anything to do with that no good horde of religionists—or anyone who had anything to do with the foolish doctrines of the Anointed One.

The overnight rains had cleaned the dust from the street and since it wasn't cold enough to freeze, the hope of a distant spring scented the air, cutting through the February haze like a scythe harvesting winter wheat. Aaron stayed behind Jonathan, though he could have taken the hill in half the time. He skipped over a puddle that Jonathan slowly stepped around, and he kicked through a second puddle, just missing his father and splashing the cold water onto the adjacent wall. Jonathan turned his gaze onto Aaron's water-soaked sandals, telling him with his eyes that he was a reckless child, but he didn't offer any scolding. He didn't need to. And though Aaron was no child, he'd seen that look before and he quieted his childishness. He reached nineteen years last week, he walked without the shame of crippled feet, and he couldn't keep from at least tapping his toes over the smooth cobblestones and revel in his pain-free stride.

Aaron must have looked an oddity—quietly clicking his thick-soled leather heels to the rhythms of his thankful heart—but except for Jonathan, there was no one about at this hour to think him odd, and he splashed through another puddle, this time steering the spray away from Jonathan's view. He was healed! No longer would he have to hobble to the shop with the help of crutches or ride the mule to go where his feet could not take him. They were covered with skin, the white scars turned pink as a newborn's flesh, and the bleeding stopped. His toes wiggled under the leather sandal straps, his heels bore the brunt of his weight without complaint, and his arches cushioned each step like the stretching of a rope bridge—the skin and sinew giving way under the force of each stride but never tearing. There was not a single shot of pain, and he followed Papa to work without a hesitation in his stride, no hitch in his gait, nothing that gave any hint he'd spent the better part of the past year hobbled and without hope of walking again. Healed he was! And, despite Papa's grimness this morning, Aaron walked like the giddiest of children, his cup running over with thankfulness to God for the blessing he'd received in the name of His son, Yeshua. It was that name that had power to grant him two whole feet and no matter how often Jonathan reminded him he could not speak of it in their home, there was nothing to stop him from praising that name from his heart. A small rock lay on Aaron's path beside a water cistern overflowing from the overnight rains. He flicked the rock

with his toe, lifting it in the air and landing it dead center in the
cistern, stirring the still water just as his soul had been stirred by the
blessings of heaven. Thank God he was whole again!

Jonathan led the way past the oil vendor's shop at the top of High
Street and around the corner onto Main, staying on the left-hand side
by the perfumery and as far away from the gates of Josiah's pottery
yard as he could walk. He didn't acknowledge the potter's gate with a
glance nor lift his nose at the scent of charred rubble lingering on the
breeze circling about the wall, and he certainly wasn't about to stop
and say to Aaron, look son there sits the potter's yard—poor soul,
awful thing that happened to the man. Jonathan was not about to turn
even a solitary glance to pay his respects to the ruins of Josiah's estate.

Jonathan tucked his chin beneath the collar of his tunic and kept
walking. It was enough he thought the potter a Rekhabite, but that
was no reason to avoid the man's property now that he was dead. And
it wasn't really Josiah's firing yard anymore now that he left everything
to his servant Mima, though Aaron still called it Josiah's pottery. The
kiln chimney hadn't bellowed smoke in months; the high roof of the
estate on the skyline above the whitewashed wall was gone, replaced
by the uneven edges of the mud-brick roof of servants' quarters at the
back of the lot. The selling tables had yet to appear outside the gate.
Mima, the potter's maidservant, vowed to continue selling Jerusalem's
finest bowls, cups, saucers, and bottles, but there hadn't been a
delivery of white sand, red clay, or wood since the devastating fire.
Mima may be a good pot seller, but what did she know about
managing a kiln? She'd never overseen a firing yard full of turners,
wedgers, and claymen to say nothing of finding the money to pay
their wage, and there was no telling how much of that was lost in the
fire that took the life of Josiah the potter and his . . .

Aaron lowered his head. He couldn't say her name; he couldn't
even think it. That would only take him back to the day he lost . . .

Cursed heart of his! Why must Rebekah's memory cause him such
pain? She was gone and he had a lathe to sharpen, three copper bowls
to mend, and that was more than enough work to keep him in stride
with Papa, at least until they were level with the main gates to the
pottery yard. They stood half open, the charred wooden planks
hanging on their hinges and the rubble of fallen stonewalls framed

between the gateposts. The winter rains had spread a black sea of soot over the ground and the burned cedars were skeletons dangling dead branches over the collapsed estate home. It was an eerie, ugly resting place, but it was Rebekah's and Aaron let Papa go ahead, his footsteps trailing off into the cool morning, while he stayed to pay his respects.

It wasn't really his heart he cursed; it was his feet. Aaron was whole, but he was only half a man. The God of Heaven had made it so. He walked without crutches and for that he should shout God's praise from every rooftop in the city. Aaron removed his toque from his head, held it in front of him like a priest offering a prayer, and let his sandy brown hair fall over his brow, hiding the tears that streamed down his cheeks. Did not heaven see he walked alone? Rebekah was gone and he knew no power that would heal his broken heart. It was his feet God cured—but would He please take them back and give him Rebekah? He saw her face in the morning light before he woke each day and he knew heaven suited her well. She was free of this earth while Aaron was bound to it with a debt to pay. He was to wait and watch over the life of the prophet Lehi, and he was left to do it alone.

"Son, we have a customer to meet." Jonathan came back down the street and stood at the corner in front of the stonemason's shop, but Aaron didn't budge at Papa's suggestion they move on. He kept his gaze on the gates to the pottery yard and when he brushed the tears from his cheeks, Papa turned away. Jonathan didn't let his heart mix with any part of this pain, but Rebekah deserved a moment of respect and Aaron stayed a little longer to reverence her memory and watch the last withered leaf fall from the oak tree and come to rest on the burned soil where she once lived.

"Son?" Jonathan spoke with his gaze turned to the ground. "We'd best be going."

"I'm sorry, Papa, I didn't mean to lag." Aaron cleared his eyes with two quick blinks. "I was resting my feet."

Jonathan stabbed the tip of his sandals at the cobblestones. "I can wait if you like."

But he really couldn't. There was something in his stance, the way he kept his head down and never glanced across the street toward the pottery, something about the burned-out property that bothered Jonathan, and Aaron would have asked what troubled him so, but that would only rile his temper. Papa knew the potter was a Rekhabite and though he never said it aloud, Aaron could see he wanted nothing more than to let the memory of Josiah and his daughter die with them. And since there was more than enough bad blood between Aaron and Jonathan on the matter of the prophets, he decided it best not to spill more.

"I'm fine now." Aaron pulled the toque over his ears and headed down Main Street, but not with the same clip in his stride.

The smithing district was a haunt, without another soul about but Jonathan and Aaron to venture among the ruins of the burned and broken shops. No one ever came here except to order smithing work or hunt old bricks and scraps of iron hidden among the rubble. They did get a visit last month from an Egyptian blacksmith inquiring about the property on the corner, the one without a chimney or roof, with only a west-facing wall still standing. It was the least expensive shop, but when Papa said he'd have to pay a hefty sum for it—three talents of silver—the man left without asking about the cost of making repairs on the open hearth, if you could call the mound of broken brick in the center of the foundation a hearth. Losing the war to Babylon brought a number of changes to the city, and purchasing property was among the most miserable, though Aaron never remembered paying anything to the Council of Elders to buy the smithy. There was never a scribe who bothered to come by the shop to make an accounting of what was owed and there had never been a collection notice delivered to the house. It was Aaron's duty to account for the money they earned at the shop, and never once did he set anything aside to pay the Elders for the property, nor did they ever pay any tax on the blacksmithing work they sold. Jonathan said it was because he was an Elder and Aaron didn't pursue the matter. Who was he to question the business arrangements Papa made with the council? If they didn't want money for the property or any of the tax from their blacksmith shop it was all the better. They could use the money for something other than paying the council's wage.

The incline in the road flattened in front of the shop and Aaron turned his gaze to the mud brick spires of the twin chimneys. Aaron was the firemaster, and nothing hampered a good fire more than a poorly vented chimney. The chimney bricks were covered with white plaster and at this hour they stood cold and waiting for the touch of his hand to kindle a flame and start the smoke filtering out the spouts. Jonathan never told Aaron how much he paid the brickmason for the plaster, didn't tell him what he paid the carpenter for wood to repair the doors, and never a word about the final price the Elders set for the property.

A man stood in the doorway of the shop, waiting for them. He leaned one shoulder against the wood planks, his legs crossed and his hands on his hips. He wore high-cut leather riding boots laced a thousand times up his lower legs. Well, not a thousand times, but there were more laces and polished leather wasted on one boot than there should have been strapped to the legs of ten cavalrymen. He had a warm, black cape strapped over his shoulders and when he saw them he untied it and draped it over his arm, showing the silver stripes of his military tunic that graced his powerful arms. A gold chain decorated his collar, though you could hardly call it a decoration with how taut it pulled on his thick neck, and rose and fell with his breathing like a noose. Before Daniel joined the military he never wore anything tight around any limb, no belts, no bracelets, nothing that would get in the way of his wrestling. But the strongest men in the military wore chains of gold, so he was going to have to like these trinkets strapped about his neck, the rings on his fingers, the sword at his side, and the dagger strapped about his bicep.

It had been six weeks since Daniel was sent on a border patrol and the dust-and-salt-covered horse that stood tied to the post near the door was ready for a good rest in the stables. Daniel grinned, his white teeth showing through his dark skin. It was winter and there was no reason for his face to be tanned so dark nor his black hair to have a reddish tint to it, but riding beneath the eastern desert sun and watching the movement of Babylonian troops in that part of the kingdom had bronzed him a shade more than most this time of year. And with so many Babylonian soldiers for the Hebrew army to watch over, there was no telling how long Daniel would be home nor how much darker his skin would grow.

Daniel raised his cloak-covered arm. "Early as usual, Papa."

"Son!" Jonathan took him in his arms. "You're home."

"For awhile." Daniel straightened his tunic and tucked the end of it under his belt. "Until I get my next assignment." He slapped Aaron on the back. "You're walking well."

"I'm healed."

"You still believe that?" Daniel's grin widened, his chapped lips nearly cracking. "Some things never change."

"Your horse must be thirsty. I'll water her." Aaron reached for the reins, but Daniel grabbed him, his powerful arm turning Aaron's tall frame back around to face him. He said, "I asked you a simple question, do you still believe in all that . . ."

A mule cart clattered down the street, drowning out the stern words of Daniel's speech. It was made of dried, yellow olive wood, but the vineyard master wasn't seated on the stoop. Sariah, the wife of the prophet Lehi, held the reins. Her dark, black hair was pinned up behind her head, she wore a hint of red pomegranate on her lips, and white powders dusted her cheeks.

"There's a woman you would do well to shun." Daniel threw his cape over his shoulders and the ends of it snapped in the air near Aaron's face. "She'll only cause you problems."

Aaron stepped in front of Daniel, shielding him from Sariah's view. It was Daniel who had thrown her to the ground in front of Lehi's estate at Beit Zayit, and he wasn't about to let the sight of him cause her any worry. He left Daniel and Papa by the shop and hurried across the street, his stride as strong as the concern in his voice. He said, "You shouldn't have come alone."

"Nonsense." Sariah tied the reins to the front board. "I love a solitary ride through the hills."

"Where's Ishmael?" Jonathan crossed from the shop, his arms folded tight across his chest and his voice gone low like the growl of a dog.

Daniel stood behind Jonathan, his dark eyes peering over Papa's shoulders. His grin was gone, replaced by a scowl that furrowed his brow. His jaw was set and he spoke between his teeth. He said, "Has Lehi had anymore visions? I'd like him to ask God a few questions for me."

Sariah didn't answer Daniel, didn't even glance his way. She handed Jonathan a jar of olives pickled in hot herbs and onions. "You must be Jonathan, the man Aaron has told me so much about."

"I'm his father."

"Very good to meet you, sir." Sariah offered her hand and waited for Jonathan to help her out of the cart, but he wouldn't take it, wouldn't even help the poor woman from the stoop. He was a stubborn man, but there was no reason not to offer Sariah a proper greeting. She may be the wife of Lehi, but she was not a prophet.

Aaron quickly helped Sariah from the cart and when she stood on the cobblestones her head hardly cleared the level of Jonathan's shoulders. Aaron said, "This is— "

"I know who she is."

Daniel leaned his head in and tapped his finger to the side of his head. "She's married to that madman."

"I've not had the chance, until now, to thank you for sending Aaron to work at our plantation." Sariah smiled up at Jonathan without the least bit of annoyance pursing her lips or narrowing her gaze. Her bright blue eyes shimmered in the early-morning shadows. "You've raised a fine— "

"Aaron works hard."

Sariah took Jonathan by the hand and shook it as vigorously as an olive picker shakes a branch at harvest time. "He certainly does."

Jonathan quickly pulled free. He said, "What brings you here?"

"I have something I want you to look at." Sariah scurried around to the back of the cart with the same stride she always used about the plantation when she was about to surprise Lehi with one of her discoveries. She leaned over the backboard, rummaged about the jars of olives, her head bobbing above the level of the sideboards and her hands moving quickly over the sacks of grain until they stopped on a wooden bow. The narrow timbers sprouted out of the handgrip into the shape of a half-moon, but without a string to draw them taut it was a very narrow half-moon. There was a crack in the upper arm of the bow and it didn't look like it could endure a full draw without breaking in two. She handed it to Jonathan and said, "Can you help me?"

Jonathan said, "We're not carpenters."

"Of course you're not." Sariah laughed, her voice filling the street with the brightness of a flute. It was the same cheeriness Aaron had known during his stay at Beit Zayit and it touched his soul with the warmth of her presence. She said, "This may be a ridiculous idea, but Nephi is a strong boy and getting stronger all the time and I thought you might be able to— "

"Strong?" Daniel stepped out from behind Jonathan, his shoulders squared to Sariah and his thick arms folded across his chest.

"Nephi doesn't have the strength to stay in a wrestling pit any longer than a child."

Aaron said, "Let her speak."

Sariah said, "I was hoping you could fashion a bow out of steel—one so strong it will never break."

Steel? Aaron stepped down along the cart and stood next to Sariah. That's what he'd been telling Papa for more than a year—they should be the ones to smith the first-ever bow of steel. It would be stronger and finer than any wooden bow and every bowman, military captain, and nobleman in the world would come to their shop in search of the secret of its making.

"That's foolishness." Daniel took the wooden bow from Jonathan and held it up to Sariah. "There's not a soldier in any army in the world who uses a bow made out of steel."

"That's exactly why we should smith one." Aaron plucked the bow from Daniel's grip and ran his hand over the long arms. "Couldn't we at least try?"

Jonathan rubbed his brow, his glance flitting from Sariah's expectant look, to Daniel's stiff standing frame, and back again. "I don't think we could make this work."

Aaron said, "But if we did, and I think we can, then it would mean— "

"We could lose a month of steelmaking."

"Have a little faith in your son," Sariah said. "The two of you can make a bow of steel if you work together. Why, I'd say you could make a carriage out of steel if you put your mind to it."

"A carriage out of steel?" Daniel spoke with a laugh cutting across the harsh tone in his words. "What kind of foolishness is that?"

Sariah took Jonathan by the hand and patted the back of it like a mother encouraging her young. "Isn't this exciting? We're doing something that has never been done before." She held Jonathan's hand in a firm grip. "Don't worry about any loss. I'll see that you're paid well no matter if it turns out or not. Aaron's a bright lad and I don't doubt he gets his cleverness from his father. Now tell me, when did you say you could have it done?"

Aaron turned his gaze into the boxcart to hide his grin. There was not a man or woman alive who could speak to Papa like Sariah spoke to Jonathan, especially with Daniel's callousness spoiling his temperament. It was as if Grandmother had been resurrected and returned to lecture her son and she expected Jonathan to be an obedient child. Sariah had no right to speak to Papa like that, but she was ignorant to etiquette, blinded by her kindly manner that she doled out with an evenhandedness that warmed the hearts of her friends and her foes. Sariah kept patting Jonathan on the hand and telling him what a wonderful thing he was about to smith, and her words softened Papa's heart enough that he said, "When did you want it by?"

Aaron leaned against the boxcart. This morning Papa wanted nothing to do with Ishmael, but now he was negotiating a bow.

Sariah said, "Can you have it by Passover?"

"That's just over a month from now. I don't think we could have— "

"Of course you can."

"But . . ."

Sariah said, "It's a gift for my youngest. Nephi turns sixteen during the Passover celebrations and I do so want to surprise him with it." She tugged on Jonathan's hand enough that he followed her to the front of the cart and she had him help her up onto the stoop. "I don't want you telling Sam about this."

Jonathan said, "I don't really ever see the boy to say anything about— "

"If Sam hears of this he'll not stop talking about it and the surprise will be over. That boy keeps a secret like a sieve keeps water." Sariah reined the cart forward and came around, headed uphill toward Main Street. She pulled up next to Aaron and said, "The boys practice with their bows every evening right before sundown. You'll want to stop by and fit Nephi with a good grip, get a sense for how he shoots and the length of his draw."

Jonathan said, "I don't think that's possible right now."

"Of course it is." Sariah pulled on the reins and started the mule lurching forward. "Nephi's not such a suspicious lad Aaron can't size him up and keep the secret from him," she called over her shoulders, her body rising and falling with the spring of the cart. "Remember, no one is to know about this, not until Passover."

The cart clattered to the top of the hill and turned onto Main Street, headed for the West Gate before Daniel said, "This is foolishness. If you knew what I knew, you'd be done with the olive oil merchants for good." He mounted his brown steed and galloped down into the lower city, the animal's hooves pounding the stone as he went.

Aaron didn't speak; he couldn't. Not with Papa standing beside him still rubbing his brow. This wasn't the first time he had reservations about smithing for the olive oil merchants and now there were many more reasons not to allow Aaron the chance to craft a bow out of steel. He should have told Papa that it would be the finest invention they had ever come up with, the greatest feat of any blacksmith in the world. But Jonathan didn't want to hear his pleadings; Aaron could tell by the way he stared into the narrow alley at the bottom of Water Street long after Daniel had turned into it.

"You'd better come along, son." Jonathan crossed to the shop, unlatched the door and before going inside he said, "The woman wants her bow by Passover."

CHAPTER 4

"Eat your fill my little ones."

Mima set the tray of seeds and dried figs on the floor of the pigeon coop, yanked her thick arm out, and shut the wicker door. None of the birds got away, at least for now, but with such a poorly crafted cage there was no telling how long she'd be able to keep them inside. The coop was held together by cords she found in the manger, rusted nails she pried from the charred remains of a chair, and pieced from left over wood in the firebox—small lengths of tinder that would never be used to fire any more pots, at least not any pots crafted by Josiah the potter or any of his servants.

Mima was not a carpenter and this was not a rock dove's roost; it was a potter's yard. She glanced about the empty precincts. It was a fine pottery yard, except for the pile of rubble and ash along the north side that was once the potter's estate. And it was a shame there weren't any workers still drawing a wage on the potter's treasury, then she could have had them build this pigeon's coop instead of assembling the thing herself. But Mima was alone, the only caretaker left on the property and Josiah's dying wish was that she care for these pigeons as a mother tends her young. It wasn't really his dying wish. Josiah was alive and living with Rebekah at the secret city called Qumran on the shores of the Dead Sea, but it was his most earnest desire and she guarded these pigeons with her life.

Mima and her three pigeons took up residence in the mud-brick servants' quarters after the fire. It didn't possess the charm of the potter's estate, but what it lacked in appeal, it made up for in sheer size. And thank heavens there were six hearths or she would have caught a death of chills from the winter cold. The chimneys sprouted from the flat rooftop like watchtowers looking down over the pottery yard. There was one rising above the roof of the main room, two above the kitchen, and three in the sleeping rooms built to house the turners, wedgers, claymen, and the kilnmaster. She let all the help go after the fire with a promise she would send for them when the work resumed. But she never told them that the firing yard would never produce another piece of pottery, at least not under her ownership. Josiah and Rebekah were gone and she would follow them to Qumran as soon as she sold the property and disposed of the potter's holdings. And until she left the city she was Josiah's eyes and ears, informing him of any danger that could come to the Rekhabites.

It shouldn't be too difficult to sell the pottery yard. The kiln hadn't suffered any damage in the fire. There were three good-sized piles of clay, another of white sand, and the turning and wedging tables sat waiting for a new potter to come and make his pots. The only difficulty would be finding a buyer who could afford such a fine piece of land in the center of the city. She'd have to sell it quietly, without Laban finding out until after it was done and she was gone. Such a pity to sell this place with high, whitewashed walls surrounding an acre of memories. It was within these grounds that she raised Rebekah from a babe into a lovely woman, and she'd spent the better part of her life serving master Josiah. He wasn't really a master. He was like a brother, always keeping her welfare utmost in his thinking and giving her the most treasured prize of all—an understanding of Yeshua the Anointed One. There was nothing that brought more peace to her soul than looking forward to the coming of the Messiah, and she had Josiah to thank for that.

Mima tapped the side of the coop, but none of the pigeons looked up from pecking at the seeds and lapping at the small water bowl. They were filthy little beasts, but she treated them like her own; and since Josiah and Rebekah were the only family she knew, these pigeons would have to fill the emptiness for now. She didn't take well to animals, but there was something about these gray and blue-feathered creatures that captured her heart, something deep in her soul that told her to care for them well.

Mima wedged a twig in the latch to keep the pesky pigeons from pushing open the coop door and sneaking out. A child understood the meaning of a firm hand across the backside, but a pigeon? There was nothing worse than chasing down the little creatures. They hopped about the yard and hid in the smallest nooks and crannies and they didn't have the sense to mind. If she told them to eat they cooed, if she sang them a song they ignored her melodies and waddled to the back of the coop to preen, and if the shadows fell across their perch, they fluttered about inside until she moved them to a warmer spot in the yard.

These pigeons were a bother, but she suffered their fickleness in silence. Well, maybe not entirely in silence, but since she was the only one living on the property, she could choose her words. It was the cleaning that brought out her most colorful language. If the pigeons didn't mess their coop so much she wouldn't have reason to scold them and threaten to let them live in their own mess. But these pigeons were raised for flight, not food, and she made certain they lived in the most habitable accommodations. They were her charge, and though they were the culprits behind her vulgarity, she would endure them as long as they had power to save the Rekhabites from the wrath of Captain Laban.

Mima moved the coop out from the shadows of the back wall and let them preen their feathers in full view of the morning sun. The coop came level with her eyes, and since she was only as tall as she was wide, she had to lean up on her tiptoes to tap on the side and get them to look at her. She had taken a liking to them, though the stirring within her whispered of a bond deeper than simple fondness. She had the power to keep these pigeons alive from day to day with seeds and water, and the pigeons had the power to deliver messages tied to their legs. They were messenger pigeons, trained by Josiah to fly to Qumran in less time than it takes to cook a lentil soup in the hearth. She would have sent a good many messages to Josiah and Rebekah, but she couldn't, not if she wanted to have them around in case of more desperate times. There were only three birds in her care, and once they had flown the coop, she'd not get them back without riding to Qumran for them. These birds only knew to fly one direction, and as soon as their flight was finished they didn't know the way back to Jerusalem.

Mima glanced up at the morning sun hanging in the eastern sky. Rebekah and Josiah were out there somewhere, hiding beneath the rays of a desert sun and all she could do was pray for God to keep them safe until she could come to them and see to their needs. They had no one to prepare their meals, clean their home, or wash their clothes. Rebekah was not the most experienced housekeeper and Josiah had never peeled an onion or seasoned a cut of lamb in his life. And though there was hardly a need for a maidservant in the desert, when they were reunited she would find a way to prepare a meal of lamb and lentil soup in their camp along the shores of the Dead Sea. And she'd be with them just as soon as she saw to selling the property and got out from under the watchful eye of Laban and his men. He could never find out that she'd masterminded Josiah's escape. Laban had murdered men for lesser indiscretions, and the sooner she was away from his scrutiny the better.

The pigeons quieted their cooing, and in the stillness of the pottery yard Mima heard the echo of Josiah's sweet voice. He was directing the wedgers to mix in more sand and the turners to take their place at the spinning tables. Mima turned her ears toward the front gate. His voice sounded so real, so close. It was as clear and strong as . . .

"I have a place for you, Mima."

It couldn't be Josiah marching through the open gates of the pottery yard. He crossed through the rubble of the potter's former residence and raised the powdery black ash in a cloud around him like a ghost returning from the dead. It certainly wasn't Josiah. She was daydreaming and in her haste to spin around and greet the stranger, her arm brushed the coop, and the green and red bead bracelet around her dark-skinned wrist caught on the rough-cut ends of the wood slats and pulled the rickety wicker crate to the ground in a cracking of slats and small timbers. The birds fluttered about, and the one named Isabel hopped through the half-opened wicker door and stretched her legs. Jeruzabel and Samantha followed, but Mima caught them by their tail feathers and returned them to the cage.

Isabel waddled over into the rubble of the potter's home and Mima had to dirty herself in the black ash, crawling about the piles of broken brick and calling for Isabel to come and perch on her hand. She was cooing at Mima when the stranger said, "I have a place for you."

She glanced up to find him hovering over her. He wore a tight-fitting gray tunic with a black cloak that wrapped about his shoulders and hung down past the silver chains and leather pleats of his kilt. It was Captain Laban and his stout frame and straight jaw hardly moved when he said, "I've come to take you away from this . . ." He stabbed the toe of his boot into the ash. "This dreary place."

"Captain, sir." Mima pulled her green shawl tight over her shoulders and across her front. Her hands were covered with black ash and they soiled the cloth with handprints. "You needn't worry about me. I have plenty of wood for the fire, there's more than enough room in the servants' quarters, and I haven't had any trouble with thieves about the place." She leaned forward to snatch the pigeon from between a charred roof beam and a pile of toppled bricks, but the bird jumped from her reach and she ended up with a handful of ash. "Silly bird, come back here this instant!"

"Look at you, crawling to catch your lunch." Laban jumped after the bird, his long, powerful stride lifting him over the pile of bricks like a jackal chasing down its prey. He landed near the pigeon and his quick hand caught hold of its tail feathers. "I have a place for you to live where you'll never have to worry about feeding yourself again." He held the bird's neck between his fingers.

"Not Isabel!" Mima plucked the bird from Laban's hand. "Don't hurt her."

"You have names for your food?"

"Only my favorite meals." Mima stroked the pigeon's head and didn't say any more about Isabel, not if she wanted to keep Laban from asking more questions about her messenger pigeons. He could never know that she planned to use these birds to warn Josiah. Mima said, "What were you saying about this dreary place?"

"I have more work for you."

Mima held the pigeon close. What poor timing this was. All she wanted to do was sell the pottery yard, pack her things and get out from under the scrutiny of the very man who was hiring her to do another evil deed. She said, "More, sir?"

"I'll pay you twice what I paid you to get rid of the potter."

Mima pulled her shawl up around her neck, the ashen handprints filling her with the strong smell of an old fire. If Laban only knew the details of how she'd gotten rid of the potter, he'd not pay her a shekel. She said, "Can't you find another to do this?"

"There's no one like you."

"Thank you, Captain." Mima nodded and smiled a weak smile. "But I'm not up to— "

"All you have to do is keep an eye on Miriam."

"The queen?"

"That's right." Laban adjusted his cape about his shoulders. "No fires, no deaths, nothing but watch the queen for me."

"I hardly know the woman."

"I'm hiring you as her handservant."

Mima tucked the pigeon under her arm. "Does she approve?"

"I hire the help at the palace." Laban set his hands on his hips, his cape flowing down over his elbows. "You'll keep a room on the fifth floor, directly across the hall from the royal family. You'll eat with Miriam, help her dress, do her hair and whatever else handservants do."

"That's the work I was trained for."

"It isn't the work I'm paying you for." Laban took Mima by the arm, pressing her bead bracelet into her wrist. "The queen should do nothing without your knowing every detail."

"Exactly what details am I watching for?"

Laban glanced around the empty yard. There was no one about to overhear them. "I believe Miriam is the palace informant."

Mima caught her breath. How did he know that? Miriam had some contact with the potter, but Josiah had covered that as innocent pot buying. It was Mulek who did the informing, delivered messages and spied on men at his mother's request. They worked together and though Mima knew about their work, they didn't know that she knew. To Miriam and Mulek, Mima was simply the potter's maidservant. Mima said, "Queen Miriam a spy; that's impossible."

"I used to think that myself. But not anymore, not since the coronation." Laban tightened his grip on Mima's wrist. "Uriah's trial is coming, and if Miriam is the informant I think she is, she'll do anything to save him, including giving herself away."

Mima pulled free. "I'm hardly someone Miriam would trust."

"It should be a simple matter to gain her confidence. You'll be with her constantly."

"Why me, Captain?"

"You've proven yourself loyal."

Mima started toward the pigeon coop. She stepped around a charred doorframe and past a pile of blackened brick. "I burnt this place to the ground because I was selfish, not because I was loyal."

Laban followed alongside Mima, kicking away the burned timbers from his path. He pulled out a talent of silver, the five-sided coin glimmering in the sunlight. "This should satisfy your selfishness."

"It's a start." Mima snatched the silver piece from Laban's palm. If he only knew how wrong he was to hire her. Mima and Miriam were Rekhabites, bound together by a belief in the Anointed One, and in these days of trouble, the Messiah was the only one who could be trusted. It wasn't the best timing, to be sure, but by putting off the sale of the property and delaying her flight to join Josiah and Rebekah at Qumran, she could be of some help to those who needed it most.

Mima said, "I'll need something to win the heart of the princes."

"Exactly what sort of something?"

"Pigeons." Mima stopped in front of the coop, the birds cooing at her arrival. She took Isabel out from under her arm. "These should do."

Laban threw the pleats of his cape back over his shoulder, his powerful chest pulling on the cloth with each breath. "We have enough of them flying about the palace to entertain you and the royal sons."

"Then you won't mind a few more."

"Be at the palace gates the first of the week and I'll see that you and your . . ." Laban glanced at Isabel, cuddled between Mima's hands. "Your friends are shown to your room."

Mima waited until Laban disappeared onto Main Street before she hurried inside the servants' quarters. She skirted past the hearth, ducked beneath the beam of a small doorway and came into a small, musty reading room where she kept a supply of Josiah's writing things. There was a stylus, bits of leather, a small bottle of ink, and string. She guarded them here, never knowing when she might need them and this matter required her first message to Qumran. She scratched the stylus over the leather, certain to mention Aaron, the son of the blacksmith—news that would interest Rebekah—followed by a careful explanation of exactly what she needed them to do to aid in her plans at the palace. She ended her message with the most important phrase of all—*Send them all immediately.*

Mima folded the note around Isabel's leg, tied it secure with string, then carried her to the door and threw her into the sky. She fluttered about the branches of a Joshua tree, perched on the back wall, glanced at Mima and then she was away, soaring over the pottery and headed east toward the Dead Sea. Heaven be praised! The bird could actually fly the right direction, just like Josiah promised she would.

Mima hurried across the yard as Isabel flapped her wings and rode the rising current up the face of the Mount of Olives. She pulled up at the back gate of the property and watched Isabel fly past the summit out of sight beyond the crest of scrub oak that rimmed the top of the hill. Isabel was gone and Mima prayed she found Josiah in the desert.

"Do you know what this means my little ones?" Mima stuck her fingers through the slats in the coop and stroked the heads of the remaining pigeons. "We're moving to the palace."

* * *

"Do you hear?" Rebekah shook the end of her broom at the sand. She was surrounded by countless dunes with uncountable, filthy, dirty, impossible-to-sweep grains that found their way inside the tent no matter how tightly she tied the flaps or staked the cords to the ground. "Don't come back inside or I'll fire you into a pot, I will!"

The tent stood on the brow of a hill above the Dead Sea, with rocky bluffs rising behind it and the tents of Rekhabite families arranged in neat rows on either side. Down the rise, three women stopped gathering kindling and stood to watch Rebekah shake her broom at the ground and shout. And when she spied them staring, she offered them a weak smile, a hasty good morning and quickly went back inside, pulling the tent flaps down behind her. What was she doing, talking to the sand like that? She leaned against the center tent pole and stared. Was this desert wilderness turning her into a fool? She'd never known a sane woman to scold the sand, at least not in public and she went back to sweeping the grains off the hard-packed dirt floor of her new home.

A breeze picked up off the beach, hurried up into the rocky bluffs and carried another gust of sand inside the tent. Oh bother! Why did she take the time to clean anything in this desert? The wind off the

Dead Sea pelted the tent with sand last night and now it was blowing under the pegs at the base and leaving a layer of grit over everything. The boys in the tent next door said it was only a nuisance in winter, but the woman across the way said the winds were just as strong during the summer and at this rate Rebekah was due to sweep the entire beach before spring. She brushed the last of the sand out the door and ordered it never to return, but she said it under her breath and kept her insanity to herself.

Rebekah folded her father's sleeping mat and stacked it near the back of the small animal hide tent. There was enough room to store the blankets behind the horse saddles and she fluffed two sleeping pillows as large as she could and made them over into dining chairs. They were pieced together from goatskins and stuffed with dried cottonwood seeds and since they had nothing else in this deserted place to make dining comfortable, the pillows kept her and Josiah from sitting on the cold, hard ground to eat their food.

Josiah was gone out to see if there were any fish to be netted in this desolate sea they called dead while Rebekah stayed behind to prepare the same meal they'd eaten every morning since coming to these desperate circumstances. She dragged the half-full sack of wheat from behind the saddlebags and spooned out three measures to make flat bread and not a spoonful more—not if the wheat were to last until Josiah made a trip to Jericho. The wheat was poorly milled, without leaven, and it didn't make the best tasting bread, though it did have the power to keep her from going faint between meals.

Rebekah sifted the milled wheat and picked out the largest bits of chaff. If only Papa would catch some fish this morning, then she'd have the energy of spirit to endure living in a musty tent away from the comforts of their life in Jerusalem. But Papa had been setting nets for a month and he'd gotten nothing. If he didn't catch any fish today, she had a mind to dig through the sandy beaches and see if she could find any shellfish and make a meal of them, no matter how unclean they were. It wasn't such an awful breach of the law in exchange for a full stomach, though she was certain there was nothing living in the sands of this awful desert wilderness.

Rebekah poured a portion of water into the bowl and mixed it into the wheat. It was the only bowl Josiah allowed her to bring from

Jerusalem. And since Papa hadn't fired any new pottery, hadn't built a turner's wheel or started on the foundation of a kiln, this mixing bowl was destined to be her only bowl for a very long while. She threw in a pinch of salt—the one ingredient she never lacked in this barren place along the shores of a salt sea—and a hint of basil before reaching out the tent door and dropping the dough onto the cooking stones in the center of their fire pit without leaving the confines of her tent. It was better that she didn't make another appearance until her neighbors forgot that she'd lost her mind over a few grains of sand.

Josiah would be back from the sea soon and he'd tell her that they were going to live as fine a life here as they had in Jerusalem and he'd say it without a fish to show for his morning's work. He'd not caught a single fish since coming here and it didn't seem there were any to catch in this sea of salt. Didn't he remember how fine a life they left in Jerusalem? No, they hadn't left it, they'd burned it to the ground—a five-bedroom estate home with a dining room large enough to seat twenty, a kitchen, store-rooms, and wine cellars—and escaped to live in this, this . . .

Rebekah pushed the hair from in front of her eyes with the back of her wrist. She shouldn't let the rigors of this wilderness beset her. They had wheat for bread and thankfully their little settlement was set at the headwaters of a small spring with enough drinking water to support all two hundred and seventy-two of them. It wasn't cool like the waters that flowed from the Gihon Spring in Jerusalem and it had a bitter aftertaste, but thirst had a way of making the poor water pure.

She put away the sack of wheat and began packing the floor. It was a ritual she performed every morning before the first meal of the day—sprinkle water over the dirt, take off her sandals and walk about like a flat-footed fowl. It wasn't the prettiest of bird ballets, but it packed the dirt tight in place and no one could see her waddling about except for . . .

The neighbor boy? What was he doing, standing at the entrance of the tent peering in at her? He'd caught her dancing like a duck and there was nothing she could do, but keep dancing. "Good morning, sir." She finished a pass down one side of the tent and started up the other. He was her closest neighbor, and he lived with his father and three brothers in the tent just around a stand of rocks. He was a tall boy, thin as a door-post, with dark-blonde hair, blue eyes, and he was the image of . . .

Rebekah turned away from his grin and hurried another pass over the floor. She could never look at him for very long, especially when he was looking at her. He was the image of Aaron; he talked with the same steady pitch in his voice, and he walked with the same buoyant stride as she imagined Aaron would if he could, and some day she prayed he would. She closed her eyes and she could see Aaron, walking to the blacksmith shop with the help of crutches, suffering in silence the pain that must still haunt his burned feet—pain that she would never understand. Not once did he ever call attention to his crippled feet or declare that he could not endure his lot in life, and it was a pure shame to think she couldn't endure hers. Rebekah lowered her head. Forgive her, God, for complaining about her new life at Qumran.

The neighbor boy pulled back the flaps and stood to his full height, his face disappearing above the level of the roof. He was exactly as tall as she'd remembered Aaron to be—three cubits and two hands. He said, "Are you all right?"

"Me?" Rebekah rubbed away the blush that flashed across her cheeks. "Why would anything be wrong?"

"I heard an awful cry."

Rebekah covered her bare feet with the hem of her robe. "It was the sand."

"The sand?"

Rebekah stepped back into the shadows of the tent, to hide the blush she could feel flashing across her cheeks. "That's right."

He turned his head to the side. "You're certain you're all right?"

Rebekah offered a weak smile. "I'm perfectly fine."

"If there's anything . . ." He backed from the door. "Anything at all I can do for you, please ask." He took another step and his feet came down around the bobbing head of a pigeon. What was the bird doing pecking about the door of her tent? The fowl should have skittered away at the first brush with the neighbor boy's boots, but it stepped inside, groused about, then waddled back outside as if it knew the way. The tent wasn't much larger than a pigeon coop, but she'd never known a wild bird to seek refuge inside a tent.

There weren't any pigeons nesting in the cliffs above camp. The men had snared as many of them as possible for food, and the rest had headed south for the winter, away from the stir of humanity. This one must have gotten lost and it would certainly end up skewered over a fire pit if it didn't fly away soon. A narrow black beak sprouted from its face with a white band of flesh at the base. It craned its neck and peered with a single teardrop yellow eye, then quickly turned again to stare with the other. It had a cap of gray-blue feathers and a brilliant run of purple down the front that turned to dark blue near the bird's legs—long spindly legs except the left one where a small roll of parchment was tied with a . . .

Why didn't she recognize Isabel's gray tail feathers splotched with dark blue sooner? Rebekah raised her hand for the neighbor boy to keep still. It was the first of Papa's messenger pigeons to find its way from Jerusalem with word from Mima, and she wasn't about to let anything frighten it away. She knelt down beside the bird and reached out to let her jump onto her palm when the neighbor boy fell on it with both hands, caging it against the ground. He said, "I got it!"

"Let her go!" Rebekah slapped the back of his hand. "She isn't an ordinary pigeon."

"She's dinner."

Men. Why did they always think with their stomachs? Rebekah peeled back the neighbor boy's thumbs and the pigeon stuck its head out, cooing loud and pecking at his hand. She took Isabel from him, picked away the knot in the string and removed the note, quickly reading Mima's pen strokes that unfolded in her hand.

All was well in Jerusalem. Nothing but the estate home had burned in the fire and Mima was living in the servant's quarters at the back of the estate. There was one thing that she should know about Aaron. Oh my. Rebekah glanced up from the note. It had news about Aaron and she quickly folded it in half. She couldn't stay inside the tent to read the rest. She had to go to her secret place, away from the musty smell of hides and the watchful eye of the neighbor boy who did not understand her joy.

"I have to feed the pigeons." Rebekah hurried out with Isabel in hand and left the neighbor boy standing at the entrance. She sprinted up the rise, picked her way over the crags and twists in the outcrops beyond camp and came onto a path leading up five steep switchbacks and out onto the summit above the Dead Sea. She walked along the ridge top toward the pigeon coops, the tent city of Qumran spreading out below her. There were forty-seven brown, animal-hide dwellings, raised on poles that stuck out the rooftops like spears pointing toward heaven. The tents sat on a swell of earth away from the open beach and protected on every side by rocky cliffs in a secluded alcove. They were organized in rows around the center of the community, each tent door opening onto the main building. It wasn't really a building, with half the foundation yet to be laid and not a single stone above ground level. But Papa called it a building and from this height the rooms were set out like an architect's drawing. There was foundation stone laid around a large room at the east end for the community to gather for meals, and half the foundation was set in place around two small changing rooms that opened onto an out-of-doors washing pool. And one day there would be a canal running from the spring that bubbled at the base of the cliffs down through a series of pools in the heart of camp—the first pool for drinking water, then one for baptism, and the last ones for bathing and livestock. But until the men of camp lined a canal with stone and sealed it to keep the water from seeping into the sand, there would never be any flowing water.

Up here, above camp, she was free of the putrid smell of stagnant brine that hovered along the west shores of the Dead Sea every morning and poisoned the air down low with a foul odor after a night of wind. Her hair came up off her shoulders, and the loose linen in her robe pulled taut about her legs like the open sails of a ship returning to port, but Rebekah was not headed home. Not now, not ever. They had left the city of their God, never to go back, and the note delivered by this pigeon was her only tie to the life she'd left behind.

They were safe here along the brackish waters of the Dead Sea. Qumran—the city of salt—was a suitable prison for Rebekah's heart and she would grow old here, never to return to the city where she left her love. It was a cruel twist of fate that separated her from Aaron and she had died twice for it—once when she faked her fiery death, and again when Josiah told her that she could never see Aaron again. Josiah had begged the blacksmith's mercy in her behalf, but Jonathan would not hear a voice from the grave and sent Josiah away telling him he could never reveal to Aaron that Rebekah was alive or Jonathan would see the Rekhabites hunted like outlaws. Rebekah was dead and the blacksmith would keep her buried from his son.

Two cages crafted of thin timbers and lashed together with cords, stood on the edge of the outcrop. Three pigeons hopped about inside the first cage, their purple, blue, and white feathers gleaming in the morning sun and their wings flapping about ready to take flight and deliver their messages to Mima. The other cage was empty. Josiah prepared it for the birds he left with Mima, the ones he'd trained to fly from their pottery yard to this hilltop coop, thirty miles away from the trouble they left in Jerusalem.

Rebekah leaned against the coop, opened the message, and began to read: *the God of Heaven has worked a miracle for your beloved Aaron. His feet are well and whole and he walks without crutches.* Rebekah glanced up into the sky above Qumran. It was a clear day with white clouds flowing across the blue heavens and a large yellow sun rising over the Dead Sea. She tried to brush the tears from her checks, but they kept coming and her shoulders began to shudder with the pain she'd kept hidden from Josiah, but up here, away from the watchful eyes in camp, she could mourn her plight. Aaron was whole and for that she thanked God. If only she had lived in a different time. Moses had only Pharaoh's army to reckon with, but she would never see Aaron again, the blacksmith had made it so, and for that she must suffer a thousand plagues for her exodus and drown her sorrow in a sea of tears that would not part. She shouldn't regret so deeply her loss, for all was not lost. But how could she trust the Healer's art, and through Him learn to love again?

Rebekah turned her gaze back to Mima's note. There was more, and it was of the utmost importance that she follow the instructions without fail. She pried open the coop with the messenger pigeons trained to fly to the pottery yard, lifted them out and threw them into the sky. In a flutter of feathers they were away, turning immediately west toward Jerusalem, and Rebekah couldn't keep her hopeful heart from flying with them. If there be wings to carry prayer, let them take flight and bear this up to the throne of heaven.

Dear God, would she see Aaron again?

Slippery little creatures! Josiah quickly drew his fishing net out of the water hand-over-hand and found the reason for its emptiness. The net had caught on a piece of drift wood and cut open a hole the size of a melon, but he could hope it was the teeth of a large fish that got away, though it didn't seem there were any living creatures in these desolate waters. There had to be some fish and though he had little skill in fishing, he was determined to be the first to catch one and provide a decent meal for his daughter. At least that's what he'd tell Rebekah when he got back to the tent without anything but a branch of drift-wood to show for this morning's work. There had to be something fit to eat swimming in these waters and as soon as he mended this net he'd try farther down along the shore, over where the beach ended and the bluffs turned into the sea. He could stand on the outcrop and cast his net into the deep blue pool that didn't look to have a single bit of sea grass coloring the water green; or maybe he'd move north where the flat beach didn't have near as much salt caked along its shore.

Isaiah said that the people of God were to prepare the desert for the coming of the Messiah and make it blossom like a rose. Josiah pried the driftwood out of the net and threw it out onto the parched beach. There was not a rosebush to be found in this wilderness and not another soul living within twenty miles of Qumran. No bedouin tribesmen came this way in search of grasses to feed their livestock. There was barely enough fresh water gurgling from the spring near camp to keep alive the families he brought to this place, and even if Josiah could find enough water to reap a harvest, there was not a seed that would grow in these salty soils. It didn't seem this desert would ever blossom with anything but thistle and thorn, no matter how strict Josiah was to obey the law of Moses. If this was not the desert Isaiah intended or the time for the advent of heaven, could they at least ask for a little rain to ease the burden of their exile? That would be blessing enough and Josiah would let another generation wait on the roses.

Josiah pulled his empty fishing net from the water and dragged it up the salt-covered beachhead. Maybe Rebekah was right; maybe there weren't any fish to be caught in this salt-laden sea, but he wasn't about to give up on their hunger until he was certain. Josiah was a potter, not a fisherman. He would build a kiln one day and train wedgers and turners to work the clay, but there was little rush in this desert land where the only deed more lifesaving than finding food was finding God. It was Josiah's wisdom concerning the law and his teaching of it that brought these families to live in this place and they found much more comfort in his words than they ever did in a new pot.

Josiah untied the bandana from around his neck and laid it on his head like a mop rag, with a rim of gray hair trimming the sides about his ear. His hair had grown long enough to comb over in place of the bandana, but he preferred the coolness of a bald head to the constant combing that style required, and he adjusted the cloth over the tenderest skin on his scalp. It was more than enough protection against the winter sun, and he didn't need a hat to shade his cherry red cheeks nor a cap of hair to save him the pain of sunburn. Josiah was dressed in a short brown robe that covered his knees. Rebekah said it made him look younger; but he didn't need youth. He wanted freedom, and the day he came to Qumran he traded the long black robes of an Elder for the garments of a desert nomad, and these quaint clothes suited him much better than the elegant attire of Zadock's council. Something about the wealth and power of a man's fashion didn't sit well with his common sensibilities and Josiah was happy to retire the costume of his former life. He would not dress another day after the manner of the Chief Elder and play the man's desperate game of pitch and toss. Rebekah was his only child and he would not risk her life for another day of opulent city living.

Josiah rolled the net into a ball, threw it over his shoulders, and trudged up the hill and onto the sandy plateau of camp where the tents of his neighbors were set in neat rows like the main street in Jerusalem; and since every resident at Qumran came from the capital, there was a certain comfort in modeling this place after the city of God. There were the oblong tents that belonged to the two stonemasons, the accountant's tent set with new poles whittled from the dead branch of a Joshua tree, the cobbler's round tent and then three more that belonged to the baker, the scribe, and the tanner. Josiah's tent was the last one in the row, the one at the far end, over below the bluffs, and he started down between the other dwellings toward home.

Josiah was the leader of this community of city dwellers without a city. They were nomads by choice, come to live the law of Moses as they saw fit, and they looked to Josiah to teach them that law. He'd brought a copy of it from his treasury—nearly four scrolls with the sayings of

Moses written on them. There was not another soul among the Jews at Jerusalem as well versed in the law as Josiah. He understood it better than any lawyer, but that was no reason for the people of Qumran to look to him to teach them the ways of God. He was a man of faith, but he was not a prophet. If only Josiah could know the will of God concerning the Rekhabites. It was the prayer he offered every morning before leaving his tent and every evening before falling off to sleep. Would God please direct them? Josiah stopped beside the outcrop of rock near his tent and scanned the small desert community. The soil was barren here, the water poor, but they would grow to love it. They would stake their claim to these rocks, build a city out of this sand, and store in the caves above their homes a record that they lived and looked forward to the coming of their Redeemer—the Anointed One!

Josiah adjusted the net on his shoulders and headed around the outcrop of rocks to his tent. Rebekah would have morning meal ready by now and he stepped to the entrance of the . . .

Rebekah? Josiah dropped the net in the sand. Not the pigeons, girl! He started on a dead sprint for the path leading up to the ridge top. The pigeons were trained to fly to the pottery yard, and once they were away there was no getting them back, not unless he made a trip to Jerusalem and brought them back in a cage. The little creatures only knew to fly one way, but there she was, throwing the birds to the sky and watching them go.

Josiah climbed the switchbacks and came out onto the bluff above camp, the hem of his robe flapping against his thighs. He marched toward Rebekah with the fury of a thunderhead before the storm. "What have you done, girl!"

"He can walk, Papa. He can walk." Rebekah leaned against the pigeon coop with her gaze turned to the sky. She'd taken the tie out of her hair, and the breeze lifted it about her cheeks and caught the strands in her tears. Her deep brown eyes had gone a shade of red and when she turned from looking after the flight of the pigeons, he felt the pain of her gaze on him.

"What are you talking about?" Josiah grabbed for her arm. "Who can walk?"

Rebekah raised a leather parchment in her trembling hand and tried to speak, but her voice caught.

Josiah took it from her and when he read the message from Mima and the urgency in her words, he understood Rebekah's pain and he let go of her arm and his anger.

He held the note between his fingers and slowly read the first line. Mima had pressed hard with the pen and it was difficult to read all the words, but he could make out most of them. The prophet Uriah was in prison awaiting trial at the hands of Zadock, and Josiah was the only man who could match the Chief Elder's understanding of the law. Mima was moving to live at the palace and she would be there during the trial. Would he please send all the pigeons immediately so she could train them to fly there? It was an odd plan; there had never been a defense mounted for anyone accused of a crime by a lawyer in exile, but if Mima believed his skill in the law and his understanding of the mind of Zadock could help the prophet Uriah win his trial, then he was willing.

When Josiah reached the end of the message about Aaron and his feet Rebekah said, "Don't you see? It's a miracle."

Josiah folded the note in his hand. Poor girl. She had endured the loss of love all this time in silence and when he told her the blacksmith refused to tell Aaron she was still alive, she'd kept it in her heart without burdening him with her pain.

Josiah said, "That's right, my love. God is a God of miracles."

Rebekah fell into his arms.

CHAPTER 5

Daniel tore loose the knots sealing shut the elephant-hide quiver. He was to care for his arrows like a mother cares for her newborn and there was not a day that Daniel didn't fletch or sharpen them. The plumes were to be cleaned before archery training and he quickly reached inside to get the—

Cursed arrowhead! One of the stone-tipped points pierced his skin just below the thumb and split open his palm—the same arrowhead he'd sharpened early this morning on his father's grinding wheel. Why didn't he pack the arrows with the plumes up? He ripped a swath of cloth from the front tail of his military tunic and wrapped it around his hand. He'd get an earful from the quartermaster for ruining the shirt, but he wasn't about to lose a chance to learn the arts of bowmanship from the finest archer in the kingdom because of a bloody palm. He tied off the bandage with a pin-knot. The wrap would keep him from losing his grip on a bow, and he could endure the pain for a morning of shooting as long as it didn't ruin his aim.

Daniel tucked the torn end of his tunic out of sight under the belt of his kilt. He couldn't keep it from the eyes of the quartermaster forever, but Daniel's military appointment would be coming from Captain Laban any day and he'd not return the shirt for washing until then—commissioned officers with their own regiment didn't answer to the quartermaster for anything, and as soon as Daniel was assigned to duty he could do as he pleased with his tunics.

He reached his hand inside the gray leather quiver—this time without so much haste—and carefully took out the first arrow. The plumes were the last things he had to clean before training began, and if he didn't hurry he'd not be ready when the master archer arrived. The arrow had a long willow shaft, with three red stripes painted across the belly and a double-sided arrowhead sharper than any blade Daniel had known. He'd sharpened daggers on the grinding wheel and forged blades of the sharpest steel, but never anything as piercing as these arrows and he was happy to have left his blacksmithing life for a chance to learn the art of shooting them.

There was never a day Daniel apologized for trading his forging hammer for a weapon or giving up the tempering heat of the open hearth for training at the military grounds. There was no regret in his soul—he did not want to go back. Mama would have him follow in Aaron's footsteps, but his brother had chosen an outlawed path and Daniel would not limp down the same ridiculous road. Aaron's feet had healed themselves, but his mind was forever hobbled and if he did not waste his life away in the company of fools like Lehi, his brother would lose it in the foolish traditions of an unseen God. Daniel knelt in the red clay of the military training grounds, balanced the arrow across his thigh, and poured green cedar tea over the plume. It was the only proper way to clean them; just as there was only one proper course for Daniel—the path of a military officer—and he had the strength of his arm and the captain of the guard to thank for his place in Judah's army. Daniel could see the light in Laban's eyes whenever he wrestled. He had the same agile footwork as the captain, with thick arms and broad shoulders strong enough to throw the largest men across the wrestling pit, and the heart to take on any challenger and win. Daniel was the first wrestler to show the same promise as the captain; he was Laban's prodigy and for that he counted his blessings more times than a priest blesses an offering. He was the surrogate son Laban did not have and there was no faster way to rise through the ranks of the military than by the captain's adopting grace. Daniel was Laban's chosen and when the captain of the guard was no longer able to lead, he would be Laban's anointed one.

The green tea dripped from the end of the arrow and Daniel worked the liquid up the rigid end of the quill and over the soft feathers, coating them with a thin layer of oil to keep away the mites that preyed on the bright green, red, and yellow pheasant plumes. There was nothing worse than flea-bitten feathers and Daniel wasn't about to let his newly acquired arrows lose their balance because of a few flaws in the plumes—a commissioned officer couldn't be seen with a poor weapon. Daniel fanned the plumed end of the arrow in the breeze, drying the green tea and sealing the feathers with protecting oil. The plumes flashed their brilliant colors and in the silhouetting light of the early morning sun he could see the perfection in the feathers. There was not a single ragged end, no gnawed tips, and not a single crack in the quills. He stroked the weapon with his good hand. Someday he'd be an officer as true as this arrow—fierce, feared, and without a flaw.

The tall cedar doors of the main entrance groaned open and the clicking of officers' boots echoed from within the stone passage leading into the yard. They were measured steps, the same calculated stride Daniel had come to respect since the first day he came to these grounds to watch the wrestling. The object of his admiration appeared beneath the span of limestone block that arched above the way into the training grounds. Captain Laban wore a leather vest draped over his officer's tunic, and he strapped thick leather guards up the inside of both arms to protect against the recoil of a bowstring. He stood like a warrior prepared to do battle and scanned the training ground with a gaze as dark and penetrating as a hawk. His nostrils blew steam into the morning cold with a regular, pulsing rhythm, hiding the line of beard that came to a point at the tip of his chin. He'd cut his hair short, not like the young men of Egypt with their bald heads, but shorn like sheep at sheering time, his black hair bristling on end like the spines of a porcupine. Laban was a powerful man, with thick arms and wide shoulders and he stood as balanced as a man with perfect aim would stand. It was the stance of a master archer and Daniel straightened at the sight of him, pinning his shoulders back, spreading his feet to the same width as Laban's, and holding his hands at his side like the captain before nodding a greeting to the greatest archer the kingdom had ever known. Bowmanship was Laban's other talent and he could shoot an arrow as true as he could wrestle a man to the ground—at least that's what the other soldiers said. To wrestle like the captain was a dream beyond anything Daniel could hope for, but to learn his talent for a bow was to become a legend like Captain Laban was a legend. And of all the soldiers in the military he'd taken Daniel as his apprentice.

Captain Laban carried a full quiver of arrows on his back—the same willow-shafted, pheasant-plumed, red-belly-striped arrows he gifted to Daniel after his return from Elephantine. Said he deserved them because of his military skills. *Skills?* Daniel was the least seasoned cavalryman to be issued a horse and he 'd never strung a bow or wielded a sword. If Daniel hadn't captured the prophet Uriah, Laban never would have wanted him back nor trusted him with the secrets of his archery. Two bows hung crossways over Captain Laban's shoulders. They were fashioned out of the forgiving wood of a young blackwood tree, the only wood that could stand the pull of an archer's string and not break. Bows made from cedar were too weak, and bows from olive wood and willow too brittle, but a well-crafted bow of blackwood lasted a lifetime so long as it was kept oiled and away from the cold winter air.

Neither of the bows could be for Daniel's lesson; they were too fine for an apprentice. The newer bow was made of thin strips of blackwood pressed together in an elegant curved shape with horse gum and tree sap, just the right angle to bear the pull of a deep-drawn arrow.

Daniel quickly arranged his cleaned arrows back inside his quiver and put away the jar of green tea as the captain crossed the grounds. Laban said, "Hang this near the heat of a fire every night till spring. That should be enough for the new wood to cure."

Daniel hefted the wooden arms of the new bow between his hands like a priest holds a babe before circumcision. "This is for me?"

"You've earned it."

"But sir, I haven't done anything that— "

Laban handed over the weapon. "I wanted you to be the first to string her up."

Daniel ran his hand over the length of the curved blackwood, sanded to a smooth finish. A handgrip was cut halfway down the bow and when Daniel picked it up his thick fingers fit perfectly into the shape of it. The wood was new, he could tell by the strong, pungent smell—like walking through a seaside forest in his former home of

Sidon after a rain—and it mixed with the horse gum and filled the air with the scent of a new bow.

Daniel dug his thumbnail into the wood and pulled up a moist sliver. "The wood's still young."

"Don't worry, son. You'll not have any trouble with her; she can endure the pull of your arrows." Laban crossed his powerful arms over his chest and nodded. "I got my first blackwood bow when I was your age." His gaze was fixed on Daniel but he was looking past him and for a moment he could see himself when he was Daniel's age—a young, seventeen-year-old man with dark, black hair, a fresh young face with hardly a growth of beard, and eyes filled with the passion to become the kingdom's strongest wrestler and finest archer. It was the same passion that flowed through Daniel's veins, and with each beat of his heart he could feel its fervor.

Daniel held the bow up to the sun and let the newly cut and carpentered grains catch the morning light. "I don't know what to say, sir."

"I say it's time for your first training." Laban slipped his bow off his shoulders and held it up next to Daniel's. They were the same size, with blackwood shaped into identical curves, notches cut the same width, and three red, painted stripes to match the stripes on the arrows. "If you want to become a great archer, you have to learn on the finest bows." He looped a string around the lower notch of his bow then held it in the sand with the back of his leg while he looped the upper notch. Daniel did the same to his bow, arching its long arms back like a catapult loaded and ready to launch a fireball over a fortress wall.

Laban turned sideways toward the target—a sack of wheat hanging from a rope—and inched his left foot forward, just far enough to give him a steady stance but not put him off balance. He stood as motionless as a lion before it strikes, and when he let go of the string, the bow snapped straight and the arrow disappeared. Daniel couldn't see it go, but he could hear the shrill sound of it piercing the morning air and echoing off the walls before landing square in the middle of the target, its red and yellow plumes sprouting out from the sack of wheat.

Laban said, "Pull the bowstring back level with your nose and don't release the arrow until you've found your balance and you have the target fixed in your mind. It's all in your— "

A flock of winter geese flew overhead and immediately Laban fell silent. He quickly notched an arrow and drew his bow as fast as lightning strikes, though lightning was never as steady nor sure as Captain Laban's aim. His arrow hit the lead bird and before the carcass reached the ground, he strung another arrow and struck a second fowl. His shot was sure, and his agile feet were light on the ground and Daniel added the Captain's skill with a bow to his growing list of the man's virtues. No, not virtues—they were gifts and Laban possessed them in full measure, the same gifts Daniel was blessed with as long as he had Laban to teach him how to reach down inside his soul and bring them out.

Laban said, "Aim high and sight three fingers above the target or your arrow will end well short of the wheat sack. And don't over draw. The bow is strong, but it isn't made of steel."

Made of steel? Daniel took an arrow from his quiver and notched the plumed end to the string. His brother was the only one he'd ever heard speak of a bow smithed of steel. Aaron talked about it endlessly—said that one day bowmaking would bring more business to their shop than smithing swords. But Aaron was dreaming—if he thought he could ever craft a bow out of steel. No, he wasn't dreaming, he was a fool. There had never been a bow made of steel and there never would be, no matter how many times Aaron claimed he was going to smith a metal bow as a gift for Lehi's son—Nephi, the one Daniel had beaten in a wrestling match. Sariah said Nephi was a fine archer, but he was really a spoiled child with a fool for a father. Daniel drew the bowstring a bit tighter and he could feel the power of the weapon vibrating in his palm. Why did Aaron ever make the plantation owners his friends? They were the wrong sort of people, no matter how much wealth they had gathered in their years of olive oil selling.

Laban said, "How is your brother?"

"Aaron?"

"That's right, the crippled one."

"He isn't crippled anymore, sir." Daniel slowly drew the plume end of the arrow level with his nose and sighted down the shaft. "His burns have healed."

Laban lowered his voice to a growl. "Was it a miracle?"

"No, sir." Daniel answered quickly, his voice barking with resolve. There was no mistaking his tone; he did not want Captain Laban to think he believed in such foolishness as heavenly visions and miraculous healings. That was the stuff of Rekhabites and any tie with that rabble would keep Laban from granting him his first assignment as a fully commissioned officer. Daniel said, "Aaron's feet healed themselves no matter what he says about— "

"About Lehi?"

Daniel glanced up from sighting down the shaft. "You know about that?"

"I know everything, son. It's my job." Laban stepped close, enough to run his fingers lightly over the drawn string in Daniel's bow. It was a perilous place to stand, but the captain understood the recoil of a bow, and if he wanted to position that close so be it. Who was Daniel to deny him his risk-taking? Laban said, "What else does Aaron say about Lehi?"

"My brother is a fool to believe anything that man says." Daniel steadied the bow in his hand and adjusted his aim until the arrow was pointed well above the level of the sack of wheat—about the right arc to cross the distance to the target and not fall short in the sand. "All that about seeing visions and such, sir. Its nothing but the foolish imaginings of a visionary man—he's nothing but *pequeah*, sir."

Laban leaned in to inspect Daniel's draw. He said, "Did Aaron say anything about Lehi's lineage?"

Lineage? Daniel kept his head steady and didn't look at Laban. The captain's relationship to Lehi was the secret he'd heard the night he fell drunk in the Jawbone Inn—the secret Laman, Lemuel, and Laban didn't know that Daniel had overheard. He said, "Aaron's never said anything about such things, sir."

"You're wrong."

A cold sweat wetted Daniel's palms. How did Laban find out that he knew the prophet Lehi was his cousin? He said, "Wrong about what, sir?"

"Your draw. It's all wrong. Sight a little higher or you'll never get the arrow across the yard."

"Yes, sir." Daniel raised his aim. The captain's questioning wasn't about his family ties to Lehi, at least he thought it wasn't until Laban walked a circle around Daniel like a tailor measuring him for a garment and said, "I want you to watch your brother for me." He pulled on Daniel's shoulders until they were straight as hewn timbers, stabbed his toe at the back of Daniel's boot until he got the right stance, and adjusted the angle of Daniel's elbow until it was as straight and true as a carpenter's plumb.

Daniel said, "What am I watching for?"

"Anything that has to do with Lehi. Do you understand? I want to know what your brother knows about the man."

Daniel nodded slowly and sighted his arrow another two fingers higher in order to . . .

What was he doing? He didn't need to adjust his aim for the length of the yard. The target stood a hundred paces away and he had more than enough strength to send this tiny little arrow screeching there. He lowered the bow and sighted the tip of the arrow straight at the sack of wheat.

Laban said, "That's too low, boy, raise your sight."

Daniel inched the string past his nose, level with his ear. The top arm of the bow bent back into his brow and the bottom arm pushed against his hip.

Laban said, "Steady, son, or you'll break the bow."

The bow was made of the finest hardwood and there was no way Daniel could break it. He drew the plumed end of the arrow past the level of his shoulder and then he drew it bit more until he could feel the power inside the blackwood shaking the handgrip like a tree branch in a strong wind.

"Daniel!" Laban reached for the bow. "That's too deep a draw, you're going to— "

A horrible crack splintered above the sound of Laban's words. The bow arms snapped and the arrow fell to the ground. Daniel turned his head as the jagged ends of the broken bow flew past, missing his jaw and stabbing into the sand behind him. Except for the stinging red line across his arm and shoulder where the bowstring snapped against his skin, Daniel wasn't hurt. He walked slowly toward the crippled weapon. The arms had shattered near the handgrip and splinters hung about the cracked ends. He was a fool for not listening to Laban. He'd broken the captain's bow and there was no magic he could conjure to put it back together again.

Laban marched to Daniel's side, ripping his leather cloak off his shoulders as he came and throwing it at Daniel's feet. "Why didn't you obey me?"

"Well, I . . . I didn't think the bow would— "

"There's no excuse for this."

Daniel lowered his head. "It won't happen again, sir."

Laban leaned his head in next to Daniel's ear. "There won't be another time!" He pushed his face up next to Daniel, his eyes narrowed and his shoulders hunched forward. "My word is the only word you're to obey."

"Yes, sir." Daniel kept his head down.

"I'm the only man you're to take orders from, do you understand?"

Of course he understood. Daniel wrapped his hands into fists at his side and his shoulders bristled with the embarrassment at the thought of losing the captain's trust.

"Not even the king's orders have power over mine." Laban pressed Daniel's jaw between his thumb and fingers. It was a powerful grip and it puckered his lips and pressed his mouth against his teeth so that he couldn't speak. "Do you hear? You will listen only to me if you're to be the first officer of my fifty."

Daniel pulled his mouth free and rubbed the pain out of his cheeks. This was a test—Laban's harsh words, his intimidating stance—to see if Daniel could be trusted. It had to be if he was offering Daniel an assignment. He said, "Your fifty, sir?"

"I'm forming a company of special guards based at my estate, all fifty of them young, strong soldiers, the best recruits I've ever trained, and all of them loyal to me." Laban dug the heel of his boots into the ground. "I want all the men to report to you."

Daniel held his arms behind his back and pushed his chest forward. He was to be the first officer over a special unit of soldiers. A smile pulled at the corners of his mouth and he forgot the pain in his jaw. This was the assignment he'd been waiting for and he said, "I've only ever been loyal to you, sir."

"This isn't like other military duties." He turned and paced a few steps and then came back to Daniel, the sunlight splitting through the short hairs on his head and silhouetting his broad shoulders. He laid his hand on Daniel's shoulder. "I'm giving you this assignment because

I . . ." He paused for a moment, glanced up at the sky, and when his gaze came back to Daniel he said, "Because I trust you like a son."

Daniel held up the broken bow and stared at its splintered pieces with the drawstring coiled about the wood like a knotted web that had power to bind Daniel to the captain. "The bowstring didn't break, sir."

"It never will, son. I won't ever let it." Laban stepped close enough to Daniel that he could feel the pulsing of his breath on his face and the heat rising from his body. "I did the same thing when I was your age and I have this to show for it." He leaned his head back and let Daniel see what pain the pent-up power of a breaking bow could inflict on a man. There was a scar at the base of his chin nearly two fingers wide and it ran from his neck and ended in the tuft of beard on his chin. "I was like you. Strong, stubborn, and the first time I drew a bow I was foolish enough to believe I could draw it straight at the target. I nearly killed myself." He rubbed the deep scar. "You can only draw a bow as far as it's willing to bend and no farther, and that's how I want you to lead this company."

"How's that, sir?"

"The public will see you protecting my estate and policing the city, but there will be times when your work must be done in secret." Laban took the broken bow from Daniel's hands and stared at it, his gaze drifting over the hobbled weapon. He lowered his voice to a whisper and said, "You'll have to endure a good deal of strain. Certainly more than this bow can endure."

"There's a bow that can endure a good deal more than yours, sir." Daniel took back the broken bow and it fell limp over his hands.

"That's impossible. This bow is made of the finest woods there are."

"Have you ever tried a steel bow, sir?"

Laban said, "I didn't know there were artisans with such skill."

"There is one." Daniel held the bow to his chest, took a deep breath, and blew the warmed winter air over his fists. He said, "My brother."

"Aaron?"

"He's working on a bow of steel."

Laban quickly reached for his purse. "How soon can he have it finished?"

Daniel lowered the broken pieces of the blackwood bow to his side. He was at the shop yesterday when Aaron finished the design for the steel bow. He said it was certain to be a success and he was going to start smithing it as soon as he could smelt some steel. The jagged edges of the broken blackwood bow brushed against Daniel's thigh, but he didn't flinch. How could he tell Laban that Aaron was crafting a steel bow as a gift for Nephi, the son of the olive oil merchant? There was no way he could convince Aaron to sell it to Laban, no matter how much the captain offered for it. It was an impossible situation with only one solution if Daniel were to remain in the captain's good graces. Daniel would watch over Aaron and when he finished smithing the metal bow he'd take it from the shop and deliver it to Laban, with or without Aaron's blessing.

Daniel said, "I'll see that you get your steel bow."

CHAPTER 6

Jebus, chief scribe of the treasury at Fort Lakhish, pushed open the archives door and light from the stairwell filtered into the basement vault ahead of his stride. He didn't bother to trim the lamp at his writing table until he was certain there was enough ink for the day's work. He headed across the archives on a dead march toward the inkwells and immediately banged his knee against the protruding leg of his three-legged writing stool. Cursed Moriah! He bent over and rubbed the joint, but it didn't rid him of the pain and he loathed the day he took on his new apprentice. Moriah always left the leg of the writing chair in the way and if he'd told the boy once, he'd told him a hundred times: put the stool under the table with the legs flush with the edge of the desk. But there it sat, protruding nearly a fist's length. Jebus pushed it in place before continuing toward the inkwells, this time with a slight limp in his right leg. He'd have a swollen-reddish welt on his knee before lunch, and by morning it would be a dark-purple mass from thigh to shin no matter if he soaked it all night in powders. Jebus bruised easily and tomorrow he'd have to wear his long kilt to hide the ugliness, the one he never wore because the leather wasn't tanned and it scratched his white, spindly legs until they turned red.

Stupid boy. Why were the peculiar scribes always assigned to Fort Lakhish? Jebus had never apprenticed a new one that didn't possess some odd behavior and Moriah was no exception. He spent far too much time perfecting his pen strokes until they were as neat and flowing as an artist's rendering. And he was anything but quick to finish his work. He never made a final copy on leather parchment without writing a draft—sometimes two and three—on potsherds. Why just yesterday the boy finished off a basket of broken pottery and when he was done transferring the document to papyrus he threw the clay pieces over the west wall without salvaging a one. Did he think broken pottery grew on olive trees? At this rate there'd be a pile of potsherds stacked high enough for an attacking army to march over the wall on the remains of his writing without so much as a rampart, a ladder, or a climbing rope. Moriah had reduced the bin of potsherds to nothing and there was not a woman at Lakhish clumsy enough with her bowls and plates and water jars to keep him supplied. There were no more potsherds left for him to waste at his leisure and Moriah would have to collect all he could from the rubbish bins of the city if he wanted to do anymore rough drafts of his writings. Jebus pulled the hem of his kilt down over the swelling knob on his knee and continued his limp toward the inkwells. Why did Moriah make his life so uncomfortable?

Jebus moved down past a stack of empty repository urns set on a shelf next to his writing table. They'd been sitting there for over a week, their wide lips staring at him and begging him to finish the monthly reports. It wasn't his fault the urns weren't sealed and archived with the others. He'd finished with the first draft of the report yesterday and he, with the urns, waited for Moriah to make copies. Jebus winced at the pain in his knee, but kept hobbling across the archives. The boy was far too meticulous to finish the reports in less than a week. Didn't he understand he wasn't making copies for the king of Judah? These were military logs and no one ever had need to read them twice. There were shelves upon shelves stacked to the ceiling in this underground vault and no one had ever come to review any of them, at least not in the seven years Jebus had been chief scribe of Lakhish. If Moriah understood that these records would be sealed in jars and never opened again, he'd do his job with a bit more haste and not waste his time on pretentious scripts with pompous flowing lines and conceited curlicues. That kind of excess was better suited to the documents of royals and Jebus had never learned that art, nor did he have need to learn it. Military records were just that—military— and he didn't require the refined frills of an overly schooled scribe to understand patrol reports, gate entry logs, or the mail from Jerusalem.

Records were records, not art, though he did have Moriah record the fort's tax collection onto clay tablets. That was a more long-lived document than the papyrus Jebus used to record the location of dried wells along the Arabian Peninsula or log the nationality of merchants that caravanned past Lakhish each month. But then, what did anyone care if there were twelve Egyptians, fifteen Arabians, eighteen Jews, and a host of Babylonian merchants traveling the trade route? Treasury documents were a different matter and they were engraved in clay, no matter how Babylonian the practice. The Babylonian accountants required it and since Judah was a vassal state, Jebus complied with the request and assigned Moriah the task.

Moriah was the only scribe at the fort who could calculate the exchange of Hebrew talents into Babylonian gerahs and he wrote their language as well as he inscribed his own tongue. It was an insufferable talent that Jebus suffered once a month when the tax reports were due to the Babylonian escritoires. Jebus told his Babylonian counterparts that *he* prepared the records and shipped the tax across the desert by caravan. That was half true—Jebus did oversee the shipment of taxes to Babylon. No need to tell them that he couldn't even read their language, let alone prepare the tax records. And yes, credit should be awarded where it was due, but in Moriah's case, he didn't need any more, not if he were to get between the doorposts of the archives each morning. Arrogance swelled a man's head, to say nothing of his character, and Jebus would not allow that in any of his scribes, apprentice or not. Pride was the demise of all good men.

Jebus turned past the storage shelves, and the light from the stairwell faded, but there was still enough for him to check the new pens stored on a wooden tray, their delicate metal-tipped ends wrapped in linen. He ran his hand over the drying leather parchment hanging from a dowel while counting the stacks of papyrus just received from Egypt in yesterday's caravan shipment. Jebus stooped to check the bottom storage shelf before moving to the inkwell. The heavy sandstone lid was sealed to the jar—just as Moriah was supposed to seal it—with a covering of beeswax not less than three barleycorns thick to seal in the moisture. Jebus pried it off to find the clay covered by a moist cloth and sprinkled with just the right concentration of water to keep the clay overnight. It was stored properly in the bottom of the vat, or at least as properly as an apprentice could. No it wasn't proper—it was perfect. Was there nothing Moriah did poorly? Even the clay was mixed to a fine texture, formed into a circular loaf without any flat sides, and the seal of a lion's head sculpted over the top in Moriah's flowing hand. That was too much. There was no good reason to inscribe the king's logo on new clay, no matter how official a document it would become once the boy finished forming the tablet and writing the tax records over it. Jebus dropped the lid back into place and smeared the beeswax over the seal. The boy remembered every detail that even the most experienced scribes forgot. But this was an archive that was not accustomed to such fastidiousness and if Moriah were here Jebus would tell him that he didn't need to waste his precious time on details. There were menservants to do that work for the scribes and he could make better use of the day if he were to . . .

"Who goes there?" Moriah appeared at the door, the light from the stairwell angling down over his dark black cap of hair that hung in thick curls at his ears and bobbed over his brow. "Show yourself or I'll call for the guards."

The thick cedar door had come half-closed on its own weight and Moriah pushed it open against the wall with his shoulders and stepped past. He was carrying a single scroll and he held it out like a sword before slowly entering. He blew back the longest curls that fell into his deep blue eyes and jabbed the end of the scroll at the shadows ahead of his cautious stride. He pointed the dowel down along one wall where Jebus was standing in the shadows, and when he didn't see him he turned his weapon to point across the expanse of the treasury, his stance tight and his body positioned like a lion ready to pounce. He said, "Show yourself!"

Jebus rapped his fist against the writing table and Moriah jumped in the air and spun back around, stabbing the scroll at the sound of his tapping. Moriah said, "Who goes there?"

What was the boy doing? Did he really think there was anything worth stealing in this archive? They kept military documents in this treasury, not gold, and the only things worth stealing were the silver-tipped writing pens. But since they were stained with years of black carbonized ink, the pens weren't worth the cost of coal it would take to build a fire hot enough to melt them down and sell them at market.

"Put that down before you fall and hurt yourself," Jebus said.

"Is that you, Jebus?"

"Of course it's me. Who did you think it would be at this hour?"

Moriah relaxed his scroll against his side. "You said you wouldn't be arriving to the archives today until well after— "

"Light the lamp, boy. I can't see a blessed thing in here." He barked the order, his voice groaning across the darkness between them, brash and very much out of place in the close confines of this basement vault. "You should have had the lamps lit before I arrived."

"I'm sorry, sir."

"Get about your duties, before I have to report your laziness."

Moriah crossed to the tallest writing table and began with Jebus's lamp first, before moving to the other four tables and then to the hanging lamps down along the wall, lighting each one in turn until the flickering flames cast a steady light and the archive began to glow with an orange timbre. It was a cheaper grade of lamp oil that darkened the light, something they never used on the upper floors of the palace fort, but it had an affection that warmed the underground vault, despite the constant cool temperatures.

Moriah wore a long Persian kilt of fine linen that reached to the middle of his shins. It was the one given him by his teacher when he passed his final tests as a scribe—first in his class of forty. There was no reason to own such fine clothing. Moriah was a military scribe and there was no future beyond that. He'd never find work in a merchant house or be considered for employment in the temple courts, despite dressing the part. The collar of his white shirt buttoned tight around his neck and the full sleeves were pressed and pleated and narrowed at the cuffs like the scribe of a wealthy businessman. Jebus turned his gaze back to the clay vat. The boy was anything but wealthy, though with his tall stature, narrow jaw, and fine-lined nose he could be mistaken for Zedekiah, king of Judah. Wouldn't that be something— the king of Judah scribing in the archives of Fort Lakhish?

Moriah said, "You're earlier than usual, sir."

"I know what time it is." Jebus rubbed the sleep from his eyes. "Just don't be late again."

"I'm not expected here for another hour, sir. No one is."

"If you're not here before I arrive, then you're late." Jebus marched to the inking table and found the wide-lipped mixing jar leaning up against the wall and without its covering. It was just as he'd expected. Moriah had left the lid off the new ink last night and now it was gone—evaporated into the cool musty air of the vault before any of it got into the small clay inkwells set in a row of five and waiting for the other scribes to come and dip their pens and push them over papyrus. Jebus took the mixing jar by the handle and shook it. "Look what you've done, boy. The ink's gone dry." He took out three measures of coal, one of iron, and another of lime from the bins above the inking table. And with a flat-headed hammer, he crushed the rock to a fine powder.

Moriah came down past the storage shelves and stood across the table from him. He asked, "Do you really think we need all that?"

"Of course we do." Jebus scooped the powdery mixture into the jar, added a shot of water and three spoons of resin to give the ink just the right thickness to stay on a pen long enough for a scribe to affix it to potsherds and parchments, but not so much it turned to glue and stuck like jam to the stylus. "Your companions will be arriving to begin their work soon and I don't want them dallying about without anything to do."

"They've never needed that much ink, sir, not even on the busiest of days." Moriah scooted the five inkwells across the table. They were shaped like perfume bottles—round, fat, and with a hole wide enough to hold a pen upright. But without the pen sprouting from the brim, the light of the lamps sparkled across the surface of the ink and it was obvious they'd been filled with a fresh supply.

"When did you . . . ?" Jebus lowered the mixing jar to his side. The inkwells had more than enough to last the day.

"Earlier this morning," Moriah said, "Before going to the kitchens to eat with the soldiers."

"I knew that."

"Yes, sir." Moriah leaned over the table to see the half-mixed ink sloshing about at Jebus's side.

"I was only making certain we had enough. It's going to be a very busy day."

"You didn't mention any new work."

"That's because there isn't any to mention." Jebus jabbed the mixing jar at Moriah, the ink splashing over the lip and dripping over his fist. "You never know when Lord Yaush or any of his captains will need something done. A good scribe is always prepared, and don't you forget that it's better to have ink than to risk, risk . . ." He kept shaking the jar. "Well, you know, not having it."

"I'll be sure to keep a good supply on hand from now on, sir."

Jebus handed over the mixing jar and wiped his hand clean on a towel. "Here, you finish with this."

Moriah placed the scroll on the table between them and began to mix the ink with a long toggle while Jebus examined his writings. "I finished it last evening."

It was a papyrus scroll, the brown skin gone browner under the glow of the orange lamplight and its tassels a shade redder. It was scrolled tight about the dowels and sealed with a dab of wax.

Jebus lifted it slowly off the table, split open the wax with his thumbnail and unraveled it between them, shielding him from Moriah's expectant smile. It was the first copy of the watchtower logs and it was finished. The entries were numbered and listed by day and each one in Moriah's masterful strokes. The letters were formed without a flaw; the lines were straight and the edges of each squared with the line above. It was a fine job. No, not fine; it was exceptional. It should have taken Moriah at least three days, and with this careful penmanship, not less than a week, but Moriah had finished it in one. Jebus slowly lowered the scroll, the smiling face of Moriah rising to view above the top dowel. Was the boy waiting to be congratulated for his work? He was hired to make copies, but before Jebus could remind him of that the sound of hurried footsteps echoed in the stairwell and a tall, wide-shouldered man stepped through the narrow door.

It was Lord Yaush. He was dressed in his formal governor's robes—a high white collar buttoned tight around his neck, a long black cape with a pattern of gold leaves embroidered across the back like a cornucopia of fig and olive and palm branches. His full head of black hair was touched with the slightest hint of gray about the ears; just enough to make him look wise, but not weak, and he combed it off his brow, away from his serious brown-eyed gaze. He hurried over to Jebus, a box of leather scrolls weighing down his stride. He set them on the inking table and said, "I need copies of these."

"Lord Yaush, sir, you didn't need to deliver these. I could have come to your office and— "

"How long will it take?"

Jebus rummaged through the leather parchments. There were eighteen perfectly good letters; all of them done in the finest tanned ox hide. "These are a very good quality, sir. No need for copies. They should last a very long time without any—"

"How long?" Yaush spoke in quick breaths, his chest rising and falling with each phrase.

"Well, I, suppose it depends on what sort of copies."

"Clay tablets."

"Are you planning to send them to Babylon?"

"I want them on the finest clay you have."

Jebus said, "I just mixed some last evening and I can start on them immediately if you like."

"Not you." Yaush stepped past Jebus and stood beside Moriah. He laid his hand on the boy's shoulder and said, "I want you to copy these."

"Sir." Jebus leaned over the inking table. "If you're in a rush, Moriah takes far too long." He waved his hands in the air. "The boy makes drafts of all his work, spends hours perfecting every pen stroke." He patted the side of the scroll box. "Why, it will take him days to finish with all these."

Yaush held Moriah by his writing hand. "Will you see to it, son?"

Son? When had Yaush ever called anyone by that name, except Setti? Jebus said, "But, sir, I'm—"

"I said the boy is to make the copies."

"But . . ."

"Don't question me on this, Jebus. I don't want you hurt."

"How could these scrolls hurt me?"

Yaush didn't answer his question and Jebus had no way of knowing what the commander meant. There was little pain in any of the work they did in the archive, except for a few cramped fingers and a hangnail from time to time.

Yaush turned back to Moriah. "Will you do it for me?"

Moriah bowed quickly. "I'd be honored, sir."

Yaush pushed the box of scrolls into his hands and said, "You're to end all other duties and spend your time with these letters only." He pointed to the far side of the archive. "I want you to work over there, away from the others."

Jebus said, "There's no desk over there."

"Give him yours. And see that he has a good lamp. I'll have the maidservants bring him plenty to eat and drink. I don't want him wasting time standing in line at the kitchens." Yaush ran his hand through his hair. "Are there any questions?"

"Just one, sir." Moriah came around the inking table. "Shall I have Jebus check my work before I bring it to your—"

"No!" Yaush barked the order and there was no misunderstanding the command. No one was to read the letters except Moriah, and he was allowed only because he was the scribe assigned to the task. Yaush gripped his robe near his belly, creasing the cloth in a web of wrinkles down his front. He turned to Jebus and said, "You must trust that it's best this way. Is that clear?"

Jebus didn't answer Yaush immediately. He drew his lips together until the bottom one buckled under the weight of his anger and the top one was lost in his nostrils. It was all he could do to restrain himself from staring at Moriah. If his gaze lingered too long on the boy's head, he'd bore a hole through it. Not a large one, just a precise one, through which he could remove Moriah's talent for writing and languages and replace them with a large measure of guile. If there was anything Jebus couldn't stand it was a talented youth who wasn't full of himself. Who did he think he was, arranging personal work with Lord Yaush? The commander had never spoken with the boy until now and Jebus could only assume Moriah had gone to him, without his permission, and begged for an assignment away from the drudgery Jebus dispensed. And if he'd spoken privately with the commander, he would have told him everything. Jebus turned the full force of his gaze onto Moriah and let his stare do its blessed boring. Moriah was a rat—he'd told the commander he was a better scribe than Jebus and that Jebus treated him like a fool. Sucking the boy's mind clean would be a fitting revenge. But since Jebus could no more remove Moriah's brain than camels could fly, he'd claim all the credit for Moriah's copying of the commander's letters. It wasn't right for an apprentice to be honored without Jebus receiving his due. He forced himself to turn his gaze back onto Lord Yaush.

Jebus said, "Everything is perfectly clear, sir."

CHAPTER 7

Hannaniah hid the restless dove beneath the cavernous cuffs of his priestly robe. He couldn't let the temple patron—a poor shepherd from the hill country—see him breach the law of preparation, but a sacrifice of such small proportion was hardly worth his effort and he wasn't about to waste his time on this dove.

Hannaniah was the most senior altar priest, the son of Azur the prophet and he couldn't break the law of Moses in public. A complaint about unorthodox preparing of dove and pigeon offerings would tarnish the good family name and he made certain the shepherd couldn't see. Sacrifices were to be prepared without blemish and without broken bone, but Moses never had to suffer the preparation of a fidgeting fowl spraying blood on his white clothing and risk staining a finely tailored robe.

Hannaniah forced a smile to the shepherd standing across the altar from him. Couldn't he have at least brought a yearling to sacrifice? A lamb? Anything larger than this dove! If he were Moses, he'd not allow the man to replace a ram or a goat with this inexpensive sacrifice, no matter how poor the shepherd. The breast meat on a dove had a good flavor, but Hannaniah's portion was such a pittance compared to what he'd take home if the shepherd had brought in, say, a yearling, there was little reason to want to perform a sacrifice of such small proportions. If Hannaniah had written the law it would have been lambs and nothing else. There was not a simpler animal to prepare for sacrifice and there was always plenty of good meat to feed the patron and the priest. Lamb was always the best meal after a hard day of offerings.

Holding the bird out of sight between his thumb and forefinger, Hannaniah snapped its neck with one quick twist. The cooing stopped, the fowl fell limp in his hand and he quickly set it on the altar stone before the shepherd could see it wasn't alive. He had to dispense with this sacrifice quickly if he ever hoped to be on to the next one where he could make a good wage for the day, and the only prudent choice was to break the tiny bird's neck and get on with the rite—the lesser parts of the law be cursed!

Hannaniah slit the dove's throat with a quick stroke of his knife. He dangled the carcass over the basin and let the blood drain from its lifeless body without the bird convulsing, something that plagued the other priests who didn't have the sense to keep themselves unspotted. Not a single drop of blood marred Hannaniah's sleeves, soiled his silver threaded sashes, or stained the jeweled vestment strapped across his chest. He ran his fingers along the brim of his miter cap. Good. It was dry and he could hold his head high without worrying that the white cloth in his headpiece was splattered with blood. There was nothing worse than believing you were clean only to have a fellow priest point out later that you were as unclean as the rest of these patrons that filed through the temple courtyards. There were only two more sacrifices after this dove offering from the old shepherd, and once Hannaniah was finished he could go home without a blemish on his garments while the other priests were as stained as sinners on the Day of Atonement.

Hannaniah had a white beard that really wasn't white, though after two washings in lime powder his hair had turned as pure as the driven snow. The caustic powders were hard on the skin, but a burn on the scalp and two more on the chin were a small price to pay for homage. Hannaniah stroked the long strands growing from his chin and resting on his chest. Beards—especially long white ones—were a mark of wisdom and there was no doubting Hannaniah's distinction. He was a priest of the wisest class, and as long as his fellow priests believed that myth there was nothing to keep him from washing his hair in lime and shying away from the sheers except to trim the ends.

Ten years Hannaniah had nurtured his growth into a full, white beard, more than enough time to craft his own rules for dove and pigeon sacrifices. Hannaniah never strayed from the procedures for lamb sacrifices brought to the temple by the working class, and he'd never done anything but orthodox preparations for ram and ox of the wealthy class, but this shepherd's dirty little fowl was a different matter and he bent the rules to keep his garments white. God approved of cleanliness before obedience and if this poor substitute for a good yearling had any power to point a man's soul forward to the coming of the Messiah, what did it matter if a few bones were broken along the way as long as Hannaniah kept his garments clean—especially if the soul Hannaniah was pointing forward belonged to a dirty old shepherd who smelled like he hadn't bathed since the day he was born.

The old shepherd was poor to be sure. He was dressed in a tattered brown robe with dust-covered sandals and a turban of rags wrapped around his head more times than a rope maker wraps his cords. He smelled of lamb, not perfume, and there was no doubt he spent his days herding sheep in the hills surrounding the city, or worse, following the roving herds of bedouin sheep in the deeper parts of the southern desert. No patron ever presented fowl for sacrifice unless they couldn't afford anything larger, and at least this shepherd had enough respect to bring a dove instead of a dirty, gray pigeon. Hannaniah cleaned the blood from the knife and hung it on a hook beside the cutting stone. How he detested preparing pigeons. There was not another sacrifice filled with as much disease than the bluish-gray bird and if this old shepherd were anymore destitute, Hannaniah would have to suffer pigeons instead of doves, the sickliest of all sacrifices.

The old shepherd followed Hannaniah across the open courtyard, down past the twelve oxen bearing the washing pool on their backs, over beyond the main doors of the temple, and pulled up beside the stone altar. Hannaniah placed the dove among the hot coals and quickly repeated the blessing he'd uttered a hundred times before about the similitude of this sacrifice symbolizing the great sacrifice of the Messiah—something the old shepherd was certain not to understand—and ended with the plea for the Messiah to come quickly and save Israel. He turned the bird with a skewer, basting it with animal fat for good eating and letting it roast to a tender brown. He stirred the metal rod through the hottest coals, lowered his voice to a whisper to keep the other priests from hearing and said, "For the right price I can add a prayer that will save you from the fiery darts of the adversary."

"What was that, sir?" The old shepherd stepped closer, his face red with the glow from the coals.

"The adversary, old man." Hannaniah kept his gaze on the roasting dove. "For a piece of silver I can save you from hell and for two more I can divine your future on earth."

The old shepherd pushed away from the altar like a burned child. "Soothsaying is forbidden by the—"

"Call it a wise investment."

"An investment in what?"

"Your future." Hannaniah spoke loud enough to silence the shepherd, but not so loud to draw the gaze of the other priests. Soothsaying wasn't the most honorable of professions, especially for a Levite, but the few shekels he made for his altar work weren't nearly enough to provide the kind of life Hannaniah deserved, and he deserved a life better than his prophetic father before him, God bless his soul. He said, "Don't you want to be saved from your sins?"

The shepherd said, "You could do that for me?"

"Penance is what I do best." Hannaniah waved the skewer like a magician's wand, the red-hot tip filling the distance between them with smoke. "I've been absolving men all my life." He turned his gaze to the tattered leather purse hanging from the shepherd's belt. "For the right price I can do any divine task."

The shepherd handed over three shekels. It wasn't near the right price and it wasn't everything the shepherd had, not by the tinkling that filtered from his purse on his movement, but Hannaniah snatched the money from him just the same. He could add this to the day's soothsaying collection—nearly ten pieces of silver since midday meal. Not a bad wage when the other priests got a few shekels and some cuts of roasted lamb and bullock from the day's sacrifices. For three shekels Hannaniah offered the old shepherd some words of absolution to get him nodding, told him he'd be saved in the kingdom of heaven to bring a smile to his face, and without charging another shekel he added a bit of unadulterated soothsaying, telling the shepherd he'd sell his herd for twice what he paid and with the profit he could trade his tent in the desert for property in the city.

The shepherd's grin faded. He said, "I don't own a tent."

"You will very soon, my friend." Hannaniah stabbed the skewer through the flesh of the dove and turned it again. Didn't the shepherd know that Hannaniah was the finest soothsayer in Jerusalem? He promised riches to any who would pay him and he did it for half what he charged wealthy men of the upper city. There was not another priest who could sooth a sinner's future as eloquently as Hannaniah or peep beyond the wide pillars of heaven and speak to spirits long since dead. And as long as this shepherd was willing to pay for his sooth-saying, he'd put on a show. Last week Hannaniah made forty pieces of silver for telling a jewel merchant that he would remarry after the sudden death of his first wife—twenty pieces when he divined the upcoming marriage prospects, and twenty more when the merchant returned to the temple and told Hannaniah that he'd found a bride. Hannaniah lifted the dove from the coals with a skewer, turned it over and let the other side roast. He was the finest soothsayer in Judah, and not another soul accused him of anything but . . .

"I know what you're doing."

Hannaniah spun around, the tip of the skewer pointing at his accuser. He would have silenced the man with it if not for the gold amulet hanging from his neck and the stately black robe flowing from his shoulders and swallowing his arms in wide cuffs. The charge against him fell from the lips of Zadock, Chief Elder of the Jews, and he stood near enough to the altar for his ears to catch every word he'd spoken to the shepherd. His dark-eyed gaze followed Hannaniah like a shadow. It was too late to explain his soothsaying; the Chief Elder had already heard and he was going to throw him out of the temple, strip him of his priestly robes, and have him arrested. There was no other reason for Jerusalem's most noble prince to visit Hannaniah than to catch him in his crimes. He could make a run for the temple gates. There were enough patrons milling about the grounds to lose himself until he reached the entrance and the Chief Elder was a frail-looking man, not the sort who could stay with him on a chase through the streets of Jerusalem. He could get to his home, gather his things, and be gone from the city in search of a new life. If Zadock were as merci-less as he'd heard, Hannaniah would have to shave his beard, let it grow back in black and full, and change his name to something common like Joshua or David. Hannaniah laid the skewer on the edge of the altar and turned toward the nearest gate when Zadock stepped across Hannaniah's path. Zadock said, "You'll not get far."

Hannaniah ushered the Chief Elder to the other side of the altar, the hot coals separating them from the temple patrons. "I can explain myself."

"There's no need."

"I'm not what you think I am."

"You're everything I'm looking for." Zadock reached for Hannaniah's purse. "Maybe more."

"I'll never do it again; I swear on the grave of Moses." Hannaniah handed over the money he'd gleaned from a full day of soothsaying. "Here, take this and I'll never desecrate the altars of the temple again."

"Keep your money." Zadock folded his arms across his chest. "You have a gift." He rubbed the gold amulet between his fingers. "You're a tall, domineering man. Your manner of speech is stirring and . . ." He stroked his chin with his forefinger. "When you prophesy, your words are believed."

Prophesy? Zadock couldn't be serious. Who would pay to hear him prophesy a call to repentance when the divining of future wealth was a much more flattering proposition? And why would he call the wrath of heaven down on the sins of his customers when blessings kept them coming back for more soothsaying? Divining the future was a business, and he couldn't afford to give up his livelihood to save a few souls with prophetic utterances, to say nothing of the hatred prophets endured at the hands of the unrepentant. There was never a worse time to be a prophet in Judah, unless the rewards outweighed the risks and it would take a good-sized prize to tip the scales in that direction. Hannaniah wiped the sweat from his brow. He'd made a good living from soothsaying, but he never meddled with false prophecies. Better to break the lesser parts of the law for a few pieces of silver, and if he were beaten with a few stripes in heaven he would endure it and cry all is well in Zion. But clothing his words in the robes of prophecy was simply bad business.

Hannaniah said, "I divine the future for money, sir, but I don't prophesy."

"How much?'

"A few times a day, you know, for anyone who is willing to—"

"Money, you fool." Zadock dropped his arms, and his amulet dangled free from the end of its gold chain. "How much money do you make from your soothsaying?"

Hannaniah pulled out ten pieces of silver from his purse. "I do twice this on a good day."

"I'll pay you tenfold that for the right prophecies."

"I'm not a prophet."

Zadock produced a talent of gold from inside the cuffs of his robe and pressed it into Hannaniah's hand. "You are now."

"What sort of prophecies do you want from me?"

"Not here."

"Then where?"

"The king is calling for a meeting of the people to discuss the Babylonian tax." Zadock glanced about the courtyard filled with patrons. "I want you to declare a tax revolt and prophesy that it will lead to the freedom of this people from bondage."

"I can't do that."

"And why not?"

"It could cause another war with Babylon."

"I'll worry about those details."

Hannaniah held the gold talent against his palm. It was a few words for more money than he could earn in a lifetime of soothsaying. "How often will I have to do this?"

"I'll need your services from time to time." Zadock spoke quickly. "But if you're good, there's more where that came from. He hurried to a side door and disappeared into the alley leading around behind the back side of the temple and it was done. Hannaniah had work divining the future that would pay him more than he'd made in all his days. He was no longer a soothsayer begging coins from temple patrons.

Hannaniah was a prophet of God.

CHAPTER 8

Laman followed Captain Laban's instructions exactly, despite the cold drizzle and patches of fog that had power to turn him back toward home. He reined past Jerusalem's east gate, down through the Kidron Valley, then turned onto a narrow trail winding up the hillside through a thick stand of olives. The trees framed the way like a spider's web of branches, filtering what little glow of late afternoon hadn't already been dimmed by the gray sky. The canopy of leaves never fell from their branches during the dark months. They kept their green color and curled up against the winter cold like a cocoon waiting for the warmth of spring to uncurl them before another growing season arrived. A low fog shielded Laman's view of anything but the rise and fall of his horse's head trotting up the mist-covered path in front of him, pressing up a steep incline, around a sharp bend, and then onto a stretch of . . .

Laman pulled up, his steed rearing on its back legs. Why didn't the captain tell him the trail dead-ended in a rocky outcrop? He spurred around, the haunches of his horse brushing hard against the trunk of an olive growing up beside the trail's end. It was a poorly kept tree, its branches overgrown with failed grafts and it had gone wild like so many of the trees in the upper parts of this vineyard. This wasn't Beit Zayit; it was the Mount of Olives overlooking Jerusalem.

Laman pulled a white cloth from under his belt and waved it over his head. He wasn't surrendering; he was signaling the captain of his arrival, but it did seem odd that Laban would order him to wave a

white cloth like a vanquished foe when all the captain need do was
wait beside this olive tree until he arrived. Laman immediately
lowered the cloth and swung down out of the saddle. He leaned his
thick shoulders against the knotted bark of the olive. Did he really
need to meet with Captain Laban again? Laman had already answered
his questions—his father Lehi knew nothing of their common
lineage—and there was no reason for him to be summoned here on
this cold afternoon away from the warm fires of the plantation house
to answer questions he'd already answered countless times before. It
didn't matter that Lehi and Captain Laban were cousins and Laman
was going to tell him flat out that he was a fool to worry so much.
Well, not exactly a fool. The captain was too powerful a man for
Laman to call him anything more damning than, say, a nervous soul.
Laman straightened against the gnarled bark of the olive tree and
rubbed his hands together. That's exactly what the captain was, an
anxious, fretful man without the sense to see—

"I see you've made yourself comfortable." Captain Laban stepped
from the undergrowth of the vineyard like a spirit from a cave. He
was on foot, leading his white Arabian behind him. His captain's
uniform was covered with a black cloak and it lifted on the misting
air with his long strides.

Laman stood away from the tree trunk, the white cloth hanging
from his hand. "I haven't been here long."

"I know." The captain reached out and rubbed the white cloth
between his fingers. "Is your brother with you?"

"You told me to come alone."

The Arabian stuck its nose over the captain's shoulder and he
shoved it aside. "You'll need Lemuel's help if you're going to keep
your father from finding out."

"We've been over this." Laman widened his stance. "My father
knows nothing about—"

"About Uriah?" The captain brushed away the rain that had
collected on his shoulders.

"What about him?"

"Your father's not to defend him."

"Lehi isn't a lawyer."

"That didn't keep him from staying Uriah's execution."

Laman shook his head slowly. "King Zedekiah did that."

The captain ripped a graft from the olive tree and pointed the end of the thin, withered branch at Laman. "I want you and your brother to keep Lehi away from Jerusalem until the trial is over, is that clear?"

"And if we fail?"

"There isn't room for failure, not this time." The captain raised his voice, the sound of it shaking the leaves and raining down a mist over them.

"Lehi doesn't obey me; he's my father."

"Reason with him."

Laman took a long breath, and when he blew it out he could feel some of the strain of his father's religion leave him. He said, "How do you reason with a man who dreams dreams?"

The captain raised his beard in a subtle smile. "I know some men who can inspire your father to listen to you."

"Lehi's got more than enough inspiration, maybe too much."

"My men can purge that from him."

"He's not the sort of man to give up his faith."

"I didn't say he would." The captain started down the hill, leading his horse through the swirling mists that hung over the trail. "I only want to convert him into a zealot more to our liking."

"There's nothing I like about any of this."

"You will." The captain kept walking down the path. "As soon as you see what my men do."

Laman followed him down the path to the brow of the hill. "What are you planning?"

The captain spoke over his shoulder. "I don't want your father's foolish beliefs getting in the way of Uriah's trial." He stopped before heading into the thick growth of the lower vineyard. "I'm going to swap his faith for fear."

CHAPTER 9

Ezekiel, the kingdom's chief lawyer, pushed his pen over the ledger without looking up at the Babylonian courier. The Babylonians' courier stepped into Ezekiel's tax collection office from the Citadel Building lobby, his boots clicking over the stone floor. By the hollow sound they made, they were cobbled of ox hide and poorly nailed in place. The door latched back in place and the courier said, "Hail, sir! I have a delivery from the court at Nineveh."

Ezekiel pushed his pen over the ledge without looking up and continued transferring the tax records onto the new parchment. Did the courier say delivery or misery? There was no telling by the way he pronounced his faltering Hebrew, and listening to his thick accent was a wretched curse. He slurred the word "hail" with "delivery," held his tongue to the roof of his mouth on the phrase, *the court at Nineveh*, leaving no doubt he was from southern Babylon, or at least from among the less-educated class of the capital city.

It didn't really matter what the man was saying. Every delivery from Nineveh was a miserable mix of Babylonian protocol, and this mandate was no doubt like the hundred other demands from the scribes in the Babylonian capital. Ezekiel dipped his pen and continued copying the tax records. Why must he suffer these constant interruptions from foreign soldiers? If the Babylonians hoped to rule the vassal state of Judah for any length of time, they should send emissaries who could speak the language of the conquered instead of sending a constant stream of letters, proclamations, and scribal procedures in the company of men with the education of mud-brick masons.

Ezekiel learned the language of the Assyrians by age twelve, the tongue of the Athenians by fourteen, and he could read and write Babylonian as if he were born Chaldean. It had taken him forty-seven years to rise to his station among the most learned of all the Jews, and though he would have preferred to keep his knowledge to himself, King Zedekiah needed a man he could trust and he appointed Ezekiel to the dual post of chief lawyer among the Jews and chief accountant over all the taxes of the kingdom. Ezekiel added a curlicue to the last number in the ledger before moving down to the next entry. He could have had a much larger office on an upper floor if he requested it, but he preferred the confines of this tax office. He didn't need a room with a balcony terrace in order to account for the king's wealth. These small confines suited him fine, away from the pressures of men who savored the public's eye like a dog savors rotten meat. Ezekiel did without the trappings of his office.

The Babylonian courier slapped his fist to his chest, leaned over Ezekiel's desk and said, "Do you hear, sir?"

Of course he had heard him. It was impossible not to with the courier standing close enough that his breath steamed across Ezekiel's face. The man had eaten one too many artichokes on his journey from Babylon, and Ezekiel had a mind to tell him to back away from his desk, but he couldn't. It wasn't his place to order the man not to breathe on him. He was here to serve.

Ezekiel rolled his ledger around a dowel, fastened the end of it with a dab of clay, and pressed his ring into the soft center, sealing it with his insignia—a rendering of a moneychanger's scale, the rod balanced on a fulcrum and the money bowls hanging by chains from both ends. It was the perfect seal for his post as chief lawyer and chief accountant of Judah. He was overseer of all the tax collectors in the kingdom, his word on points of law was final among lawyers and there was not a kinder gesture from the king to mark the fairness with which he oversaw his high position in the treasury than the stamp on his silver ring. Fairness was the incarnation of his tenure as chief tax collector and a blessed remembrance to his wisdom as chief lawyer.

The courier said, "I have a letter from the from the king of Babylon."

Ezekiel pushed his ledger aside and glanced up at the man. He was dressed like all Babylonian military men: a dark blue tunic with a tight collar around the neck and silver buttons down the sleeves from shoulder to cuff. He retrieved a tablet from his pouch and laid it on Ezekiel's writing table. It was cast of grayish white clay and not nearly as large as the hundreds of other documents that passed through this office from the scribes and accountants of Babylon. It was barely two hands long and one wide, but king Nebuchadnezzar's taxmen didn't need much space to write the final cost of losing the war. Ezekiel carefully pried back the seal, lifted away the cover protecting the penned words imbedded in the dried clay, and read the order of taxes to be collected by his office and sent to the court of Nebuchadnezzar. The king of Judah was to pay tribute to Babylon of one quarter of a merchant's profit, one-quarter of a farmer's harvest, one-quarter of a manservant's wage, and one-quarter of all of Judah's increase.

Ezekiel set the tablet down. A one-quarter tax? That wasn't an impossible tariff, not compared to what he'd expected from the Babylonians. They were tyrants, at least that's what he'd been told about King Nebuchadnezzar and his court, but he couldn't be near the tormentor he'd been made out to be with a paltry one-quarter tax. This was hardly the yoke promised by the prophet Jeremiah. Why, a vassal tax this low was a gift from heaven and it would be a simple task for his tax collectors to do their work. Ezekiel would raise the total to, say, half a man's income, send a portion to Babylon and keep the rest for king Zedekiah, his court, the military, and of course a portion for the Council of Elders—Zadock was certain to press him for a very generous share.

"That's certainly a hefty sum, my good man." Ezekiel came around the table and stood beside the courier. He shook his head. "I don't know if our people can endure under such a burden."

The courier smiled and said something about Ezekiel paying the sum in full or Babylon would return with her armies, but he spoke with such a heavy accent all Ezekiel could understand was a word or two about his nation being the most powerful on earth. Ezekiel nodded with each of the courier's forced Hebrew phrases. Why did the Babylonians always deliver speeches? Couldn't they just do their business and get on with it instead of standing to attention and spouting national pride like a flood from an eternal fountain? The courier ended his words by saying something Ezekiel understood. "You're to deliver the tax to Nineveh."

Ezekiel said, "That's where I always send it."

"It's to be sent when you celebrate the Passover in two months time."

Ezekiel returned to his desk and took out a writing stylus. At least the courier knew the Hebrew feast day, though he pronounced the name poorly. It was Passover, not Phaash-hoover. Ezekiel said, "I'm never late with the tax." He set the courier's clay tax tablet near the edge of his writing table with a stack of other tax documents, lowered his head into the lines of accounting records, and let the courier see himself out the door and into the sea of lawyers, noblemen, and merchants that flooded the Citadel Building in late afternoon.

Ezekiel had land documents to prepare and barely enough ink in his bottle to finish all of them before the end of the day. He penned the official description of the land owned by the royal house of Judah onto the parchment. The Elders of Gilded disputed the parcel and Ezekiel carefully plotted the boundaries of what the crown owned— from the summit of Mount Shiloh, south along the banks of the Jordan to the first tributary, then west to Wadi Al Shalom. That was a legal description of land purchased by King Solomon and passed from father to son for a thousand years, and Ezekiel wasn't about to let a handful of Elders from a small village fifty miles north of Jerusalem cause a stir over it. It would be royal land for another thousand years, or at least as long as Ezekiel oversaw the royal family's holdings.

Long afternoon shadows fell faint across the windowsill high on the inside wall of the tax collection office. The accountants and scribes in adjacent offices put away their scrolls and capped their inkbottles, but Ezekiel couldn't leave until he finished the copies of the water-rights agreement. It was a short document, and he could prepare three copies long before his wife finished preparing the pheasant and yams for supper. She always fixed the same food the evening of the Sabbath, and he could smell the sweet aroma in his mind and see her seated at the table with their three children waiting for him to come home and enjoy a meal together. Ezekiel hurried through the agreement to water-rights on a tributary of the Jordan north of Jericho, his lone lamp lighting the edges of his parchment, but lacking the power to find the far reaches of his office and chase away the dark shadows that gathered in the corners.

The lobby of the Citadel Building stood quiet, with only a handful of merchants still milling outside his door finishing the last of their business. The scratching of his pen streamed out into the lobby and mixed with the hushed bartering voices of the last day of the week. He finished the first copy of the water-right agreement and started with the second when a man stepped inside the office, shut the door and locked it behind him. His head was down so that the black and white shawls streaming from under his turban hid his face, but there was no doubt about his intentions. He was staring at the tablet in the corner of Ezekiel's writing table, the one left by the Babylonian courier. He said, "Is that the levy?"

His voice was thin and rasping and immediately Ezekiel knew the man hidden behind the shawls. Before him stood Zadock, Chief Elder of the Jews.

Ezekiel rose from his chair. "How can I help you, sir?"

Zadock reached for the tablet. "Are you the only one to have read this?"

Ezekiel straightened the pleats in his robe. "There aren't many in this office who can read the writing of the Babylonians, sir."

The Chief Elder walked around the writing table and stood beside Ezekiel. He ran his long, thin forefinger over the uneven surface of the clay and when he reached the first mention of a one-quarter tax, his head came up slowly. He said, "I want you to change this."

"I'm sorry, sir. We don't set the tax in this office. The Babylonians do that."

"I want the one-quarter to read three-quarters."

"I told you, sir. We don't set the—"

"You'll do as I say if you want a seat on my council."

A seat on the council? That was the last thing Ezekiel needed. He wasn't given to public office and didn't have the temperament to sit on Jerusalem's governing council. He preferred this small office away from the stir other government posts incurred. He said, "What was that, sir?"

"You heard me." Zadock inched the tablet toward Ezekiel. "Change this tax levy to read three-quarters and you'll have the post every nobleman in the city covets."

Ezekiel said, "A three-quarter tax is an unbearable sum."

"This is a Babylonian tax, isn't it?"

"Well yes, but . . ."

"Then let the Jews in Jerusalem believe the Babylonians set it that high."

"I can't do that."

"You have a pen, don't you?" Zadock pointed to the clay stylus laying beside the inkwell.

"Shouldn't we discuss this with King Zedekiah?"

"I've all ready done that."

"The king approves of this?"

"I take care of the king's most troubling matters."

Ezekiel glanced about the office. It was empty, but he lowered his voice the same. "Does the king know what a stir this will cause?"

"I'll worry about that. All you need do is prepare to fill the potter's seat on the council."

"The potter's seat?"

"That's the only vacant one I know of."

"But sir, I really don't have any interest in—"

"We'll be working together for a very long time and its best we begin on good terms."

"What terms, sir?"

"I'm not be questioned."

It was impossible to know if the Chief Elder was talking about the change to the tax notice or the seat of the Second Elder on the council, but since the man was staring at him with penetrating dark eyes, it was best he not inquire further. Ezekiel gathered some white-colored sand, a wedge of gray clay and a cup of water. He combined them in a mortar bowl, mixing the fine white sand into the clay with the short end of the pestle until it was nearly the same color as the tablet, but stopping short of a perfect match since wet clay was a bit darker then dry clay, and there was no room for error. Zadock insisted that when the clay dried, no one was to know Ezekiel had changed the Babylonian levy.

Ezekiel said, "Why don't you promote the Third Elder to the potter's post?"

"The money changer?" Zadock offered a faint smile. "There's not a soul in Jerusalem who trusts the man."

Soul? That was an odd choice of words for the Chief Elder. Ezekiel said, "Surely there must be other Elders on the council you trust to fill the vacancy."

"I don't trust anyone." Zadock turned his gaze onto Ezekiel. His eyes were dark and impossible to read. He said, "You would do well to remember this advice."

"What advice, sir?"

"Trust only me."

Ezekiel used the tip of a knife to chisel away the words "one-quarter" from the tablet, then filled the holes with clay before carefully etching the word "three-quarters" into the fresh clay and searing it dry over the heat of his table lamp. He said, "What are the king's orders for the surplus?"

"What surplus?"

"Well, sir, if my calculations are correct and we collect three-quarters of a man's income, pay the Babylonians only a quarter, there should be a rather large sum left over."

"Your tax collectors will never collect this tax."

Never? Ezekiel handed the tablet to Zadock for inspection. Why would the Chief Elder bring word to raise the levy on a tax he never intended to collect?

"I'll take this for the king to review." Zadock brushed his fingers across the perfectly altered clay. "Have your tax collectors post a copy of the levy on the doorpost of every citizen in Jerusalem."

"Every doorpost?"

"Deliver an official notice to the members of the Council of Elders, all the officers of the military, and every nobleman in Jerusalem."

"But, sir." Ezekiel tapped the tip of his writing pen on the table. "We've never taxed them before."

"Put my seal on every notice."

It was an odd request. No, not odd, it was foolish. Why did the Chief Elder want to send a notice to every house in Jerusalem with his name on it, informing the citizenry of an increase in the tax levy? That was something better left to the military—men who carried swords and were trained to defend against the anger that was certain to come from such a proclamation. Zadock was raising the tax for no reason, blaming it on the Babylonians who had asked a reasonable sum, and the Chief Elder never intended to collect any of it.

Ezekiel put away the mortar and pestle. "There will be such an outcry against you as you've never known in the city."

"That's exactly as I would hope." Zadock's head came up and the ends of his shawls fell from his shoulders and down the back of his robe. He gripped the edge of the writing table with both fists. "And when they come to me I'll tell them that it is the tyranny of Babylon that has sent this scourge upon Judah." He tapped the clay tax tablet where Ezekiel had altered the words with new clay. He said, "This never happened."

"What never happened?"

Zadock offered to shake his hand, but Ezekiel didn't put down his writing pen. Zadock said, "I can see you're going to make a fine Second Elder."

Jonathan the blacksmith waited in the shadows behind a tall stone pillar, away from the merchants crowding into the Citadel Building lobby. The sun was setting over the western hills and the last orange light filtered through the half-open doors, casting an eerie glow over the men milling about the chamber and conducting their hurried business, in a rush to finish before the Sabbath. They spoke in hushed tones that echoed off the marbled walls and high ceiling.

It had been three months since Jonathan finished smithing Laban's sword, and he was to meet Zadock here to collect for his work. A merchant passed near the pillar and Jonathan wrapped the black and white shawls of his calling close to his face. Why did Zadock choose such a public place to do their dealings? They could have done this at the blacksmith shop, or in the council chambers— anywhere but the lobby of the busiest building in the city. Jonathan had done his work in secret and he expected to be paid in secret, not from the visible funds that sat on the money-changing table in the center of the lobby. It wasn't right for strangers to make an accounting of his private wage.

The money-changing table was nothing like the ones in the market with rickety legs and a set of worn weights that couldn't measure the difference between a full-grown hen and its egg. This table was hewn of heavy oak, its legs were sturdy, and when the silk trader leaned against the edge of it, the table didn't budge, not even a wobble on the stone floor.

The money changer sat in a high-backed mahogany chair. He wore a large black robe with the cuffs rolled back and tied about his elbow with cords to keep any coins from slipping beneath his sleeves. His fingers were ringed in gold and the bands clinked against the coins he was counting—ten pieces of silver for the silk trader. He placed them in the man's leather purse, noted the exchange in his ledger and then stood from his chair and announced that the Sabbath was upon them and he would be closing soon. It was Jonathan's good fortune that not another soul approached the table, and when the businessmen in the lobby began to file out, he stepped from behind the pillar. Finally. He could see to getting his money without sacrificing his privacy.

Jonathan approached the table and before he could inform the money changer he was to meet Zadock here, the Chief Elder appeared in the doorway leading from the kingdom's tax accounting office. His long fingers were cupped in front of his pleated robe, and he walked toward Jonathan with a rigid stride that lifted the black shawls about his gaunt features.

Zadock called across the lobby. "I have your gold, blacksmith."

Of course he had it; that was the reason for their meeting, but must he speak so loudly? Jonathan turned his gaze to the floor, deflecting the stares that turned his way. The Chief Elder had never spoken of their business in public, but his squawking attracted a crowd of merchants to the changing table.

Jonathan said, "Is there another place we can do this, sir?"

"Nonsense." Zadock raised his hands to the men gathered around the table. "I want everyone to meet the city's finest blacksmith."

Jonathan spoke into the collar of his robe. "I don't need an introduction."

"Gentlemen." Zadock cleared his throat. "The blacksmith has earned a place among our most noble citizens." He stood beside the money changer, his hand on the backrest of the changing seat. "Go ahead, give the man his due."

A wooden box sat near the back of the table. The seams between its planks were riveted in place with metal pieces and the latch was sealed with a brass lock. The money changer opened it and removed a tray of gold coins, the appearance of so many talents stirring a rush of hushed whispers.

Zadock said, "Is twenty talents correct?"

Must he say it aloud? Jonathan dug the heel of his sandal into the stone floor. Zadock knew exactly how much he was to be paid; they agreed on the sum the day he began work on Laban's sword.

"You had best count them." Zadock pushed the gold across the table.

"Inside here?" Jonathan's gaze passed over the faces of the merchants gathered about him.

"That's right."

"But, sir . . ."

"Do it." Zadock spoke with a firm, steady voice and Jonathan obeyed, quickly fingering through the coins, turning the lion-headed side over to reveal the inscription of the tribe of Judah, then stacking the twenty coins one atop the other. It was more gold than he'd ever seen and the wine merchant started to whistle louder than a river crane, but only until Jonathan shot a penetrating glance in his direction; then his whistle died between his lips.

Jonathan said, "Everything's here."

"Not everything." Zadock leaned over the table and snatched back all but five of the talents. "That should take care of the tax."

"What tax?"

"The Babylonians get three-quarters of all you earn." Zadock slowly moved out from behind the changing table and the merchants parted to let him pass.

A perfume merchant dressed in silver-threaded robes stepped forward. His fingers danced about his face as he spoke. He said, "That can't be. No one can bear such a burden."

The silk merchant quickly hid his purse under his belt. The coins jingled and he raised his voice to cover the noise. He said, "This is an—"

"An outrage?" Zadock said.

"It's an impossible tax to pay."

"I hoped you would feel that way." He squared his shoulders to the merchants. "All of you should feel cheated."

Jonathan said, "How can a man support a family with this kind of burden?"

Zadock hid his hands beneath the pleats in his robe. "Five talents of gold should keep you a good while."

"I was thinking of these men." Jonathan glanced about the lobby, and the merchants began to speak in low tones and there was no doubt about their dislike. They did not want to pay three-quarters of their income to the Babylonians.

"That's noble of you." Zadock handed the gold to the money changer. "Make a record that the blacksmith has paid his tax."

Jonathan stepped to the money-changing table. "This kind of tax must not be allowed to stand."

"That's right my good blacksmith, that's exactly right." Zadock lifted his hand from the money box and motioned to the merchants. "All of you should stir the anger of your fellow citizens."

"You don't mean that." Jonathan slowly shook his head. "You don't really want that kind trouble from the princes and nobles of the city."

"Honorable men should stand against unfairness." Zadock smiled softly, the delight pulling at his cheeks. For some odd reason the Chief Elder enjoyed announcing the tax—a burden so heavy that at its very best obliged citizens of Jerusalem to talk of revolt against Babylonian rule.

"Good day, blacksmith." Zadock tucked the moneybox beneath his arm and started out the main doors of the Citadel Building past the other merchants. "Good day to you all."

CHAPTER 10

Taxes?

Laban ripped away the notice nailed to the back gate of the estate and held it up to the midmorning sun. What was this, a joke from the Chief Elder? He would have thrown the parchment into the gardens and let it molder in the frosty soil till spring, but it had Zadock's official seal at the bottom and there was no doubting the levy had come from him. He slapped the parchment across his palm. Three-quarters of all his income! What kind of foolishness was this?

Laban stormed onto Market Street without changing from his morning robe—a black-dyed linen wrap with a border pattern sewn of fine gold threads. The wide collar flapped open across his chest, the robe untied from neck to navel and only a narrow black sash around his waist to keep what little modesty Laban had from turning to outright impropriety. His unlatched sandal straps slapped free against the cobblestones of Market Street, the sound of them turning the heads of shoppers passing by his gate. Laban quickened his stride, his head held high and his thin line of beard set firm along his jawline. What were these women staring at? Hadn't they ever seen a man's bare chest before?

The midmorning winter walk was cold, but no colder than the words Laban had for Zadock. He tightened his grip on the tax notice until it was a sweaty ball of leather in his palm. It was an insult to send a tax collector to his estate with an assessment. Since when did the council charge the captain of the guard? Laban gleaned his livelihood from the tax—he didn't pay it. The shoppers jumped from before his stride like seawater cut asunder by the prow of a great ship, their basket-laden heads bobbing in his wake. Three women lost their purchases, spilling wheat and oats and barley over the street, to say nothing of losing their heads judging by the squealing that accompanied Laban's sudden appearance. Shoppers! Didn't they have the good sense to mind the balancing of their purchases instead of gawking at him and losing their baskets?

Laban ducked into the shadows of the government arch, the stir he'd started echoing off the stone overhead and chasing him out of the market and onto the quiet of King Street. He turned immediately up a narrow path of a hundred flat-stoned steps where not a ray of winter sun found its way down past the stone arches spanning the path. Only the dim glow of the sky lighted this place obscured by overhanging balconies and four-story rooftops and buildings that stood close enough that Laban could reach out and touch the stonework, iron-barred windows, and metal-plated wooden doors of the wealthy men of the upper city's east side. These estate owners were just like Laban—above the common man's tax and Zadock had no right to . . .

What was this? Laban stopped outside the door to the first estate. Nailed to the ornate oak plank was a notice just like the one wadded in his palm. He glanced up to the door of next estate, and the next and the one after that. Every door had a tax notice nailed to the front and Laban brought his gaze back to the crumpled ball in his hand. The notice he'd gotten on his gate was not an ill-timed joke or an accounting mistake by a new tax collector. It was a tariff for every nobleman in Jerusalem and there was no doubt Zadock had made a terrible mistake. No, not a mistake—he was a fool. Did he think he could send the tax collectors to every prince and noble in the city and not reap a firestorm of protest? And worst of all, he'd sent them to his own neighbors as if they were common men, not worthy of a say in the sudden change in the collection practice. The Chief Elder would never walk this street again without the need for a troop of soldiers to protect him from the indignation that would surely follow after ordering a full tax on men who were accustomed to a privileged rate. And if Zadock needed protection, Laban certainly wasn't going to provide it, not if the Chief Elder insisted on applying this outrageous tariff to him.

Laban marched up the street toward Zadock's home. It wasn't really a street, since not a single wheeled cart could climb these steps. It was a lane, a narrow footway hardly wide enough for the horse that stood tied to a post across from the third estate, and there was even less space for the merchant selling beans from the saddlebags of a mule. Laban skirted past the man and his beast without returning his greeting or his smile. What was a merchant doing selling beans here? There were less than fifteen estates in this expensive east side district, hardly enough business to make door-to-door peddling up a steep incline of steps worth the effort. And if the bean seller ever reached the dead end at the top of the lane he'd find the estate that belonged to the man who was going to tax three-quarters of his earnings. No, not tax, he was going to steal three-quarters of every workingman's profits. Curse Zadock! What was he thinking, raising the levy this high? They'd agreed on half of a man's income—a quarter of it sent to the king of Babylon as tribute and then a portion more to pay the military a meager sum and take care of the king and his court. But three-quarters of a man's income? That was more than any common man in Jerusalem would stand for, and Laban was anything but common.

Zadock kept a two-story estate at the top of the lane, but it stood in the shadows of much taller estates; the Chief Elder was believed humble by his neighbors. Laban reached the Chief Elder's door and pounded his fist against the oak planks. If only his neighbors really knew what sort of humility the Chief Elder possessed. Zadock lived alone except for a small contingent of three maidservants to do the work of cooking and cleaning, and a single manservant to trim the gardens, repair the clay roof, and see that the property didn't fall into disrepair, though one man was hardly enough to look after an estate quarried of limestone. The mortar between the slabs in the front façade was cracked and the winter rains from last evening pooled at the base and seeped into the foundation, though there was little need to worry about flooding or mold. This was the outside wall separating the estate from the street, and though it was built to look like part of the residence with barred windows and a balcony overlooking the street, it was nothing but a faked front of brick and mortar and the water would only irrigate the soils of the gardens that lay on the other side. Zadock preferred to live away from the noise of his public, and though there was little traffic on this lane, he had a replica home front raised to match the front façades of the other estates in this district, while his residence stood back off the street nearly twenty paces.

The bolt clicked open, the door in the fake wall inched open and the maidservant said, "The Chief Elder wasn't expecting anyone this morning."

"He'll see me." Laban pushed open the door and knocked the maidservant back into the barren soils of the garden, picked of every legume and onion. The Chief Elder didn't plant flowers in his garden. There was no reason to impress his guests since he never invited anyone to his estate. Even Laban had only come here twice, and then to stand in the street and peer in while the maidservant fetched the Chief Elder.

"Wait here." The maidservant stood in Laban's path. "I'll ask if the Chief Elder will see you."

"He'll see me." Laban pushed her out of his way.

"But, sir, you can't." The maidservant hurried alongside him. "He's not dressed for the day." She reached for the latch to shut the main door to the house, but Laban pushed her aside and flung it open.

A heavy lemon scent of myrrh rose from the brass incense burner that stood in the entry. It was a one-legged stand with a corroded brass bowl attached to the top and it smoldered with burning ingots and split the air with a plume of myrrh-scented smoke. Three more incense bowls hung from the rafters, freshening the air of the second-floor mezzanine, their red coals peering through the haze. Laban scaled the stairs through the smoke and turned into the Chief Elder's anteroom, a small quarters with deep-red tapestries hanging from the walls, a tall-backed sitting chair crafted of dark woods, and a red cushion fluffed and waiting for Zadock to sit on it and pick up the scroll of the laws from the reading table and begin his studies.

Laban brushed past the reading table and into the Chief Elder's dressing room. It was a narrow space leading to Zadock's sleeping chamber, with just enough room to hang his robes and turbans and sashes. Seven robes hung from hooks on the wall, each one weaved with the same black pleats and stiff collar with sleeves and hems of identical lengths. Why did he need so many robes of the same style? But then, fashion was not one of Zadock's passions. Opposite the robes stood shelves of turbans and headpieces, each one pointed like the horn of an ox, and beside them sat neatly folded stacks of white and black shawls and sashes. So many pieces of clothing, yet they were all similar. The Chief Elder could wear the same clothing for months and never have need of a washwoman.

"Good morning, Captain." Zadock stood in the darkest corner of the dressing room, fitting a shawl over his gray hair and letting it fall down over his shoulders. "I expected you earlier."

"You did?"

Zadock stepped around the rack of gold amulets and the glow of the lamp turned his white complexion a deep yellow. "You should have gotten word about the— "

"What's the meaning of this?" Laban held out the ball of leather that was the tax notice. "Was it something you ate?"

Zadock raised his left eyebrow. "We have a trial to win, Captain."

"Curse you Zadock, I came here about the tax, not Uriah's trial."

"You're angry."

"Of course I am."

"And we can only pray the rest of the city will be as angry as you."

"You're a fool."

"I am, and you'll thank me for it."

"I'd rather hang you." Laban began to pace between the shelves of shawls. "Everyone will want to hang you for this. You should know the nobles are not accustomed to this kind of treatment."

"And when they voice their anger, I'll suggest to King Zedekiah that we not pay the tax to Babylon."

"What has gotten into you?" Laban knocked a stack of black shawls to the floor. "You're going to start another war."

"Our war, Captain, is with the queen. The Babylonians are simply a . . ." Zadock ran his tongue over his lips before he said, "A diversion."

"Curses, Zadock; they have thousands of soldiers stationed near our borders and none of them are commanded by Miriam. It wasn't the queen who sent us this insufferably high tax."

"She certainly didn't." Zadock slowly fitted a turban over his brow, careful not to wrinkle the black shawl that streamed out from under it. "I did."

"You what?"

"I was there when the Babylonian levy arrived at the tax office." Zadock tucked his gray bangs under the brim of his turban. "And I had it changed from a one-quarter to a three-quarter tax."

"What were you thinking?"

Zadock checked his reflection in the sheet of polished brass hanging on the wall. "The increase is large enough to outrage the citizens of Jerusalem, don't you think?"

"Does the king know about this?"

"He will in due time. We're going to involve him at every step in returning the tax to one-quarter and he will come to view us as his most intimate and loyal advisers."

"I don't understand why you're doing any of this."

"You will."

Laban shook the tax notice at Zadock. "This has nothing to do with Uriah's trial."

"Have you forgotten about the Lakhish Letters?" Zadock powdered his already pale nose. "They have evidence that could lead to us."

"You're not planning to use them at the trial, are you?" Laban's harsh voice fell quiet on the clothes that hung from the hooks on the walls, muting the force of his words. "You can't let anyone read them."

"No one ever reads any of the documents stored in the archives at Lakhish, but . . ."

"But what?"

Zadock said, "I have to prove Uriah was a thief."

"You have Lord Yaush as a witness." Laban played with the sleeves of his sleeping robe. "The commander's testimony should be enough. He caught Uriah intercepting my letters."

"Uriah's lawyers could ask for them."

"Uriah doesn't have any lawyers, and as long as his father still believes he's hiding in Egypt, Uriah will never have anyone to defend him."

"He has Miriam."

Laban straightened to his full height, his shoulders went rigid, and the knot in the sash tying his robe at the waist came loose. "She's not a lawyer."

"She's the queen of Judah and she could convince her husband to have the Lakhish Letters brought to Jerusalem."

"No one defending Uriah will ask for them, not as long as they believe the letters will prove Uriah a thief." Laban quickly retied the sash tight about his waist. He pulled the open flaps of his sleeping robe across his chest like formal military dress. "I can have Daniel destroy the letters."

"Not that." Zadock raised his hand and pointed his long forefinger at Laban. "Not unless this fails."

Laban let go his hold on the robe and the lapels fell open. "Unless what fails?"

"The tax." Zadock took the notice from Laban and picked at the corners with his long fingernails until they lifted up and he unraveled the mass. "We need King Zedekiah to believe our words over Queen Miriam's if we have any hope of victory in this trial."

"There you go again, worrying about the king's marriage."

"As should you." Zadock spoke quickly, his words pulsing from his mouth. "We have to prevent the queen from bending Zedekiah's ear." He sat in a short-legged chair and latched his new leather sandals about his feet. "Do you have spies watching her?"

"One. Mima has agreed to it."

Zadock leaned back in the chair. "Get her in place immediately. If we're to win a judgment against Uriah we must know everything Miriam says to the king."

"We can watch her, but we can't keep her from talking to the king. For the sake of Moses, Zadock, they're husband and wife."

"We don't need to keep them from talking to each other." Zadock rubbed the ring finger on his left hand. "All we need do is keep Zedekiah from believing Miriam."

"I wasn't sure until now." Laban leaned against the clothing rack. "But you have gone mad, haven't you?"

"If I have, it's only for want of convincing the king that Uriah is worthy of execution." Zadock tucked the ends of his shawl under the collar of his robe. "That time will come when we're rid of anyone who can hurt us and I want you to start with Jeremiah." Zadock handed over a parchment with instructions to Laban regarding exactly how he was to take care of the prophet. There were a thousand soldiers Laban could send to do this deed, but the Chief Elder's instructions were certain. Laban was to deal with Jeremiah on his own.

Zadock said, "Make sure no one sees you go to Jeremiah's home. I don't want anyone to suspect you of anything."

"Why me?"

"You're the man who banished him from Jerusalem, aren't you?"

"But . . ."

"It's only right that you finish what you began."

Laban said, "I don't need this."

"Do it soon, Captain, while I see to replacing Jeremiah with a prophet more to our liking."

"What are you talking about?"

"Hannaniah, of course."

"The priest?"

"Not for much longer." Zadock picked the string of a lemon rind out from between his teeth. "He's going to make a much better prophet than anyone God would select."

Laban scratched his beard. "How can Hannaniah help us win Uriah's trial?"

"Trust me."

"I trusted you to win me the throne, but Zedekiah and his sons are still alive and well."

"Be patient."

"For how long?"

"Until Zedekiah stops believing that what Miriam says holds any shred of truth."

"And when will that be?"

Zadock stepped across the narrow dressing room to Laban's side. "The moment he stops loving her."

"That's impossible." Laban retied the sash about his waist, tighter than the first time. "Neither of us can work that miracle."

"Miracle, Captain?" Zadock pushed his turban up off his brow. "I didn't think you believed in such nonsense."

"You know what I mean. Zedekiah adores Miriam."

"That's about to change." Zadock removed the ring from his finger and dropped it on the ground, the gold band tinkling against the stone. "The moment King Zedekiah stops loving Miriam you'll see how easily he agrees with our case against Uriah."

"You're a fool." Laban silenced the gold ring with the tip of his boot. "You can't stop him from loving her, and even if you could it will have little bearing on Uriah's trial."

Zadock smiled and his gaunt cheeks lifted away from the high bones on his face. He said, "Miriam and Zedekiah's love thrives for one reason; destroy that and we gain the king's ear."

Laban took back the tax notice and wadded it in his hand, the way he wadded Miriam's veil the evening he found the torn end of it stuck in the gatepost of the palace livery stables and determined she was the informant he'd been hunting all these months. He said, "What are you planning to destroy?"

"The very thing that gives life to their love." Zadock crossed the dressing room. He stood in the incense that hung like a fog about the door and before he disappeared into the hallway he said, "Trust, Captain. We'll destroy their faith in each other."

CHAPTER 11

Elizabeth clutched the knife. It was not a simple thing to keep a secret from Papa, but if she were to come to know the peace of heaven Zoram knew, she had to sneak the ores from her father. She spread her robe over the length of the kitchen table, flattened the pleats and pulled away the sash about the middle. Her long, black hair fell into her eyes and she flicked it out of the way of her scheming and cut a slit along the hip seam wide enough to fit two bars of copper and one of silver—just the right proportion for another brass plate. The wooden legs wobbled with each stroke of the knife and she wedged her foot against them to keep from waking the family.

It was because Zoram exhausted all his money buying ore from miners in Bethlehem that Elizabeth was sewing a secret pouch into her robe, her fingers dancing a needle and thread along the slit and disguising the cloth of the pouch beneath the seam line. She was to meet Zoram at the shop this morning with enough ore from a miner friend of the family to smith another brass plate. What she didn't tell Zoram was that Papa was the miner and she was taking the precious metals from her father's stores. And since no one, not even Zoram, knew of her thievery, she made the slit just the right size to fit the copper and silver beneath the linen and not leave any visible traces of the opening.

Certainty was a blissful way to live, but Elizabeth was not blessed with that kind of contentment. She was like the cords of a rope-maker—draped between opposing hooks of Zoram's faith, and obedience to Papa. She was pulled from both ends and twisted again and again, and she could only hope that when the twisting and pulling was finished she was the cord binding the opposing ends together with a measure of the promised tranquility of heaven. She'd prayed to know if Zoram's belief should be her belief, but until this morning she'd done little to prove her faith. If the whisperings of the Spirit judged in favor of her helping Zoram and she came to know the peace of his Messiah, there would not be a happier soul under heaven and she would bind her heart to his. But if her pilfering created confusion in her soul, she would close her heart to him and search for another. She had endured too long without the peace of heaven in her breast and if she did not obtain her own witness, she would have to endure without the company of Zoram.

A tickle scratched at the tip Elizabeth's nose and she wrinkled the end of it, sniffling but not sneezing. That would only raise Mama out of bed. Ruth could hear a cough from twenty paces, a sneeze from forty, and her children's whimpers from the other side of heaven. Well, maybe not heaven, but three nights ago she heard Elizabeth get out of bed once for a drink of water and again for a blanket. Why did mothers always have the keenest sense of hearing?

Elizabeth held the robe up to the small oil lamp. Perfect. The pouch was hidden from view and there were no visible cuts along the seam. Her hand fit inside with just enough space that the linen didn't ruffle when she pulled it free. The threads held and the linen pouch was sturdy enough to bear the weight of the ores. This was the robe Mama had woven for her and she wanted to run up the stairs, wake her, and tell her the secret she kept—that she was helping Zoram because she must know about his Messiah, the one the prophets called Yeshua ha-Mashiakh—Joshua the Anointed One. But that was blasphemy, not to be spoken in this house. Elizabeth could only pray that if Mama heard her get out of bed this morning, she would count it as the getting of another glass of water or the fetching of another blanket and never discover that her daughter was helping the prophet Jeremiah with his plates of brass.

Another tickle played at Elizabeth's nose and she held her breath, waiting for it to pass. Why did she always sneeze in the early morning? If she'd gotten a good night's rest she wouldn't have to hold her breath to keep from waking the family, but how could she sleep with so much pressing on her mind? She wiped away the tears before they ran, not that the streaking mattered. She didn't have time to powder her cheeks with abalone dust, color her lips with red pomegranate rouge, or perfume her robe with flower-scented waters. Hopefully Zoram wouldn't notice. He was to meet her in the street outside the shop. It was dark there and he would never see her unkempt appearance nor suspect she'd taken the ores from inside.

Elizabeth slipped her arms through the armholes and fitted the robe over her head. When her gaze cleared the lace collar, she found Sarah seated halfway down the steps. The girl's arms were wrapped around her shins and her chin was planted in her knees. How did she get there without making a sound? Elizabeth hurried over and said, "What are you doing up at this hour?"

"Watching you."

"You should be in bed."

Sarah's light-red curls bobbed about her ears. They were really brown, but over the winter they'd taken on a reddish hue and Mama said Sarah was going to grow up the image of great-grandmother, with short red bangs hanging over her high brow, a short nose that turned up whenever she was angry, and a shorter temperament to go with them.

Sarah pressed her chin into her thighs and said, "What did you do to your robe?"

"I was cleaning it." Elizabeth smoothed the pleats about her hip and to be sure Sarah didn't notice the pouch, she spun about like a mincing maiden and said, "Doesn't it look wonderful?"

Sarah spoke in a muffled voice, her knees pushed against her jaw, smoothing the sharp edges of her words. She said, "It would look better if you didn't use a knife to clean it."

Elizabeth quickly put away the knife and threads. "How long have you been sitting there?"

"Long enough to know you didn't clean any spots from the linen."

Elizabeth set her hands on her hips. Why did she have to have a sister? Aaron and Daniel and Joshua would never bother to get up at this hour, no matter how much stirring she made. And if they did, they wouldn't know to ask about her robe. Boys didn't know the first thing about clean robes or weaving or any such thing.

Elizabeth had to keep Sarah from saying anything that would raise suspicions, but she couldn't simply ask the girl not to tell Mama. Swearing her to secrecy was like telling a fox where the rabbit's den was hidden and she'd be up the stairs waking the family as soon as Elizabeth was out the front door, spouting to them about the pouch she'd sewn into the robe. She had to think of a diversion. She draped a thick winter shawl over her shoulders and started across the room to the front door. She said, "I'll be back before anyone's awake."

Sarah said, "Where are you going?"

"I won't be long." Elizabeth unlatched the front door and glanced back into the kitchen. "Zoram is coming to work at the shop early today."

"I knew it." Sarah grinned between the posts in the banister and squealed like a mouse. She said, "You're going to meet him and you're doing it alone! What will Mother say?"

"Quiet or you'll wake her." Elizabeth shook her finger. "Promise me you won't tell a soul."

Sarah inched down to the bottom step. "You were cleaning your robe to see Zoram, weren't you?"

"It isn't any of your business why I was cleaning my robe." Elizabeth turned the latch on the front door. "Promise me you won't say a word."

Sarah slumped back down on the step and buried her grin in her lap. "You can trust me."

But Elizabeth couldn't, not Sarah. The girl never kept a secret, but thankfully she believed this robe cleaning was about courting and had nothing to do with creeds. She couldn't keep the girl from waking Mama and Papa, but at least she'd not tell them about the secret pouch, not when she believed this was about meeting Zoram. That was a giddy secret, and though it was sure to bring a lecture on the respectability of a proper woman, she could endure it as long as there were no questions about why she went to see Zoram. She didn't want to lie to Mama about stealing ore from Papa, not when the lie was to cover a blessed act.

Elizabeth quietly latched the door behind her and left Sarah sitting on the step. Well, she didn't exactly leave her sitting. She could hear the girl climbing the steps to their mother's bedroom, and Elizabeth had little time if she were to get the ore from the shop and meet Zoram in the street before Sarah roused Mama and Papa out of bed. She hurried to the gate and let herself into the street with as long a stride as the hem in her robe allowed. No one could see her getting into Papa's bins.

Not even her trusted Zoram.

The overnight rains thawed the frozen dirt in the coal yard into a sea of mud and with the cloud cover gone it was a very cold sea. Zoram steered the pushcart through the mire. A stack of coal for the smelting oven rose above the sideboards and the weight forced the front wheel into the soft earth. He pushed down on the handles, popped the wheel out of the rut and started it moving again, careful not to lose the load. There was nothing more difficult than firing a muddy load of black coal and if he wanted to get the smelting oven heated before Aaron and Jonathan arrived, he was going to have to start with clean fuel.

Winter mornings were better spent in a comfortable leather chair set beside a freshly kindled fire in Laban's treasury with a pen and papyrus calling him to work, not pushing a cart across the dark reaches of the Blacksmith's coal yard, ankle deep in muddy ice water and wearing a short leather kilt no less. He should have dressed in something warmer, but once the oven was stoked and the shop crackled with the stifling heat of steelmaking, a short kilt would make smelting sufferable. Zoram was contracted by his master Laban to work here two days each week, and though he was indentured to Jonathan for a year of labor, working at the shop did have its advantages. He could smelt whatever he liked as long as he finished before steelmaking began, and twelve months was more than enough time to smelt the brass plates his father, Jeremiah, needed.

The cart fell into another puddle, the wheel raising a spray of dirty water across his face and sinking axle-deep in mud. What a mess! If he'd wanted morning to arrive with a wet start, he'd have poured a bucket of clean water over his head rather than endure the filth that now covered him. He pressed his thigh against the backboard of the pushcart. The axle squeaked like a quail caught in a snare before sinking out of sight. Zoram put his shoulder against the backboard, but when he heaved, the wheel pushed deeper, and the cart went over, spilling coal over the front board and pulling Zoram with it.

Zoram fell forward, his hands out to break the fall, but they didn't keep him from the tomb of mud that received his body from head to foot. The mud was as cold and wet as any sepulchre, and only Zoram's ears were spared from burial, sprouting just above the mud like a rabbit sitting in its hole. His nose sank three fingers deep, his cheeks stuck to the surface of the mud, and when he heard a sweet woman's voice calling him he kept his face in the ground. Please let her pass him by unnoticed. He couldn't answer her call no matter how insistent the greeting, not with his mouth full of mud and his eyelids forced shut against the mud. This was a poor way to greet someone and, no matter what the woman calling to him from the back door of the shop said, he couldn't show his face—

This was not a good morning!

"Good morning, sir!" Elizabeth stood between the doorposts and peered across the coal yard. A strange man lay face down in the mud, his arms stretched above his head and his long, bare legs sprawled behind him. She never would have seen him there, but when she arrived and found the front door to the shop unlatched and a horrible noise erupting in the back, she hurried to see what raised such a stir.

Elizabeth should have gotten the silver and copper from the ore bins and hidden it in her secret pouch before helping him to his feet. But she couldn't just leave him facedown in the mud without checking to see if he was breathing. What if he died there while she was busy stealing the ore? Thievery she could live with, but letting a man die—well that was a sin she could never be rid of and she hurried across the yard, skirted a puddle, and tiptoed around a pile of iron tailings to get a better view of the man.

There was no way it could be Zoram. The stranger was dressed in a kilt and tunic, and Zoram didn't own one, thank heavens for that.

At least she'd never seen him in anything but a white robe and turban. Mud stains on white linen were impossible to get out. And though Zoram's wash was none of Elizabeth's worry, she couldn't keep from concerning herself with the smallest details of his life.

Elizabeth picked her way over to the edge of the deep puddle. It was absolutely not Zoram. He didn't have broad shoulders or strong arms like this stranger and though Papa said blacksmithing was toughening Zoram, it couldn't have toughened him that much. Elizabeth pulled up a few strides from the fallen man. Thankfully Zoram was far too sensible a man to dress in such skimpy clothing on a chilly winter morning. Only a madman would dare wallow about in a perfectly strange pit of mud with nothing but a kilt to cover his legs and a short tunic over his torso. Elizabeth lifted the hem of her robe and leaned over the stranger. "I say, good morning, sir."

"Not exactly a good morning, Elizabeth." The stranger lifted his head from the puddle, the whites of his eyes blinking above his mud-plastered cheeks. He was masked behind a thick layer of wet earth with stalks of straw hanging from his chin. He smiled and there was no mistaking his straight white teeth. It *was* her love and when he blinked his green eyes she couldn't help but catch her breath and say, "Zoram, is that you?"

He rolled over in the puddle, the front of his kilt sticking to his thighs, and his tunic matted to his stomach. He reached out his hand and said, "Help me up, would you?"

She certainly would not! She couldn't take his hand, not with it covered in mud. She stepped back onto firmer ground and said, "What are you doing out here like this?"

Zoram stood and wiped the mud from his face, but it only smeared about his eyes and turned him into something of an owl peering through dark bands of mud-feathers. No, he didn't look like an owl; he was dazed and he had the look of a man smitten by a rod. He pulled the mud-soaked tunic away from his belly. "I was heating the ovens."

How could he heat the ovens out here? Elizabeth glanced toward the shop. The smelting oven was inside and there was no reason to be wallowing in the mud unless he'd gone mad. Elizabeth held her hand to her cheek. Oh my, that's exactly what had happened—Zoram had fallen in the mud, hit his head and he wasn't at all certain where he was; she could tell by looking into his dazed eyes, gone wider after such a fall.

Elizabeth raised her hand. "How many fingers am I holding up?"

Zoram squinted in the darkness. "I can't tell."

See there, she was right. He'd been knocked senseless. She ran her hand through his hair, searching for a lump, a swell, a soft spot on his skull that would give reason to his insanity, but all she could find were clumps of mud. She said, "You poor dear, it must have been a horrible fall. You can hardly see."

Zoram spit the foul-tasting stuff from his mouth. "Mud, Elizabeth."

"I know, everything's a blur right now, but the dizziness will pass, I'm sure of it." Her hand stopped on a small bump at the back of his head. This had to be the reason for his odd behavior, at least she was certain it was until the bump came lose between her fingers and a rock fell from the mud on his head. Everything was clear now. Her Zoram had fallen and hit his head on a rock. She came back around and studied his brow, searching his face for a trace of blood, a cut, anything that would explain Zoram's madness, but she found nothing but mud. She said, "Do you know what day it is?"

"It's not what you think." Zoram shook his head and the mud flew off his bangs and sprayed across Elizabeth's face. She stepped back from the pushcart, her sandals slipping down the edge of the puddle and sinking into the soft ground. It was the lowest point in the yard where all of last night's rain had pooled. She reached for the sideboard of the cart, but she was too far away to get hold and all she could do was swing her arms, fighting to gain her balance.

Zoram leaned over to take her in his mud-covered arms and lift her to drier ground, but this wasn't how she had pictured it. Their first embrace should be a sweet moment, not a dirty one with Zoram smelling more like sewage than spice and she wasn't about to let him take hold of her, not while she was wearing her new robe. He'd only stain the white linen. She said, "No, Zoram, not like this." But Zoram snatched her from the edge of the puddle and lifted her off her feet, his white-toothed smile shimmering from behind muddy lips like a conqueror bearing the spoils of war. She squirmed and he tightened his grip against her fighting. His strong arms and quick footedness had saved her from falling into the mud, and after a moment more of fidgeting she relaxed and let him nestle her to his chest, the warmth of his body comforting her against the cold morning air. He'd dirtied her robe, but the feel of him close to her was worth the stain, and she could remove the mud with a bucket of lye and a good washboard.

Zoram turned to carry her away from the puddle's edge when a bat flew over the wall and came at them. It was an ugly, dirty animal with its wings fluttering about. Papa said he'd gotten rid of the bats, but obviously not all of them. Thank heavens Zoram had the sense to duck out of the way. His sudden movement lifted the pleats of Elizabeth's robe into his face. She quickly leaned forward to pull the cloth away from in front of his eyes, but her stirring forced him to lose his footing and he slipped back into the puddle, his feet sinking into the muck.

"Zoram!" Elizabeth wrapped her arms around his shoulders. "What are you doing?"

His right foot slid out from under him and with only his left one to steady both of them, they began to tip like a great cedar in a forest, felled at the trunk. Elizabeth tightened her grip around his shoulders, or was it his neck? It must be his neck. She was climbing up his body in search of higher ground and he was choking on his words telling her to let go of . . .

They fell into the mud—together.

Aaron peeled the blanket from his face. What was that sound? A drop of water trickled off the edge of the shop roof and collected on the timber joist before falling onto his makeshift bedroom—a lean-to of sticks covered with leather hides. It was the night rains and Aaron turned onto his side and tried to forget he was sleeping on the hard cobblestones of the alley next to the shop, standing guard for thieves that were certain never to appear.

There was no reason for Papa to send him out here every night for the last week. They lost some copper and silver bars from the ore bins a few months back and again last week, but Papa could have miscounted their stores. The locks on the shop doors were never broken, the latches never forced and not even a babe could wiggle through the narrow window vents. The only other entry was the chimney if it were possible for a man to get through a pipe two hands wide and shimmy down into the smelting oven—an impossible feat for the most nimble of prowlers. Aaron pulled the blanket up under his neck. There were no thieves and he was going to tell Papa he wouldn't spend another night out here in the alley without more reason than a single missing bar of . . .

A fluttering of air streamed past Aaron's face. He threw off the blanket and jumped to his feet. Bats. The flying rodents streaked past him in the darkness, their wings brushing his head. Papa said he'd gotten rid of the creatures, but the blacksmith shop stood halfway between caves on the Mount of Olives and a large patch of wild chokecherry west of Jerusalem, and there was nothing Papa could do to keep the constant stream of bats from flying this way between dusk and dawn with a supply of fruit stuffed between their cheeks.

Aaron wrapped the blanket over his head to keep the bats away and let the cloth hang down, the end of it dancing at his toes—ten perfectly pink, healthy toes, strapped into new leather sandals and all of them without a single scar to remind him of his smithing accident. He never could have spent the last few nights out in the cold March weather if he were still crippled. He stomped his feet on the ground to take the chill out of them when he heard another rushing sound. The bats were gone and he pulled the blanket back from his ears. It wasn't a rushing of winged creatures at all. It was some sort of splashing and it filtered over the wall from the coal yard. He cocked his ear and there it was again, louder than before. It filtered over the wall accompanied by the unmistakable sound of voices.

Papa was right. It was thieves. What a fool he was for not hearing them sooner. He never should have fallen asleep and he hurried down the alley, around to the front, and found the door ajar. Cursed hoodlums! They'd pried the lock and gotten into the shop and now they were in the coal yard rummaging about. Aaron slipped inside and quickly hid between the wooden ore bins before the outline of a dark-clothed figure stepped in from the coal yard, his gaunt form framed between the posts. He wasn't a large thief. He stood two hands shorter than Aaron and his shoulders were as narrow as a bird's breast. He walked with a short, timid stride and when the intruder stepped past his hiding place, Aaron leaped on him, catching him around the waist and pulling him to the ground. They rolled three times and butted up against the ore bins in a flurry of arms and legs. Aaron wrestled to the top, pinned the man's hands to the ground and started to swing his fist when the thief said, "Aaron, what in the name of Moses are you doing?"

"Elizabeth?" Aaron lowered his fist. Was it really his sister trapped beneath him? He couldn't be sure until Zoram appeared with an oil lamp, the light splitting the shadows and angling down over the forging table, its orange glow falling on Elizabeth's mud-splattered face. Her new robe was covered with brown earth, her sash clotted with mud, and her long, black hair was matted to her face. She was as unrecognizable as Zoram with only the pink of his lips and whites of his eyes visible through a mask of mud that caked his skin.

Aaron folded his arms across his chest. This was perfect. He wasn't going to let this moment pass without a measure of teasing. Elizabeth would never explain herself out of this if Mama found out. Ruth was not one to allow improper courting of her eldest daughter and finding these two in the dark and covered with mud was about as improper as anything Aaron could remember. And if Papa found out about this, there would be no end to his lecture. He wouldn't stand for a breach in courting etiquette, no matter how much he'd come to trust Zoram with the matter of Elizabeth's tender heart.

Aaron said, "I know everything."

"You do?" Elizabeth rubbed the mud from her hands. "I can explain."

"There's nothing left to explain."

Zoram said, "I know this looks a bit odd."

"A bit odd?" Aaron winked at Zoram. Of course it looked odd. Aaron raised his hand to shield his smile from the lamplight. He said, "Wait until Papa hears about this."

"Aaron, no." Elizabeth inched back against the ore bins. "Promise me you won't tell Papa about the— "

"Tell me what?" Jonathan stepped in from the street. He was dressed in his smithing apron. His black hair was combed back off his brow and the sleep of morning weighed down his eyelids. He stepped past the tool rack, around the open hearth, and stopped at the back door. "What happened to the load of coal?"

"I'm sorry, sir." Mud dripped from the ends of Zoram's hands. "The cart got away from me."

Aaron said, "Elizabeth was— "

"We slipped." Elizabeth jabbed Aaron in the side. "I was helping Zoram with the coal and we fell in the mud."

Jonathan came back inside the shop. "You'll want to be more careful next time."

That was all Papa was going to say? Aaron came around next to Jonathan. Aaron said, "At first I thought they were thieves." He set his hands on his hips. "You could imagine my relief when I found it was only Elizabeth and Zoram behind the shop, alone." He held onto the word "alone" long enough for it to sink into Papa's consciousness, but at this hour Jonathan was only conscious of firing the ovens, and he headed out into the muddy coal yard to fetch in a load of coal without another word about Elizabeth's indiscretion.

Aaron stood in the doorway watching Jonathan pull the cart from the mud, but he kept Elizabeth in view. The mud hung in clumps from her pleats, but she didn't brush it away. She slowly stepped away from door, inching back against the ore bins. She reached behind her back into the first one and pulled out two bars of copper and slipped it into something like a purse stitched beneath the muddy hip seam of her robe.

Elizabeth said, "Shouldn't you be out there helping Papa with the coal?"

"Papa doesn't need my help." Aaron kept facing out the door, but he could see her working the silver bin. It stood a little higher than the copper and it was the only one Papa locked for safekeeping. Elizabeth kept her back to it, her gaze on Aaron, watching his every movement and never knowing that he could see her watching him. She rose up on her toes and felt about with her hand until she found the latch, unlocked it with Papa's key and removed a single bar of silver, as subtly as a thief in the night, placing it in her pouch along with the copper. She was lowering herself from her toes when Aaron turned from the door and caught her dropping the bar into her pouch, the metal flashing in the dim light.

Aaron came down along the forging table. "You're the thief I've been waiting to catch."

"What are you talking about?" Elizabeth stood away from the bins.

Aaron said, "Give me the ores you took from the bin."

"Aaron," Zoram said. He stood between them. "It's not what you think. Your sister's been getting me some ore from miners in Bethlehem." He turned to Elizabeth. "Isn't that right?"

Aaron said, "She may be getting ores for you, but not from any miners in Bethlehem."

"That's enough teasing." Zoram pressed his lips together, hiding the whiteness of his straight teeth. "We should help your father with the ovens."

"I'm not teasing." Aaron reached for the hip seam in Elizabeth's robe and began feeling for the ore hidden beneath the cloth. "How do you explain her hiding these?"

"Stop that." Elizabeth pulled her robe free of Aaron's grasp and the metal gave up a muted clang.

"Elizabeth?" Zoram stepped closer to her, his dark, curly hair flopping over his brow. "The ore for the plates came from miners in Bethlehem. Isn't that right?"

Aaron said, "What plates?"

Elizabeth backed toward the front door, shivering from the ice-cold water and mud that soaked her body. Her long, tangled hair hedged about the neckline of her robe. She said, "Zoram made brass plates to record—"

"Elizabeth!" Zoram followed her to the front door. "Don't say anymore about the plates."

"We can trust him."

Aaron said, "Brass plates to record what?"

Zoram said, "No, Elizabeth, don't."

Aaron said, "Tell me!"

"I can't." Elizabeth disappeared into the street, with Zoram following her.

Aaron pushed out the front door and found Elizabeth standing across the street emptying the contents of her pouch into Zoram's hand. She was speaking quickly, pleading with him, her words lost in the rush of whispers that filled the morning air with her haste.

Aaron started toward her and immediately she fell silent. He said, "I saw what you did inside."

"Not another word about this, do you understand?" Elizabeth jabbed her finger at Aaron like a mother chiding her young. "I don't want you saying anything to Papa."

Aaron pulled up a good distance from Elizabeth. When did she become so bold? She should be offering him an explanation for her thievery or at least begging him not to go to Papa with it, but instead she was telling him to keep silent. Wasn't this his witty older sister who preferred reading to shopping? The shy girl who lowered her gaze in the company of men and strangers? But Aaron was just beginning to understand that Elizabeth hid her feelings and her doings in a silent world, one that she was not about to let him enter, at least not now.

Aaron slowly stepped toward her. "What's gotten into you, Elizabeth? You can't take the ore from Papa, not without his blessing."

"You don't understand."

"I'd like to."

Elizabeth took Zoram by the arm and they stood together like two pillars of mud. "This is between us."

"Not when you steal from our shop, it isn't."

"Oh, Aaron, please!" Elizabeth gathered the hem of her robe off her ankles. There was little reason to keep the mud-covered cloth from dragging under foot, but she did it out of habit, just as she was blindly giving Zoram these ores without regard for their business. How did this green-eyed lad with black, curly hair convince her to steal from her own family? If he needed money to purchase ore for brass plates he could pay for it. Zoram made a good wage working for Laban.

A tear ran down Elizabeth's cheek and he reached to brush it off her rose-red skin, but she turned away. "Please Aaron, don't say anything to Papa."

"Why are you doing this?"

"Because I must." She hurried down the street and out of the smithing district, her dirty robe dragging on the stone.

"Elizabeth!" Aaron started after her. "Tell me what you're—

"Let her go." Zoram took Aaron by the arm. "She'll tell you when the time is right."

"When will that be?" Aaron pulled free. "Once she's stolen all the ore from our shop?"

"Trust her."

"With what?"

Zoram lowered his voice. "With all your soul."

What did Zoram know about a man's soul? He worked for Laban. Aaron said, "I don't need your help."

"You needed me the day your feet burned."

"What are you talking about?"

"I was on an errand with my father to come by your shop the day you were burned." Zoram moved closer, but Aaron backed away from him. Zoram said, "You were nearly unconscious and I—"

"I wasn't unconscious." Aaron rubbed his brow. "I remember everything."

"Do remember how I lifted your feet out of the molten ore?"

The memory of his accident was like a distant dream. He hadn't seen everything that was going on around him. He could only remember faint glimpses of the man who gave him the blessing but he would never forget the words he spoke. Aaron said, "Who told you about my accident?"

"There's a reason I wear long, white sleeves everywhere I go." Zoram pulled back the cloth of his tunic and wiped away the mud. His skin was pocked with scars from the wrist to the elbow. He said, "You were screaming in pain when you kicked the hot metal onto my arms."

Aaron shook his head. "I did no such thing."

"That was right before you lost consciousness the first time."

"The first time? What are you talking about?"

"I held your head to keep you from shaking and bathed your feet in cold water." Zoram moved around next to Aaron. "You came around long enough to hear the blessing."

"This is some kind of trick. I remember the man's voice and it wasn't yours. What does this have to do with stealing ore to make brass plates?"

"It was my father's voice you heard. He was there with me. We came to inquire after Jonathan's skill in making plates of brass." Zoram spoke with a firm voice. "My father blessed you that your feet would be healed to save the life of a—"

"Your father?" Aaron lowered his head. "Who is your father?"

"I can't tell you that."

"And why not?"

Zoram reached out to take Aaron by the hand. "He'll tell you when's he's ready."

Aaron pulled away from Zoram's reaching. How could he trust him? He was part of their lives—especially Elizabeth's life—but he was Laban's servant and there was no reason to trust him with anything to do with the prophets, anymore than he should trust Elizabeth to tell Papa about the ores she'd taken from the shop.

Aaron said, "Until you trust me with your father's name, I can't trust you."

"Here, take these." Zoram offered the copper and silver Elizabeth left with him. "I'm not a thief and I'll see that you're paid for any ores you're missing."

"Keep your money." Aaron pushed Zoram's hand out of the way, knocking the bars to the ground.

There was too much at risk to take a chance on believing Zoram and it was best to err on the side of reason. Zoram could have pieced together what he knew about Aaron's feet from talking to Elizabeth. He could be spying on their family and there was good reason for Laban to want to know about them with Papa serving on the Council of Elders, Daniel in the military, and Aaron with ties to Lehi. What a fool he was. It was his duty to watch over Lehi, and if Zoram was part of a threat to the prophet's life, then he could never be trusted. Aaron left Zoram picking the ores off the street and started out of the smithing district. He had to find out from his own flesh and blood if Zoram was telling the truth.

Aaron went after Elizabeth.

Ruth pushed aside the thick canopy of winter curtains and let the warm breeze draft into the kitchen. It wasn't really warm, but since this was the first morning in three months that didn't chill her to the bone, she aired out the musty scent of winter and waited in the gray dawn for the sun to light the courtyard.

Ruth leaned a jar out the window and filled the water clock to overflowing. She dipped out two and a half cups to bring it level with the line etched just below the brim and tossed away what she didn't need. If only she could dip out the trouble in their family as easily as the overflow from the clock. Jonathan sided with the Elders, Daniel with Laban, and she could never tell them that she believed the words of the prophets. She would gladly toss this conflict from their lives like the overflow from the clock. Ruth leaned against the sill. These troubles were flesh of her flesh and bone of her bone, and she couldn't rid herself of her kin as easily as unwanted water, or root them out like weeds from her garden.

The first rays of morning fell over the water clock and Ruth uncorked the spigot in the bottom. Large drops clung to the red clay bucket like dew on a stand of ripening winter wheat before dropping to the ground below the kitchen window—the faint splashing reminding her of the promise of peace. that came to those who took upon them the name of Yeshua. How she longed to find that peace and she reached out to let the droplets wash over her hand as if they had power to cleanse her of her troubles. Not a day passed that she didn't raise her prayers to heaven and beg the Almighty to guide her to the life-giving waters of the Anointed One. Jonathan was a good husband and Daniel a fine son, but they did not seek the same waters of faith. Their hearts were impossible captives and she could neither fight their war for them nor carry their wounded souls back across the battle lines to the safety of her heart. She could only stand by and watch their faith slowly trickle away like water from the bottom of the clock, and pray one day they would stop the cork and collect within the well of their hearts the redeeming waters of her new faith.

"It's time, Ruth."

The deep voice drew her gaze away from the water clock to a man standing in the courtyard. She dried her hand and held it over her brow to shield the morning sun. She said, "Time for what, sir?"

The stranger stepped to the window and immediately she recognized the prophet Jeremiah's plain brown robe and his beard that reached well past his collar. His uncombed gray hair capped his head and curled about his ears like vines on an arbor pole. This was the man banished by Laban for preaching in the city. He had saved Aaron from the smelting oven and had given him a blessing of healing, and for that she was thankful, but he was also the one who told her that Jonathan moved his blacksmithing business to Jerusalem to help with the smithing of brass plates. How could he think such a presumptuous thing? Jonathan came from Phoenicia to start a new blacksmithing business among the Jews. No, it wasn't presumptuous of Jeremiah to think such a thing; it was impossible. Her husband was not one to change his mind and he'd already taken sides on the matter of the prophets. The name of Yeshua the Anointed One was not to be spoken in this house and there was little reason to believe he would ever lend a hand to an outcast holy man like Jeremiah—not if he preached that God would raise up a Messiah among the Jews to be the savior of the world.

Ruth said, "This isn't a good time to speak with my husband about blacksmithing."

Jeremiah held his hands beneath the clock and washed them in the cold water. His skin was worn, calloused from years of vineyard keeping. He said, "I came to see about matters of your soul."

Her soul? When did anyone worry about her salvation? Ruth had only ever met Jeremiah once. It was a brief encounter months ago in the market, hardly enough time for her to share anything about her most private worries.

Jeremiah said, "I know the desires of your heart. I've seen you mourn with Queen Miriam when she mourned and I've seen you comfort her when she was in need of comfort." He stood to the window, his head silhouetted by the morning sun. "You're willing to bear the burdens of others, aren't you?"

"Well, I . . ." Ruth lifted her hands from the sill. "Of course I am."

"It's time for you and your family to take the name of the Anointed One upon you."

"You don't understand." Ruth backed away from the window, the light moving off her face. How did Jeremiah know about her deepest hope? She'd only ever spoken with Miriam about her desire to gain the blessed promise of the Holy Spirit, but her family wasn't ready to enter the waters of the washing pool, at least not her entire family. She glanced toward the gate leading in from the street. There was no sign of Jonathan returning for morning meal, but if the fires were set at the shop and there was nothing for him to do but wait for the ovens to heat, he could return at any moment. How would she explain the prophet at their home; or worse, what if Jeremiah spoke to him about baptism? She could never tell her husband about her witness of the Anointed One, not now, maybe not ever, and if she couldn't do that then she certainly couldn't make a covenant to stand as a witness of God, not in these times and certainly not in this place. Ruth said, "You had better go."

"If you're to find any peace in these troubled times, you must turn your burdens over to the Lord." Jeremiah leaned over the sill, his kind brown eyes peering in at her. "Only He can make them light."

Ruth pushed a chair out of the way of her retreat, the wooden legs grating over the stone floor. She would give anything to have the burdens of these troubled times made light. All she'd ever prayed for was for their life to be good and for Jonathan's heart to soften and for Daniel to end his admiration of Laban, but the heavens had not moved on those matters. Ruth shielded her face with the back of her hand, and shook her head. "This isn't the right time for your preaching."

"You need the strength that comes from baptism."

"We're not ready for that right now."

"There's little time left before you will stand as witnesses."

Ruth came up against the table, the hardwood stopping her retreat. They had already risked so much. Didn't Jeremiah see the divide that threatened to destroy her family? If Ruth were to keep them from splintering like so many other families in Jerusalem, she had to remain in the middle; and baptism was not a fence-sitting rite. She rubbed away the worry that furrowed her brow and said, "We've not been summoned by any lawyers."

"The witness that comes with baptism is what will save Jonathan and Daniel." Jeremiah dipped his hand inside the clock and slowly stirred the water about; washing it against the sides of the clay bucket like the constant, gentle flowing of a stream along the shore. "Isn't that what you've been praying for?"

Ruth came back to the window. How did he know that was what Ruth hoped for? She said, "Miriam told me that peace was the blessing that comes from baptism."

"That's part of it." Jeremiah nodded and the ends of his graying beard brushed over his chest.

"What else is there?"

"Baptism is the gate that will open your life onto . . ."

The pattering of footsteps sounded at the front of the gate and Ruth said, "Come inside. You can't be seen out here." She left the window, ran through the kitchen, and met Jeremiah at the back door. He stepped inside as the front gate swung open, the wood planks banging against the posts. Whoever it was, they were in a hurry and Ruth left Jeremiah in the kitchen and went to the main room in time to open the front door for Elizabeth to stomp inside. Her face was covered with thick, brown earth except where tears had cleaned streaks down her cheeks. The pleats in her robe were matted together with mud that not even the most experienced washerwoman could hope to scrub away.

"Elizabeth?" Ruth picked at her sleeve, pulling the muddy cloth away from her skin. "What's wrong girl? What happened to your robe?"

"It's Aaron." She held her hand to her mouth and hid her trembling lips. "He, he . . ." Her voice was lost in a quiet sob.

Aaron marched through the open door, his shoulders forward and his sandy brown hair rising off his head with each step. "Why don't you tell us why you're stealing ores from the shop?"

Ruth said, "Elizabeth, is that true?"

Zoram hurried up the steps and inside the main room. His dark skin was hidden behind a darker covering of mud, but his straight white teeth and curly hair were as unmistakable as his slender, upright stride. He held out the bars of copper and silver to Elizabeth and said, "Why didn't you tell me these came from your father's stores?"

"I couldn't." Elizabeth held her hand to her mouth. "Not until I knew for certain that I should be like you."

"Don't say that, Elizabeth." Aaron stepped between them. "Zoram works for Laban."

Elizabeth touched Aaron on the arm. "Zoram is the reason I know."

"Know what?"

"That I should take upon me the name of Yeshua the Anointed One."

Ruth took Elizabeth in her arms. It didn't matter that she was covered in mud and bathed in awful-smelling waters. Her daughter had gained the blessed witness of the Anointed One and that was the testimony she prayed all her children would find. Ruth held Elizabeth's trembling body close. She said, "Is baptism what you want?"

Elizabeth turned her mud-stained gaze to Ruth and nodded. "More than anything else, Mama."

Zoram lowered the ores to his side. "I'm sorry I didn't understand sooner."

Aaron stepped in next to Zoram. He said, "How can anyone of the house of Laban be happy about baptism? Laban murders Rekhabites."

"Zoram is of my house." Jeremiah entered from the kitchen. His voice was deep and resonating like thunder against the walls of the main room.

"Jeremiah? What are you . . . ?" Elizabeth rushed over and fell against him, trying to push him back into the kitchen. "Don't show yourself. No one can know about you; it will only hurt Zoram."

"Aaron already knows." Zoram pulled Elizabeth back.

Ruth touched Zoram on the arm. "Why didn't you tell us before now?"

Elizabeth said, "It was his position in Laban's treasury we were trying to protect." She took Zoram by the hand. "If Laban finds out he's the son of Jeremiah, there's no telling what he would do."

Jeremiah said, "You can blame me for this. I never should have risked your lives with the making of brass plates." He took the ores from Zoram and placed them in Aaron's hands. "Take these back to your father and I'll find another way."

Zoram said, "Papa, there is no other way. Theirs is the only black-smith shop in the city."

"We'll help you." Aaron returned the ores to Jeremiah's hand and clasped the man's worn skin in his grip. "It was you, wasn't it? It was these hands that healed me."

"I gave you a blessing in the name of the Anointed One." Jeremiah stepped a circle around Aaron, his gaze turned down to inspect Aaron's feet, his lips lifting into a smile with each stride. "But it was God who healed you, not me."

"It isn't finished." Aaron lowered his voice to a whisper. "I still have one thing left to—"

"There's more required of you than saving the life of a prophet."

"What else is there, sir?"

Jeremiah laid his hand on Aaron's shoulder. "It's time you stood as a witness of God."

Ruth said, "Aaron, no, not yet. The time isn't right."

"The time will never be right." Aaron marched to the front door and peered out into the morning. "Not in this city."

Ruth wrapped her arms around herself. "I could never bear to see you suffer more."

Jeremiah turned his gaze from Ruth to Aaron and finally settled on Elizabeth. "If you have faith unto baptism, no evil will prevail against you."

Elizabeth stepped forward, the pleats of her muddy robe brushing against Ruth. She said, "Can we, Mother?"

Ruth gathered Aaron and Elizabeth in her arms. They were ready for this, but what about Daniel and Jonathan? Would this baptism split their family with a divide so great she would never be able bridge it? She said, "The two of you can do this, but I can't."

Aaron said, "You must."

Elizabeth said, "Why won't you join us?"

Ruth nestled Elizabeth's head against her neck and pulled Aaron in close enough that she could feel his chest rise and fall with his breathing.

Ruth said, "Not without your father."

CHAPTER 12

Daniel pushed open the gate to Laban's estate with one hand and he held a document close to his vest with the other. The parchment was tied with cords and sealed with Captain Laban's own monogram—the first assignment for his company of fifty—and he wasn't to open it until he got inside the estate and met with his men for the first time. Daniel stood in the entrance, blocking the gate from closing. He ran his hand over the parchment, the uneven wax seal holding it shut. These orders were for Daniel and his men and he fought to keep a smile from rising to his lips. He'd been in the military less than a year and he had command over fifty, and not just any command. His men were to guard Laban's estate, police Jerusalem, and carry out the most difficult missions—the ones no others in the military were to know about. Daniel was commander of Laban's elite, personal guard.

The outdoor lamps lighting the courtyards of Laban's estate burned with a welcoming yellow glow that chased away the dun of winter, casting a warm light over the gray, stone walls, rooftop parapets, and arching balcony windows of Daniel's new residence. This was his home now, the headquarters for his company of fifty, and he kept a private room on the upper floor with a fine bed and a cedar desk and maidservants to do his bidding, and he already knew what he would bid them do. After meeting with his men, he'd have the maidservants draw him a warm bath scented with frankincense, and while he was bathing he'd have them serve him a shot of wine and a roasted leg of lamb dipped in garnish and served with a round of bread. Daniel closed the gate behind him, the post rattling against the latch, and the cold evening wind whistling through the bars. No, he wouldn't trouble the maidservants for a shot of wine and a garnish; he'd demand they bring a tankard full of strong ale and he'd have them baste the lamb until it was cooked to the bone with the flavor of his favorite herbs, and the bread would have to be soft without any hard kernels left after the winnowing. Daniel was the commander of Laban's fifty, and the captain said he could have whatever he pleased, whenever it pleased him.

The courtyard was exactly as Captain Laban said it would be—empty—with no watchman to ask the nature of Daniel's business. He stepped to the empty watchmen's post beside the gate. The high wall and overhanging ledge sheltered him from the wind that rasped through the leaves clinging to the front-facing façade of the estate, and it would have blown out the fire burning in the cauldron next to the watchman's stoop if not for the tall clay rim protecting the flames. There hadn't been a watchman for nearly two days, not since Laban sent all the soldiers back to their regiments. The captain was replacing them with Daniel's company tonight. He stuffed the sealed document under his belt, the end of the parchment scratching against the cloth in his tunic. They would live here at the estate, eat in the kitchens, stand guard over the property, and always be ready and waiting to do Laban's bidding.

Daniel pulled off his new leather gloves, stuffed them under his arm, and held his hands over the cauldron fire burning in the watchman's stoop, his fingers moving with the shifting flames but never able to catch a steady stream of warmth. The gloves were made of finely tanned hides, stitched with silver threads and issued to him this afternoon by Laban. The captain said Daniel would need them for tonight's meeting, said he wanted Daniel's new company to respect him and there was no better way to earn the reverence of the tough-minded, rough-edged men Laban had assigned to this new company than by the strength of Daniel's arm and the fineness of his dress. Daniel rubbed his hands together, blew the warmth of his breath between his cupped fingers and pulled the gloves back on over his hands. He had more than enough strength to impress his men. Why, he could lift two of them over his head and throw them across the courtyard if he needed to make a show of strength, but until Laban issued him his new riggings, he was desperately lacking in costly apparel.

Daniel scaled the steps of the main porch, the tail of his cloak snapping at his knees. It was woven of black sheep's wool with silver clasps about the collar and a matching tunic pulled taut about his thick shoulders, but it wasn't so uncomfortable that he couldn't enjoy the reverence it inspired. The boots were worn and the heels didn't click over the stonework and up to the main door like new boots should. Laban had offered to replace them along with the other clothing, but Daniel had refused. He wanted nothing on his feet but the alligator skins he'd gotten on his trip to Egypt. The boots were a sign of good luck from his first mission, when he captured Uriah, and Laban allowed him to wear his superstitions on his feet.

The ready room stood at the end of the hall and the loud talk of men streamed from inside. Daniel pushed the door wide open, rousing his men to attention. Fifty pair of eyes followed Daniel's slow stride to the center of the room, the men pushing back to let him pass. They hardly fit inside the stuffy room, their thick frames pushing against each other and crowded three men deep, the damp, warm air filling the room with their eagerness for their new assignment. They were mostly young soldiers, reassigned from every infantry, cavalry, and fort across the kingdom and they were selected for the strength of their arms and their skill with weapons. And since Daniel didn't see Captain Laban among their number, there was no better time than now to let his men know that he was in command of this company. He leaned his face in next to a soldier and said, "What's your name?"

The soldier pinned his shoulders back. "I don't have one, sir."

"You what?"

"That's right, sir. I don't have a name."

"What kind of an answer is that?" Daniel yanked his cape off his shoulders and draped it over his arm. "What's your rank, soldier?"

"I have none, sir." The soldier forced his chin down hard with each word.

"I want your name and your rank. That's an order."

"I can't, sir."

"And why not?"

"I have other orders."

"From whom?"

"From me." Captain Laban stood beyond the line of soldiers, warming his hands over the hearth, his dark skin taking on a red glow from the fire. What was he doing here? Laban had given Daniel written orders with instructions that he wasn't going to be at this meeting.

Daniel said, "Sir, I didn't expect you."

"There's something I want to tell your men." Laban scratched his beard with his forefinger and turned his gaze over the fifty men, their bodies stiff as boards and their ears cocked to the captain's words. He said, "None of you have a name except for the ones Daniel gives, no rank except what he assigns. You have no past and your only future is what Daniel tells you. You're to obey him without question, and when I leave this room you will have no other commander. The only contact you will have with me will be through this man." Laban shook Daniel's hand. "Congratulations, Commander. It's time you and your men got along with the business at hand." He pointed at the sealed document stuck beneath Daniel's belt. "Read it before the night escapes you."

Daniel turned on the heels of his old boots, the alligator skin striking a familiar squeak. He walked to the table opposite the hearth, spread the scroll over the wood planks, and began to read. It was a short message, not more than a few lines and it gave only brief details of a very odd mission, nothing like what Daniel expected. He and his men were to go and return before sunrise. They were to disguise their faces and wear nothing that may link them to Laban. They had one mission to accomplish and Daniel slowly rolled the scroll around the dowel and placed it under his arm. He said, "We ride to Beit Zayit tonight!"

A thin covering of perspiration blanketed Sariah's brow and she quickly dabbed it dry on the bed sheets before placing her feet on the cold, stone floor. She wouldn't lie in bed a moment longer and let this sickness grow worse, not with Lehi sleeping beside her. He'd spent yesterday digging about the trees in the middle vineyards with Ishmael and if she'd known that a few hours of hard labor would cure the restlessness that plagued him since his first vision, she'd have put a shovel in his hands and sent him into the groves to work out his prophethood weeks before. He came home last evening with calluses on his hands, sweat soaking his tunic, and a tired smile on his face—something she hadn't seen for two months. He took a hot bath—something she wished all her boys would do more often—and fell into bed earlier than usual, and Sariah wasn't about to wake him to tell of her midnight illness. It would pass as soon as she got some fresh air. She stood away from the bed and rubbed the pain in her side. It must have been something she ate at evening meal that caused the queasiness, though there was no food that had the power to upset her with such fury as the . . .

Not another cramp! The pain shot through Sariah's stomach and she bent over, her hand against her side and her lips pressed shut to silence her gasps. What was it that caused her such pain? No one else in the family was sick; she'd taken nothing but the sweetest water and not less than once a day she ate a dried fig picked from the large tree in the gardens and stored in a sealed jar in the pantry and there was not another fruit that inspired good health like a fig. There was simply no excuse for her to be sick except for her concern over her husband.

Sariah came around the bed and stood over Lehi. He'd been still for hours without turning onto his side or tossing about, and she immediately placed her palm on his chest to check his breathing and feel for the beating of his heart. She nearly lost him the day he arrived home from Raphia, threw himself down on this bed and didn't get up for three days. He said it was a vision, that God bid him read from the *Book of Heaven*; but no matter what sort of book it was she wasn't going to let him do that again. Lehi was not allowed to pass from this life without saying good-bye. He may be master of Beit Zayit, but she was master of his well-being and dying was not something he could do without her permission.

Lehi was still breathing and Sariah pulled the blanket up about his neck and tucked it beneath his gaunt chin, but she kept her hand firmly planted on his chest, measuring each steady heartbeat by the gentle quaver that pulsed through her palm. Thank heaven it wasn't like before, when Lehi returned from Raphia and there was hardly the faintness of life in his chest. He was tired tonight, that's all it was and his stillness had nothing to do with another vision or she'd shake him until he opened his eyes and asked her why she was acting like such an odd goose at this hour of the night. Then she would think of some peculiar answer like his snoring or he was too close to the edge of the bed—anything to make sure that she wasn't going to lose him again, not even for three days. There was nothing that inspired more fear in her soul than his reading from the *Book of Heaven*. Sariah took a deep breath. Let him read from the book of life—their happy, prosperous life at Beit Zayit—and leave the *Book of Heaven* to another prophet.

Lehi's dark, black hair fell down into his eyes and she slowly lifted the ends back and ran her hand over his brow. He was a hard-working soul and even in the dead of winter his skin was tanned from working about the plantation. Who would have ever thought that this man with wind-blown red cheeks, a tuft of black beard at the end of his chin, and a deep, soothing voice would attract the notice of heaven? Prophet was a calling better suited to holy men, not businessmen, and there was no telling the problems his vision could cause for their olive growing and oil pressing, to say nothing of her peace of mind. Lehi was her husband, the same kindhearted, simple man she'd known since the day Sariah's mother told her that she would marry the ten-year-old, dark-headed, green-eyed lad that lived over the hills at Beit Zayit. Mother was right; Sariah had married the man of her dreams, but those childhood dreams were nothing like Lehi's vision of reading from the *Book of Heaven*—a dream that could become a nightmare for this family.

"Is there a reason you're pinning me to the bed?" Lehi slowly opened his eyes and looked down his nose at her hand set square in the middle of his chest. "Or is this a dream?"

"It certainly is not." Sariah took her hand back. "I was only fixing the blankets around you. I do hate it when they wander off during the night, especially with the cold spell we've had."

Lehi kept his shoulders pressed against the pillow, but he didn't need to lay like that. Sariah hadn't pressed that hard; she wasn't large enough to pin his shoulders down. Lehi said, "Do you press this hard when you tuck the grandchildren into bed?"

"They don't squirm nearly as much, dear." Sariah hid her hand beneath the pleats in her sleeping robe. "And they're good to sleep through the night without waking."

Lehi said, "I don't sleep well with an owl watching over my every breath."

"Don't worry about that." Sariah patted him on the arm. "There isn't an owl that could endure your snoring."

"Nor any that could endure your worrying."

"Someone has to." Sariah pushed against his side, scooting him toward the center of the bed. "You could fall on the floor if you insist on sleeping this close to the edge."

"That isn't what upsets you." Lehi wrapped his body in the blanket from neck to foot and it was like watching a priest wrap a body for the sepulchre. He said, "It's the *Book of*—"

"Don't say it." Sariah leaned over the bed. "I don't understand any of this and I don't want to."

"I've tried to tell you about the sweetness of the words I read in the—"

"Lehi, please."

Sariah pressed her fingers to his lips to stop his speech, but she couldn't hold them there forever, not after his vision. No matter how much she hoped to hush the opening of his mouth, there had never been a silent prophet, not after seeing what Lehi had seen and reading what he had read from the *Book of Heaven*. Her husband was destined to call men to repentance, but must he go to the Jews at Jerusalem? There was not a more stubborn lot than the people in the capital and it would be a simpler task to part the Red Sea or have the desert stones spew forth drinking water than to point out the errors of the ways of the Jews.

"I don't want to hear about your vision of the book." Sariah wrapped her arms around herself like an apron holding in the pain that gnawed at her stomach. "Not right now."

Lehi said, "What's wrong, Sariah?"

She couldn't tell him. It would only sadden him if he knew she dreaded the bitterness of his prophethood. Lehi had been carried away in vision like the ancient prophets; that was the holy part of his calling. But must Sariah also suffer the bitter taste that came with reading from the *Book of Heaven*? It was filled with the prophecies of the Anointed One—that the Son of God would come down to earth and dwell in a tabernacle of flesh and suffer for the sins of man and break the bands of death and be resurrected—and Lehi was to teach those words to the people of Jerusalem. He said they were sweet to the taste, like a honey finer than anything prepared from the plantation hives, but it wasn't the sweetness of the word of God that caused Sariah to fear. Every prophet since the world began wrote of the bitterness that followed tasting the sweet words written in the book, and Sariah held her hand to her stomach. The sharp pain had gone, but there was still a nagging inside her, like the sickness ancient prophets suffered after they came to understand their mission written in the *Book of Heaven*. It wasn't long ago, back in the days when Sariah's grandmother was a girl, that an angel took burning coals from the altar of the temple and placed them on the lips of the prophet Isaiah to purge his mouth of sin and prepare him for preaching the words of the Anointed One. Isaiah heard the voice of the Lord, just as Lehi heard it, and the Lord asked Isaiah whom He should send just as the Lord had asked Lehi, but Sariah did not want her husband to answer as Isaiah had answered. Must she stand silent and let Lehi say, *here am I Lord, send me?* That's what worried her most, that Lehi, after having tasted the sweetness of the word written in the *Book of Heaven*, would do as all the prophets before him had done without any thought of the bitterness it would cause him. The words of the book may be sweet to the taste, but once they settled in Lehi's belly and he came to know the bitterness of rejection and persecution and even the threat of losing his . . .

Another sharp pain shot through Sariah and she bent over, gripping the bed sheets into a wadded cloth. She couldn't tell Lehi what was wrong. If he understood the pain his calling caused her, it would only make his nights more restless.

"Sariah?" Lehi sat up in bed. "Tell me what's wrong, my dear."

"Nothing at all." Sariah let go of the sheets and stood back from the bed.

"Are you ill?"

"Look at you." Sariah lowered her hands to her side, away from her stomach. "Worrying over nothing."

"You're not feeling well; I can see it in your face."

"I'm hungry." She really wasn't, not with another cramp shooting through her stomach, and she started for the bedroom door.

Lehi said, "Where are you going?"

"To get some lemon tea."

"At this hour?"

"It's just a midnight craving." Sariah rubbed her side. "Nothing that a good broth won't cure."

Sariah hurried across the room, unlatched the door and went out in search of a remedy for the pain in her stomach. The mezzanine above the main hall was dark, without even the light of the moon shining through the canvas-covered windows and lighting the vaulted ceiling of the anteroom. She leaned against the banister, waiting for the cramp to pass and allow her the dignity of walking down the stairs under her own power. A fever she could walk with, but the cramping was better suffered holding onto the polished wood banister. It wasn't really a fever that burned through her body, but whatever it was, she'd lost a good night's sleep over it along with her appetite, except a fetish for pickled olives. That was the remedy she needed. Not a strong lemon tea or a broth of soup, but a few olives from the pantry, the ones sautéed in vinegar, flavored with diced onions, and soaked in a mild bath of saltwater. That's exactly what she needed and she stood away from the banister and started for the stairwell. The thought of any drink or food left her weak, but the hope of a pickled olive calmed her troubled stomach and she found her way down the stairs and turned into the shadows of the hallway leading to the kitchens. It was an odd sort of hunger, but she'd be rid of these cramps and sleep through the night if she could satisfy her craving.

The double doors to the kitchen creaked open. The large clay bowls were still arranged on the kneading tables where Sariah had left them last night, waiting for morning and the stir of her hand to fill them with flour and water and make dough for the ovens. The stone floor had dried after she helped the maidservants mop the goat's milk spilt by a grandchild too young to carry the cup. The plates and bowls and saucers stood on the drying shelves, the last drops of water falling into a puddle on the table below them. The kitchen was in order except for the smell of burned wood from the double hearths that stopped Sariah in midstride. She caught her breath to keep the scent from causing another cramp. The smoke lingered in the air, and in her condition, everything that had the power to make her ill remained far too long for her liking. She should have known last night while preparing evening meal that it wasn't the smoke back-drafting from the ovens that sent her out of the kitchen for a breath of air. It was the beginnings of this illness and with a bit of luck and a few olives she'd be over it soon. Sariah crossed to the pantry over beyond the bins of dried fruits. She reached up onto the shelf, felt with her hand past the bottles of nuts and figs, down along the plank where she'd placed the last half-full jar of . . .

Where were the pickled olives? She felt about the shelf. There was empty space where there should have been a large jar. It couldn't have been Laman; he didn't like pickled olives. And Lemuel and Nephi were never good at lurking about, finding where she hid the delicacy. Lehi never bothered to lurk. He insisted Sariah let him eat them in full view until she wrestled them away from him and hid them here on the highest shelf in the pantry, behind the nuts; though when she put them up here last evening she noticed Sam was waiting beside the ovens with one of his grins. That's who it was; Sam had stolen them after she put them here. Sariah turned out of the pantry, crossed the kitchen, and found her way back down the darkened hall to the front door of the estate. That boy was going to be the death of her. Well, maybe he wasn't going to drive her to the grave, but he was going to force her out into the night to get another jar from the storehouse.

Sariah hurried down from the porch and past the fountains in the main plaza. There was a light in the upper chamber of Uncle Ishmael's home. The poor man was up with a cold or the flu or what-ever ailed him in the cold months. Thank heaven winter was all but gone and he would start sleeping through the night. The cobblestone lane wound down a sloping incline and Sariah followed it to the bottom of the hill before turning onto a path through the oldest vine-yards, the first ones Lehi and Ishmael planted. She lifted the hem of her sleeping robe out of her stride, stepping through the soft, moist earth between the rows of trees.

Storehouse number three stood in a small clearing near the back of the old vineyard. It wasn't really the third storehouse. It was built long before the others, but it was the smallest one and Nephi called it number three. There was no reason for him to store anything but oil here, except that Sariah insisted he keep her pickled olives, not because she trusted them in his care—she didn't trust any of her sons with the pickled olives—but the storehouse was always locked and since she knew where Nephi hid the key, she allowed him the honor of guarding them here. The walls were fashioned with thick slabs of limestone to preserve the cool ground against the heat of summer and keep out the freezing cold of winter. It was dug into the side of the hill with only the front façade of stone to give away its location hidden amid the trees.

Sariah turned over a small stone set on the ground beside the chest-high cedar door, found the key and let herself inside, the moist air rushing past her cheeks. She skirted around the clay cisterns to the small shelf on the wall without waiting for her eyes to adjust to the darkness. She knew exactly where the pickled olives were stored and she went straight to the jars, took one down and went back out into the night, locking the door behind her and stowing the key under the rock. At last, she had some pickled olives and she broke the seal and reached her fingers inside. The olive was soft and the light taste of vinegar and oil was just what she needed to chase away the cramping and stave off her craving. She hadn't felt like this since before Nephi was born and immediately Sariah dropped the half-eaten olive back into the jar.

It couldn't be. She wasn't with child, was she? Sariah held both hands over her womb and pressed lightly. It had been long enough she'd forgotten how she should feel, but something deep inside whispered she was carrying a baby. She leaned back against the storehouse door, took the pin out of her hair and let the long, black locks fall down over her shoulders. A baby? Sariah let her gaze wander out over the trees in the old vineyard. This is where she brought Rachel, Leah, Laman, Lemuel, Sam, and Nephi to hide among the trees and climb the branches, their eyes filled with the pleasures of childhood. That's what she enjoyed most about motherhood—the light in her children's eyes and the laughter—but it was time to give that up for the joys of grandmotherhood, and it didn't seem possible she would have the strength to give birth to another child she could call her own.

It had been fifteen years since Nephi was born and she was without a spring in her step like when she was a young mother, but there was nothing that had power to warm her soul and give purpose to living than the promise of holding a new life in her arms, and she would find the strength somewhere. She'd have to remove all the linens and blankets in the room next to her bedroom. There was just enough space for a cradle, a good supply of fresh air and sunlight from a small window, and close enough she could hear the baby cry from her bedroom. She'd have to recruit the help of her daughters to weave clothing for the infant and they'd have to make new blankets—there had never been a baby born in her family without a stack of finely woven linens to wrap about the new arrival.

Another mild cramp tightened her womb, chasing away the warm feeling that filled her soul. She'd given birth to six children, but she'd also lost two, and the cramping frightened her. She started back through the vineyard, the jar of olives tucked beneath her arm, her feet carefully picking her stride over the uneven soil. The moon was nearly full and its brightness filtered through the grove and cast an eerie glow through the branches of the old vineyard, lining Sariah's way with crooked, thin shadows like the lines of a spider's web. The trees in this grove were thicker than in other vineyards. Their woody trunks were gnarled and twisted into shadow-filled holes large enough to hold Sariah's fears of losing this baby. If she could, she'd leave her fears inside the dark hollows in these trees and not let Lehi's prophethood frighten her into having any more cramps. She couldn't, not if she wanted to keep this baby.

A blood-curdling, warlike cry echoed through the vineyard, and the outline of torch-bearing men entering from the road like foot soldiers on the front line of a mighty army brought Sariah to a stand-still. One of the intruders threw his torch into the air, the orange flame falling through the branches of the olives like fiery rain from heaven. It hit the gnarled trunk of an olive tree a few paces from where she stood, spraying sparks over the ground and lighting the tinder at the base of the tree. Sariah quickly kicked dirt over the flames, killing it in a swirling cloud of black smoke. Another volley of orange flame streaked through an opening in the branches, the oil-soaked rags on the end of the torch bursting apart like burning feathers, some falling on the hem of her robe and lighting the cloth on fire.

Sariah pressed the burning cloth against the cool ground to smother it before running back to the storehouse for cover. The clearing was dark without the orange flames that streaked through the vineyard. She found the stone where she'd left the key, turned it over, but it was nowhere to be found. Where did she put it? This was the stone where the key should have been; she was certain of it, and she ran her fingers through the moist soil, searching for the brass key. She crawled to the next stone, one hand holding the jar of pickled olives and the other turning the stone over and sifting through the soil for any sign of the key amid the flashes of flames lighting the ground around her. She turned over another stone, then another, and still no key. Was she losing her mind? She crawled to the door, scooping away the loose soil, frantic to find the key and get inside and wait out the deeds of these men. Then she could return to the estate in safety. Sariah felt along the threshold of the storehouse, her small fingers trembling over the stone entrance.

"Did you lose something?" The cold metal of a knife stung across her neck and the putrid breath of a drunken man froze her in place, his coarse whiskers rubbing against her cheek. His voice was gruff and he lifted her to her feet with such quickness the blade cut into the skin across her throat. He turned her around with his thick arm and studied her from the hem of her robe to the crown of her head. His face was painted black, and only the whiteness of his teeth showed in the flaring light of the sky. He held the storehouse key between his thumb and forefinger, the brass catching the light of the fires.

Sariah said, "Who are you?"

"Do you like the fire?" He ripped away the cloth of her sleeping robe, baring the skin of her shoulder. "We're going to burn it all down."

"Why are you doing this?" Sariah lifted the cloth back in place and stepped away from the sharpness of his knife.

"We're going to scare the prophet." He pulled at her robe, tearing free the sash about her hips.

"Leave me alone!" Sariah pushed his hands away from her.

"Death to the prophet." His speech was slurred and he waved his knife at her like a wild man. He was drunk and when he reached out to take her in his arms, Sariah slapped him across the face.

"You fool!" The man swung his fist, striking Sariah across the cheek, fracturing the bones in her face. She fell back, holding her nose, waiting for him to come close. He was within her reach, one hand waving the knife and the other holding onto the brass key when she swung the pickled olives at him, cracking the jar open on his head and sending him reeling to the ground.

Sariah sprinted out of the clearing, the torn cloth of her robe flapping about her shoulder. She reached the road and pulled up behind the trunk of an olive tree. The shooting pain in her face filled her eyes with tears, but she wasn't blinded by it and she could see the band of horsemen that lined the edge of the old vineyard, their animals snorting the cold air, their hooves pawing the cobblestones, and their sleek necks facing the stately grove of trees like a cavalry ready to ride against an enemy. They weren't soldiers, not with the dark clothing they wore and the black ashes that hid their faces. What evil brought these men here? This vineyard was nothing more than dormant trees without a single olive hanging from their branches and there was no reason for a band of outlaws to want to destroy them.

The lead rider reined down between his men, lighting their torches from his, the orange flame casting an eerie light over his broad-shouldered frame. He ordered some into the vineyard on foot to light fires while the others threw their torches high into the branches, and there was nothing Sariah could do to stop the volley of fire that arched through the sky and landed inside the vineyard—not if she didn't want to risk her life and the life of her unborn baby.

The cries of the drunken man she'd left near the storehouse filled the air and there was only one thing she could do to save herself from his search. She darted from the vineyard, one hand pressed against her stomach and the other reaching ahead of her stride, carrying her up the rise in the lane toward the main courtyard of the estate. She had to wake Lehi and her sons and get them to come put out the fires and, God willing, they could save her and the old vineyard from these intruders.

Sariah was at the top of the incline when the lead outlaw ordered her to stop. She kept running, her feet pushing against the uneven cobblestone. Dear God, let her reach the house safely! She was nearing the fountains when the pounding of horse hooves reached her hearing. The lead outlaw pulled alongside Sariah. He was hunched forward in the saddle, his black-painted face twisted into a scowl and a torch in his hand. Sariah cut over to the fountain, the horse's wide, powerful body missing her, and its hooves clapping past.

The outlaw came around, his boots digging into the horse's flank, his body arched over its mane. He came at her straight on, his horse hitting Sariah in the side and knocking her to the ground. She landed on her back, her hand pressed to her stomach and her head snapping against the hard, unforgiving cobblestones, splitting open a wide gash. The outlaw jumped from the saddle and stood over her. The rushing in her head blurred her vision, but she knew the penetrating, brown-eyed gaze of the man above her. It was Daniel, the brother of Aaron. His face was black with soot and he was wasn't wearing the military uniform she'd seen on him the last time he came to the estate, but she would never forget the sight of him forcing Aaron to stand on his burned feet in this square and answer the questions of Captain Elnathan.

The other riders came in behind Daniel and circled their horses around Sariah's fallen body. She was trapped there, surrounded by a cavalry of men.

Daniel said, "It's you again, old woman."

Sariah said, "Daniel, why you?"

"She knows you, sir." One of the riders slid out of the saddle, his sword drawn. "I'll silence her."

"Stand down!" Daniel gripped the man's sword arm. "She's going to tell Lehi what he needs to hear."

Sariah sat up, her hand pressed to the gash in the back of her head, slowing the blood that ran down her neck. "Tell him what?"

"You see this?" Daniel pointed down the lane, toward the growing fire that filled the old vineyard. "Your husband will lose more than his precious olive trees if he does anything to help Uriah win his freedom."

A powerful cramp seized Sariah's womb, more violent than any she'd endured through the night. She groaned and turned her gaze to the moonlit sky. Not the baby, dear Lord, not the baby.

The moon went dark.

CHAPTER 13

Eliza, wife of the prophet Jeremiah, tied down the grapevines farthest from the house, the ones beyond the brow of the hill near the back of the vineyard. She carried a handful of cords cut from the tanned leather hides hanging in the stable and bound the flapping vines into place against the worn arbor poles. The fall harvest just past was a wet one, leaving the grapevines with far more winter length than their tendrils could keep pinned down, and the gangly things danced in the cold north wind like a stand of winter wheat. Well, they didn't exactly dance. The lanky vines were far too woody to do anything but flail about until she made her way down the arbor and tied them in place; and if she could shed a few of her fifty-one years she'd make her way with more spring in her stride. Eliza wrapped the end of one around the arbor and lashed it to the pole. Jeremiah didn't ask her to help with her feet the way they were—swollen from the cold weather—but she wasn't about to let him do it alone. Eliza pressed another vine against the arbor with her thumb and tied it down with a cord. If she hadn't left a pot simmering on the hearth and come outside to help, Jeremiah would have caught his death of cold before he ever finished, and God would never forgive her if she let one of His prophets freeze to death, no matter how ridiculous it was to be out in the middle of winter tying the vineyard. Eliza steadied herself against an arbor post and bent over to rub her ankles, but all the rubbing in the world wouldn't rid her of the pain, not until she got inside a warm house where she could soak her feet in salts.

The winter in Anathoth was colder than in Jerusalem and Eliza pulled the ends of her shawl tight around her ears, raised her collar under her chin, and rubbed her hands for warmth. Why did Jeremiah pick a cold February afternoon like this one? He was working on the other side of the rise. She couldn't see him beyond the swell of earth obscuring her view, but he was there, she could hear him talking to the grapevines—something about holding on until their spring flowers filled the arbors with the scent of their blooming. And he said it with such a poetic ring, it was hard to believe that he was sad today. Jeremiah rarely said a word among the date trees lining the road, and she never caught him conversing with the melons in the patch behind the house. But the grapes were a fruit of a different vine and they drew his conversation the same way Zoram did whenever he came home for a visit. And though this fruit could never replace Zoram's dry wit and easy manner, at least they gave him something to talk to. The pitch in Jeremiah's voice didn't rise or fall or sing with the usual cheerful senti-ment. It was his lonely voice, the same forlorn tone he'd used with the grapevines since Captain Laban banned him from preaching in Jerusalem—a banishment that kept him from seeing Zoram—and in his exile he addressed the grape arbors as if they were his children.

Children? Eliza shuffled down the row to the next loose vine. They only had one child, and before they adopted Zoram, Jeremiah talked to the grapes—a forgotten habit that reappeared the day Laban found Jeremiah in Jerusalem's upper city market, embarrassed him in front of a crowd, and sent him packing back to Anathoth. Poor Jeremiah hadn't slept a wink since. Eliza blew warm air over her hands before holding the next vine steady against the pole with her thumb. Silly goose. Jeremiah shouldn't let his loneliness for Zoram drive him to talk to these woody grapevines. Thank heavens Eliza didn't suffer from the same malady; she wouldn't allow herself that fancy. And as soon as they finished with the arbors she'd insist Jeremiah come inside to eat a helping of lamb stew and reminisce about their son. Stew was Zoram's favorite meal, prepared with lentils and a thick broth seasoned with just the right herbs. Eliza wrapped the flailing vine around a post, tied it down with the thickest cord in the bunch and smiled to herself. She'd left a large pot of stew simmering over the hearth; there was enough to feed three and though she'd never say it aloud, she prayed the smell of it would bring Zoram home for a visit. That was all either of them could hope for. They couldn't risk going to the city to see him and the only man they had to thank for their exile was . . .

"Laban!" Jeremiah yelled the captain's name. His head appeared above the arbor along the brow of the hill, bobbing like a pomegranate thrown into a pond. He was sprinting toward her, his graying hair flying on the wind and his red cheeks puffing for air and when he reached the arbor he climbed it in stride, his robe catching on the vines, but not tripping him and certainly not slowing him. Eliza leaned on her toes against the arbor pole and waited for him to race through the last stand of grapes. Where did he find the legs to run like that? He hadn't moved that fast since the day they were married.

Jeremiah cried, "Run for the house, my dear; get inside before he arrives."

Before who arrives? Eliza glanced about the vineyard and found no one but the two of them among the grapes. She'd grown accustomed to Jeremiah's odd sense of humor, but had he lost his mind this time? It was one thing to talk to the vines, but must he run about the vineyard yelling the captain's name? His outburst bordered on madness and it was a good thing none of the neighbors were out in this cold or she'd hear about his insanity at the well first thing in the morning. Drawing water was the best place to find out the news of Anathoth, and she prayed that her husband didn't become the most talked about story of the day.

Eliza said, "What in heaven's name has gotten into you?"

Jeremiah ducked under the last arbor and came up beside Eliza. His face was red as a cherry and his breath a flash of steam shooting from his mouth. She was about to insist he go in out of the cold when the reason for his insanity turned onto the road from town. Captain Laban was perched in the saddle of an Arabian, its white coat and braided mane flashing between the fig trees lining the road. He turned down the arbor toward them, the horse threshing the soft ground with its hooves.

Eliza dropped the leather cords at her feet. Had someone revealed to Laban that Jeremiah had visited the city? If she'd told her husband once, she'd told him a shekel's worth of times not to break his banishment and sneak into the city, but he refused to listen to her advice. Eliza held her hand over her heart. What if it was about Zoram? What if Captain Laban had found out the secret—that their only son was the keeper of the keys to his treasury? That was a secret that could reap for them a whirlwind of trouble, and Captain Laban was the sort of storm they would not endure without a good deal of suffering.

Laban was still a good ways off when he pulled up, got down out of the saddle and walked toward them, slowly guiding his horse between the arbors. What was he walking for? There was plenty of room for him to ride his horse, and though it would pack the soil about the roots and stunt the growth of the grapes, Laban was not the master of this vineyard, and God willing he would never be the master of any vineyard. He was captain of the guard and the man never got down out of the saddle to lower himself to the level of commoners. Without the height the horse added to his stature, Laban was another man—a thick-armed, broad-shouldered man—but much less over-whelming than he would have been sitting above them on his mount. It wasn't nearly as hostile an arrival as the last time Laban came to their home wearing a dark cape, jumping the arbors, and pounding at the door to their home with the fury of an entire army packed into his fist, but Eliza stepped behind Jeremiah all the same, took him by the arm and held him close, like a protecting armor that could keep her from whatever tempest blew in with their uninvited guest.

Captain Laban lowered his voice, carefully pronouncing each word with an educated Hebrew accent. He said, "Good afternoon to you, my good lady," and he held onto the last letter of "lady" like a well-trained gentleman.

Good Lady? Eliza held her hand to her cheek. The captain had never offered her a greeting, especially one spoken in such a kindly tone. The last time he came to visit he forced himself inside with his sword and threatened her husband with pain of death if he didn't anoint his famed blade. And why he would ever want another blessing for a sword that had been anointed by the hand of Joseph, she didn't know. There was not a finer blessing that could be given than by that ancient prophet, but Jeremiah had obliged the captain and she was pleased to have her husband counted with Joseph of old.

Laban took Eliza by the hand, bowed as if she were some sort of royalty and said, "I hope I haven't come at a bad time."

Of course he had. Laban was not welcome here and anytime he came was a bad time. Eliza's hand began to tremble in his, but she dared not take it back. Better to let Laban offer whatever odd greeting he came to offer, than risk rousing his rage. He was not a man she dared trifle with and if he desired to show her some respect, she knew better than to refuse it. His hand was warm and sweat from the hard ride streamed off his face and into the thin beard that graced his straight chin. No, it didn't grace his chin; nothing graced Captain Laban, no matter how stately the cloak that hung about his shoulders or how brilliant the brass buttons that flashed in the afternoon sun. He brought his head up from bowing to Eliza and the scent of perfumes rose up off his short, fresh-cut hair like a field of blossoming flowers. The captain was bathed and shaved and dressed for a formal visit and she and Jeremiah were the reasons for his grooming.

Laban turned his gaze to Jeremiah and said, "Very fine vineyard you have here, sir."

Jeremiah pulled Eliza back, away from Laban's reach. "What do you want with us?"

Laban raised the collar of his cloak around his cheeks to keep warm against the cold wind, the steam of his breath shooting from between the part in the cloth. "There must be hardly any work to keep you busy this time of year."

Jeremiah said, "We have plenty."

"Certainly not enough to keep you from visiting Jerusalem."

Jeremiah stepped toward Laban, his shoulders back and his head raised. It was the same posture he took whenever he had rebuke on his mind, and Eliza could only pray that whatever came out of his mouth wouldn't anger Laban. Jeremiah said, "It wasn't vineyard keeping that banned me from the city."

Laban said, "I was drunk and I should have known better than to—"

"You threw me from my cart and kept me from preaching the word of God to His people." Jeremiah stepped to the Arabian and tapped the tip of his sandals at the animal's hooves. "You nearly crushed my head with these."

"I lost my mind that day." Laban stroked the Arabian's mane until she offered a contented grunt. "I've come here to ask you to—"

"Your mind isn't the only thing you—"

"Jeremiah." Eliza tugged on his arm. "Let the man speak."

Jeremiah's jaw stiffened and he lowered his gaze away from Laban, but at least he didn't say any more. He didn't need to, not with Captain's Laban's mouth drawn tight and his shoulders hunched forward like a leopard ready to leap.

Laban said, "I see you haven't lost any vigor for your preaching." He steadied his mount, stroking the animal's coat, and spoke in the same kind tone he'd used with Eliza. But he wasn't really kind. He hesitated on the word *preaching,* and it wasn't difficult to hear that he was masking his hatred for Jeremiah's work behind his flattering words. Laban said, "I like your spirit."

But he didn't, not entirely, though Eliza was pleased Jeremiah didn't notice, at least until he raised his gaze from staring at the ground and said, "You mock God, but His prophets will not be silenced."

Eliza tugged on the belt tying Jeremiah's brown working robe about his waist, but it didn't keep him from pulling free and pushing on the Arabian's neck. The animal sidestepped out of the way, her hooves coming down over Laban's boots and forcing the captain to jump out of the way to keep his feet from the crushing blow.

Laban said, "I'm trying to be civil." Laban's words rushed from his mouth in a flurry. He threw his cloak back off his shoulder, exposing a dagger beneath the belt of his kilt, but when Eliza began to back away he calmed his words and half covered the weapon with his hand. He said, "I was hoping we could find some peace between us."

Jeremiah said, "If it's civility you want, you should begin by removing my banishment."

Laban lowered his head and softly agreed.

"And if it's peace you want, you'd invite me back to the city to preach the word of God to his—"

"I told you, *we've* already done that." Laban gritted his teeth when he spoke, like a child forced to grant the wishes of a boy he did not want to play with. But since there was no one else with Laban, Eliza had no way of knowing who his *we* included.

The deepest lines in Jeremiah's brow softened. He stepped back from Laban's horse and said, "You'll let me come back to Jerusalem?"

Eliza came around next to her husband. Why had the captain ridden to Anathoth to lift Jeremiah's banishment? There had to be a reason. Laban was not the sort of man to change his mind with regard to any prophet, least of all Jeremiah, not unless there was a reason, and she couldn't help but ask, "I want your word you won't harm my husband if he returns to the city."

Laban smiled, the point of beard at the end of his chin pushing up about his lower lip. "*We* want nothing more than to have your husband preach his gospel in Jerusalem."

"You and who else, sir?"

Laban mounted his Arabian with one strong leap. He was a large man, but he had such power in his legs that he pushed his body up off the ground with the ease of a leopard climbing a tree to wait out its next prey. He righted himself in the saddle and said, "I speak for all the people of Jerusalem when I say we have need of your husband's words of peace now more than ever." He reined about between the arbors, the Arabian's haunches pushing Eliza back against the poles. "There's talk of revolt."

"Not another war." Eliza took her husband by the hand. It had only been a year since the Babylonian army was camped about their vineyards, waiting for the siege on Jerusalem to do its evil work. Blessedly the city fell within a few weeks or they'd still be suffering from the thousands of foreign soldiers who turned their vineyards into battlefields.

Laban lowered his voice as if the grapevines were spies with power to hear what he was about to say. "It's because of the tax."

Jeremiah said, "Have the Babylonian tax collectors come?"

"They won't need to." Laban inched forward in the saddle, the well-oiled leather hardly creaking under his powerful frame. "The revolt will come before they ever collect their first shekel."

Jeremiah peered up at Laban between the horse's ears. "I've not heard anything of the sort."

"You will." Laban prodded his mount forward, pushing the animal's head into Jeremiah's chest. "As soon as word of the high tax spreads, every citizen in Judah will beg King Zedekiah to break the yoke of the Babylonians."

"How high a tax?"

"Enough for Zedekiah to consider another war."

"He can't break with Babylon, not yet."

"He can do anything he likes." Laban wrapped the end of the reins around his hands like a coiled serpent. "He's the king."

"You must tell the king he can't do this." Jeremiah leaned against the side of Laban's horse, his hand on the captain's boot. "God has spoken otherwise."

Laban sidled his horse away from Jeremiah's reach. "I don't think Zedekiah is concerned about what God has to say on the matter." He turned his head down, his lips hidden behind the level of his brow, and the tip of his black beard was the only thing Eliza could see moving as he spoke. He was hiding something, but since she couldn't see his face or look into his eyes, there was no telling if it was his story of tax revolt or his profession of newfound faith in God that was not to be believed.

"This is certain to fail." Jeremiah stepped close to the horse again, this time leaning against its flank but not touching Laban. "The Jews are to be subject to Nebuchadnezzar until this generation passes away."

"I was hoping you'd say that. My men are not ready to fight another war." Laban couldn't keep a smile from spreading across his face, a grin as wide and curved as the moon at midsummer night. But this was not summer and his expression was not one of relief, at least not any sort of relief Eliza had ever seen. It was a mischievous grin, like a little boy plotting a hideous hoax. Laban said, "It will take some powerful preaching to convince Zedekiah against mounting a revolt."

"God bless you, Captain, for ending this peril before it happens." Jeremiah reached up to take Laban by the arm, but he steered his horse away from Jeremiah's reach and there was no mistaking his refusal. He did not want a prophet to touch him.

Laban said, "I'm leaving the resolution of this peril to you, not to God."

Eliza leaned back against the arbor and let Laban rein past. He jabbed his boots into the haunches of his Arabian, spurring the animal to full gallop, its hooves kicking up a flurry of mud and dead brown grasses across her robe. She was right. Laban may have come quietly, but a quiet leaving was not in his nature. He was captain of the guard and there was no reason for him to acquire common graces. But as long as he was using whatever influence he could conjure to convince the throne not to start another war, she would endure the man's poor manners. Eliza brushed the mud from her robe. There had been more than enough blood shed over these lands, and raising another army to keep from paying tax to Babylon was too high a price to spill more; and any man—even if it were Laban—who sought peace above war was worthy of her patience. If Laban had come seeking Jeremiah's counsel, and the message from the Almighty was for Judah to be yoked under Babylonian bondage for a generation, who was she to question the messenger? Her husband's banishment had been lifted, and though something deep inside her said she shouldn't allow him to return to the city, there was nothing she could do to keep him from preaching his next sermon—Judah was to remain under Babylonian rule. And though Eliza feared for Jeremiah's safety, she had to find the faith to allow him his calling. He was chosen and there was nothing she could do to change that. Eliza brushed the flecks of mud off her cheeks and combed three strands of straw out of her long brown hair. She did not curse God for taking her husband from her, but she did question the Almighty from time to time.

Must she trust her husband into the hands of Laban?

CHAPTER 14

Zedekiah entered the royal court by the back door to keep from causing a disturbance, but it was no use. The scribe saw him sneak inside and the man fell to his knees on the marbled steps, his voice ringing about the stone columns and domed ceiling. He cried, "Hail, Zedekiah, Great King of Judah!"

Zedekiah lowered his head and walked directly to his throne. Must the scribe make such a show? There was nothing more disturbing than a greeting like this one. A simple good afternoon without so much groveling would do, but ever since the coronation, Zedekiah walked the halls of the palace with servants falling to their knees and offering a string of greetings that would make an ox blush.

The scribe laid his scroll on the steps and said, "Have mercy on your humble servant."

Mercy? Zedekiah sat on the edge of his throne and arranged his cape over the backrest. The scribe didn't need mercy; he needed a muzzle. Zedekiah planted his elbows on the armrest. If only God had chosen another to govern His people, Zedekiah wouldn't have to endure this spectacle. He motioned for the scribe to rise and stand with the other four men waiting in the wings to discuss the business of the day. "Can we begin?"

The scribe held out a document—something about the royal herd of sheep and goats wintering in Moab. What did Zedekiah know about shepherding in the eastern province of the Moabites? The straight-cut ends of Zedekiah's brown hair brushed the collar of his new clothes. Miriam insisted he dress in a coat of white cloth with gold-thread-trimmed cuffs, and buttoned so tight across his chest he couldn't fill his lungs with any measure of breath. It was Miriam's way to keep him from dozing on the throne, something she caught him doing nearly every afternoon about this time. The business of these scribes was certain to bore him to sleep today, but he would not be caught snoring in public, not with Miriam's choice of a stiff-collared tunic sprouting above the neckline of the tight-fitting coat and squeezing away any thought of nodding off.

Zedekiah took the scroll from the first scribe, signed his name and affixed his seal, and it was done. The royal treasury was to pay the Moabites for grazing rights through the end of the winter. That wasn't so difficult, was it?

The second scribe scaled the steps to the throne and fell to his knees. "Hail, Zedekiah, Great King of—"

"Let me have that, would you?" Zedekiah took his scroll and turned his gaze into the writing. If another of these scribes fell to his knees, Zedekiah was going to outlaw the practice and nail a proclamation to the doorpost of this court, informing all who enter that the next one to call him *Great King of Judah* would be sent to prison.

Zedekiah unrolled the second scroll. It was longer than the first, but not any more complex. He wouldn't have any trouble deciding on the titles of noblemen in Shiloh or the birthrights of squatters on their land, though neither matter had the appeal of an afternoon stroll in the gardens. The sunlight streamed through the window and beckoned him to leave these chambers and enjoy the first good day of late winter; only a few patches of ice remained along the shaded side of the arbors. He'd spent the winter locked away in the musty confines of this chamber and any chance for a walk in the half-frozen courtyards was better than this. Zedekiah signed his name at the bottom next to his seal. The men of Shiloh would be known as viceroys and the squatters on their land could stay until spring.

The chief accountant was next, but before he could scale the steps with his ledger or open his mouth in greeting, Zedekiah said, "Not another step!" He leaned against the backrest of the throne and closed his eyes. "Stand there and read the figures to me."

"Out loud, sire?"

"That's right." Zedekiah's head came to rest against the ornately carved wooden lattice. He folded his arms and said, "And do it in your best voice."

The accountant spoke without raising or lowering his pitch. It was a relentless droning of the harvest listed in baths of grain per acre, taxes collected from every merchant class in the kingdom, imports of gold, exports of oils and furs, and fees on foreign caravaners. Zedekiah began to nod off somewhere between the amount of wheat collected from farmers near Debir and the number of sheep added to the royal herd in Ramah. Wasn't there someone else in the kingdom better suited to hear these issues? What he wouldn't give for an aide, a counselor, anyone to inform but not coddle him. He needed an advisor, a man he could rely on in matters of state, but since there was no one who had earned his trust, he was destined to spend today as he had nearly everyday since the coronation, mulling over details of kingship. The accountant's monotone voice continued detailing the shipments of oats and barley received at the palace last month, the number of vats of olive oil in reserve and the sacks of figs left from last year's stores. Zedekiah's eyelids fluttered shut, his head listed to the side, and in his half sleep he could see the door at the far end of the chamber swing open and the soft golden glow of late afternoon forming a halo around—

Miriam? What was she doing here? She'd caught him snoring and he righted himself, adjusted his tight collar, brushed his hand through his hair, and squinted across the chamber to see the queen in the entry wearing a white summer robe of thin linens, the hem brushing her ankles. Her long brown hair was braided down past her shoulders, with a red and green linen scarf holding the bangs back off her brow. A light shawl was wrapped about her neck. It draped over her straight shoulders and hung down past the mittens that warmed her hands. Her clothing was not nearly warm enough to venture outside, but there she stood, dressed for a summer walk through the gardens in the middle of winter.

Miriam held Benjamin by one hand, Dan by the other, and Mulek stood beside her. The boys were dressed in kilts, not the sort of clothing that would keep them from a runny nose, but then Zedekiah wasn't to worry about the princes' maladies. Miriam attended to them and let Zedekiah busy himself with the tasks of kingship no matter how much he preferred the duties of fatherhood to the trappings of royalty.

Zedekiah left the accountant reading from his scroll and hurried across the chamber. When he arrived at Miriam's side she said, "I caught you."

Zedekiah pulled on the collar around his neck. "Do you really think it possible to sleep in this?"

"Papa?" Benjamin tugged on his arm. "Can we play the hiding game?"

Miriam said, "He learned his numbers to ten this morning and I told him that we would hide in the gardens and see if he could find us." She took Zedekiah by the hand. "He won't play without you."

Benjamin said, "One, two, three, four . . ." He stopped, his small brow furrowed and his thin lips mouthing his guess on the next number, but not uttering it aloud. Ben never was a child to make a mistake in front of anyone and though he was only four years old, Zedekiah saw himself in his son's predicament. He had the same penchant for public correctness when he was a lad. He leaned over, patted Benjamin on the shoulder, encouraging him on to five when Mulek stepped in behind the boy and cried, "One!"

Benjamin grinned and said, "Two, three, four . . ." His cap of sandy brown hair bobbed at the recitation of each number and he pronounced them in perfect diction, though far too slow if he ever hoped to reach ten before Mulek started him over. The poor boy was lost in a never-ending maze, cursed by the very brother he trusted to help him to the end. It was an amusing thing to watch the boy chase back to the beginning like a dog chasing its tail, never catching it, but thinking he was getting closer. Ben was to eight when Dan leaned forward and said, "One!"

Ben followed with, "Two, three, four . . ."

"Boys." Miriam touched Mulek and Dan on the shoulders. "You're his brothers."

And that's exactly what they were doing—acting the part of mischievous older brothers and Ben was the object of their amusement, his tiny fingers held out to count in front of him and his tiny lips trembling, not knowing if they should curl up into a giggle with his brothers or fade into a frustrated frown. When Ben finally reached ten he said, "See, Papa, I will count while you hide in the gardens."

Miriam pulled on Zedekiah's arm. "Will you come with us?" She stood on the top step of the chamber, half obscuring his view of the scribes standing near the throne and the accountant holding his ledger and waiting for Zedekiah to return. "It shouldn't take long."

"Please, Papa," Ben jumped up and down, his too-large-for-a-little-prince sandals slapping the ground with the wallop of a mule whip.

Zedekiah called across the chambers to the scribes, telling them they were finished for the day and he would continue their business tomorrow. Without waiting for a response he escorted his family out of the palace.

The last light of afternoon angled down over the high garden walls and warmed the brick along the west façade of the palace. The fountains gurgled from half-frozen spouts with pointed icicles hanging into the pools. Benjamin was the first into the yard, racing to the bench in the center of the grounds with steam pulsing from his mouth. He lowered his head, folded his arms, and immediately began his count.

"One." Benjamin's tiny voice pierced the cool air.

Miriam said, "Follow me."

"Two." Benjamin rubbed his eyes with his fists.

Miriam spoke softly. "We have to hide together or he'll never have the patience to find all of us."

"Three."

Miriam led them around the corner of the palace to a dark spot below the eave of a balcony. It wasn't really a hiding place, and except for the shadows, they were standing in full view of the gardens. But it was the perfect place for Benjamin to find them and since he wasn't the most able finder, Zedekiah and the princes didn't object to Miriam's selection.

Zedekiah stood against the wall with Miriam next to him and Mulek and Dan leaning their heads against his side to keep out of the light. He wrapped his arms around them, their closeness warming him. Couldn't Benjamin count to a thousand and let him savor this moment with Miriam and his two eldest sons? How long had it been since he held them this close? The duties of kingship had taken him away from them far too often and he was thankful for the chance to play this childish game.

Benjamin's tiny voice echoed from around the corner. He was to seven, but struggling to remember the next number.

Zedekiah leaned forward and cried, "One!"

There was a long pause and then the high-pitched voice of Benjamin returned his father's count with, "Two, three . . ."

"Zedekiah . . ." Miriam poked her elbow into his side. "You're worse than the boys."

It was a mischievous thing for a king to do to a prince, but it just might do little Benjamin some good to learn early in life not to trust everything he heard. Otherwise the boy would end up like a puppet on the end of a string, marshalled about by men who had no business influencing his decisions, trapped in a never-ending game of hide and seek.

Zedekiah laughed and pulled Miriam close, her braided hair falling over his arms. The scent of her perfumes filled him with the sweetness of her presence and for a moment he forgot he was king of Judah and put out of his mind that he had a nation to rebuild after the war. He had Miriam, and he held her close to him. His children were healthy and well schooled by their mother. They were a family, and Zedekiah could only thank heaven for that. He'd lived a God-blessed life and his greatest blessing was the companionship of Miriam, the love of his life.

Miriam said, "What are you planning to do with Uriah?"

Zedekiah leaned over to study her eyes, but with the shadows obscuring her face, he couldn't see her feelings, only listen to them. "Why do you ask?"

"No reason." Miriam spoke soft and slow, the way she did whenever she was concerned about something. "I was only curious."

She wasn't, not really, not by the way she hung on each word. Zedekiah said, "I've never known you to be curious about anything." He pulled back her braid and touched his finger to her cheek. "What are you trying to tell me?"

"Hush, dear." Miriam touched his lips. "Benjamin is nearly finished counting."

Zedekiah raised his voice and said, "One!"

A long silence followed, broken only by Mulek and Dan's giggling at their younger brother's predicament and then Benjamin's tiny voice trailed around the wall. "Two, three . . ."

Miriam didn't elbow him this time. She said, "I worry about Uriah down in the dungeon."

"He'll be fine until the trial."

"How can you be sure?"

"Laban assures me he's well taken care of."

"Laban?" Miriam's body tensed in his arms. "I don't trust him."

"He's a fine officer."

"He was supposed to summon Uriah's father to find a lawyer and I have yet to see anyone come forward to defend him." Miriam shook her head and her braids fell across her face, but they couldn't hide the compassion in her voice. She did not want Uriah to be treated poorly. Miriam said, "Shemayahu would have come to see his son long ago if he knew he was in prison."

"How do you know Uriah's father?"

"Well I . . ." Miriam pulled Dan's mittens back down over his hands and tightened Mulek's collar about his neck. "I'd hope that any father would come to the aid of his son."

"Don't worry yourself about this." Zedekiah held Miriam close to him. "Laban has taken care of it; he told me himself."

Miriam said, "Is it possible that Laban is lying?"

Zedekiah let go of Miriam. Those were harsh words and he fell quiet with only Benjamin's frustrated counting to fill the silence. Had Miriam forgotten that it was Laban who came to her aid when thieves entered the palace during the coronation and it was the captain who stood waiting to protect them at every turn? Miriam was a good woman, but her motherly instinct was playing on her emotions, and until she came to appreciate Laban's faithfulness, he would keep silent his disagreement on the matter. There was plenty of time for her to change her mind about the captain of the guard. They were young to be king and queen of Judah. They'd never been tutored in the practice of royalty and until they knew their way about the maze of kingly and queenly duties that befuddled them at every turn, time was the only thing in their favor.

Benjamin's soft, almost inaudible footsteps came down along the wall of the palace and Zedekiah pulled his family back out of the sunlight that angled lower in the sky and threatened to give them away. Good for little Benjamin. He'd finished counting and he was searching for them, the pitter-patter of his small sandals moving slowly toward the side garden. He was walking—not running—an odd thing for the little boy who moved and talked and ate at the pace of a gazelle, except of course when it came to boiled fish. Benjamin would have nothing to do with the delicacy, no matter how much the cooks doctored it to look like sweet bread. Zedekiah turned his gaze to the sound of Benjamin's coming and smiled across the courtyard to welcome . . .

Zadock? What was he doing in the gardens? Benjamin's footsteps fell carefully behind the Chief Elder, his head lost behind the rise and fall of Zadock's pleated robe. The boy didn't squeal his delight at finding his family hiding in the shadows, not with a stranger walking with him. He bolted past the swirling hems in Zadock's clothes and nestled his head in his mother's side.

Zadock was dressed in his usual black-robed attire, but he was wearing a gold amulet instead of the usual silver one and he was without his turban. His gray hair fell over his brow and poked about his ears in an uncombed mass. And when he spoke his shrill voice echoed off the underside of the balcony. "I didn't mean to interrupt you during such a . . ." He stopped well before the shadows of their hiding place and said, ". . . an intimate moment."

"What is it you want, sir?" Zedekiah stepped out from under the balcony ledge.

"I have something you should see."

"Can't it wait?"

"I'm afraid not." Zadock held up a folded parchment, drew back his forefinger and let the soft leather fall open. "You must see this."

Zedekiah quickly skimmed the document and read; *the Babylonian levy shall be three-quarters of a man's income.* "That's impossible. When did this arrive?"

"The tax collectors posted the notice last evening immediately after the Babylonians delivered it."

"Why wasn't I informed first?"

"Forgive me, your majesty, but I did this for your sake." Zadock moved his long, bony finger down the tax notice to where his name and seal were placed beside the amount of the levy. He'd signed the most distasteful document in the kingdom, the one parchment that had power to raise the wrath of the people more than any other and he was claiming it his own. Zadock said, "I didn't want you to suffer the unpleasantness of raising the tax."

Zedekiah said, "That's noble of you, sir."

Miriam left the princes standing in the shadows of the balcony—as far away from the Chief Elder as she could leave them—and came alongside Zedekiah, leaning over his shoulder to read the document.

Zedekiah said, "Wouldn't you agree, my dear?"

Miriam lifted the hem of her robe above her feet and said, "I have to take the children inside."

"Don't go." Zedekiah took her by the arm. "We'll be finished with this in a moment."

Miriam's smile faded, replaced with a sullen look, and she spoke in her nervous voice, the words spilling from her. "I really must go; the children are getting cold and I have to draw a bath for Benjamin and they haven't eaten since—"

"Since when did the cooks charge you with feeding the princes?" Zedekiah cleared his throat and tapped his right foot on the ground, the way he always did when he wanted her to agree with him or at least obey him.

"Zedekiah, please." Miriam pulled free of his grasp.

Zedekiah folded the tax notice in half and gripped it in his palm. Why was Miriam so fidgety? It wasn't like her to act like this. He'd never known her to be a nervous woman. She was as well-spoken, strong willed, and forthright as any lawyer in his court, but now she shrank from even addressing him in the presence of Zadock. For the sake of heaven, couldn't she at least stand by his side and smile at the man? No, not for the sake of heaven—for the sake of his throne she should be civil to the most powerful man in Jerusalem. He lowered his voice and slowly said, "I want you to stay here."

"I'm sorry, sire." A smile tugged at the corners of Zadock's lips and his gaunt cheeks stretched across his cheekbones. It was a very weak smile, almost indiscernible, but it was a smile. "I didn't mean for this matter to cause hard feelings between you and the queen."

"That's kind of you, Lord Zadock." Miriam pulled the collar of her thin linen robe tight around her neck, her gaze directed away from him. She glanced at the setting sun and said, "Don't you think it a bit too cold to conduct business outside, especially at this hour?"

It wasn't too late, at least not by Miriam's usual comings and goings and Zedekiah had no way of knowing why she wanted to leave

with such haste. She was never concerned about the coolness of the
weather or the lateness of the day, not when it came to a walk in the
gardens, especially with him, but he could see the apprehension in her
posture and she did not want to be out here. Was it Zadock's signing
of the tax notice that bothered her? The tax was an unbearable thing,
but they had expected something like this and she didn't need to
concern herself with the business of the kingdom. She had the children to look after and that was more than enough without
concerning herself with the public welfare.

Zedekiah reached for Miriam's hand. Her grip was rigid and her
skin cold. He said, "We'll finish with this now."

Zadock said, "If you'll have me, sire, I'll oversee the tax."

Zedekiah said, "I can't ask you to do that."

"It's the least I could do for you and your wife."

"You see there." Zedekiah patted Miriam on the arm, but her body
didn't soften. She was filled with an angst he'd never known in her
before. He said, "The Chief Elder is only worried about our welfare."

Zadock said, "There's going to be an uprising against this tax, sire."

"Laban and his men can deal with that."

"That may not be wise." Zadock spoke slowly, his shoulders
forward. He said, "I suggest we encourage a revolt."

"You what?" Zedekiah let go of Miriam's hand.

"That's right." Zadock nodded and his gold amulet bobbed at the end
of its chain. "We should consider not paying the tax, at least for now."

"We can't do that, not with the Babylonian armies patrolling our
borders."

Zadock said, "A revolt should give me enough power to negotiate
a lower, more equitable tax."

"You're not serious, are you?" Zedekiah rubbed the concern
deeper into his brow. "You're willing to negotiate with the
Babylonians?" He shook his head slowly. "They're not known for
their patience on matters of tax. You'd be taking your life in your
hands if you approached them with this."

"That's a risk I'm willing to take." Zadock bowed and the cuffs in his
robe lifted about his wrists. "I'm sworn to serve the throne, your majesty."

"You're a fine man, Zadock, a fine man indeed and I'd be honored
to have you oversee the tax." Zedekiah shook the Chief Elder's hand.

Zadock's grip was weak, his fingers reaching around Zedekiah's wrist with the strength of a dead fish, but he wasn't weak, not by governing standards. Zadock was the most influential man in the city, next to Zedekiah of course, and if Miriam were to be believed, he'd grown to be more powerful. Zedekiah shook for an uncomfortable length of time and then he shook a little longer. What did Miriam know about government? She lived in a world ruled by intuition and in these difficult times her suspicions would only divide loyalties. Zadock was a uniter, a man willing to shoulder some of the burdens of kingship. Finally, Zedekiah had an aide he could trust with his burdens, a counselor who understood the troubles of leadership, someone who could guide him in matters of state. He said, "We should speak with the people about this, make some sort of announcement."

"I've already taken care of that." Zadock rubbed the end of his amulet between his fingers. "If you read the tax notice carefully, you'll find it declares the last day of the month for a gathering." He turned to Miriam and said, "We'll need you to stand with your husband that day. All of Judah will want to know that you support the king in this matter."

Miriam said, "Have you gotten approval for this?"

"Your husband seems to agree, my lady." The Chief Elder took back the tax notice and held it up to Miriam. "And there isn't a soul in this city that won't favor a revolt against a burden as impossible to bear as this."

Miriam lowered her head. "I was referring to God's approval, sir."

"Of course you were." Zadock stepped back, the hem of his robe brushing against a lone juniper. "And there's no one more able to pray for our success in this matter than you. You will remember us in your prayers, won't you?"

"Isaiah prophesied that our bondage was to last seventy years." Miriam played with the sash on her robe, but her voice was steady. "By my count we have sixty-nine remaining, sir."

"I didn't know you were so versed in dead prophets."

"No more than you, I'm sure."

Zadock said, "Wouldn't you agree it best to consult with living prophets on these matters?"

"Certainly." Miriam let go of the bow in her sash. "I didn't know there were any you trusted."

"I hope you don't mind, sire." Zadock stepped past the juniper bush and positioned himself next to Zedekiah. "I've already taken the liberty to speak of the tax with the prophet Hannaniah."

"Hannaniah?" Zedekiah folded his open-cuffed arms across his chest. Who was this prophet named Hannaniah? He'd never heard of him before.

"That's right sire; he's been schooled by the temple priests since he was a lad. He's a very bright man, with a good knowledge of the law and he's certainly one we could trust to receive guidance from heaven."

The click, click, clicking of boots echoed from the main gardens and before Zedekiah could ask anymore about this new prophet Hannaniah, Captain Laban turned the corner, came down along the hedge and stepped between a line of rose bushes. He was dressed in his captain's uniform, a long cape streaming out behind his powerful stride. He stopped beside the Chief Elder and said, "Have you told the king about Uriah?"

Miriam stepped close enough to Laban that the skirts of her robe brushed against his legs and she looked up into his bearded face. "Is there something wrong with the man?"

"Nothing that should concern you, my lady."

Zedekiah said, "What is it?"

"I moved him to the upper prison, washed him, and fed him some good broth." Laban removed his helmet and held it at his side, the leather chinstrap playing about his hand. "I believe he's in the best of spirits for trial."

"Trial?" Zedekiah crossed to Laban's side. "I haven't arranged for his trial."

"I think it's best we conduct it at the east gate." Zadock circled around behind the king. "The council always conducts its public trials beneath the arch of the east gate."

"I suppose that would be acceptable."

Miriam said, "What about Shemayahu?" She stepped in front of Laban and Zadock, her braids lifting off her shoulders and fluttering the ends of her red and green scarf at her cheeks. "You can't begin the trial until Uriah's father provides for his defense."

Laban said, "I haven't seen the man."

"Did you notify him?"

"Of course, my lady." Laban tightened his grip on the helmet. "That's the usual protocol for a trial like this."

Miriam said, "That's odd."

Laban said, "There's nothing odd about military protocol."

Miriam held the sash in her robe. "There is something peculiar about a father who refuses to come to the aid of his son. Wouldn't you agree, Captain?"

"I don't concern myself with the welfare of traitors." Laban let go of his helmet, catching it by the chinstrap before it fell to the ground.

Miriam said, "When did you send notice to Shemayahu?"

"I don't remember." Laban tapped the tip of his boot on the stone. "Two months ago, maybe more."

"You're certain?"

Zedekiah said, "Miriam, the good captain has already answered your question."

Zadock said, "We should move forward with the trial, wouldn't you agree, sire?"

Miriam touched Zedekiah on the arm. "We'll have to appoint a lawyer for Uriah."

"That's for Uriah's family to decide, not the throne." Zedekiah took Miriam by the arm, but she pulled free and said, "Is that your final word?"

Zedekiah didn't look at her. He said, "I can't change the law for one man."

"Very good, your majesty." Zadock nodded. "I'll begin making arrangements for the trial immediately."

Laban bowed his powerful body before turning on his heels and starting out of the gardens in company with Zadock.

"Can we play again?" Benjamin hurried out from under the protecting shadows of the balcony with Mulek and Dan slowly following behind him. The littlest prince covered his eyes with his hands and said, "One, two, three . . ."

What was he doing, beginning another game of hide-and-seek at a time like this? They couldn't play again, not with Miriam's lips drawn together in a tight frown. She was upset; he could tell by the way she stood staring at him long after the Chief Elder and Laban disappeared out of the garden. What was he to do? Zedekiah was like little Benjamin, counting with his hands over his eyes, but never reaching ten. He was chasing his tail in search of a solution that could never please both Miriam and Zadock. He couldn't simply change tradition and hire a lawyer to defend Uriah, not without the blessing of Uriah's father—to say nothing of offending Zadock. The Chief Elder had offered his services with the Babylonian tax, and his expertise would prove to be invaluable. And though he was assigned to prosecute the case against Uriah, he could be trusted, no matter how much Miriam believed otherwise.

Zedekiah couldn't keep from feeling Miriam's gaze on him and maybe Benjamin was right, maybe another game of hide-and-seek would ease the tension between them. He leaned over and placed his mouth beside Benjamin's small ear. The boy was nearly finished counting, his tiny fingers spread apart and his eyes peering between them.

Zedekiah said, "One."

Laban latched the garden gate shut behind him and leaned against the post. He didn't usually linger about the courtyards of the palace, but with Zadock pulling up in the shadows of a tall oak growing near the front wall, he couldn't simply walk past, offer a courteous good evening, and take his leave. Laban stepped beneath the barren branches of the tree, the trunk filling the space between them. He set his arms behind his back and pushed his chest forward. He said, "That went well, don't you agree?"

The shawls beneath Zadock's turban hung down over his ears. "I want Ezekiel informed of the details of Uriah's trial."

"Why the chief lawyer?" Laban spit on the ground. "I thought you were going to prosecute the matter."

"I am, and that will leave the duty of directing the trial to the Second Elder on the council."

Laban scratched the back of his neck. "You're not going to make Ezekiel the Second Elder?" He raised his voice, the force of his words shaking the branches above him. "You can't simply raise him to that post. We don't know him well enough and you don't want anyone to cross you like the potter. What will the other Elders say? He's too young to be an Elder."

"I'll do as I please."

"Do you trust him?"

"I don't need trust, Captain." Zadock spoke slowly. "Ezekiel knows the law as well as anyone. He's the perfect replacement for the potter."

"You don't need a replacement; you need a man to direct the affairs of the trial in your favor."

"Ezekiel will steer the trial wherever I tell him." Zadock held the iron bars in the fence surrounding the palace gardens. He said, "I want you to make sure Uriah's father doesn't hurt us."

"You didn't really believe me in there, did you?" Laban raised his hand toward the palace gardens. "I didn't send any notice to the man. Shemayahu doesn't know that his son is held in our prison. He thinks Uriah's still hiding somewhere in Egypt."

"I know that." Zadock wrapped his long fingers around the iron bars and peered between them, back into the palace gardens where the royals played. "And so does Miriam. You heard what she said."

Laban played with the tip of his black beard. "What can she do to us?"

"She'll find a way to bring Shemayahu here."

"She's only a woman."

"That woman, Captain, is the reason you're not king of Judah." Zadock's voice was as thin and rasping as the leaves that skittered across the stone path leading from the gardens. "See that you deal with every lawyer in the city the same."

"The same as what?"

"The same as the innkeepers. Any lawyer who accepts even a shekel's worth of work to defend Uriah will have to answer to me." Zadock stepped farther back under the tree, beneath the long shadows of the palace wall.

"What *about* the innkeepers? What do *they* have to do with this?"

Zadock came around the trunk of the oak and stood in front of Laban, his dark eyes opened wide and his thin nose pointing up at him. "There will be no place for Shemayahu or any of his house to lay their heads. There will be no food to give them strength and not a single drink of wine to calm their thirst, and any innkeepers who do otherwise will lose their inn. Is that clear, Captain?"

Laban leaned against the tree trunk, his arms across his chest and his head back. "Why do you fear Shemayahu?"

"You're the one who should fear him." Zadock pushed away from the garden gate, the bars groaning in their moorings.

"I don't fear an old man from Arim. Nothing of any consequence has ever come out of that village."

"Fear, Captain, will keep you from repeating your mistakes." Zadock passed his tongue over his dry lips. "And you will do well to fear Shemayahu."

The sun fell below the western hills and the lengthening shadows chilled the courtyard. Zadock pulled the collar of his cloak about his neck, rubbed his hands together, and continued. "If Shemayahu comes to the city, make sure his visit is short and unpleasant. There is to be no room in any inn for him."

"Do I look like an innkeeper to you?"

"I don't care how it's done; just make certain no one takes in Uriah's family."

Zadock lifted the hem of his flowing robes off the ground and headed for the front gates of the palace, but before he disappeared around the wall Laban said, "Where are you going?"

Zadock said, "I have a Second Elder to appoint."

CHAPTER 15

The reading chair stood in the center of the library, collecting the heat of a dying fire. Ezekiel fitted himself into the angle of it and let the flickering red glow from the hearth warm his face, relax his eyelids, and slowly carry him off to . . .

No, not sleep, he wasn't going to let the warmth lull him off to dream the frightening dream that haunted him every time he nodded off. He forced open his eyes, draped a scroll between the armrest, and began his nightly review. Debtor's law this evening—obligations on land over fifty acres were due the first of each month, the middle of the month for labor of more than a day's work, and anything owing on property was to be blessed by the temple priest before it was paid on the last day of the . . .

What was that? Ezekiel turned in his polished chair, the sleeves of his robe sliding over the slippery surface. He set aside the scroll and peered between the carved wood backrest like a prisoner peering between iron bars. There was no one in the library—no maidservant bringing him tea, no manservant making rounds of the estate—and he settled back into his reading chair and spread the scroll out in front of him, the top stick resting on his knees and the bottom stick pressed against his belly. He rolled down past the writings about debts on gold, silver, and precious stones. He hurried through the words about debts on wheat and barley and finally stopped turning the sticks at the writings about fines: any debtor who cannot pay his due shall incur a fine of not less than three mina coins for every seven days the balance remains unmet, except for debts owed in the seventh year when the balance is to be forgiven and the debtor freed from his obligation. If a debtor died in prison before paying his obligations, it fell to his extended family to . . .

A noise sounded among the rafters and echoed about the cross-beams like the lift and fall of linen robes. It grew louder, like evening winds bearing down on the outside wall of the library, and the timbers overhead creaked under the force of the gale. It was the sound of a hundred flying creatures landing on the rooftop, and when the shutters on the highest windows burst open Ezekiel raised his hands to protect himself from the winged cherubim flying inside, carrying a book from heaven with warnings of the destruction of Jerusalem written across its pages. The cherubim demanded he eat the writings. It was an odd thing to do with a book from heaven, especially prophecies as dreadful as these, but they were the word of God and like honey to the taste, at least they seemed as sweet as honey until he swallowed and his stomach tightened with illness. Two more angels appeared beside his chair, each one carrying a scroll wrapped around a stick. No, they weren't angels, they were men and the first one carried a stick with the record of the Jews. Ezekiel leaned over the armrest in his chair to get a better look. He knew the second man, he'd seen him somewhere before, but no matter how hard he tried to remember where, he couldn't place a name with the man's face. The second man was carrying a second stick with the record of the house of Joseph of old who was sold into Egypt and his history was written into the parchment.

The men handed over their scrolls and when Ezekiel took hold of them the leather from one stick fused into the fibers of the other. The scrolls were one in his hand, like water from two rivers joined as one. Ezekiel asked the men what this meant. Why were these sticks of Joseph and Judah joined like this? What good could come of mixing the writings of Judah and Joseph? He turned in his chair to ask them, but a voice thundered louder than the rushing of the cherubim wings, ordering him to stand on his feet.

Ezekiel came out of his reading chair, the scroll of debtor's law falling from his lap and landing at his feet. He blinked twice and glanced about the library. The windows were closed, the men standing beside his chair were gone, the cherubim nowhere to be found, and the rushing wind silent. Ezekiel wiped the sweat from his brow. What a fool he was. He'd fallen asleep and allowed himself to suffer the same confusing dream he had every night for months. He reached down to pick the scroll off the floor when he spied a man standing in the entry to the library.

"What are you doing there?" Ezekiel left the scroll at his feet. "Who let you in?"

"The maidservant said I should meet you here."

Ezekiel rubbed his brow. "Do you have an appointment?"

The man stepped into the room and the light of the lamp fell across his wide shoulders and short, black hair. He had a straight jaw and a powerful neck and Ezekiel immediately recognized Jonathan the blacksmith, the Twelfth Elder on the council. Jonathan's cheeks and thick arms were smeared with ash. He smelled like smoke from an olivewood fire and there was no doubt he'd come from hovering over the heat of an open hearth.

Jonathan wore a thick leather kilt about his hips and a leather apron over a gray tunic. It was an odd choice of clothing for an Elder, but then Ezekiel never understood why Jonathan was appointed to the council. The Babylonians may have deported some of the educated men of the city, but there were certainly more than enough left that the Chief Elder didn't need to bring a common artisan into his council. Jonathan's only distinction was his knowledge of steel—he was the only Jew who knew the secrets of smelting the metal—but that didn't merit a seat on the council, unless there was something about the blacksmith's steel making Ezekiel didn't know.

Jonathan removed his toque from his head and held it between his hands like a priest offering a prayer. "I'm sorry to bother you."

"You gave me a start, that's all. I shouldn't have been so, so . . ."

"So afraid?"

"You didn't frighten me." Ezekiel came around his reading chair. "What brings you here at this hour?"

Jonathan held out a gold amulet, the metal shimmering in the light of the fire. He said, "The Chief Elder wanted it delivered immediately."

Ezekiel took the amulet and held it in his palm. The metal was still warm, the heat of the forging fire still trapped within the finely crafted gold. He held it up to the light of the lamp and slowly mouthed the words of the inscription. Ezekiel's name was etched into the precious metal next to his title—Second Elder of the Council of Elders at Jerusalem. He cradled the amulet with both hands. Why must the Chief Elder promote him ahead of the other Elders? Zadock didn't need Ezekiel on his council. It was a promotion he did not want, and with rumors of a tax revolt spreading about the city like wildfire he should avoid any ties to Zadock. He held the gold chain and let the amulet swing from the end of it. He said, "What do you think of this?"

"I used the purest gold, sir." Jonathan stuffed his toque under his belt. "There's not a flaw in the smelting and— "

"No, no, not the smithing. Your workmanship is more than fine." Ezekiel shook the amulet by the chain. "The words, blacksmith; what do you think about my appointment?" He leaned forward. "Doesn't it bother you?"

"Should it?"

"I'm not a member of the council and yet Zadock places me ahead of you and the others. That should anger you."

"Better you than I, sir."

"What do you mean?"

"Well, you know the law better than most." Jonathan nodded. "I'm pleased with your appointment."

Pleased? Ezekiel held his hands under his chin. The blacksmith had every reason to loathe him, but instead he was content to let Ezekiel have the post. "What about the other Elders? Do they share your enthusiasm for this?"

"I'm a blacksmith, sir." Jonathan brushed the ash from his arms. "There isn't a lot I share in common with the other council members."

"I see." Ezekiel rubbed the amulet between his fingers. The blacksmith was right. He wasn't a merchant like the others, but his honesty was refreshing. Ezekiel said, "Have you no desire for the highest seats on the council?"

"I have more than enough trouble taking care of my family." Jonathan shook his head. "I don't need anything more."

Ezekiel carefully fitted the chain over his head and let the amulet play about his chest. He said, "Did the Chief Elder say anything further about this?"

"There was one thing."

"Go on."

"I don't know exactly how to tell you." Jonathan lowered his gaze. "It isn't my place to deliver such messages."

"What is it, blacksmith?"

"These are Zadock's words, not mine."

"Get on with it."

"You're to keep the amulet as long as . . ."

"As long as what?"

Jonathan cleared his throat. "As long as no lawyers assist Uriah's father in the upcoming trial. No one in the city is to defend him."

"I can't threaten lawyers to refuse work."

"The Chief Elder didn't use the word threaten, sir."

Ezekiel lifted the amulet away from his chest, the gold catching the light of the lamp and reflecting its yellow into Jonathan's eyes. "And if I refuse to keep lawyers from defending Uriah?"

Jonathan's dark hair fell into his eyes, and he quickly pushed it back off his brow. "I can take the amulet back if you like."

Ezekiel let go of the amulet and it fell against the pleats in his robe. "Tell Zadock he shouldn't expect me to force his will on the lawyers in this city whenever it pleases him."

Jonathan nodded and started for the hall, but Ezekiel took him by the arm and said, "What is it like?"

Jonathan pulled his ash-soiled arm free. "What was that, sir?"

"The council." Ezekiel stood close enough to feel the warmth rising off Jonathan's body. He lowered his voice to a whisper and said, "What is it like sitting in judgment with the Elders?"

"You've seen many more trials than I ever will."

"I've never sat in judgment."

Jonathan stepped back. "Casting a vote against a man's life isn't a pleasant thing."

Ezekiel nodded. "Then you believe Uriah is innocent."

Jonathan stared back at him, his eyes wide as an owl in the dark of night. "Do you?"

Ezekiel said, "You voted to execute Uriah."

"I voted the way Zadock wanted me to vote."

"Will you do the same in this trial?"

"It doesn't matter how I vote. Zedekiah has the final say about Uriah now."

Ezekiel started back around the reading chair to sit down, but pulled up when Jonathan said, "There's another thing you should know about the amulet, sir."

"What's that?"

"The Chief Elder said you would need it in order to preside over Uriah's trial."

"Exactly what does he mean by preside?"

"I'm not versed in the ways of trials." Jonathan rubbed his hands together. "But isn't it the usual way of things to have the Second Elder direct the affairs of a trial when the First Elder is prosecuting?"

Ezekiel waved him off. "Zadock doesn't want me to direct Uriah's trial."

"You're more than qualified."

"I can't favor Zadock over Uriah."

Jonathan said, "That's something you'll have to speak to Zadock about."

The wooden rafters creaked and Ezekiel glanced up at the vaulted ceiling. There was no rushing of wings, no flying cherubim, and no voice thundering him to his feet. This was not a dream no matter how much he wished it were. He did not seek this post of Second Elder, but for some odd reason Zadock wanted him there. Did the Chief Elder think him qualified for the post, or did he want him close enough to keep his eye on Ezekiel? He said, "Can I ask you a difficult question?"

Jonathan shrugged. "I don't know if I have the answer."

Ezekiel stood beside his chair and played his fingers over the hard wood in the armrest. "Do you think it possible for Jerusalem to be destroyed?"

Jonathan backed into the hallway and the lamplight moved off his face. It was impossible to see his reaction and Ezekiel said, "Is there something wrong, blacksmith?"

"Nothing, sir, it's just that . . ."

"What?"

"This seems a matter for the military and I have little experience making war."

"I wasn't asking about warfare." Ezekiel stepped toward Jonathan. "I was asking if you believe it possible for God to remove His protection of this Holy City."

Jonathan spoke slowly. "This isn't a matter members of the council usually consider."

"The prophets consider it, at least I hear them preach it more than I ever remember them doing."

Jonathan said, "I really should go."

"I have reports that Babylonian soldiers are gathering in the eastern borders to ensure we pay our tax to Nebuchadnezzar."

Jonathan said, "You don't really think they would destroy the city over unpaid taxes, do you?"

"I don't know what men will do for money."

Jonathan placed his toque on his head and pulled it down over his ears. "Do you believe them?"

"The reports are from reliable sources near Jericho."

"No, sir, not the Babylonian army. I meant the prophets." Jonathan cleared his throat. "Do you believe what the prophets are saying?"

"I suppose that depends if this city has lost its holiness."

Jonathan inched down the hallway. "Has it?"

"Time will tell, sir."

Jonathan started toward the front door, but before he turned out of sight Ezekiel said, "Prepare yourself and your family, blacksmith."

Jonathan came back to the library entrance. "Prepare them for what?"

Ezekiel returned to his reading chair and pressed the amulet against his chest. He was the newest member of the council, appointed by Zadock to the seat of the Second Elder, but must he keep this post? He stared into the fire, his mind returning to the words written on the scroll of his dream. A tax revolt was possible and if the Babylonians came against the city, he with Zadock would be the cause of it. Ezekiel spoke over his shoulder. "These are the very worst of times, blacksmith. The very worst."

Ezekiel let Jonathan find his way out.

CHAPTER 16

Queen Miriam left her sons to finish their dinner, with instructions to the maidservants to see them put to bed before she returned—and heaven willing she got back before sunrise. She selected the midnight-black steed from the palace stables for its speed over long journeys. There was not another horse in the royal herd that could run in the shadows of night and not be seen, nor any with the stamina to carry her to Arim and back before dawn. She was racing the sun and thanks be to heaven it was the middle of winter with dawn long enough away that she dare leave the city and visit the home of the prophet Uriah. No, not visit. Not even Uriah's father, Shemayahu, could know that she came in the dark of night with a message that had power to save his son. It was best he believe a military courier delivered the double-sealed document she was about to forge.

Miriam led the steed into the yard, latched the waist-high gate behind them, and started on her way down past the stalls of forty horses stabled behind wooden slats and peering at her. They pawed straw with their hooves, pushed on the gates with their muzzles, and shook their manes, as if to warn her of the perils of her plan. Miriam pulled the collar of her riding cloak up about her cheeks, but it didn't shield her from the stares of the other horses, their eyes gleaming in the moonlight and their breath snorting from their nostrils and pulsing over the top boards in a stream of thick steam. It was her good fortune none of these animals could speak, or they'd convince her not to ride into this trouble. Let God save Uriah while she saved herself and her sons by doing nothing that would stir Captain Laban's suspicions. And though their snorting and stomping was loud enough to roust the stablemaster from his quarters, she'd sent over a delivery of wine from the palace cellars, undiluted with even a single portion of water. It was strong drink, one to be frowned upon, but it had power to cast a deep sleep over any man with a penchant for intemperate ales, and the master of this yard was just such a man, to say nothing of the stable boys he employed.

Miriam hurried past the peering herd, turned the steed out the gate of the livery and the silver coins in her satchel jingled against the supple leather. Two talents were more than enough for Uriah's father, Shemayahu, to hire a fine lawyer to defend his son. Miriam tightened her grip on the reins. Her hands were God's hands on earth, her good deeds His good works, and with that bit of inspiration from heaven she was moved to help Uriah despite the Hebrew law that allowed only family to appoint a lawyer. She wasn't breaking the law; she was making certain Shemayahu got this money along with a notice advising him of the trial. The poor man didn't even know his son was to be tried—Laban had seen to that—and all Miriam could do to correct the captain's silence was to give notice for him.

Miriam turned the steed through the gate and across the military grounds toward the single-story, mud-brick offices at the far end. The iron bars covering the small windows were spaced with such narrow gaps that it was impossible for a sparrow to shimmy through, let alone Miriam. But she had a key. No, not one key—she'd taken thirteen keys from her husband's vault and they clanged at the end of a chain. With a little luck one of them would unlock the building and another the door to Laban's office. She left the steed tied to a post, quietly guided her feet up the steps and tried the first key—a long brass one with two teeth. With a silver, spoon-shaped end, it wasn't the sort of key that would open a military building, but she wasn't in such a hurry she couldn't try all of them. The key fit poorly in the latch and when she turned it, the pin held fast. She forced the lock, but it didn't budge and she went to the second key on the chain. It was as long as the first, but not nearly as thick. This one would open the door, wouldn't it? She turned it, but again it failed to free the pin. The third and fourth keys fit into the latch, but the teeth were all wrong and the front door held firm. It was the ninth key that finally let her inside.

Captain Laban's chambers stood at the end of the hall past the commissary and across from the lobby. A brass plate with his name etched into it decorated the front door. Two side doors emptied into narrow hallways exiting the building, one returning to the training grounds and the other leading onto the wide cobblestone road of King Street. Miriam tried three keys before finding the one that opened the office. She quickly entered, locked the door behind her, and kept the key that had power to let her out again pinched between her thumb and forefinger.

Miriam lit the lamp that hung on the wall beside the door, and the light spread over Laban's empty desk. Where did he keep the double, sealed scrolls? Laban wasn't a scribe, but certainly he kept a few of the double, sealed documents in his office she could use to craft this notice. There were leather parchments stacked in the shelves on the opposite wall, each one with the captain's military seal on it. There were short sheets for letters on another shelf, maps nailed to the wall, and a good many documents bulging in the mail pouch hanging from a peg, filled with letters from the many outposts across the kingdom. There were more than enough empty scrolls waiting to be filled with whatever messages the captain of the guard delivered, but they were not the sort of scrolls she needed and she could only believe that she'd sneaked into Laban's chambers for naught. What was she doing here, locked inside without any double scrolls?

Miriam came around the desk and her leg brushed against a shelf nailed halfway down the sideboard. It was hidden from view, but within reach of anyone sitting in the captain's chair. She sat and let the yellow lamplight filter down over a double scroll of virgin papyrus, a stylus, and a full bottle of ink. At last! She'd found what she came for. The double scroll was the most official of documents and she couldn't have hoped for anything better than this to ensure the authenticity of her forgery. The papyrus unraveled with a scratching noise over the wooden desktop and Miriam kept the ends from curling back into her writing by setting the keys at the top and the inkwell at the bottom. There was a long cut across the belly of the sheet and it would have come in two if not for a small tab of papyrus connecting the top and bottom of the scroll. She stirred the pen and began to write her message across the bottom portion below the cut, imitating Laban's hand as best she could; *Be informed that Uriah, son of Shemayahu, is held in the palace dungeons at Jerusalem, awaiting trial for the crime of treason. You are hereby notified to provide for him a lawyer in his defense.*

Miriam repeated the message a second time on the top portion of the scroll exactly as it appeared on the bottom. She signed Laban's name and scrolled the copied portion down to the cut between the two halves before folding it back on itself until it was a tiny wad of papyrus and she could seal it with three daubs of wax and tie it with cords. It was an odd-looking thing, the bottom portion of the scroll laid out across the writing table with her forged message in thick black ink and a copy of it reduced to a clump of wax-sealed, string-bound papyrus no wider than the stub of her thumb and attached to the top of the original by a small tab of papyrus like a wart on the face of her flowing Hebrew script. There was no better way to preserve the integrity of a document and when Shemayahu removed the wax on the sealed portion, untied the cords and compared the copy to the unsealed words of the scroll he would believe it an official proclamation from Captain Laban himself.

Miriam loosely scrolled the unsealed bottom portion around the sealed copy and stood, pushing the chair back and grating the legs over the stone floor. Perfect! She had her double-sealed document, informing Shemayahu of his son's imprisonment. Miriam was reaching for the inkbottle to put it away when footsteps fell in the hall. Who could that be? The last officer left here hours ago and there were no maidservants in this place. Soldiers didn't need anyone to clean up after them, and there wasn't any reason for anyone to want to come back here after a day's work except for . . .

No. It couldn't be Laban, not now. The footsteps drew closer and Miriam quickly stood away from the desk, her elbow tipping the inkwell and staining the bottom of the letter with splotches. What a fine mess she'd made and no time to clean it up and hide her doings in this chamber. She stuffed the notice under her arm and turned her ear to the sound of a hand testing the latch. Thank heavens she'd locked it or she'd be found out. She hurried to the side door and lifted the chain of keys to the dim light. Not another guessing game. She had to divine which key unlocked this latch, with little margin for a poor choice.

She picked out a long, brass key with four wide teeth and an ornately decorated finger hold. Just the sort of key that would open a . . .

No, not that one. That was a key that would open the royal vault or the great palace hall, but certainly not the side door to Laban's chambers. She let it fall back with the others, ran her fingers over three more, and settled on a plain-looking iron key without any etchings to set it apart from the other twelve keys. This was a key that would open an obscure side door—it had to be. There wasn't time to test the others, not with the latch to the front door of Laban's chambers clicking open with a piercing ping, the sound of it echoing across the room and taking Miriam's breath away. She forced the iron teeth into side door latch.

Dear God, let this be the right one!

Laban gripped the latch to his chamber door, turned a shoulder to the wood planks and readied for a fight. There was a creature inside, there had to be with the clinking of a cup or a bowl or some sort of pottery tipping over. They were the sounds of a thief and it was a good thing he'd come back to return a pair of boots to the commissary or he'd never have been in the hallway to hear.

Laban pushed open the chamber door. It banged against the lamp hanging on the inside wall and smothered the flame to darkness. In the vanishing light he saw a dark cape flying about the form of a shadowy figure escaping out the side door. The room went black. Laban started after him, but ran into his desk. He braced his fall with his hands on the desk and smeared them into some sort of liquid. The weight of his body cracked a leg on the desk, rocking it to the side and dropping him onto the floor. Cursed desk! He jumped to his feet and made it to the side door, but it was locked from the outside. He felt for the small key he kept on a chain about his neck, but with his wet, sticky hands he couldn't get hold of it. Godforsaken key! He quickly retraced his steps past the broken desk, out the chamber and down the narrow hallway into the yard. The thief was riding out the back gate of the training grounds on a horse from the royal stables. How did he let the man get away like that? But at least there was no reason to worry. He stored nothing of value in his chambers and the foolish thief would have nothing to show for his work—no gold, no silver, no precious stones—nothing to repay him for his nocturnal plunder, except to sit on Laban's chair and pretend to be captain of the guard, and . . .

Laban raised his hands to the moonlight. Was it an accident his hands were covered with dark, black ink? The stains were the kind that kept on the skin for days and he'd have to go about the city with soiled hands. He rubbed away what he could in the dirt and marched back inside, stopping at the side door. There was nothing odd about the entrance and he ran his stained hands over the wood planks. There were no marks indicating the posts had been pried away. He tried the latch. The brass handle was secure, the bolts were snug, and when he finally got hold of the key with his ink-covered hands and fitted it into the latch and turned it, the pin clicked just as it should. There was nothing about this door that could aid his investigation except that it was locked.

How did a thief get a key for his chambers?

Miriam reined to the summit beyond Hebron and surveyed the valley below. An icy spring bubbled beside the road and she let her mount lap water while she studied the torches atop the walls of Fort Lakhish flickering on the horizon at the far end of the valley. The outline of its turrets and towers covered the distant hill with the shadows of a mighty fortress standing against the moonlit backdrop of southern Judah's hill country. Her gaze fell from the fort, back down the valley to the small congregation of buildings nestled amid a thick forest at the base of the trail. Qiryat Ye'arim—the city of trees— and there was no doubt where it got its name, with cedars sprouting along the narrow lanes and footpaths of the town like tall bottles of wine on a dusty cellar shelf, hovering over the ninety-seven mud- brick homes that turned this forest into a thriving village with moon- beam shadows of gray streaming down through the branches and onto the square rooftops.

Miriam spurred away from the spring and back onto the trail, the horse kicking up dust behind them. She leaned forward in the saddle and held the stirrups against the animal's flank, pressing through a stand of scrub oak and splashing through the creek bed three times before the trail leveled and they galloped into the east side of Arim—the village of the prophet Uriah's birth—where she could leave her forgery on Shemayahu's doorstep and forget that she ever delivered it.

Miriam left her mount tied up behind a stand of date trees and crossed the road to Arim's only inn, where Shemayahu lived with his daughter-in-law and three grandchildren in the upper rooms. She pushed open the gate and quietly made her way past the porch benches to the front door. The inn was locked and the windows were dark. Good. Everyone was asleep. She set the sealed scroll on the porch, tucked silver coins inside and made a fist to knock on the door, but she couldn't just wake the family and hurry away—not with the impression that flooded her mind, telling her that this was not the right thing to do.

Not the right thing? How could saving Uriah's life be wrong? But the impression was powerful enough to turn her back down the porch with the notice and the money in hand. What was she to do if not leave this for Shemayahu? She'd ridden through the night to deliver them and now she was abandoning her mission. She was to the bottom step when her foot brushed against the stack of empty wine bottles set beside the porch, knocking them over and shattering them on the courtyard stones. She began gathering the broken pieces when she heard someone stir in the bedroom window above her.

What was that? Shemayahu pulled the blanket off his face and blinked in the darkness. No, not the wine bottles. The breaking clay crashed on the steps below his narrow bedroom window and stirred him from his dreams. Foolish wild creatures! Why did they have to prowl about late at night when he didn't have the strength or the presence of mind to chase them away with the end of a broom? If they came about the inn by afternoon, he'd be ready for them, but the vandals didn't do their meddling during the day and it was his own fault for leaving the wine bottles on the front porch where they could get at them. Well, it wasn't entirely his fault. His grandsons, Benuriah and David, were to put the empty bottles in the wine cellar before bed, and they'd gotten all but the last stack of them stowed.

Another burst of breaking pottery cluttered the air with a loud crashing. That wasn't the sound of squirrels or varmints or rabbits, not by any stretch. It was too loud for anything smaller than a goat and Shemayahu turned on his side, his ear toward the window. Could it be the scapegoat?

How many times did Shemayahu warn the town priests not to let the goat go on the Day of Atonement last October? That was a ceremony better left to the priests in Jerusalem, not the small hamlet of Arim. If it was the scapegoat that had gotten through the gate and onto the porch, Shemayahu was going to charge the priests for the broken wine bottles and insist the animal be taken off the streets once and for all!

Shemayahu sat up in bed and listened in the dark for another sound of the goat stirring outside. He didn't mind that the local Elders celebrated the Day of Atonement the same way the priests in Jerusalem did by placing all the sins of the people on the head of a goat and sending it off into the desert with a red ribbon tied around its neck warning everyone it was not to be bothered. And though they couldn't offer a second goat as a sacrifice on the temple altar like they did in Jerusalem, it was their faith that kept them looking forward to the day when the Messiah would atone for the sins of the people. But this was Arim, not Jerusalem, and when the local priests released their own goat, it was the beginning of a celebration Shemayahu would never forget, no matter how hard he tried. The stubborn animal never carried the villagers' sins farther than the end of Main Street before it sauntered back into town right in front of the inn and no one dared chase it away, not with the foolish belief that bothering the animal would bring all their sins back upon their heads, no matter how sincerely they had repented.

Shemayahu ripped the blanket off his legs, but didn't turn out of bed, not with the cold floor waiting to receive his feet. Better to wait and listen to hear if the goat had gone than to endure the chill of the wood slats for no reason. If the goat was still wandering about the steps he was going to capture the pesky creature and have it butchered. The scapegoat may be a sacred animal, but Shemayahu had lived with its prowling and bawling and scavenging for six months and this was the last straw. He rubbed the sleep from his eyes. A scapegoat was supposed to take the sins of the people into the wilderness, but this scapegoat had taken the streets of Arim and the animal refused to give them back.

Shemayahu waited in the darkness without moving. It was the middle of the night and waking to the noise of a stubborn goat was not a pleasant dream, not when sleep was the only time he could forget the ache of sixty-seven years nagging at his bones. Shemayahu had deep-brown eyes fixed above his gaunt cheeks like the entrance to an owl's roost—alert in the most tiring of times. His hands weren't worn like those of other men his age who spent their lives in the vineyards about Arim, gathering grapes for the pressing stone. Shemayahu inherited his inn from his father and he lived his life pouring wine, not harvesting it from the vine or pressing it underfoot. But now, the curse of not having an heir wearied him more than the harvest ever could.

Shemayahu swung his legs out of bed and sat on the edge of it with his feet dangling above the floor. He reached for the lamp beside his bed, but with the shaking in his hands he missed and had to steady himself before trying again. The shaking had plagued him since last week when he slipped carrying a keg of wine from the storehouse and hit his head against the bar. The cut measured three fingers long and he hid the ugly gash under a bandage. The swelling had gone down, but the bruising still colored his brow a dark purple. The doctor said it would go away soon, but it didn't seem he would ever rid himself of the shaking. He took the lamp by one hand and carefully struck the flint. It didn't light and he would have tried again, but he dropped the flint and had to step down on the cold floor. Cursed fool he was! He crawled about the floor, feeling for the flint in the shadows like a blind man. If he hadn't hit his head in the first place, he'd not have to endure the shaking that shuddered through his arms. He could hardly pour a cup of wine for patrons to say nothing of crawling about the floor like a babe. But he'd chosen the life of an innkeeper and he wasn't allowed to be old anymore, not with his son, Uriah, gone. If only he were here, none of this would have happened.

How he longed to have Uriah's steady hands do the work about the inn. It had been seven months since Shemayahu began shouldering the burden of his fleeing son. And then there was Uriah's wife, Deborah, and their three children. They were sleeping down the hall, and he crawled about the floor quietly searching for the flint to keep from waking them. That poor family had lived far too long without a father to see to their support. And since someone had to look after them, Shemayahu had donned an innkeeper's apron every day since the day Uriah escaped into Egypt, and he served customers with a smile and a prayer that somehow, someway God would bring his son home from the land of the pharaohs, forever safe.

The sound of footsteps and the tinkling of the scapegoat picking up the broken clay filtered up from the porch. That was impossible. A goat didn't have hands, no matter how sacred an animal it was. There was someone at the door and if the stirring on the porch below proved to be Uriah, then Shemayahu could give him back his apron and let him carry kegs from the cellar while he held his grandchildren on his knee. Wasn't that what he was supposed to do when he became a grandfather—sit on the porch of the inn and in the twilight of his days let the sun warm his soul with the joy of his family?

Shemayahu found the flint, lighted the lamp, and started toward the window.

He said, "Uriah, is that you?"

A light appeared in the window above Miriam. She dropped the potsherds, the already broken clay crashing to the ground in tiny fragments. She hurried across the street, mounted up behind the date trees and leaned forward in the saddle, pushing aside the branches to see a gentleman with graying hair push open the front door and step onto the porch. Shemayahu carried himself with a bent-over posture, a long sleeping robe trailing behind his stride. He raised his lamp to the sky, repeating Uriah's name, and when no one answered his call he mumbled a curse on the soldiers who had chased his son into Egypt. Immediately Miriam knew she was right to come here with a forged letter from Laban. She clutched the undelivered notice in her hand. Laban hadn't informed Shemayahu of his son's condition and he was still looking for Uriah to return home from Egypt without any notion that he'd been held in prison these past months.

Shemayahu gathered the potsherds into a rubbish pile, offered another, not-so-calloused curse against the scapegoat and disappeared inside, clicking the bolt in place behind him, the harsh sound echoing across the street, piercing Miriam to the very center. How she wished she could be Shemayahu's proxy. She would run back to the inn, and tell Shemayahu that she would willingly take all the anguish Laban and others like him had caused and carry it as far away into the wilderness as she could. She had news of Uriah, and though she could not free Uriah from prison, any news was better than not knowing. That's exactly what she was going to do! She slid out of the saddle and started out from behind the trees when a powerful impression filled her soul, stopping her from taking another step and telling her that the message she carried was to be delivered, but she was not the one to deliver it. Miriam leaned against the side of the horse, her body weary from the lack of sleep and the long ride. She held the doubled, sealed scroll to her breast. If she was not to deliver this message, then who? She stroked the horse's neck. If Uriah were to have a lawyer, then Shemayahu was going to have to find one for him. Why couldn't she simply leave this notice on the doorstep, be done with her mission, and head back to Jerusalem?

Miriam slowly pulled herself back into the saddle, the skirts of her robe covering the horn. She leaned forward, pressed the horse's mane between her fingers, and stared through the fig branches, beyond the wall of the inn, down along the gentle tree-lined slopes above Arim that gave way to a rocky ridge lining the valley all the way to Fort Lakhish sitting atop a distant hill, its towers and parapets twinkling with burning torches like tiny stars raised in the night sky. Lakhish was like a city of refuge, floating above the . . .

Was that her answer? Lakhish was not the city of Hebron or Golan or Kedesh—cities Moses appointed for refuge—but there was something about the fort that filled Miriam with hope for Uriah. The prophet hadn't taken anyone's life, but he did need refuge from the vengeance of Laban and Zadock. Miriam guided her steed out from behind the fig trees and onto the dusty road in front of the inn. Was she to deliver this notice to Fort Lakhish? The impression was unmistakable and when she spurred her heels into the horse's flank and raced west through the dark streets of Arim toward the fort, her questioning heart flooded with peace. Her journey wasn't finished until this notice was delivered to Shemayahu; and if God wanted another to do that, then so be it. It was not her place to question His will, only to obey and leave the rest in His hands. She tucked the double-sealed notice under her belt and leaned forward in the saddle. God had prepared another to deliver this notice to Shemayahu and do something she could not.

Find a lawyer to defend the prophet Uriah.

CHAPTER 17

Mima placed the linen-covered pigeon coops on the front steps of the palace, hunched her shoulders forward, and set her hands on her hips, ready to ward off any who dared offer to carry the birds to her room. If the palace help found out she was sneaking pigeons inside, they'd send her away and tell her never to come back, no matter that Laban had given his permission to bring them here. A dirty fowl had no place in the king's residence and her only recourse was to cover them with a thick cloth cut from the curtains of her quarters and sewn to fit over the wicker cages.

The palace butler opened the main doors before Mima could knock. He was baldheaded with curly, white hair dressing the sides of his head, and gentle brown eyes, hardly the sort of man Mima should fear. But until she got these pigeons past him, he was the enemy. He didn't offer a word of greeting or ask the nature of her business. She was the queen's handservant and there was no way the butler could mistake her black skin and tightly curled locks of hair, to say nothing of the girth she carried about her middle. She had the power to knock the stoutest palace guard off his feet with one good swing of her belly, and if he made the slightest advance on her pigeon coops, she'd slap him with it. Well, maybe not with her belly, but she'd think of something to keep him from finding out what she concealed in these wicker baskets. The coop on her right hand was filled with outgoing pigeons that knew the way to Qumran, and the one on her left hand was for incoming pigeons just arrived from Josiah and Rebekah, and the sooner she got past the butler and up to her room to begin training them to home to her new quarters, the sooner she could send for Josiah to come pick them up and take them back to Qumran.

Mima plucked the coops from the porch and waited for the butler to stand aside, but he didn't move and thankfully the birds kept quiet, the darkness under the linen keeping them from cooing and scampering about. The butler stood in the doorway with his mouth hanging half-open and his wide eyes grown wider. Must he stare at her like that? Mima was wearing red-and green-striped clothing that dressed her stout frame in bright, spring colors. The cloth was wrapped about her like a scroll with knots tied at the small of her back and high on her hip—not the most modest thing she could have worn on her first day at the palace with the sheer cloth pulling tight across her chest, but if it served to distract the butler's attention away from the pigeons, then her less-than-modest dress had served its purpose. Thank heaven for Ethiopian fashion.

"May I come in?"

The butler closed the doors and quietly latched them in place. He said, "Follow me."

"I can find my way, sir." Mima marched past him and into the lobby. The walls were decorated with red and gold tapestries hanging above an assembly of spears and swords with enough pointed tips and blades to slice every roasted lamb, sheep, and pheasant from here to Egypt. And those hanging lamps—they gave off enough heat to bake an entire year's worth of bread in one afternoon. But since Mima wasn't hired to do any of the cooking, she wouldn't chide anyone for wasting so much oil to light an empty lobby. Mima reached the main stairs and stopped. Who on earth would want to live a hundred steps above ground?

Burning frankincense scented the upper floor and the tartness of it livened Mima's legs so that she didn't stop until she reached the top. She was out of breath, but no so much she couldn't offer a silent prayer, asking heaven to bring her into the good graces of Prince Mulek and Queen Miriam. She had to gain their confidence if she had any hope of helping the prophet Uriah. The tables near the landing were set with vases of evergreen boughs and pinecones that mixed with the pungent frankincense. When Mima passed by, the strong scent filled her with the hope that somehow, someway, God would see that all went well with her first meeting of the royal family.

Four bedroom doors stood open along the length of the hall and Mima didn't bother to lean over the railing, call after the butler, and ask him which one was hers. It certainly wasn't the room on the right, not with an army of maidservants bustling about the quarters changing bedsheets and pillows, sweeping the polished stone floors, and picking away the lint that had gathered on the rugs at the entrance to the expansive bedroom chamber that could only belong to the royal couple. The next room had two very small beds stuck against opposite walls and a host of wooden blocks neatly stacked below the windows, and there was no way this was for Mima. She could no sooner fit in a bed that size, than she could swim across the Galilee without sinking to the bottom, and there was no doubting that the smallest princes, Dan and Benjamin, lived here. Two rooms remained at the end of the hall, one for her and the other for Prince Mulek. Mima stepped past a maidservant polishing the bench seat and stood between the open doors. She closed her eyes, guessed that she should have the bedroom on the right and then turned that way with the pigeon coops swaying at her side and the . . .

"Guess again."

Mulek stood in the doorway she'd selected, his thin body leaning against the frame. He'd been waiting there, watching her foolish guessing game. He said, "This one's mine."

Mulek was dressed in a purple tunic, a gold emblem sewn across the chest and his thin arms sprouting out the short sleeves that barely covered his bony shoulders. He'd grown taller since Mima saw him last, the end of his tunic hardly reaching his belt, and his leather kilt falling well short of his knees. He was going to be as tall and elegant as his father, maybe even more elegant, what with his mother's delicate eyes, narrow nose, and those high, rose-colored cheeks that bespoke a regal heritage. His hair had grown in, though it was still too short to tell if he had the curls and waves of the queen, or the straight, over-the-brow hair of his father.

"You're to board in that room, across the hall." Mulek pointed to the open door. "They moved the other chamber servant to another floor to make room for you."

"My, my." Mima set the coops on the floor beside her feet. "Since when do I merit my own room?"

"Laban insisted you have a private room on the same floor with my mother." Mulek peered at her, his eyes narrowed like a soldier standing guard, and the only thing he had to protect was his mother. He said, "How much is he paying you?"

"Well I . . ." That was an odd question for such a young boy to ask. She said, "I don't suppose any more than the other help?"

That wasn't exactly the case. Laban had offered Mima a full talent of gold to watch for any evidence of the queen's spying, and it was a good thing the captain didn't know that Mulek was the one he sought. The prince was an elusive informant, but until now, he'd moved between the palace and potter's home without suffering the captain's suspicions and if he was to be watched, there was no telling what harm awaited the boy's missteps. Mima should have told Mulek right then that she knew he was the palace informant, that he was the one Laban hated above all others, but this was not the right time to confess her allegiance to the Rekhabites, not in the middle of the hall with maid-servants scurrying about and Mulek standing there, wearing his suspicions of her like a poorly crafted mask. She took a deep breath, forced a smile and said, "What a wonderful time we're going to have."

Mulek folded his arms across his chest. "I know why you're here."

"Of course you do." Mima patted him on the head. "I'm to look after you and your mother."

Mulek ducked his head away from her patting. "He told me everything."

Mima lowered her voice. "Who told you?"

Mulek stepped around Mima's large frame and into the hallway, headed toward the open bedroom door. He said, "Bring the pigeons and follow me."

How did he know about the birds? They were hidden under the linen and none of them had made the slightest cooing, but she picked them up and followed him.

The ceiling in Mima's new quarters reached two stories above the floor. The walls were finished with white stone; the mortar sparkling with the sheen of crushed minerals. Large windows framed the bed on each side and Mulek untied the cords holding the shutters in place and pulled back the wooden slats to let the morning sun filter in with the breeze. He took the pigeon coops from her hand, set them on the windowsill and removed the linen covering. "Mother made sure you got the room with plenty of windows and directly over the main gardens. She said it would be easier to train the pigeons with the gardens close by."

"How do you know all this?"

Mulek opened the wicker door on the first coop and set the pigeons on the window ledge, letting them preen on the sill and flap their feathers in the morning sun. He said, "Are these the pigeons you're training to home to the palace?"

"Well yes, but . . ." Mima grabbed two of the birds. "You can't let them out like that, they'll fly away."

"No they won't, they know you." Mulek took back the pigeons and set them on the sill with the others. "They know the smell of your hair and the look of your face and the sound of your voice, and if you teach them how to find this window ledge, they'll risk their lives searching to come home." He ran his fingers over their gray-blue feathers. "They always come home." He spread chopped figs along the sill. There was nothing that guided a pigeon home faster than the promise of sweet-tasting figs, but how did Mulek know that? He was a prince, not a bird trainer. Mima had seen Josiah train the birds, yet she didn't know half what Mulek knew.

One of the pigeons began to peck at the fruit and immediately Mulek whisked it up from the ledge. "This one already knows the windowsill." He stuffed the bird under his tunic. "You stay here while I take her to the gardens and see if she can find her way back."

"Stop right there, young man." Mima hurried over and stood in the door, blocking his way into the hall. "You're not going anywhere until you tell me who taught you to train pigeons."

"I did."

A man stepped from the shadows in the corner of the room, over beyond the vanity. His face was shrouded behind the lace that draped the bed's canopy in a cascade of white cloth.

"I sneaked the bird trainer in." Mulek stuffed his hand beneath his shirt and stroked the pigeon. "There isn't a sewer or water tunnel I don't know about."

Mima came around the bed to get a better view of the man. She knew his stature—the way he held his shoulders back, his hands resting on his hips, and his chin pushed forward. He was dressed in a brown robe, the same one he'd worn the day he escaped into the desert. His skin was tanned and his cheeks were gaunt, nothing like the well-fed, round-faced man she'd sent to Qumran three months ago. There was no way he could be here and she wouldn't believe it until the he removed his hood, exposing his bald head.

"Josiah?" Mima held her hand over her trembling lips. If Laban or Zadock found out he was alive, they'd put him in a grave from which he could never return.

Josiah said, "Mima, you look good."

"Good?" She shook her fist at him. "Is that all you can say after all the worry you've caused me? I've never looked worse. I haven't slept for months worrying over you and now you come back to Jerusalem under the worst of circumstances and you have the nerve to tell me that I look good."

"Mima." Josiah took her in his arms. "You never looked better."

A tear fell down Mima's cheek and she dried it before it fell on Josiah's shoulder. She said, "How is Rebekah? I do so miss the girl."

"I'm well, Mima." The door to the changing room inched open and Rebekah stepped out. She was wearing a plain brown cape over her worn, white robe, the same robe she'd worn the day she left Jerusalem, and it had gone gray from the blowing sands and dirty environs of Qumran. Mima could only see the hem beneath the brown cloak, but there was no doubt that Rebekah was in need of a new robe. The girl shouldn't have to wear such clothing, not when Mima kept a closet full of Rebekah's robes—the finest Josiah's money could buy. And that poorly woven cloak was simply a disgrace. The threads were coarse and the stitching uneven and Mima was ashamed to have her in such threadbare cloth. The cloak didn't do justice to Rebekah; it was far too plain for a woman of her beauty. Rebekah still had wide, penetrating eyes and her smile was like the sun rising over the Mount of Olives. Her long brown locks were braided with a silk ribbon. The brown color of her hair had gone light from so much sun and the ends were frayed, but a good soaking in olive oil would cure that. Her skin was fair but dry, and Mima touched her hand to the girl's cheeks. Parched they were, and her lips chapped. Mima warned her a thousand times there was nothing that could rob her of her youth faster than the desert winds— always blowing, always dry—and they'd sucked the water from her skin like a vulture sucks the meat off a carcass.

Mima said, "I've got just the right oils to take care of your skin, and I'm going to draw a warm bath and have you soak in it until your nails soften up. There's nothing that— "

"Mima," Josiah said, "we can't take a bath here."

"And why not? There's plenty of bath water." Mima pulled Rebekah into her arms and she felt the frailness of the girl's body against her. She never was one to eat her fill, and three months in the desert hadn't given her anymore of an appetite. "I'm going to take you down to the palace kitchens, do you hear, and see that they feed you."

"I'm fine, really." Rebekah's voice was like a flute and it was playing the most beloved music of all—the music of Mima's adopted family, the only people on earth she called kin, but it wasn't entirely a happy sound. There was something in Rebekah's voice, the way she forced her smile. She never remembered Rebekah speaking with her chin down and her gaze holding to the floor like a lost sheep.

Mima said, "What is it girl? It isn't like you to be so, so . . ."

Josiah said, "So heartsick?" He took Rebekah by the hand. "I'm going to stay with Mima and Mulek and begin training the pigeons and I'll let you go as long as you mind me."

"But, Papa, I—"

Josiah placed his finger to her lips. "He's not to know about us."

Rebekah took a deep breath. "Is there no other way?"

"No one is to see you. It's too dangerous. You must obey me on this."

Josiah helped with the hood of her cloak, hiding her beauty behind the ugly cloth like a death mask hides the face of the departed, and immediately Mima knew where Rebekah was going. She was off to see the son of the blacksmith.

From a distance.

The burning ingots of hard coal heated the air inside the smelting oven like the desert sun heats the image of a mirage, blurring Aaron's vision of the smelting mold sitting in the center of the oven. It was like looking through the puddles in a pond, but there was nothing cool or refreshing about the white-hot heat backdrafting out the open door and raising Aaron's hair off his brow. He got hold of the smelting mold with tongs, inched it out of the oven and started toward the forging table, carrying the hot metal like a priest bears an incense burner in a funeral procession. The pungent odor of the hot metal pricked his lungs just like the day . . .

Aaron took a deep breath, the bitter scent filling his soul. Why did he think of Rebekah's funeral now? He'd smelted steel for three months without suffering the memory of that day, but with the low hanging smoke lifting off the metal and swirling about him, the remembrance of that evening came rushing back. He carried the incense burners down Main Street that night, walking ahead of the wooden box with her remains, then down Water Street to the crypt in the cemetery on the hills west of the city, and it was no longer the hot air backdrafting out the open door of the oven that blurred his vision. Aaron tried to keep the smelting mold steady while he dried a tear on the shoulder of his tunic, but the molten ore spilled over the side and Aaron jumped out of the way of the smoldering metal. He ducked to miss the rough-hewn wooden crosspiece that hung in front of the forging table. He really didn't need to flinch, not with the thick leather sandals latched to his feet, the ones Papa purchased from the cobbler back when he couldn't walk on his own power. He swore he'd never wear the unforgiving leather and thick soles. It was Rebekah who insisted he wear them, the same wide-eyed, dark-haired woman who gave him courage to believe the words of Lehi; and if it weren't for her faith he would never have gained enough of his own to be healed. Aaron stepped around the fiery ore on the floor. Rebekah wasn't alive to share her faith with him and he didn't have enough of his own to beg the Almighty to heal him twice in the same lifetime.

Aaron set the smelting mold on the forging table and pinched a half measure of black ash between his fingers, sprinkling it over the metal. There was nothing better to chase away the haunting memory of Rebekah's death than throwing himself into his work, and this was going to be a steel like none other he'd smelted before—forgiving enough to endure the pull of an archer's draw without cracking. A full measure of ash was far too much for anything but brittle steel. He'd already discarded two rounds of smelting, neither of them with the right strength and suppleness for a steel bow, and if Aaron didn't get it right, he may never be able to craft his invention in time.

Aaron let the fine grains of ash fall over the metal and work their magic, adding just enough strength for the arms of a bow to keep their shape, but not so much that the metal wouldn't give. He leaned in and blew the ash evenly across the surface, his lips carrying a silent prayer that this invention would remove the pain of the past and bring him to live in the present. But it didn't seem he would ever forget.

Rebekah's memory haunted the deepest recesses of his soul.

Daniel turned his horse off Main Street and down through the blacksmithing district. A long, thin plume of white smoke rose from the chimney. He'd come at smelting time—the only time the oven vented smoke as clean as fresh-fallen snow—and with a little luck Aaron would have found the right mixture of ash for the steel of a bow and Daniel could tell Laban that it wouldn't be long before he'd get his new weapon.

The smithing district was quiet except for the soft falling of sandals on the cobblestones. A woman picked her way along the edge of the lane, skirting around the bricks of fallen walls and placing her small sandaled feet between the large stones pulled up during the war to weaken the foundations. She stepped over the half-burned roof beam that stuck a good cubit into the lane, and climbed over a pile of broken brick before she crossed to the open door of the shop with the hood of her cloak pulled close to her face.

Daniel quickly steered into the alley across the street, hiding himself behind a crumbling column of stone that was once the east wall of a blacksmith shop and watched the stranger peer inside the shop. She was a slight woman, with an old, brown cloak draped over her shoulders. It was a tattered thing, with runs in the cloth and frayed ends about the hem, and no one but the poorest beggars wore such ragged attire. Her hair was uncombed and it wound out from under her hood and hedged about her neck like the tentacles of a weed. No, not a weed. Her hair was far too dry and sunwashed to be anything but dead thistle. Daniel patted the horse's side to quiet her. What would a beggar woman want at the blacksmith shop? There was no food to ask and she couldn't want any brass; you couldn't eat metal. Daniel leaned forward in the saddle, tightened his grip on the reins, and he was about to trot out from the cover of this half-fallen wall and shoo her away when she pulled back from peering inside the shop and he caught a better glimpse of . . .

No, it couldn't be Rebekah. The spirits of the dead didn't sneak about to haunt the ones they knew in life. And even if the dead could raise themselves, they didn't come back to beg alms. Daniel rubbed his eyes with both hands. There was no way the woman standing at the door of the shop was Rebekah.

Was there?

The rough-hewn wood of the doorpost dug into Rebekah's hand, but she wouldn't pull back from spying until she'd taken in a full measure of Aaron. Moses said to write the words of God on a parchment and nail it to the doorpost, but there weren't any parchments hanging from the entry of the blacksmith shop and if she wasn't hiding from Aaron, she would have posted the words of her heart where all who came in and went out could touch them and offer a prayer asking heaven to keep the words of God always on their lips.

Rebekah leaned far enough around the doorpost to see that Aaron's smithing apron was far too large for his thin frame. Didn't he know the extra leather wrapped his long, bony body like a vine wraps an arbor pole? If she could, she'd size it to fit him like the robe of a king. And then there was his hair. Why didn't he have the sense to comb it in place? His sandy brown locks stuck up off his brow like a horse's mane. He always told her that it was from sweating all day at the blacksmith shop and there was nothing he could do about it, but she knew better. The simple sight of him standing by the forging table was as refreshing as a drink of cool water on the parched desert of Qumran and she leaned in farther, careful not to attract his attention. Oh how she loved him! This was a time to dance with the pleasure of seeing him again, a time to laugh a girlish laugh at being so near, but she couldn't, not when her heart mourned their separate lives. Would she ever write on a doorpost that this painful season had passed—that whatever purpose heaven had for her broken heart had been fulfilled?

Rebekah's knees went weak and she pressed her body against the doorpost, the unforgiving wood keeping her from falling inside. She would gladly be his tailor to dress him, and his cook to see that he was well fed, and his handservant to comb his hair and care for his every need. He was the man who had kept her from fear and held back despair, and she belonged next to him. Before she left for Qumran she thought she loved him, but in the desert she had come to cherish his thoughtful manner and his calm, untroubled soul that spilled out of him in a low, soft voice and filled her with peace. Rebekah turned her ear toward him, but there was only the tinkering of his blacksmithing and the quiet, steadiness of his breathing, and not a word from his lips to remind her of the sound of his . . .

Rebekah gasped—it was true, Aaron could walk. He was standing over the forging table, tapping his foot to the rhythm of his whistling. He was healed and Rebekah couldn't get her hand over her mouth to keep the surprise from rushing out of her and turning Aaron's glance toward the door. She pulled behind the doorpost, her back flush against the outside wall. He'd seen her—not her face—but he'd felt her presence; she was certain of it and she picked up the hem of her robe and hurried away from the blacksmith shop, the ends of her tattered, brown cloak swirling behind her. Papa warned her not to let Aaron see her and she ran away from him as quickly as her feet could carry her, but she couldn't take everything with her.

She left her heart on the doorpost.

Aaron turned from the forging table to see a shadow pass across the doorpost. It couldn't be Papa, not unless he'd come back early. Jonathan had left for the mines this morning, and it wasn't Daniel. He never came by the shop since he started living at Captain Laban's residence. The move didn't seem to bother him, though there had never been an officer assigned to do the trivial work of a watchman.

Aaron took another pinch of ash between his fingers and lightly salted it over the metal, waiting for whoever stood outside to come in, but when the breeze was the only thing to blow through the open doors, he walked to the entrance, cleaning his soot-covered hands on his leather apron and straightening the collar on his tunic.

The street outside the shop was empty with only the sound of footsteps trailing away from the shop door. Aaron leaned his shoulder against the doorpost and watched a woman scurry up the hill toward Main Street. She was nearly out of sight, over the crest of the hill, but Aaron caught a glimpse of her. She had a familiar way, her shoulders leaning into her stride, one hand holding her cloak across herself and the other hand working at her side, just like . . .

No, it couldn't be Rebekah. She was gone and he'd never get her back, but he couldn't keep from saying, "Rebekah, is that you?"

Of course it wasn't her and he reached his hand against the doorpost to steady himself. It was his heart playing tricks on him, and he was about to return back inside when, on the sound of his voice, the woman shuddered under her brown cloak and broke into a dead run up the brow of the hill. He'd seen Rebekah run from him once before, that day at the Pool of Siloam when he begged her to leave her father's religion. He couldn't prove it, but somehow he believed the fire that killed her was the work of men who hated her faith. There was a certain familiarity about the woman in the brown cloak, but he was a fool to think it was her. Rebekah was dead and he shouldn't let his heart prod him to follow after a ghost, though he couldn't keep from untying his smithing apron and throwing it back inside the shop. He wasn't going after the stranger; he was simply standing away from the doorpost to get another glimpse of her.

The woman wasn't running from Aaron, she was a beggar and she was running for fear of being caught with food stolen from the market, or coins from a blind man's purse, or bread from a baker, though she did possess the same carriage and stature as Rebekah. He could not let her turn the corner onto Main Street without following. He was still in love with Rebekah's memory and he threw down his smithing robe and sprinted from between the doorposts.

He would not let his season of mourning end.

Rebekah didn't break stride at the sound of Aaron's voice. She pushed past a line of pack mules, dodged between a cart filled with figs, and a woman carrying a water jar on her head and skirted along the opposite side of Main Street before turning up Milo Hill, through the gates of the upper city and into the market.

Aaron would recognize her unless she got rid of this brown cloak, and Rebekah quickly pulled it off and threw it on the ground to be trampled underfoot, and then hurried across the market to stand with shoppers crowding around the cart of a grain merchant. She asked three measures of wheat and another of barley and when he told her he had plenty of wheat but his servants hadn't arrived with the barley, she said she would wait. She didn't have any reason not to stand there with her back to Milo Hill and pray that Aaron didn't . . .

Oh dear, there he was, his face visible above a sea of hoods and hairpieces and dodging the tall baskets bobbing atop the heads of a hundred women. His face was covered with ash, the sweat streaming from his brow and streaking his face. He was hunting for her and when he pushed through the market toward her, she turned back to the grain cart.

Aaron said, "Rebekah, is that you?"

She could hear him step up behind her and she gripped the sideboard. What was she to do?

Aaron said, "Excuse me, could I have a word?"

He'd found her and Rebekah let the veil of her hood fall from in front of her face. She was about to turn around and greet him when Aaron's hand fell on the shoulder of the woman standing next to her. She had light brown hair tied about an ivory bar, much the way Rebekah wore her hair before she left the city. She was the same height as Rebekah, with the same narrow shoulders and thin nose and when she turned around Aaron said, "I'm sorry, I've mistaken you for someone." His voice was soft and low and he tried to step back, but the swelling crowd pushed him against Rebekah. She kept her head turned down toward the grain cart. It was a brief touch, but she could feel the lifelessness in his body and his defeated voice drew tears from her eyes that fell quietly from her chin onto the bed of the grain cart.

Aaron stepped back and said, "I didn't mean to trouble you."

Rebekah leaned over the sacks of wheat. She said, "Sir, how long until your servants arrive with the barley?"

Her inquiry didn't send Aaron away immediately. She could feel him standing behind her, his tall frame casting a long shadow. Aaron said, "Excuse me, I don't mean to bother, but have we ever—"

"She's dead!" Daniel reined through the crowd, his horse pushing aside the shoppers and his arrival turning Aaron around. "You'd better get over her before you go mad."

"Didn't you see her?" Aaron stepped toward the horse.

"She's no more alive than you are dead." Daniel reined in close, the horse's wide body separating Rebekah from Aaron. "You carried the incense burners at her funeral, don't you remember?"

Aaron lowered his head and rubbed his brow. "I haven't slept much since then."

"It's time you turned your mind to other things."

"What else is there?"

Daniel slid down off his horse, his boots planting firm on the cobblestones. "How is your bow making coming along?"

Aaron started past him. "I have to get back to the shop."

"I asked you a question." Daniel grabbed him by the tunic and pulled him in close. "And I want an answer."

"Fine, it's coming along fine." Aaron spoke in a low voice and there was no doubting the confusion that filled his mind like the mixed-up hair that stuck up off his brow.

"How long will it take you to finish it?"

"I . . . well, I'm not sure." Aaron backed away from Daniel before turning around and pressing slowly through the crowd, his sandy head of hair disappearing down Milo Hill. Rebekah would have watched long after he was gone, but she couldn't, not with Daniel reaching down and picking up her cloak off the street. He held it up, the tattered cloth draped like a spider's web in his hands. And when his head came up, he turned his dark-eyed gaze on Rebekah and smiled. She pulled her hood close about her face and stepped behind the canopy of the farmer's cart, her shoulders pressed against the stone wall and her breath caught in her throat. Dear God, no. Don't let this be.

Daniel knew.

CHAPTER 18

"Potsherds!" Jebus knocked on the door, rattling the planks. "Potsherds for the archives!"

It was the last house on the street, the one that belonged to the second lieutenant of regiment seven, and if his eldest daughter, Beulah, didn't have any broken pieces of pottery in her rubbish bin, he was going straight back to the archives and tell Moriah to find another to do this work. Jebus was chief scribe at Fort Lakhish and it was demeaning enough to have Moriah appointed to make copies of Commander Yaush's letters; he didn't need to be out hunting the city for potsherds under orders from an apprentice. He spent the better part of the afternoon canvassing the homes on the southern tier of the city, the only ones Moriah hadn't already bedeviled with his potsherd scavenging. Moriah's insistence on making rough drafts and copies of copies was going to be the death of him, it was! Why, if that boy had his way, he'd write down every recipe the palace cooks conjured, make three copies and pass them about the kitchens before making corrections for a final draft only to throw them in the rubbish. He was frittering away ink they couldn't spare, to say nothing of wasting potsherds.

The door creaked open and Beulah stood in the entry holding her baby brother in one hand while keeping a three-year-old from hiding in the skirts of her robe with the other. She had long, black hair braided down past her ears, and dark eyes to match. Her robe was freshly sprinkled with perfume and the hastily placed white powder on her cheeks had gotten on the collar of her robe. She'd dressed so quickly before answering the door that her feet were bare. Her toes poked out from under the hem of her robe and there was no doubt that Beulah was a perfect name for the girl, *married* was the only name that fit her—*marriage* was what this girl was looking for. She leaned past Jebus to scan the street, searching for Moriah, the eligible young scribe that had caught her fancy and said, "Isn't Moriah coming today?"

"I wish he were, my lady."

Beulah rubbed the baby's head. "What did you say you were after?"

"Potsherds."

"You must work for Moriah."

Work for him! Jebus straightened his collar and pulled the cuffs of his tunic down about his wrists. Did he really look like an apprentice scribe? There was not a more stinging insult than to be thought of in the same breath as Moriah, not since the young scribe had won the good graces of Commander Yaush and taken over his treasury. He lifted a leather satchel in the air between them and shook it. He said, "Potsherds, my lady."

"Where is Moriah today?" Her lips turned down into a soft frown. "My little brothers do so enjoy the man. He has such a warm soul."

Jebus spit on the cobblestones. She was hedging the truth; she had to be. It certainly wasn't her little brothers that enjoyed Moriah's company, not nearly as much as Beulah. Jebus spoke through his teeth and said, "We don't have time for souls."

"Oh my, you scribes are an amusing lot."

Jebus cleared his throat like a juggling master before a performance. "We entertain when we can."

"You know something . . ." Beulah patted Jebus on the arm. "The more I'm around scribes, the more I think it would be a fine profession for my little brother." She shifted the baby onto her other hip and raised his tiny hand. "What do you think, does he have the fingers to write as well as Moriah?"

"Very promising, miss, very much indeed. Now do you have any—"

"Moriah's very talented, you know." Beulah leaned farther out the door, her gaze sweeping the street for any sign of him.

"He has his weaknesses." Jebus began tapping his boot on the cobblestones. What did she see in Moriah? The boy was an apprentice scribe, earning half the money Jebus earned, and she spoke of him as if he were a nobleman.

Beulah said, "Are you sure Moriah isn't coming?"

"Potsherds, my lady. That's all I need."

"I didn't have any the last time Moriah came by, but I sneaked into the kitchen and broke one of my mother's old pots."

"I can wait." Jebus lowered the bag to his side.

"I didn't say I had another pot I could break."

Jebus forced a smile. "It's for Moriah."

"Oh really?" Beulah lowered her baby brother to the floor and sent him crawling off with his brother. "Wait right here." She disappeared into the shadows. A loud crash echoed from inside, and when she came back to the door she dropped four pieces of broken pottery into his satchel. "Imagine that, I found a cracked bowl." She followed him down the steps and into the street, her bare feet pattering over the cobblestones. "Would you make sure to tell Moriah where you got the potsherds?" Beulah brushed the ends of her braids back off her shoulders. "With my little brothers playing about the house, our pots are breaking all the time."

"That's a shame, my girl." Jebus kept his gaze turned to the ground, hiding the frown that puckered his lips like a lemon. What spell had Moriah cast over this woman that she would want him as a suitor? "I wouldn't wish so many broken pots on any house."

"It isn't a curse." Beulah smiled. "There isn't anyone at Lakhish that minds helping Moriah."

There she went again, praising the boy for no reason. Someone was going to have to put Moriah in his place, and if no one else did, then Jebus certainly wasn't going to pass up the next opportunity.

He said, "Good day, my lady."

Moriah worked his pen over the potsherds, copying the eighteen leather parchments onto the rough-draft surface of broken pottery. He began transcribing Commander Yaush's letters early this morning, before the hearth in the center of the treasury warmed the air, and he had to drape a blanket over his shoulders to keep his shivering from turning his letters into illegible drivel. The other scribes had come and gone for the day, but here he sat, still hunched over his writing, the oil in his lamp nearly gone, the cuffs on his white shirt rolled up past his elbows, and his legs stiff from sitting on the stool. He was a tall boy, and though his feet touched the ground, he hadn't moved from this spot but twice, once to get a drink and again to stretch. Moriah rubbed his thighs. If he didn't finish with the rough draft soon, he'd never be able to straighten his legs again.

Moriah blinked the blurriness from his eyes and kept the pen moving. He was nearly finished copying all the lines onto the potsherds and then he could tell exactly how many clay tablets to prepare. And if he kept using a small script and no punctuation, it didn't look like he'd need more than three clay tablets for the final draft.

He reached the end of a sentence, and instead of inserting a blank line, Moriah wrote the Egyptian phrase, *khpr-n*, to quickly separate one thought from another. Even the most poorly trained scribes knew to use the phrase—*and it came to pass*—to save space in their writing. It was a tool Moriah borrowed from Egyptian hieroglyphics and it fit seamlessly between the thoughts in the Lakhish Letters without disturbing the flow in the document—much better than the space-consuming jots and tittles of Hebrew grammar—and no one would ever notice, their eyes passing over it like an ink-dot on a sheet of papyrus.

Why did the Egyptian scribes always find the most efficient ways to write? They were the best schooled; they had a command of language like no others in the world and all because of simple improvements in writing like *it came to pass*. Moriah dipped his pen in the well, let it take on more ink, quickly scribbled down *khpr-n* between two phrases, and went on with his transcribing—the entire potsherd draft a continuous line of writing with nothing but *it came to pass* to divide the thoughts on the page. If he could, he'd leave this treasury to apprentice among the scribes of the Nile, instead of biding his time in the musty confines of this place under the tutelage of Jebus, a man who didn't even hold his pen correctly. But he was committed to work here for not less than three years and he was going to have to make the best of his apprentice-ship, no matter how much the man loathed him.

Moriah tapped the tip of the stylus against the rim of the inkbottle and penned the next line, inserting *khpr-n* between the line about Uriah's guilt as a traitor and the one about Uriah delivering Judah into the hands of the Babylonians. Moriah lifted his pen from the potsherds, rubbed his eyes, then read the line again. Uriah, guilty of treason. How could that be? He checked the original. It was there on the page in Captain Laban's own hand and there was more. Uriah was a saboteur and his preaching of peace with Babylon had weakened the resolve of Laban's military men during the war. Moriah slowly copied the Hebrew words, not because he wanted to make perfect letters, but because he did not want to form them at all.

The broken potsherds were arranged like a great puzzle into the shape of a large tablet, the pen catching on the jagged and broken edges, but the words Moriah penned on them were more puzzling than fitting the pieces together. Why would Captain Laban write such damning things about Uriah? Moriah pushed on through the letter, copying each word as the captain had written them. Laban accused the prophet as an accomplice with the Rekhabites, a liar guilty of reviling against the throne, and a turncoat profiteering on the blood of his own people. Moriah put down the pen and stared at his draft on potsherds. Why would Commander Yaush want a copy of these falsehoods? Uriah was a God-fearing prophet and Yaush a God-blessed military man and there was no reason to preserve these lies on clay tablets.

The door to the treasury pushed open and Jebus walked in, the end of his new leather kilt flapping against his skinny, white legs. He marched over to Moriah's writing table, but pulled up well before he was close enough to read from the potsherds. At least the man had the sense to obey that part of Commander Yaush's orders. Jebus was not to read anything Moriah transcribed—the Lakhish Letters were for his eyes only.

Jebus raised his satchel and said, "Is four enough?"

Moriah checked the letter he was transcribing. It was the last of the letters from Captain Laban, and four potsherds should be enough space for him to finish. Then he could begin preparing clay for the tablets. He said, "That should do."

"I don't see why you have to make so many copies." Jebus glanced at the potsherds on the writing table. "You could have gone straight to making tablets."

"I didn't know how large to form the words."

"It's simple." Jebus clucked his tongue as he spoke. "You write until you're finished, and if you run out of space you fashion another tablet."

"But—"

"I know what you're going to say; you want everything to look perfect." Jebus scratched the side of his face with his fingertip. "Well, we don't have time for perfect in this treasury, and if Commander Yaush hadn't told you exactly how to copy his letters, I'd never let you waste your time or our potsherds on such frivolous writings. We have letters and notices and a hundred other things to put our potsherds to good use and we don't need to make a rough draft only to have you throw them over the east wall to rot in some scribal rubbish pile." He emptied the leather bag into Moriah's hand, the four potsherds clattering in his palm.

Moriah said, "Where did you get these?"

"I found them in the street." Jebus spoke quickly, cutting the words of his speech short. He said, "A pot must have fallen off a potter's cart on the way to market."

Moriah examined the broken clay pieces. These potsherds didn't come from a potter at all. The exterior of each piece was hand painted with three blue lines, and there was no mistaking the mark of the household of the second lieutenant from regiment seven—the father of Beulah. Moriah didn't say anything. It would only upset Jebus and the last thing he wanted to do at this hour was listen to another of his lectures. It was always better to keep quiet than endure his tirades. Moriah went back to his stool, placed the four potsherds at the bottom of tablet number three and pushed his pen quickly over them, copying the final lines of letter number eighteen onto the . . .

Moriah lifted his pen from the potsherd, dripping ink off the tip and splattering the planks of his writing table, but he didn't bother to return his pen to the bottle. He was staring at the last line on the letter. It couldn't be. Captain Laban would never write something like this.

"What is it, boy?" Jebus bit on his thumbnail. "What are you looking at?"

"Nothing, sir." Moriah quickly dabbed up the ink with a cloth, pulled the leather parchment of letter number eighteen close and leaned over it to keep Jebus from reading what no man should read, not unless he wanted to bring the wrath of the captain upon himself. "Nothing at all."

"How long until you're finished?" Jebus inched closer to the writing table.

"Sir!" Moriah held up his pen. "You're not to read from the letters."

Jebus leaned against the writing table, his wide-eyed gaze moving quickly across the potsherds. He took the cloth from Moriah and feigned cleaning the ink that had splattered on the tabletop, but his gaze was still focused on the writing. He said, "Will you be joining the other scribes for evening meal?"

"I have clay tablets to prepare." Moriah covered the last line with both hands.

"You work too hard, boy."

Jebus marched out of the treasury, but before he scaled the steps Moriah said, "Thank Beulah for the potsherds."

The hall outside the treasury fell silent and Jebus's head poked back around the plank. "What was that?"

"I said good evening, sir."

"That's what I thought you said." Jebus disappeared behind the wooden planks, his footsteps quickly tapping up the stairs and out of the archives.

Jebus hadn't seen the worst part of the letters, the curse that Laban had written against the crown, at least Moriah hoped he hadn't. No one could know that Laban had written his desire to *curse the princes of Judah and their father with them.* Jebus wasn't one to keep a secret and if he read any part of the letters and thought it had power to bring him money or enlarge his reputation among the noblemen, he wouldn't hesitate to pass along what was written. Moriah spread soft, gray clay over the table, rolled it flat with a wooden pin to the thickness of a finger. He cut away the edges, forming it with a curved top and straight sides before taking out a stylus and transcribing the writings from the potsherds onto the first of three clay tablets. The Lakhish Letters had secrets that should go to the grave unspoken. Moriah glanced at the door to the treasury where Jebus had gone out. Hopefully he hadn't read anything.

The letters contained a curse with enough power to dig a man's grave.

The owl living in the Joshua tree outside the front gates of Fort Lakhish had caught its fill of mice and finished annoying Setti with its hooting hours ago. The faint glow of morning touched the heavens east of Lakhish, the stars fading into a dark blue canopy of sky. The valley below the fort stood quiet. There was no movement along the road and the approach to the lower gate was clear. Setti leaned over the edge of watchtower number one, cupped his hand to the side of his mouth and cried all was well. His deep, powerful voice pierced the quiet of night like a cock crowing before dawn and the sound of it stirred the watchmen under his command to attention along the catwalks.

Setti crossed to the bastion side of his tower and leaned over to see inside the high-walled corridor that led from the lower to the upper gates. The torches lighting the passage were flickering and three had gone cold. The quartermaster was going to have to soak the wicks longer before he set them out for the night or they were certain to fail inspection.

There were no arrivals during the night—no deliveries of food, no regiments listed in the return log, and none scheduled to depart until the next watch. The evening was ending as peacefully as it had begun, with the gateman at his post leaning over the draw wheel in the same bent-over, head-down, shoulders-forward position he'd taken a few hours back, fighting the sleep that overpowered even the strongest men at the end of the watch.

"Setti, let me up."

It was a whispered voice, like the rustling of leaves in the breeze, and it was coming from inside the bastion just below Setti's watch-tower. He squinted through the dimness to see a tall, thin man standing at the bottom of the steps leading down the inside wall to the cobblestone corridor. He was dressed in a wrinkled, white tunic, his sleeves rolled up past his elbows and the tails untucked from his matching white kilt. A linen sack rested in his arms and when he started up from the bastion floor, the contents rattled about inside.

"Moriah, how did you get inside here?" Setti checked his log and when there was nothing listed for the night watch he stuffed the parchment under his arms and said, "No one's allowed in the bastion until after sunrise."

"Just let me onto the catwalk leading to the east wall, will you?" Moriah reached the top of the steps. His eyes were red, his hair uncombed, and he looked like he hadn't slept for days. He started along the bastion wall toward the watchtowers above the upper gate.

"Hold on there. You can't just go where you please, we have regulations." Setti grabbed his helmet from off the hook on the inside wall of his tower. "What are you doing here?"

"Cleaning up some things from the archives." Moriah held the bag close to his chest, the contents tinkling with each of his quick strides. "Rubbish, that sort of thing."

"Garbage at this hour?" Setti stopped well before the watchtower at the top of the bastion. "You have to have an order to come up here. Who sent you?"

The guard manning watchtower number six stepped out from his post, blocking Moriah's way onto the catwalk. He folded his arms across his chest and said, "Is there something wrong, Captain, sir?"

"Moriah!" Setti rubbed the back of his neck. "Who sent you?"

Moriah stood still, the bag held out in front of him like a priest holds a vessel of sacred olive oil. He said, "I'm on an errand for Commander Yaush."

"My father sent you?" Setti came up alongside Moriah. "Is this about the letters?"

"Are you going to let me pass or not?"

Setti waved the watchman back onto his tower, told him to be at ease, and then he followed Moriah onto the catwalk that arched over the upper gate, down along the top of the north wall to an empty archer's station before turning onto the east wall that wandered along the brow of a steep hill. A breeze blew up the face of the wall and over the catwalk, raising Setti's hair off his brow and whistling past his ears.

Moriah pulled up near a stone parapet and pulled at the cords sealing the bag shut. The contents jingled about like muted cymbals and when the cords came loose and the bag fell open in Moriah's hands, Setti saw the reason for this early-morning march along the catwalk. It was filled with broken clay, the red hue visible under the soft light shimmering in the sky before dawn. Moriah turned the bag over and let the potsherds shower to the ground, falling quietly among the tall, soft grasses that grew up in the no-man's-land between the lower and upper walls of Lakhish—a place where no one would every disturb them. He took a deep breath, folded the bag under his arm, and started back down the catwalk, leaving Setti leaning over the wall, staring over into the vacant land where he'd rid himself of the potsherds.

What was it that caused Moriah to act so oddly?

CHAPTER 19

The prophet Jeremiah lifted the ox yoke to his shoulders, draped his arm over the unyielding limbs of the wood, and marched through Jerusalem's east gate. The yoke was rough-hewn from cedar wood and the deep notches cut into the ends were ready to receive leather riggings, though this harness would not see the back of an ox or feel the tight knots of a farmer's reins—at least not today. It was a heavy thing to carry on his shoulders and he walked with a bent-over stride. This long timber was meant to be strapped about the shoulders of an ox, not carried on the back of a man; but he brought it all the way from Anathoth to remind King Zedekiah and all the Jews at Jerusalem that God intended for them to suffer the yoke of Babylonian rule for seventy years, and he wasn't going to let the weight of it keep him from making that clear. The Jews weren't beasts of burden, but until they saw beyond the size of their treasuries and loved their fellowmen more than they loved their increase, God would not free them from the Babylonian yoke. And if that meant paying a three-quarter tax, then so be it.

Jeremiah limped down Main Street and turned up Milo Hill into the upper-city market. He stayed in the shadows along the stone wall and gates and shop fronts, keeping away from the hurry of so many headed to the government district to hear news of the tax. No, they weren't headed to hear about the tax; they were going to see if the rumors were true—if King Zedekiah was really going to mount a revolt against the Babylonian levy.

The crowd swelled, doubling in size with so many narrow streets and footpaths emptying into the market. A merchant pushed past Jeremiah, elbowing him in the stomach and knocking the air from his lungs. He cursed Jeremiah for carrying the yoke of an ox on his shoulders in the crowded marketplace and he shouldered Jeremiah into a wheat vendor's cart, forcing him to his knees, skinning them red on the rough stones and ripping the cloth of his already-torn robe. He should have slapped the merchant across the backside, looked him in the eyes, and told him what he thought of his intemperance, but he couldn't. He was come to speak the words of the Messiah and he stayed down while the merchant grunted his disgust and damned him for his foolishness before disappearing back into the crowd.

Jeremiah pulled himself up by the sideboard of the wheat cart, righted the yoke over his shoulders, and pressed on through the market—around a group of accountants discussing the tax, past a horde of merchants complaining they could not give up so much of their income to the Babylonians, and in behind a platoon of soldiers guarding the entrance into the government district. There were a good many more guarding the government district than he'd expected, but he had just started past them when the quiet voice of the Spirit begged him not to go further. He leaned against the cool stones in the archway, away from the hurry of the crowd. Why shouldn't he walk past the soldiers? They couldn't put him in prison. Captain Laban had ended his banishment and he was free to come to the city, but the still voice in his soul constrained him to stay put a while longer.

God would prepare the moment for him to speak.

Laban rushed down from the balcony above the main gates of the temple and came in behind the platoon of soldiers guarding the entrance into the government district. He pushed past the lieutenant and studied the gathering crowd. Where was Jeremiah? They couldn't start without the prophet; Zadock wouldn't allow it. Without Jeremiah they would never expose the queen and her association with Rekhabites.

Laban peered down through the archway and onto Market Street. Just as he thought. There was a steady stream of merchants and nobles heading toward the government district, but no sign of Jeremiah in their number—not a single dusty farmer robed in brown cloth with worn, leather sandals. Laban quickly went over each face passing out of the shadows and into the sun-drenched courtyards outside the walls of the temple. There were wealthy men sporting expensive, pleated robes, polished leather latched about their feet, and enough jewelry to play out every gold mine between here and Bethlehem, but there were none among their number resembling Jeremiah with his graying beard and drooping, brown eyes.

"Lieutenant!" Laban pushed past the nobles and came in next to the officer in charge. "Why haven't you sent a report?" That's the least he could have done for Laban's peace of mind. Couldn't he see how important this was? Laban hadn't told the lieutenant exactly why he should watch for Jeremiah, but there was no excuse for his negligence. Laban was the man's superior officer and he was to do the captain's bidding without fail.

"There's nothing to report, sir." The lieutenant stepped forward.

Laban said, "I'll be the judge of that. I want a report."

"We haven't seen him."

Laban slapped his fist to his breastplates. "Is that all you have to say?"

"I suppose I could have sent word that there was no word to be sent."

"Fool!"

"I'm sorry, sir." The lieutenant stepped back from the force of Laban's words. "It won't happen again."

"Not you." Laban spit on the ground. "Curse the prophet Jeremiah."

The lieutenant said, "I could send a man to Anathoth and fetch him here."

Laban turned his gaze past the lieutenant and onto a man standing in the shadows. It was Jeremiah. The captain quickly turned away and faced the sunlit square; he didn't dare stare and risk chasing Jeremiah away. He was standing against the stone bricks on the far side of the archway and he was carrying the yoke of an ox over his shoulders like a slave. No, not like a slave. It was a long timber, and he had his arms draped over it like a criminal strapped to a board before he's hoisted up and martyred for his crimes. It was an odd thing for Jeremiah to carry about the streets, but if the man wanted to act the part of a condemned man, so be it. Let him crucify himself, as long as he took Miriam with him.

Laban returned up the steps and came out on the portico above the east wall of the temple overlooking the crowded street. The royal couple had arrived with a troop of palace guards and a contingent of maidservants to do whatever bidding royals bid their help to do. King Zedekiah stood near the front, his purple robes draped over the railing and his scepter tucked beneath his arm, the diamond-butted end sparkling in the shade of the temple pillars. His hair was cut straight across his brow and when he turned to speak to the queen it danced above his eyes. Miriam stood with her hands folded in front of her white robe sequined with abalone shells that sparkled from shoulder to hem. The queen's long, black hair was braided into a veil, and her straight thin nose and cheeks had taken on the redness of the cool day. She had fair skin and wide, brown eyes worthy of a goddess and Laban was a fool to believe they could keep the king from trusting such beauty. Zedekiah stood beside her, his hand on Miriam's shoulder and his ear turned to hear whatever whispered words fell from her red lips. Laban adjusted his brass helmet forward over his brow, the red plume falling into his line of sight. Why did he ever listen to Zadock? They could never destroy the trust between the royal couple and Laban should stand to the railing and cry to the crowd below that the tax had been reduced to a quarter of a man's income and tell them to forget this nonsense of a tax revolt and return to their homes without further—

"Did you find him?"

Zadock's rasping voice pierced the silence and Laban turned to find the Chief Elder standing with the brim of his turban pulled down over his brow to shield his white skin from the sun. He didn't do well in the afternoon heat, and though there was little warmth on this cool February afternoon, he scowled at the brightness and gripped the pleats of his robe about his stomach like a sick patient.

Laban directed him down the railing, away from the hearing of the royal couple. He said, "Jeremiah's here."

Zadock leaned over the railing, the breeze lifting the Chief Elder's black and white shawls up off his shoulders. "I don't see him."

"He's right below us."

"You had better not be wrong about this." Zadock pulled back from leaning over the railing and tapped his fingers on the capstone, his nails clicking against the brick. "Jeremiah must speak out against—"

"Jeremiah is the least of our worries." Laban drew his shoulders back to attention, the brass breastplates pulling taut against his chest. "It's going to take more than a tax revolt to keep Zedekiah from trusting Miriam."

"Everything is going according to plan."

"Whose plan?" Laban removed his helmet and stuffed the red-plumed headpiece under his arm. "Do you really think a few words from a man like Hannaniah can divide Zedekiah and Miriam?"

"Hannaniah will do more than divide them." Zadock cupped his long-fingered hands together. "His words should be enough to begin the process." He pointed to the back side of the balcony. The holy man Zadock had hired stood in the shadows of the temple pillars, and when the Chief Elder motioned for him he hurried over. He wore the colorful girdle of the high priest over his white, priestly robe. He wasn't the high priest; why, he'd not been promoted beyond the rank of officiating at the altar, but in these days, wearing the right clothing had a powerful effect over men and the high priest was happy to loan his clothing for a price. The girdle had twelve stones tied like an apron across Hannaniah's chest, and a white mitre cap sat atop his hair. He was a young man, but his white beard was more than enough to convince this gathering of his wisdom, though all he need do was convince King Zedekiah that he was a prophet and that God had spoken to him of a tax revolt. Hannaniah had the right lineage. He was the son of the prophet Azur, he began his studies in the temple at age twelve, and he was hired to carry out the duties of a priest at the young age of sixteen, a good four years before most men are considered for that service. He was a tall man and his height commanded an unspoken respect.

Zadock took him by the arm and pulled him close. He said, "Are you ready?"

"Where did all these people come from?" Hannaniah stuffed the ends of his fingers beneath the girdle of precious stones. "You didn't tell me I had to convince so many I was a prophet."

"You're good with people; that's why I hired you."

"One at a time, yes, but not the entire city."

"Tell them what they want to hear and they'll call you a prophet." Zadock nodded his head as he spoke. "You've been doing that all your life."

"This is different." Hannaniah took deep breath. "This could cause another war."

"Let me worry about that." Zadock shook him by the arm. "Just remember that God has spoken to you and you're an instrument to communicate the will of heaven. You're a prophet and you have to make certain that the king believes you're called of God. Do you understand that?"

"I thought it was the people I was to convince." Hannaniah stepped to the railing, his gaze directed out over the crowd that had swelled to over ten thousand, the sound of their voices filling the balcony with the low rumble of their presence. King Street swarmed with men all the way to the steps of the Citadel Building. Men spilled into the alleys boarding the temple gate, and stragglers entering the government district climbed the outer walls to gain a view of the proceedings, only to be chased away by the soldiers guarding the balcony, while others scaled onto the rooftops like little children sneaking into a feast celebration.

Zadock said, "Once you win these people over, Zedekiah will believe you to be a prophet and Jeremiah a soothsayer."

Hannaniah primed his collar about his neck. "Is there a reason you want me esteemed above Jeremiah?"

Zadock said, "That's what I'm paying you for."

The white ends of Hannaniah's beard bristled about his straight lips. "Thus saith the Lord God of Israel."

"That's right, and as soon as you promise these people deliverance from the tax, they'll proclaim you a prophet of God and forget the nonsense Jeremiah has been spouting since before the war."

Zadock turned his gaze across the balcony toward King Zedekiah. He was crossing toward them, his long train spreading over the rough stone and the gold in his crown glowing amid the shadows. He escorted Miriam at his side, her hand atop his. The crowd of maidservants and guards surrounding them parted to let them pass, their slow stride and erect posture as royal as were their pressed and pleated garments.

"Good afternoon, sire." Zadock lowered his head.

"Is this the man you spoke to me about?" Zedekiah inspected Hannaniah's bright, white robes.

Zadock said, "This is the prophet, sire."

Hannaniah bowed quickly and kissed Zedekiah's hand. He said, "By the grace and power of God I've been blessed to see the destiny of our people."

Zedekiah took back his hand. "Let's hope it's a pleasant one."

"Precisely, sire." Zadock spoke with a shrill voice like wind whistling through a bare storehouse. "We're gathered to hear the will of heaven on these matters. Our nation depends on it."

Zedekiah took the Chief Elder by the arm. "Are you certain we're doing the right thing?"

A thin smile lifted at the corners of Zadock's mouth. "The will of heaven be done, sire."

"That's all I wanted to hear." Zedekiah glanced at Miriam, but she didn't respond to her husband's probing gaze, didn't even blink. Her face was half hidden behind the lace and linen of her intricate white veil—the same veil she'd worn the day Laban found shreds of it caught in the gate of the livery stable. Laban rubbed the cloth of his tight-fitting tunic between his fingers. How did the queen mend her veil so quickly that night without leaving a trace of torn cloth? It had to be the same veil she wore today, and with her eyes hidden behind the patterns in the lace they were impossible to read.

Zadock led the king to the railing and they looked over the throngs gathered below. He said, "All of them are here to have their king save them from the Babylonian tax."

"Save them?" Zedekiah shook his head slowly. "You're not serious about a tax revolt. I thought you were going to negotiate with the Babylonians?"

"I wouldn't call it a revolt." Zadock held the railing with one hand and placed the other beneath the pleats of his robe. "I need the weight of the prophets and the king of Judah behind me if I'm going to negotiate with the Babylonians. If they understand we're united in this, they'll revise their levy down to one-quarter of a man's income."

"It's still a revolt, no matter how we use it against them." Zedekiah turned his gaze over the gathering crowd. "We'll not survive another war."

"We can't live like beggars for the rest of our lives. We must have some power to negotiate." Zadock turned to the crowd, his robes pressed against the railing and the brim of his turban pulled back to let the sun cast a golden glow across his white skin. He raised his long-fingered hand in the air and waved to the crowd. He cried, "Hear me now, people of Jerusalem."

The street quieted and the men in the crowd turned toward the balcony.

Zadock said, "The king of Babylon has commanded us to pay him three-fourths of all our increase."

A resounding cry filled the street and echoed up along the building fronts. The crowd began to sway, raising their hands overhead and chanting, "Death to Nebuchadnezzar! Death to his taxes!" Two boys scaled the wall of the Citadel Building, stood on the third-story ledge, and lit afire the ensign flag of Babylon, waving the burning blue cloth on the end of a pole.

Zadock spoke above the rhythm of their chanting. "Your king has pleaded with God to deliver us." He brought Hannaniah to the railing. "And here is the reply from heaven." He took Hannaniah's hand in his and raised them together. "I bring you word of your deliverance!"

The chanting broke into cheers that rang off the temple walls and reverberating about the balcony.

Hannaniah waited for the cries to calm to a low rumble before he said, "Thus saith the Lord of Hosts. Within the space of two years, the God of Israel will break the yoke of Babylon, and all the captives that have been taken out of our land will be returned." He motioned to the temple behind him. "And all the sacred vessels the armies of Nebuchadnezzar took for the spoils of war will the Lord God return to—"

"Amen to your words, for I will not hear anymore of them!"

The lone cry of a man rose up from beneath the balcony, like a wild beast howling at the moon. The crowd parted and in its wake marched the prophet Jeremiah, brandishing the yoke of an ox over his head like a giant sword. "Amen, I say! Enough of this!"

Jeremiah reached the center of the street and turned to face the balcony, his eyes open wide and his hair blown up off his head like the mane of a lion. He said, "Hear now the words that I speak." He lifted the yoke onto his shoulders and carried it about like an ox. "The prophets before me prophesied of the war and of our bondage to Babylon. How is it that Hannaniah now speaks of deliverance and of peace when the ancient prophets declared we would suffer captivity?" The crowd pressed in on Jeremiah, but he drove them back, clearing a circle around him with the ends of his yoke. He raised his gaze to the balcony and said, "If Hannaniah is truly sent of God, then we will wait for two years for this peace and deliverance to come to pass, but we should not anger the Babylonians by refusing to pay their tax."

Hannaniah hurried down the steps from the balcony. He waded through the sea of men surrounding Jeremiah and when he reached the prophet, he stripped the yoke from his shoulders and said, "Thus saith the Lord!" He raised Jeremiah's yoke over his head and brought it down with a resounding crack against the cobblestones, splintering the wood in two. "Even so will I break the yoke of Nebuchadnezzar, king of Babylon."

The crowd erupted, throwing their tax notices into the air and surging forward, pressing against the gates of the temple and chanting their agreement with Hannaniah's declaration—God would deliver them from their oppressors.

Laban retreated from the railing and hid deep in the shadows over beyond the giant pillars where Miriam wouldn't see him watching her. He couldn't let her see him take note of her escape. The queen slowly backed away from the railing, leaving Zadock and her husband to accept the cheers from the crowd. She hurried to the maidservants, borrowed an old, brown shawl to cover her white veil—the tattered ends of it hiding the abalone sequins that shimmered on her shoulders. She was disguising herself, but she could never hide from Laban. He was watching her every step.

Miriam darted down the steps and pushed her way through the throngs. Foolish woman. She was falling into their trap just as Zadock said she would. Laban marched out from behind the pillars and sidled in next to Zedekiah. The king waved his scepter to the revelers in the street below, the diamond-butted end reflecting the sunlight over their faces. Laban pushed the end of the scepter aside and said, "Sire, is that your wife?"

"Miriam's right here, Captain." Zedekiah reached down along the railing for her hand and when he couldn't find it he turned about, searching the balcony for her. He said, "Where has she gone?"

"I believe that's her now." Zadock pointed to the woman picking her way through the crowd toward the prophet Jeremiah. Her white veil hung out from under the ends of the brown shawl, bobbing like driftwood among the sea of dark robes and darker-haired men.

"That's her but . . ." Zedekiah stuffed his scepter beneath his arm. He leaned forward, the breeze lifting his straight hair up off his brow. He squinted into the sunlight. "Where's she going?"

Zadock raised his hand to his brow, shielding the sun from his eyes. "She must have business with the prophet Jeremiah."

"That's foolishness; she doesn't have business with . . ." Zedekiah turned from looking over the railing. "She wouldn't do something like that, not without speaking to me first."

Zadock said, "Jeremiah has ties to the Rekhabites."

Zedekiah lowered his voice. "What are you saying?"

"Only what I hear in the street, sire." Zadock bowed. "The Rekhabites listen to Jeremiah's words and they heed his preaching. He's not one of them, but he is very much part of them."

"Miriam would never . . ." Zedekiah turned back to watch her cross the square. "She has nothing to do with the Rekhabites. I'm certain of it. We have no secrets."

Laban said, "None, sire?"

"That's right. She would have told me if she had anything to do with the Rekhabites."

Zadock set his hand on the railing next to Zedekiah's. "Everyone has their secrets, sire."

"Not Miriam." The pace of Zedekiah's speech quickened and he shook his head. "She doesn't keep anything from me, especially something like this."

"I'm sure its nothing." Zadock straightened his robe over his shoulders. "At least nothing that she wants to share with any of us."

Miriam pushed a merchant aside with one hand and forced two dancing men out of her way with the other. What an awful time to venture into the street with Laban and Zadock and—heaven help him—

her husband watching the street from the balcony, but she couldn't let the prophet Jeremiah leave without speaking with him. She had to know if Hannaniah spoke for God. If he were indeed a prophet, she'd rejoice with the rest of the men in this crowd, but if he were not, she wouldn't let her husband be led astray by foolish preaching. This was a matter that had power to bring another war to their homeland, and she would not let her husband make a poor decision on the advice of Zadock.

A drunken nobleman rushed toward her, fell to his knees, took her by the hand and in a voice strong enough to attract the gaze of everyone within twenty cubits, cried his thanks to her for delivering them from the Babylonians. Must he draw attention to her like that? Strong drink reduced the most educated men to fools. She freed her hand from the nobleman's grasp before he could press his lips against her skin and soil it with the wine that soured his breath, then quickly left the nobleman to grovel on his knees. She turned past an abandoned mule cart and came onto the spot where Jeremiah was picking up his broken yoke. Hannaniah was gone, disappeared into the crowd with no sign of his white beard or priestly robes visible among the masses.

Miriam gathered a piece of broken yoke and handed it to Jeremiah. She said, "Excuse me, sir. Would you hear a question?"

"My lady." Jeremiah fell to his knees, but Miriam quickly said, "No, not here. This isn't a good time for introductions." She took Jeremiah by the hand and raised him to his feet. "Tell me, sir, is it true? Is Hannaniah a prophet of God?"

Jeremiah's gaze moved past her and his eyes took on a brightness she'd not seen before. It was as if he was listening to words she could not hear from someone she couldn't see, and she turned to see who had wrested his attention away from her. It was a clear day, not a cloud in the sky and there was no one but the dancing merchants and noblemen in the street—none of them paying any mind to Jeremiah or trying to speak with him, but there he stood, staring up through the bright rays of afternoon that shined down on him. And when Jeremiah came back to her and she felt the penetrating spirit of his gaze on her, he said, "God has spoken." He turned a full circle, his gaze searching the faces in the crowd. He said, "Where has Hannaniah gone?"

There was no sign of him near the gates to the temple, and there was no one wearing anything as bright as his clothing on the Citadel

Building steps. He was gone, at least that's what it seemed until Miriam spied Hannaniah's white beard and white-robed frame down near the government arch on the other side of the square. She said, "He's there, sir."

"Hannaniah!" Jeremiah held the broken yoke up to the sky, the splinters splitting the sunlight and casting a jagged-edged shadow over the cobblestones. "Hear what I have to say!"

Must he speak that loud? The revelers backed away from Jeremiah's thundering voice and left Miriam to stand next to the prophet alone. She played with the ends of the borrowed brown shawl, holding the cloth close to her face and backing to the edge of the crowd to find cover.

Jeremiah's sudden outburst drew the gaze of her husband from the balcony; at least it appeared he was looking down on Jeremiah and she certainly didn't want him to see her here. Zedekiah leaned forward, his hands gripping the railing. Zadock and Laban stood beside him, the Chief Elder speaking into his ear and the captain standing erect, the beginnings of a smile playing at his lips. It was the same smile she'd seen on his face the day he marched into her bedroom with the torn piece of cloth from her veil; and thanks be to heaven she'd had another identical veil or she never would have been able to discount his suspicions as the foolish imaginings of an overzealous soldier. But suspicions followed the criminal and Miriam was of all women most guilty. She'd kept hidden what she knew of Laban's association with robbers at the coronation, for he would kill the Rekhabites and she was one of them.

Hannaniah ended his conversing with friends and looked up. He called through the crowd and said, "What do you want with me now, old man?"

"You have broken these yokes of wood." Jeremiah raised the splintered timbers into the air. "But the Almighty will make for His people yokes of iron to put around their necks that they may serve Nebuchadnezzar, king of Babylon."

"Don't be a fool. *My* words are the will of God, not *yours.*" Hannaniah raised both hands and shook them to the rhythm of his words. "God will not suffer this people to pay tax to Babylon."

Jeremiah said, "You make this people to trust in a lie."

"I don't have time for your charades." Hannaniah started down the street toward the archway leading out of the government district and into the market.

"Hear me out!" Jeremiah raised his voice and silenced the last of the revelers. He said, "Thus saith the Lord!"

Hannaniah pulled up just inside the stone archway, but he didn't turn around. He stood with his back facing Jeremiah, his hands stuffed beneath the pleats of his white robe, his body silhouetted by the shadows and when he spoke, his words reverberated inside the passageway. He said, "Tell me, what does God say?"

Jeremiah dropped the broken yoke to the ground. "This year you shall die because you have taught rebellion against the Lord."

Miriam leaned up on her toes to see Hannaniah disappear into the shadows of the archway. She was right; he had prophesied falsely and Jeremiah had cursed him with an awful cursing—that he would die for telling lies in the name of God. There was no doubt that Zadock had hired him to do this soothsaying. Why didn't she see the Chief Elder's hand in this before now and save her husband the confusion of counsel from two conflicting prophets? These were different times than when Isaiah walked the streets of Jerusalem, when the kings of Israel sought the prophet's wisdom at every turn. Miriam couldn't simply invite Jeremiah to the palace for tea and explain his doctrines to Zedekiah, but somehow she had to convince her husband that he should trust the man and not listen anymore to Laban or Zadock or their soothsayer Hannaniah.

Jeremiah placed his arm on Miriam's shoulder. He said, "Does that answer your question, my lady?"

It did, but it was cause for so many more. Miriam checked the balcony. Her husband was watching and she quickly stepped back from Jeremiah's grasp. She lowered her head without answering and turned up the street, pushing through the crowd and out of sight of the balcony. She wasn't betraying her husband's trust; she was trying to help him. But could she ever tell him that? And if she did, would he believe her? Zedekiah had always trusted her, and after today she prayed he still would. Then she prayed one more thing—that he would never ask if she were a Rekhabite.

She could never lie to him.

CHAPTER 20

Shemayahu set down the rack of wine bottles on the porch next to him and let the warm morning sun take the chill out of his bones. He didn't bother to invite the caravaners plodding past with their camels to come inside and enjoy one of his ales. Better to let them proceed on their way in a cloud of dust while he rested. He'd spent the morning hauling bottles from the cellar and there was still time for a nap before patrons began filing into his inn for a shot of gooseberry wine. Shemayahu leaned back against the outside wall of the inn, his hands behind his head like a pillow, softening the bricks. It wasn't really Shemayahu's gooseberry wine. His son, Uriah, devised the recipes—none of them stronger than goat's milk—and the patrons confused the sour taste for the bite of intemperate ales, no matter how many times Shemayahu insisted it was no stronger than muddy water from the well on the flats south of town. He stretched his legs out in front of him and yawned. He wasn't going to get up off this step until his feet were rested and ready to stand behind the bar and serve his customers.

A man dressed in a dark robe reined his brown steed through the gate. It was a powerful beast, not like the poor stock owned by vine-yard masters, their animals working the land with sagging haunches and the life in their legs spent. This horse bristled with power, its legs full and fleshed with the strength of a mighty breed, and Shemayahu would have thought him a courier if not for the second horse he led behind him on a rope. Shemayahu stood on the porch, but didn't come down the steps. Couriers didn't ride the hill country with two horses, not when they hardly had room for a mailbag. The second horse was of the same stock as the first, its leather saddle strapped in place and waiting for a rider to mount up, take the reins, and ride faster than the wind. There were not two young steeds as well bred and finely groomed as these among the stock of any of the vineyard keepers, caravaners, or shepherds that frequented the inn.

The stranger's head was covered with a black linen hood so thick that not a ray of light found its way beneath the cloth. The ends of it were pulled forward down over his brow and the sides came in around his cheeks, but he couldn't hide his straight chin and piercing, brown eyes behind the hood. The stranger's thick robe clothed him like a cloud shrouds a rugged mountain peak; they swirled and folded about his powerful shoulders and tied under a narrow sash at his hips before spreading out over his thick legs. His riding boots were polished and laced up to his knees. There was no dust on them from the north country, no sand from the southern deserts, not a single sign to tell where he'd come from except for the military brand that stuck out from beneath his saddle. The word Lakhish was burned into the animal's flank, just behind the haunches, and Shemayahu could only believe that this man was from the cavalry at the fort. The stranger didn't appear to be a solider, though he sat in the saddle like a man who knew the ways of horsemanship.

Shemayahu slowly came down the steps. He said, "We're not open till afternoon."

"I didn't come for a drink." The stranger's deep-throated voice growled from behind the hood of his robe.

Shemayahu righted his aching back and pulled his shoulders straight. "If it's trouble you bring me and my house, sir, I'll have you know that I—"

"I bring you this." The stranger reined in next to Shemayahu and held up a doubled, sealed scroll, the sort of letter sent between nobles and delivered by courier. But Shemayahu wasn't a noble, and by the expensive dress worn by this stranger, he was no courier. He placed the sealed document in Shemayahu's hand, motioning with a gentle movement of his fingers to open it.

Shemayahu unraveled the unsealed portion and began to read over the carefully penned words, notifying him that his son was in prison. But that was impossible. Uriah was in Egypt and there was no reason to believe he'd been captured. He kept his head in the scroll and said, "Where did you get this?"

The stranger leaned over the saddle and picked away at the sealed portion of the scroll, breaking away the wax seal, untying the cords binding the leather, and unfolding the tightly packed edges of the second scroll. It was a perfect copy of the original with Captain Laban's name penned across the bottom. Shemayahu held the scroll to his breast, the soft leather playing against his throat. He lowered his voice to a whisper and said, "Dear God, not this."

"There's only one man who can save your son." The stranger threw the reins of the second horse at Shemayahu's feet and left the expensive animal in the yard.

Shemayahu held up the reins. "Sir, your horse."

The stranger pulled up in the street, but didn't turn back. He was facing the hills beyond Arim where the trade route did not go—only a narrow winding trail to carry travelers through the backcountry where there was nothing but dry mountain valleys and a few water-filled wadis to give life to the olive orchards of vineyard keepers in the lands west of Jerusalem. He said, "There are no lawyers in Jerusalem who will defend your son. Captain Laban and the Chief Elder have seen to that." He raised his deep-throated voice loud enough to shake Shemayahu to the very center of his soul. "If you want to see your son alive again, you'll get on that horse and come with me."

The arms of Aaron's old wood bow rose and fell with the rhythm of Beuntahyu's steady stride. It was lashed to the saddlebags along with a quiver of arrows. A heavy jar of bowstring resins sat atop the weapon, pressing it against Beuntahyu's haunches like a millstone on a grinder's wheel. Well, maybe not a millstone, but there was no doubting Aaron's burden was heavy. He was to fit Nephi for a bow without giving away the reason for the measurements. And if Nephi found out Aaron was smithing him a new bow there'd be no way to keep Sariah from throwing him into the sea with a millstone tied about his neck.

Aaron couldn't finish forging a bow until he knew how tall to
fashion the arms and how wide to cut the grip and the only way to
get a fair measurement was to hold this wooden bow up to Nephi's
frame, have him heft it, string it with a good horsehair and sight it on
a target. And he couldn't simply have Nephi hold the bow while he
took the measurements, not if he were to keep from ending up at the
bottom of the Galilee. Millstones don't float.

Aaron eased on the reins and let Beuntahyu stretch her stride into
a full gallop. She was home here among the vineyards, with a blanket
of deep wintergreen covering the hillsides, the scent of fresh-cut
winter grasses and the smell of . . .

What was that?

Aaron pulled up and Beuntahyu shook her head against the pull
on her bit and whinnied her complaint at the sudden stop. It was the
smell of a fire that brought Aaron around and when Beuntahyu got
wind of it she raised her nose to the scent of burning wood and turned
her ears to find the crackling sound of a brush fire. Aaron didn't have a
sense as fine as Beuntahyu's to pick out the burning, but he didn't need
it. It hung on the air like an unseen fog, the smoldering smell seeping
into the cloth of his tunic like a wine stain that would never wash out.
Aaron leaned forward in the saddle and spurred Beuntahyu down
through the vineyard-laden hills, searching row after row for smoke or
flames or any sign of fire among the wintering trees. They flew over
the creek bed still flowing from winter rains and past the pressing yard.
The smell of burning wood was thickest near the servants' quarters
along the cobblestone road, and when they came round past the last
white-plastered home Aaron found the reason for the smoky smell.

The oldest grove at the plantation—the one with olives as sweet as
figs and oil as pure as heaven—was burned black, the scorched branches
splitting the morning sky. The charred remains of olive trees lined the
lane all the way to the estate homes. Aaron turned Beuntahyu in a circle,
inspecting the remnants of the dead grove. It couldn't have been Uncle
Ishmael. He cursed wild olives with a fiery vigor, but this vineyard was
anything but wild. These were the first trees planted at Beit Zayit and
they never produced anything but the finest fruit. Aaron turned down
through the rows of burned-out stumps and skeleton trees—Beuntahyu
picking her hooves through the black soot that blanketed the ground.

There was not a green-leafed tree left standing, no birds perched on the branches, and not a single sound of life except near the back of the vineyard, over near the storehouse. The roof was burned out, the front wall was slumped forward, and the foundation stones were cracked beyond repair. The door hung on one hinge, the planks charred, but not fallen away, and it slowly inched open ahead of Nephi's stride, his thick arms wrapped around a leaking oil cistern, the clay vessel scorched black and cracked from the heat of a great fire. It had been nearly three months since Aaron had seen his friend. He'd grown taller and his round cheeks had flattened against the bones in his face.

Nephi set the cistern down and stepped to the bow sticking above the saddlebags on Beuntahyu's backside. He said, "Do you fancy yourself an archer?"

Aaron got down from the saddle, the ash lifting in a plume around his sandals. How could Nephi ask such a thing with the vineyard destroyed and fifty broken cisterns stacked outside the storehouse and leaking spoiled oil over the ground? Aaron said, "How did this happen?"

"It's nothing we can't repair." Nephi unlashed the bow from the saddlebags and wrapped his hand around it. Aaron should have taken better note of where the lower arm of the bow reached below Nephi's knee and where the upper arm reached level with his brow, but he didn't bother, not with the horrors of a fire that destroyed everything, including the oil Nephi was to care for.

Aaron said, "Tell me about the fire."

"There isn't anything to tell." Nephi notched an arrow and stretched the bowstring to a full draw with an effortless pull, his back arched and his shoulders forward. He landed the arrow square in the burned-out trunk of an olive tree. "Did you see that, right in the center of the trunk?"

Aaron said, "The entire vineyard is lost."

"We're going to repair everything and forget this ever—"

"Repair it?" Laman stepped from the shadows of the vineyard, pulled the arrow out of the trunk and walked the plumed shaft toward them, his leather boots sinking into the black ash up past his ankles.

Nephi said, "Did you finish checking the trees in the vineyard? Are there any we can save?"

Laman brushed past Nephi without answering his question. He snatched the bow from him, notched the arrow he'd pulled from the tree and pointed it at Aaron. He said, "You and your brother planned this, didn't you?"

"Daniel?" Aaron backed away from the sharp-pointed tip. "What does he have to do with this?"

"Don't play the fool." Laman inched the bowstring back to a full draw. "You and your brother set this vineyard on fire."

Nephi said, "Put that down. You're going to hurt someone."

Laman said, "You want our land; that's why you did it, isn't it?"

Nephi reached for the bow. "Stop this. Now."

"Not until I get the truth." Laman stepped away from Nephi's reach, the arrow still aimed at Aaron. "You and your injured feet and your God-given powers to save my father's life. It's all a lie to madden Captain Laban until he takes away our land."

Aaron was trapped between Beuntahyu's powerful body and the threat of Laman's arrow. He said, "What are you talking about?"

"My father was a fool to think you could bring us anything but pain." Laman's oil-covered forefinger slipped off the bowstring, but he kept the arrow drawn in place with his other fingers. "How did you do it—dip your feet in sheep's blood or did you cut them with a knife to make us think you were injured?" He stepped closer to Aaron, the shaft aimed between his eyes. "That's what it was. You cut your feet just enough to bloody them and fool my poor mother into thinking you needed her powders and lotions. You nearly had me believing your story with your crutches and bleeding and pretending to be the man from my father's dreams." The arrow rose and fell with Laman's heavy breathing. "Captain Laban believes my father unfit to own this land and he'll take it away from us unless you reason with Lehi, tell him that it was all a lie, that your feet never needed healing, that there never was any pillar of fire. My father isn't a prophet. Do you understand that? He's not a prophet." He raised his voice and said, "Say it was a lie!"

Nephi stepped between them, his gaze turned down the arrow's shaft and into Laman's dark eyes. He said, "Why don't you believe father?"

"Back away. He's going to confess his lies to me, you'll see." Laman pushed Nephi aside and took aim at Aaron. "You convinced my father he'd seen a vision, didn't you?"

Aaron said, "I didn't convince him of anything. I didn't have to."

"Don't lie to me." Laman's arms began to shake. "You got him drunk with wine until he couldn't tell the difference between a sunrise and a vision of heaven."

Nephi said, "Why don't you put that down and we can talk about this?"

"I'm finished talking." Laman waved Nephi off with a quick glance and leaned the bow in close to Aaron's head. "I won't let you steal this land from us, not any of it. No one will drive us from Beit Zayit. Do you hear me? No one will."

"Son!" Lehi dropped a cistern at the storehouse door, cracking it open and spilling oil over the entry. His black hair was mussed up off his head and there was no doubting that Sariah hadn't dressed him today. She'd never let him attend to his chores without combing his hair.

Nephi lowered his voice to a whisper. "Let go of the bow before father finds out what you've said."

"It's time he learned what sort of man he trusts with his life." Laman didn't move his sight off Aaron "Tell my father it's all a lie or I'll—"

"What's going on here?" Lehi came alongside Laman, the hem of his robe brushing the ash-covered ground.

"Morning, Father." Laman slowly relaxed his draw-arm.

"What are you doing, son?"

"I finished checking the grove. The trees are burned clear to the lake."

"What about the old tree in the clearing?" Lehi shook his head and mumbled something about the tree growing here long before he and Uncle Ishmael planted the grove. He said, "Is she gone?"

"She was the only one that survived."

"Thank heaven for that." Lehi patted Laman on the arm. "You know better than to point a drawn bow at a man."

Laman said, "I was adjusting the sight."

Aaron said, "I'm fine, really I am."

"That's easy for you to say." Laman threw the bow at Aaron's feet. "It wasn't your vineyard that was burned to the ground."

An unsettled silence fell across the ashen grove and Aaron would have let it distill a while longer, but he couldn't; he had to ask, "Is it true? Did my brother Daniel do this?"

Lehi said, "It's not going to happen again."

Laman said, "This won't be the last time. Not unless you stay away from Uriah's trial." He wiped his ash-covered hand across his brow. "You saw what they did to Mother and they won't stop there."

"No more harm will come to her." Lehi sighed. "I'll not allow it."

Aaron said, "What happened to Sariah?"

Laman said, "What does she matter to you?"

Aaron slapped his hand against the charred stump of a dead tree. "Tell me she's all right."

Lehi said, "It's nothing that won't heal with time."

"Heal?" Laman kicked at the ash, raising a cloud around his boots. "Look at this vineyard and tell me what happened to Mother isn't any worse."

Aaron turned his gaze out through the black remains of trees that stood on the barren ground like dead corpses waiting to be buried. The vineyard was black and without the promise of new life. Aaron said, "Can I see her?"

"Bring Beuntahyu up to the house." Lehi turned in the ashes, his sandals hidden beneath the black stuff. "We'll talk inside." He started down through the line of stumps and burned branches with Nephi and Laman walking beside him. Aaron followed them onto the main road with the smell of ash lingering well past the last stand of soot-laden trees. They turned up the hill past Ishmael's home and Aaron was tying Beuntahyu to the main gates of the estate when a brown steed raced down through the south vineyards and into the courtyard. The rider covered the distance at full gallop, his body leaning over the saddle. He was an older man with graying hair and he didn't slow until he pulled up next to Lehi. Between short breaths he said, "You're the one we came to speak with."

"You and who else, sir?" Laman leaned forward to see past the man's brown steed, but there was no one riding with the stranger.

"The man right behind . . ." The stranger turned in the saddle. He said, "He was right behind me, I'm sure of it. He was wearing a costly riding robe and his saddle was sewn with precious stones like the riggings of a nobleman."

"Send him away, Papa." Laman leaned against the main gate, his arms folded across his chest. "We get beggars through here all the time."

"I'm no beggar."

Lehi said, "Perhaps you lost your companion along the trail."

"That's impossible." The stranger turned his horse in a slow circle, searching the south slopes of Beit Zayit for the other horseman. "He had a good sense for a horse and he knew every back-country trail between here and Arim."

"Arim?" Laman stood away from the gatepost. "You're from Arim?"

"That's right. We rode through the night and my companion was right behind me when we came over the last hill and down through the vineyards; I'm certain of it."

Laman said, "What was his name?"

"He didn't say."

Laman spit on the courtyard stones. "You rode all the way from Arim with a man you don't know?"

"I had no choice. He told me there was only one man who could help my son."

Laman said, "Who's your son?"

"I was afraid you would come here." Lehi walked around in front of the stranger's horse. He said, "You're Shemayahu, the father of Uriah, aren't you?"

"How did you know that?"

Lehi said, "Your friend gave you this animal, didn't he?"

"Well yes, he did."

"And he didn't ask a shekel in return, did he?"

"Nothing, sir."

"He brought you here through the back country to keep Laban's men from seeing you."

"That was his reasoning."

Lehi said, "What else did your friend tell you?"

"That you knew the law well enough to defend my son."

Lehi took a deep breath. "I thought that might be the reason you came here."

"How do you know all this?"

Nephi stood beside Lehi, his thick hand on his father's shoulder and his black, curly hair waving on the breeze. He looked up at Shemayahu in the saddle, his deep blue-eyed gaze penetrating the distance between them like the rays of the sun. He said, "My father's a visionary man."

"This is foolishness!" Laman worked his lower lip between his teeth. "You came alone."

Shemayahu said, "I told you how it was, sir."

"Not the whole truth, you didn't." Laman marched to Shemayahu's horse. "You stole this animal and now you want us to believe that someone gave it to you. You're nothing but a thief and I should turn you over to the king's army and see you beheaded." He ran his hand down along the animal's coat and when he lifted the saddle blanket and exposed the military brand of the governor of southern Judah burned into its hide. He said, "You rode here on a horse stolen from Fort Lakhish."

"I rode here, sir, to take care of this." The stranger took out a doubled, sealed scroll and let the leather fall open in his hand. It was an order for trial. Uriah stood accused of the crime of treason and Shemayahu was to find a lawyer to speak in his defense or he would have to do it himself. He said, "Your father is the only man who can save my son."

"That's another of your lies." Laman slapped Shemayahu's horse on the backside, startling the animal enough that she reared on her front legs. "Get off our land."

Lehi calmed the horse with a stroke of his hand. "That will be enough out of you for one day."

Laman said, "I'm trying to protect us."

"The man who brought me here . . ." Shemayahu reined his horse about to face Lehi. "He said you were like my son, that you had power to call my son's captors to repentance because you had read from the *Book of Heaven*."

Laman said, "There never was a *Book of Heaven* nor a second rider." He turned around, his dark gaze moving quickly from Lehi to Nephi before stopping on Aaron. He said, "Don't you see? This man's like all the others who want to take our land from us and strip us of everything that's ours."

Shemayahu got down off his horse and bowed his graying head to Lehi. He handed over the trial notice and said, "Will you defend my son?"

Lehi said, "I'm not a lawyer."

"You know the law as well as any."

Laman said, "You can't do this, Father. Not after what happed to Mother."

Before Lehi could say more, a nursemaid burst onto the balcony above them. She stepped through the window of the bedroom chamber that belonged to Lehi and Sariah, carrying a water basin against her hip and a white towel over her shoulder. Her face was drawn out and white, the lines beneath her eyes darkened with the fatigue that comes with caring for the ill. She said, "Come quickly, sir. It's Sariah."

Lehi pulled free of Shemayahu's grasp and started up the steps. "We'll have to discuss this later."

"Please, sir." Shemayahu followed him through the iron-barred gate and up the garden path. He stopped on the porch and said, "Have mercy on my son."

"And you, sir, must find some mercy for my family." Lehi disappeared through the tall cedar doors of the estate.

Nephi, Laman, and Shemayahu slowly found their way inside, leaving Aaron to linger in the courtyard with Beuntahyu. He secured the saddle bags, checked Beuntahyu's shoes, and was lashing a water skin around her muzzle to let her drink when he caught sight of a horseman hiding among the burned olive trees over where the old vineyard gave way to the estate gardens. His face was shrouded behind a large hood that came to a point at the top, but in the dark shadows of the burned trees it was impossible to see any more of his dress or know how fine a horse's riggings he owned. He was leaning around a blackened trunk and when he felt the wonder of Aaron's gaze, he quickly came around on his mount and disappeared out the back of the vineyard raising a thick cloud of ash behind him. Shemayahu wasn't lying.

There *was* a second rider.

The window overlooking the old vineyard was covered with a thick cloth, but not thick enough to keep back the foul air that seeped round the seams and filled the dimness of the reading room with a vision of what lay beyond—a hundred olive trees lost to fire and forty more with their tender branches singed bare of buds for the coming season.

There was not another place where Aaron could find peace away from the wary eye of Laman and wait for word on Sariah except here in the reading room. He stood beside the shelves, the light of a single oil lamp flickering over the sealed jars of accounting documents, drawings of desert trails, recordings of family histories and more writings on the law and words of ancient prophets than he could read in three lifetimes. Down at the far end where the light faded into the shadows, one of the scrolls lay open atop the other parchments, the top dowel pulled back. It was made of new leather and the smell of it filled the room with the scent of a tannery. It was the account of Lehi's dream after he returned from Raphia, the words written in Lehi's hand, his flowing pen strokes running across the soft leather without a single blotch of ink to mar the parchment, as if the unerring hand of angels had penned them. There were neither misplaced words nor misspellings and each phrase began with the proper Egyptian and-it-came-to-pass punctuation.

Aaron let the bottom dowel reach down past his knees and began reading: *I, Lehi, being overcome with the spirit, was carried away in a vision.* Aaron traced his finger over the words as he read. *And I saw the heavens open and God sitting upon his throne, and His son, the Holy One of Israel, the Messiah descending out of the midst of heaven. And I also saw twelve others following him. And the first one gave me a book. And I did read that not many years should pass away before the Babylonians would return and destroy Jerusalem and take many captives into their lands and . . .*

Not another war. Aaron had heard the rumors in the markets— about the tax revolt angering the Babylonians and rekindling the war—but until now those rumors were nothing more than hearsay, not the stuff of prophecy. Aaron rolled the scroll up around the dowel and walked it across the room toward Lehi's reading chair where he could sit and collect his thoughts. The chair stood in the center of the reading room, beneath the domed part of the ceiling, and Aaron slowly lowered himself into the angle of it, his long legs stretched out in front of him, his shoulders pushed against the cushion, and the top of his sandy, brown head lost below the level of the high back. How could this be? A war with Babylon would be the end of their blacksmithing, dashing any hope of building a business among the Jews.

The reading room door creaked open behind Aaron, but he kept still, not saying a word, not making a sound. He hunched down in the chair and waited for the tall, thin frame of Lemuel to pass behind him and step to the shelves. Lemuel started with the top scroll on the stack of parchments, reading the first lines, and then discarding it for the next one. He finished rummaging through the scrolls and began unsealing the jars, pulling the writings from inside the belly of the deep red clay containers, quickly reading through the first words before sealing them back inside. He was to the last jar at the far end of the shelves when Aaron held up the scroll and said, "Is this what you're looking for?"

Lemuel dropped the jar, the lid rolling along the shelf until it came up against a protruding timber in the joints. He spun around, his thin face hardly visible among the shadows. His cap of black hair was filled with lengths of straw, and his tunic was covered with horse-hair from the curry brush. Lemuel was the stablemaster and he brought the remnants of his work and the smell of the barns with him. His long arms were stiff boards at his side. "Where did you get that?"

Aaron sat on the edge of the reading chair. "Have you read this?"

"I haven't time for my father's ramblings. You'd think he'd have the sense to make better use of tanned leather. He writes down everything that comes into his head." Lemuel pointed toward the shelves. "All sorts of odd things, little details about our family and his life—you know, petty things. He's been doing it for as long as I can remember."

"These aren't petty things."

"Give me that." Lemuel snatched the scroll from Aaron and stuffed it under his arm. He worked his lower lip between his teeth. "Ever since the day my father had his, his . . ."

Aaron said, "His vision?"

"I was going to say, ever since our shipment of olive oil returned from Raphia without reaching Egypt, my father spends a good deal of time here reading the words of ancient prophets, maybe too much time. He thinks he can find the answer to his troubles in the words of dead men."

"Why don't you tell me what troubles you're talking about?"

"Visions, dreams, thinking he has power to speak with heaven." Lemuel gripped Lehi's scroll with both hands. "Oh, but then I forgot, you believe in angels."

"Doesn't any of this matter to you?"

"What matters is our land." Lemuel leaned over the chair, his damp breath flowing past Aaron's cheeks. He said, "I don't have to tell you that my brother Laman's right when he says Captain Laban fears my father."

"Captain Laban doesn't fear anyone."

"What do you know about fear? You didn't find your mother lying in her blood in front of the house and you didn't choke on the smoke of a raging fire while the heat seared your skin and you couldn't run for the river because if you stopped digging trenches the fire would spread up the hills and burn every olive tree on the plantation." Lemuel nodded as he spoke. "That's the sort of fear we live with every day and it won't end until my father stops spreading foolish things around like this, this . . ." He took the scroll out from under his arm and shook it at Aaron. "My father has to stay put and keep quiet until Captain Laban forgets about us."

"You're wrong." Nephi stood in the doorway of the reading room, the collar of his tunic pulled up around his thick neck. "You and Laman are both wrong. Father's been called to warn people of another war and the sooner you stop scaring the family, telling them we're going to lose the plantation, the sooner he'll be about his business."

"I didn't set the vineyard on fire." Lemuel turned his narrow-eyed stare on Aaron. "His brother did."

Aaron said, "I'm sorry for whatever Daniel's done to hurt you."

Nephi said, "Daniel didn't hurt us nearly as much as Lemuel's lack of faith."

Lemuel said, "What do you want from me?"

"Tell Father that he's free to go to Jerusalem." Nephi crossed the room, his long, powerful legs pulling his blue kilt taut across his thighs. "Tell father that all will be well if he goes to Jerusalem."

"We'll never be safe if he goes to the city." Lemuel threw the scroll on the ground and it rolled open at Nephi's feet. "They'll kill him. Don't you understand? They'll kill all of us."

Nephi picked the scroll off the floor and held it against his chest, the soft, blue cloth of his tunic folding down over the penned words. "No one's going to kill anyone, not with the tender mercies of God watching over us."

"Tenderness?" Lemuel pushed his chin down into his chest and laughed. "That won't save father from a merciless man like Laban."

He walked to the cloth-covered window that obscured his view of what lay beyond. "We don't need any Babylonian soldiers to destroy this place." He pulled away the curtain, exposing the burned trees that loomed beyond the gardens. "Laban will do it for them."

Nephi said, "Nothing's going to happen to our land."

"You and your misplaced faith. What has it ever gotten us?"

"God will make us mighty to endure this."

"I thought you were a sensible boy." Lemuel ripped the leather scroll from Nephi's grasp and pointed the end of it at him. "God isn't going to fight a war for us."

"He'll make us mighty."

"Mighty for what? Fighting the entire Babylonian army? You really are a fool."

"Somehow, someway, God will find a way to make us mighty." Nephi leaned out the window, his hands planted on the ledge. He turned his gaze to the sky and said, "Mighty—even unto the power of deliverance."

The thin lace canopy hanging between the bedposts wasn't thick enough to shroud Lehi's view of Sariah lying in her bed, the life slowly seeping from her womb. It was death that stained her sleeping robe dark red, and their unborn child was to be the worst casualty of the fire that destroyed the old vineyard. The nursemaid pealed away the bloodied wraps before cleaning Sariah's skin with perfumed waters and wrapping her loins.

Dear God, don't let her lose this child. Lehi pulled the canopy down to keep from seeing anymore and rubbed the lace between his fingers. Sariah had decorated the bed with this cloth, sewing it with delicate white threads; and if the flowered patterns had power to save Sariah the pain of losing this child then he'd travel to the Orient and find the finest lace known to man and fill this bedroom chamber from floor to ceiling with it. What else could he do? He'd made the bed a comfortable place to heal, stuffing the mattress cushion with new wool as soon as the doctor said Sariah was to stay down, no walking, no lifting, nothing that would strain her, but he couldn't help the nurse-maid attend to the bleeding. It was too painful to watch. Sariah wasn't to sit up except to eat, no deep breathing, no crying, and certainly no sudden movements of any kind. Lehi pressed the lace canopy against his cheek. What would he do if she lost this child to a sigh or a sneeze or, heaven forbid, a laugh that he could have prevented?

Lehi slept on a reed mat thrown on the floor beside the bed to keep his tossing and turning from bothering Sariah's rest. He wouldn't sleep in another room and leave her unattended, no matter how uncomfortable the stone beneath him. He would be by her side every moment, and if not him, then the nursemaid, and if not her then Rachel or Leah or Laman or Lemuel or Sam or Nephi. Lehi spread his arms, gripping the bedposts on either side. They'd lost two little ones before their oldest, Rachel, was born, but that was so long ago Lehi had forgotten the pain until now.

A gasp carried round the bedpost and Lehi stepped down along the sideboard to see the reason for the hurried breath. Thank heavens it was the nursemaid and not Sariah. She was replacing the bandage on the back of Sariah's head and the sight of so much dried blood caused the gasp. The blow to Sariah's head was healing slowly, but the bouts of trembling and the vomiting were a horrible strain. Sariah's hair on the back of her head was gone, shaved to the skull, and the nursemaid quickly dressed the gash with a thick linen bandage, rubbed some olive oil into her scalp to keep her skin from chaffing and slowly lowered her back onto the pillow. Her broken nose was tender. The swelling was going down, but the bruising below her eyes was still a deep shade of purple.

The nursemaid said, "She's sleeping now. When your voice carried up from the porch and Sariah heard you speaking with that man, well, she got out of bed mumbling something about you having faith in your-self. I tried to stop her, but she wouldn't listen to me. She could hardly stand on her own, what with all the shaking and her weakness. She used that to steady herself." The nursemaid pointed to the cane leaning against the side of the bed. "She didn't get but two steps before she fell to the ground." The nursemaid's voice caught. She brushed the tears from her cheeks and tried to explain more, but all she could do was mumble between her tears something about the pain Sariah must be suffering.

Lehi escorted the nursemaid out of the bedroom, helping her with the oils and wraps and bandages she carried on a tray. He quietly closed the door behind her and came back to the bed, sponging water over Sariah's feverish brow. How did he ever let this happen to her? He should have been there to protect her, to keep her safe. He put away the sponge and dried her head with a towel. It was his meddling with the captain of the guard that brought this horrible curse upon Sariah, and now Shemayahu had come to beg his help with Uriah. Hadn't he done his part? Was there no one else who could assist Uriah?

Lehi laid his hand on Sariah's head to pronounce a blessing. He closed his eyes, waiting for the inspiration of heaven, but there was no prompting, no promise of healing, no divine words of comfort, nothing but silence. He wanted to tell her that she would be healed, that the life within her womb would be preserved, but he couldn't, not without the consent of heaven. He lowered his head and waited for the revelation to distill upon his mind like the dew from heaven, but he had no clear vision of what blessing God reserved for Sariah.

"It's a test." The calm, steady voice of Sariah filtered up from the pillow and her eyes opened.

A test? Lehi peered between his outstretched arms. What was she mumbling about?

"It's a test of your faith." Sariah raised her hand to the open window. "I tried to go to the balcony to tell you, but the cane gave out." She reached over the side of the bed and took hold of the end of it. "I'm going to need a stronger one to get downstairs for evening meal."

Lehi took back the long piece of blackwood with a brass tip nailed to one end and a hand piece whittled on the other. He said, "It wasn't the cane, dear."

Sariah smiled up at him. "I'm healing very well, you know."

Lehi straightened the sheet along the side of the bed, folded it under the blanket and tucked it in place beneath the mattress. He didn't usually notice the details of housekeeping, but it was better to make the bed than to tell Sariah that the nursemaids believed she was going to lose the child. He said, "Can you eat? There's a lamb cooking and some fresh bread in the kitchen. Rachel and Leah were over this afternoon baking."

"Did they use the newly milled grain from the last bin on the bottom shelf?" Sariah sat up on one elbow. "The bread never turns out as well when they use the other."

"I'm sure they did just fine." Lehi laid her back down in her bed. "They're your daughters."

"Why don't you sit down here?" Sariah touched the edge of the bed with the palm of her hand. "I want you to tell me about the visitor that came today. Did you invite him to stay?"

"I'll ask him."

"You should help Shemayahu."

"There isn't much that escapes your hearing, is there?" Lehi sat next to her, his hand on her stomach and the cuffs of his gray working robe falling over the sashes of her sleeping robe. "I told him I'm not a lawyer."

"You're better than a lawyer."

"I've read the law, studied it since I was a boy, but you know I've never argued it. I've never stood before a court and—"

"You don't need to be a lawyer, my dear. You're a prophet, and at Uriah's trial you'll deliver God's word to every nobleman and commoner in Jerusalem."

"My dear Sariah." Lehi lifted the soft black strands of hair off her brow and peered into her eyes. "You don't really believe that, do you?"

"I believe God chose you because of your faith, not because of your learning or your understanding of the law." Sariah narrowed her gaze, if it were possible to narrow an already focused stare, the light in her eyes concentrated on Lehi. She said, "God's testing the depth of your conviction and if you want Him to heal me you'll . . ." Sariah arched her back and she took a sharp breath, but she didn't cry out.

Lehi stood quickly. He said, "Sariah, what is it?"

"It will pass." Sariah slowly let her body back down onto the mattress. "I'm fine, really I am." She touched her hand lightly over her stomach before adjusting the bandage wrapped around her skull. "My suffering is a test of your faith."

"What am I supposed to do?"

"You've read from the *Book of Heaven* like all the ancient prophets before you."

Lehi shook his head slowly. "It said nothing about losing a child or defending a man before the king."

"You know what you have to do." Sariah swallowed hard and her tongue passed over her dry lips.

"You need some water." Lehi crossed to the pitcher on the table, poured a glass and walked it slowly back to her "This should take care of your thirst."

Sariah pushed the drink from her lips. "If you want this baby to live, you'll go to Jerusalem with Shemayahu."

"I was a lucky man the day God led me to you."

"Does that mean you'll help Shemayahu and his son?"

Lehi stepped back from the bed, the light from the window casting a soft, yellow glow over Sariah. "I have to do what's best for you and our family." He turned and started for the bedroom door.

"Lehi." Sariah spoke in her firm voice, stern enough to turn Lehi around in the doorway. She tucked the blanket up around her neck and said, "You're not the only one in this family permitted some revelation."

Shemayahu stood in the anteroom, waiting for Lehi to come down. It wasn't as comfortable a place to wait as the sitting room with its soft cushioned chairs, but he wouldn't leave this spot below the doors to Sariah's bedroom until he got Lehi's word. He rubbed the talent of gold between his fingers. It was given him by the horseman who brought him here and as soon as Lehi promised to defend his son he would see that Lehi got every shekel of it. The plantation owner was a wealthy man, but a talent was a fine gift for what he was going to do for Uriah.

The door to Sariah's room creaked open and Lehi slowly made his way along the mezzanine hall, his hand groping for the railing, and his oil-stained working robe weighing down his stride. Shemayahu walked in stride below him. He peered up through the hanging lamps and dark wood banisters. He said, "Sir, have you any word about my son?"

"We should eat first." Lehi kept walking. "Evening meal should be ready soon. Why don't you wash up and we can speak in the reading room?"

"I've already washed."

Shemayahu reached the bottom step the moment Lehi arrived at the landing at the top of the stairwell, the two of them facing each other with only the run of stairs spanning the distance between them.

Shemayahu would have knelt and begged Lehi for his help, but he was an old man with slumping shoulders and a crooked back and the best he could do was hold the end of the banister, turn his gaze up and wait.

Lehi glanced back at Sariah's bedroom door. He said, "This is a bad time for our family."

Shemayahu nodded. He understood bad times. He'd spent the better part of six months waiting for his son to return. How many nights had he worn his knees against the floorboards beside his bed, praying for God to bring his son home? Shemayahu held the gold talent in his palm. He said, "This is to thank you for helping my son."

Lehi started down the steps. "There are a good many lawyers in Jerusalem who will defend your son for a hundred times less than that."

Shemayahu let go of the railing and stepped back from the bottom step. He didn't need any other lawyers. He needed Lehi.

Lehi reached the floor, one hand still clinging to the banister. "It shouldn't take you more than a day to find a lawyer sympathetic to your son's plight."

Plight? What was he talking about? This was no plight. This was his son's life. Shemayahu said, "The horseman, the one who led me here, he told me if I wanted to see Uriah free I should come to you."

"He was wrong."

Shemayahu backed away, crossing the anteroom with the gold talent held out in his palm and then he backed one more step into the front door, the full force of his body running up against the timbers and knocking the gold talent from his hand. The coin rolled across the anteroom and fell in the space between them, spinning on its end.

Aaron closed the door to the reading room and left Nephi with his brothers. The murmur of voices filtered down the hall from the anteroom, and he turned down the corridor and into the front entry of the estate to find Lehi at the base of the stairs and Shemayahu with his back pressed against the tall timbers of the main door. They stood facing each other and neither man spoke a word, but Aaron didn't need to hear what they were discussing. Shemayahu pushed his brow down into his eyes and pressed his shoulders against the door. Lehi's head was down and he rubbed his hands together. Neither man moved to collect the talent spinning about on the floor. It was more money than Aaron had ever seen and it flashed its golden light over the floor. Aaron bent down to pick it up when Lehi said, "It belongs to Shemayahu."

Shemayahu said, "I can't take it."

Lehi crossed the room, took the gold talent from Aaron and added another from his purse. He said, "Use this to find a good lawyer."

Shemayahu turned away and faced the closed door. He spoke into the timbers. "I came here begging your help, not your wealth."

Aaron stepped back to let the men finish their discussion. He inched in next to the tall Egyptian urns and let the bright blue porcelain hide his intrusion. They were two men burdened with protecting their families. Zadock and Laban had evil plans against Shemayahu's son, and somehow that evil had found its way to Beit Zayit, brought here by Daniel. Aaron gripped the rim of the vase. Cursed brother of his! Daniel had done more than burn a vineyard and injure Sariah. He came in the night with fear and planted it in Lehi's heart, Aaron could see it in the man's face, the way the outside edges of his eyes turned down and his strong, wind-burned hands trembled.

Shemayahu unlatched the door and stepped onto the porch and Aaron leaned around the urn to see past Lehi. Shemayahu didn't speak another word. He got onto his military-issue horse and bolted onto the road leading out of Beit Zayit, the animal carrying him as fast as its legs had strength.

Lehi stood in the doorway long after the sound of Shemayahu's horse faded into the late afternoon. He kept his head down and he rubbed his hands together as if he were washing them in a large basin, though there was no water or perfumes or soaps to wash away the fear that soiled them.

Lehi said, "I can't endanger my family."

CHAPTER 21

Ruth pushed back the thick canopy of curtains covering the kitchen window and let the cool evening breeze draft the fire. She should be joyous. Elizabeth and Aaron were to be baptized tonight, but she couldn't keep the fear from stalking the peaceful corners of her heart, and she returned to the hearth to lean over the boiling pot of water and draw out a spoonful of cheer. There was nothing that had the power to restore her soul on a cool evening than a sip of hot tea steeped with mint. Oh, that her worries could evaporate like the cloud of steam rising from the pot. She took the tea from the hearth and fished out the bundle of leaves before stirring in a spoonful of honey and sneaking another taste. Perfect. The mint had done its blessed work and they'd have a fine tea to chase away the chill of wet clothes after the baptism. And hopefully that was the only suffering Aaron and Elizabeth would have to endure for their new faith. Ruth poured the steaming brew into a clay jar and wrapped it in three layers of cloth like a babe in winter. It was a good mile walk to the secret washing pool on the farmer's flats south of Jerusalem, and this hot tea was going to stay hot long enough to warm them after coming out of the cold baptismal waters. Ruth placed the jar in the wicker basket along with blankets, two large drying towels, a jar of oil to rub their skin before going down into the water, a bottle of rose-petal perfume to freshen them afterward, and, of course, the baptismal robes with white pleats to place over Aaron's shoulders and an embroidered collar to accent Elizabeth's delicate features.

Ruth crossed to the foot of the stairs and called to Joshua and Sarah, asking them if they had changed into the black cloaks she'd laid out for them. She waited by the steps until she heard their muffled replies— Joshua's robe was tight about the neck but Sarah was going to help him dress. Ruth told them to hurry. They were to stay the night with the carpenter's wife and she would be along to collect them any moment. There was not another woman in the lower city they feared more than she. Not less than once a day she passed by their gate on her way to her home across the street. She had crooked brown teeth, a mole on the end of her nose, and the sight of her sent Joshua and Sarah running for home, but she was a kindly woman Ruth trusted with her children.

Ruth returned to the hearth to add a log to the fire when a high-pitched rasping broke the silence and Ruth spun around. Somehow Joshua had sneaked down the stairs and stood behind her. He pulled on his collar with both hands, his voice a faint wheezing. He said, "Is my face blue enough?"

"Joshua!" Ruth hurried to his side. Of course the boy's face had gone blue; what did he expect with the cloak tied about his neck that tight? She pulled loose the knots and said, "What are you thinking, son? You could choke to death."

"Sarah did it." Joshua coughed. "She said the carpenter's wife was afraid of children with blue faces and if I didn't turn blue she'd eat me for dinner."

Sarah slowly came down the steps. Her red hair was tied behind her ears and her freckles shimmered in the lamplight. "I didn't say she'd eat him."

Ruth set her hands on her hips. "Exactly what did you say?"

"I never used the word dinner."

Joshua rubbed his neck. "She said I wasn't all the way blue and she tied three more knots until I couldn't—"

"Did not."

"Did so."

"That's enough." Ruth took Joshua by one shoulder and Sarah by the other. "You're going to have to get along this evening. You have no other choice."

"I always get along." Sarah reached over and patted Joshua on the head.

Joshua said, "She's touching me."

"That's enough." Ruth sent them back to their room to finish dressing, with the same lecture she'd given them that morning—they weren't to speak to the carpenter's wife about Ruth's journey out of the city—and they disappeared beyond the level of the landing, their heads nodding to the rhythm of Ruth's warnings. Why didn't her children fear the things that could hurt them most? Sarah screamed at the sight of a frog, turned red near a garden snake, and cried at the first sign of a split in her robe. Joshua walked on the opposite side of the street from mules, held his hands over his eyes when he stood on a cliff, and cried whenever Sarah came near him with a stick. But they were ignorant of danger, without the slightest fear of the evil that had power to tear this family apart. Ruth would have taken Sarah and Joshua with her to the washing pool, but the Spirit of heaven filled her heart with the warning of danger and begged her to leave them with the carpenter's wife, and she obeyed.

The hot steam filtered from the lip of the tea bottle and Ruth stood next to the basket with cork in hand waiting for it to lessen. There was no reason to let her foolish, misplaced, motherly fears keep them from going to the secret washing pool, but she wasn't about to leave her youngest here unattended—not if the Spirit of God told her otherwise. Ruth placed the cork in the mouth of the tea bottle and that was the end of it. She'd not let worry get in the way of an evening as important as this. God would watch after the blessed ritual of Aaron and Elizabeth's baptism and keep all of them safe.

Wouldn't He?

Prince Mulek pushed Benjamin's chair closer to his plate, pinning his little brother between the backrest and the edge of the table. Benjamin could reach the plate without Mulek moving him closer, but Mother was waving the end of her long finger at him and he knew exactly what that meant; he was to keep Benjamin from squirming or she'd have him take the boy back to his room and there wasn't time for that, not if he was to play sick sometime after the main course was served, but not so soon after that he couldn't blame it on something he ate. Mother gave him strict instructions before dinner—he was to cover their departure with a sick stomach and keep father from suspecting anything.

The dining table was the largest one in the palace with as many polished hard wood timbers stretching over the frame as there were in the main doors, and if it were tipped on end it would reach up into the vaulted ceiling well above the hanging lamps. The table stretched from the hearth on one end, the flames dancing their yellow light onto Mother, all the way to the other side of the room to the stone head of a lion hanging from the opposite wall, just above Father.

Mulek set his elbows on the edge and cupped his cheeks in his hands, waiting for the maidservant to deliver his plate, and hopefully the cooks hadn't put lentils in the soup this time. They knew how much Mulek hated the long narrow pods with flat little seeds inside, but they never were able to hide the taste by cooking them in lamb or boiling them with fish, and they always filled his plate to overflowing with the awful legume. They said he was going to end up thin as a rail just like his father, but that didn't scare him into eating lentils. What did the cooks know about being thin? Every one of them was as wide as this dining table was long.

Mulek leaned around the tall brass goblets and peered past the pot of herbs, over toward the head of the table where Zedekiah sat, playing his fingers over the soup spoon. Papa hadn't said a word since taking his seat. He was never quiet at evening meal, but this evening he was nothing but silent. He leaned back in his chair and stared at Miriam, not saying a word, not changing the tight-lipped look on his face, and not once running his hand through his brown hair like he usually did when he had something to say to Mother. Tonight he didn't speak a word about the work of being a king, didn't pat Benjamin on the head, or toss a piece of honeycomb to Dan who had a sweet tooth that was sure to rot before he reached his eighth birthday. Father didn't even glance at Mulek, say his name or ask about his writing lessons with the scribe from the temple. Mulek finished the day with perfect penmanship on clay tablets, and the scribe said he could begin with ink and parchment tomorrow, but Father wasn't the least bit interested. All he did was fold his arms over his chest, tap his foot against the stone floor in a slow, constant rhythm and stare down the length of the long table at Miriam, a certain hesitation filling the empty space between them.

Mother didn't return Father's stare and she breathed a sigh when the first of five cooks lumbered through the side doors leading from the kitchens with their meal—roasted quail with bread stuffing, figs, a good helping of nuts and, without fail, a large bowl of lentil soup disguised beneath diced onions and mushrooms. He couldn't see the lentils on the surface, but they were there. They had to be. It was the largest cook who served Mulek his food and she smiled a wicked smile when she set the steaming bowl in front of him, her lips rising to expose a gap between her front teeth. It was her—the evil cook he'd seen in his dreams. No, not his dreams, this was the cook of his nightmares, the one he'd seen in the evening shadows while he slept, sneaking lentils into all his meals. The cook patted Mulek on the head, wished him to enjoy what she'd prepared, and then withdrew back into the kitchens like a fox to its hole to prepare dessert, but he wasn't about to touch the soup, no matter that he stirred it about with a spoon and couldn't find any lentils floating in the milky broth. She'd ground them into the soup. That's how she tried to poison him, hiding the lentils in the thick soup like mortar between bricks, and all it would take is one bite for him to prove it. He pushed the bowl away and it would stay there until he finished his meal. There was no better way to make himself sick than lentil soup, and Father wouldn't suspect anything if Mother hurried him out of the dining room for some air and a visit to the doctor after eating the soup from the evil cook.

Mulek drew the plate of quail close, put the knife to the bird and was about to cut away a slice when Miriam leaned over her food and said, "You'd better eat your soap, dear. The cooks will have dessert ready soon."

Eat his soup? Did she have to remind him he was to get sick so soon? Mulek had spent the afternoon running about the gardens, climbing the trellis to the roof above the west wing, and he needed something to fill his belly before he made himself sick. There was nothing he liked better than roasted quail served with bread and he would have reminded Mother of that if not for the look on her face. Her brow was furrowed, her eyes open wide as an owl, and there was a slight trembling playing at her lips. She wasn't worried about Mulek eating his fill, not really, not by the way she was stealing glances at Father. She was telling him to get along with getting sick.

Zedekiah ran the tip of his knife over the quail, but didn't cut into it. He was playing with his food, the long cuffs of his blue evening robe hiding the blade down to the point. He said, "Aren't you hungry tonight, son?"

Of course he was. Couldn't Father tell by how quickly he cut into the quail? He stuffed the first slice into his mouth and tried to answer while he was chewing on the warm, brown meat, his muffled words lost in the large room.

Miriam said, "It isn't polite to speak with your mouth full."

Mulek swallowed hard, but before he could offer a respectful, yes, Mother, Zedekiah said, "Leave the boy alone."

Miriam said, "I was only trying to—"

"I know what you're trying to do and I don't like it."

Mulek didn't cut another slice, not if it was going to cause his parents so many harsh words. He'd never known them to argue, especially over his table manners, and he immediately put down his knife.

Miriam said, "It isn't like you to speak like that in front of the children."

"It isn't like you to hide things from me." Zedekiah pushed his plate aside, the quail sliding onto the table. "What were you thinking, talking to the prophet Jeremiah in public? He has ties to the Rekhabites."

"Is that such a bad thing?"

"They're traitors to the kingdom, all of them."

Miriam said, "You've been listening far too much to the Chief Elder's babblings."

"Are you defending the Rekhabites?"

Mulek leaned against the backrest, his glance flitting between Father sitting stiff and erect in his chair and Mother with her shoulders forward, her head half down, and hovering over her food. A flash of cold sweat streaked across his brow, but not because they were upset with him. It was the prophets that caused this quarrel and a shot of fear tore open a hole in his stomach wide enough that he would have fallen in if not for the armrests. He grabbed hold of them, keeping himself from reeling to the rise and fall of his frightened stomach and praying that nothing came of Father's heated inquiry. Zedekiah wasn't supposed to know about their dealings with the prophets and even less about their association with the Rekhabites. Mother said it was too dangerous for him to know.

Miriam said, "Speaking to the man is nothing out of the ordinary." She played with the edge of her plate. "He's a prophet."

"If he is, he's a false one."

"How can you say that?" Miriam dropped her knife and it clanged until she smothered it with her hand. "If anyone is guilty, it's that man Hannaniah."

"I didn't accuse either of them of false prophecy, nor did Zadock." Zedekiah pulled his cuffs back off his wrists.

Miriam said, "The Chief Elder can't be trusted."

"What do you mean, not trusted?" Zedekiah stood, the train of his robe brushing the backrest and his voice echoing about the dining room. "The man is only trying to help us."

Miriam daubed her lips with the end of a napkin. "I'm sure he paid Hannaniah more than enough for his trouble."

"Are you accusing Zadock of soothsaying?"

Miriam turned her gaze into her food. "Have you tried the quail?"

"I'm not hungry tonight."

Not hungry? Father was a thin man, but he didn't get that way by starving himself. Mulek had never known him not to have an appetite as large as two kings, and he never could tell where it all went. Father's legs were thin, his stomach straight as a board, and he could only believe that he hid what he didn't like behind the tapestries hanging on the dining room walls, something Mulek only did with lentils, and thank heaven they were low-hanging tapestries or the maidservants would have found him out long ago.

Miriam said, "It wouldn't be the first time Zadock paid men to speak for God."

"Enough of this foolishness!" Zedekiah came down along the table, brushing past Mulek's chair and sidling in next to Miriam. He raised his voice louder than Mulek had ever heard him speak and he leaned his face in next to Miriam like a mother scolding a child. He said, "You had better have good evidence of this before you go about accusing Zadock of hiring a soothsayer."

Mulek pushed his plate of quail over next to the bowl of lentil soup. He didn't need any of it to make himself sick. His parents' harsh words were more than enough to tighten his stomach and make it growl, not with the rumblings of hunger, but with fear. Mulek bent over and groaned. "Mother, I'm ill."

Zedekiah said, "See there, you've made the boy sick with your behavior."

Mulek pressed his hand against his stomach. The pain was real and it twisted his insides until he couldn't breathe. He said, "Mother, I think there's something wrong with me."

Miriam hurried to his side. She said, "Mulek, is it your food, dear?" She glanced at Zedekiah. "I think it's something he ate; you know how he hates lentil soup." She pushed the bowl out of Mulek's reach and pressed the back of her hand against his brow. "That's exactly what it is and he's gone white in the face because of the soup."

Zedekiah said, "He'll be fine. He's a strong boy. Lentil soup never killed a soul."

Miriam took Mulek by the hand and helped him down from his chair. "I'm taking him outside for some air."

Zedekiah didn't offer to help. He stood between Dan and Benjamin, his hands firmly planted on the backrest of both chairs. He said, "Let the maidservants take care of him. We haven't finished."

"The boy needs his mother right now." Miriam's body stiffened and she tightened her grip around Mulek's cold hand. She said, "I think it best we discuss this later, once you've had a chance to calm down."

"I may never calm down about this."

Father was right. He never would, not if he found out that Mulek and Mother were Rekhabites. It was something they kept from him, not because they didn't trust him, but because Mother said it would keep Father safe if he didn't know. It was a secret Mulek was sworn to keep, but holding it inside, away from the ears of his father, made his stomach churn and he leaned against Miriam's side, his head nestled against the skirts of her robe, his body gone limp against her side.

Miriam hurried Mulek across the dining room, but before they turned into the hall leading to the main doors of the palace, he glanced back at his father. Zedekiah leaned over Mulek's soup. He stirred a spoon through the bowl.

He said, "This isn't lentil soup."

The red-hot rod slipped from the tongs and crashed to the ground. Aaron was a fool not to keep a firm grip and he clamped down hard, quickly raising it from the stone floor to keep Papa from coming over to see why all the clanging. It was time for Aaron to be on his way to the washing pool south of the city, but he couldn't just pick up and leave with so much work unfinished, not without good reason. And joining the Rekhabites was not a topic he cared to discuss with Jonathan.

There were no deep red streaks running along the length of the rod, not a single white band about the belly and Aaron quickly set the tip against the round surface of the granite bending stone, hammering with measured strokes and filling the shop with the ring of his careful work, the noise keeping Papa from reminiscing over Daniel's forging skills. Aaron stepped closer to the table. He didn't need Daniel or his strong arm to help with this invention. He was going to finish it on his own, and he kept the hammer dancing over the metal, slowly bending the first of four arcs into the narrow rod just like the bends he'd seen on Assyrian bows, but with one difference—this bow was not formed in the wood-bending, brine-water vats of boat makers; it was smelted in the heat of Papa's oven and forged by the power of Aaron's hammer and if he could bend it without folding the metal in on itself, he'd have a weapon more powerful than the finest ever made—he'd have the first four-curved bow. Well, maybe not the first, but there was none other made of steel, and as long as Papa allowed him to pursue his creation, he'd call it the only one on earth.

Sweat dripped from the end of Aaron's nose, but he didn't wipe it dry. The metal was losing its malleable red color and he hurried his hammer over the rod, bending the beginnings of the small curve at the top of the bow to hold against the pull of a horsehair bowstring. He flipped the rod over and started two large, half-moon counter-curves along the belly, angling the bend to just the right pitch to power an arrow a hundred cubits farther than the strongest bow. The metal for the handgrip didn't need his forging and he skipped over it, turning the rod again and quickly tamping on the small arc near the bottom before the heat was gone from the metal. Then he lifted the bow to the yellow lamplight and sighted down the length of it. The small arcs near the ends were hardly visible, but the two large bends in the center stood a good two fingers off the line—not a bad bend for the first pass, not bad at all. The metal bow was taking shape without any of the cracks that ruined thin metal rods like this one, and the tug of a smile pulled at his lips. He didn't need any help from Daniel. The steel he'd smelted was as pure and supple as the skin on a newborn babe, the forges were angling without any cracks, and he stuck the bow back into the fire.

The sound of Jonathan rummaging through the pile of unfinished blacksmithing work due for pickup in the morning didn't have power to turn Aaron away from staring into the burning coals of the open hearth. Tinkering was Papa's way of telling him to put away his invention and help finish what couldn't be left until tomorrow. They had to fit wooden handles on the stub-ends of the brick mason's trowels, temper the brass ends of the baker's oven paddles, and sharpen the stonecutter's dulled chisels before first light, but Aaron ignored Papa's poking about and stirred the rod through the coals, raising a cloud of ash to shroud the distance between them. There was enough work stacked on the shelf to keep Papa busy for a good two hours, and Aaron couldn't lend a hand if he hoped to keep Papa here while he sneaked to the washing pool.

Aaron lifted the heated bow from the hearth, but before he passed it over the bending stone a second time, he held the metal rod in the air. Smoke streamed off the charred end and the red glow warmed his face. Tonight he was going down into the waters of the washing pool to make firm his disposition to live right. No, not disposition; this was more than a promise to keep a calm temperament and possess an upright character. Aaron was making a covenant to live right in return for the promise of a life guided by the steady promptings of the Spirit of heaven.

Aaron stretched the bow out in front of him, the smoke swirling off the end of the metal. The hot white haze encircled before trailing up into the ceiling and dying among the wooden rafters. No, his baptism wasn't a welcome into a fold. He was entering by a gate that opened onto a long road of honorable living and there was only One who could unlatch it and start him on the road to a new life. Aaron was to take the name of Yeshua upon him, to always remember Him, to stand as a witness of Him at all times and in all places, and he prayed the gift of the Holy Spirit would sear the testimony of the Anointed One deep enough into his soul that he could never deny the path he'd chosen, no matter how difficult that may—

"You've lost the heat, son." Jonathan marched to the forging table, his sudden arrival chasing away the last of the smoke. "What are you doing, fanning the metal in the air like that? You know not to cool your forging."

Aaron said, "I was inspecting the angles."

"Not while it's hot." Jonathan rubbed the back of his neck. "You raise the metal to the air once you've finished a pass with the hammer, not when it's just out of the fire. Why don't you put that bow away and get some—"

"I don't need Daniel's help." Aaron doused the bow in the water cistern, the steam rushing past him in a sputtering blast. "I can do this myself."

"I was going to tell you to get some rest." Jonathan pressed his lower lip between his teeth. "You've been working too hard on that bow of yours." He leaned over the forging table, his palms flush with the wood planks. "I want you to go home."

"You want me to do what?" Aaron came back around the forging table and stood face to face with Jonathan.

"You heard me." Jonathan's gaze flitted about the shop like a speck of ash thrown off by the hearth. "I have this feeling you should go home."

Feeling? Papa never spoke about his feelings. He was not a man given to things of the heart, or at least he never spoke of such things. Papa couldn't mean to send Aaron off with so much unfinished work stacked on the shelves, not unless he was following the same peaceful voice Aaron heard. It penetrated deep into his heart, urging him to share the details of his baptism and not worry about what Papa might say. The spirit of God had softened Jonathan enough that he was ready to be still and know that God was God. Aaron folded his arms and sat on the footstool that stood next to Jonathan. He took a deep breath and began to tell him that . . .

What was he thinking? He couldn't say anything about his baptism. Papa wouldn't listen. He had no sympathy for Rekhabites, and if Aaron mentioned the name Yeshua the Anointed One, he'd raise Papa's anger. That name wasn't to be uttered in their home. If he couldn't speak it he certainly couldn't tell Papa what name he was taking upon himself. There was no power that could soften Papa's stubborn heart; not even Aaron's love could alter his will. He offered his love to Papa the night he joined Lehi's caravan—and for what? It didn't soften Jonathan's heart then and the gentle promptings of the Spirit weren't going to soften his heart now. He'd not risk telling Papa anything that could provoke his anger and he backed toward the door, untying his smithing apron with each step.

Jonathan followed him to the door. "Son, maybe I should . . ."

"Should what?"

"Maybe I should come with you."

Come with him? He couldn't let Jonathan do that. He said, "I'll have your dinner sent from home." Aaron reached for the latch. Why did he make such a foolish offer? There would be no one at home to bring him his dinner. Aaron handed Jonathan his smithing apron, turned the latch, and went out into the night before Papa could say another word.

The evening air rushed through the linen of Aaron's tunic, but it wasn't cool enough to rid him of the burning deep in his soul, begging him to go back inside and tell Jonathan about his baptism or risk losing more than the promised blessings of the Spirit for a season—he could lose his life.

The sound of the stonecutter's chisels against the grinding stone cut through the stillness of the evening. Papa was back at work, all was well, and Aaron hurried up the hill away from the sound of it. He was free to make his way through the shadows that lurked about the broken-down shops of the smithing district. Tonight was appointed for Aaron's baptism, and he wouldn't let Papa change that. He lengthened his stride, slapping the bottoms of his sandals against the cobblestones, but the scuffling didn't drown the still voice telling him there was evil hidden in the darkness of Jerusalem's streets. Evil with power to . . .

Stop it! He wasn't letting foolish fears keep him from the waters of the washing pool. He lowered his head and pulled the collar of his tunic tight around his neck. There was nothing out here in the streets that could kill him. He was to be a witness of the Anointed One, not a martyr.

The faint sound of Papa's tamping on the stonecutter's trowels reached his hearing and he stopped beside the toppled wall of a burned-out smithy and leaned against the splintered wood of a broken gate, his gaze turned down the hill toward the shop. Lamplight streamed out the front doors and cast a golden glow over the street. It was the only bright spot in the district and it begged him to go back and speak with Jonathan about his baptism. But it didn't make sense to tell Papa. Aaron had a plan and he was going to carry it out.

Aaron went home.

The willow tree hung over the back wall of the captain's estate like a tired beggar, pleading with Elizabeth to give up her wait in the cold night air and go on with her baptism without Zoram. She paced beneath the haunting sound of the bare branches rustling against the capstones along the top of the wall, rubbed the warmth back into her arms, and prayed that Zoram's tardiness was not a bad omen—she couldn't go to the washing pool without him.

Zoram was to meet her here, but the only companions she'd attracted were a flock of sparrows come to this tree to celebrate spring on a night cold enough to silence their singing and drive away any cheer she hoped to gain from this baptism. Elizabeth reached the far end of the wall, turned and paced back down along the length of it, pulling the ends of her black lace shawl close. Everything she wore was black—the ribbon in her hair, her robe, the sash tied high on her hips, even the patterns sewn into lace. No one would see her on the flight to the washing pools, but there would be no flight without Zoram. What was keeping him? It couldn't be the monthly accounts. He told her he'd finished those records the first of the week. The taxes were figured, the servants were paid on time, and Laban should thank him and send him from the treasury with an extra shekel for his timely labors, not keep him well after a proper hour doing whatever work captains bid their scribes to do.

The back gate to the estate stood deserted, without the usual pair of watchmen standing guard, and Elizabeth stopped long enough to peer between the slats. No one. Not a solitary soul walked the garden paths winding in and out of a maze of buildings and walls. He wasn't coming and she was going to have to do this baptism without the comfort of the man who had lighted her soul with faith and brightened her mind with an understanding of the Anointed One.

Elizabeth turned from the gate, but before she started toward home she spied a man keeping in the shadows of the buildings across the street. He hesitated beneath the canopy of the perfumery. He peered through the darkness and when Elizabeth asked, "Who goes there?" He started toward her. He was dressed in white robes with a short, white vest wrapped over his tunic—the tassels whipping about his elbows with each hurried stride. The breeze caught under his white turban and immediately she recognized Zoram's quick hand holding it fast to keep it atop his head.

Zoram was dressed wrong. They were to wear their darkest clothing, nothing that would hold the light of the stars like Zoram's bright clothing. There had to be a reason he was dressed like this and it no doubt had something to do with his unsettled manner, his gaze darting about the street, and his long strides carrying him with a hurry she'd not seen in him before. He didn't offer a word of greeting and when he reached her side he took her by the hand and started up the hill toward the government district, passing by the back gate to Laban's estate as if he were a stranger there.

Elizabeth said, "Mother and Aaron are expecting us."

"They'll have to wait."

Wait? It wasn't like Zoram to keep mother waiting—he was a man of the finest etiquette—but since he was also filled with the spirit of mischief she determined it best to play along with his teasing. She laughed softly and said, "We really should head toward home. They'll be waiting on us and I do hate to keep them—"

"It isn't safe for us there."

Not safe at home? Elizabeth pulled free of his grasp. She stood in the middle of the street, the breeze lifting the hem of her robe about her ankles. She said, "We're going to the baptism, aren't we?" She forced a smile, but when Zoram didn't return her gesture she said, "Tell me everything is going as we planned." She gripped the skirts of her robe and said, "Tell me no evil has come to my family."

"I'm sorry, Elizabeth. I went hunting for your brother to warn him."

"Warn him of what?"

"I don't know exactly how to say this, but . . ." Zoram removed his turban and ran his hand through his curling locks. "We must stay away from your home until after the hour of baptism has passed."

"What do you mean, stay away?" Elizabeth slowly shook her head, searching Zoram's green eyes for the reason behind this madness. "There isn't a safer place in all the earth than my home."

"Not on this night."

Elizabeth said, "I thought this baptism was what you wanted for me."

"We'll have to find another time. I have this feeling that—"

"I don't want to hear about your feelings. I want you to come with me before Aaron and Mama leave for the washing pool." Elizabeth straightened her shawl over her shoulders. "Are you coming or must I do this alone?"

"Don't go." Zoram's voice was firm, but there was a pleading in his words that she'd not heard before and she turned away before he could see the tears streaking her cheeks with uncertainty. Why did Zoram refuse to come with her? He'd not given her any reasoning other than his feelings. She quickly wiped the tears from her cheek. "Why do you refuse to come with me? Do you fear Laban so much you dare not—"

"Don't you understand?" Zoram lowered his head. He said, "God is the only one I fear."

Daniel tipped his head back to get the last drop of wine before throwing the bottle in the haystack just outside the horse stables. The glazed pottery crashed against the hard-packed dirt and sent his mind spinning at the sound of it. Strong drink was not allowed in the livery, but he could saddle his steed just fine—no matter that he'd downed two bottles in the wine cellar and another on his way over from the main house. He shuffled inside the barns and got the saddle down from the rack. Laban didn't mind Daniel drinking from his private stores as long as he didn't make a fool of himself in front of

the men, but what did the captain know about foolhardy drinking?
Last week Daniel found Laban at the front gate sleeping off his
intemperance in the middle of the morning, and no one spoke a word
about Laban's foolishness. He walked the saddle over to his horse—a
young steed from the royal herds wintered at Jericho with a fighting
spirit and speed like the wind—and rigged the saddle with two
leather straps under the steed's belly, leaving some play in the stirrups.
His legs were stronger than most and he needed a good two fingers of
play to ride with any comfort.

Daniel pulled himself up into the saddle and rode into the yard with
a firm grip on the reins. Tonight was the first in two months he was free
of his command and he was headed to the Jawbone Inn to waste away
the evening and forget his duties overseeing the soldiers about the estate,
even the gardener picking through the bushes on the far side of the yard
carried his lamp like a watchman and wielded his hoe like a sword. He
stood to attention when Daniel reined past the sycamore trees. He was a
strong boy, but he didn't have quick enough feet or nimble enough
balance to stay with Daniel in the wrestling pit. No one under his
command did. Daniel beat him in a match this afternoon and now he
was making good on their bet—a full night of gardening duties. He'd be
pulling weeds until the cock crowed or at least until he rooted out every
last thistle in the gardens. Daniel kept his horse trotting toward the front
gate, but before he was out of earshot he told the soldier to be sure and
spade out the weeds growing near the back gate, over beyond the
servant's quarters where no one ever saw and the light of day never
reached. But if anyone ever did venture that way, the thorns made for a
terrible eyesore and the work would keep the boy busy for another hour.

The watchmen at the front gate knelt on the ground playing pitch
and toss and they didn't stand to attention until the last one had his
turn. Daniel tossed them a coin, told them to pitch one for him and
see that he got the winnings when he returned. These men weren't
trained for greeting guests and if they weren't the finest swordsmen
and archers in the kingdom, he'd have the whole lot of them court-
martialed. Daniel was training them to do Laban's biddings, not stand
watch and he forgave them their insubordination just as long as they
put an arrow on any mark Laban asked of them. He dug his heels into
the animal's haunches, turned into the street and started toward the—

"Whoa, there!" Daniel veered hard to keep from running over the beggar darting across his path. Cursed woman! Why didn't she look before she crossed his way? The sun had set, but it wasn't so dark she couldn't see him coming out the gate. She drew a child by the hand, pulling him out from in front of the horse's hooves.

The woman said, "Excuse us, kind sir."

Excuse us? What kind of street urchins used that sort of language? Daniel came around hard to see they were all right, but the horse's whinnies hadn't stopped them from continuing down Milo Hill. Daniel leaned forward in the saddle, squinting into the evening shadows. The woman should have at least stopped and explained herself after cutting across a soldier's path, and not just any soldier. Couldn't she see Daniel was an officer and deserved the respect due his rank?

Daniel cantered down the hill, keeping a good distance behind the night travelers, but not so far back he couldn't study them. These weren't normal urchins working the streets after dark despite the heavy bag the woman carried over her shoulder. She had a strong, erect stride, unhampered by what she carried. She dressed in a dark, black cloak, her head down, her face hidden beneath the hood of her robe. Daniel let out the reins and pushed his horse a little faster, closing the distance between them, but not so close as to give away his curiosity. The woman's long, black hair was drawn back off her brow with a gold band and she had a string of pearls about her neck. The hem of an elegant purple gown sneaked out from beneath her black cape and showed at the cuff and collar. She was perfumed and bathed and the scent of a wealthy woman carried on the air like the first roses in springtime. There was no doubting she'd come from an important affair in the upper city. The boy was a tall, thin lad with the same posture as his mother. He was wearing a purple tunic of the most expensive linen. He had a narrow nose and thin red cheeks, and his hair was cut straight across his brow just like the prince of Judah, but it couldn't be him, could it?

The woman had said "kind sir," and her voice sang with the same softness he remembered the queen having, her Hebrew falling from her lips with the accent of the educated class. She let go of her hood for a moment, letting free the cloth that cloaked her face. She had a high brow, her cheeks were red from the frosted air, and when he caught a glimpse of her profile he could see the gold chain that shimmered about her neck.

It was Miriam, but what was the queen of Judah doing without a troop of soldiers to protect her after dark? It was Miriam and Prince Mulek; it had to be them. There was not another family in all of Judah with the elegance of pleated capes and silver hems in their clothing.

Daniel followed them down Milo Hill and onto Main Street and when they stopped in front of the potter's burned-down property, he quickly reined into an alleyway and watched the two royals mill about the charred gate waiting for . . .

Aaron? What was he doing meeting royals at the potter's residence? It had to be him with his tall, skinny frame and those frail arms hanging at his side, swinging to the rhythm of his long strides. Aaron never left Papa to finish the day's work alone, but there he was, reaching an arm around Mulek and taking Miriam by the hand. How did Aaron know them? Mama had done some weaving for the queen, but Aaron was no weaver and there was no reason for any royal to want to speak with Aaron. Daniel quieted his horse so that he could hear their faint voices. The queen didn't feel right about what they were doing, but Aaron insisted that all was well and they should bring the disguises and meet Ruth at their home.

Daniel brought his steed around and spurred deeper into the alley, crossing behind the square brick homes of the lower city neighborhoods and down a footpath that emptied into the alley behind his home. He had to see what sort of a visit these royals were paying, and he jumped from the saddle and climbed the back wall.

The lamps were lit in the kitchen and Mama worked in front of the open window. He couldn't tell exactly what she was cooking; there weren't the usual aromas filtering out the window, but it had to be something good. Nothing Mama fixed tasted badly, except, possibly wild herbs, and even then, she had a way of making the unpleasant portions of a Passover feast palatable. It had been months since Daniel had eaten one of Mama's meals and he would have marched through the front door and given her a kiss on the cheek and asked if he could stay for evening meal, but not now, not with the royals meeting Aaron at the potter's residence with designs on coming here.

Daniel hurried across the courtyard and crouched in the darkness below the window. It was the perfect watching place. He could see the front gate, hear everything that went on inside the home, and if need be, he could raise his head and steal a glance of the main room. The captain told him the queen was not to be trusted and if there was anything he could learn about the woman and her son, he'd report it. He was duty bound, and he would lie in wait to see exactly what service he should provide—no matter that this was the home of his flesh and blood. He was sworn to obey only one master.

Captain Laban above all others.

Darkness filled the kitchen window like a troubled soul and Ruth prayed there was nothing in the shadows of the night that could harm her children. The fire in the hearth was burning out and Ruth pulled the thick drapes across the opening to slow the draft. Her youngest were gone with the carpenter's wife with orders not to speak a word about the baptism. The tea was in the basket on the kitchen table and she took a seat beside it, her elbows set on the wood planks, her hands cupped under her chin, and her gaze flitting about the room in search of something to pass the time. Aaron and Elizabeth were late and she had nothing to do but wait until they arrived.

Ruth's gaze rested on the bundles of wild herbs hanging from the hooks above the hearth waiting to be chopped into a garnish for Passover. It was a good chore to keep her mind from wandering back to worrying, and though Passover was still a good month away, it didn't keep her from taking down the bundles of wild herbs and preparing them for the feast. Dried horseradish had the look of withered white carrots and the smell of bitter onions, and tradition required she prepare it into a garnish and serve it in haste, not chopped and ground a month ahead of time and stored away to wait for the feast day. But she spread the tubers over the table just the same and cut away the leafy tops, the bitter smell of the herbs reminding her that tonight she had chosen to be passed-over for baptism while she watched Aaron and Elizabeth blessed with the spirit of their new faith.

If spring had come earlier this year, Ruth wouldn't bother preparing dried herbs from last season—there would be more than enough growing along the banks of the Gihon Spring to pick and chop and make a garnish for the meals of Passover—but with the winter as cold as this one had been, there was no telling if there would be any bitter herbs growing in time for the feast and it was better to have put some away from last year than not have any to remember the day Moses freed the Hebrews from the bitterness of their Egyptian bondage in search of this promised land.

Ruth turned her ear toward the door, listening for the sound of her eldest children, but it was only the creaking of the ceiling beams and the rush of the breeze about the hinges of the front door. Elizabeth was in the upper city waiting for Zoram to finish his work in Laban's treasury, and Aaron was at the blacksmith shop smithing metal for an invention he was making—said it was going to be the finest thing he'd ever crafted. He was to leave Papa at the shop with a good two hours of work to keep him busy and meet here with the others before taking separate flights to the washing pool on the flats south of Jerusalem.

Ruth dropped a horseradish, but quickly picked it up before it was too long on the floor and she had to throw it out. What if they were followed tonight? She steadied the horseradish between her fingers and cut away the skin. She shouldn't think such evil. God would protect them, wouldn't He? She turned the herbs over and cut away the skin on the backsides. Why did she let these whisperings get the best of her? There was not a better night for her eldest children to be baptized. Jonathan had plenty of work to keep him busy until well after they returned from the washing pool, and Daniel hadn't been home from Laban's estate for a month. There was nothing to stop them from sneaking out of the city unless it was the feelings of her heart, and she put them away privily. Her misgivings were not permitted to overshadow this happy night.

Ruth set the skinned horseradish in a mortar bowl and ground them with a pestle, raising a fine powder in the air and filling her eyes with the sting of Passover. Since the day her children were old enough to tell her of their likes and dislikes, they never hesitated to rail against horseradish at Passover. But no matter how much they complained, she was going to see they ate the awful stuff and enjoyed it. What did they know about awful-tasting food anyway? She'd spoiled them far too much last Passover with a sweet haroset of apples, walnuts, dates, and raisins ground into a pudding and sprinkled with cinnamon, and though it was to remind them of the mortar their forefathers made to cement the bricks in pharaoh's palaces and pyramids, the only thing her children remembered was how much the haroset sweetened the aftertaste of the horseradish.

Wild horseradish garnish at Passover was in remembrance of the days when Israel lived in bondage, and she couldn't simply rewrite history to coddle their tongues and spare them a taste of slavery, though tonight Aaron and Elizabeth were to learn of a different flight from bondage. Ruth kept the pestle crushing about the bowl, her tears running off the end of her nose. She should be happy for their newfound faith, but she was to remain in a land of bondage without the promised blessings of the Holy Spirit as her constant companion. Ruth brushed her cheeks to make sure the tears welling in her eyes didn't fall. All she wanted was for her family to be together—not divided by the evil that raged in the city. If this rite of baptism had the power to bring her family together, or at least begin that eternal bond, she could not deny her children that blessing. But she was like the Hebrews in the days of Moses, her spirit enslaved until Jonathan joined her exodus. She would not go down into the waters of baptism without him.

The front door flew open, the wood slats banging against the inside wall. Who could that be entering the house with such fury? She'd taught her children better and she sneaked along the kitchen wall and peered around the pillar separating her from the main room. Elizabeth hurried in with Zoram at her side. She should know better than to behave so brashly, and Ruth was going to have to refine the girl's manners if she ever hoped to catch a young man with Zoram's education. Ruth cleaned her hands on her apron. Well, maybe catch wasn't the right word, but Elizabeth certainly was fishing. The girl fretted about the house all day, wondering if he was going to come at all and she spent a good two hours washing her hair, perfuming her robe and pacing about like a caged animal. Ruth stayed hidden behind the pillar and watched Elizabeth walk to the center of the main room with a confident stride, her hand in Zoram's hand. She was a pretty girl. No, she wasn't a girl. With Zoram at her side she was a proper-looking woman, with wide, brown eyes and narrow lips that were turned up into a broad smile, an expression that didn't come easily until Zoram stepped into her life.

Zoram wasn't dressed in dark clothing and Ruth was going to have to find the man something to put over his white robe and turban if they were to walk unnoticed through the farmers' flats south of the city. He could leave the turban here, no matter how much he needed it to keep his curly hair in place, the ringlets dancing over his eyes, playing at his ears, and covering the collar at the back of his neck. Ruth couldn't have found Elizabeth a finer suitor. Not that he'd expressed a desire to marry the girl, mind you, but there was no mistaking the affection that lighted his eyes whenever he was in Elizabeth's company. They were a noble couple, their hearts guided by wisdom and their love tempered by the reverence of heaven, and Ruth could only hope that this baptism would bring their two hearts closer, with the same oneness she prayed would someday grace her marriage to Jonathan.

Elizabeth said, "Mama, where are you?"

Ruth hurried back to the bowl of bitter herbs before she said, "In the kitchen, dear."

Zoram stepped into the kitchen ahead of Elizabeth and stood beside Ruth without saying a word about the oddness of preparing a garnish a full month before Passover, and she added restraint to her list of the man's admirable traits. He was going to make a fine suitor and as long as he didn't point out her peculiar habits, she'd approve of any marriage arrangements he proposed. Not that he'd made any such suggestion, but there was certainly no doubt he would one day soon.

Ruth poured the horseradish into a jar and sealed the lid with a smattering of beeswax before asking Zoram to set it on the highest shelf in the kitchen. She said, "Preparing this garnish may seem a bit odd, but I had to do something to stay busy until we left."

"Oh, Mama!" Elizabeth stood in the kitchen entry, her body trembling. She said, "We aren't going tonight."

Ruth hurried to Elizabeth's side and pulled back the strands of soft, black hair from her face. "What is it, girl?"

"It's, it's . . ." Elizabeth brushed away a tear.

"It's my doing. I want you to come back with me to my quarters until this passes. You'll be safe there." Zoram leaned over the kitchen windowsill and peered into the courtyard. "Something isn't right. It's too dangerous to go through with our plan tonight.

Ruth stood beside Zoram. How did he know the depth of her fears? She'd sent Sarah and Joshua with the carpenter's wife because of her dread, and now Zoram was dredging it up from deep in her soul and she could feel it encircling her breast like a weight bearing down against her breathing. She said, "If you know what evil comes this way, tell me what it is."

Zoram stepped back from looking out the window. "I don't know."

"Then why do you frighten us?"

Zoram touched Ruth on the hand. "I don't mean to cause you any fear."

"You certainly haven't brought us any peace." Ruth stepped to the kitchen table and began sorting through the basket. She didn't need to check—the tea and rubbing oils were properly packed, and the white clothing and towels were neatly folded, but she had to busy herself with something and she kept her hands moving over the contents.

Zoram said, "I don't know what to say, except I have a feeling it isn't safe."

Ruth pulled her hands from the basket. She understood what he'd felt but couldn't say. She'd felt the same voice. "Go on."

Zoram removed his white turban and placed it under his arm. "It speaks with a voice strong enough to constrain me to say it's too dangerous for us to go to the washing pool." He stepped back from looking out the window. "We have to leave immediately. It isn't safe here either."

That was the same inspiration Ruth felt, but until now she'd believed it was her motherly fears preying on her mind. She said, "What about Aaron? We can't leave without him. He'll think we've gone to meet him at the washing pool." Her voice caught and she held her hand to her mouth. She said, "He's suffered too much in his short life. I won't let him suffer anymore."

"He'll be fine, Mama." Elizabeth found Ruth's cloak hanging from a hook on the wall. She said, "God wouldn't fail to warn Aaron."

"I hope you're right, dear." Ruth patted Elizabeth on the arm. "And I hope he's wise enough to listen to his heart."

Ruth left the lamps burning and the piping hot mint tea in the basket on the kitchen table and followed Zoram and Elizabeth into the night. The lamplight may chase away whatever evil passed by her home, but the tea was a complete waste. It would never warm her children after their baptism. Ruth started past the gate, but before going into the street she turned back.

There was not a soul about the house to drink her tea.

The light from burning oil lamps streamed through the windows and the crackle of a hearth fire greeted Aaron at the front gate. He ushered the royals toward the house, the orange light falling on Mulek's new growth of hair, cut straight across the brow like his father and no longer shaved like an Egyptian prince. Aaron hurried the boy with his mother inside the main room and sat them down in the large bench seat with a folded blanket for a cushion.

Miriam said, "We'll have to split up to keep from drawing attention. You'll go with us and your mother and Elizabeth will take another way out." Miriam set down her bag, untied the cords and pulled back the cloth. There was a brass helmet inside, a red plume, a sword, a leather kilt with silver studded pleats, and a purple sash palace guards wore about the waist. She said, "This should be enough of a disguise to get you through the government district without any of the other soldiers asking you questions. We'll take the narrow gate beyond the palace. Do you know the entrance?"

"I'll follow you."

"You'll have to lead out, and with so many soldiers in that district, you can't be asking us questions. It wouldn't look right. You have to know the way." Miriam helped Aaron with the sword before turning to Mulek. "Did you bring it, son?"

The prince pulled a small scroll from under his tunic and laid it on the table. It was a map of the upper city along with every footpath and road through the lands south of the city. "The washing pool is right here." He traced his long, thin finger over the contours of Main Street, up through the government district, around the north wall of the palace, and down a narrow alley to the gate, then every turn and twist in the countryside to the secret washing pool. He said, "We'll take the main road three miles south, then follow the stream down through a stand of willows another mile and a half." His voice was steady for such a young lad, but he'd been tested more than most boys his age and he spoke with a calm manner better suited to men three times his twelve years. "It's near the back of a pasture and with lambing season near, it's full of sheep."

Aaron said, "You certainly know the way."

"I could never forget. It's where Mother and I were baptized." Mulek felt under the collar of his tunic and when his hand came up empty he said, "Mother, we have to go back; I've left it."

"You don't need it, son."

"I can't go to the washing pool without it."

Aaron said, "Without what?"

"His charm." Miriam pulled Mulek close to her. "It was given him the day he was baptized to remind him of his promises." She reached her hand across the table to Aaron. "And tonight you and Elizabeth will do the same, God willing." She helped Aaron tie the chinstrap in place and the sash around his waist. "Now fetch your mother down to see this map before we're on our way."

Aaron stood at the base of the stairs and called for Ruth to come down, but there was no stirring in the rooms on the second floor and he called again. He started up the stairs and he was halfway to the landing when the sound of footsteps in the courtyard drew Aaron's gaze to the kitchen window. He came back down and leaned out. The gate was still latched, there was no sign of anyone about the yard and he pulled the curtains back.

Daniel? What was he doing along the outside wall of the house, his thick shoulders pressed against the stone like a thief in hiding? He smiled in at Aaron, his white teeth shining in the moonlight and the metal studs in his leather tunic scratching against the stonework. He came to the window, his wide body framed by the sill, and when he leaned his head inside, the smell of strong wine came with him. His voice was low and his tongue hung on every word. He said, "Hello, Aaron."

"What are you doing, sneaking about like that?"

"I was hungry."

Hungry? Three months had passed without Daniel ever once stopping by to enjoy Mama's cooking, try some of her bread, or join the family for a meal.

Daniel peered past Aaron to the basket sitting on the kitchen table. "Is there any food in—"

"There's nothing." Aaron stood between the basket and the window, blocking Daniel's view. He took out the white baptismal clothing his mother weaved for him to wear and stuffed the garment beneath his tunic. The cloth bulged at his belly, but it was better to wear it like this than take a chance on Daniel seeing it. He pushed the reeds in the top of the basket together to hide the pot of tea inside. He turned around and said, "There's not anything in here for you."

"What about Mama's pantry? Is there any food in there I could—"

"Not now." Aaron stood in front of a kitchen chair, the baptismal clothing pushing his tunic over the backrest like a sack of wheat. He said, "Mama's not here to fill your belly."

"I know that."

Aaron smoothed his tunic against his stomach. How did he know Ruth was gone?

Daniel came around to the front door. Aaron hurried to meet him outside and keep him from coming in to see the royals, but Daniel sauntered into the main room before he could get to the door. Mulek pulled his collar up and Miriam lowered her head, but it was too late. Daniel had seen them in the full light of the burning lamps.

Daniel bowed to Miriam and said, "Your Majesty, I didn't expect to see you here."

"Leave them be." Aaron marched to Miriam's side. "They're my guests, not yours."

"I'm sworn to protect them." Daniel reached to pat Mulek on the head. "Isn't that right, boy?"

Mulek ducked away from Daniel's hand. "We can manage on our own."

"You weren't planning on going anywhere on such a cold night, were you?" Daniel ran his hand over the soldier's stripes in Aaron's disguise. "My men have orders to kill commoners dressed in military clothing."

"He was only trying it on." Miriam stood from the bench with an unmistakable concern lighting her eyes. She tugged on the sleeve of Aaron's tunic and said, "Have your mother take in the sash three fingers and add another to the length of the cuffs." She lifted the skirts of her robe and started for the door. "That should do for the men who are going to wear that about the palace."

Daniel stood in front of the door, blocking Miriam's retreat. "Since when does the queen of Judah hire out the weaving for the palace guard?" He leaned against the planks in the door and removed his leather gloves one finger at a time. "And at such a late hour, my lady."

Miriam said, "This is the best time to find your mother at home, Lieutenant."

Lieutenant? Aaron stood beside Daniel. No one ever called his brother that, at least not in this house. Aaron said, "She doesn't need you or your questioning right now."

"She needs more than a few questions, brother." Daniel stuffed the gloves under his arm and walked to the kitchen. He pulled the basket close and began piecing through the contents.

Miriam stood across the table from him. She leaned forward and said, "Do you know where your mother's gone?"

"I thought you were leaving?" Daniel kept his gaze in the basket. "You've finished with your business haven't you?"

"Don't speak to her like that." Aaron stood at the head of the table. "Have you no respect?"

Daniel tilted his head over the basket and smiled in at the contents. "I'll speak however I please."

Miriam said, "Tell us where Ruth is."

Daniel looked up from the basket. "Mama left in company with Zoram and Elizabeth."

Aaron leaned over the table. "Did she say where they were headed?"

Daniel poured a cup of tea from the jar, the steam rising past his lips and into his thin line of beard. "They said something about taking a long walk south of the city."

Aaron stood back from the table. Mama was already gone to the washing pool and they were going to have to hurry to meet her there. He turned to Miriam and said, "Can I see you to the palace, Your Majesty? It isn't safe for you to be about the city alone after dark."

The queen nodded and quickly tied her cloak around her neck "I suppose I can come back another day to speak with your mother."

Aaron escorted the royals to the front door, but stopped short when Daniel called to him, his powerful voice resonating through the house. Daniel raised the steaming cup of tea to Aaron and grinned. "Mazel Tov, brother."

Jonathan heated the brass oven paddles over the open hearth, searing a coat of lacquer into the metal before setting it aside. He didn't use the water bath to cool the brass. Quick-cooled lacquer never lasted more than a year, and if these baker's paddles were going to carry the mark of his hand, he was going to see they endured a lifetime of bread baking without losing their shine. The trowels were next. He'd fitted the wooden handles in place and all that remained was to set the stub-ends with a fixed double joint to keep the wood from prying away from the metal. He held a supply of nails between his lips, set one of them alongside the joint and lined the hammer square with the head when the clapping of horse hooves sounded in the street and the muzzle of a young brown steed poked its nose through the doorway.

Jonathan set down the hammer and side-stepped around the end of the forging table with the nails still stuck between his lips. He pushed the horse's head aside and found Daniel high in the saddle, his eyes filled with a wild light and the ends of his short-shaved beard gleaming in the moonlight. He sat straight, his shoulders back, and when he came around, his leather boots brushed against Jonathan's ribs.

Daniel said, "I'm on my way to report to Captain Laban."

Jonathan wiped his hands clean on his leather apron. Why did Daniel bother to stop by to tell him that? The boy hadn't stopped by the shop in more than a month to tell Jonathan anything. He moved the nails to the side of his mouth. "Report what, son?"

"Aaron." The horse whinnied and Daniel jabbed her with the blunt end of his heel until she quieted. "He's joining the serpent people."

Jonathan spit the nails from his mouth. Not an hour ago, he was thinking he shouldn't be so hard on Aaron and his beliefs, that he should find out what fired his faith, but not any longer. He'd lost Daniel to soldiering and wasn't about to let religion turn Aaron's heart away from the shop. Blacksmithing was the weld that bound this family together. Jonathan ground the nails into the stone with the sole of his sandals. Cursed Rekhabites! He was going to have to act quickly. If there was anything that could draw his sons back to blacksmithing it was prosperity. Riches would temper Aaron's faith and soften Daniel's military dreams; and if not—well, there was always Joshua. His youngest didn't suffer the same delusions. Joshua was Jonathan's insurance against the future, a last hope to keep alive his blacksmithing birthright if he failed with Aaron and Daniel. Was it too much to ask that the ways of the father live on in the son—any son?

Daniel said, "Aaron's headed to meet the Rekhabites at a washing pool south of city, says he's going to be baptized by one of their prophets."

"Your brother's doing no such thing. He lost interest in those zealots after Rebekah died. He's not even mentioned the name of . . ."

Daniel said, "Yeshua the Anointed One."

Jonathan scanned the empty street. There was no one about to hear the name of the God of the Rekhabites. He said, "You're not reporting any of this to Zadock or Laban."

"It's my duty."

"Your duty is to this family."

"Aaron's not worthy of your good name."

"I'll decide that." Jonathan reached to pull Daniel from the saddle, but the boy yanked on the reins and spooked his horse. The animal reared on her back legs and threw Daniel from the saddle onto the cobblestones. He was shaken, but nothing was broken and before he could stand, Jonathan mounted the horse and headed for the east gate with Daniel shouting for him to come back, but he couldn't.

Not until he stopped Aaron.

Zedekiah pushed Miriam's scarves off the shelf and into a heap on the floor of her dressing closet. He poked them with the silver-studded toe of his boot, but there was nothing hidden among the lace and linen. He felt through Miriam's sleeping robes and squeezed the cloth like a cook kneading dough. Her dinner and day robes hung from the hooks along the wall and he quickly rummaged through them like a common thief searching for a money purse. There were no notes stuffed into pouches, no stash of jewels or money or secret documents, not a single clue to her odd behavior. It wasn't like

Miriam to keep things from Zedekiah, but if she wasn't going to confide in him then he was going to find out her secrets on his own.

Zedekiah carefully folded the scarves and placed them back onto the shelf, arranging the blue ones at the bottom of the stack, the red ones in the middle, and the white ones on top. They were to be left as he found them. Miriam could never know he'd searched her things. It was best if she believed she had his complete trust.

There was no sign of anything out of order among the perfumes and creams on Miriam's vanity, and not a single clue to her peculiar doings among the documents she kept on a shelf opposite the bedroom door. Zedekiah turned into the hall and passed Mulek's room on the way to the back stairwell. The lamps were lit in the boy's chambers and Zedekiah stopped beside the doorpost and leaned around to see inside. If Miriam was hiding something from him, Mulek's room was a much better place to keep it. His sandals fell quietly on the Persian rugs just inside the entry and he ducked below the level of the windows gracing the west wall to keep from being seen in the gardens below. He shouldn't worry about being seen in here. It was a common thing for him to pass through his son's room, though his search was anything but ordinary.

Zedekiah fluffed the mattress and found nothing but goose feathers. The closet shelves were filled with Mulek's folded tunics, purple robes, and leather kilts. He ran his hand over the clothes and his fingers brushed against something hidden between the folds in one of the tunics. It was the size of a fingernail with a hard, polished surface like a gem or a trinket from a necklace. He pulled it out, held it up to the light and found . . .

A tiger's tooth? What was that doing among Mulek's clothes? Zedekiah had given it to him on his eleventh birthday and if the boy was going to hide it from his brothers, he shouldn't put it here. It could fall between the wood slats behind the shelves and be lost forever. Under any other circumstance he would have taken the tooth and told his son he wouldn't get it back until he found a safer place to hide it, but there was no way Zedekiah could explain how he came across it except that he was searching for evidence of his mother's deceit. He quickly returned the tooth between the tunics and smoothed the wrinkles out of the cloth. There was no proof that Miriam was up to any pretense. She may be acting peculiar but he'd been married to her long enough to know she was capable of harmless peculiarities.

Zedekiah started back around the bed when he bumped up against a small table crowded with trinkets. A bowl of arrowheads sat next to a stack of feathers and a bag filled with colored rocks. It wasn't that long ago when Zedekiah collected boyhood treasures and sailed cucumber boats in the palace fountains. He ran his hand over the bag of rocks, checked the bowl of arrowheads, and was just reaching for the longest feather when his elbow knocked a sealed wooden box off the edge. The lid cracked on the hard stone and the contents spilled onto the floor. There were three silver coins, a brass button, the blue shell of a robin's egg and . . .

What was that glittering in the lamplight, splitting its rays into reds and greens and yellows? Zedekiah pushed aside the button and seashell with his finger and fished out the thin brass chain with a single charm of a serpent dangling from the end, the curves of the snake reflecting the light. He held it up and stared at it like a man caught in a soothsayer's spell. What evil curse caused Mulek to keep such a thing? This was the mark of the Rekhabites—the sign of rebellion and mistaken beliefs in a Messiah, and Mulek had no business keeping it.

Zedekiah rubbed the brass charm between his fingers. He could hope this was an innocent curiosity of youth, but he would wait and watch to see if Miriam or Mulek gave him reason to believe otherwise. He'd seen Miriam speaking with the prophet Jeremiah, but there could be another explanation for their public meeting beyond the treachery this charm implied.

"Sire."

The familiar grating, high-pitched voice of Zadock rang from the hallway. What awful timing—Zadock, his most trusted member of the Council of Elders, Laban, the captain of his military, and Daniel, the boy Laban said was his finest young officer under his command, marched through the open door. Laban and Daniel were dressed in thick riding cloaks and boots laced up their shins while Zadock wore his usual black council robes.

The Chief Elder came around the bed. He said, "There's a serious matter that requires your attention."

"At this hour?"

Zadock said, "It can't wait."

"Why is there always something that can't wait?"

"I'm sorry, Your Majesty." Captain Laban stepped past Zadock, the polished brass on his breastplate gleaming in the lamplight. He said, "It has to do with Rekhabites."

"Can't you and your men deal with those zealots?" Zedekiah tucked the charm under his belt and walked into the hall with the men following him. "I've never fancied them as large a threat as you gentlemen have."

Zadock said, "You believe they're heretics, don't you?"

"Of course I do." Zedekiah kept his thumb under his belt, holding the serpent charm in place. "I simply don't have the time to concern myself with their harmless doings."

Laban said, "I'd hardly call them harmless."

Zadock said, "They're traitors to the kingdom."

Zedekiah reached the main stairs and started down the first flight. "Some of them possibly."

Zadock hurried down the steps alongside Zedekiah, his robes swirling about his sandals. He said, "All of them are rebels who should be dealt with."

Zedekiah stopped on the landing above the main lobby. The smell of bread pudding filtered up from the dining room. It was his favorite, filled with nuts and bits of dried mango and plenty of dates, and it was his best excuse to retreat from these men with the charm hidden beneath his belt. He said, "My youngest sons are waiting to have dessert with me in the dining room."

Zadock said, "Can it wait, sire?"

"I don't like eating my pudding cold."

"You may not have an appetite once you hear this news."

"Exactly what is this about?"

Zadock hovered one step above him, with Lieutenant Daniel coming up on his left and Captain Laban on his right. He said, "It's your wife. We have word she may be contacting the Rekhabites this evening."

Zedekiah turned to the railing and leaned out over the main lobby. He said, "What are you saying?"

"A Rekhabite washing rite, sir." Daniel stepped in next to the king. "The queen may be attending one this evening."

"That's foolishness." The pointed end of the charm dug into Zedekiah's thumb. He said, "Where did you hear such a thing?"

Daniel said, "I can take you there."

Zadock said, "We hired an old shepherd to lead us to the washing pool. He says the Rekhabites go there from time to time late in the evening."

Captain Laban said, "I took the liberty of preparing your horse, sire. We're saddled and ready to look into this."

Zedekiah pushed away from the railing and marched down the last flight of stairs. The Chief Elder was right—this was a matter that couldn't wait on bread pudding. He crossed the hall to the double-wood doors at the main palace entry, but didn't push them open. He said, "If you're right and my wife is attending this Rekhabite ceremony, what does it mean?"

Zadock opened the palace door and the cool night air rushed inside. He said, "Your wife, sire, could be the palace informant."

The washing pool stood hidden among the rocky parts of the pasture surrounded by a stand of willows. Aaron waited beside the tree with the thickest trunk, watching for any sign of his family. He was dressed in the delicate white linen baptismal clothing mother had woven for him. It was a one-piece tunic that pulled over his head like a newborn's robe and she said it would remind him of birth into a new life. It smelled of rose petals and Aaron held it to his nose and breathed the fragrance. He was ready for a new life, but he wouldn't go forward with this rite until Mama arrived with Elizabeth and Zoram.

Aaron pushed aside the branches and peered across the flats spreading out below the rise. Where were they? They should have been here hours before, but all he could see in the moonlight was a herd of sheep grazing on brown grasses. There was no stirring among the animals to give him any hope they were coming. Water gurgled down from the top of the pasture and collected in a small creek bed winding through the willows. It passed beside Aaron on its way over an outcrop of rocks before dropping into the washing pool in a gentle spray of cool water. The pond was a man-made reservoir fashioned of timbers and packed mud like a beaver's dam, backing the water deep enough for baptism. It wasn't as fine as the washing pool on the temple precincts, but it was faith he needed in order to take upon himself the name of Yeshua, not a polished brass bowl.

Jeremiah stood at the edge of the pool, waiting for Aaron to join him, but he wasn't going down in the waters until his family arrived. He scaled the rocks above the pool and took a seat beside the royals. Mulek's long legs hung down over the edge of the rock, the sole of his sandals brushing the top of the water. He dipped his toe under, stirred it about, and when he saw Aaron staring at him, he turned his gaze back to the water and stirred it again. Queen Miriam sat with her hands in her lap, her legs together and her feet resting on a pedestal of stone. She said, "Could something have—"

"Don't say it." Aaron held his hand up. He couldn't bear to think anything had happened to them. If he'd only told Papa about his baptism he would have gotten home in time to meet the others and none of this would have happened. Jonathan would have listened to him, he was certain of it; the Spirit begged Aaron to confide in him.

"I'm sure it's nothing." Miriam reached over and took Aaron by the hand. "We can wait a while longer."

Aaron said, "What will your husband do when you don't return immediately?"

"We'll think of something to tell the king." Miriam pulled Mulek in next to her. "Won't we, son?"

"I can't let you stay any longer."

Jeremiah came up the rise from the edge of the pool. He said, "You came here to be baptized, didn't you son?"

Aaron rubbed the back of his neck. It wasn't supposed to be like this. Elizabeth was to be baptized with him and Ruth was to stand on the banks with towels and hot tea and enjoy the spirit of the occasion. He said, "I can't do this without my family."

"You're making a covenant with God, not with anyone else."

Jeremiah led Aaron down along the bank and into the pool. The water crept up no farther than Aaron's thighs, but the cold forced the air from his lungs. Jeremiah took him by the hand and called him by his full name—Aaron Ben Jonathan the Blacksmith. He spoke with a deep, solemn voice and told Aaron he was baptizing him by the authority of the Almighty as a witness that Aaron was entering into a covenant to serve God so that the Spirit of heaven would be poured out upon him and that—

"I can't do this." Aaron pulled his hands from Jeremiah's grasp. "I should have listened."

"Listened to what, son?"

"I should have told my father about this."

"You can tell him once you're home."

"It's not that, sir. Something's gone terribly wrong and it's because I didn't listen to the promptings of the—"

A horse thundered among the willows and a steed appeared from between the trunks of two trees, headed toward the washing pool at full gallop. The animal jumped the rocky bank and came down hard, splashing Aaron and knocking Jeremiah off his feet. The rider came around and immediately Aaron recognized Papa's angry face in the moonlight. How did he find this place?

Jonathan leaned over the horse's mane and told him to get on, but Aaron backed away, the hem of his white clothing floating atop the troubled surface of the water. "Papa you don't understand."

"I understand plenty." He reined the horse alongside Aaron. "Now get on before you make more of a fool of yourself."

"He's not made anyone a fool, sir." Miriam stood on the rocks above the washing pool, her face half hidden behind the hood of her robe. She held Mulek next to her, her hand over his face, hiding him from Jonathan. "Let your son do as he pleases."

"Who are you to tell me what to do with my family?" Jonathan reined to the outcrop below Miriam, the thick legs of the horse cutting a wake through the water. He said, "I nearly lost this boy to a Rekhabite woman who—"

"I'm not a boy, Papa." Aaron slapped his fist against the surface.

"She stole your heart, son." Jonathan raised his voice to the queen. "And I'm not about to let another woman like you ruin his life."

"Rebekah didn't steal my heart." Aaron trudged through the water. He reached for Jonathan's leg. "I gave it to her."

"She's dead now, son." Jonathan reined away from Aaron's grasp and pulled him forward into the cold water. "And its time you let her faith die with her."

Aaron stood, water dripping from the end of his nose and spitting off his words. "I'm not going anywhere." He wiped his lips with the back of his hand. "I came here to be baptized and I won't let you keep me from it." He turned back through the pond toward Jeremiah. "No one is going to stop me."

"You'll do as I say!" Jonathan reined alongside Aaron, took him by the arm and with one mighty heave pulled his lanky body onto the back of the horse. He kept Aaron trapped under his arm and turned his voice to the trees lining the pool. He said, "There will be no baptism tonight or any other night, do you hear me?"

Aaron said, "I heard you the first time and—"

Jonathan's rough hand covered Aaron's mouth. He reined to the other side of the pool. "No one in my family has anything to do with Rekhabites or the prophets. Is that clear? No one. I'll not allow it!"

Jonathan was speaking to a crowd that wasn't there, at least not anyone Aaron could see, no one but the lambs in the pastures beyond. He was gone wild, calling to the trees lining the washing pool as if they had ears to hear and eyes to see. He reined out of the pool and through the willows at full gallop and it was impossible to jump from the horse. They rode through the pasture, out through the herd of lambs, and onto the road headed back to Jerusalem before Jonathan spoke. His voice was firm and it didn't rise or fall with his words. Anger robbed the kinder passions from his speech and he told Aaron he was not to be baptized—not now, not ever, not as long as they lived under the same roof. He was the head of this family and his will was to be obeyed.

Aaron didn't answer. He lowered his head and let the rise and fall of the horse shake him to the very center. Mama was right; he should have gotten Papa's blessing, but what harm was there in letting Aaron follow his faith? Tears fell down his check and onto Papa's back, soaking into the cloth of Jonathan's tunic. He'd lost his chance to reach Papa's heart, a chance that would never come again, but Aaron would not lose hope in the promise of a new life. Maybe Papa was right; maybe they couldn't live beneath the same roof any longer. It was time to find a place where Aaron could live his faith as he saw fit—

Far away from here.

Zedekiah stayed level with the other riders until the trail narrowed through a gully and forced the company into a single-file line. He sidled his horse in behind the old shepherd and didn't allow Zadock or Laban to get ahead of him. If Miriam was out here, he was going to be the first to see her with the Rekhabites.

The old shepherd led them down a rocky ridge into a creek bed, then upstream alongside the water's edge. His tattered robe smelled of sheep and scented the night air with the pungent perfume of his shepherding. He carried a staff he said was for luck, though they didn't need any tonight. The man said he knew where the secret Rekhabite washing pool was hidden among the rocky swells and shallow ravines of these pastures and he was going to sneak them in the back way. There were Rekhabites practicing their washing rites tonight and he was going to lead them to the exact spot or return the twenty pieces of silver the Chief Elder paid him to guide them here. He swore he would, with one hand on his lucky staff and the other raised to the starry night.

A line of willows appeared on the horizon and the old shepherd swung down from the saddle. They were to follow him to the top of the rise on foot and not speak a word. The washing pool was on the other side of the trees. He waited for Zedekiah to stand close to the willows before he lifted the branches aside and let him peer into the clearing.

A dam stood just beyond the trees with a pool of water backed up behind the fallen timbers. Water spilled over an outcrop on the far side and standing atop the rocky bank was—

"Do you see her?" Captain Laban crowded in next to Zedekiah. "Where is she?"

Zadock said, "I'm sorry, sire. This is most unfortunate."

"I don't need your pity." Zedekiah stepped aside and let them see. There was no one there, nothing but freestanding trees sprouting from crags in the rocky outcrop.

"That can't be." Zadock stepped back from the willows. "Where is she?"

Daniel marched to the pond, splashed along the shore and came back through the willows. He said, "They have to be here somewhere."

"I've seen enough." Zedekiah started down the rise to his horse.

Zadock followed behind him. He said, "There's been a mistake."

"You're right." Zedekiah mounted his steed and leaned over the saddle. His wife wasn't the palace informant. He said, "The old shepherd owes you twenty pieces of silver."

CHAPTER 22

Aaron prodded Beuntahyu forward, but she would not enter the narrow red rock passage at the summit. She backed away from the shadow-filled opening, raised her head to the breeze and whinnied. What was she afraid of? She shouldn't be so temperamental about returning to her home. The wide-open olive vineyards of Beit Zayit stood on the other side of this cool damp chasm, but she shook her nose at the air filtering through from the other side and tried to turn back down the winding trail toward Jerusalem. Aaron jerked the reins and kept her facing the passage. There was no finer place for her to run free, and in winter, when the world was dressed in dormant brown grasses, the dark green canopy of leaves covering the plantation hills was a positive comfort.

Beuntahyu reared back on her hind legs. The saddlebags shifted across her backside and hung low on her haunches. She tried to come up again, but Aaron took out the slack in the reins and kept her down. Wonderful, just splendid! They were stuck at the top of this mountain, neither of them willing to go home. Aaron stroked Beuntahyu's muzzle and told her it would only take a moment to trot past the high rock walls to Beit Zayit, but they weren't turning about and heading back to Aaron's home—not now, maybe not ever. Didn't she understand that? They weren't going back to Jerusalem.

Aaron shifted the saddlebags back into place, and the smithing tools inside the leather pouch gave up a soft clang. Aaron didn't steal them from Papa, though he did sneak them from the rack near the front door of the shop this afternoon when Jonathan wasn't looking. The forging hammer, tongs, small pickax, and shovel belonged to

Aaron, and hopefully Papa wouldn't notice they were missing until he was far enough away to be free of his father's tyranny. Rebekah was dead and there was nothing to keep him in Jerusalem and endure Papa's order that he end his ties to the Rekhabites—he wasn't to speak about them as long as they lived under the same roof.

Aaron brought Beuntahyu around and waited for her to calm in the shade of a Joshua tree growing up beside an outcrop of rock before he dared try another approach. But they weren't going back. He had to find a place where he could follow the quiet dictates of his heart and Beit Zayit was the place to start. He didn't plan on asking Lehi for work, and he couldn't stay with them for more than a night or two. The plantation was too close to home, and Papa would come looking here for him, but he could get advice from Lehi before moving on. There was not another soul who understood Aaron's plight better than Lehi. The man was running from Laban just as Aaron was fleeing his father's domination. Well, maybe Lehi wasn't running, but he was hiding from the Elders, staying out of the public eye and avoiding Laban in order to keep his family and his property safe. Lehi could offer Aaron some advice before he headed into the hill country south of Beit Zayit, show him the lay of the land, and maybe provide him with a good map. No, it wasn't advice he needed and he knew the land well enough to find his way. He came to Beit Zayit to get Lehi's approval before he left home in search of the freedom to follow his faith. He was doing the right thing and there was no doubt Lehi would agree. He had to. Running away from home was Aaron's best choice.

There were ten measures of flour packed inside the saddlebags next to the smithing tools, a bit of salt, some dried lamb, a sack of wheat, another of barley, and one more of figs. Aaron left five shekels in the pot on the kitchen table to pay for what he'd taken from the pantry. It was enough food to last him until he found work as a traveling black-smith and he prayed that when Mama found it missing, her heart didn't break. She wouldn't know immediately he was gone, not nearly as soon as Papa would see the tools missing. Aaron was a worthless coin fallen through a small hole in the bloated purse of Papa's heart—made rich from his dealings with the Elders—but Mama wasn't so occupied with the business of blacksmithing that she wouldn't soon forget the loss. With any luck she'd replace his absence with the daily pull and tug of the purse strings of her heart—the riches of Elizabeth's growing affection for Zoram, Sarah's precious fits of girlishness, and young Joshua's prized adventures were more than enough to help her forget any pain he caused her. And maybe, just possibly, one day she'd add to her purse the same treasure Aaron left home to find. Maybe Mama would be blessed with the treasures of baptism, too.

Aaron clicked his tongue and pressed Beuntahyu into the narrow passage. She stutter-stepped before relenting to his strong hold on the reins. They were halfway through when Aaron pulled up. The reason for Beuntahyu's resistance stung his lungs and forced a cough from deep in his throat. Aaron sat straight in the saddle. It was a stifling scent, but where was the bad air coming from? He wiped his eyes and peered down through the rocky passage to the far end where the shadows gave way to a dirty, gray light. The smothering smell of burning wood filtered in from the other side and Aaron trotted Beuntahyu through the growing cloud of smoke and out onto the hills above the plantation.

A hundred small fires burned along the slopes of Beit Zayit. Aaron brought Beuntahyu around in a wide circle, scanning the vineyards below. The hillside was covered with a thick black vapor and it turned the afternoon sun into a fiery orange ball. No, not another arson! He couldn't let Lehi lose more of his vineyards and he stabbed his heels into Beuntahyu's side, sending her galloping down through the fog of smoke.

The creek running through the middle vineyards had a good supply of water and Aaron pulled up beside the bank, jumped from the saddle with a water skin in hand and filled it full before leaving Beuntahyu on the road and starting into the middle groves.

There were no flames among the rows of trees, no fires burning about the trunks or leaping across the branches, at least not until he reached the far side where a fire burned inside a ring of stones. The blaze had the strength to jump the rock wall, spread across the dry grasses and destroy the olives. Aaron emptied his water skin on it, raising a shot of steam into the air, but making little difference in the fire's size or intensity.

A long branch lay nearby and he dragged it over and beat on the fire, scattering burning branches and covering himself with ash. He brushed the charred bits of black from his brow and stepped closer, hovering over the fire like a woman before a hearth—a very hot, very fierce hearth.

The flames flared on a breeze and Aaron jumped for cover in a knee-high trench dug about the roots. It was a firewall; it had to be—why else would the plantation servants dig a long, narrow pit about the roots of these olives other than to save them from burning?

Tears stung Aaron's eyes, but it wasn't from the smoke. There wasn't enough of it swirling about his head to cause so many tears. He wiped them away and when his vision cleared he found Ishmael hovering above him, seated on a brown steed. His angel-white hair and beard were filled with flecks of ash, and his brown work robe was dirtied from the smoke of the fire. He carried a long pruning knife in one hand and a stack of dead wood in the other and there was no doubt he was clearing the ground to keep the fire from spreading.

Aaron said, "How much of the vineyard is lost?"

"Lost?" Ishmael inched his mount closer. "We haven't lost any, son."

"That's good news." Aaron waved the branch in the air. "Where's the worst of it?"

"The servants had a terrible time down in the lower vineyards. The smoke hovers there in late afternoon when there's no breeze and it makes if difficult to throw any more wood on the fire."

More wood? Why would Ishmael want to throw more wood on the fire? Aaron lowered the branch to his side. Maybe feeding a fire would burn it out. He said, "Do you know who set it, sir?"

"Well, I did, son." Ishmael reined over to the flames and dropped his load of branches into the fire. "I've been up since dawn kindling these fires, with the help of some of the men of course. You don't think I could raise this much smoke on my own do you, boy?"

Aaron dropped the branch and let it smolder on the ground beside the trench. "You what?"

"I had a little help from the servants." Ishmael cleared his throat. "You don't think I could—"

"Not that, about the fires." Aaron gazed up at Ishmael from the pit. "Why did you set the vineyards on fire?"

Amusement pulled at Ishmael's lips, lifting his beard around a smile and revealing his straight, white teeth. He said, "Its pruning time, son. Didn't I teach you about that the first time we met?"

"You gave me a lecture about the pace of growing sweet olives, sir."

"Ah, yes, the one about the roots and branches; I remember it well." Ishmael leaned back in the saddle. "Did you learn anything from it?"

"It was all about the art of growing roots and branches at the same rate, but never anything about setting the vineyard on fire." Aaron rubbed the back of his head. "You never said anything about that."

"That was a lecture for the growing season, son." Ishmael shifted in the saddle. "Do you see anything growing around here?"

"There are a few young and tender branches, sir."

"There are at that, son, but this is pruning time, not growing time. We've nearly cut away all the old woody branches from the vineyards and thrown them into the fire to be burned." Ishmael reined in under the nearest olive tree, stood in the saddle, and reached up into the tops of the branches. His horse stayed steady while he cut away some of the gnarled old wood. He threw it down into the fire, dusted his hands and told Aaron that he had to cut away the branches that didn't put out much good fruit anymore. He lowered back into the saddle and said, "If we don't prune the old branches every spring they take the strength of the roots for themselves and—"

"And the fruit turns bitter." Aaron smiled up from the trench. "I remember that much, sir."

"No, son, this isn't harvest time, it's pruning time." Ishmael shook his head and flecks of ash fell from his blackened beard. "It's the young and tender branches of new growth we worry about this time of year." He reined in his horse around the base of the tree, peering up into the branches, looking for more old wood. "No need to worry about how fast the branches and roots grow until the early summer." He circled around the tree before sidling in next to the trench. He leaned over the saddle and said, "The first pruning of the year is all about new growth. We cut away some of the old branches, dig about the roots, and nourish them with rotten olives; then we pray for one more thing."

Aaron said, "Sweet olives."

Ishmael worked his fingers through his beard. "You really should stay with your blacksmithing, son, you're very good at that."

Aaron shrugged. "I spend a good deal of time over a hot oven, sir. It doesn't allow for much time cultivating olives."

"I wouldn't expect so." Ishmael pointed his pruning knife at a small branch sprouting from the top of the trunk. "We dig and dung and nourish with rotten olives and if we're lucky we get some young and tender branches like that one."

Aaron lifted his feet, shifted his weight, and immediately the air stung his eyes. There was no reason for it to nip at him. The smoke had shifted, but the stinging was stronger than before. He brushed away the tears, but it didn't rid him of the terrible smell coming from . . .

Aaron glanced at his feet. He stood ankle deep in the dregs of rotten olives, the awful smelling stuff stinging a stream of tears from his eyes and down his cheeks. He lifted his sandals and kicked them clean. He said, "These olives smell like—"

"It's pigeon dung, son."

Aaron jumped from the trench and dragged the bottoms of his sandals through the dirt.

"There isn't anything better than pigeon droppings." Ishmael inched forward to examine the trench. "Once every three years is about the right timing to convince a tree to put out some tender shoots in spring." He laughed and it was like the hooting of an owl, rising from deep in his chest and filling the grove with the happy sound of his presence. "You picked the wrong year to be jumping in these trenches."

Aaron slapped his sandals against the trunk of the olive, spraying the wood with a dirty white residue. He said, "Is Lehi about?"

Ishmael turned down the row and started out of the grove without answering.

Aaron said, "Where are you going?"

"Back to the creek, son." He kept his horse moving slowly through the smoke. "You don't think I'm going to take you to see Lehi smelling like that, do you?"

They reached the main road and Aaron washed his sandals before getting up into the saddle and riding alongside Ishmael, down past the corrals, beyond the pressing yard, through the village of servant homes, and out beside the clear water fountains in front of the estate where the scent filtering from the kitchen hearths replaced the awful memory of dung with the pleasant welcome of evening meal.

The main house stood quiet among the dormant gardens except for a stand of green cedars growing on the shady side. The front doors were open, but there was no stir of anyone about. The balcony shutters of Sariah's bedroom were drawn open and the stout frame of Isabel, Ishmael's wife, passed in front of the window. She carried a bowl of steaming hot water and a linen towel draped over her shoulder and she bent out of sight over Sariah's bed before she spied Aaron looking in at her. Why hadn't Sariah healed? She was a strong woman and she didn't lack for the will to get well. She had the finest doctors to tend to her and there were a host of maidservants to look after her needs.

Aaron slowed in front of the main gates. He said, "How is she?"

"My wife's a good nursemaid."

Of course she was, but that wasn't what Aaron asked. He said, "What about the baby?"

Ishmael turned his steed toward the path running to the back of the estate. He said, "Sariah's picked out a name."

That wasn't what Aaron asked. Ishmael was avoiding his questions. Aaron said, "Then the baby's going to be fine, is that what you mean?"

Ishmael didn't answer and Aaron hurried Beuntahyu along and caught him where the path dipped down into the side yard. He said, "What name did Sariah choose for her baby?"

Ishmael kept his horse moving down through a stand of trees and past the smithy. He didn't speak a word in reply, but his silence was all the answer Aaron needed. Sariah was going to lose the child if she hadn't already. Cursed Daniel! If he wasn't working for Laban, Sariah wouldn't be up in that bed suffering the loss of her unborn.

The gardens behind the estate stood empty. There was not a soul strolling among the hedges—no one to hear the babbling fountains that watered the rose bushes, no one to see the new buds waiting to blossom and no one to take word inside that Sariah's beloved birds had returned from wintering along the shores of the Great Sea and filled the willows at the back of the gardens with the fluttering of feathers and the chirping of spring.

Aaron said, "Sariah should never have bothered to choose a name for the child."

"Don't talk like that, son."

"It's true, isn't it? There isn't going to be a baby, is there?"

Ishmael began to answer, but the sound of cheering carried through the willows, scaring the birds from the branches and drowning Ishmael's words amid a flood of flapping of wings and chirping. The sound drew Aaron through the trees to an open gate and he reined Beuntahyu between the posts. It opened onto a fenced meadow that stretched out to the shores of Lake Beit Zayit with a constant breeze rolling off its blue surface.

Rachel, the eldest daughter of Lehi, stood a little ways down from the gate. She wrapped her babe in a blanket and steadied herself against her sister Leah's shoulder. Leah held her son, Simon, by the hand. The boy still had a thatch of hair that refused to sit down on his scalp, and freckles that dotted his cheeks like the stars of heaven. He spied Aaron sitting in the saddle and tried to get away from Leah, but she kept a firm grip on the boy and thanks be to heaven for that. The last time Simon got loose, he ran about the dining room and skidded across the floor, sticking his nose in Aaron's feet to see the reason for grandmother Sariah's prayers. On this visit he'd no doubt want to see if Sariah's prayers were answered. They were, but this was not the time for Simon to examine Aaron's feet.

The four daughters of Ishmael—Nora, Abigail, Hannah, and Mary—sat a little farther down on the whitewashed planks of the fence, their knees under their chins and their feet lodged between the slats to keep them from falling back into the gardens. It was a perfect perch for a good view and they had reason to stand watch over the meadow, or at least keep an eye on the men standing among the dead grasses of winter. The archers were their future husbands.

Abigail suddenly straightened on the fence, raising her head. It was Lemuel's turn to shoot at a sack of wheat hanging from the branch of a lone olive tree in the middle of the meadow and she wasn't about lose his thin body behind the narrow arms of his bow, not by the way she set her hands on her knees and leaned forward on the narrow plank of the fence. Lemuel sighted down the shaft and Abigail craned to see past her sisters. Lemuel checked the straightness of his aim and Abigail nodded her approval. Lemuel drew the bowstring back and Abigail's hands shot up off her knees ready to clap, her sudden movement forcing her back. She teetered, her arms waving about, and she would have fallen from the rail if her sisters hadn't grabbed her by the sash and kept her perched alongside them.

There was no reason for Abigail to clap in approval of Lemuel's shooting, not by the way he prepared his arrow. Aaron wasn't an archer, but he'd studied the art of bowmanship and Lemuel was not a patient shooter. He crowded the plume end too close to his cheek and when he let go, the feathers brushed his face and steered the arrow off course. It landed a good five paces shy of the wheat sack, the shaft shattering in the rocky soil at the base of the olive tree.

The daughters of Ishmael turned back to their quiet conversations without raising a single cheer—everyone but Abigail. She jumped from her perch, clapped like a gushing patron at a story telling and she would have kept clapping if Nora, her eldest sister, hadn't ordered her back to the fence. Nora kept her voice low, but not so low Aaron couldn't hear her lecture Abigail with the sternness of a mother watching over her young. A bad shot was to be forgotten, not applauded, and if Abigail had any intentions on becoming a good wife she should remember not to stir Lemuel's frail sensibilities. He didn't take well to public loss and she should know better.

Hannah was the quiet sister, though she did giggle when Sam pulled an arrow from his quiver, kissed it, and held it up to the late afternoon sun. She was a good match for the third son of Lehi who never suffered a loss for words. He called across the meadow and told Hannah there was not an arrow that could fly as true as his heart, and judging by the poor grip he used, there was no doubt of that. His voice carried on the breeze and he offered a wager—a kiss if he hit the sack square in the belly, but Hannah would have nothing to do with that gamble no matter how sure the bet. Sam wasn't a superstitious soul, not with the family's business dealings and the accounting ledgers under his charge, though he was nothing but foolhardy with his archery. He quickly drew without taking aim and let go. The arrow caught the fringe of the sack, but passed through and landed a good ten strides beyond the target. Sam bowed and Hannah giggled. He marched over, took her by the hand and she let him hold it awhile before pulling free like a proper woman should. She turned her blue eyes and thin red lips into the shoulder of Abigail's robe and giggled until Sam turned back across the meadow to join his brothers, the breeze bending the brown grasses against his stride.

Beuntahyu whinnied and shook her muzzle when Laman appeared with a long bow strapped over his shoulders. She hadn't forgotten the man's poor stable manners, and the sight of him made her powerful body bristle. Nora was nothing but soft on Laman. She held the top board of the fence with both hands and kept her gaze on Laman, and when he glanced her way, she nodded discreetly, her chin tucked against her neck and her head hardly moving; but it was still a nod of approval for the man she was promised to marry.

Laman lifted his long bow out in front of him, his hand steady and his stance wide and when he drew the bowstring, his back arched with the power of a mighty man. He let go and his arrow raced through the air, but he'd over pulled and it went high, running through the top of the sack, up where the cloth was gathered into a knot. A muffled approval distilled over the gallery like a cold spray of water. Laman cursed his shooting, stabbed the end of his bow into the ground and stared at the target long after it stopped swinging. He'd missed the center.

Mary, the youngest daughter of Ishmael, was the only sister to keep still when her promised took aim. Nephi pulled an arrow from his quiver, but Mary stayed with her arms folded and the white hood of her robe pulled close around her dark hair. Nephi notched the bow to the string, but Mary didn't lean forward from the fence and stare.

Nephi was dressed in a new light blue tunic and kilt that dwarfed his large frame. The wide collar of his tunic fell below his breastbone with enough room for his chest and shoulders to grow strong and straight without having to replace the shirt. The cuffs came well past his wrists and made it difficult for him to get a good hold on the grip. They sagged about the bowstring and he had to brush them aside to keep the cloth from catching in his draw. At a few weeks shy of sixteen years old, Nephi was growing fast enough that there was good reason to weave his clothes this large. In the short time since Aaron had last seen the boy, his round cheeks had flattened against the bones in his face, his shoulders were thicker, his neck wider, and his legs had lengthened enough that he walked with a stout stride. He was growing exactly as Aaron expected he would and he was going to be a good fit with his new steel bow—not perfect, but by the time Nephi was Aaron's age the bow would fit like a well-tied turban. It was unfortunate Aaron didn't have it with him. It would no doubt improve Nephi's shooting. Aaron was certain he'd crafted it with the right blend of metals, and it was a shame he'd never finish the bow.

He still had a horsehair drawstring to weave and a quiver of arrows to fletch, but the invention Sariah had hired him to craft would never be ready for Nephi's birthday. Aaron wasn't going back home.

Nephi assumed a steady stance. He paused with the arrow drawn and he sighted longer than any of his brothers. He was a patient archer and when he let go, the arrow sailed straight to the heart of the sack of wheat, piercing a hole in the center and freeing the grain to trickle from the bag.

Lehi appeared from behind the line of Ishmael's daughters. He'd been watching from the shadows of the willows, but there was no mistaking his resolute stride across the meadow. He was dressed in a red-and-black-striped robe and when he arrived at the sack of wheat he didn't pull Nephi's arrow from the target and declare him the winner. He reached up into the branches of the lone olive tree, cut away the last old growth, and raised it overhead, announcing that pruning time at Beit Zayit was over and, like every year, an olive branch was the prize offered for the winner of the shooting contest for which there was still no champion, not until the last shooter had a chance.

Lehi pointed the olive branch at Aaron and said, "Come out here, son."

He didn't really want Aaron to shoot, did he? Aaron knew the nuances of bowmanship, he'd studied the archers' grip, the balance of a good stance, and the proper pull of a bowstring, but studying archery did not make him an archer. He'd never shot an arrow and he kept out of sight among the willows until Ishmael swatted Beuntahyu on the backside and sent them trotting into the meadow.

Aaron got down out of the saddle. He said, "I don't know the first thing about—"

"Try this one." Nephi handed Aaron his bow.

"I've never done this before."

"It's simple, really." Sam sauntered around behind Aaron, leaned over his shoulder and pointed his forefinger at the target like a carpenter sights down a plumb. He said, "All you do is hit the sack."

What did Sam know about simple? He'd missed the target by ten paces. Aaron fished an arrow from Nephi's quiver, notched it against the string, spread his stance even with his shoulders and turned his left hip to the target. He drew the bow arms to just the right arc and then he sighted down the shaft, waiting for his body to still and the tip of the arrow to stay on the target before releasing his fingers and flighting the arrow across the meadow.

A cry, ten voices loud, scared the birds from the willows. Aaron raised his hand to his brow, shielding his eyes from the rays of the setting sun, and peered at the sack of wheat. His arrow hit dead center, shattering Nephi's arrow and knocking it to the ground.

Lehi presented Aaron with the olive branch. He said, "We have a winner."

"It was luck, sir."

Sam said, "You could make a good deal of money with that kind of shooting." He stood next to Aaron and scratched his chin with the tip of his finger. "What am I saying? I could make a good deal of money wagering on your shooting. They have a traveling circus. Have you ever thought about—"

"Sam." Lehi held up his hand in front of the boy. "Let him alone."

Aaron handed the bow back to Nephi. He said, "I didn't come here to shoot arrows."

Laman stepped around in front of Sam. He said, "What did you come here for?"

Lemuel let out a high-pitched laugh. He spoke through his merriment. He said, "The boy came to bring us more trouble."

"Is there something wrong, son?" Lehi took the olive branch from Aaron. "What's troubling you?"

"I'm leaving and I won't be coming back anytime soon."

Laman folded his arms across his chest, then said, "That isn't such troubling news."

"Enough, son." Lehi stepped between them, blocking Aaron's view of Laman. He said, "Is your father leaving the Council of the Elders to move his blacksmithing to another city?"

"No, sir." Aaron rubbed the back of his neck. "I'm leaving the shop. I'm going to make a life of my own away from here."

"What does your father say about this?"

"He doesn't know." Aaron lowered his head. "He wouldn't let me go if he did."

Lehi laid his hand on Aaron's shoulder. "Your father needs you right now."

"He doesn't need me." Aaron backed away from Lehi's grasp. "He doesn't need anyone. He's stubborn, and hardheaded and—"

"And obstinate." Lehi nodded slowly. "And unforgiving, and demanding, and unreasonable, and . . ."

"You obviously understand why I'm leaving."

"How could I not understand?" Lehi turned his gaze onto his sons. "I have four sons of my own and every one of them have said something like that at one time or another; isn't that right boys?"

Sam and Nephi smiled, Lemuel shrugged, and Laman kept his arms folded across his chest.

Lehi said, "I thank God everyday they're still here with me. They're healthy and hardworking and I couldn't ask for finer men to call my sons." He walked a line in front of them, his hands behind his back like a proud father. He stopped next to Laman and said, "Thank heaven none of them have run away."

Aaron said, "I'm not running away."

"What do you call this?" Sam pointed to the packed saddlebags tied to Beuntahyu's haunches. "A one-day supply of food?"

"I'm only seeking refuge."

Laman said, "Not here you're not. We don't want you on our land."

Aaron turned away from Laman's harsh words. He said, "I'm going to find refuge from my father just like you've found refuge here at Beit Zayit away from Laban and Zadock."

Lehi said, "I'm not hiding from them. I'm—"

"You're doing exactly as you should." Laman's deep voice thundered across the meadow. "The moment you go to Jerusalem Captain Laban will destroy us."

Aaron said, "You haven't gone to Jerusalem since the fire, have you?"

"He hasn't and he never will." Laman stepped between Aaron and Lehi. "None of us are going to Jerusalem until everything returns to the way it used to be."

Aaron said, "When will that be?"

Laman said, "As soon as Uriah's trial is over."

"Nothing will ever be the way it was, son." Lehi lowered his head and his voice was soft as the breeze that crossed the lake. "Unless the Jews return and repent and seek the Anointed One with a broken heart, there is little hope for Jerusalem."

"I don't want to hear anything about destruction." Laman raised his thick arm to Lehi. "That kind of talk got Uriah branded a traitor and thrown in prison."

Lehi said, "That isn't why Uriah's in prison."

Laman rubbed his fingers together as if they were soiled. They weren't, but he kept rubbing them to the pace of his quick speech. He said, "Of course that's why Uriah's in prison. He's a traitor, plain and simple."

"There's another reason, something deeper than what Zadock shares with others," Lehi said.

Laman said, "This is foolishness."

Lehi replied, "We're going to pay a dear price for whatever evil he keeps hidden."

"We've already discussed this a hundred times and nothing's changed." Laman shook his head. "Jerusalem will never be destroyed, not as long as Captain Laban keeps a strong army about to defend the city." He turned his gaze onto Lehi. "We'd all do well not to speak rumors. It will only anger Laban and you saw what he did to Mother."

"Laman's right, sir, and I'm doing the same." Aaron leaned his tall frame against Beuntahyu's side. "I'm leaving Jerusalem to find some peace."

"Listen to me, son." Lehi took Aaron by the arm. "You can't leave your father."

"You're not going to stop me, are you?"

Lehi tightened his grip on Aaron's arm. He said, "There's something you must know about Jonathan."

Aaron pulled free. "There's nothing more to know about my father."

"Hear me out."

Aaron checked his saddlebags and adjusted the stirrups. If Lehi had something he should hear before heading out, he was willing. He said, "What is it I should know?"

Lehi waved Ishmael over and the vineyard master galloped across the meadow, tearing up the grass in his wake. Lehi said, "Have you finished pruning the House of Israel?"

Ishmael said, "Every tree in the vineyard is done except that one."

"Perfect." Lehi stepped past Aaron and mounted Beuntahyu with a quick leap into the saddle. She didn't balk a single step and she grunted her approval at his sitting in the saddle and taking the reins. Lehi leaned over and offered Aaron his hand. He said, "Are you coming?"

"Coming where?"

"To prune an old olive tree."

Aaron rubbed his brow. What kind of counsel was this? He said, "I didn't come here to learn vineyard keeping, sir."

Lehi reined around in front of Aaron. "There's something you should know that only a very old olive tree can teach."

Aaron swung up behind Lehi and wrapped his arms around his sturdy frame. "There's nothing about vineyard keeping that will change my father's heart. He's a stubborn man."

"This isn't about vineyard keeping. Its about your future and your father's future, and it's something you can only know by going deep into a vineyard cultivated with a fine old olive tree." Lehi started Beuntahyu galloping across the open meadow toward the burned trees of the old vineyard. He said, "Its written in the branches of the House of Israel."

Where was Aaron? Jonathan stacked the wood in the firebox. The boy was at the shop early this morning kindling the ovens like a good firemaster should, but he'd not been back since midday meal, leaving Jonathan to sweep the floor and scoop the ashes out of the open hearth. It was Aaron's task to clean up at the end of the day, but since he'd already finished sharpening the knives, filling the cooling cistern with water, and cleaning out the smelting oven for tomorrow's steel-making it wasn't so much work that Jonathan couldn't sweep up for him. Aaron didn't say he was going to pick up work from patrons in the city and he hadn't gone on deliveries—none of the finished work was missing from the shelves.

It was early to end a workday. The sun hung in the western sky and the last warm rays of the day filtered through the open door, but they didn't have power to chase away the isolation of working alone. Jonathan untied his smithing apron, hung it on the peg next to the door and . . .

Where were Aaron's tools? Jonathan lifted the tail of his smithing apron. The rack where Aaron's hammer and tongs should be stood empty. The pickax was gone and the shovel wasn't leaning against the wall. Aaron couldn't have gone to the mine to get more coal. The bins were full and there was no reason to take hammers and tongs to dig in the ground. Jonathan let his smithing apron back down over the empty rack. He stepped into the street and locked the shop door. He'd been hard on the boy, but Aaron wouldn't run away would he? Jonathan pulled the collar of his tunic up around his neck and started out of the smithing district. He had to pick up a broken oil vessel from the temple priest and stop by the brickmason's shop to see about his cracked trowels before heading home, but he couldn't stop thinking that Aaron might have left home. The boy wouldn't do such a foolish thing without asking Jonathan's blessing.

He wouldn't allow it.

Charred trees stood at the entrance to the old vineyard like black skeletons, reminding Aaron of the fire that burned this place to the ground. Ash still stood in pockets over the earth and the remnants of burned branches hung over Aaron, filtering out the sun. If Lehi wanted to teach Aaron a lesson in pruning he shouldn't have brought him here—there couldn't be an olive tree left alive in the old vineyard; at least it didn't seem possible until the desolation gave way to a clearing near the heart of the blackened grove.

A large olive tree grew in the golden light of sunset. It stood far enough away from the other trees that none of its branches were singed and its leaves were free to turn from the dark green of winter sleep to the bright emerald color of spring. The tree had a thick trunk as wide as three horses standing side-by-side. The gnarly wood twisted up from the roots like the worn face of a wise old man watching over this vineyard. It grew among these burnt remains of dead trees, quietly putting forth its young and tender branches and renewing the life that was stolen from the other trees.

"She's the oldest in the vineyard." Lehi reined a circle around the trunk with Aaron holding on about his waist. He said, "It's the only one my grandfather cultivated on this land."

"Bless his soul." Ishmael pulled in beside them. "He named her the House of Israel. I didn't understand why when I was a boy."

Aaron leaned around Lehi's shoulder to get a better view. The tree didn't look any different than any other olive except for the wider trunk and thicker wood, and she did stand taller than most, but beyond that there didn't seem to be any reason to give this one a name—especially such an odd name like the House of Israel.

Aaron said, "Do you understand now?"

"It's part of a story, boy." Ishmael pulled on the end of his beard. "A story told by the prophet Zenos. Do you know it?"

"I'm sorry, sir." Aaron shook his head. "We don't speak much about prophets in our family."

Lehi swung down from the saddle. He gathered tinder out of the dry grasses and kindled a fire. He said, "It's more than a story."

"Amen to that, cousin." Ishmael tied his horse to a branch on the tree and helped gather some sticks to add to the fire. "It's prophecy, pure and simple."

Lehi stirred a stick through the growing flames. "Ishmael and I were young boys when grandfather taught us the story. We were too young to understand it then, but he promised that as we grew older we'd come to see in the story the history of our people from the time Abraham made a covenant with God." He pulled the stick from the fire and pointed the red-hot end of it into the dusky sky. He said, "It's our history from the days of Abraham all the way through to the end of the earth."

Aaron got down from the saddle and tossed a stick onto the flames. "History has little to do with my father."

The sun fell below the western hills and a chill swept over the vineyard. Lehi said, "These are dangerous times, son."

"And," Ishmael added, "your father is in the middle of that danger."

Aaron threw another stick into the flames. "I don't know what you're talking about."

"You have to listen with your heart." Ishmael crouched close to the fire and reached his hands over the flames. He began humming softly, though there wasn't a melody to his singing. He kept his gaze fixed on the fire and repeated a chant or a poem or some sort of hymn. It had a slow, methodical rhythm and the words came from deep in his throat, saying that these were the words of the prophet Zenos—an allegory of an ancient prophet who likened the House of Israel to a tame olive tree which a man took and nourished in his vineyard.

Lehi spoke with Ishmael still chanting softly beneath the normal level of his voice. He said, "The story of the olive tree begins with Abraham." He stepped to the House of Israel and ran his hand over the gnarled wood of the trunk. "The day God made a covenant with Abraham that all the people of the earth would be blessed through his seed was the day this olive tree was first nourished among our people."

Ishmael didn't look up from his stoop in front of the fire. His voice was steady and the lyrical words flowed out of him as if he'd uttered them a thousand times, the soft rhythms of his chanting telling of an olive tree that grew, and waxed old, and began to decay. And the Lord of the vineyard said he would prune it, and dig about it, and nourish it that perhaps it would shoot forth young and tender branches, and not perish.

Lehi reached up and took hold of a young branch sprouting from the bark, up where the trunk of the ancient tree split into many branches. He said, "This tree used to put out a good many young branches in spring, but it's beginning to decay."

Aaron stepped in next to Lehi. "Can you save it?"

"I think it's dark enough." Lehi scanned the sky. "After sundown is the best time to cut out a graft." He took out a small knife, scored the young and tender branch with a v-shaped cut at the base where it sprouted from the trunk and slowly pulled it away from the mother tree. He carried it over to Ishmael's horse, found some olive pulp in one of the saddles bags and packed the scored tip of the branch with a mass of green mush. He said, "That should keep this graft until we find a wild olive tree that will take it."

Aaron scratched the back of his neck. "Why a wild tree, sir?"

"There's no better way to tame a wild tree than with a graft from a good tree like this one. And there are no sweeter olives on the plantation than the fruit of this tree." Lehi wrapped a patch of burlap around the olive pulp and tied it off with a string. "You'd be surprised how many wild olives take hold here on these lands. Ishmael will find a good place to graft this one and preserve the fruit of the House of Israel. And I'll have Ishmael bring in some of the young branches from a wild olive tree and graft them in here." He patted the old tree on the trunk. "That may just be what she needs to keep her from decaying."

Aaron said, "You don't mean to put a wild graft in your finest tree, do you?"

"It's the only way to rid the tree of decay and bring her back to putting out sweet olives on all her branches."

Aaron tossed another stick into the fire, careful not to disturb Ishmael. Why were they telling him about the prophet Zenos and his allegory? It didn't have anything to do with Aaron leaving home to start a new life, and it certainly didn't have anything to do with his father, at least he didn't think it did until Lehi dusted his hands clean, sat Aaron down on a rock near the fire, and told him that the grafting began a hundred and twenty years ago among the Hebrews who lived in the northern kingdom. After the Assyrians conquered the north, they deported thousands to nations along the northern coast of the Great Sea. Lehi held the tender graft with both hands, the burlap wrap poking between his fingers. He went on about the Assyrians importing people from other nations and bringing them to Israel to live alongside the Hebrews in the north. It was like grafting wild and tame branches all about the vineyard and the deportations didn't end with the Assyrians. A good many Jews were taken last year after the war with Babylon and there was no telling how many more Jews would be deported from Jerusalem before the grafting of the House of Israel was finished.

Aaron picked up the young and tender branch Lehi had cut from the trunk. He ran his hand over the burlap cloth that held the olive pulp against the scored end. He said, "Do you really understand all that history from a story about a vineyard master caring for his olive trees?"

"And a good deal more, son." Lehi took the young branch from Aaron and walked it over to Ishmael's horse. He hid it in Ishmael's saddlebag and quickly tied the leather flap, sealing it out of sight. He said, "There are to be others, a very small number of Jews—some of the most important young and tender branches cut from the tree— that the Jews at Jerusalem may never know about."

"What others?"

Lehi said, "That's another part of the story of the olive tree, son."

Ishmael raised his voice. Not so loud to drown out Lehi, but enough that there was no mistaking the words of the allegory, Ishmael slowly chanting that this branch would the Master of the Vineyard hide in the nethermost part of his vineyard to preserve the good fruit of this dying tree in a distant promised land.

Lehi kept his hand on the saddlebag where he'd hidden the graft and slowly stroked the leather. It was an odd thing to do and Aaron said, "You know who those others are, don't you?"

Lehi nodded slowly, but before he could say anything Ishmael stopped his chanting and looked up from the fire. He said, "You shouldn't concern yourself with our troubles."

Their troubles? What did Ishmael's troubles have to do with Jews hidden in a distant promised land that no one at Jerusalem knew about?

Ishmael said, "The parts of the story you must know about are in the main branches, son."

"A story about an olive tree isn't going to change my father's heart." Aaron kicked at the tip of a log burning in the fire and raised a rush of sparks. "Especially one written so long ago by a prophet named Zenos. My father isn't given to believing such things."

Ishmael said, "You can never leave your father until after . . ."

"After what?"

"Listen, boy. Listen with your heart." Ishmael settled his gaze back to the fire. He leaned forward, the light of the flames casting a golden glow over his white beard. His head was steady and his lips hardly moved, but the chanted words of the allegory resonated from deep in his soul, saying, "after many days the tree put forth somewhat a little, young and tender branches, but behold, the main top thereof began to perish and it grieved the master of the vineyard that he should lose this tree. And he plucked off those main branches and cast them into the fire."

Lehi quietly scaled the trunk of the olive tree without troubling the rhythm of Ishmael's chant. He climbed as limber as a child at play, his strong arms pulling his wiry frame into the branches. He pruned away the old wood, threw it down and whispered for Aaron to burn it. They had to burn these cut branches or they'd send out shoots and take root and cumber the ground of the vineyard with wild olives; and the last thing they wanted was for the main top of a decaying tree to take hold in the ground. Lehi cut away the last of the withered old wood before jumping from the branches and coming down next to Aaron. He threw the gnarled length of olive branch into the fire, then said, "This is your father's destiny."

Aaron stood up from the rock. He said, "My father isn't an evil man."

"Didn't you listen to the story, boy?" Ishmael stood from before the fire and turned the full force of his wide-eyed gaze onto Aaron. He spoke quickly, his breath rushing from deep inside him. He said, "The main top of the branches, son. They've gone bad and there's nothing the Lord of the Vineyard can do but cast them into the fire to protect his vineyard and keep the fruit from going bad."

Aaron said, "What are you saying?"

"It's already begun." Lehi leaned a hand against the trunk of the House of Israel. "Zadock controls the Council of the Elders and there's no telling how long it will be before . . ."

Aaron said, "Before what?"

"I'm not certain, but I have this feeling that will not leave me. If I only had some document, some evidence that could help me understand why I feel this way about Zadock and Laban."

"Feel what way, sir?"

"I can't explain it except to say that they will be the undoing of Zedekiah and the only way to stop them is to cut the main branches off and throw them into the fire." Lehi gripped the gnarly bark of the House of Israel. "Otherwise, Jerusalem will be destroyed."

"That's impossible." Aaron walked to the fire and stared into the flames. "Zadock's one of the king's trusted advisors."

"That trust may doom the king."

Aaron folded his arms across his chest. "Zadock's doings have nothing to do with my father."

Ishmael said, "He's part of the Council of the Elders."

"My father's not done anything wrong. He's not like Captain Laban or Zadock."

"The prophet Zenos said the main top of the tree will perish." Ishmael stood next to Aaron. He said, "Your father will perish with them."

"You don't mean that." Aaron backed away from the fire. "You don't think he's going to be killed." He turned to Lehi. "That isn't what you mean."

Lehi said, "Go back to your father. He needs you to show him the way now more than he's ever needed you."

"But I . . ."

"Go back and help him."

"Help him do what?"

"The first day we met I knew you would save my life." Lehi held Aaron's hands in his. "But your father's life is more important than mine."

Aaron said, "My father won't leave the Council."

"Don't give up on him." Lehi's eyes filled with a certain light. He said, "The Lord will soften his heart *again*."

Again? How did Lehi know Aaron had squandered his first chance to share his faith with Papa? Aaron untied Beuntahyu from the tree and swung up into the saddle. He didn't tell Lehi about the neglected promptings he'd dismissed in the shop the night of his failed baptism, but somehow Lehi knew enough to say the Lord would soften Papa's heart *again*. Aaron backed Beuntahyu away from the old olive tree and Lehi walked alongside, telling Aaron the Lord would bless him if he chose wisely, but there was no choice to make. Jonathan would never listen to anything about Aaron's faith. He thanked Lehi for his words, but he couldn't go back and tell Papa about the allegory of the olive tree. Jonathan didn't have the patience to listen to a prophet—living or dead. Aaron was to return to Jerusalem and see to his father's safety, but Jonathan would only dismiss his concerns as the foolishness of a zealot. No, he wasn't to see to Papa's safety. He was to see to his salvation, but Papa didn't want salvation; he wanted a successful blacksmith shop and there was no use returning to help a man who would not be helped.

Aaron thanked Lehi once more before reining out of the vineyard. His saddlebags were packed, he was ready to take his leave and as soon as he reached the road he was going to turn south out of Beit Zayit into the hill country and not have to endure seeing Jerusalem again. He was going to . . .

What was that? He heard his name and he pulled up to look back over his shoulder. Lehi and Ishmael were gathering the last branches from the ground and throwing them into the fire, raising a burst of flames into the evening air, neither of them making any gesture to call him back. That was odd. He was certain he'd heard his name and he prodded Beuntahyu forward, guiding her across the ash-covered ground. They were to the main road when Aaron heard his name again, this time louder than the first, but when he looked about there were no servants riding past, none of the sons or daughters of Lehi or Ishmael. There was no one to speak his name. He was alone and it was nothing more than his imagination.

Aaron didn't turn south toward the hill country. The trade route was an easier ride and he'd go back the way he came and take it south instead of traveling lands he didn't know well. He started up through the vineyards and Beuntahyu lowered her head and pushed her shoulders forward, raising a sweat on her coat and carrying them to the summit. Aaron spurred around before passing to the other side of the cliffs. The sun was gone and he could see the smoldering fires that dotted the vineyards and gave light to . . .

He heard his name a third time. It was as clear as the fresh air rising up from Lake Beit Zayit and pushing away the cloud of smoke from the pruning fires. It came to him in a flash, like the streaking of a falling star painting a glimmer of light across his mind, and he understood that the only way to save his father from the Elders of the Jews was to help hide the young and tender branch, like the one Lehi had cut from the House of Israel and placed in Ishmael's saddlebag. Aaron leaned forward in the saddle and peered down at the old grove. He couldn't see Lehi from this distance, but the light from the fire he tended flickered among the burned trees in that part of the vineyard. Lehi was the young and tender olive branch Aaron was to help hide in the nethermost part of the vineyard. That's what God was telling him and immediately Beuntahyu bristled beneath Aaron. Somehow she sensed the stiffness that pierced Aaron's body to the very center like a hot iron on tender skin, searing deep into his soul. God expected him to help hide Lehi in order to save his father from the Elders of the Jews, but there was a price he would have to pay. Aaron had suffered burned feet, he'd endured the loss of Rebekah, but this hiding of a tender branch in the nethermost part of the vineyard was going to bring him more suffering than he'd ever known before.

Aaron reined about and raced Beuntahyu through the narrow red rock passage. She entered without balking, her muzzle pushed down into the rhythm of her gait. They came out the other side and traversed the winding trail without breaking stride. Aaron let go of the reins after the last switchback and Beuntahyu galloped through the sagebrush and onto the wide, sandy path of the trade route stretching across the plateau. He could ride north and be back in his former home of Sidon in three days. He was known there and he could start work immediately in the shop of one of Papa's friends. He could go south through the hill country and travel to Egypt and see a land he'd only heard of from caravaners and sailors.

Jerusalem's walls and towers and parapets stood on the horizon, decorated by a hundred oil lamps twinkling through open windows. The moon rose above the skyline, casting a soft, white glow across the rooftops. Somewhere below one of them stood his father, waiting for him to come home. It would be simpler to find another home away from this place where he could live without the promise of more pain. Aaron dug his heals into Beuntahyu's haunches and started her running north, up the sandy trail away from Jerusalem. He could be in Sidon by week's end and leave his worries behind.

Aaron wasn't willing to suffer that much for his father.

Ruth untied the last dry tunic, folded it with the other clothes and took down the rope hanging across the courtyard. It was late to be taking down the wash. The sun had set and the cool night air sent shivers through her bones, but she couldn't leave the clothes hanging outside overnight to collect the dew. Aaron was going to need a clean shirt for work at the shop, and Joshua would bring the line down—clothes and all—with his romping through the courtyard first thing in the morning if she didn't remove it now.

The gate swung open and Jonathan stepped in. He didn't usually come home until later and she didn't have his supper ready. The lentils and onions were boiling, but she couldn't add the cut lamb to the stew until the water was lower in the pot and it was sure to be an hour before she was ready to serve him his food. Jonathan wasn't accustomed to waiting and Ruth gathered the clothes into the basket and started to coil the rope.

Ruth said, "You're home early tonight."

"There wasn't much to keep me at the shop." Jonathan scanned the shadows until he found her.

Ruth began to coil the end of the rope around her arm. "I won't have dinner ready for a while yet."

"I'm not hungry."

Not hungry? There was never a time when Jonathan wasn't hungry, even when he was sick he found a way to eat something. Jonathan walked to the far end of the courtyard and picked up the other end of rope. He began wrapping it around his arm, the two of them slowly coming together with each coil. His brow was furrowed like it was whenever he was deep in thought and when he reached the end of his rope and stood next to her, Ruth said, "Is there something troubling you?"

"Nothing." Jonathan took the rope and told her he'd carry it inside. He stuffed the coil under his arm. "Have you seen Aaron?"

"I thought he was with you." Ruth peered around him to the gate, but there was no one. Jonathan had come in alone. She said, "What is it Jonathan? Is there something wrong?"

"I don't know, I . . ."

"Evening, Papa." The voice came from the back of the courtyard, over beyond the dried leaves of the grape arbor. It was Aaron, his tall, thin frame standing among the olive trees like a young branch growing in spring. He'd been there watching them take down the clothing and when he stepped forward he was leading Beuntahyu by the reins. Ruth didn't remember hearing him get the horse from the small stable behind the house, but there he stood, Beuntahyu rigged, the saddlebags packed and ready for a delivery of blacksmithing work or a trip to the mines or some sort of journey. She said, "You're not going anywhere until you've had your dinner."

Jonathan slowly walked to Aaron. He stared at the boy for a moment then passed his hand down along Beuntahyu's powerful haunches to the saddlebags. He unlatched them and rummaged about until he found a forging hammer. He turned it in his hands, the moonlight reflecting off its shiny head, before returning it to the leather pouch and tying it shut.

Jonathan said, "The boy's not headed anywhere tonight."

That was odd. Ruth lifted the clothesbasket to her hip. Why on earth would Aaron go to the trouble of saddling his horse when he wasn't going to take her out?

Aaron laid his hand on Jonathan's shoulder, his fingers trembling just enough to ruffle the collar of his father's tunic.

He said, "You're right, Papa. I'm home for the night."

CHAPTER 23

Where was that leather satchel? Josiah rummaged about in the darkness of the dressing closet just off Mima's palace bedroom. She said the satchel was under the linens on the second shelf, but he could feel nothing large enough to sneak forty-seven scrolls of the law out of the Citadel Building in the middle of morning.

The closet door inched open and light streamed in. It was Rebekah and she was standing in the full light of morning, the rising sun shining through the slats in the shutters and silhouetting her rose-colored robe. Her hair was braided around an ivory bar and the soft light turned the brown strands to gold. She gathered her eyebrows together and held her lower lip between her teeth. "Did you find it?" She hesitated on each word, a certain heaviness weighing down her speech. There was no mistaking her apprehension. She did not want him to go to the Citadel Building, no matter how many times he'd told her that he had to have a complete copy of the law. He didn't have a library at Qumran, only a few scrolls, and if he was to defend Uriah by messenger pigeon, he was going to have to build a library in the desert.

Josiah pushed aside a stack of blankets and felt along the wooden shelf until his hand brushed over the coarse hides of the satchel sewn together with a thick stitch. There it was, just as Mima had promised—a satchel large enough to carry the law. He pulled the strap on over his shoulder, the pouch coming level with his hip and extending a full cubit ahead of his stride. The brass latches were strong, the top flap secure, and he rested his elbow on it. This would make stealing the law much less difficult than hiding it beneath his robe or carrying the scrolls out of the Citadel Building in full view of the guards—to say nothing of any of the Elders who may be about the place. He said, "You stay here and make sure Mulek and Miriam take the pigeons for one last flight. I don't want any of our messages lost."

"There's not been any problem with their training. We could leave immediately without another pigeon run."

"Why are you so anxious to leave the city?" Josiah scratched his bald head. "I thought I'd have to carry you back to Qumran in shackles."

"It isn't safe for us here anymore."

"It was never safe for us here."

Rebekah picked up the coop off the floor and said, "We could be gone before midday."

"I have to get the scrolls and . . ." Josiah took the coop from her and set it back on the floor. "We've not released them from outside the city."

"They're smart little creatures." Rebekah stuck figs through the wicker bars of the cage and the pigeons began nibbling their breakfast from between her fingers. "They can find their way to Mima's window without another day of training."

"Not Samantha." Josiah reached inside the cage and felt about until he got hold of Samantha around the body. She had a bright blue head with a longer-than-usual yellow beak, and the long white stripe down her back didn't fade into the gray feathers when she fluttered about. It was a distinctive marking that none of the other pigeons had and there was no mistaking Samantha from among the other birds.

Josiah stroked her head until she began to coo. He said, "This one's never been very quick to find her way home."

"You know she's lost her left eye. She doesn't see everything the others see. That's all it is."

"I hope you're right." Josiah rubbed the soft feathers above Samantha's iron-red eye. She had lost her eye on one side, but she didn't need her sight to cross the thirty-five miles of sand between Qumran and Jerusalem. Like all pigeons, Samantha was blessed with a bit of iron lodged in a sack at the base of her eye. It was like the pointer on a compass, guiding her straight and true across the open countryside back to her home, the pull of the earth like a magnet drawing her from any quarter in the world. Josiah examined Samantha's single eye. The lid drooped and the empty socket was grown over with a thin layer of skin. She could get to Jerusalem without any trouble, but could she find her way about the city to Mima's window? It was the last leg of the journey that worried Josiah. The other two pigeons had sight in both eyes, and once they arrived at Jerusalem they could find their way among the maze of streets and buildings and stone-walled courtyards, back to Mima's window ledge. But Samantha didn't see all the landmarks that passed below her flight.

Ever since Josiah returned to train the pigeons, he'd sent Mulek out into the gardens every day with the birds to let them loose so they could fly back to Mima's windowsill. Isabel was the first to find her way. It must have been her appetite that drew her back so quickly. She could smell the bits and pieces of figs from every corner of the palace gardens and after some prodding, Jeruzabel and Samantha followed. Josiah started to worry about Samantha the day he sent Mulek outside the palace grounds to let them loose again. Samantha never came back and the prince found her fluttering on a window ledge on the other side of the palace above the storehouse grounds. But since that day she had been perfect, finding her way home on her own, without any help from the other birds. Mulek released them on Main Street, then down in the lower city along Water Street, and finally at the Pool of Siloam, the farthest point south where pigeons flying from Qumran would come over the wall and enter the city. What they had never done was release the birds beyond the south rim of the Mount of Olives, and today was their last chance to see if they recognized the walls of Jerusalem when they cleared the last hill on the mount and started up the Kidron Valley. Josiah kissed Samantha on the beak. He said, "Come home today, girl. We don't have time to come looking for you."

Rebekah said, "We should take the pigeons and leave. The birds know their way about the city and it's . . ."

"It's what?" Josiah returned Samantha to her cage and latched the door shut.

"Laban's men are everywhere inside the Citadel Building. You'll never get up to the council chambers and back without someone seeing you."

"I've never had any trouble getting in and out unnoticed."

"That was before you were dead."

She was right. This was the first time Josiah had left the confines of Mima's quarters, and if anyone recognized him it would be a resurrection of unpleasant proportions. Josiah was a well-regarded man in Jerusalem before his death. It was his notoriety among commoners and noblemen that forced him to hide in this palace bedroom for nearly a week, eating whatever food Mima scavenged from the kitchens and never venturing near the open windows to gather the pigeons from their daily training flights. He was a dead man, and he could no more lift his head among the citizenry of Jerusalem than a ghost could march down Main Street on a feast day without drawing attention—though he'd never known a ghost to have a round face, cherubic red checks, and graying tufts of hair circling the top of a very bald head like his. He pulled on the hood of his robe and pushed his collar up past his cheeks. He said, "We're blessed no one has seen either of us since we came back."

Rebekah returned to feeding the pigeons without saying another word. It wasn't like her not to carry on a conversation until well after every morsel of thought was consumed, or at least picked-over enough that their discussion looked like a pauper's table without anything left to chat about. But there she was, crouching over the pigeon coops, her fingers finding their way through the wicker and not paying any heed to what he had to say.

Josiah said, "It's a very good thing we haven't been found out."

Rebekah took a fig from the bowl, broke it into pieces and kept feeding the birds, her back still turned to him. Josiah ran his gaze about the bedroom, stopping once on the window with its large metal latches and again on the locked door leading into the hallway. Mima left it that way when she went out this morning with the same instructions as every day—they were only to open the door after three knocks and the sound of her voice uttering the password: onion. It was an odd password that they really didn't need. There was no mistaking the sound of Mima's voice, but as long as the password comforted the woman, Josiah endured her attempt at secrecy. He said, "I suppose it would be difficult for anyone to find us here."

Rebekah nodded. "I suppose."

Josiah tapped the side of the leather satchel that pushed against his hip like a woman's wash basket, a very large one with enough room to carry the clothes of a house with ten children all the way to the Jordan River and back. He said, "I'll return as soon as I fill this with scrolls."

He crossed the room and unlatched the door. He was heading into the hall when Rebekah said, "Daniel saw me."

Josiah stood in the doorway. "The blacksmith's son?"

"I'm not certain he saw me, but . . ."

"But what?"

Rebekah folded her arms across her chest. "I was in the market, trying to keep Aaron from spying me and then he came along and, well . . . I thought he was gone, but when I turned about our eyes met and he may have recognized me."

"Is that why you're so anxious to leave the city?"

"We could be on our way now, without worrying about whether Daniel saw me or not." Rebekah lifted the coop by the handle. "You don't need the scrolls. You know the law better than any lawyer."

"Those pigeons won't help us without the scrolls." Josiah uncovered his head. "There may be some obscure precedence of law I don't know about, some odd ruling by an ancient king, or a verdict by the council from years gone by that I've never heard of, and knowing it could help win Uriah's freedom. I have to study every scroll." He leaned over and patted the top of the wicker coop, stirring the pigeons with his rocking of the cage. "These *angels* will bring whatever help I find in the scrolls to Uriah's trial. They're Uriah's *messengers*."

"Let me come with you." Rebekah took hold of the bedpost, the long wooden piece shaking in her hand. "I know my way about the Citadel Building."

Josiah checked the hallway. There were no maidservants cleaning the royal chambers across the hall and the doors to the bathing and dressing rooms were shut. He pulled his hood close against his face, but before going out into the hall he glanced over his shoulder. Rebekah stood beside the wicker coop holding the pleats of her robe. She needed some words of comfort, anything that would keep her from worrying over him as much as he worried over her, but all he could think to say was, "See that the pigeons are back and ready to leave for Qumran when I return." He went into the hallway, latching the door behind him to keep Rebekah safe within, but what he didn't know was that leaving her in Mima's bedroom with the pigeons was more dangerous than anyplace he could hide her.

The birds could give them all away.

Chief Elder Zadock carried the last stack of scrolls across the large chamber, his sandals shuffling over the marbled floor and the quiet sound of his footsteps fading amid the arches and beams of the high ceiling. The sweet scent of frankincense burned from the brass bowl near the window, a plume of smoke rising up and disappearing through the silk curtains on the balcony. Zadock studied best with the room perfumed, and he left word with the Citadel Building guards that he was not to be disturbed until he finished reading for the day. The watchmen with their constant checking and re-checking were not only a bother, but Zadock lost a good twenty shekels worth of frankincense every time they opened the main doors and let the breeze blow the scent right out into the street. Did the watchmen think Zadock could afford to perfume the entire city?

Zadock dropped the armful of scrolls on the council table next to the others—forty-seven in all—and returned to his red-cushioned chair. He unraveled the first one, pulled the wide sleeves of his black robe back to the elbows and laid his long, thin arms over the parchment. Treason was Zadock's only charge against Uriah and he had to find another of equal gravity to ensure Uriah didn't escape the trial with anything less than a sentence of death. The man had to die in prison along with what he knew about Captain Laban. Lehi could never know he was the rightful heir to the brass plates and the sword of Joseph—that was a secret to be sealed in Uriah's grave.

Zadock leaned forward in his chair, his gaze moving quickly over each line in the scroll. He spent most mornings sequestered in the council chamber reading through the law, searching for vagueness, points of ambiguity—any technicality he could use to ensure Uriah's death sentence. The man preached in favor of the Babylonians and he fled to Egypt to escape punishment, but that wasn't enough to prove him guilty. The most damning evidence against Uriah was the letters locked away in the basement vaults at Fort Lakhish. Uriah intercepted the military documents en route to the fort and Governor Yaush had seen him do it, but Hebrew law required two witnesses, and though Yaush was to testify, Zadock could never bring the Lakhish Letters to trial as the second witness. No one could know what they contained—there were enough subtle references dropped into Laban's letters that an intelligent lawyer could uncover their plot to assassinate King Zedekiah. Zadock couldn't destroy the letters until the trial was over, their very existence upheld Governor Yaush's testimony, but they were to be kept at a distance. No one could study them, no one was to read them, and they weren't to be brought to trial; the risk of being found out was too great. Zadock removed his turban and shawls and set them on the chair beside him. Lord Yaush's testimony was going to have to be enough to convince King Zedekiah of Uriah's treason, and if he could keep Uriah from hiring a lawyer there was a chance Uriah would never ask to see the letters at trial. Yaush could testify he'd seen Uriah intercept the letters. He could also testify that the letters were safely locked away in his vaults, and Zadock would prove his case against Uriah with a single witness.

Zadock finished the first scroll and he quickly moved on to the next one. He thumbed through the stack of scrolls, past the ones recording the days before the kings when judges ruled Judah. The second stack were scrolls recording the interpretation of the law during King Solomon's rule, three more from the days of King David, and one each from the rule of Kings Asa and Jehoshaphat. Zadock stopped his long, bony fingers on the scroll from the days of King Hezekiah one hundred and twenty years ago and pulled it from the stack.

It was an obscure scroll, one he'd never read, but if there was anything that could help him, he had to know. Zadock unsealed it, rolled it out on the tabletop and leaned over the parchment. It was written in old Hebrew by the prophet Micah, but not so old he didn't understand the colloquialisms of a time gone by. The scroll began with the usual long-winded salutation about the word of the Lord that came to Micah the Morashite in the days of Hezekiah, king of Judah, which he saw concerning Jerusalem. There was a long tirade about the fall of the northern kingdom that fell during Micah's life and then a good many lines about destruction and the usual drivel of wars and calamities, but nothing that could help Zadock in his trial against Uriah. At least it didn't seem there was anything until he reached the end of the third section of writing where Micah the prophet said that Zion would be plowed like a field, and Jerusalem should become heaps, and the mountain of the house—Solomon's temple—would be destroyed.

That's what Zadock needed. Blasphemy was the charge he could use against Uriah. There was no law against a man predicting wars and destructions and scourges against the people of Judah, but preaching the destruction of Jerusalem was forbidden and speaking that the temple, the very house of God, was to be destroyed, well that was a crime worthy of death. Zadock skipped down the parchment to where the Elders of the Jews brought Micah to trial before King Hezekiah, charging that he said Jerusalem and the temple would be destroyed. Zadock held his forefinger on the line to keep his place. Why didn't he think of this sooner? Zadock had a good case for treason, but if he could trick Uriah into speaking against Jerusalem and the temple he was sure to add blasphemy to the man's list of crimes.

Zadock inched to the edge of his chair. He had to know the result of Micah's trial and he quickly read on, searching for King Hezekiah's verdict. If Micah was found guilty, then the possibilities for success against Uriah were growing. He set his elbows on either side of the parchment and rested his brow in his hands. The main doors to the chamber inched open.

"Zadock, sir. You're to come immediately."

It was Daniel, the new officer Laban appointed over his fifty. He stood at the far end of the council chamber, his hand on the butt of a newly issued sword, and his chest heaving for breath from climbing the stairs to the council chambers. He pulled his dress blue tunic taut by the tails, his thick shoulders pulling the shirt tight about the collar. His voice boomed about the room with the authority of a commanding officer, but for all the strength of his arm and the confidence in his manner, he was going to have to learn some protocol. Zadock was to be addressed as Lord Zadock and then only after a proper bow, and Daniel had done neither. Why was it so hard to train soldiers these days?

"What is it?" Zadock rolled up the scroll of Micah and set it atop the others. The outcome of Micah's trial held the key to building a case for blasphemy against Uriah, but studying it was going to have to wait until after he dealt with this interruption. He said, "I left orders I was not to be disturbed by anyone."

"Captain Laban sent me."

"What does he want now?"

"I'm not exactly certain, sir, but he said it was urgent." Daniel straightened against the tall cedar door, his shoulders back and his chest pushed forward. "He needs you at the stables immediately."

"Stables? Curse him, why does he always want to meet at the stables? It has such an awful smell and . . ." Zadock blew out the flame in the incense bowl and scowled at the glow of morning light that shone through the silk curtains. "Have you looked outside?"

"I walked here straight from the palace. Is there something I should have seen?"

"The day, boy, did you see what kind of day it is?"

"It seems fair enough."

"I don't like fair." Zadock parted the curtains. "There's far too much sun." He pulled the curtains shut, the silks streaming on the breeze. "If I must attend to the multitude of Laban's urgencies, we shall do it by way of the alleys. There's more shade along that way."

"Very well." Daniel held the chamber door open. "Shall we go?"

The boy wasn't a complete loss. He was learning some etiquette. Zadock placed his shawls over his graying hair and fitted the turban in place before turning into the hall. He headed toward the back of the building, away from the main stairs when Daniel said, "Sir, that isn't the way to the main doors."

"There's another way out that only a few know about. If you're going to work with Laban and me it's time you knew about it." Zadock motioned for Daniel to follow him. He led him around a wall of stone that looked to be a dead end, but hidden behind a tall, standing urn filled with palm branches was an opening that led to the top of a stairwell, spiraling down twenty turns to the main floor. It was like the entrance to a catacomb with a low-lying ceiling and narrow walls cut through the rough-hewn stone. Zadock pointed down the stairs and told Daniel he was to go first. He said, "I don't like anyone walking behind me."

Zadock followed, one hand on his turban to keep it from coming loose against the low-lying stones, and the other feeling his way along the wall. He said, "What could be so urgent that Laban needs to speak with me now? He knows I'm busy."

"It was something about pigeons." Daniel disappeared around the curve of the stairwell and Zadock hurried his stride to keep up, but not so fast that he lost his footing or his turban. Daniel said, "I really didn't understand any of what the captain was talking about and when he ordered me to fetch you, I came right away."

"Pigeons?" Zadock followed Daniel around two more flights, each one with a narrow window cut through the stone to allow in some air to freshen the musty smelling place. "Why pigeons?"

"He didn't explain any more than . . ." Daniel stopped without giving notice and Zadock ran up against him, his chin poking into the boy's rigid back. Zadock righted himself, straightened his robe over his shoulders, and said, "What is it, boy?"

"It's just a, a . . ." Daniel turned sideways and there, standing in front of Zadock was an old manservant trying to get past. He was wearing a tattered brown robe with the hood pulled across his face. He slapped a large leather satchel that hung at his side and said, "I have the council chamber to clean."

There was a familiar tone to his voice. It was deep but cheerful, and it had a rhythm that turned Zadock's gaze onto him. He would have spoken to the man or at least asked his name, but there wasn't time. Daniel had already pushed down around the next turn and Zadock did the same, turning sideways to let the old man by, but when they brushed robes the man's hood pulled to the side and Zadock caught a quick glimpse of his profile. No, it wasn't even a glimpse, it was a flash of the man's countenance. He had red cheeks and a nose that turned up shorter than most. Somewhere, deep in Zadock's memory, he knew the man, but he couldn't remember exactly where. It wasn't like Zadock to take note of the help; he didn't have time to worry about the men and women who cleaned up after him, but there was something about this manservant and he stopped on the stairwell and watched him turn out of sight.

Daniel came back up the stairs. He said, "Do you know the man?"

"Why do you ask?"

"No reason. I saw him leave the palace about the same time I did."

"What was he doing there?"

"I suppose he cleans the chambers in both buildings."

"I didn't know we shared the same servants with the royal family."

"Do you want me to go back up and see to him?"

"Enough about the help." Zadock spun around, the hem of his robe lifting about his feet. He said, "What was that you were saying about Laban's pigeons?"

Mima set Dan and Benjamin in the chairs facing the open window and told them not to say another word about her green and yellow skirt that wrapped about her middle like a Persian juggler. And if they giggled one more time about the matching scarf around her brow and the brass baubles hanging from her ears she was going to make them take another bath. If there was ever a signal fire or a warning flare that could be seen at midday she was it, and these boys were going to have to endure her until their mother returned. Miriam was gone with Mulek to release the pigeons, and tending to these boys was the least she could do to make certain the birds had one last flight from outside the city walls before Josiah and Rebekah left for Qumran.

Mima placed a bowl of figs on the sill between Dan and Benjamin and told them not leave their chairs until they were finished or they'd turn into pillars of salt. And when Dan threatened to get down and make another mess with his collection of colored rocks he'd scavenged from the banks of the Jordan River, she reached into her pocket and produced a piece of rock salt she'd taken from the kitchen, telling him it was the leftovers from the cobbler's son and if he didn't mind her and stay put, he was going to end up just like the boy she held in her hand— a pitiful little white mineral fit to be crushed and sprinkled over dinner.

Mima stumbled over the colored rocks strewn across the floor. She caught herself against the bedpost and told the boys they were going to have to keep their room better. They giggled and she told them she could touch these rocks and turn into an evil toad and eat them, but when her skin didn't turn a wart-laden green and her tongue didn't grow long enough to catch flies, the boys turned back to the bowl of figs—one for Benjamin and three for Dan. These princes were not the easiest lot to entertain, to say nothing of the difficulty of scaring any sense into them.

Mima was setting the rock collection on the shelf when Captain Laban marched through the bedroom doors and ordered her to follow him. He gave her only a moment's notice to find a maidservant to watch over the boys, before repeating his demand that she come immediately. If she wasn't working for him, she would have told him exactly what he could do with his demands. He led her on a hurried march, down the back stairs and through the kitchens without taking even a breath of midday meal—something Mima could never do and she paused at the door long enough to sniff at the air—lamb with a hint of basil.

Captain Laban turned down the hall and out into the palace store-house, moving at such a frantic pace Mima lifted her skirts out of her stride to keep from going down. She wasn't about to fall twice in the same day and what an awful landing she'd make in the puddles from last night's rains. A woman of her size would break clean through the cobble-stone, and they'd never find her planted twenty cubits deep with the dark mud masking her black skin. There was hardly a dry place to step among the wine merchants and wheat vendors hauling their goods inside the storehouse, but Laban insisted she keep up. She jumped the puddles, skirted past the mule carts, and ducked into the archway after him.

Laban stopped in the shadows. He peered out the other side, into the sun-drenched corrals of the palace livery. He said, "Do you see that?"

She saw it, and she bit her lip to keep from saying that everything wasn't as it appeared. The stone archway framed the sight of Miriam standing near the first stall, her hair pulled back and tied behind her head with a pink bow. She wasn't wearing riding boots or a cloak, but she directed the master of the livery like the captain of a cavalry, telling him to saddle Mulek's horse with a medium chair-saddle and tie the stirrups up high for better control. Miriam was wise not to ask for a horse of her own. She was a skilled rider and she was sure to glean Laban's suspicion if he knew.

Mulek stood beside Miriam, his new riding boots reaching up past his knees. He was carrying a pigeon coop with Samantha, Jeruzabel, and Isabel fluttering about inside.

Laban said, "Tell me what you know about that?"

Mima sighed. Why did he have to inquire about the birds? She said, "Miriam doesn't really know anything about riding, sir. She's just going to walk alongside the boy while he learns to handle a horse."

"The pigeons, tell me about the pigeons. The boy takes them everywhere."

"He enjoys the birds." Mima glanced back toward the palace. She said, "I have Miriam's other children to look after." She lifted her skirts and started out from under the archway, headed back toward the palace, but Laban took her by the arm and pulled her back to his side. He said, "I've seen the boy release the pigeons in the palace gardens day after day." He turned the full force of his gaze onto Mima. "I spied him last week releasing them in the streets of the lower city."

"It's child's play, nothing more, Captain."

"You're certain?"

"The boy's fascinated with the birds. He takes them out to see if they can find their way back to my window. He won't be still until he's tried them from a new spot each day."

Laban pulled on the tip of his beard. He said, "Do they find their way home?"

"You didn't really bring me all the way out here to discuss pigeons, did you?"

"He must be training them."

"To do what? Fly back to my window?" Mima shook her head, her thick curls of black hair bobbing over her scarf. She said, "I brought the birds to the palace to get close to the boy. Miriam never lets him out of her sight, but now she lets him come to my bedroom and play with the birds, alone."

In company with Daniel, Zadock turned into the archway. He had a narrow stride and he would have toppled over on the least bit of breeze had there been any blowing. He stepped past Mima without according her the least bit of a glance and squinted up at Laban. His thin voice echoed through the archway. He said, "What is it that couldn't wait till evening? You know how I hate going out during the day."

Laban said, "I was wrong to send for you."

"Wrong about what?"

"The pigeons." Laban pointed toward the livery where the stable-master was strapping the pigeon coop to the saddlebags of Mulek's horse. "I was worried about Mulek's pigeons."

"You sent for me to tell me the prince has a new pet?" Zadock threw his hands in the air. "You're losing your mind, Captain."

Daniel leaned forward to peer into the light of the livery stables. His voice was soft. He said, "I thought I was losing my mind when I saw the potter's daughter."

Zadock slowly turned his head, the shawls of his turban not moving from off his shoulders. He said, "You saw who?"

"Rebekah, sir." Daniel turned back from staring into the livery long enough to say, "The potter's daughter, you know the one, the dead girl." He turned back to watch Mulek fussing with the reins of his horse and Miriam checking the stirrups and riggings about the horse. They were about to take their leave and Daniel said, "Does the queen know how to ride?"

Zadock came around in front of Daniel, blocking his view of the livery. He lowered his voice, the shrillness reduced to a rasp. He leaned forward and said, "Are you certain you saw Rebekah?"

"I didn't really see her. I thought I saw her."

"Did you follow her?"

"I tried, but when I got through the crowd she was gone." Daniel scratched the side of his head. "Or she was never there to begin with."

"Tell me, boy." Zadock took Daniel by the arm and shook him. "Was it her or not?"

"It was like seeing a ghost if that's certain enough for you, sir." Daniel pulled free and straightened the cloth of his sleeve. "It wasn't anything that should—"

"Get your men and meet me at the Citadel Building." Zadock started down the archway, the sleeves of his robe flapping about his wrists.

Daniel said, "What is it, sir?"

Zadock stopped at the end of the archway, where the light met the shadows. The Chief Elder didn't go out into the sun immediately. He stood there, his face shrouded by the light streaming down behind him and casting only shadows across his face. He said, "The old manservant in the stairwell, the one with the leather satchel. I remember his voice now. It was Josiah the potter."

Laban said, "That's impossible; we buried him and his daughter months ago."

"Had you read the prophecies of the Rekhabites you'd know something about resurrection." Zadock snapped his fingers and sent Daniel marching from under the archway to muster his men to the Citadel Building. When the sound of his leather boots faded around the corner, Zadock said, "Are you coming, Captain?"

"I have business to attend to other than chasing ghosts." Laban started toward the livery stable. Miriam and Mulek were leaving the yard by the far gate and before Laban disappeared into the mass of stable boys running buckets of water and delivering hay to the stalls, he said, "I'd like to see exactly where Miriam and Mulek are headed with their pigeons."

Mima stayed beneath the archway long after Zadock and Laban had left. Her heart was filled with indecision and her legs would not carry her. Should she warn Miriam that Laban was following her, or should she go fetch Josiah out of the Citadel Building before Daniel and his men descended on him? The Chief Elder was breathing life into Josiah's dead soul, and as soon as he was gone from the city the suspicions would die with his departure. Mima started toward the livery, but stopped before passing from under the arch. Something whispered that she wasn't to go there. She hurried back down to the other end, but when she turned toward King Street there was still no peace in her breast—she was not to go to the Citadel Building, no matter how dangerous things had become for Josiah. It wasn't until she turned back through the storehouse yard that the indecision left her soul. She plodded through the puddles, in through the kitchens and up the stairs to her bedroom. She knocked on the door—three taps followed by the password: onion. Rebekah didn't answer and when Mima tried the door, the latch fell open in her hand.

The bedroom stood empty, a draft sneaking through the shuttered window and lifting the white linen curtains. She threw them open and scanned the sky for the pigeons, but they were not circling above the palace. She leaned out and checked the stone ledge, but still no birds. Rebekah was to collect them as soon as Mulek and Miriam released them, but Rebekah was nowhere to be found. Mima came back inside and checked the closet, looked under the bed. There was no sign of anyone—no pigeons, no potter, and no Rebekah. Mima leaned against the bedpost. There was nothing she could do but wait here and, heaven willing, it would be a short wait.

The Chief Elder's hunt allowed little time for error.

Daniel threw open the gates of Laban's estate and ordered the watchmen to sound the first call—three long blasts on the shofar horn to assemble his swordsmen—the sound of it echoing off the high stone walls before dying in the gardens. Eight soldiers filed out of the servants' quarters, with two more joining them from inside the estate. When Daniel saw them he turned about-face and started around to the back of the estate shouting orders at his men who were still strapping on their swords and pulling on their shirts. They were to capture an intruder at the Citadel Building and there was no room for error. Whoever it was, he was a master of disguise—he'd eluded them once before, but not again. The last time he was sighted he was wearing a tattered brown robe with the hood pulled up over his balding head. Daniel led them out the back gate and onto Market Street, shooing the shoppers out of his way like a seasoned officer, though these women didn't obey like good soldiers and he pushed them aside to open a path for his men. They filed under the government arch, two abreast, and fanned out onto the square in front of the Citadel Building. Daniel sent three men to the alley with orders to come up the back stairs and meet them at the council chambers. He stationed two more on the front steps telling them to look for a brown-robed man with a large leather satchel over his shoulder. He pushed open the main doors, the long wood planks banging open against the inside wall. His men followed him inside, their boots thundering over the stone. The echo of their swords unsheathing from the leather casings sounded about the lobby, startling the accountants and businessmen out of their path. Daniel scanned the faces retreating to the edges of the lobby, searching for Josiah the potter, and when he was certain the brown-robed man wasn't among their number he took their search up the main stairs.

They were to the third floor and panting for breath when they came across a woman hurrying down. She had a white shawl over her head and another covering her face so that her eyes were the only things visible between the wraps. She wore a delicate light-blue linen robe with sashes and bows, and the cloth was perfumed with the finest scents. And except for her large stomach, she was a well-proportioned woman with a strong gait. There was no doubt she was a noblewoman and when she lowered her head and tried to pass, Daniel ordered his men to let her be. He didn't bother to ask her name or the nature of her business in the building, and he started back up the steps.

Daniel rounded the last turn in the stairwell and found Zadock on the landing, his finger pressed to his lips, and there was no doubting his silent command. They were to slow their climb, hold their swords close against their stomachs, and still the leather straps about their helmets. When Daniel cleared the last step, he found the reason for Zadock's silence. A man stood at the far end of the hall, pulling on the locked doors of the council chamber, testing them, prying at them to come open. It was the potter and he was dressed as Daniel remembered him—an old brown robe, the cloth tattered, and the hood rising to a point at the top.

Daniel motioned with his fingers for two men to stay on the landing while the others followed him. He came up behind the potter, the tip of his sword stretched out level with his head. He said, "Step away from the door."

The potter slowly came about and there, standing before Daniel was a noblewoman, her dark braided hair spilling out of her hood and her red cheeks lifting into a smile. She pushed the tip of Daniel's sword aside and said, "Are you the one they sent to let me in?"

Zadock pushed past the circle of soldiers. He said, "Who gave you that robe?"

"This thing?" The woman removed the thick outer robe, revealing the elegant silk dress that fell from her shoulders and tied about her hips with flowing sashes. "The manservant with the large satchel gave it to me." She dropped the robe on the floor in front of Daniel and smiled at him with her pomegranate-red lips. "My husband is downstairs taking care of some business, something to do with taxes."

Daniel picked the robe up off the floor. "I asked you, who gave you this?"

"I met the manservant in the hallway and he told me they wouldn't allow any women on the council chamber balcony, and since I've always wanted to look over the square from up here, he was kind enough to loan me—"

"Curse him!" Zadock pushed the woman aside, unlocked the chamber doors and stormed to the council table. He said, "He took them."

"What is it, sir?" Daniel came up behind the Chief Elder.

"The law, it's gone." Zadock ran his hands across the empty tabletop. "Every last scroll."

Daniel crossed to the balcony and held the silk curtains aside for Zadock to pass. They leaned over the railing and searched among the white-robed priests filing out of the temple gates and the legion of businessmen and lawyers scaling the steps of the Citadel Building for any sign of . . .

"Over there." Daniel pointed up King Street. A mule cart rolled over a white cloth and the wheel threw it up into the air. It was the one the potter had over his head and it fluttered back to the ground to be trampled underfoot by the mule. Daniel turned his gaze farther up the street and spied the woman's outer robe—a light blue cloth with bows and ribbons. It lay in a heap along the walls of the palace and beyond that, up near the main gates was another white wrap. Daniel pulled back from the railing, but before he could say anything Zadock said, "Send your men to meet me at the palace. I'm going to see that they search every room. If the potter's alive . . ." He stuck his hands beneath the pleats in his black robe. "I'm going to right that error."

Daniel started back through the council chambers. He said, "I'll have my men at the main gates."

Zadock stood on the balcony entrance, the silk curtains lifting about his turban. "Send your men, but you go to your brother and tell him that Rebekah is alive."

"We don't know that."

"That's precisely why I want you to tell him. If it was Josiah who stole these scrolls then they're both alive and your brother is the one man who would know it."

"Aaron won't trust me with that."

"He doesn't need to; he'll tell you everything you need to know by his passions."

"What passions?"

"The fury of lost love burns in your brother's heart." Zadock passed his tongue over his parched white lips. "If Aaron grows angry at the news you bring him then you can be certain that Rebekah's dead."

"And if what I say doesn't anger him?"

"Then you can be certain he's hiding the knowledge that Josiah and Rebekah are alive."

"You don't know my brother. He's not quick to anger."

"He loved her, didn't he?"

"Well, yes, but . . ."

"Then he'll tell whether or not Rebekah's alive without ever telling you. Now go!" Zadock raised his hand in the air, the sleeve of his black robe flapping about his wrist. "Find out if Rebekah and her father are alive."

Miriam led Mulek's horse down through the stand of sycamore and locust, the first buds of spring fattening on the leafless branches. Jerusalem's south wall rose above the trees, each giant stone as large as an elephant and stacked one upon the other into a great cliff. It didn't seem possible that the prophets were right, that the city of Miriam's birth would ever be destroyed. This was the Eternal City, the city of God and she turned her gaze away from the high parapets and ensign flags flying atop the wall.

Mulek's head bobbed like driftwood on the Galilee, his thin body swaying about at the whim of the horse's powerful stride and his speech littered with stuttered phrases. He never spoke clearly when he was riding, his chin shaking about and his body bouncing in the saddle. Blessedly the coop hadn't come loose from the saddlebags. She'd tied them down with a good many pin-knots and there was no way they were going to come free. The pigeons weren't to be released until they were beyond the hills—out of sight of the wall of the city—and if the coop fell to the ground the weak wicker would never hold and the birds would fly away home without a good test of their steering senses.

The road turned away from the city and up a rise out of the Kidron Valley. They were alone without any mule carts raising miserable clouds of dust, and no rocks strewn about to hinder the horse's stride. A grove of cedar with thick, green branches cast a shadow across their path, hiding this stretch from the view of the city walls. It was the perfect piece of road where no one could see them running the horse at full gallop. Miriam should have known better than to ride in daylight on a public road. The queens of Judah did not ride on the back of a horse, but she wasn't like other royal wives. She checked to make sure they were alone and then she quickly pulled herself into the saddle, took the reins in both hands with Mulek nestled between her arms and they were away, galloping through the cedars, the sweet scent of pine filling the air. Miriam leaned forward, her chin nestled on Mulek's shoulder and her braided hair lifting on the air. They were free, if only for a moment, from the watchful eye of—

What was that running through the trees? Miriam pulled up and came around, her gaze quickly moving among the cedars lining the road. Was it another rider following them?

Mulek turned in the saddle. He said, "What is it, Mother?"

"I don't know. I thought there was a . . ."

"A what?"

"It's nothing, dear." Miriam slowly reined into the trees. It was a dense grove, with low-lying scrubs and tall cedar casting a deep, cool shade over them. She said, "Shall we have a look?"

"We can't ride through there, not with all these trees."

He was right, but that didn't keep her from the challenge. Miriam told him to hold on and spurred the horse forward, jumping three bushes, dodging a wide limb, and racing down a ravine and over a creek bed. A wall of rock stood along the far bank and Miriam pushed the steed over it, the animal leaping into the air with the strength of ten men and landing atop the outcrop with the precision of a bird landing on a window ledge. The steed climbed the embankment, grunting to the top and Miriam held onto the horse's mane to keep Mulek from falling off and pulling them both to the ground. If there were a horseman following them, she'd lost him among the pines. They came onto a clearing of sagebrush and brown grasses and Miriam brought the horse around, facing back toward the city. They'd come around the bend, the Mount of Olives shrouding their view of the city walls.

Miriam tied the steed to the trunk of a cedar while Mulek unlashed the coop from the saddlebags and set the birds in the middle of the clearing. He opened the wicker gate, took out the pigeon named Jeruzabel and lifted her to the sky. He said, "Find your way home little creature." Jeruzabel leapt from his hands and soared south toward Bethlehem. Mulek leaned up on his toes, his gaze following her route. He said, "She's going the wrong . . ." Before he could finish, Jeruzabel came around in a wide circle, her head down and her wings riding on the breeze. Josiah said the pigeons were guided by a compass of sorts planted deep in their eyes, and if he was right then Jeruzabel had gotten her bearings and the compass was pointing her beyond the Mount of Olives toward home.

Mulek released Isabel next. She fluttered up into the branches of a cedar and peered down at them. She preened a moment, turned her head about, and then she was off in a flurry of feathers, flying low over the trees toward Jerusalem and disappearing out of sight.

Samantha was the last pigeon Mulek took from the coop. He stroked the white band of feathers on her back and told her she could find Mima's windowsill all by herself, he was certain of it. He raised her to the air and—

"Are you enjoying your morning ride through the hills?" Captain Laban reined out of a dense stand of cedars, his white Arabian chafing at the bit and arching her braided mane against his pull. She was a beautiful beast with powerful legs, a well-curried coat, and a saddle with silver studs and emeralds sewn into the leather. He said, "I had no idea you could ride a horse like that, my lady."

Miriam hurried to Mulek's side and held the boy as close to her breast as he was holding Samantha to his chest. "We're enjoying our ride, thank you, Captain."

"You really should tell me when you leave the palace. It isn't wise not to have you and the boy accompanied by some of my men." Laban patted the Arabian on the neck. "It isn't safe outside the city walls. You could end up dead like the potter." He spurred over next to Miriam. "Did you hear about him? I received a report that Josiah the potter may still be alive."

"I wouldn't doubt it."

Laban leaned over the saddle; close enough that Miriam could feel his breath across her face. He said, "Doubt what, my lady?"

"The potter was a persistent man in life. I would expect his spirit to be as unrelenting in death."

"This isn't a matter for humor."

"I don't find any of this amusing, Captain."

Laban sat up in the saddle. "They're searching for the potter as we speak."

"You're wasting your time. The man's dead." Miriam led Mulek around to the other side of her brown steed away from Laban's view. She quickly unlashed the saddlebag and retrieved a small papyrus, a length of string, and a stylus with just enough dried ink in the tip to scratch a few legible words. She said, "The potter's been dead for months and I think you should let his memory die with him."

"I curse his memory." Laban reined his Arabian around, leaving Miriam out of his view long enough for her to write the only thing she could think to save the potter, before dropping the stylus on the ground and holding the note in the palm of her hand. Laban came full around and said, "If we find him alive, he'll pay for his treason."

"I'm sure you'll see to that." Miriam took Samantha from Mulek and nestled the bird against her chest. She worked the note around the pigeon's leg and with her forefinger and thumb she secured it in place with the string. She said, "Is there a reason you bother me with the details of the potter's death?"

"His life is what should bother you."

"Captain, I'm on an outing with my son, if you don't mind." She handed Samantha to Mulek. "There you go, son. Why don't you release her?"

Mulek lifted Samantha to the sky, but she didn't take flight. She sat in Mulek's palm, her head turned to the side and her one eye focused on Laban. She shook her head, preened her neck, and then stared again at the captain. Mulek poked the feathers on her underside, but she refused to fly.

Laban reined over and snatched the pigeon from Mulek, gripping her about the breast. Her legs poked through his gloved hands. The knot in the string came loose, leaving the note holding on with only one strand. Laban said, "You have a lot to learn about releasing a bird."

Miriam said, "He enjoys playing with the fowls, Captain."

"He should learn to deal with them better." Laban held Samantha over his head. He said, "See here, Your Highness. This is how it's done." He threw Samantha into the air and she immediately flapped her wings, the note flailing loose about her leg and certain to come free before she reached the palace. Samantha rose above the trees and disappeared beyond the branches, and Miriam prayed that the note would hold until she arrived at Mima's window. And since this was Samantha—the pigeon with a single eye—she added a second prayer.

Help the bird find Mima's window.

Cursed coal bins!

Daniel peered through the fine powder floating about the shop. It had to be the bins. Nothing dirtied the air with filth as much as stocking them with coal. Another cloud of coal dust bellowed across the blacksmith shop, so thick Daniel held his breath until it settled enough that he could see Aaron at the far side, one hand tilting a basket of coal into the bin and the other hand holding a white cloth over his mouth. It wasn't really a white cloth, not with all that soot blackening it with dust from the mines south of Bethlehem. Aaron had been gone with Papa for a week on a journey that should have taken them two days, but without Daniel's arms to work the pickax and shovel, the mining of fuel required more time than before. Daniel leaned against the doorpost and folded his arms across his chest. It wouldn't be too many years before Joshua was old enough to help in the shop. He was nearly seven and by the time he was nine he could spend a half day here, and by the time he was twelve he'd be putting in as many hours as Daniel did when he was the same age as the little—

"What are you doing here?" Aaron peered through the dust-ridden air.

"Nothing, really. Thought I'd stop by and see how the work was coming along."

"What inspired your curiosity now?" Aaron finished pouring the last of the coal into the bin. He waved his hand through the air to clear it. "You haven't been by in months."

Daniel stood away from leaning on the doorpost. "It's about Rebekah."

"Hand me that would you?" Aaron pointed to the tongs hanging from a peg on the wall. "What about her?"

Daniel walked the tongs over to Aaron. "I have some news."

"Why don't you let the dead rest?" Aaron lifted a long red rod from the coals of the open hearth and laid it out over the forging table. It was the steel for the bow, it had to be by the shape. It looked to be a good quality. There were no dark spots in the redness—a sure sign there were no cracks in the metal. Aaron had done a respectable job with the smelting, but he wasn't a forger, at least not as fine a forger as he. Daniel could curve the arms of the bow to the prefect arc in one day and save having to heat and re-heat the metal and risk cracking it. But Aaron, well, there was no telling how many times he'd have to heat this rod and hammer it into the perfect shape. And then there were the odd ideas Aaron had about the shape of the bow. He wasn't going to forge it into the usual half-moon arc. He was determined to recurve the arms into the shape of Assyrian bows, but those were made of wood and there had never been a recurved bow made out of anything but wood curved and shaped in the shops of ship-builders—the only men on earth who knew how to bend and soak and bend again the wood of cedars into the shape of Assyrian bows. And there was no way Aaron could work that same magic with his bow. He'd have to heat and hammer for weeks only to weaken the metal with cracks and there could be nothing worse than a fissure in metal that was intended for a bow. With the added pull of an archer's string, a single crack was certain to break the bow on the first draw.

Daniel said, "Do you need some help?"

"What do you care about blacksmithing?"

"Laban's interested in your invention."

Aaron said, "I haven't invented anything."

"A steel bow could bring you a good deal of money."

Aaron steadied the tip of the red-hot metal against a rounded stone and brought the hammer down over it, forcing the metal to take on the shape of the granite. He said, "This bow isn't for sale."

"If Captain Laban likes it, you could make these for his army. It could mean a good deal of work for the shop."

"This isn't for Laban or his army."

"I'm just telling you that—"

"I thought you had some news about Rebekah."

Daniel came around the forging table and faced Aaron across the width of it. The hot metal cast an orange-red light across Aaron's face. Sweat dripped down the end of his nose and he shook it away before bringing the forging hammer down hard, the head ringing against the metal until it fell silent and he lifted it for another stroke. His eyes were riveted on his work and Daniel leaned his head in and said, "Rebekah is alive."

Aaron didn't move his gaze away from his work, didn't even put down the tongs. He raised the hammer overhead and said, "Did you tell Mama?"

"Is that all you can say?" Daniel grabbed the edge of the forging table with both hands. "I tell you that Rebekah is alive and you can't say anything?"

Aaron brought the hammer down with the same steady stroke. "I'm sure Mother would like to know."

"I thought you loved the girl?"

Aaron held his lower lip between his teeth and worked the hammer over the hot metal, curving the top arm to the shape of a large round stone. It wasn't near enough of an arc for a good bow, not by any stretch, but it did have the beginnings of one. Aaron was bending the metal just enough to get the arc started, but not so much that he cracked it and wasted the steel. He had three more stones laid out on the table, each one with a deeper curve to it and he was going to forge his bow in stages, like a wise forger would if he were to attempt something that had never been attempted before. A little at a time was the only way to bend steel without breaking it.

"You're doing fine with that bow. Real fine." Daniel left the forging table and started for the shop door. Zadock was right. Aaron was hiding something. He didn't even flinch at the mention of Rebekah. He didn't even care, and there was nothing he cared about more than the potter's daughter. If Aaron had shown a little anger or even a little interest in the news, Daniel would have believed the girl was dead, but not now, not by the way Aaron was hiding his emotions, keeping back what he knew about the girl.

Daniel stopped at the door before going out and glanced back at his brother. Look at him, standing at the forging table, wielding the hammer against the metal. He was hiding something, he had to be. Aaron wasn't one to keep a straight face unless he was he feigning his indifference. He brought the hammer down again and again, pounding harder and harder bouncing the metal bow up off the curling stone before hurling the hammer across the shop, landing it against the side of the smelting oven and opening a crack in the bricks. He spun around, his eyes swollen with tears and said, "What do you know about love? Have you ever lost something that meant more to you than your own . . ." Aaron waved his hand at the stripes on Daniel's military tunic. "Than your own good fortune? Have you ever loved something that much and had it taken away from you?" His words shot from his mouth with such force that his chest heaved for breath. He fell to his knees on the hard stone floor, his fists raised to the sky like a man offering a prayer, but this was no prayer. He was at war with the Eternal and his tears poured over his cheeks. He said, "Dear God, why?"

Daniel backed out the door of the shop. He'd never seen such sorrow and anger welling up from Aaron's soul and he turned into the street and hurried away from the shop, Aaron's sobbing chasing him up the hill toward the palace. He had to tell Zadock. Whoever the Chief Elder was hunting, it wasn't the potter.

Rebekah and Josiah were most certainly dead.

"I thought Rebekah was with you." Mima leaned out the window and searched the sky for pigeons. She said, "The bedroom was empty when I returned."

"I told the girl to stay here and collect the birds." Josiah laid the satchel of scrolls on the bed and came around next to the window. "We have to leave the city immediately."

"Not without the . . ." Mima shielded her eyes from the sun and peered into the sky. "There's the first one."

Jeruzabel circled above the palace. She came around twice before diving to the window ledge and fluttering to a stop next to Mima.

What a fine bird she was and Mima stroked her across the back feathers before drawing her inside and placing her in an basket with a bowl of chopped figs and covering her with a lid made of reeds. Mima searched the sky for the next bird, but there was no sign of the others and she came back inside and closed the shutters. "You can't go without the other pigeons. You're going to need all of them."

"We go as soon as Rebekah arrives." Josiah went to the bedroom door, peered out into the hall and came back. "There's no telling what Zadock will do to find us."

"He's not certain you're alive."

"I know the man." Josiah rubbed the tuft of hair above his right ear. "He won't stop until he's certain we're dead."

The fluttering of feathers sounded at the window and Mima pushed open the shutters to find Isabel waddling along the stone ledge. She was out of reach and refused to come back. Stubborn little fowl. Didn't she understand there was little time to waste with Laban's men searching everywhere? Mima leaned onto the sill, her belly pressed against the stone ledge and scooped the bird up with both hands. Two pigeons home and only half-blind Samantha left to arrive. Mima searched the gardens for her. The poor girl always hung about the branches of the sycamore trees and waddled about the fountains before she found her roost, but she was nowhere to be found among her favorite stopping places.

"This much I know." Mima placed Isabel in the basket with Jeruzabel. "God will see your only daughter and my last pigeon back to us safely."

The last time Aaron came here, he carried the burned remains of Rebekah and Josiah in a wooden box. The place of the sepulchres stood on the west slopes of the Hinnom Valley, rising out of the narrow canyon like a sanctuary overlooking the west gate of Jerusalem. A hundred tombs dotted the rocky hillside that was the resting place of the city's wealthiest families.

A footpath wound up the hillside past the sepulchre that belonged to the moneychanger's family, then around the switchback to the tomb of a gold merchant and his wife, then down the right fork and across the face of the hill to Rebekah's tomb. Her name was chiseled into the large round stone sealing the entrance, along with her mother's and Josiah's names and the inscription—*sleep well till we meet again*—arching across the top. Aaron pushed against the stone, his shoulder turned into the rough chiseled surface and his hands bearing against the sheer weight of it. He dug his feet into the ground and heaved again. He had to get inside and prove that Rebekah wasn't alive, that nothing but death had separated them. Daniel was wrong; she was dead, and no matter how much Aaron wished him to be right she would never leave this place until the day of resurrection. The stone didn't budge and Aaron backed away, his chest heaving for breath. He would never go inside this tomb and see that she was there, and he was left with only the memory of others to recount to him the story of her fiery passing.

A run of weeds grew around the base of the sepulchre and Aaron rooted them out. He should have come here more often and done the work Rebekah couldn't do for herself, but before today he didn't have the courage to stand outside her tomb and wish to God things were different. He should have prayed that prayer, but in the months after Rebekah's death he'd petitioned heaven so many times he feared tiring the Eternal with his repetition.

The flowers growing up either side of the sepulchre were Rebekah's work. She told Aaron it was the least she could do to honor the memory of the mother she never knew. Before Rebekah died, she came here often to pay her respects and care for the grounds. She had a gift for growing flowers and if it hadn't been for her careful nurturing, the potter's estate never would have had any color gracing its arbors and porches, or any ivy growing up the walls and hanging about the trellis.

The first buds of spring were fastened on the ends of the stems, the petals of each flower tightly packed like great teardrops with only a thin line of color visible near the top. Aaron plucked a white rose and pulled back the petals until the pristine color filled his hand. It had the same innocence he remembered in Rebekah's eyes, the same freshness that scented her hair, and when he ran his fingers over it, it was like touching her gentle spirit. Aaron breathed in its fragrance before carrying it around to the front of the tomb and planting it in the loose soil at the base of the sepulchre in memory of Rebekah. He plucked another rose from the bushes—a light yellow blossom—and when he forced open the petals, there were dark shades of orange like the shades of doubt that clouded his soul. He ran his finger over the darkest portion. He didn't pray about Rebekah anymore. His heart was darkened with too much sadness to ever hope he could hear her bright voice from heaven. It only left him empty and without an answer and he took the flower to the front of the sepulchre and planted it in the ground next to the white one. This rose was for him—for his enduring wish that he could see her face one more time and tell her that he loved her. He turned the darkest petals toward the opening of the tomb, and if she ever showed herself from inside this crypt she would know that he'd been waiting on her.

A red rosebud grew on the highest stem, the long, prickly length of it winding up around the edge of the sepulchre and Aaron leaned up on his toes to pluck it off and bring it around front. It shimmered in the morning sun and cast a deep red glow across the other blossoms. Of all the colors of a rose, Rebekah would have preferred this one. She always said a red flower was for love and he planted it between the others. The white rose was for Rebekah and the yellow rose was for Aaron, but the red rose belonged in the middle—there was no other place for it, not if Aaron were to honor Rebekah's memory. The red rose was for the love between them.

A meadowlark chirped in the branches of the locust growing out of the rocky hillside just above the tomb and when Aaron lifted his gaze to the sound of the bird he spied a woman through the branches. She stood at the top of the trail looking down at him. She was wearing a dark robe, the hood pulled across her face, but she had the same form as Rebekah and her eyes were the image of Rebekah's eyes.

Aaron ran up the trail around two more switchbacks to the top of the hill where the sepulchres gave way to a graveyard with hundreds of headstones marking the resting places of commoners. The woman was gone from the brow of the hill and he called Rebekah's name, but his cry was lost in the wind whipping across the plateau. He scanned the rocky hilltop and there, toward the far side he spied the woman kneeling beside a grave, dressing the headstone. He skirted past a low-lying wall of stones, around the grave markers, down a small incline, and came in behind the woman. He stood over her, his hand above her shoulder, but not touching her. He said, "Rebekah?"

The woman stood slowly and her hair was the first thing Aaron noticed. The brown locks fell out of her hood and about her shoulders. They were braided with an ivory bauble and pink ribbon just like Rebekah wore and Aaron couldn't keep from whispering her name. He said, "Rebekah, you're, you're . . ."

The woman turned to face him. She had Rebekah's deep brown eyes and her high cheeks, but it wasn't Rebekah. She held a bunch of wild yellow poppies and said, "Can I help you, sir?"

Aaron backed away with both hands up and told her there was nothing she could do for him. He turned back through the graveyard, his feet carrying him quickly over the rocks, the wind drying what remained of his tears. He veered off the trail around the first switchback, his feet pushing loose rock over the edge. He righted himself with help from the limb of a scrub oak and climbed back onto the trail, running down along the face of the hill, his arms swinging wild and his hair rising off his head with each hurried stride. The trail turned sharply across in front of Rebekah's sepulchre and he was moving too fast to keep his footing.

Aaron fell face first, his long body sprawled in the dust. The rock in the path tore at the flesh in his hands and bruised his belly and his fall raised a cloud of brown earth that filled his eyes like salt in a wound. He blinked away the dirty tears until he could see Rebekah's tomb.

A single red rose stood at the entrance.

Zadock stood on the main stairs of the palace anteroom with Laban's fifty assembled before him. He raised his hand to silence their murmuring and the men stood up from leaning on their swords with their shoulders back and chests forward. The giant oil lamps of the anteroom reflected the yellow glow off their brass helmets and breastplates.

Zadock said, "There's a man in the palace. He has a bald head with graying hair about his ears and he answers to the name Josiah the potter. I want you to find him."

The soldier in the first rank stepped forward. He glanced at his men before saying, "Is there a reason you need all of us to hunt down a potter, sir?"

"He isn't a potter." Zadock turned his gaze across the marbled floors of the anteroom, past the royal family crest that hung between two pillars, then up along the mezzanine and stairwells leading to the upper floors. If the potter was inside these halls, he needed every one of these fifty to do more than keep him from escaping—they were to use their swords to get rid of him. The law allowed for the killing of robbers on sight, without trial. To be accused as a robber was to lose any protection under the law, and Josiah the potter deserved none. He was no better than an outlaw and Zadock brought his gaze back to bear on the soldiers. He said, "The man is a robber."

A cheer rose up from the soldiers like the growl of a hundred lions rising up to pursue its prey. The hunt was on. They lifted their swords overhead, the pointed tips and sharp blades rising and falling with their rabid cry.

"There are to be no prisoners—not the potter and not anyone hiding him; is that understood?"

Another cheer filled the chamber and the men hoisted their swords higher.

Zadock pointed to the first rank of ten. "You search the catacombs and dungeons. And you there, secure the main floor." He dispatched ten men to the west wing in a scuffling of leather boots, ten more to the kitchens and gardens, and the rest he sent marching up the stairs to the mezzanine level where the palace help made their quarters. They were to secure every room and ferret out every hiding place in the palace until they did away with the potter.

Zadock crossed the anteroom and slowly pulled open the door to the royal chambers. Except for the light streaming through the large window at the far end beyond the king's throne, the room stood dark. He could wait for word here, away from the stir of the hunt. He closed the door behind him, but before he found a suitable place to relax, a scuffling echoed about the chamber. Zadock stepped behind a pillar and watched a young woman pull herself over the window ledge. She was silhouetted by the light of day filtering in behind her, the shadows covering her face. She wore a rose-colored robe and she had long hair braided down the back, but beyond that there was no telling who it was. She crept across the chamber, her sandals falling quiet on the marble floor. She paused at the door, peered into the anteroom, and then she was gone.

Zadock came around the pillar and hurried after her. He stepped into the anteroom and scowled at the light from the large windows and giant oil lamps, his hand cupped over his brow. Where had she gone? The main hall was empty, the archways leading down the east and west wings were silent, and the mezzanine overlooking the ante-room was empty. He was about to return to the royal chamber and find a seat in the dark where he could rest when the sound of footsteps echoed in the stairwell above him. He climbed a few steps, leaned back to get a view of the stairs winding around to the upper floors and there, on the banister, he saw her hand. She was carrying two roses, one white and one yellow, and when she came around the next flight he caught a glimpse of the girl. Could it be his good fortune? Was that really the sweet, cherubic face of Rebekah, the potter's daughter, climbing the steps? It was only a short view of her, her face passing beyond the banister, but he turned his ear and listened for her foot-steps. She climbed about three more flights and then out onto the top floor where the royal family made their home. Zadock held the pleats of his robes with both hands. Miriam! She had to be the one harboring Josiah and Rebekah. There was no one else in the palace who would do such a thing, at least not anyone who lived on the upper floor.

Zadock called for the men from the gardens and kitchen to follow him up the stairs. He gathered the soldiers searching the halls of the mezzanine level, and the fifty men started up the main stairs in a resounding march.

The upper-floor hallway where the royal family lived stood quiet. The urns were filled with flowers, the floors polished and the expen-sive aroma of frankincense scented the air, but there was no one about to enjoy the fragrance.

Zadock stationed a rank of soldiers on the landing at the top of the stairs and sent another rank down the hallway to the back stairs. There were only two ways down from the top floor of the palace, and he sealed them both off with orders not to let anyone pass without his permission. He led the rest of the troop to the first bedroom, the one that belonged to Miriam and Zedekiah. They were to start here and work their way down the hall to the last room until they found the potter. He reached for the latch, but the door came open before he could turn it and King Zedekiah stood in the entry, tying the sash on his black morning robe, the gold threaded hem grazing his knees. He was like the dark walnut wood doorposts that rose up on either side of him—tall, thin and without a single blemish in the finish. His skin was covered with olive oils, his hair neatly combed forward over his brow and his young face was freshly washed. He said, "I didn't call for any soldiers."

"Your Highness." Zadock bowed quickly. It was better to feign his patience for royalty than risk offending the king with his hurry to find the potter. He said, "I didn't know you were in."

"Where else would I be? This is my home."

"We have a problem."

"It looks more like a war." Zedekiah turned his gaze over the rank and file in the hallway. He said, "Since when did you become captain of the guard?"

Zadock forced a thin smile. "There's been a breach of the palace security."

"What sort of breach?"

"Josiah the potter. He's somewhere on the upper floor."

Zedekiah rubbed his oil-covered brow. "This isn't a graveyard."

"I believe the man's alive and he's come to the palace to disrupt the trial." Zadock peered around the doorpost of the king's bedroom. "Do I have your blessing to make a search?"

"Do you really expect me to allow our living quarters to be turned upside down in search of a ghost?"

"We have to be certain."

"Of what?" Zedekiah folded his arms across his chest. "The man is dead."

"The trial, sire." Zadock lowered his voice to a near whisper. "It's only a matter of days before it begins and we can't let anything disrupt it."

"I never thought the potter to be a threat in life and now that he's dead . . ." Zedekiah raised both hands in the air. "I doubt him any more of a threat."

"We shouldn't take any risks."

"Search if you must." Zedekiah stepped aside. "But don't make a stir." He glanced at the soldiers waiting to search the floor. "I don't want to be disturbed anymore than I have to be."

Zadock assigned a rank to Mulek's chamber, another to Dan and Benjamin's quarters, and he led the rest of the men into the king's bedroom chambers. If there were anyplace Zadock would find Rebekah and Josiah it was here in the room the queen shared with her husband, and since she was gone on a ride with her son and his pigeons, he could search without her meddling. He ordered the soldiers to check the windowsills and make certain there was no one hiding on the ledges. Zedekiah's clothes were laid out on the bed—a blue kilt with a matching vest and white tunic, a golden sash for his waist and a pair of knee-high boots with more laces than a man should have to tie in one day. The soldiers checked beneath the mattress. They searched the dressing rooms, marched through the washing room where steam from the king's hot-water bath filtered back into the bedroom. There was no sign of the potter and Rebekah hiding in the steamy precincts of the wash room, nothing in the closets and hallways of the bedroom chamber. Zadock stormed back into the hall, the click of soldier's boots following him. The reports from the princes' rooms were the same—no sign of anyone. No maidservants, no royals, and certainly no dead potter and his daughter. Zadock scanned the hallway. Where had Rebekah gone? He'd seen her hurry up the steps and disappear onto the upper floor landing carrying a bouquet of white and—

That's what he was looking for. On the floor, fallen beneath a mahogany wood table he spied a yellow rose petal. He hurried over and picked it up. He was right. She came this way, but where?

The small door to Mima's room stood at the far end of the hallway, hardly visible between the arches supporting the vaulted ceiling and hidden behind a stand of pillars. Zadock moved closer. She was his spy in the palace and there was a chance she'd seen something that could help his search. He made a fist and pounded on the thick wood planks.

Maybe Mima could shed some light on Rebekah's disappearance.

"Open up in there."

A shrill, high-pitched voice penetrated the wood slats of Mima's bedroom door like a piercing winter wind. She was to unlock immediately, but she couldn't, not until she hid Rebekah and Josiah. She motioned them to the window and helped Rebekah onto the ledge, her thick, black hand steadying the girl at the hip, but it was no use. Rebekah couldn't keep her balance on the narrow ledge outside the window unless she gave up the yellow and white roses she carried.

Mima said, "I'll take care of them, dear."

Rebekah held the roses close to her breast.

"Listen to me, girl." Mima lowered her voice to a whisper. "You can't get a good hold on the window ledge with flowers in your hand."

Rebekah let her have them and then she was gone out the window. Josiah climbed onto the ledge behind her and they were safely in their hiding place, if you could call perched on a narrow piece of stone five stories above the palace gardens a safe place to hide. Josiah stood with his back to the stone wall, his shoulders pressed against the limestone and his feet flat over the narrow ledge, balancing himself against the pull of the earth. Rebekah was turned the wrong way with her stomach flush with the wall, but at least she couldn't scare herself looking down into the gardens. The girl's feet were trembling, the leather on her soles shaking against the stone. Mima had little time to comfort the girl with more than a quick nod and a forced smile. The girl was losing her composure and if Mima didn't answer Zadock's knocking and get him on his way quickly, Rebekah was going to scream; or worse, she was going to fall. If Zadock found them, he'd not hesitate to push them to their deaths and call it an accident.

Mima came back inside and straightened her green scarf about her brow. She tucked the tails of her low-cut blouse beneath the waistline in her skirt and offered a short prayer for God to keep them safe. She set the yellow and white roses in an empty vase on the table beside the door before unlocking the latch.

The Chief Elder pushed Mima aside and marched around the bed, taking up a post below the window, the light of midday streaming over his pointed turban and soaking into the dark fibers of his robe like water into a sponge. He said, "Have you seen them?"

"Seen who, sir?" Mima brushed the tight curls of thick black hair from in front of her eyes.

"The potter and his daughter."

"Are you feeling well, sir?" Mima looked into his dark eyes. "Josiah and Rebekah died in the fire."

"The home may have gone down in flames, but . . ." Zadock pulled away the blankets on Mima's bed and pushed the mattress to the floor. He peered at the empty space between the slats and the floor. There was nothing there but a little dust and he threw the blankets over the emptiness. He said, "Are you sure the potter and Rebekah were inside the estate when it burned?"

"I locked the doors to the dining room. They had no way out."

"Is that all you can tell me?"

"Their bodies were buried in the sepulchre west of the city. You were there; you saw them seal the stone across their grave."

"I heard the mourners and I saw the wooden coffins, but the bodies . . ." Zadock kicked over the wicker basket, freeing Isabel and Jeruzabel. "I never saw their remains."

"They were burned badly, sir." Mima went to her knees and gathered in the two birds. "There wasn't much to see beyond a few charred bones."

"They're here somewhere." Zadock turned to the window and set his hands on the sill. "I can feel it."

"There's no one here but me and these birds." Mima returned the pigeons to the makeshift coop. She replaced the bed cushions and folded the blankets. She said, "I would have seen them if they came this way."

"If the potter escaped your scrutiny the first time, he can do it again." Zadock leaned his head out the window, the top of his turban brushing against the half-open shutters. He said, "The potter and Rebekah are here and I'm going to—"

A flapping sound carried on the air just outside the window and Samantha flew straight into Zadock's turban, forcing him back inside, and dislodging his turban in the process. She flopped on the window ledge, the distinct white stripe on her back catching the sunlight. She gathered her bearings and jumped to flight, circling the room and careening past Zadock's head. She fluttered about the bedposts, circled the room again, and headed straight for Zadock. The Chief

Elder ducked out of the way, and Samantha flapped through the ratted thatches of his gray hair before coming to rest on the sill.

"Foolish bird!" Zadock replaced his turban. "Is she blind?"

Mima picked her up and stroked her wings. Thank heavens she arrived when she did. Mima turned Samantha's bad eye to the Chief Elder. She said, "Only on this side, sir."

Zadock straightened the pleats in his robe. "How do you put up with such stupid animals?"

"I use them to entertain the princes."

"Better you than I."

Mima opened the door to the coop and reached Samantha inside, but she jumped from her grasp and came to roost on the windowsill. Of all the places in the bedroom, why did she have to roost near the hiding place?

Zadock plucked her from her perch. He held her by the ends of his long fingers like a frightened child, his nails digging at Samantha's wings. He said, "Where shall I set her?"

Mima didn't answer. Not with the piece of papyrus hanging from the end of Samantha's foot. It had come open in flight and the words penned in Miriam's hand were visible: *Sneak Josiah and Rebekah out of the city! Zadock hunts them!*

If Samantha had only arrived moments earlier she could have sent the potter on his way, but the note could only harm them now. Mima reached to take her back, but she fluttered under Zadock's stiff grip and her sudden movement dislodged the note, sending it fluttering to the floor, the words face-up.

Zadock and Mima both bent down to pick it up when Daniel marched into the room, his powerful body brushing Mima aside and pushing her back against the bedpost. The tip of his boot pinned the note to the floor and covered the words. Daniel said, "The potter is dead."

Zadock came up without the note. He handed the pigeon to Mima and said, "Is that what you told your brother?"

"That's right, sir. When I told him Rebekah was alive, he did just as you said he would." Daniel stepped closer, the sole of his boot hiding the note from view. "Aaron was filled with more anger than I've ever seen in a man."

Mima stepped to the window, the width of her black-skinned body pushing Zadock and Daniel back from the sill and blocking their view of the ledge. She pulled the shutters closed and locked the latch. She said, "We don't want the pigeons to get out, do we?"

"I'm sorry for the trouble, woman." Zadock pressed his thin lips together. "I was wrong to think you let the potter escape."

Mima turned around, her back pressed against the shutters and Samantha cooing in her hand. She said, "No trouble at all, sir."

Daniel bent over, picked the note out from under his boot and said, "Is this yours?"

Mima snatched it from him before he could read it. She thanked him and stuffed it under the neckline of her low-cut blouse where not even Daniel or Zadock dare retrieve it. They hadn't found anything that would lead them to believe Josiah and Rebekah were alive; at least that's what she believed until Zadock stopped at the door before going out into the hallway. He pulled out a single rose petal and held it up to the yellow rose sprouting from the urn on the table. It was a perfect match.

Zadock said, "It's early for roses."

CHAPTER 24

"I'm closed!"

Pella pushed his broom toward the faint sound of footsteps outside the front door of the Jawbone Inn. Who could that be at this hour? He'd sent away the last soused soldier a good while ago. The mugs and glasses were washed and stowed, the wine cleared, and all he had left to do was set the stools up and mop the floor before climbing the steps to his room, forgetting he was an innkeeper until morning. It couldn't be a traveler wanting a room, though he wouldn't mind the money. Of the five rooms on the second floor, a merchant from Megiddo occupied the first one on the left and a gold trader from Tanis took the other across the hall, leaving three empty, and vacancies weren't good business no matter what hour of the night he had to fill them. Most travelers never bothered to stay overnight in the upper city where rooms were twice the cost of lower city inns, except on feast days when there was never room at any inn.

Pella set the last stool upside down on the bar and pushed the broom over the floor and in behind the wood pillar beside the door. It couldn't be a traveler walking up the steps to the inn—no one ever traveled this late on an early spring evening; it was too cold and too dark. And anyone wanting a room at Pella's inn would knock before trying the latch, or at least give a clap, or call a greeting, or anything to announce his arrival, unless this comer had intentions of keeping himself concealed. Pella pushed his broom into the corner and whisked away the dust that collected there. What was he thinking?

Thieves didn't rob his inn; they came here to get a drink with the money they pilfered.

It couldn't be the night watch. The two boys on duty came by earlier; they always knocked and he'd sent them away, as he did every evening, with a round of cheap wine and a plea that they keep an eye on his inn. The price for a bit of extra security was always two bottles, though there was no need to protect the Jawbone. Not with a regiment of Captain Laban's men stationed across the street at the training grounds and another twenty guarding the palace up the hill from the inn, but to be sure, he stood to the door with his broom pointed at the wood planks, the stiff reeds in the end of it his only protection.

The intruder clicked the latch not less than ten times, no doubt checking to make sure he could enter quickly. But the door pushed open so slowly that the thick leather straps lashing the frame to the post hardly squeaked about the hinges. It was like a ghost coming to haunt the inn, though the only spirits that frequented the Jawbone had been corked into a bottle and hauled to the cellar hours before. If it was a thief, he didn't seem to be in a hurry, and when he did enter he'd have to deal with more than a broom-toting Pella—he'd have an entire regiment on his hands. The Jawbone held a special place in the hearts of soldiers and it would only take one cry from Pella to bring them running to his rescue. Well, maybe it wasn't a special place in their hearts, but he did have the allegiance of their bellies. And maybe it would take more than a single cry at this hour to raise them out of bed, but they would come and they'd risk their lives to save the stores of wine he kept in the cellar. Drinking was a hallowed event for soldiers at Pella's inn, and the wine he served was downright sacred. But no amount of reverence could calm Pella's suspicions. The cold night air swept in with the opening door like an invisible fog and Pella was alone with only a broom to stop the intruder.

"Who goes there?" Pella stepped into the draft and raised the end of his broom to the door. It flew open, the planks slamming against the doorstop. Pella jumped back and cried, "Thief!" He stuck the end of his broom into the face of the no-good, lurking, cunning, thieving . . .

Eight-year-old? The intruder couldn't be a day over that age with his bright, young face, innocent green eyes, and naive smile to calm the depths of Pella's suspicious heart—if you could call him an intruder at all. The end of the broom covered the boy's upper lip like a mustache and his nose was lost among its reeds. He raised his hands in the air and said, "Benuriah!"

"What are you talking about, boy?"

"My name, sir. You asked who goes there." Benuriah's thin, small voice was muffled behind the broom. He glanced over his shoulder into the night and when he turned back, he returned his face into the reeds exactly as Pella had stuck them. With his hands still raised over his head he said, "You can call me Benuriah, kind sir."

Kind sir? Pella dropped the broom to his side. Who was this boy of such refined manners? Pella had rarely been called "sir" in all his days of inn keeping and never in the same breath as "kind." And he was not given to the company of children, though in the case of this brown-headed marvel he'd make an exception. It wasn't often anyone understood what kind of man Pella was and the title "kind sir" suited him just fine. He deserved a little respect after thirty-two years of pouring wines for thankless soldiers, even if the admiration came from a boy who didn't stand any taller than a bar stool and had not the sense to wipe his running nose.

"You gave me a scare. Does your mother know where you are?" Pella leaned on the end of his broom. "What are you doing out at this hour?"

"A room, sir." Benuriah held out three pieces of silver. "Do you have any left for the night?"

"You want a room?"

"That's right." Benuriah ran the back of his hand beneath his nose and sniffled. His cheeks were red from the cold and his fingers poked through the holes in his linen hand warmers. He said, "Are you full?"

"You're too young to be wanting a room."

"It's not only for me." Benuriah reached into a small leather purse and pulled out more silver coins pinched between his thin, white-cold fingers. "We can pay whatever you ask."

"Put that away, son." A woman hurried from around the corner of the inn where travelers tied up their animals. The hem of her robe dragged behind her, the cloth clutched by the tiny hand of a three-year-old toddler. She carried a newborn in her arms, wrapped in white linen, and the two large satchels hanging from her shoulders weighed down her stride. She took the coin purse from Benuriah and placed it beneath the sleeve of her traveling robe. "We can't afford anymore than three pieces of silver. We don't know how long we're going to stay." She straightened her robe on her shoulders as best she could with a babe in her arms and the heavy bags over her shoulders. She offered her hand to Pella and said, "I'm Deborah. You've already met Benuriah." She glanced at her feet. "This is David and . . ." She checked beneath the blanket. ". . . The new arrival doesn't have a name, not until her father sees her and decides on a fitting one."

Pella drew the door full open, stepped from the warm glow of the inn and peeked beneath the cloth. He was not given to showing his emotions over anything, but the adorable little girl sleeping beneath the linen invited his admiration. He touched her nose with the tip of his finger and stroked her soft cheeks. Why hadn't the father seen this babe? Deborah didn't offer any explanation why her husband lived in Jerusalem, while they lived far enough away to require a room at his inn and Pella didn't want to pry, though he couldn't keep the word scoundrel from conjuring deep in his thoughts. Any man who could bear to part with such a lovely brood must be a good-for-nothing rascal, to say nothing of being absent for the infant's birth along with not providing a decent dwelling somewhere in the city for them to lodge. Pella said, "I'm sure your husband will be pleased to see you."

"If he'll see us at all."

Pella was right. The father of this child was a scoundrel to be sure. That's exactly what the man was. What father wouldn't want to see this fine family?

Deborah said, "I pray every night he'll see us." Her smile faded and her chin began to quiver, though the tears misting her eyes couldn't hide their deep brown beauty. They were wide and filled with a determined light, despite the cold night that chilled her cheeks red. She had a high, strong brow and with her hair pulled back under her hood she was ready to face a raging torrent, though the weather was calm and these little ones were hardly a handful. Well-mannered was the best word for them, what with Benuriah calling him "kind sir" and David not complaining about the cold that forced him to stomp his sandals over the stone and wrap his face in the wide sleeves of the cape Deborah wore over her robe. She reached beneath the linen to find the baby's tiny hand and press it between her fingers.

"Please come inside." Pella took the satchels from Deborah and started toward the door. "You can warm yourselves beside the fire while I get you something to eat."

Deborah said, "That's very kind of you. It's been a long journey from Arim."

Pella pulled up, stopping well before reaching the threshold. Did Deborah say she hailed from Arim? He kept facing the open door, not turning back to let them see his face. He was not a good bartering soul—he'd never had the stone face of one—and he didn't want Deborah to see the concern that tugged at the corners of his eyes and furrowed his brow. He asked, "Are you from Qiryat Ye' Arim?"

Deborah's voice brightened. "Do you know the place?"

Pella spoke over his shoulder. "We get a lot of soldiers in here who've spent time at Fort Lakhish."

"We know all about soldiers, don't we boys?" Deborah ran her hand over Benuriah's hair, his head nodding in answer to her question. "My husband with his father own the only inn near Lakhish and we serve more soldiers than do the cooks in the fort's kitchens."

The inn near Lakhish? Pella wiped his hand across his face, smoothing his brow and calming the twitch about his eyes. Could these be the rogues Captain Laban warned him to watch for? He turned about in the doorway and studied each of them from head to toe—Benuriah's smiling face, David hiding among the pleats of his mother's robes and Deborah with her babe. Captain Laban didn't say it would be a family from Arim, only that he should watch for an older gentleman named Shemayahu with graying hair. Pella scanned the street. It was empty and there was no one with them that met that description. Why, there was no one else with them at all. They were alone and hopefully they would remain that way. These couldn't be the people Laban had told every innkeeper in Jerusalem to turn away, though the similarities were difficult to ignore. The prophet Uriah operated an inn with his father from Arim, but there could be other inns in that town other than Uriah's couldn't there? Deborah's satchels hung heavy in Pella's hands, but he didn't set them down. He stared at his newly arrived guests. Laban's instructions were clear. He was to deny Uriah's father, Shemayahu, a room. The man was not to be allowed even the slightest respite. Pella was to make sure Shemayahu's life was uncomfortable enough that he would not endure a long stay in the city. But these young boys and their mother were hardly the sort he should make uncomfortable, and they certainly hadn't arrived in company with anyone who remotely resembled Shemayahu.

Pella said, "I'll prepare three beds."

"Could you make it four?"

"Do you really need one for the baby?"

David stepped from his mother's skirts and said, "It's for grandfather."

Deborah pulled the boy back. She said, "My father-in-law. He shouldn't be too much longer." She moved her babe to the other arm. "He's arranging a visit with my husband."

Pella said, "A visit?"

"My husband, he's a . . ." Deborah glanced away from Pella's stare. "He's a prisoner."

Pella softly said Uriah's name, but not so soft that Deborah didn't hear him. Her head came up and her eyes were wide and hopeful. She said, "Do you know him?"

Pella said, "You'll have to forgive me."

"There's not been any offense taken, sir."

"I don't mean you any ill, but . . ."

"But what?"

Pella dropped Deborah's satchels onto the stone porch and they hit with a deadened thud. He backed into the warmth of the inn, his glance darting between Benuriah's smile, David's pulling on Deborah's hem, and the small babe beneath the linen. He couldn't allow their need to alter his obligations. They may be travelers from another city, but he was a resident, a citizen of Jerusalem and he had no choice than to reach for the latch and shut the door if he wanted to keep Laban's men buying his wines. Pella said, "There's no room in this inn."

The wood planks came between them.

The sun angled its early-morning rays down along the alley wall of the Jawbone Inn and chased away the cold of evening. Shemayahu spent the night on a mat with little power to cushion the uneven rise and fall of cobblestones that jabbed into his sleep and stiffened his joints. He was too old to be outside in cold weather and his grandchildren too young, but there was no other place in the city they could go—not a single inn would take their money—and he wrapped his arm over Benuriah and David to keep them from shivering until the sun did its blessed work and warmed their bed. Benuriah curled his knees up into his chest and David reached for Shemayahu's hand, mumbling that he was cold and begging for grandpa to come close. They had endured the night with their tired bodies huddled against the wooden gate of an upper city estate and nothing but a mule blanket thrown over them.

Deborah lay awake, her head propped against the last gate where the alley dead-ended into a high wall. She held her babe close to her body to keep the infant from freezing. It was impossible to know if her eyes were swollen from lack of sleep or from crying away the night. It wasn't an easy thing to have her three young children sleep in the streets of such a large city, to say nothing of her husband imprisoned for reasons even Shemayahu didn't understand.

The tapping of metal-shod hooves sounded at the entrance to the alley and Deborah pulled the blanket over the newborn's face before raising three fingers, telling Shemayahu there was more than one man coming up behind him.

"Wake up, old man!"

Old man? Shemayahu let go of his grandsons and rolled over to see the giver of the insults. His eyes didn't focus well in the morning and the pain of stiff joints, made stiffer from the cold air, didn't make sitting up any easier. He pushed his hair out of his eyes and peered up at the stout soldier in the saddle above him, with riders flanking him on either side. The soldier's thick arms and square shoulders were silhouetted by the light of dawn. His face was a shadow, except for a thin black beard that lined the edge of his dark, tanned jaw before disappearing into shaved sideburns. He had a short sword holstered at his waist. His crocodile-skin boots and snakeskin belt left no doubt that the man had traveled to Egypt, or had at least traded with merchants of the Nile delta.

The lieutenant's men called him Daniel. He had the straight chin and the square-boned cheeks of a powerful man, and he sat three hands taller than the two cavalrymen flanking him. Or was it his thick neck sprouting from strong shoulders that made him seem taller than the others?

Daniel jabbed his heels into the horse's haunches and came around to the other side of Shemayahu. He wore the stripes of a lieutenant, but he couldn't be an officer; there were no lines around his youthful brown eyes and not a single furrow worrying his brow. The military didn't let boys lead their men, at least not the military Shemayahu had known all his life. But then these were changing times and with Laban as captain of the guard there was no telling what storms of change he would brew.

One of Daniel's cavalrymen leaned over his saddle and said, "It's them, sir. Right where the innkeeper told us we'd find them."

The second cavalryman reared his mount, the horse's hooves clawing at the air and clapping back onto the stone. He raised the brim of his helmet and said, "I'll take word to Captain Laban. He'll want to know about this and I'll—"

"You're not going anywhere." Daniel leaned over and took the soldier's horse by the bridle. "If anyone's going to inform Laban, it'll be me, as soon as I'm certain this is the man we're looking for. Is that clear?"

"Yes, sir, but . . ."

"But what?"

The rider lowered his voice. "We're to drive them from the city."

"I know our orders." Daniel turned in his saddle, his crocodile-skin boots squeaking against the stirrups. He inched his mount in next to Shemayahu and said, "What are you and your family doing here, old man?"

Shemayahu rubbed the pain out of his knees. The journey through the pass near Hebron and down into Bethlehem hadn't been kind to the swelling. Five days it had taken him to return to Arim from Lehi's plantation, gather his son's family, and walk them to Jerusalem. And after refusal at every inn he had a mind to go back to Arim, but he couldn't keep these children and their mother from seeing Uriah. They had lived too long without the peace of a good father in their home and he wasn't taking them back without Uriah in their company, no matter how difficult the chore.

"I asked you a question." Daniel leaned over the saddle. "Tell me what you're doing here or I'll run you out of the city."

"You'll do no such thing." Deborah stood, rocking her babe in her arms. "We have every right to be here, don't we, Papa." She tipped her head to Shemayahu. "Go on, show him."

Shemayahu should have gotten onto his feet with the help of his cane and addressed the lieutenant, but he stayed sitting next to his grandsons—he wasn't about to use the cane like a crutch and give Daniel reason to call him "old man" again. He didn't need a cane to hold himself upright against the pull of teetering bones. He only ever used it to lengthen his stride, and he'd use it over Daniel's head if the soldier didn't show a bit more respect to him and his family.

Shemayahu raised his head and said, "Are you with the palace watch?"

"It doesn't matter who I'm with."

"It does if I have this." Shemayahu held up a double-sealed leather scroll for Daniel to read, the notice inviting Shemayahu to hire a lawyer and bring him to visit his son in prison. Captain Laban's signature lettered the bottom of the scroll.

Shemayahu stood, his head coming level with Daniel's knees. He said, "I'm Uriah's lawyer, sir."

Daniel snatched the notice from Shemayahu and quickly read over it.

"You see, there . . ." Deborah walked around in front of Shemayahu. "We were ordered to visit my husband by your commanding officer."

Daniel kept his gaze turned into the words on the scroll. "Captain Laban would never write something like this."

"He did and he sent it to us by courier." Deborah grabbed for the notice, but Daniel reared his horse and the animal's hooves drove her back against the alley wall. The baby began to cry, but that didn't keep Deborah from righting herself and saying, "We're not leaving this city." She pushed the horse's muzzle aside. "Do you understand me? You can deny us lodging and food, you can run us through with your horses, but you'll not be rid of us until I see my husband." Her lower lip began to tremble but she didn't shed a tear, not with Daniel staring down at her. She swung at him with an open hand and Daniel raised his boot to push her away, his heel in line with the babe's head.

"Deborah!" Shemayahu stepped between the boot and the babe, taking Daniel's heel in his back and falling into Deborah. They went to the ground, the baby bawling, Deborah crying, and Shemayahu groaning.

Daniel said, "You men keep watch over them until I get back." He galloped away, leaving Shemayahu and Deborah in a heap on the alley floor and taking with him the only hope they had of seeing Uriah.

Daniel kept the prison notice.

Zadock stood on the steps below Zedekiah's throne. He pushed his black turban forward like an impatient child. He didn't have time to wait on the king to finish speaking with his wife about their children. She was a woman and she could tend to their education without conferring with her husband on every matter. They were discussing a new teacher for Mulek, music lessons for Dan, and a new writing slate for Benjamin. For the love of Moses, didn't the king of Judah have better things to concern himself with than a writing slate of clay? And if that wasn't bad enough, one of the court scribes stood in line ahead of Zadock, waiting to take down a letter to the Elders in Hebron.

Zadock reached over the scribe's shoulder, took the pen from his hand and whispered, "You're out of ink."

The scribe reached for the small inkbottle in his other hand. He said, "I have a good supply of—"

"I said, you're out of ink." Zadock snatched the inkbottle from him, hid it under the pleats of his robe. He said, "Off you go and get some more before I have you imprisoned for using inferior ink on the king's letters."

The scribe scurried across the chamber, and the sound of his shuffling sandals raised Zedekiah's gaze from his deliberations with the queen. He said, "Where is he off to?"

"Ink, sire." Zadock kept his hands hidden beneath his robe. "He forgot his good ink."

Zedekiah stood from his throne and left Miriam standing behind the backrest. He said, "What brings you to see me?"

"Uriah's trial, sire." Zadock forced his lips together. "It's time."

Miriam hurried from behind the throne. "Have you any word from Shemayahu?"

"We can't wait any longer for Uriah's father to appear out of nowhere." Zadock shook his head. "The man isn't coming."

Zedekiah said, "Who will defend Uriah?"

"He can do that himself. He's educated, he knows the law and . . ." Zadock cleared his throat. "No one knows his guilt better than he."

Miriam didn't deny Zadock's maligning. She started down the steps and Zadock moved aside to let her pass. She crossed the chamber, staying in the shadows of the tall pillars and she was to the doors on the far side before Zedekiah said, "Miriam, where are you going?"

"The children." She reached for the latch. "I have to see Mulek."

Zedekiah said, "About what? His new teacher?"

Miriam turned her gaze onto Zadock. It was a penetrating stare, as if she could see through his lies and he turned his head down away from her glaring. Miriam said, "I have more important things for the boy to concern himself with."

Miriam left the chamber.

The throwing ball had a magical appeal and the only thing Mulek had to do was toss it in the air and his brothers followed him down the corridors of the east wing like a piper enchanting them with a melody. The ball wasn't a flute, but it had power to entice Dan and Benjamin outside to play. It was made of the finest linens, dyed with an expensive red color and tied together with gold chains to keep its round shape—just the sort of toy fit for the prince of Judah, at least that's what Papa told him the day he brought it home from his trip to the Orient and gifted it to Mulek on his eleventh birthday. He hardly ever brought it out of his bedroom where he kept his finest toys, but today there was reason to take it out and Dan and Benjamin followed Mulek out the garden doors and into the bright morning sun, asking him if they could play catch with the ball forever and Mulek told them they could, but not nearly as long as the last time they played forever. What he didn't tell them was that mother had sent him to spy and they were his cover. Dan and Benjamin were too young to under-stand the secret work Mulek did for his mother and they were happy to follow him down the steps, past the hedges and through the rose garden. They hurried down along the row of purple maples that weren't really purple this time of year, but since Mulek's brothers only knew to call the stand of dwarfed trees on this end of the gardens by their late summer color, he told them to follow him that way.

Benjamin was dressed in an old kilt Mother said could endure his playful spirit as long as she tied it tight enough so it didn't fall off his thin, four-year-old frame. The double knots bulged at his waist and made him walk with an odd stride, but they kept the kilt from slip-ping down around his ankles, and with a bit of luck they wouldn't cause a scene in the main courtyard. Mother said they weren't to attract attention while they played, and a prince without clothes was just the sort of notice they were to avoid. Dan reached over and picked at the knots tying Benjamin's kilt and Mulek told him to leave his brother be. There was nothing worse than Benjamin running through the palace grounds with nothing on but a smile. Not less than once a day the boy slipped off his clothes and streaked through the palace raising a stir among the maidservants. It was such a common occurrence that the palace help called Benjamin the prince without any clothes and Mother was determined to break the boy's dreadful habit before his next birthday or she'd have to lock him in his room until he learned to stay dressed.

There was never a worry Dan would keep his kilt around his hips where it belonged. He was a seven-year-old with the sensibilities of a man. He had dark-brown hair that stuck up off the top of his head like a rooster's crown no matter how many times it was combed and oiled in place, and with the breeze blowing through the gardens, every lock on his head stood on end. Dan had cherry-red cheeks and his eyes were greenish brown—a color Mother said was adorable. Mulek glanced at Dan. What sort of color was adorable?

Mulek was the first to reach the last maple tree and turn down a narrow path leading between the junipers—the hair on Dan's head bobbing above the level of the bushes and the clapping of Benjamin's too-large-to-stay-on-his-feet sandals filling the main courtyard with the sound of their arrival. They came onto the square beside the fountains and Mulek immediately pulled up. The reason he'd lured his brothers here to play was leaning against the iron bars of the main palace gates. Captain Laban was exactly where mother said he'd find him—one hand gripped about the gatepost and the other stuffed beneath the shimmering brass of his breastplates, and when he shifted his weight, the clanging of his armor chased the sparrows out from under the clefts in the stonewall. He was speaking to the other reason Mother had sent Mulek to spy. Chief Elder Zadock stood inside the gates, the cloth on his black turban gathering the heat of the morning sun and the iron bars casting striped shadows over his white complexion. The air was filled with the singsong of his high-pitched voice, but he was speaking through the shawls that fell from his turban and the cloth muffled his voice so that he was impossible to understand from where Mulek stood.

Mulek inched over and took up a post close to Laban and Zadock. He made his first throw to Benjamin, the boy lifting his arms in the air only to have the colorful ball hit him square in the brow. Benjamin giggled and Mulek kept one ear turned to his soft laughter and the other cocked to the rise and fall of the Chief Elder's voice. Whatever it was he was discussing with Laban, it wasn't for everyone to hear, not with him speaking through his shawls and Laban throwing glances toward the watch post, and keeping his men at a respectable distance.

Benjamin picked the ball off the ground, ran half the distance back to Mulek with his cheeks full of air and his arms swinging wild and when he released the ball it went straight to the ground and rolled the full length of the courtyard. Mulek didn't pick it up. He let it run through his legs and roll closer to Laban and Zadock before retrieving it and taking up a post a little closer to the captain. Mulek had to keep an innocent face for as long as God required it, and in the company of Dan and Benjamin, Laban would think him a harmless child at play. Laban didn't know it, but Mulek was the one the captain hated above all others—the one he hoped to capture.

Mulek was the palace informant.

"I met with the king early this morning." Zadock adjusted his turban forward onto his brow and pulled his collar over the ends of his graying hair. He leaned in next to Captain Laban and said, "We begin the trial in three days."

"Did you convince him to hold it at the city gates?"

"Zedekiah wanted to do it in his palace chambers, but I insisted otherwise. If he wants the Elders on my council to serve as his jurors, it will have to be at the east gate where we conduct all our public trials."

"And he agreed?"

"You know Zedekiah; he's as naive as a child." Zadock cleared his throat. "Have you paid the nobles to attend the trial?"

"Four hundred and all of them with good strong voices." Laban slapped his fist to his chest and his breastplates clanged against his powerful body. "Zedekiah will think all Israel wants Uriah dead when he hears them chanting for his life."

Zadock said, "I want everyone in place well before the arguments begin. Uriah's friends are not to get close enough to be heard, is that clear? The defense isn't to get any support from the crowd."

Laban said, "I didn't think Uriah had any lawyers."

"He doesn't. Not one has come forward to defend him." Zadock nodded, the point of his turban throwing shadows over the courtyard stone. "Just this morning Zedekiah appointed Uriah to defend himself."

Laban smiled. "It's going to be a short trial."

"It will as long as . . ." Zadock passed his tongue over his lips.

Laban said, "As long as what?"

"As long as no lawyers come forward to help Uriah, otherwise it could . . ."

A cloth ball glanced off Zadock's turban, the gold chains clanging against the Chief Elder's stiff headpiece before falling to the ground. It was made of finely weaved red linens. Zadock had never seen such an expensive toy, but he didn't pick it up. He hadn't time for a playful soul as a boy and he wasn't going to sully his hands with the foolish preoccupations of childhood. He stuffed his fists under the pleats in his robe and turned his gaze out over the courtyard to see the princes of Judah in their play clothes.

Mulek hurried over, his short dark hair playing about his ears. He pushed past Laban with his gaze turned down onto the ball. He said, "Excuse me sir, I missed the throw."

Zadock said, "You most certainly did."

Laban said, "Do you want me to get rid of them?"

Mulek's head shot up, his wide eyes peering up at the Chief Elder. Foolish boy. Must he look up with those large, brown eyes, pleading his case? Didn't he understand Zadock was the Chief Elder and he had neither the patience nor the sensibilities to endure the play of children and the loud prattle that came with such trivial pursuits? Mulek should at least have the sense to throw his ball elsewhere, but then he was the prince—a young one at that—and there was little harm in having him nearby. He was too young to understand the gravity of Zadock's conversations or the complexities of his plotting. And just look at the boy's mournful eyes. He was a puppy, not a prince, and an innocent like him couldn't bring any hurt to Zadock. Mulek was a naive, pathetic boy like his father and thank heavens he would never become king and mire the kingdom with the foolish doctrines of goodwill and kindness. The boy didn't have the backbone to govern, and Zadock, with Laban's help, would see that neither he nor his father would rule for any length of time.

Zadock didn't have time to deal with Mulek and his father right now, not until they dispensed with Uriah. He was the man who knew too much. No, Uriah wasn't a man; he was a nuisance, a very dangerous irritation who possibly knew enough to implicate them in their attempt on the lives of the royal family and the sooner they silenced him, the sooner they would be safe from anyone finding out their ties to Shechem and his band of robbers. Those fools! If they'd been successful at the coronation, he wouldn't have to worry about Uriah or the king.

Zadock raised his hand to Laban and said, "That boy is a weak little imp, a harmless child. Let him play with his brothers." He offered Mulek a nod of the head—the closest thing to a bow he could muster for a prince who would never be king. He said, "God speed, prince of Judah."

Mulek snatched the ball from the ground. He said, "Thank you, sir," and hurried back to throw the ball to his brothers.

"There's something about him," Laban said. "I don't know what it is, but there's something very, very . . ."

"Zadock, sir! Captain Laban!" Lieutenant Daniel galloped up the street and came around. He pulled off his helmet, his long, black hair falling down into his eyes. He sidled in next to the iron bars and leaned over the saddle with a leather scroll in his hand. He said, "We have a problem at the Jawbone Inn."

"At this hour? None of my men drink before midday." Laban stepped to the bars. "What company is he from? I'll see that his commanding officer is informed of the—"

"It's Uriah's father, sir."

"What!"

Daniel's horse sidestepped away from the sound of Laban's outburst. He said, "Shemayahu's here, sir. In Jerusalem."

Laban stuck his face to the iron bars. "Who sent for him?"

"You did." Daniel held out a parchment. "This is your notice, isn't it?"

Laban reached for the leather scroll, but Zadock snatched it from between the bars and quickly read through it. He shook the scroll to near tearing and said, "You told me you didn't send notice to Shemayahu."

Laban said, "I didn't."

Zadock pushed the scroll at Laban. "Explain this."

Laban read through it and when he finished he rubbed the back of his neck and slowly said, "I don't have an explanation, except . . ."

"Except what?"

"Well about a month ago, maybe longer . . ." Laban turned his gaze toward the archway leading from the palace to the military grounds. "It was late one evening. I happened to return to the military offices and I came across a thief. I chased him, but he got away with a leather parchment." Laban held up the scroll. "The inkwell was spilled and the pens were out and he could have used them to write this."

Zadock took the leather notice back and rolled it tight around itself. He said, "I've never known a thief to be well versed in letters."

Laban said, "I suppose not."

"You suppose?"

"What do you want me to say, that I raised the entire cavalry to chase down a man for a piece of missing leather parchment?" Laban jabbed his finger at the air and his voice was far too loud not to attract the attention of the palace watch standing at the far side of the main gates. He said, "I don't spend my days chasing after common thieves and I don't order my men to waste their time on such, such . . ."

The colored ball flew over Zadock's turban and the gold chains caught on Laban's finger, spinning round twice before coming loose and falling to the ground with a soft thud. Laban fell silent and let Mulek press past them. The boy apologized for interrupting them, retrieved the ball and once he left them in peace, Zadock said, "It was no ordinary thief that wrote this notice to Uriah's father."

"What are you saying?"

"I want you to find out who wrote this."

Laban turned toward the gate, his full brass armor reflecting the bright morning light. He called to Daniel and said, "Take us to Shemayahu now."

Zadock didn't follow Laban into the street. He stayed and stared over the empty courtyard like a lost child searching for his mother.

Captain Laban came back down from the gate. He said, "Are you coming?"

Zadock waved his hand to silence Laban, but he wouldn't be quiet. Laban said, "What are you looking at. There's nothing out there."

Zadock said, "Precisely," and kept staring about the gardens, the faint trickling of water through the fountains and the chirping of birds the only sound to be heard. It was an odd thing for the princes to abandon their play so quickly without the usual giggling and squealing that accompanied boys that age. They had gone to find other mischiefs as quickly as a cat leaps to the rooftops to prowl.

Zadock lifted the hem of his robe off the stones and started toward the gate, but the bright red color caught his attention and drew him down along the wall. There, rolled up against the stonework, was Mulek's ball. Zadock picked it up and glanced back over the empty yard again, the grounds silent of even the slightest sound of the princes running through the hedges or climbing the trees. They were gone, vanished into the midmorning light without a trace, and Zadock couldn't keep from dwelling on their sudden disappearance. He threw the colored ball back into the courtyard and let it roll across the stones and come to rest against the trunk of a small sapling before making his way out the palace gates.

Exactly what sort of game was Mulek playing?

Daniel led Laban and Zadock down King Street, past the front doors of the Jawbone Inn, and found his men standing guard at the entrance to the alley. They reined aside to let Daniel pass, telling him they left Shemayahu and his family at the end of the alley. They would have stayed with them, but the woman's child drove them away with its crying and with good reason. The shadows were filled with the bawling of a child, the cries echoing off the high limestone walls of wealthy estates. Daniel ordered his men to wait there while he led the Chief Elder and the captain up the cobblestone rise and around a jog in the lane to where he'd left Shemayahu and Deborah lying on the . . .

Where were they? Daniel ran the last few cubits to the top of the alley and there, tied to a post was a baby goat, bawling for its mother. Curses! How did Shemayahu escape the alley and leave this foolish animal as a decoy? The walls rose three stories on either side and the gates to the estates were sealed shut with metal bolts so that not even the strongest thief could break them down and . . .

The cool morning breeze blew open the last gate where Daniel had found Shemayahu and his family sleeping. The wood planks creaked open on leather hinges and when they banged against the outside wall of the estate, Daniel stepped inside.

The early flowering buds of spring filled the beds of a large garden and Daniel started past them to the door of the home when he spied a mule blanket thrown down along a run of steps chiseled into the outside wall of the home. The blanket belonged to Shemayahu. Daniel grabbed it and turned up the steps, taking two and three at a time.

The flat, clay roof spread over the expanse of the estate home coloring the top of it a deep orange. There were rows of reed mats sprinkled with nuts drying in the morning sun and a line of tall baskets. Daniel pushed the first one over, spilling the flax. He jabbed the toe of his boot at the next and the basket rocked on end, but didn't go over. That's where they were, they were hiding inside the basket and Daniel ripped away the lid and ran his hand through the white flax, but there was no one inside. He pushed over another basket, pulled free the lid on three more, but still no Shemayahu or Deborah or any of the family of Uriah. They were gone, and the only way they could have escaped was jumping from this roof to the one next door, and from there to the next. Daniel spun around, scanning the rooftops in every direction. They could have gotten down along King Street, or jumped across to the alley leading in behind the palace grounds. Or they could have gone over there behind the Jawbone where three estates were connected like a bridge behind the inn and leading the roof-runners down toward the lower city before they would ever have to leave the safety of these high haunts and climb back to street level.

Daniel held Shemayahu's mule blanket between his hands and tore it through the middle, rending the fibers with a savage tearing of the cloth. Curse Shemayahu and curse his son Uriah and curse his whole family! They'd gotten away and now Daniel had to tell Laban he'd failed. He started back down the steps to the alley without any prisoners, but he was not without a firm resolve.

He would find Uriah's father and bring him to Captain Laban.

Surprise was the only way to take an enemy, and Sarah hid behind the trunk of the largest olive tree in the yard, clutching a goose feather like a soldier holds a weapon and waiting until Ruth filled the water jar from the cistern and disappeared inside the house. Finally! Joshua was left to himself without Mama's protecting graces. This was her chance to settle the score, the one she'd promised to tally after Joshua ate her figs at breakfast.

Sarah stepped out from behind the tree, pointed the tip of the feather at Joshua and said, "Off with the robber's head!"

"No, don't use the feather! Not the feather!" Joshua jumped to his feet, waving his arms. "Your hair will turn red if you tickle me with the feather."

Red? Her hair was already red, and it wasn't getting any redder, no matter how many times she chased Joshua about the yard. If she were a boy she'd wear a turban to hide its brightness, but no matter how often she played in the mud with Joshua or collected frogs along the banks of the Gihon Spring, she was still a young lady and she was obliged to wear her hair for everyone to see—to endure the stares of black and brown headed women like a prisoner caged by her beauty, no matter how many women thought her hair ugly. Her red hair was beautiful; Papa told her so. He also told her that every time she teased Joshua or let her strong-willed temperament rear its head, her pretty red hair turned a shade of deep, ugly red. What did Papa know about little girls and red hair? She'd spent every morning this week chasing Joshua around the yard with a stick and her hair was still the same color.

"I show no mercy for your kind."

Sarah cut off Joshua's retreat into the house and he turned back into the olive trees. He said, "You can't use the feather. It's against the rules."

Sarah said, "I make the rules in this kingdom." She waved the feather ahead of her and followed Joshua down the row of olive trees. If she didn't tickle him until he cried for peace, there was no one else who would. Joshua ran faster than most little boys and he had her to thank for that. She cornered him at the end of the row between a stack of empty baskets and the water trough, and pressed the tip of the feather to his nose like a soldier points the tip of a sword at the heart of a prisoner. She said, "I have you now, evil robber, down on your back and close your eyes."

"Never!" Joshua giggled and tried for her feather with both hands.

"I said, down on your back." Sarah pressed her lips together and furrowed her brow seriously enough that he did as she said without her having to take him by the shoulder and force him down. Silly boy. He never could tell the difference between her make-believe serious face and her real mad one. She leaned over him, her lips resisting the powerful tugging of a smile, and quickly fluttered the plume about his nose until he sneezed and giggled and tried to shield his face with his hands, and then she tickled him some more. She reached to pull up his tunic and tickle his belly, but Joshua rolled over, his face in the soil and his giggles blowing dirt out from under his planted face. Sarah rolled him over on his back, pinned him to the ground with her foot, and danced the feather about his chin.

"No, Sarah, please, stop it now!" Joshua grabbed for the feather, missed, and grabbed again. On his fourth try he snatched it from her hands, jumped to his feet and ran out of the olive trees waving the captured weapon over his head and hollering his victory before disappearing inside the house.

Sarah fell to her knees, red-faced and laughing, and she would have stayed there a good while if not for the figure crouched on the wall above her. She fell quiet and quickly stepped back against the protection of a tree trunk, the gnarled and twisted olive bending around her like a wooden fortress. How long had the stranger been there, bent over and prowling with his knees up in his chest like a lion ready to pounce and his face hidden behind the canopy of olive leaves that turned a shade of deep green in winter but never fell to the ground? Sarah leaned out from under the thickest branches to see him more clearly, but he moved down the wall behind another branch, his face still hidden behind the winter foliage, with only the sunshine to outline his form against the cover of leaves. He reached his hand out to test the branches and then leaped from his perch.

A pair of costly gazelle leather sandals crashed through the canopy, breaking a long branch with a thundering crack. They were attached to dark-skinned legs that had grown too long for the silver-studded kilt that wrapped around the stranger's hips. His purple tunic caught on the limb and he pulled it free as he fell through the air and landed as nimbly as a robin in the garden, his knees bent and his arms out for balance. If there were any who could inspire intrigue for the daring and mischief of robbers it was this intruder. But he was no robber. Sarah knew him the moment his long-boned body broke through the branches.

Mulek no longer looked like the baldheaded son of an Egyptian governor. He'd not shaved his hair over the winter and the cap of locks that coiled about his ears and flirted with his brow was a style fit for a Hebrew prince. His new hair framed his high cheeks and elegant thin nose and when she felt his gaze on her and the wonder of his eyes, she turned away and waited for the warmth of a blush to finish flashing across her cheecks.

Mulek said, "I need your help."

"My help?" Sarah stepped back against the trunk of the olive tree and laid her hand on the gnarled bark. "Whatever for, sir?"

"Can I trust you?"

That's what a friend was for and Sarah hardly knew the prince. She said, "We're not friends."

"I need more than a friend."

How could Sarah hope to be more than a friend to the prince of Judah? She'd watched him from a distance and then only in the company of her mother when they delivered weaving to the palace. Sarah lowered her gaze to the ground, not because Mulek wasn't handsome, but because she was the daughter of a blacksmith and a weaver and she could never hope to enjoy the company of royalty. Mulek would make a faithful friend, but they were born of different circumstance and she would never be anything more than a commoner and he a prince. She would speak to Mulek when spoken to, but she could not be his friend. Sarah would never chase Mulek about the yard with a feather.

Sarah bowed. "Good day Prince of Judah."

Mulek took her by the hand and raised her up. "We haven't time for that sort of thing. We have to save them."

"Who?"

Mulek led her out of the trees and across the courtyard to the front gate. "You have to promise you'll tell no one but your mother what I'm about to show you."

"There's nothing outside this gate but cobblestones."

"Promise me."

Sarah pulled free of Mulek's grasp and set her hands on her hips. "Not until you tell me what I'm promising."

"Your mother said you had a wild spirit like no other child." Mulek's nose twitched when he grinned. It was an expression that said he understood her stubborn spirit and he wasn't about to let her get the best of him.

Sarah said, "That isn't entirely so." She looked away from his piercing stare. He was right about her wild spirit, but not in the company of strangers. Outside the safety of her family she was happy to be seen and hardly ever heard. Sarah searched the yard for Ruth, but she hadn't come back out to refill her jar with drinking water. Where was she when Sarah needed the comfort of her protecting graces or at least her pleated skirt to hide from the gaze of this royal son?

"Is this about more weaving for Mother?" Sarah started toward the house. "I can call her and tell her that you're here to—"

"This has nothing to do with weaving." Mulek took Sarah by the arm and brought her back to the gate. His blue eyes were filled with a serious light and there was no doubt about his concern. "Can you come and go without being seen by anyone?"

Sarah nodded. No one ever took notice of her going in and out of the house. She was a forgotten child, lost between the elegance of the woman Elizabeth had become, the miracle of Aaron's healing, the handsomeness of Daniel's soldiering, and the preciousness of her little brother's antics. And though she tried to act as precious as Joshua, he was the only one the women in the market pinched on the cheek and rubbed on the head—the little creature had fooled everyone! But why did Mulek care if she came and went without being seen? This was all very strange and she said, "Is this some sort of game?"

Mulek stepped next to her, his long body hovering over her and his shadow darkening her face. He said, "Saving Uriah's life is no game."

Sarah's chest tightened and she held her hand to her heart. What danger lurked on the other side of the gate? The wood planks stood in the full sun collecting the heat of the day and Sarah leaned against them to chase away the chill that filled her soul.

Mulek reached his young, soft hands to her cheek and lifted her gaze up to meet his. He said, "I don't mean to frighten you."

Sarah straightened her shoulders. "I'm not afraid."

"Then you'll do this?"

"I'm ready." Sarah stood away from the gate, blew the red hair back off her brow and said, "Go ahead and open it."

The moist air filtered up from the wash basket like steam off stone after a summer rain. Ruth carried the wet clothes across the main room toward the front door. She'd spent the early morning washing, and all that was left to do was hang the wash out to dry. The dust from Jonathan's Elder shawls came out nicely, the spots in Elizabeth's robe were gone, and she'd gotten all the stains out of the children's clothes except one. It didn't seem the mud in Joshua's white tunic would ever come out, no matter how many times she passed it over a scrubbing board or covered it with enough lye powders to take the skin off a mule's backside. The lye never failed her, but when it came to Joshua's clothes, it didn't matter that she used fire from the hearth. They never cleaned up like the others. Just moments before he'd come running into the house, the front of his tunic stained with dirt, and when she asked him what he'd gotten into, the boy blamed Sarah for the mess, said she'd forced him to the ground with a feather. Ruth shifted the basket to her other arm. Didn't the little rascal know that she could tell when he hedged the truth? What sort of boy would go to the ground under threat of a feather, and from his sister no less?

Ruth sprinkled the basket of clothes with perfume from her homemade stores—one shot of rose petal essence and two of wild mint. They weren't strong like the frankincense perfumes purchased at the market, but they lasted just as long and there was never a day when her family didn't thank her for the finely scented clothes. Well, maybe they didn't actually thank her, but she knew they were grateful by the way they sniffed at the collars and held the cloth to their nose to take in the freshness, at least everyone but Joshua. That boy could no more smell a fine scent than he could sit still and eat his dinner.

Ruth lifted the heavy basket and swung the door open, the weight of the wet clothes slowing her stride. She had crossed to the clothesline hanging between two olives trees near the back of the yard when she saw Mulek at the front gate with Sarah. That was odd. What was Mulek doing here speaking with Sarah? There was no reason for him to come to their home unless . . .

Ruth dropped the wash basket and started over. Mulek would only ever come here if there were trouble, and immediately she prayed a silent prayer that whatever the reason for his coming, it wasn't something they couldn't endure. Mulek opened the gate before Ruth could get there and standing in the street was a mother clutching a babe in her arms, two boys holding to the skirts of her robe, and an older man standing behind them, stealing hurried glances over his shoulder.

Mulek said, "This is Uriah's family."

"What!" The word escaped Ruth with such force it turned the gaze of all to her. Why did the prince bring them here? Ruth stepped past them, peered into the street to be certain no one was watching, and then ushered them inside their gate and latched it behind them. Didn't Mulek know there was not a more intolerable place he could bring Uriah's family than to the home of one of the Elders? They'd already voted to take Uriah's life once and Jonathan was going to sit on the jury with the other Elders at the next trial and it wasn't wise for them to come here. There was no telling how Jonathan would react to these people. She nodded, but it was impossible to remove the fear she could feel pulling at her cheeks and tightening her brow. She managed to say, "What a lovely family."

Mulek introduced the strangers and said, "They haven't a place to stay. There's not an inn that will have them and Mother said you would board them."

Ruth undid the strings on her apron and let it fall down over her outer robe. Didn't Mulek understand what he was asking? Jonathan would never allow it.

Mulek said, "Mother will want to know if you can put them up during the trial."

Ruth didn't answer, and in the long silence Benuriah said, "Does this mean we have to sleep in the street again?"

David said, "No, don't let the soldiers chase us again, not the soldiers."

"Sleep in the street?" Ruth held her hand to her mouth. "Don't tell me that's where you've been staying."

Deborah said, "Only one night."

Ruth patted David on the head. "What about the soldiers, son?"

Shemayahu said, "This morning a young officer held us under guard in an alley of the upper city, and when he went off to fetch the captain of the guard this boy found us and . . ." Shemayahu laid his hand on Mulek's shoulder. "He brought us here."

"A young officer found you?" Ruth held her hand to her breast. "What was his . . . "

Mulek said, "It was Daniel."

Ruth lowered her head. She said, "I'm sorry, so very sorry."

"There's nothing you can do about that evil man." Deborah held her baby close to her bosom. "Why, he nearly hit my little girl with the heel of his boot and if it weren't for Shemayahu there's no telling what hurt he would have done to her." She pulled her shoulders back and raised her chin. "If I didn't have this babe to watch after I would have gone after that soldier with both my fists and he'd not forget the lesson I'd . . . ."

Mulek tugged on Deborah's sleeve. He said, "Daniel is Ruth's son."

"Your son?" Deborah relaxed her shoulders and fiddled with the cloth covering the baby's face. "I'm sorry. I didn't mean to suggest that—"

"You poor dears." Ruth turned to see the worried faces of Uriah's family. She couldn't deny them a place to rest, and she pulled Deborah and the children close to her and took Shemayahu by the hand, leading them toward the house. "Come inside and I'll get you something to eat. It's nearly time for midday meal and my husband, he should be along any . . ." Ruth fell silent. What awful timing. Jonathan didn't usually come home at midday, but this morning before he left he told her not to bother bringing him his lunch. He wasn't going to fire up the smelting oven or the open hearth, and he could leave the shop and come home today without wasting any firewood.

"Is there something wrong?" Deborah quickly dug into her purse. "We can pay whatever you ask. We only need lodging for as long as my husband's trial lasts and then we'll . . ." Her voice broke and she brushed away the tears.

"Put that purse away." Ruth pushed Deborah's hand aside. "You're not going to pay for lodging in this home."

Mulek said, "What shall I tell Mother?"

"Tell her all is well."

Mulek picked up the wash basket Ruth had dropped. He said, "It isn't really well, is it?"

"If God is willing . . ." Ruth took the basket from him. "We'll make it well."

Jonathan pushed through the gate and into the courtyard. The smell of midday meal filtered from the kitchen window and he took a deep breath. Potato stew was simmering in the hearth, he was certain of it. There weren't many foods he could detect, and when he was hungry everything Ruth prepared warmed his palate, but there was no doubt this was potato stew—not to be confused for a watery soup of potatoes and broth with a hint of basil. This meal was a thick goat's milk potato stew seasoned with onions and mushrooms, and the scent mixed with the fresh bread cooling near the window and filled the courtyard with the call to midday meal.

Jonathan crossed the courtyard in less time than it takes a hungry bear to climb a tree, pushed open the door and said, "Ruth, I'm home."

There was no answer and not a sound to tell him there was anyone afoot. He closed the door slowly, crossed to the kitchen, and there sitting in silence around the table were the unfamiliar faces of two young boys, a woman with her baby, and an older man. Joshua and Sarah sat opposite them and Elizabeth was serving a plate of bread. Ruth stood at the hearth stirring the potato stew and when she felt the wonder of his puzzled gaze, she turned around, the ladle still in her hand, and said, "Oh, Jonathan, you're just in time."

Ruth hadn't said anything about entertaining guests for midday meal. Why, they hardly ever entertained anyone in their home and now they had an entire family come to eat with them. What in the name of Moses was this about? Jonathan came around the crowded table, the silent gaze of all upon him. He slipped between the back of Joshua's chair and the banister to the stairs, patting the boy on the head as he passed, and came in next to Ruth. He lowered his voice and said, "You didn't say anything about . . ." He glanced over his shoulder and smiled at the family staring back at him like prisoners. He turned to Ruth and said, "About these, these . . ."

Ruth said, "About our guests?"

"That's right." Jonathan leaned his head in next to Ruth's. "Who are these people?"

Elizabeth leaned in, a second plate of bread cooling in her hand. She pushed her dark braids off her shoulders and said, "Shall I introduce them?"

Ruth said, "Serve the bread, dear."

"But Mama, I can—"

"I said, serve the bread, daughter." Ruth stared at the girl until she nodded and hurried down along the table to the far end and set the bread plate at the foot. Ruth hooked the pot of potato stew with the end of the ladle and pulled it from the fire. She set it on the table and said, "Jonathan, have a seat and eat something before it grows cold."

Jonathan sat across from the elderly man in the company and let Ruth fill his bowl while he broke a round of bread and sopped it full and immediately the room erupted with the pouring of stew and the tinkling of spoons against pottery and the soft breaking of bread and the sipping of sweet red wine from the cellar. It was a peaceful sound, filling the silence so that Jonathan didn't have to say anything to the strangers sharing his table. He stole a glance at the elderly man seated near him and when their eyes met he immediately turned his head back into his food.

The man said, "My name is Shemayahu."

Between bites Jonathan mumbled that he was pleased to meet him and tried to keep his food from falling back into his bowl. He scooped another spoonful into his mouth, his head still turned down into his eating. Shemayahu. The name was vaguely familiar. It had a ring to it. He'd heard it somewhere before, but he couldn't remember where.

Shemayahu said, "I really should thank you for lodging us in your home until—"

Jonathan choked on his stew. He coughed up three pieces of potato and what looked like an artichoke. He turned to Ruth and said, "You know I don't like artichokes."

Ruth patted him on the shoulder. She said, "It's just an odd-shaped potato, dear."

Jonathan nodded slowly and took another bite, his head down. After a long silence, the sounds of eating slowly returned, though not with near the heartiness as before. Jonathan sopped another piece of bread about the bottom of the bowl and he was about to ask Ruth for another helping when . . .

Jonathan dropped his spoon into the bowl and it clanged against the hard clay side. Did Shemayahu say he and his family were lodging in this house? Jonathan's head came up and he planted his elbows on the table. He said, "Are you staying here?"

Shemayahu pushed his bowl aside. He said, "We couldn't find a place in any inn."

It was odd they couldn't find lodging in any of the city's many inns. This wasn't a feast time and there wasn't any reason for the inns of the city to be full. Jonathan said, "That's unfortunate there isn't any room."

"It isn't that they're full; it's just—"

"Have some more dear." Ruth leaned over the table with the pot, her small frame blocking Jonathan's view of Shemayahu. She filled his bowl to overflowing, and when the broth spilled onto the tabletop she said, "Oh my, I'll get something to clean away the mess."

Jonathan said, "Go on with what you were saying."

Shemayahu said, "We tried to find lodging at the Jawbone Inn just last night, but—"

"Excuse me." Ruth pushed Jonathan aside and wiped away her spill. She said, "Would you like some more bread, dear?"

Jonathan sat back in his chair. How was he to carry on a conversation with their guest if he couldn't see the man, to say nothing of Ruth's constant interruptions? But he didn't begrudge Ruth her kindness. She was showing hospitality and he said, "Another piece of bread would do fine."

Ruth served him two more rounds of dark, warm bread. She said, "I told Shemayahu he and his family could lodge with us until their business in Jerusalem is finished."

Jonathan leaned past Ruth to see Shemayahu. He said, "Exactly what sort of business brings you to Jerusalem?"

"We've come to see my son."

Ruth patted Jonathan on the shoulder and opened her eyes as wide as he'd ever seen. She was telling him it wasn't polite to pry, at least that's what she seemed to be saying by the rigidness in her body and the way she held her upper lip between her teeth. Ruth was never one to meddle in the affairs of others and it was a talent Jonathan would do well to learn.

Ruth said, "It's a family matter, dear."

"I see." Jonathan nodded slowly toward Shemayahu. "I wish you the best."

Shemayahu said, "That's very kind of you."

"We can pay for our lodging." Deborah opened a small purse and held out three pieces of silver. "This should help cover the cost of the food."

Ruth said, "Nonsense, we can—"

"Three pieces of silver should do just fine." Jonathan reached over the table, took the money, and rubbed the silver coins between his fingers. He said, "For the time being anyway."

Shemayahu came around the table and stood next to Jonathan. He offered his hand and said, "Then you agree to this arrangement?"

Jonathan turned his gaze onto the babe in Deborah's arms. "The little one doesn't cry all night, does she?"

Deborah held the babe up for Jonathan to see her smile. "Does this look like a face that could cry, sir?"

Jonathan said, "She has her mother's eyes."

"And I assure you," Deborah held the babe close, "I never cried when I was her age."

Jonathan shook Shemayahu's hand and welcomed the man to his home. He turned his head back into his meal. What was he doing, renting his home to strangers? But Shemayahu's family had a need and there was plenty of room in their home to accommodate them, though there was a nagging concern lost somewhere in the back of his memory. Shemayahu. He knew that name and someday he was going to remember exactly where he'd heard it. He filled his spoon full and he was lifting it to his mouth when he pulled up, the stew balancing in front of his eyes. He'd been wrong all along. This wasn't potato stew at all! It was watery, thin-broth soup—potato soup—and not a single mushroom nor any of the goat's milk and thickening flour that made this his favorite stew. He lowered the spoon back into his bowl and broke another round of bread.

Why did he suffer such a poor sense of judgment?

CHAPTER 25

Uriah sat in the dark corner of the upper prison, his knees pulled up against his chest and a bowl of pottage balanced between his hands. It had been four months since he was taken prisoner and if his father didn't see to defending him at trial he was going to rot in this place. Uriah stirred through his food, if you could call this white paste food. He'd suffered the same bland meal every morning since Laban and his men carried him from the well of the prison, but he wasn't about to ask for something better. The guards weren't kind with the butt of a sword, though they only hit him across the back where the bruises didn't show through his ragged brown robes. They said he was to look presentable for trial and a bloodied face would bring him undeserved sympathies from the king.

There was no privacy in this square prison with four rough stone walls rising two stories above the floor. Ten tall pillars supported the high ceiling. A hearth stood along the far wall, but there had never been any wood to light a fire and dispel the chill of morning. An open washing pool flowed with a constant trickle of fresh water, but Uriah couldn't bear to lower himself into it for a bath, not with the memory of the floods he endured in the well to say nothing of the knee-high mud and the . . .

Dear God, how did he ever endure the rats?

The only light came from a solitary lamp hanging in the center of the room, casting a yellow glow over the prisoners, but Uriah stayed in the corner shadows. The guards warned him to keep to himself, away from the eyes and ears of the other men in the room or be returned to the well. Uriah slept in this corner, ate in this corner, and when he walked to the far side of the room to relieve himself in the open sewer, he drew the sharp glances of men more guilty than he.

This was the peaceable prison—nothing like the catacombs below—peopled by men who made better guests than criminals. There were no chains to bolt them to the limestone wall and not a single iron vault to hold a violent man like a cage holds a beast. These were biddable folk, serving the lightest of penalties for the least of crimes. The man seated at the head of the dining table was a tax collector, incarcerated for keeping a portion of the tax that belonged to the royal treasury, but since every tax collector kept an undue portion, this man's only crime was admitting he'd taken anything. A lawyer sat across the table from the tax collector, sentenced to the upper prison for railing against the Elders at trial. A thief sat beside him, insisting he stole nothing, and two more thieves sat opposite him, admitting their felonies and begging the lawyer to defend them for stealing a bag of wheat and a round of bread. It wouldn't be long before all of them were gone. Thieves didn't stay long in this mild prison, lawyers and tax collectors even less—a few days, nothing more—and then Uriah would have to endure the arrival of new prisoners. Twenty-five had come and gone while he languished in the shadows, and he prayed the next man through the doors was his father, come to see to his defense. Shemayahu was his only hope if he ever wanted to be free of Laban and Zadock.

The door flew open, banging against the inside wall. A troop of prison guards stormed inside carrying bottles of perfume, soaps, clean towels, and a change of clothes—a new brown robe with a wide sash, polished leather sandals and a gold headband to keep the hair back off the shoulders. The jailer stood at the front of the troop. He raised his lantern overhead and cast a light into the shadows of Uriah's corner. He said, "There he is."

The guards picked Uriah off the floor and ripped the clothes from his back, the cloth digging into his skin as it tore. They forced him across the prison to the washing pool, poured cleansing perfumes over his body, and threw him into the frigid waters. The jailer leaned over the edge of the washing pool and smiled. His teeth were filled with holes, and his speech was cluttered with whistles. He said, "I'm to have you cleaned and dressed."

The water lapped against Uriah's hips. He wrapped his arms around himself and shivered in the cold air. He shook his wet hair from in front of his eyes. "Cleaned and dressed for what?"

"Your trial, son." The jailer threw a towel at Uriah. "It begins today."

Low clouds from an overnight storm masked Jerusalem's high walls and hung about the towers, shrouding the city. Commander Yaush leaned forward in the saddle, reined his steed across the wide-open plains toward the walls, square rooftops, and majestic pillars of Solomon's temple on the distant hillside. Jerusalem stood on the horizon like a night vision, but it was no imaginary city and this ride to Uriah's trial was no dream. Yaush was called as the lead witness. No, he wasn't called—he was ordered to attend; otherwise, he never would have made the journey to participate in this nightmare. He tried to convince Zadock his testimony was of no help, but the Chief Elder told him he was the only witness, and Yaush had no other choice than to appear at trial.

The escorts who accompanied Yaush from Fort Lakhish couldn't keep up on his run across the open expanse of the valley between Jerusalem and Bethlehem; but then he shouldn't expect his wife, Sophia, and his son, Setti, to ride like seasoned cavalrymen. Sophia spent her days sewing, and Setti was captain of the night watch and very much untrained in the rigors of riding. The road turned down through a run of cedar that graced the Tyrolean Valley, and when they cleared the trees they came alongside the base of Jerusalem's south wall, its massive limestone blocks rising through the mists like the cliffs of Mount Carmel reaching above the fog-laden shores of the Great Sea.

The trial was to be held inside the city's east gate, but Yaush didn't ride around to the other side of the city and up the rampart to the entrance. It was no doubt well guarded before the trial, and the moment he arrived, Captain Laban would get word and he'd not be at liberty to attend to other business. He led Sophia and Setti west through the Cheese Maker's Valley, past a hundred goat pens, cheese vats, and milking racks, then up a rocky road between the cemetery and city walls.

Jerusalem's west gate had no archway, no wide passage with thick limestone to moor the gatepost in place, and no intricate carvings of cherubs to ask God's blessing upon the entrance. Yaush came around in front of the gate, his horse shaking its head against his pull on the reins. It was a small entrance with a single wooden door that didn't require a draw wheel—nothing like the massive double wood gates that protected the entrance to his fortress at Lakhish. This may be the city of God, but faith shouldn't get in the way of building strong fortifications. If he were captain of the guard he'd rebuild this gate to match the ones he'd built at Lakhish and protect the holiness that lay within, if there was any divinity left within the city's precincts. The gate was drawn open and stopped with sandbags and the watchman dozed against the gatepost. It was a breach in security that Yaush would never have allowed at Lakhish, but since he had to get inside without making known his arrival, he didn't reprimand the soldier for his slothfulness.

Yaush tightened his cloak around his shoulders to hide his officer's dress beneath and told the watchman he was traveling with his wife and son and they had accommodations at the Jawbone Inn. The soldier waved them through and Yaush rode down the emptiness of Main Street, past the first line of homes, before pulling up and waiting for Sophia to sidle in next to him. The ride had blown her veil off her long, black hair and Yaush would have loaned her the scarves he wore around her neck to keep her cheeks warm, but he couldn't. He had to keep his face hidden until after he met a man in the lower city.

"This should be enough for our room." Yaush handed Setti his money purse. "Take your mother to the Jawbone Inn and I'll be along soon."

"As soon as what?" Sophia leaned forward in the saddle.

"I have some business to attend to." Yaush patted his horse's mane.

"Are you going to report to Captain Laban?"

"Not now."

Sophia said, "You really should eat something."

"I'm not hungry."

"You haven't eaten a full meal in days."

"I've not had an appetite."

"This has nothing to do with your appetite." Sophia inched her horse forward. "I'm worried about you."

"I'll be fine."

"Fine?" Sophia brushed her long hair back from in front of her face. "You insist we arrive before sunrise when the trial doesn't begin for hours."

"I didn't want to keep anyone waiting."

"It's about those letters, isn't it?"

"The letters are locked safely away in the vaults."

"Tell me." Sophia reached for his hand. "What is it in those letters that has turned you into a . . . a . . . ?" She drew her hand back. "Don't you trust us?"

Setti said, "I can come with you if you like?"

"You go with your mother."

"But Papa, I—"

"I said, go with her."

Sophia said, "What sort of business are you conducting at this hour?"

Yaush couldn't tell her what he was doing and he prodded his horse into a steady trot down Water Street. He was taking a treasonous road that could be his undoing, and he'd not allow his family to follow him down that path. Betrayal was a fickle master. He pulled his hood over his head and covered his face with the black scarves.

This business was for his eyes only.

A dark morning fog hung about the palace grounds and Mulek slipped into the thick of it and disappeared down the alley along the north side. He carried a large basket made of double wicker—the strongest the palace storehouse servants weaved—and it was certainly large enough to carry out Mother's instructions. He was not to stop for anyone until he reached the bakery bordering the east gate, and then only long enough to tie the knots and set the basket in place. Mother insisted he wear a tattered robe to disguise his nobility. The hem dragged on the cobblestones and hobbled his hurried stride, but at this hour there was no fear of being sighted.

Mulek carried the basket high on his back and ran down through the towering homes of the east side neighborhoods, his leather sandals falling soft over the cold ground and the sound of his passing dying on the limestone façades with hardly an echo. The narrow footpath veered left, and when he rounded the corner he came across three nobles dressed in costly blue robes. They were headed toward the east gate and Mulek scampered into a side alley before they saw him streaking through the mists. He hurried past a line of back gates and into the next street over where he stumbled onto a group of nobles gathering at the crossroads above the east gate. What were so many well-dressed nobles doing up at this hour? They were never out of bed until the sun cleared the Mount of Olives, but this morning there was not one sleeping. He quickly backtracked through the alley and turned onto a narrow footpath. He cut across the upper city and down along the length of city wall, reaching the far side of the district without venturing through. It was the long way around, but he couldn't let any nobles see him with the basket.

The scent of new bread filled the air behind the bakery. He waited beside the back gate for his heart to slow and his chest to end its heaving, when the wood planks creaked open and the baker's flour-sprayed face poked out. He was a stout man with a belly large enough to hold forty dozen rounds of bread. He wore a white apron over his robe, the cloth splattered with dough from his early-morning breadmaking.

The bakery was lighted with lamps hanging from the crossbeams and warmed by the crackling fires of three ovens. He led Mulek through the kitchens and up a run of stairs to the roof. The air was clear up here, without any fog to hide Mulek from the view of soldiers guarding the east wall. He ducked out of sight and waited until the last watchman turned his march back toward the main tower, then scampered across the rooftop with the basket in tow. The gap between the kitchen roof and the main house was far too wide to jump, but a plank lay between the two and Mulek walked it like a bird scaling the branch of a tree. He hid behind a rise of limestone eaves until the watchman made his next pass, then ran again, his footsteps falling quiet on the soft, clay-topped building. He crawled on his belly the last three cubits to the edge and sneaked his head over to get a good view of . . .

What were all these nobles doing here at this hour? Nearly four hundred had gathered, hours before the start of the trial, and scores of soldiers were stationed at each entrance to the square. The main doors of the east gate were sealed and the gatekeeper passed travelers through the small side entrance, checking every basket and cart that passed into the city.

Mother was right—this basket was the only way in and he tied one end of the rope through the handles and wound the other end around two stone pillars like a pulley in a draw wheel, ready to leverage the weight of the basket and its contents. Mulek secured the riggings out of view of the catwalk and hurried back over the rooftop. He went out the baker's back gate, but instead of returning to the palace, he started down the back streets toward the lower city.

He had one more task to complete before his early-morning mission was finished.

Ruth left the wheat and oats half ground and stood in the darkness of the main room watching her guests sleep. Benuriah and David lay still on mats along the far wall. Shemayahu stirred beneath the blankets on the bench seat, and Deborah slept in the corner with the baby, her rest softened by the thickest blankets Ruth could find.

She should let Shemayahu sleep longer. He was an older man and he needed his rest, but he was to be ready before sunrise and she crept across the room toward the sound of his breathing. She reached to shake him from his sleep and tell him it was time to—

"Uriah!" Shemayahu ripped the blankets off and sat up, his sudden movement frightening Ruth back a step. He peered into the darkness and said, "They murdered my son!"

"It's me, Shemayahu." Ruth tapped him on the shoulder. "You're in the blacksmith's house."

"They murdered him." Shemayahu rubbed his eyes. "I saw it."

"Your son's alive." Ruth inched back to the bench. "You're going to see him at trial."

"Papa?" Deborah stirred in the corner of the room. She left the baby sleeping and stepped in next to the bench seat. "I'm here with you, Papa." She held his hand. "Everything's going to be all right. It was just another of your dreams."

Ruth said, "I can get him some tea."

"He's well." Deborah ran the back of her hand over his brow. "His dreams unsettle him for a while and then he's fine."

Shemayahu said, "It wasn't a dream."

"You were sleeping, Papa. What else could it be?"

Shemayahu stared at the floor. "It was from God."

"Don't talk like that." Deborah let go of his hand. "Nothing's going to happen to Uriah; promise me it won't."

Shemayahu slowly shook his head. "I can't promise you anything."

Ruth said, "I'm sure all will be well."

"You don't understand." Deborah held her hands to her mouth and spoke between her fingers. "Papa is like my husband."

Ruth said, "I'm sure they're both handsome men."

"It isn't that. It's his soul. God speaks to Shemayahu like he does my husband and . . ." Deborah began to cry, and through her tears she told Ruth that a few weeks ago Shemayahu foretold that a masked man riding a mighty steed would come and tell them where they could find Uriah. The next day a hooded horseman disguised behind black scarves brought them a notice telling of Uriah's imprisonment and trial, and now this—nightmares about Uriah's death, something Deborah feared but never dared speak of until now. She glanced at her sleeping baby. "He hasn't even seen our daughter."

"There now." Ruth pressed Deborah's head against her shoulder. "Nothing's happened to Uriah."

What else could she tell Deborah? Her husband was imprisoned for a multitude of crimes he did not commit and with the powerful men arrayed against him, victory was an impossible hope—her husband's accusers were not accustomed to losing. There were so many reasons for this gentle woman to give up, and Ruth pulled Deborah's shaking body close.

Ruth said, "I have some food in the other room. Dates and a warm cup of tea."

A knock sounded at the front door, cutting off Ruth's words before she could finish telling Deborah about the fresh goat's milk she'd warmed over the hearth. Ruth slowly undid the latch, the leather hinges creaking open with far more noise than new leather ever should. The door swung open against the inside wall of the main room and Mulek stood in the dark blue light before dawn. He said, "Are they ready?"

Ruth leaned outside and checked the courtyard, and when she was certain no one had followed him through the fog, she ushered him inside and closed the door. "This is too dangerous."

"It's going to work. It must." Mulek smiled up at Ruth, his white teeth shining. "God will go before us."

Ruth touched the boy on the cheek. If only she had as much faith. She said, "When do they leave?"

"We have to go now. Laban already has his men in the square and it won't be long before he places more in the side streets and footpaths near the square." Mulek turned to Shemayahu. "Are you able, sir?"

Shemayahu quickly pulled his full robe on over his sleeping garments, splashed cold water over his face from a basin in the kitchen, and hurried to the door.

"Not without us." Deborah came around the bench seat, her babe in arms and her two young boys in tow—both of them rubbing the sleep from their eyes and Deborah tying her hair back in place. "We're going with you."

Shemayahu said, "That isn't wise, daughter."

"Nothing we've done is wise, Papa, but that didn't keep us from coming here." Deborah pushed open the door and escorted her children into the cool morning air. She turned back to Shemayahu. "Are you coming?"

Mulek hurried ahead of her and Shemayahu followed, working his cane over the ground. They were gone out of the gate before Ruth could insist they eat something to take the edge off their hunger. She leaned against the doorpost and prayed Mulek was right—that God would go before them.

Mulek led Shemayahu and his family down the hill toward the Pool of Siloam. They were headed away from the trial, but they couldn't simply walk up High Street and cross in front of the east gate, not with so many nobles gathering there. Better to cut through the lower city and take Water Street to the far side. It was the long way around the city but it was the only way to avoid . . .

Mulek stopped so suddenly that his followers nearly ran into him. At this hour there shouldn't be anyone about, but there was a horseman sitting in the saddle of a mighty steed half-hidden in the alley just below the blacksmith's gate. The steed was drawn back into the narrow passageway, its warm breath funneling from its nostrils and piercing the cool air with its panting. The rider was dressed in a black cloak, which was drawn about his face to mask its features.

Mulek took Benuriah and David by the hand, slowly turned around, and whispered for Deborah and Shemayahu to follow him. There was a narrow footpath they could take and he started up the street, praying that whoever was on the horse hadn't recognized him. No one must know he was helping Uriah's family.

Mulek hurried his little company past the carpenter's home, staying in the morning mists that hung about the dark stone walls gone cold from the long night. They were to the cobbler's home when the rider burst out of the alley. Mulek tried to open the latch on the cobbler's gate, but it was locked, and their only escape was to run for the footpath two houses farther up the hill and lose themselves in the maze of paths that connected the homes and properties of the lower city. Benuriah ran alongside Mulek, his legs churning. David held fast to Mulek's hand to keep from falling. Deborah kept her babe close to her breast, and Shemayahu hurried his cane to keep up. They were only a few cubits from finding safety among the shadowed twists and turns of the alley when the masked rider cut across their path, the steed's powerful body blocking their way.

"Run, Shemayahu!" Mulek pushed on the horse. "Run for your life!"

"No, son." Shemayahu pulled Mulek back from the horse. "This man means us no harm."

How could that be? Surely a man hiding behind a cloak could bring nothing but harm. Shemayahu said, "It's you, isn't it?"

The rider nodded and inched forward, the animal's muzzle sniffing at them.

Shemayahu said, "What do you want with us?"

The rider spoke, his deep voice echoing off the walls. He said, "Where is Lehi?"

"He isn't with us."

The man leaned over his saddle, his hands tight about the reins. He said, "I led you to his plantation so you could—"

"He's not coming." Shemayahu stepped back and placed his arm around Deborah.

"Who's defending your son?"

"I am."

The man got down from the saddle, landing on the cobblestones like a seasoned rider. He stood tall; Mulek's head only reached to his stomach. His thick black cloak rode high on his broad shoulders. He spread his feet like an officer inspecting his troops and rubbed the cloth of Shemayahu's tattered brown robe between his fingers. "You'll not impress the king dressed like this."

"I don't need the clothes of royalty to free my son."

"You need Lehi." The rider let the cloth of Shemayahu's robe fall from between his fingers. "Why isn't he with you?" he asked.

Shemayahu said, "There was a fire, and his wife, she was injured and she's going to lose her—"

"I know about the fire." The rider paced in front of his horse. "This will never do. I could reason with Lehi—but you? You're Uriah's father and you'll never agree to this."

"Agree to what?"

The man stopped pacing and turned the full force of his stare on Shemayahu. "If you hope to free your son, you must do exactly as I say."

"I won't risk Uriah's life on a man who hasn't the courage to show his face."

"You don't want to know who I am."

"And why not?"

"You wouldn't trust me if you did." The man spoke in low, muffled tones through the fabric of his cloak. He said, "And you must believe that what I'm going to tell you is the only thing that can save your son."

"I trusted you once and it didn't bring me Lehi's help." Shemayahu turned to Mulek and said, "Shall we go?"

"This way, sir." Mulek started them up the rise toward the footpath, but the rider stepped in front of him and said, "There's a garrison of soldiers down that way. You'll not get a hundred cubits before they have you."

Mulek stepped past the man, sneaked down the winding footpath to a pilaster in the wall. He peeked around it and found soldiers standing watch over the back alleys of the lower city. He hurried back to Shemayahu and told him it was just as the stranger had said; they couldn't go that way.

Shemayahu said, "What is it that can free my son?"

"The letters. The ones your son intercepted en route from Captain Laban to Fort Lakhish."

"Who told you about them?"

"You need the letters to win your son's freedom."

"You're trying to trap me, aren't you?" Shemayahu straightened with the help of his cane. He said, "The letters are the reason he's a condemned man. They're the reason for this trial, and Zadock is going to use them to prove my son a traitor."

"Zadock doesn't have the letters. They're locked away in the treasury at Fort Lakhish."

"That's impossible." Shemayahu held the end of his cane with both hands. "The law requires two witnesses against my son. Zadock needs the letters to win this trial."

"He's not going to use the letters."

"And why not?"

"Because they have the power to free your son." The masked rider adjusted his cloak, keeping his face covered. He said, "There's something in the letters that Zadock and Laban fear."

"What is it?"

"All I can tell you is the key to undoing the charges against your son is in the Lakhish Letters."

"How do you know all this?"

"The same way you know your son's not guilty," he said, placing his hand to his chest. "I know it in my heart." He mounted his steed and started his horse trotting down the hill, but he pulled up at the entrance to the alley, and before disappearing into the shadows said, "Without the Lakhish Letters, you'll not defeat Zadock."

CHAPTER 26

Zadock turned down past the east gate, strode across the main square, and tossed a red cushion on the seat of his high-backed prosecution chair. He didn't sit on the woolen pillow. Etiquette required that the prosecutor stand until the king was seated for trial; and since there was no sign of the royal chariot arriving down Main Street, Zadock leaned against the prosecution table. It reached to just above his waist and the soft, hickory-wood surface stood empty, waiting for him to unroll his scrolls and make trial notes in the margins. He didn't need a table, certainly not one this large. He had nothing to spread over it.

Zadock came to trial without any of the forty-seven scrolls of the law to place atop this wooden perch. If there were any reason to suspect Josiah the potter had stolen them from his chambers, he'd rend his robe in front of the gathering crowd and curse the man to a painful death. Thievery, not ghosts, was responsible for the missing documents—some enterprising young lawyer who couldn't afford the cost of a scribe but it was not the potter, it couldn't have been. Zadock rapped his fingernails over the hickory wood. The potter lay dead in a tomb in the hillsides west of the city with his wife and daughter, and Zadock was a fool to have believed otherwise. The potter's ghost may have power to haunt his peace of mind, but a spirit could never steal the scrolls of the law. It was flesh and blood that removed them from his chambers and Josiah the potter no longer enjoyed the corporeal good fortune of a wormless body.

Zadock paced in front of his desk. He never should have insisted they abide by the custom of conducting trials at the east gate. It wasn't worth the risk to have four hundred nobles standing behind his table, voicing their support of his prosecution when there were so many other things out of his control in this open-air venue. Why didn't he concede to Zedekiah's request that they conduct this trial in the royal chambers? Within the confines of the palace, Laban's men could monitor the guests, but out here there was no controlling who came and went.

Travelers from the farthest reaches of the kingdom filled the city to celebrate Passover in three days' time, and a good many of these dreadfully curious pilgrims milled about the square. The chattering crowd stirred an echo about the limestone parapets and tall towers inside the archway of the east gate. It was the sound of too many people, gathered in too-close quarters, and Zadock had to make quick work of this trial and end this spectacle before these commoners turned the trial into a circus.

The crowd surged forward and knocked over Zadock's chair. Fools! He waved them back, picked up the chair and replaced his red cushion. Didn't they know not to press too close? He was the chief prosecutor in Uriah's trial and he was to be treated with the respect due his royal appointment. He was surrounded by this horde, and Zadock kept his head up and his gaze turned away from them. A brown-robed man stumbled at Zadock's feet. He rolled up against his prosecution table, bending its legs to near breaking.

That was it! He'd had enough of their disorderliness and he raised his hand to the soldiers assigned to hold back the crowd. He was going to see this troublemaker thrown into the catacombs beneath the palace to rot. No, that wasn't what he should do. He took a deep breath, lowered his hand, and slowly stepped aside to let the fallen man stand, without cursing his clumsiness. If Zadock was going to convince King Zedekiah of Uriah's treachery, he needed a good show and there was no better inducement than the cheers and ovations of these pathetic commoners joined with the nobles in favor of his prosecution.

A troop of prison guards entered the square with Uriah, and the noblemen jeered his arrival, but now was not the time to waste their breath. There was still no sign of the king and Zadock silenced them with a dismissive wave. They were to cheer his prosecution, not bleat like lost sheep at the appearance of Uriah in chains. Zadock sent three soldiers to pass word among the nobles that they were to hold their tongues until he signaled. They were Jerusalem's wealthiest residents and they should behave accordingly.

The guards stood Uriah in front of the lonely table, his lifeless gaze set on the king's throne, waiting for the monarch to arrive and decide his fate. Uriah was well fed. He was bathed and clothed in a new brown robe, but his face was as white as the moon. Why didn't the prison guards let Uriah outside in the sun each afternoon? He was to look healthy and robust at his trial without the slightest hint he'd been starved nearly to death in the well of the prison.

Zadock reached under his robe and pulled out the only document he had brought to trial—the prison notice forged in a thief's handwriting that looked nothing like Laban's, though the name scratched near the bottom did resemble the captain's signature. Zadock spread the parchment over the tabletop, pinning the curled end down under the inkbottle. Somehow this document had found its way to Uriah's father, Shemayahu, but he was nowhere to be seen among the commoners arriving at the square, and there was no way he could sneak into the trial. A full regiment filled the parapets and catwalk along the east gate and they stood watch on every street and footpath leading into the square. Uriah would have to defend himself. Zadock had seen to that.

Uriah's shackles were all wrong. The soldiers never should have linked his foot-irons to the metal collar around his neck, and Zadock told the prison guards to cut the chain. Better to let him look to the sky and divine whatever foolish revelation he may conjure to free himself of this mess. Uriah was not a good lawyer. He fretted far too much over salvation when he should concern himself with deliverance, and with any luck he'd convict himself by his own poorly spoken defense and rid the kingdom of another fool.

Ezekiel led a contingent of black-robed Elders through the crowd, past the scribes, up a run of steps to a porch overlooking the square, to the jury chairs set on either side of the king's throne. He was a tall, thin man, but with certain nobility in his stride. He wore a well-trimmed beard that brushed the collar of his robe, and in the light of midmorning his clothing shimmered with the look of newly stitched cloth. An amulet hung from his neck with the seal of the Second Elder etched into the metal, and the sun's rays reflected off its surface.

Ezekiel carried a long, olivewood trial staff. The top was curved like a shepherd's stick, and a gold band decorated the top. Matching chains hung from the end like vines on an arbor and they echoed like chimes on the breeze. The handgrip was well worn from years of trial proceedings—passed from generation to generation, from Chief Elder to Chief Elder. Since Ezekiel was to conduct Uriah's trial, Zadock had loaned him the venerable staff.

Ezekiel stood with one hand on his staff and the other resting on the amulet, ready to signal the trumpeters to call the trial to order, but there were no palace guards streaming down Main Street, and no banners announcing the king's arrival. Ezekiel slowly turned his gaze onto Zadock without offering a nod or a smile or any sign indicating he understood that he was to direct the course of this trial in the Chief Elder's favor. Zadock folded his arms across his chest. Was it a mistake to elect Ezekiel to the post of second Elder? The man was well suited to conduct a trial. He was the chief lawyer in the city and he'd bartered away a portion of his soul by changing the Babylonian tax levy in exchange for his seat on the council. Zadock raised his hand to welcome Ezekiel. Hopefully the man was willing to barter away the rest of his soul to keep his appointment. Ezekiel didn't return Zadock's gesture. Had he forgotten his allegiance or was he simply acting the part of impartiality? That's what he was doing—playing the part of the unbiased juror. Ezekiel could be trusted. He was the perfect choice to conduct these proceedings.

Jonathan the blacksmith was the last Elder to arrive at the square. He entered from High Street and climbed the rise at an unforgiving pace, stealing past the wheat vendor's stand and around a mule cart. Ruth followed after him. This was not a wedding and she was not an unmarried woman, but when Zadock turned the scrutiny of his gaze onto her, she hid her face behind a common brown veil and pressed in behind Jonathan like a betrothed woman obeying the rules of modesty. She reached for his arm and slowed him long enough to pick the lint from his council robe. There were no laws barring her from coming, but didn't the blacksmith have the sense to tell the woman to stay home? Thankfully she didn't share the wild Rekhabite notions of her eldest son.

Aaron walked beside his mother without the slightest sign of the limp that once impeded his stride. Jonathan should have kept his son home, along with Ruth, though the boy didn't seem to be a threat with his sandy brown hair falling over his brow and into his wide, blue eyes. There was little Zadock could do about Aaron's attendance, not with him pushing his way through the crowd toward the benches near the front. When Aaron saw Zadock's unmoving stare, he reached for his mother's hand and pressed it between his like she was a frightened child. If Aaron posed any threat, made any attempt to influence this trial, he'd regret the day he sympathized with the Rekhabites.

Elizabeth was the last in the blacksmith's family to enter the square. She held the two youngest children, Sarah and Joshua, by the hand and dragged them up the hill. Elizabeth passed the table of scribes, and the reason for her hurry sat in the last chair. Zoram raised his inked pen to the girl and she smiled. Ruth tugged on Elizabeth's arm to get her moving to their seats, but she didn't go immediately. She was speaking to Zoram. They'd not been promised, at least the blacksmith didn't mention anything about the betrothal of his daughter, but there she was conversing with Zoram in public. And if that wasn't bad enough, she reached out and touched Zoram on the back of his hand. It was a good thing the boy had the sense to pull his pen hand away, ink the quill and turn his head into his parchment before the pair caused a scene.

Zadock left his prosecution table and slowly eased through the crowd to the east gate. The blacksmith's son, Lieutenant Daniel, stood beneath the thick stone arch with a troop of men. He was a stout boy, with wide shoulders and dark brown eyes like his father, and he directed his men with a strong voice, telling them to let the merchants pass into the city without questioning them.

A bent-over beggar with a cane approached and Daniel immediately ordered his men to pull back the hood and reveal the beggar's face. It wasn't Shemayahu and Daniel let him go, telling his men that Uriah's father was younger than that. He had straight, white hair, and his cane was whittled from young cedar wood, not like this old man's walking stick, and there was one detail his men should look for above all others. Daniel pushed his helmet up off his brow and peered at the line of arrivals streaming up the approach to the city. He told his men that Shemayahu may be an old man, but he would never let them pull his hood back like the beggar. He had the strength to escape over rooftops and they were not to be fooled by his age. They should *never* allow Shemayahu to escape again, not as long as Daniel was first lieutenant over Captain Laban's fifty.

"Never, son?" Zadock's question spun Daniel around. He said, "Tell me, do you have any reports?"

"Nothing, sir. Not a single sighting. But he'll not get past us." Daniel pointed across the main square. "I have men searching everyone entering by Main Street, a full troop watching High Street, and the rest are stationed at every footpath and walkway that leads to this place."

Captain Laban reined under the archway, his Arabian flaring its nostrils with each step and shaking the silver tassels hanging from the bridle. The captain wore his military dress attire—a blue tunic with polished brass breastplates strapped to his powerful chest. He was a commanding figure, with dark eyes, a straight jaw, and thick arms. He sat high in a leather saddle decorated with silver studs and jewels.

Laban lost his balance and Zadock quickly grabbed him by the leg to keep him from falling out of the saddle. Cursed fool! Why did he always begin his drinking at the wrong time? He may be a strong man, but he wasn't strong enough to hide his ale in front of the king and this jury. Zadock came alongside the Arabian and peered up at him. He hadn't been drinking long. His eyes weren't red from a full night of revelry.

Zadock said, "I want you to sit at the prosecution table and not say a word."

Laban said, "And why not?"

"You'll fall out of your chair in the middle of a speech."

"I'll do no such thing."

"You're in far too good of spirits, Captain."

"This occasion calls for good spirits." Laban reached for the bottle in his saddlebag. "Would you like a drink of—"

"Put that away." Zadock forced Laban's hand away from the leather pouch. "We have nothing to celebrate."

"Come now, Zadock, don't be modest. You've won this trial."

"We haven't won anything."

"What with your little tax scheme and Hannaniah's acting, and the banishment of the Lakhish Letters and . . ." Laban righted himself in the saddle and lowered his shoulders. He said, "You took care of the Lakhish Letters, didn't you?"

"Calm yourself, Captain. The letters will never come to trial."

"You see there." Laban loosened his hold on the reins. "We have nothing to worry about. You'll convict Uriah of treason and—"

"Treason alone may not be enough."

"What are you talking about? Uriah intercepted my mail. We have Commander Yaush as a witness."

"You really don't understand the law, do you, Captain?" Zadock ran his hand over the horse's white coat. "We need two witnesses for a conviction."

"Shechem was there. He saw Uriah intercept my mail before it was delivered to Fort Lakhish."

"Do you really think we could bring the king of robbers as a witness?"

"What else can you do?"

"If treason fails to convince the king . . ." Zadock stroked the side of Laban's horse. "I have another charge to bring against Uriah."

"What is it?"

"I'm going to fool him into preaching."

"For the love of Moses, Zadock, Uriah thinks himself a prophet. You don't need to provoke him to preach his doctrines. He'd preach to a hill of ants if he thought they'd listen to him."

"Precisely." Zadock kept rubbing his hand over the horse's coat. "And I'm going to provide him more than a hill of ants."

Laban lowered his voice to a whisper. "What sort of snare are you setting?"

"No need for a snare." Zadock spoke softly to match the quiet timbre of Laban's questioning. "He'll catch himself in his own words."

"Excuse me." Daniel stepped in next to the horse. He laid his hand on the jeweled saddle and spoke in a hushed voice. "Is there a reason to whisper?"

"I'm certain Uriah and Lehi know my lineage." Laban adjusted himself forward in the saddle, the leather resisting his sudden movement. "If they find out I plotted to have the king—"

"Laban!" Zadock raised his voice loud enough to startle the sparrows nesting beneath the archway and scare them to flight. The captain was a fool to mention the foiled assassination. What was he thinking, telling Daniel about the attempt on the king's life? Zadock stepped in front of Daniel. He said, "The captain's been drinking and you know what stories he tells when he has too much wine in his belly."

"It isn't a story." Laban slapped his fist against his breastplates. "Lehi can't know about—"

"That's enough, Captain." Zadock raised his hand to silence him.

Daniel said, "Is there something I should know about Lehi?"

Zadock said, "All you need to know is that when Lehi comes to trial, it will end our troubles with the man."

"Lehi's not coming to trial." Laban removed the gloves and stuffed them under his arm. "He's not ventured from Beit Zayit since I ordered Daniel to burn his orchards. Isn't that right, son?"

"Yes, sir." Daniel nodded. "Lehi's not journeyed off his property in the two months since the fire."

"Fire doesn't kill rats." Zadock took out a small box, extracted a pinch of lime powder, and sucked it into his nostrils. "It merely smokes them from their holes."

Laban said, "Rats? I didn't say anything about rats."

"Look over there." Zadock put away his box and tipped his head toward the rampart leading up from the road to the east gate. Jeremiah hurried up the incline, darting in and out of the queue. His beard had gone gray over the winter months without any of the resins he used to hide himself from detection. But the man didn't need a disguise any longer, not since Laban lifted the ban on his coming. He was dressed in a farmer's robe that ended at the middle of his shins and exposed his dirty, sandal-shod feet. He'd been out in his muddy fields, no doubt preparing them for the first growth of spring, and he didn't have the sense to wash before the trial. Of all the would-be holy men this city endured, Jeremiah was the most repulsive. If God were to select a prophet, he certainly could have done better than Jeremiah. He had none of the graces of a man who would attract a following among the educated.

Laban prodded his Arabian forward. "I'll take care of this."

"Let him pass."

"You don't mean that." Laban came around, the Arabian's hooves clapping against the cobblestone. "He could ruin this for us."

"Trust me." Zadock grabbed hold of the bridle and pulled the Arabian close. "Jeremiah will do us more good than he ever intends." He waited behind the horse's wide body for Jeremiah to reach the top of the rampart and pass by the soldiers checking the arrivals. They let him through and he hurried inside the square, unaware that Zadock was monitoring his every step. Jeremiah would never know he was the reason King Zedekiah stopped trusting the queen. He was the wedge in their wedded future—a split that was going to ensure a verdict against Uriah and much, much more.

Zadock said, "Keep your eye on him and any others that surface during the trial."

Laban said, "Other what?"

Zadock came down along the side of Laban's horse. "This trial will unveil our enemies."

"You mean the palace informant."

"I mean everyone who works against us." Zadock took Daniel by the arm. He was a stout lad and his body bristled with strength. Zadock said, "Go fetch Hannaniah and bring him here."

Laban said, "What do you want the soothsayer for?"

Zadock said, "We hired Hannaniah to be a prophet and we have need of him to remind Zedekiah of his prophecies."

"What prophecies?"

"That his wife can't be trusted." Zadock turned to Daniel. "Go, Lieutenant. Bring us Hannaniah."

Daniel marched from under the archway of the east gate and into the light of midday. He pushed through the crowd and disappeared onto a side street that led into the upper city before Zadock said, "You should be more careful with what you say in front of the boy."

Laban said, "I trust him."

Zadock shook his head. "He's not proven himself."

"He's as fine a soldier as I ever was at his age. He's done everything we've asked him. What more does he have to do to win you over?"

"As long as his brother's alive, he's to be regarded carefully."

"The crippled boy?" Laban yawned. "He's harmless."

"Didn't Daniel tell you he was healed?"

"What are you talking about?"

Zadock said, "Aaron claims Lehi did it."

"That's impossible."

"What matters is that you don't trust Daniel with every detail of our doings as long as his brother associates with Lehi. Do you understand?"

"You're wrong about Daniel." Laban shrugged. "He's going to be one of us."

"We only trust those who've proven themselves." Zadock said. "Until Daniel seals his loyalty with blood, the boy can't be trusted with our most guarded secrets."

Laban said, "You're not going to order Daniel to that to his brother, are you?"

"You didn't hesitate when I ordered you to take care of your father and brothers."

"That was different. We were at war. The Babylonians killed them."

"With your help, Captain."

Laban said, "We're not at war any longer."

"You're wrong." Zadock rubbed the mane of the captain's horse between his fingers. He said, "As long as there's anyone who can stop us from gaining the throne, we have an enemy."

A bright blast on the shofar horns announced the arrival of King Zedekiah, the blare echoing under the archway. Zadock started back toward his table and Laban left his horse with the watchmen and followed to the prosecution table.

The crowd quieted when a manservant pulled back the leather flap on the four-wheeled royal chariot and let King Zedekiah step out. The straight-cut bands of his brown hair sneaked out from under his crown and he nestled his scepter along the length of his right arm. He wore a long, blue robe with a gold sash about his thin waist.

Miriam was next out of the chariot, her white robe catching the midday sun and reflecting its light onto the soft red color of her lips and the powders of her cheeks. She was pleasing to look at, though there was little more than her beauty that had power to please. Zadock had placed her throne over with the scribes, but the woman would have nothing to do with that arrangement and she ordered it set next to her husband before she took her seat. Benjamin bounded from the chariot and Mima snatched his hand to keep him close. The black-skinned nursemaid was a large woman, but she didn't lack for the quickness to look after these young royals. She held Benjamin by one hand, Dan by the other, and under her arm she carried those cursed pigeons. Why did she bring the pests here? She led the youngest two princes to their place on a bench directly behind the queen's throne and set the coop on the ground next to her feet. It was an odd thing for Mima to do, but she was Zadock's spy and if she determined it best to bring pigeons to trial and keep the princes entertained, there was no need for him to question her judgment.

Mulek was last to step from the chariot. He stayed a good distance behind Mima and his brothers, throwing his foolish red cloth ball into the air. He missed a catch and the ball rolled beneath the blacksmith's chair, but before Jonathan could get it for him, the prince crawled under and retrieved it himself. Must the boy bring a toy to every public gathering? At the winter feast he hit the high priest in the backside with a rock from his sling; last fall he dropped a handful of arrowheads into a basket of wheat during the feast of ingathering; and there was no telling what sort of mischief this red ball would cause during the trial. Foolish boy. When was he going to leave his toys in his palace chambers where they belonged? His mother shouldn't allow him in public with such undignified play-things. Mulek excused himself to the blacksmith and quickly took his place beside Mima, but the woman didn't ask him to put the ball away. She let him keep throwing it, the red cloth rising high into the air from behind the jury chairs and royal thrones before falling back to earth. If it weren't time to begin the trial Zadock would have gone to Mima and insisted she stop the boy from his childish game of catch. This was a trial, but then, what harm did a foolish little red ball present to his prosecution?

Ezekiel raised his hand and called the crowd to order in the name of Zedekiah, king of Judah, and ordered the Chief Elder to proceed with his prosecution.

"For our good and the good of our children, we must rid our land of those who would destroy us." Zadock stood beside his prosecution table, his long fingers extended over the surface. "Uriah, stands before us in chains because he would see evil done to us. He would have Judah fall by the sword."

The nobles near the front began to murmur a curse on Uriah's name. It was a low, constant rumble below the sound of Zadock's high voice and he encouraged them with a slight wave of his hand. He said, "This prisoner spied for the Babylonians."

Uriah kept his gaze turned to the ground. He slowly shook his head, his chin pushing against the metal collar around his neck. He softly said, "That isn't true. I never—"

"This man's treachery brought the Babylonian armies into our lands." Zadock pounded his fist on his table. "And they are still with us, deporting our people and taxing our property."

Uriah's hands began to tremble and his voice was hardly audible above the murmuring crowd. He said, "I didn't do—"

"And because of Uriah's doings, all of Judah suffers."

Ezekiel tapped the end of his trial staff against the ground until the crowd quieted. He said, "What charges do you bring against Uriah?"

Zadock said, "Treason."

Uriah's head came up. The scar he'd gotten the day he was captured had healed, but it was an ugly reminder of the man's struggle with Lieutenant Daniel on the shores of the Upper Nile River. It ran across his brow and into his wide, pleading eyes. He said, "Sir, I have done nothing but warn this people."

Ezekiel said, "Is that your plea? Do think yourself innocent?"

Uriah didn't answer.

"I ask you." Ezekiel tapped his staff again. "Is that your defense? Do you plead your innocence before this court?"

"Of course he does." Queen Miriam stood from her throne. "Didn't you hear him? He's innocent of any treason."

"My lady." Zadock stepped in front of Miriam. "Are you a witness for Uriah or did he hire you to be his lawyer?"

The nobles erupted in laughter and their cackling sent the queen back to her throne. Ezekiel tried to quiet them, but the tapping of his staff and his call to order had no power to contain the mirth. Zadock wasn't usually an amusing sort and he rarely found the humor in any tale, but the sight of Miriam—a woman no less—standing to defend Uriah was nothing short of absurd. The queen had no influence in the proceedings of this trial and hopefully even less in her husband's final judgment of Uriah's treason.

With the help of Hannaniah, Zadock had seen to that.

Jonathan the blacksmith didn't laugh with the crowd. He cocked his ear to a strange, but familiar voice. It called from the sky, announcing that Uriah's lawyer had arrived. Jonathan turned in his chair and scanned the catwalks. There was no one but watchmen standing at attention with their helmets strapped in place, their spears at their sides and none of them speaking aloud. The voice came again saying Uriah's lawyer had come, and Jonathan turned his gaze quickly over the onlookers standing in the second-story balconies of the homes opposite the east gate. They were laughing with the rest of the crowd, but none of them were speaking the words he heard. Jonathan leaned back in his council chair to check the outside wall of the bakery directly behind him.

Shemayahu? What was Jonathan's houseguest doing, lowering himself in a basket from the roof of the bakery? His daughter-in-law Deborah and the woman's children were with him, and if it weren't for the web of pulleys he'd rigged about the rooftop he'd not have the strength to lower such a heavy load hand over fist.

"Intruders!" Zadock silenced the laughing with his cry and hurried around the council chairs. He pointed at Shemayahu and said, "Remove that man before he harms the king!"

The palace guards formed a circle about the throne in a flurry of clanging swords and sent three men after Shemayahu, but before they could reach him, Zedekiah ordered his men to stand down. They parted, and he stepped from among his protectors. He said, "That will be all, Zadock."

"But sire, the intruders, they could harm you."

Zedekiah pointed his scepter at Shemayahu. "This elderly man isn't going to harm anyone."

Shemayahu bowed and introduced himself as Uriah's father.

Jonathan leaned forward on his chair, but not so far that the other Elders in the council noticed his curiosity. Shemayahu was the father of Uriah and he was a fool not to have recognized the name sooner. Why did he ever agree to take the man and his family into his home? If Zadock found out about his guests there'd be a good deal of explaining to do.

Zedekiah said, "Where is the prison notice?"

"He has it." Shemayahu pointed at Zadock, and the Chief Elder handed over a double-sealed leather document. Zedekiah read through it and when he reached the end his head came up, his gaze peering over the top of the document. He walked it over to Miriam and said, "This writing looks exactly like—"

"Laban's hand, most certainly." Miriam took the scroll from her husband, rolled it around the dowel and placed it on the throne, wedged between her body and the armrest. She smiled at Laban. She said, "The captain has perfect letters."

Shemayahu said, "I've come to defend my son."

"This can't be allowed." Zadock stepped between Shemayahu and the king. "This man is uneducated. He doesn't know our laws well enough. He'll add nothing but a disturbance to these proceedings."

Ruth sat on the benches just down the run of steps from Jonathan. He rose up in his chair high enough to get her attention, and when he pointed at Shemayahu all she did was shrug. They'd both been fooled into taking the man into their home and Jonathan lowered back down into his chair, his face hidden behind the backrest of the perfume merchant in front of him. What an awful chance of fate. He prayed the king would listen to Zadock and send Shemayahu away, but Zedekiah waved his scepter in the air and informed the jury he was going to allow Uriah's father to act as his son's lawyer.

Zadock said, "Sire, we follow protocol in these matters and I must insist that—"

"I said I'm going to allow this."

Jonathan sank lower in his chair. Shemayahu had paid him for a fortnight, with a promise from Jonathan they could stay longer if needed. He was going to have to find a way to break his word without dishonoring his house. No, he was going to let Ruth find a way to rid them of Shemayahu. She was better with guests. He'd have her return their money and send them on their way. Ruth would understand. Jonathan was a member of the council and a man like Shemayahu shouldn't board in his home. It offended the spirit of impartiality; at least that's what he'd tell his wife and let her take care of this mess.

Ruth was a good woman.

Where did he go? Ruth stood to find Jonathan among the Elders but his head dropped below the horizon of high-backed chairs and she lost him between the perfume merchant and the moneychanger. She leaned around in front of Aaron and Elizabeth and spied Jonathan slouched low in his chair, his black and white shawls pulled close against his face. Good. He couldn't suspect her of harboring the family of a criminal. He believed she was taking in renters for Passover. Otherwise, he'd be staring at Ruth, not hiding from her. He had a pensive, faraway look in his eyes. It was the same look she'd seen the day Elizabeth was born—he handed the girl to her, told her he had no idea how to care for a newborn, and went off to take care of his blacksmithing. This was a trial, not a birthing, but there was no doubt what Jonathan was thinking. He was going to pass the task of dealing with Shemayahu to her and when he did, she was going to make certain Jonathan kept his good name. Shemayahu had paid for lodging through the trial and they were going to honor that promise.

Ruth was going to make certain Jonathan was a good man.

Deborah helped her children out of the basket and rushed to her husband, but she wasn't as fast as Benuriah or David. The boys held fast to their father's legs and she wrapped her arms around his chained body, with their infant daughter pressed between them. Uriah hadn't seen the babe and Deborah couldn't keep her from him any longer. She had his brown eyes, his narrow nose, and thin eyebrows. They were together and the sobs choked her words.

Deborah touched the scar on Uriah's brow, her fingers trembling over his skin. "Who did this to you?"

Uriah took her hand from his brow, the chains about his wrist clanging with his movement. "That doesn't matter now. We're together."

Tears welled in Uriah's eyes and slowly trickled down his cheeks. He told her he loved her and pulled his family close against his weak body. He was thin and his grip wasn't as powerful as when he fled Arim last year, but he was alive and Deborah could only thank God for that. She laid her head on his shoulder and whispered into his ear. She said, "We don't have a name for her."

Uriah ran his hand over his infant daughter's thin head of hair. He said, "There isn't a prettier name than yours."

"When you're old, you'll confuse the two us if we have the same name." Deborah wiped the tears from her eyes. "And we're going to grow very old together."

Uriah said, "That may not be."

"Don't talk like that. You're going to be set free." Deborah held his chained hands between hers. "You're a prophet of God."

"There are prophets who are deliverers and there are prophets who are martyrs."

"I won't hear this." Deborah shook her head.

"It may be that I seal my prophecies with my life."

"I won't let you speak like that." Deborah touched her fingers to his lips. "God will deliver you."

"Deliverance does not come on this earth." Uriah held Deborah's hand, the chains pressing against her flesh. He said, "I love you dearly. Never forget that."

Three soldiers pulled Deborah back, but she didn't let go of Uriah's hand immediately, not until she told him that she could never forget his love. It was the first time she'd touched him in nearly a year and the feel of him against her side and the light in his blue eyes and the sound of his voice filled her with the memory of how much she missed the sweet savor of his presence. The soldiers led her and the children to sit on a bench behind the defense table with instructions that they were to be still and not speak or they'd be taken from the trial. Deborah agreed to behave quietly and she held her hand to her mouth to keep from crying aloud. She'd been reunited with her husband, but there was still an aching fear that filled her soul. God wouldn't take the man she loved more than life itself.

Would He?

Zadock retreated to his prosecution table and sat on his red cushion while Uriah conferred with his father. Shemayahu held his son by the arm and assured him all would be well, that somehow God would guide them—the two of them side-by-side, father and son, defense lawyer and traitor. It was a pathetic sight, Uriah sitting in chains with his family around him, and Zadock was going to make certain the young prophet never lived a day free of his shackles.

"Order, I call this trial to order." Ezekiel pounded the end of a wooden staff against the courtyard stone. He said, "Chief Elder, sir, have you any witnesses?"

Zadock said, "I call the esteemed Lord Yaush, governor of southern Judah."

Lord Yaush wore a blue military tunic with silver trim in the sleeves and around the neckline. A matching cape draped over his shoulders, and reached nearly to his boot tops. The governor's wife, Sophia, and his military son, Setti, accompanied Yaush to the front of the court before letting him pass to a small witness chair set in front of Zedekiah's throne. It was a three-legged stool with a square piece of wood nailed to the top, hardly sufficient to bear up the weight of this army general. Zadock ordered the soldiers to replace it with a larger seat with armrests. Yaush was going to be here long enough to prove Uriah's treason and there was no need for him to do it sitting on narrow timber. It was the least Zadock could do for the witness who would win this trial for him.

Yaush fitted himself into the angle of the large, hardwood chair, draped his arms over the sides and squared his shoulders level with the backrest. He said, "Commander Yaush as requested, sir."

Zadock said, "You're the governor of southern Judah, isn't that so?"

"That's one of my titles."

"You're also a military commander."

Yaush nodded slowly, his gloved hands cupped in front of him. "I have five thousand men under my command."

"Your superior officer, who would that be?"

"I report directly to Laban." Yaush nodded to the captain sitting at the prosecution table, and Laban returned the gesture, but he didn't utter a word of greeting. Yaush said, "There's no more senior officer than he."

"Lakhish is a good distance from Jerusalem, is that correct?"

"It's not too far, sir." Yaush leaned against the backrest. "It's a hard twenty-five-mile ride, but we built the fort in the hills south of Jerusalem close enough that you can see the signal fires by night and reach the city in less than a day with a good horse."

"Certainly you don't communicate with Captain Laban by signal fire."

"In times of war I do."

"And in times of peace?" Zadock paced in front of Yaush with his hands behind his back. He said, "How do you communicate with Laban in Jerusalem?"

"Courier."

"Tell me, Commander." Zadock rubbed the side of his nose, working the snuff back into his head. "What became of the courier Hosha Yahu?"

"He's dead, sir."

"How did he die?"

"He ran a knife through his heart."

"He killed himself?"

"That's right."

"Why would he do such a thing?"

"I don't know. He cried for God to have mercy on his soul and turned the blade on himself."

"Certainly you have an opinion on the matter."

Shemayahu called from the defense table, his voice echoing across the square. He raised his hand in the air. "Commander Yaush could never know what his courier was thinking."

Zadock turned to Ezekiel. "Commander Yaush was Hosha Yahu's superior officer. There's no one who knows him as well as Yaush."

Ezekiel said, "You may continue."

Zadock said, "Did Captain Laban trust Hosha Yahu to carry his most confidential letters to Fort Lakhish?"

Yaush said, "Hosha was the only courier Laban trusted."

"Isn't it possible that Uriah convinced Hosha Yahu to betray that trust and join his treason?"

"That's a lie!" Shemayahu stood from his table, the legs of his chair grating over the stone. "My son didn't convince Hosha Yahu of anything. The boy brought the letters to the inn." He pointed at

Laban. "The captain was writing lies about my son's faith and lies about his preaching, and Hosha wanted Uriah to know exactly what Laban was saying about him."

Laban stayed seated at the prosecution table, his gaze forward, his lips pressed shut. He remained silent just as Zadock had advised him. The less he said, the more King Zedekiah would believe he had nothing to gain in this matter.

Ezekiel said, "Shemayahu, you're not to call members of this court liars."

"That's what they are." Shemayahu shook his cane. "Both of them are liars."

Ezekiel said, "I'll not allow any more outbursts like this."

Shemayahu said, "But my son never—"

"Take your seat, sir, or I'll excuse you from this trial." Ezekiel tapped his staff until Shemayahu returned to his place.

Zadock stood beside Commander Yaush's witness chair, his long fingers touching the armrest. He said, "Did Hosha stop at the inn often?"

"Every Jerusalem to Lakhish ride. It was a drinking habit he enjoyed."

"It seems an odd thing for the young courier to kill himself in a town where he was born and raised. Did he have any enemies among the patrons at the inn?"

"He was a good boy." Commander Yaush nodded. "He didn't have a single enemy in all of Arim."

Zadock said, "Could it be that Hosha Yahu feared the consequences of his actions?"

"What actions are you talking about, sir?"

Zadock resumed pacing in front of the witness chair. He said, "Hosha Yahu delivered mail to the outposts along the southern trade route."

"That's right. That was his route."

Zadock said, "Didn't he carry secret mail sent from Captain Laban?"

"Confidential mail was nearly always part of Hosha Yahu's deliveries."

Zadock said, "Did he allow the innkeeper to read Captain Laban's confidential mail?"

"I believe he did, sir."

"You *believe*?" Zadock stopped pacing. "Did you ever see the innkeeper read Captain Laban's secret, confidential mail?"

Commander Yaush softly said, "I did."

"And who might that innkeeper be?"

Yaush cleared his throat. He said, "Uriah, sir."

"Tell me, Commander." Zadock raised his voice. "What is the punishment for treason?"

Shemayahu slammed his fist on the defense table. He said, "Reading a few letters from a courier's pouch does not make my son a traitor."

Zadock quickly turned on Shemayahu. He said, "It makes your son a spy."

"He never took anything to the Babylonians. He would never do that. He, he . . ."

Ezekiel shook his staff at Shemayahu and ordered him to sit down and end his tirades, while Zadock walked a circle around the commander's chair. The Chief Elder pulled on the end of his chin. He said, "Isn't it true that Uriah was known on many occasions to say that the Babylonians were certain to take our lands by force and if we rebelled against their occupation they would destroy Jerusalem?"

Yaush said, "I never heard the boy preach."

"Isn't it true Uriah preached that the Babylonians should be allowed to make Judah a vassal state, and require we pay a tax to the king of Babylon?" Zadock turned to the crowd. "A very heavy, impossible-to-bear tax."

The nobles began to murmur on Zadock's signal, their low voices raising a din of curses against the levy imposed by the Babylonians.

Commander Yaush said, "You should ask Uriah what he did or didn't preach about the—"

"Isn't it true Uriah wanted the Babylonians to destroy us, that he intercepted Captain Laban's letters in order to help them win the war against us and occupy our lands and collect taxes? Isn't that right, Commander? Isn't Uriah a traitor to our people?"

The ringing and clanging of thick metal chains filled the square and silenced the murmuring of the nobles. Uriah inched his way around to the front of the defense table, his stride troubled by the short metal lengths shackled to his ankles. He raised his brown-eyed gaze to the crowd. He said, "I never betrayed my people."

Zadock crossed to Uriah. "You preached the destruction of Jerusalem, didn't you?"

Shemayahu said, "Don't answer that question, son."

Zadock yanked on the chains hanging between Uriah's wrists. He said, "God will never allow His Holy City to be destroyed."

Uriah turned his gaze to the sky. "If the people of Jerusalem do not repent, God will remove his protection from us and then—"

"No, son." Shemayahu came around the defense table and took Uriah by the arm. "Don't say anymore. He's trying to goad you. He wants you to—"

"What will happen if God removes His protection?" Zadock pushed Shemayahu aside. "Will we fall into an eternal pit of fire or will the sun go dark or maybe the moon will turn red as blood?" He raised his hand to the crowd. "That's what men in your business say to scare their followers. What will it be from you, Uriah? Should we expect to reap the whirlwind or how about a great fire to burn us? Is that where we will find your God—in some great calamity?"

Uriah said, "You'll not find God in the whirlwind or the fire, but the still, small voice that speaks to the soul."

"Is that how God told you of the fate of the Holy City? Was it the still small voice of God that told you the Babylonians were coming to take our lands. Or was it the still small voice of your Babylonian friends?" Zadock leaned in next to Uriah, so close that he could feel the boy's breath on his face. "Tell me, prophet, how much did they pay you to spy for them?"

Shemayahu said, "Son, hold your tongue."

Zadock said, "You're a fool to think that God would let our city be destroyed."

Uriah spoke in a calm voice that mixed with the sound of the chains clanging about his wrists. "When all the faithful in this city have left, and when all who obey God and seek to live after the manner of heaven are gone from this city, then will Jerusalem be without the protection of God, and the Babylonians will destroy it."

"And what about the temple?" Zadock lifted his gaze toward Solomon's temple rising above the skyline on the highest hill in the city. "What will happen to the holy sanctuary?"

Uriah raised his arms level with his head before the chains pulled taut and stopped him from lifting them higher. "There will not be one stone left standing upon the other and there will be wailing in the streets, for Jerusalem is no more!"

The crowd's cries against Uriah filled the square. They pushed forward and the soldiers raised their spears to keep them from overrunning him. The men in the balconies raised their fists and called for Uriah's head, and the nobles joined in the chanting against him.

"Say no more, son." Shemayahu wrapped his arms around Uriah and pulled him back to his chair.

Zadock marched to Ezekiel. "I would direct you to change the charge against Uriah."

Ezekiel said, "If you remove the treason, there are no charges against the man."

"I'm adding to it."

Ezekiel said, "Adding what?"

"Blasphemy." Zadock pointed his finger at Uriah. He said, "The Holy City of God will never be destroyed, and anyone who speaks such sacrilege is worthy of death!"

A man in the balcony overlooking the square cried, "Pequeah—visionary man." The nobles pulled back their hoods and chanted, "Pequeah, pequeah, pequeah! Death to the visionary man." The chant spread through the crowd like a fire run wild on a field of dry grasses and it filled the square with the vulgar cursing against Uriah the traitor. Zadock marched to the table of scribes and peered over their writings, making certain they recorded the new charge. The trial was going according to plan. He'd made Uriah more than a traitor, and he wanted every word of it recorded on parchment.

Beheading was the punishment for either crime.

The chanting crowd covered the shuffling of Mima's skirt. She took the pen from under the cloth and scribbled a note on a small scrap of papyrus. She had to get word to Josiah. If there were any point of law Shemayahu could use to free his son from the charge of blasphemy, Josiah would know it. She felt inside the small wicker basket, found one of the pigeons trained to fly to Qumran on the shores of the Dead Sea and tied the note to the creature's leg. She handed it to Mulek and told him to release it. He threw the pigeon into the air and thankfully the chanting drowned the sound of its fluttering wings. The bird circled the tower above the east gate before taking flight over the Kidron Valley and disappearing into the hills beyond the city.

"My lady." Mima spoke loud enough for the queen to hear, but not loud enough to draw the notice of her husband.

Miriam slowly turned in her throne. She spoke in a whisper. "What is it?"

"Don't look at me." Mima quickly waved her hand until Miriam turned back. "We need some time to get word back."

"Word about what?"

"There isn't time to explain. Can you play sick?"

"How sick?"

"Sick enough to stop this trial."

Miriam held the back of her hand to her brow and groaned, but it was hardly loud enough to draw the attention of her husband, to say nothing of the closest-sitting Elders and the unruly crowd. Miriam, queen of Judah, was too refined and dignified to create a public scene, and Mima needed pandemonium. If there was anyone who could create it, she could. She lowered her shoulder into the queen's back-rest and knocked the royal seat up off its legs, throwing Miriam to the ground as she let out a loud shriek that silenced the onlookers.

Mima ran around the fallen throne with her hands over head. She screamed in her thick, Ethiopian accent. "Get me some water and a blanket."

"What is it?" Zedekiah rushed over. "What's wrong with her?"

Mima knelt at Miriam's side, her large body shielding her from the view of others. She said, "The queen's fainted again."

"Fainted?" Zedekiah bent over to take Miriam by the hand, but Mima swatted his arm and said, "Don't touch her; you'll make it worse."

Zedekiah said, "I don't remember Miriam fainting before.'

"It's her medicines. She's forgotten to take them." Mima fanned her with her hands. She said, "Where is that water?"

Zedekiah said, "I don't recall any medicines."

"The ones in the big bottles on her vanity, sire." Mima feigned to check Miriam's brow for a fever. "You've seen the white crystals and the chopped green powders and those distasteful red herbs. She's always mixing them in the morning and evening."

"Wasn't that for her skin?"

"The blue Egyptian powders are for her skin. The others are for her head, and if she doesn't take them regularly—well, you can see for yourself. The poor dear must have forgotten this morning." Mima patted Miriam's hand. "She's going cold." She rose to her knees and said, "Where is that blanket?"

Zedekiah waved the palace guards over. He said, "Help the queen into the chariot and see that she's taken—"

"No, no, you can't take her from here." Mima raised her hand, the thick undersides of her arms swaying like large sacks of grain. She pushed Zedekiah back a step. "You'll only make it worse."

"She must be moved." The Chief Elder pushed past Zedekiah, his long, frail body hovering over the queen. He said, "We can't conduct a trial with her laying about like this."

"You're not moving her." Mima shook her head and the tightly woven curls in her hair danced over her brow.

Zadock said, "And why not?"

"Why it could . . ." Mima rubbed her hand over Miriam's palm. "It could kill her! Kill her right on the spot. That's exactly what could happen."

Miriam's eyes shot open, but before anyone noticed her return to consciousness, Mima slapped her on the cheek and leaned forward to let the fringe along the hem of her blouse hide Miriam's eyes. She said, "The poor dear won't come out of this sleep until we get her medicines. It took a good triple dose last time."

Zedekiah said, "This has happened before?"

"More than I like to think, sire."

A soldier delivered a blanket and Mima draped it over Miriam's head, explaining that she had to be covered from head to toe. Her eyes were to be kept away from the light and under no circumstances should the blanket be removed until Mima returned with the medicines. She hurried to the chariot, pushed the driver off his stoop and stood on the front rung, the whip in one hand and the reins in the other. She bolted the four stallions and drove out of the square with the clatter of chariot wheels mixing with the clap of horse hooves. Mercy, what had she just done? She had to give the pigeon time to fly to Qumran, but did she have to make such a scene? Hopefully Josiah would find the fowl and send a message in return before Zadock discovered that she contrived the queen's illness. He must never know she was using these pigeons to communicate with Josiah.

She was not the bird lady.

CHAPTER 27

The cobblestones in the threshold were cracked and pitted from years of weather, and the dry shell of dead, brown thistle clung between the fissures. Daniel pounded on the gate and called for Hannaniah to open, his deep voice penetrating the gaps in the wood planks and echoing in the courtyard beyond. Hannaniah lived in a small, one-story brick home at the top of a narrow walkway of steps in the upper city. It was the last dwelling at the end of the rise, pushed up against another home like an afterthought. It stood in the shadows of tall buildings, and an archway spanned the street between two neighboring estates, filling the lowly courtyard with dark shadows at midday. Dead vines hung from the joists protruding through the stone façade and the branches of a wilted willow bent over the wall. Daniel made a fist to knock again when the latch clicked and the gate creaked half open. A woman poked her head through the opening, her uncombed gray hair falling down over her shoulders in ratted thatches. She was dressed in a sleeping robe that was wrinkled from collar to hem. Lines creased about her dark eyes when she spoke. "What do you want?"

Daniel stood at attention. He said, "I've come to collect Hannaniah."

"Tell the Chief Elder my son isn't for hire." The woman spit on the ground next to Daniel's boots. "Do you hear me? My son will never work for Zadock again." She shook her head and the ends of her gray hair danced about her shoulders.

Daniel gripped the hilt of his sword. "Don't make this difficult for me."

"It's the Chief Elder who's made this difficult." The woman started to close the gate, but Daniel forced his boot into the jamb and kept her from latching it shut. He said, "I have orders to bring Hannaniah to trial."

"I told you, boy. Hannaniah won't be going to trial. Not today, not ever."

Daniel pushed open the gate and knocked the woman to the ground. He said, "Where is he?"

"Get out! You're not welcome here." The woman used the gate to help her back to her feet. She grabbed Daniel by the arm. "This is my home."

Daniel pulled free, climbed the steps to the porch and crossed to the front door. He reached for the latch and—

"Unclean!" The woman screamed, her lungs forcing the cry from deep within her breast and filling the courtyard with the hissing of her words. She ran up the steps and fell to her knees in front of the door, one hand reaching for Daniel and the other covering her mouth. She spoke between her fingers. She said, "You can't go inside, not until the high priest comes to cleanse it."

What had happened here that required the high priest's blessing? Daniel wasn't going to let this old woman frighten him and he took the latch in his hand, but didn't lift the bolt. He said, "Is there an illness in the house?"

"God forgive Hannaniah. He was too young to know better." The woman shook her head and her long, gray hair fell in front of her face. Her body shook and her tears splashed onto the stone near her knees. She spoke in a faltering voice. "Why did Hannaniah do such a thing? We didn't need the money. He was not a prophet like his father before him."

Daniel said, "Where's your son, woman?"

She raised her head, pulled her hair back from in front of her face and brushed her tear-stained cheeks. "It's the curse of the prophet Jeremiah that did this to my son." She turned her gaze up into the shadows of the high walls blocking her view of the heavens. "Will my son ever find forgiveness?"

"I don't have time for your superstitions." Daniel lifted the bolt, but the woman pushed his hand off the latch and it clicked back into place. She said, "Don't go in there."

"Then you go fetch me your son." Daniel reached to bring her to her feet, but she pulled away from him and stood without his help. She unlatched the bolt and let the door slowly creak open. There were no burning lamps to brighten the dark shadows, and the stench of death hung on the air.

The woman said, "Fetch him yourself if you like, but I'll not go inside until the priest arrives."

Daniel stood on the threshold, his hand pushing the door fully open and his voice piercing the darkness. He said, "Hannaniah, I've come to take you to trial, sir."

"God forgive my son his false prophecies." The woman covered her face when she spoke. Tears streamed through her fingers and off the end of her chin. Her speech was muffled by quiet sobs, but her last words were clear.

She said, "His body is in the back bedroom."

CHAPTER 28

The chirping of a bird sounded outside the tent door and Josiah the potter pulled the leather flap down and tied it shut with a double pin knot. It was bad enough that he had to endure the winds that blew in off the Dead Sea in late morning and filled the air with piercing grains of sand, but must he also endure the sparrows seeking refuge from the daily rain of grit? The little fowls shredded everything with their beaks, and just yesterday a flock of the tiny birds found their way inside the tent and pecked a hole in the last sack of wheat. It would take a trip to Jericho to replace it and he wasn't going to let anymore of these creatures inside. The flap of the tent was to be kept closed, and as soon as Rebekah returned from drawing water he was going to lecture her on the matter.

Josiah ignored the cooing outside and picked up a scroll. He unrolled it over a small table built of driftwood come ashore on the salty beachhead below camp. There was too much sand in the air to read outside and he took his midday meal in here where he could eat and read the scrolls of the law—the ones he'd taken from Zadock's council chambers. There were forty-seven in all, more than enough to keep him reading for days, and if he didn't get a good start he'd not be ready to help in Uriah's trail if his help was ever needed.

Josiah swallowed the last bit of four-day-old bread left over from the last baking. It was dry and caught in his throat, and it was going to take all the water Rebekah could fetch in one trip to dislodge the crusty thing. Josiah coughed to clear his throat and pulled the small oil lamp near the scroll. The girl would be along soon enough and he turned his head into his reading—something about the lawyers in the days of the old kingdom when Solomon gathered all the tribes of Israel under his rule.

"Papa, are you in there?"

"I'm here, girl." Josiah put aside his reading, untied the flap and peered out. Rebekah stood with a jar of water balanced against her hip. The wind whipped past her head and twisted her dark-black hair into a mess of tangles. Why was the girl standing out in the wind? She was never one to let her hair go uncombed, but there she was, staring down at the ground, not pulling a hood over her head or ducking into the tent to get out of the sand.

Josiah said, "Come inside before the . . ."

The reason for Rebekah's hesitation pecked at the ground in front of the tent. The pigeon flapped its blue-gray wings, preened them, and waddled about the tent post.

Rebekah handed Josiah the water. She said, "There's a note, Papa, look. There's a note attached to the pigeon's leg."

She quickly untied the papyrus, put it under the light of the lamp and pressed the ends from curling back over the letters. She read it aloud, the breathless words spilling from her. Uriah's trial began today. Zadock had tricked Uriah into testifying that Jerusalem, the Holy City, would be destroyed and he added the charge of blasphemy to the treason. Rebekah read faster, her hurried words filling the tent with concern. There was little time to act. Did Josiah know of any point of law to help the man? Urgent reply needed.

Rebekah held out the small, tattered note and let Josiah read through it again, his lips mouthing the words. The Holy City destroyed? Why did Uriah let Zadock trick him into saying such a thing? He should have compared the destruction of Jerusalem to the burning of an olive tree or the plowing of a field asunder or the boiling of a cauldron, but in a public trial he should never say the city would be destroyed. With that many witnesses there was nothing he could do to save Uriah from the charge of blasphemy, unless of course he could find some obscure verdict that ruled otherwise and there wasn't anything in the writings of the law that . . .

Josiah fell to his knees beside his sleeping mat and rummaged through the leather pouch where he stored the scrolls of the law. There was something about a king reversing a charge of blasphemy against an ancient prophet, but where was it written? He lifted three scrolls from the pouch and set them aside. He'd read something about that recently, something about blasphemy that could aid Uriah. Amos was the first prophet Josiah read after returning to Qumran and he quickly picked up that scroll and skimmed over it. Nothing. There was not a single reference to blasphemy and he put the scroll away and hurried over the writings of Jonah and Joel and Joash. There was not a single word about blasphemy in any of them. Where was the reference he sought? He removed all the scrolls from the pouch and sat them on the ground beside his reading table. The writings in one of these scrolls had to do with the Law of Blasphemy, he was certain of it, but he didn't have time to read through all of them, not with Mima waiting for his reply. He offered a silent prayer before stooping over the scrolls and running his hand over the leather. Each one had a distinct brown color, some with worn edges and others made of new leather without a single frayed end and when his hand touched the scroll with a red tassel hanging from the dowel, his mind filled with light and immediately he remembered the day he studied from it.

The Citadel Building. That's where he'd read about the charge of blasphemy. The day he sneaked into the council chambers, this was the scroll that was left open atop the others. He'd quickly gone over it before placing it in his pouch and sneaking out of the chambers before Zadock found him there. It was the writings of the prophet Micah, a man who lived in Jerusalem a hundred and twenty years ago when the Assyrians destroyed the northern kingdom and scattered the ten tribes of Israel throughout the nations along the northern shores of the Great Sea. Josiah laid it over his driftwood table and held the lamp over the writing. He hurried down past Micah's prophecy of the last days when the mountain of the Lord's house would be established in the tops of the mountains. There were some of Micah's descriptions of the fall of the northern kingdom with Assyrians eating the flesh of Hebrews and flaying their skin from off them and breaking their bones and chopping them in pieces, but nothing about the destruction of Jerusalem.

Josiah lifted the lamp off the reading table, turned the dowels to the middle section of the parchment and read on. The tone of Micah's words changed when he wrote of these times when the Babylonians would invade the southern kingdom of Judah. There was no more about the eating of flesh and nothing about the flaying of skin or crushing of bones. The gloomy foretelling of Jerusalem's destruction was filled with prophecies about the coming of false prophets. Josiah raised his head and stared at the brown animal hide ceiling of the tent. Why would Micah write about false prophets together with the invasion of the Babylonians? It was a short passage, hardly more than fifty words, but there was no mistaking it. The fall of Jerusalem was somehow tied to the rise of false prophets and the Jews acceptance of their prophecies.

Josiah turned his gaze away from staring at the ceiling and slowly moved his finger over the writings, careful to consider each word of Micah's prophecy. False prophets would make the people of the Lord err and cry peace while the enemy prepared for war. The sun would go down over the diviner for there would be no answer from God, and they should no more have night visions. Josiah lifted his finger from the parchment. Who was this false prophet and what did he have to do with the destruction of Jerusalem?

Josiah turned the dowel, rolling the parchment to the writings near the bottom. The lettering was larger and pressed deep into the leather, the fibers torn by the heavy hand of an ancient scribe. The writings prophesied of the nobles and princes of Israel who pervert equity. They teach for hire and the prophets divine for money, yet will they lean upon the Lord and say, no evil can come upon us for is not the Lord among us?

The side of the scroll was curled up over the last of the writing and when Josiah pressed it flat against the table he found the story of the prophet Micah's trial. It was like an ancient voice speaking from a hundred and twenty years in the past. The Elders of the Jews put Micah on trial for speaking blasphemy against the Holy City, but Hezekiah, king of Judah in those days, determined the verdict and ruled that the prophet Micah was . . .

"Get one of the pigeons." Josiah pushed the scroll off the table and replaced it with a small piece of papyrus.

Rebekah said, "Papa, what is it?"

"Hurry, girl." Josiah began writing a response to Mima, his pen racing over the page. "There isn't time to explain."

Rebekah set the water jar down next to the wheat sack. "Which pigeon?"

"The strongest one."

"Samantha?"

"No, not the blind one. I don't want to take any chances with Samantha's vision. Bring Isabel. She can get word back to Mima's bedroom window without losing her way. Hurry now. Mima's waiting on us."

Rebekah left the tent flap fluttering in the wind.

CHAPTER 29

Governor Yaush leaned back in the witness chair, his movement creaking the wood joints. He didn't wish the queen of Judah any harm, but it was his good fortune that she'd fainted. Until Mima returned with the medicines there would be no more questioning. He had time to figure out how he could allow Shemayahu the chance to request the Lakhish Letters as evidence without implicating himself in all this. Yaush perched his elbow on the armrest and lowered his chin into his hand. Was he the only one who understood that the letters were Uriah's only chance at freedom?

Shemayahu sat at the defense table across from Yaush, one hand on his son's chained arm and the other holding fast to the edge of the hickory-wood tabletop. He was an old man without enough daring in his heart to jump an uncharted abyss as wide and cavernous as asking for the letters. They were locked away in the underground vaults of Fort Lakhish and as long as they remained there Shemayahu was certain to think his son safe from the charge of treason. Yaush didn't know how the letters could free Uriah, but he'd studied them for months, and something deep in his soul told him they could. If only he could get another opinion from an educated man, a lawyer, a scribe, someone who could find the one key he was missing and unlock the mystery of why Zadock and Laban feared the letters.

The royal chariot clattered into the square, and Mima jumped from the stoop before it came to a full stop, her large body bringing her down onto the cobblestones with a heavy thud. She ambled over to Miriam, raised the queen's head and tipped a drink to her mouth. It was the color of white and red herbs mixed with green powders, and it looked more like wine than medicine, but it did have the power to revive the queen. She rubbed her eyes and insisted that she was well. Zedekiah begged her to return to the palace, but she would have nothing to do with his pleading. She threw off the linen blanket, and Zedekiah hurried to set her throne back on its legs. She took her seat beside her husband with the strength of a woman untouched by the sickness of fainting spells. She told Zedekiah she was not leaving the trial until the last witness of the day had testified, and she promised Mima that she'd never forget to take her medicines again. The Ethiopian maidservant pulled her bench seat close to the queen, sat the princes down next to her and reached around the backrest of Miriam's throne to hold the woman's hand, whispering whatever words of comfort maidservants offer their mistresses.

Ezekiel stood before the court, his staff pointed at Shemayahu. He said, "Have you any answer to the charges against Uriah?"

Shemayahu crossed the court to the witness chair, his cane tapping the ground ahead of him and the afternoon sun casting his bent-over shadow across the stone. He stopped in front of Yaush, but he didn't speak. He was staring at Yaush, looking deep into his eyes. He whispered, "Have we met before?"

Not here! Yaush held his hand to his mouth like a veil to cover himself. Of all the places Shemayahu could discover his identity, why must he do it while Yaush sat on the witness chair in front of Captain Laban and Zadock? Yaush said, "I've frequented your inn with my men before."

"That must be it."

"I must protest." Zadock spoke from his seat at the table. "Shemayahu doesn't know the law well enough to ask an intelligent question."

Shemayahu ignored Zadock's complaint and said, "Commander, are you certain you saw my son intercept the secret letters Captain Laban sent to you?"

Yaush said, "That's right. It was the third day of the week, the same day Hosha Yahu always made his deliveries."

"Did anyone else see my son read the letters?"

Of course there was someone else, but he couldn't mention Shechem, king of robbers, if he hoped to keep his command of Fort Lakhish. Captain Laban had ordered him never to reveal that he'd worked in league with the man. The last Lakhish letter Laban sent to him desperately explained that Shechem had attempted to kill the royal family during the coronation and ordered Yaush never to reveal the folly of having hired the man. He was to remain silent on the matter of Shechem or lose his commission. Yaush leaned forward to see past Shemayahu and find his wife sitting on the benches beyond the Council of Elders. Sophia's hair was pulled back off her brow with a red ribbon and she sat next to Setti, his military tunic pulled tight across his straight shoulders. Yaush didn't fear losing his command of Lakhish. He could make do without the high rank and the honors that came with the post. It was his family he feared losing, and if Laban ever suspected anything less than complete allegiance in Yaush, the man wouldn't stop with punishing only him.

Shemayahu said, "Commander, was there anyone else? Did anyone, beyond yourself, see my son read the Lakhish Letters?"

Zadock said, "I fail to find anything of consequence in these questions."

"I'll tell you the consequence." Shemayahu stabbed his cane into the stone and leaned on it. "You have no other witness beyond the commander."

Yaush lowered his head into his hands. He'd spent weeks trying to help Shemayahu get a lawyer. Lehi had refused to help him and now Shemayahu refused to follow his advice. Didn't he have the sense to know what was best for his son?

Zadock spoke disdainfully. "What bearing does any of this have on Uriah's guilt? He's a traitor and we all know it."

Shemayahu said, "You have nothing but Commander Yaush's testimony."

"You know nothing about the law."

"You need two witnesses, sir."

"That law doesn't apply here." Zadock directed his words to Ezekiel. "Isn't that right, sir."

Ezekiel leaned on the trial staff. He spoke slowly. "Have you any other witness to Uriah's treason?"

"I told you, that law doesn't apply in the matter of treason." Zadock stood, his long fingers spread over the prosecution table. "Governor Yaush is one of Judah's finest military commanders. He's honest, his word is beyond reproach, and he has faithfully served our nation in times of war and peace for more than twenty-five years." He swept his hand toward the Council of Elders and the king. "This man's testimony is more than enough to prove Uriah guilty of treason." He pointed his long finger at Ezekiel. "Isn't that right, sir?"

"One witness isn't enough." Shemayahu crossed to the writing table where the scribes sat recording the proceedings. He said, "I ask that my son be released, the charges against him forgotten and—" he laid his hand near the closest parchment—"The record of this trial blotted out forever."

Zadock said, "You're a fool."

Shemayahu said, "I didn't come to trial with only a single witness, sir."

"And I didn't come to trial with only a single charge against your son." Zadock returned to his table and fitted his long, thin body into the angle of his chair. His brow wasn't furrowed and his lips were raised in a very narrow, odd-looking smile. He turned to the nobles and said, "Does anyone gathered here doubt Uriah the prophet is guilty of blasphemy?"

The nobles cheered Zadock.

Zoram hurried his pen across the parchment. The crowd's loud cheers kept Zadock and Shemayahu from asking more questions and he had time to catch up. He'd recorded most of Shemayahu's words, but once Zadock began speaking over him it was impossible to write all of the arguments. Zoram leaned over to check the writings of the other scribes. The chief scribe from the palace was still writing of Mima's return with the medicines; the chief temple scribe was appending a note on the law of two witnesses; and the scribe for the Council of Elders was dozing with his face in his hands. They were further behind than Zoram and he turned the white collar of his tunic up around his neck and went back to writing. He couldn't share with them what they missed. These were the chief scribes of every reputable treasury in the city and they would never admit they'd missed anything.

Zoram dipped his pen into the inkbottle and let the excess drip from the end before quickly recording Zadock's last comment—that this trial was about the prophet's guilt. No, he couldn't use the word prophet in Captain Laban's official record. Zoram quickly scratched out the word prophet with his fingernail, tearing away the fibers stained with his error, and replaced it with the word "accused." It wasn't really an error. Uriah was a prophet, but these were Laban's records and Zoram couldn't write that holy title without angering his master or drawing suspicion back on himself. Zoram finished recording the rest of Zadock's words—that this trial was about Uriah's guilt and did anyone gathered here doubt that the *accused* was guilty of—

"Blasphemy!" The prophet Jeremiah stepped out of the crowd and stood next to Zoram's scribe table. How did he get in here? There were hundreds of soldiers guarding the east gate, but there he stood with the yoke of an ox on his shoulders—the same yoke he had worn the day he argued with Hannaniah over the tax revolt. The timbers were split down the middle, the broken arms held together with cords.

Jeremiah wore a tattered brown working robe and the end of his long, gray beard scratched over the cloth of his limp collar. His sandals were dirtied with fresh mud from mucking about the grape arbors. Jeremiah set his worn hand on the wood surface beside Zoram's parchment, but thankfully he didn't look down or say anything that would rouse Laban's suspicions.

Zadock said, "What do you know about blasphemy, sir?"

Jeremiah said, "Oh that I had a lodging place in the wilderness. I would go far away from you." He swept his arms toward the Council of Elders seated on the porch. "For you are an assembly of treacherous men."

"We are peace-loving men." Zadock nodded to the Elders. "The council has done nothing but seek freedom from the Babylonians."

"You speak peaceably with me now, but in your heart you lie in wait." Jeremiah pointed his finger at Zadock. "You bend your tongue like a bow."

"Are you calling me a liar?"

Jeremiah said, "Uriah speaks the will of God, but you turn his words into blasphemy."

"That isn't so." Zadock slowly stepped toward Jeremiah. "No evil can come among us, for God is with us, not Uriah. And he sent us Hannaniah the prophet to prove that to all."

Jeremiah said, "Hannaniah is a diviner and he makes this people trust in a lie."

"Hannaniah prophesied freedom from the Babylonians." Zadock straightened his cuffs about his wrists. "There is no more divine news than that, unless you have something more to proffer."

"Thus saith the Lord." Jeremiah turned his gaze out over the square, his arms spanning the timbers of the yoke and his eyes filled with a determined gaze. "Seventy years will we live in captivity and if we do not repent and pay tax to the king of Babylon, this Holy City of God will be destroyed."

Zoram dropped his pen, and ink splattered over his parchment. Why did Jeremiah say that Jerusalem would be destroyed? Better to have said the Jews would be cursed or the people slain or stoned or bound and gagged and flogged to death with soft palm leaves, anything but condemning the city itself. Didn't Jeremiah know he could be charged with blasphemy and suffer the same fate as Uriah? Zoram cleaned away the blotted mess, dipped his pen into the ink again, and fixed the tip to the parchment, but he didn't join the other scribes and record Jeremiah's appearance at the trial. How could he write that his father had blasphemed the Holy City?

Lieutenant Daniel entered the square from Main Street. He didn't cross to Captain Laban and he didn't join his men guarding the square. He mixed quietly among the nobles near the front and he stayed there until Zadock spied him among the expensive silks and linens of Jerusalem's wealthiest residents.

Zadock said, "Lieutenant, bring Hannaniah over."

Zoram set down his pen, pushed his parchment aside, and leaned forward to get a better view. There was no sign of Hannaniah with Daniel. He was alone and he marched quickly across the square. He was halfway across when Zadock spread his hands to the crowd and told them that the Lieutenant escorted Hannaniah here to speak for God and prove that Jeremiah was a false prophet.

"Zadock, sir." Daniel pulled up in the middle of the court, his boots falling quiet on the stones. The crowd hushed and the gaze of all fell on him. He said, "Could I have a word with you?"

"Where's Hannaniah, Lieutenant?"

"With all due respect, sir, we should speak of this in private."

"I sent you for Hannaniah." Zadock stabbed the end of his finger into the tabletop. "Bring him here."

Daniel removed his helmet and stuffed it under his arm. He pushed his dark-black hair off his brow and stood at attention. He said, "Hannaniah is dead, sir."

The writing pen began to shake between Zoram's fingers. His father had prophesied Hannaniah's death for speaking falsely, but until now he didn't think it would happen like this, not during Uriah's trail, and he began recording it, his pen moving over the parchment, but he stopped when Zadock said, "Was he murdered?"

Daniel said, "I don't know. I didn't go inside. The house was still unclean."

"Murderer!" Zadock spun on Jeremiah, his long finger pointed at the prophet and his robes swirling about his arms. "You murdered Hannaniah."

Jeremiah said, "If you do not amend your doings, God will bring the same curse against you."

Zadock said, "Take him to the prison."

"Do with me as you wish, but know for certain that I'm innocent."

Daniel ripped the yoke from Jeremiah's shoulders. The cords binding the timbers came loose and the broken wood fell around Zoram, the gnarled lengths of olive wood covering his parchment. Zoram didn't look up from his writings. He kept his gaze turned away from the awful scene. What was to become of his father? Certainly they didn't think Jeremiah murdered Hannaniah. He may have cursed the man, but he would never hurt anyone. Couldn't they see that God had done this thing?

Daniel bound Jeremiah's hands behind his back with leather cords and tied a gag to his mouth, but before he marched him away, Zoram reached for Daniel's arm.

He said softly, "Be gentle with him."

A hand tapped Miriam on the shoulder, the thick fingers pressing against the flowing veils streaming down her shoulders. It was Mima, but Miriam didn't turn around and speak to her. She softly asked what Mima wanted and the woman sneaked a note into her palm. It was written in Josiah's hand; she recognized it immediately from the many notes they passed before he escaped the city. And there, in perfect Hebrew script was the answer to the charge of blasphemy. Miriam turned her head to the side. She coughed twice and said, "What should we do?"

Mima leaned forward, her voice strained. She said, "Have Mulek deliver it to Shemayahu."

How could she do that? She couldn't let her son run out in the middle of the trial under the watchful eye of Zadock. What if he caught him with the note?

Mima tapped her on the shoulder again. She said, "Mulek's been ready to deliver a message since we arrived this morning."

Miriam spoke through the cloth of her veil to cover her words. She said, "What are you talking about?"

Mima reached for Miriam's hand and squeezed it in hers. She said, "Why do you think I had him bring his ball?"

Zadock marched to the front of the court, raised his hands to the council and king, and was about to refute the notion that Hannaniah's death had anything to do with false prophecies when a red ball rolled off the end of the porch with Prince Mulek darting after it. Foolish child! Zadock dodged out of the way to keep from colliding with the boy. Mima never should have allowed him to bring his toys here. For the sake of Moses, she was the boy's handservant. If it were any other child, Zadock would have the soldiers remove him, but this was the royal son and hopefully the king would do something about the boy's unruly behavior. This was not the place for a child to throw a ball about, no matter that he was heir to the throne.

"Blasphemy is a serious crime." Zadock moved his gaze slowly over the Elders before coming to rest on King Zedekiah. He said, "Our law requires that anyone convicted of it is to be—"

"Free Uriah." Shemayahu's voice echoed over Zadock's words. He said, "You can't convict my son of blasphemy. The law is against you."

Zadock didn't bother to turn around and answer Shemayahu's

accusation. What did he know about Hebrew law? He was a babbling fool. Zadock waited for Shemayahu's voice to die in the crowd before he reminded the king that death was the correct judgment against a blasphemous man like Uriah.

Shemayahu said, "Are you familiar with the trial of Micah?"

Of course he was familiar with it, wasn't he? Zadock had studied every trial ever recorded on the scrolls of the law. He kept facing the king and council while he quickly recalled the details, his mind hurrying over the writings carefully etched into his memory from years of reading. Micah's trial was such an obscure bit of history that if he erred there was no way Shemayahu or any of the other Elders on the council would know it. Zadock rubbed his chin between his fingers. Micah was tried a hundred and twenty years ago for preaching that Zion would be plowed as a field, and Jerusalem would become heaps, and the mountain of the house—Solomon's temple—would be reduced to a forest of trees. Micah was guilty of blasphemy against the Holy City just as Uriah was guilty. He wasn't exactly sure of the verdict. Zadock was studying that very scroll the day the law was stolen from his chambers and he never finished reading the judgment against Micah, but there was no doubt that he was convicted of blasphemy.

Zadock turned around, the hem of his robe swirling over the cobblestones. Mulek was standing beside Shemayahu and when the prince saw the Chief Elder's piercing gaze on him, he picked up his red cloth ball, hurried back onto the porch and sat on the bench seat behind his mother's throne.

Shemayahu was reading from a small scrap of papyrus no larger than three fingers. Zadock marched across the court and snatched it from him. It was written in small, hastily drawn Hebrew script, but King Hezekiah's verdict was legible enough to read. Micah was innocent of the charge of blasphemy. The Lord repented him of the evil he had pronounced against the Holy City because it was not a crime for a prophet to speak the will of God.

Shemayahu said, "My son should be set free in the same manner that Hezekiah freed Micah."

Zadock crumpled the note and threw it to the ground. He said, "Uriah is a traitor."

Shemayahu said, "You haven't enough witnesses to prove that."

"That isn't entirely true." Zadock returned to his prosecution table and lowered himself into his chair. "But then you don't want me to send for the Lakhish Letters, do you? They'll only hurt your son further."

Shemayahu leaned his aging body against the defense table. "What are you saying?"

"Agree not to press for a second witness and I'll agree not to send for the Lakhish Letters." Zadock adjusted his shawls over his shoulders, set his hands on the table in front of him and turned his gaze onto Shemayahu. "We'll let the king determine if there is sufficient evidence to convict your son."

Shemayahu laid his hand on Uriah's shoulder. "Why do you want my son dead?"

"I want justice."

Shemayahu's gaze flitted between Uriah and King Zedekiah. He was like a fowl searching for a safe place to roost, but he'd never find one. The king was certain to rule in Zadock's favor.

Zadock said, "Tell me, Shemayahu, what would you have me do with the Lakhish Letters?"

Shemayahu scratched his fingers through his gray hair. He took a deep breath. He began to speak when a clear, strong voice rang from under the archway of the east gate.

Lehi pushed through the crowd. He said, "The Lakhish Letters are to be brought to trial immediately."

Sariah clung to Lehi's arm. She was thin, her face was pale, and there were dark circles around her eyes. She walked with her shoulders back to counter the weight of her growing womb, one hand beneath the unborn and the other pressed against the bandages wrapped around her head. She stopped in front of Zadock's prosecution table, greeted him with a weak smile, and told him she was pleased to be in his company and that nothing, not even a raging fire in the vineyards, could keep her from an occasions such as this. And, if it weren't any trouble, would he accept a gift from her? Sariah handed him a bottle of her pickled olives.

Cursed woman! What was she doing, giving him a gift from the vineyards he'd ordered Laban to burn? Zadock refused the olives. He said, "The Lakhish Letters serve no purpose here."

Sariah patted Lehi on the arm. She said, "Go on and tell the man what you told me about the House of Israel growing in our vineyard."

"I'm not a vineyard master and I was speaking to your husband, not you, woman." Zadock pulled the edge of his shawl forward to block the sight of her.

Lehi stepped between them, his stout body shielding Sariah from Zadock's view. He was dressed in a long white robe with blue satin and silk trim about the collar and cuffs. He had new leather sandals and the smell of them filled the square with the freshness of his presence. His hair was combed back and it was dark except for the touch of gray wisdom about his ears and a few white strands gracing the tuft of beard on his chin. He had deep green eyes and they filled with a certain light when he said, "We need the Lakhish Letters to prove your guilt."

"Don't you mean to say Uriah's guilt?"

Lehi didn't answer and Zadock turned to Shemayahu. "Do you really want this man to defend your son? The Lakhish Letters will only hurt your defense."

Lehi stretched his hand out toward the jury. "Zadock is like the uppermost branch of an old olive tree gone wild. The fruit he bears will bring the fall of Jerusalem and you will be lopped off and cast into the fire with him if you do not repent."

The Elders stood from their chairs, their fists in the air and their cries raised against Lehi. The crowd joined the Elders and the square erupted in a volley of shouting against the vineyard owner.

"He knows." Captain Laban grabbed Zadock by the arm and whispered in his ear. "Stop him before he tells every noble and commoner in the city about his lineage and the tax levy and our attempt on the life of—"

"Sit down before you draw attention to yourself." Zadock leaned his head in next to Captain Laban. "Lehi doesn't know anything."

"Why else would he confront us like this if he didn't know?"

"He's searching for something to snare us with." Zadock pushed Laban back toward his chair. "Now stay there and keep silent."

Zadock marched over and stood close to Lehi. He said, "Why must this people endure the babblings of visionary men? You lead this people away by the vain and foolish imaginings of your heart."

"It is not foolish to have faith in the Messiah and it is not vain to believe Jehovah will redeem the world." Lehi turned his gaze to the sky and said, "Great and marvelous are thy works, O Lord God Almighty!"

"This man is pequeah!" Zadock turned to the crowd and spoke over Lehi, his voice drowning out the man's praises. He signaled for the nobles to join him. They began with a low rumble, but the chanting grew until it filled the square.

Zadock said, "There is no redemption. We were born into the world at the pleasure of God and we are here to eat, drink, and be merry, for tomorrow we die."

Lehi raised his voice above the chanting. "The throne of God is high in the heavens and His power, and goodness, and mercy are over all the inhabitants of the earth."

Zadock said, "There is no heaven. When a man dies that is the end of him and there is nothing more than a dark night!"

Lehi said, "God is merciful and he will not suffer those who come unto Him that they should perish!"

"Enough of your arguing!" King Zedekiah stood from his throne and stepped to the edge of the stone porch, the train of his cape following behind his stride.

The chanting subsided and in the silence Zadock bowed. He said, "If it pleases the king, will you decide the guilt of Uriah and end this matter?"

Zedekiah said, "It pleases me to adjourn this trial for three days."

"For what purpose?"

"There will be no decision until I see the letters." Zedekiah turned to Commander Yaush. He said, "Take Lehi with you to Lakhish and bring me the letters."

Shemayahu said, "I must protest, sire. I don't trust these men."

"Then go with them if you must." Zedekiah pointed his scepter at Yaush. "See that you bring me the letters."

"We can't wait three days." Zadock walked to the center of the court. "That will be the eve of Passover and there won't be room in this square to conduct a proper trial. The city will be overrun with travelers come to celebrate the feast."

"Then we'll finish this trial in my palace chambers, but it will be done before the sun sets on Passover. I will not celebrate this nation's deliverance from bondage with Uriah sitting in my prison." Zedekiah marched to his chariot, and pulled himself up on the stoop. Before ducking beneath the leather canopy he said, "Until midday on the eve of Passover, gentlemen."

Queen Miriam followed Zedekiah into the chariot with the royal sons, with Mima following behind them.

Captain Laban stepped in next to Zadock. He said, "You told me the Lakhish Letters would never come to trial."

"They won't."

"What do you call this?"

Zadock said, "Where's your horse?"

Laban pointed out his white Arabian tied up next to the guard station. "Why do you ask?"

"You're to ride to the caves in the hills east of the city."

"You want me to find Shechem?"

"That's right."

"You've gone mad. There are a thousand caves in those hills. I'll never find him."

"The moment you get close to him, he'll find *you*." Zadock pointed his long finger at Laban. "Tell him to destroy the letters."

"Shechem can't get inside Lakhish. No one can get inside the fort without entering by the bastion."

"Let Shechem worry about the details. That's what we pay him for." Zadock waved his hand in the air. "Now go quickly, before Commander Yaush and his company return to the fort."

Zadock pushed through the crowd to the east gate and watched from beneath the shade of the archway as Laban spurred across the Kidron Valley, up a narrow trail into the Mount of Olives toward the hills east of Jerusalem. He had to see that Shechem destroyed the one thing that could ruin their alliance.

The Lakhish Letters.

CHAPTER 30

A small corral with a stable and watering trough stood back off the road. It was half hidden in a grove of cottonwoods and scrub oak below Jerusalem's east gate. Lehi paid the stable boy two shekels for watering his horses and tending them during the trial. He helped Sariah up into the saddle and stood beside her animal to steady it. Late afternoon brought with it the cramps and sickness that had racked her body since the vineyard fire and he stilled the horse to keep from adding to her pain.

Lehi was to meet Commander Yaush and Shemayahu here and depart for Fort Lakhish, but before they arrived he had to make arrangements for Sariah's lodging. She couldn't make the journey to Lakhish and he wouldn't risk sending her home to Beit Zayit, not in her condition. He rubbed the horse on the muzzle and told Sariah he never should have allowed her to come—the ride was too hard on her. She didn't answer and Lehi knew better than to say anymore. She was in enough pain. She didn't need to deal with his mild rebukes and he lowered his head and offered a silent prayer that God would provide for Sariah while he traveled to Lakhish. The inns in the city were full and there was no one he could turn to for help, at least not anyone he trusted. They had no family in the city and though Aaron was a good friend, he couldn't ask the boy's help. His father would never allow Sariah to lodge with them.

The wide, black-skinned form of Mima, the queen's handservant, made her way down the rampart from Jerusalem's gate. She pushed through the crowd, hurried around a slow-moving mule cart with the hem of her colorful red and green skirt dragging in the dirt. She should have raised it off the ground, but her hands were busy with a small wicker coop. She stepped around the cottonwoods growing up in front of the corral and marched straight to Lehi. Was Mima the answer to his prayers? Could she care for Sariah while he was gone to Lakhish? She was the former handservant for Josiah the potter and she was well trained in the care of a woman. Lehi reached for his purse. Five pieces of silver would be more than enough for the three days' care. He held the coins in the palm of his hand and waited for Mima to come around the bend in the trail and step into the clearing in front of the stables.

Mima spoke with a mild Ethiopian accent. She held out a cage with a pigeon jumping about inside and said, "If there's anything you don't understand about the Lakhish Letters, this pigeon can help you."

Lehi peered between the wicker bars. Did she really mean to say the pigeon could help? He said, "Does the bird read?"

"Of course not." Mima lowered the cage to her side. "What kind of fool do you think I am?"

Lehi said, "Why don't you tell me more about the bird?"

"I don't have time for this." Mima quickly glanced over her shoulder. "They'll grow suspicious if I stay too long."

"Who will grow suspicious?"

"Listen to me." Mima took Lehi by the arm. "I was Josiah the potter's maidservant. Do you remember him?"

"He was a fine man and a student of the law."

Mima said, "He understood it better than anyone in Jerusalem."

"It was a shame to lose him to that fire."

"We didn't lose him." Mima leaned her head in. "He's still alive."

Alive? The man's funeral was three months back and there was no doubt this woman was still grieving. He said, "It must be painful for you."

"Didn't you hear me?" Mima waved the coop about and the pigeon fluttered its wings. "I told you he's alive and this bird can take a message to him."

Nodding, Lehi spoke slowly. "Certainly it can." The messenger pigeon must be part of some sort of Ethiopian grieving ritual he'd not heard of. He said, "Does it deliver the messages to heaven?"

"What sort of question is that?" Mima pushed her red and green bandana back off her brow. "It flies the messages to Josiah's camp."

"Camp?"

"That's right."

"Exactly where is this camp?"

Mima glanced about, her gaze flitting over the travelers passing along the road. She lowered her voice to a whisper. "I can't tell you. No one can know where he's gone. If anyone finds out, they're certain to go there after him."

Lehi worked his chin between his thumb and forefinger. Didn't this woman understand that heaven was not a camp and it certainly wasn't a secret? Josiah had died and gone there, and every soul on the face of the earth was certain to follow when they died. Lehi took a step back from Mima. Was this the sort of woman he wanted to trust with the care of Sariah? Mima wasn't grieving. She'd completely lost her wits.

Mima said, "If you have any trouble understanding the Lakhish Letters, Josiah can help." She pressed the wicker cage into Lehi's hands. "Send him a message with this pigeon."

"Have you done this before?"

"Of course I have. I sent him a message just today."

"And he answered you?"

"Within the hour."

"And you think Josiah will get word back to me as well?"

"He won't reply to you. Josiah only answers me."

Lehi bit his lower lip to keep from smiling. "Of course; I should have known that."

"You send him a message, he sends me the reply and I get word to you." Mima removed her bandana and brushed her hand through her thick curls. "Do you understand how it works?"

"I understand perfectly." Lehi couldn't return the pigeon to her. There was no telling how a woman in her condition would react if he refused to take the bird and he tied the cage to his saddlebags. He could never leave Sariah in the care of such an odd handservant. How did she ever get work with the queen of Judah? Lehi slipped his silver coins back into his money purse.

Mima and her pigeon were not the answer to his prayer.

Aaron hurried out of the east gate and down the rampart to the Kidron Valley. Where were Lehi and Sariah? There was no sign of them walking among the mule train packed with sacks of grain, and they weren't riding with a large group of pilgrims headed south toward Bethlehem. Aaron offered a silent prayer that somehow God would lead him to them and let him ask Sariah if she was going to keep her child. If there was anything he could do to ease her pain he would, but not a single rider in a caravan of perfume and oils resembled Lehi. And the woman riding in a chariot with two drivers at the front of the band of merchants was too tall and overdressed to be Sariah.

Aaron dodged around a farmer's cart, stepped in past a beggar asking alms and pulled up on the dusty shoulder of the road, his sandals sinking into the fine powder and filling the gaps between his toes with the sandy, warm earth. He held his hand to his brow to shield his eyes from the late afternoon sun so he could search every face that passed, but it was no use. Lehi and Sariah were not among the thousands leaving the city. They'd gotten away too quickly after the trial and there was no hope he'd find them now. Aaron started back up the road past a stand of cottonwoods. How would he ever know if Sariah was well and ask her if there were anything he could do to help ease her . . .

Aaron's heart told him to turn around, but he kept walking. There was nothing beyond the stand of trees but an animal stable set off the main road and there was no reason to look there for Sariah. He pushed his sandals through the dirt, lifting a cloud of fine dust around his legs when the thought came to him again. If he were to help Sariah all he need do was turn around and . . .

Aaron peered through the low-lying branches of the cottonwoods. Was that Sariah sitting in the saddle of a brown steed with her hand on her stomach? Aaron skirted about the trunk of the largest tree and turned down a dirt path leading to the stables. Lehi was holding the reins of Sariah's horse and Aaron sprinted over, waving his hands in the air.

"The baby . . ." Aaron reached the clearing in front of the main corral and leaned one hand against the side of Sariah's horse. He spoke between gasps for breath. He said, "You're going to keep the baby, aren't you?"

Sariah nodded. She said, "God willing, son."

Aaron took Sariah by the hand and his words rushed out of him like water through a broken dam. He told her how he'd worried for her life, and for the baby's life, and that her recovery was an answer to his prayers. Nephi's bow was nearly completed. The horsehair bowstring was done, the forging finished, and if he worked hard the next few days he'd have it polished and ready by Passover. Sariah thanked him, but her voice was soft—nothing like her usual robust chatter. She was ill; he could tell by her pale complexion and the slight trembling in her hands.

Lehi stepped between them. He said, "Do you know of a place she can lodge three days while I'm away at Lakhish?"

Aaron said, "The inns are filled for Passover."

"I knew that."

Aaron ran his hand through his hair. He couldn't invite Sariah to stay with his family. Papa would never allow it. He was already upset about Uriah's family lodging with them. Aaron took the reins to Sariah's horse. He said, "She can stay with us."

Sariah said, "What will your father say?"

"We already have five houseguests that aren't to Papa's liking." Aaron took the horse by the reins. "One more shouldn't make a difference."

CHAPTER 31

The ride from Jerusalem tired Setti, but it had been a full week since he'd captained the night watch and with the sun already set over the western hills and the shadows of evening descending over the watchtowers and parapets of Lakhish, it was his duty to stay with his men and watch the fort until sunrise.

Setti circled down past his father, told him he was taking command of the night watch and he wasn't going to let Yaush or Sophia convince him otherwise. What would his men think if he rested the night while they stayed on the wall? He leaned over his saddle, kissed his mother good night and told her to sleep well before reining back to let Shemayahu and Lehi pass into the high-walled corridor leading to the upper gates. The sound of their hooves echoed through the passage before falling silent and safe within the precincts of Lakhish. Once they were inside, Setti put himself to the task of checking the lower gate.

The day's runoff pooled about the foundation stones and if it turned much colder there was a risk of ice. Setti got down from his horse and kicked at the puddle with the tip of his boot. This time of year the thawing and freezing of spring was a gate's worst enemy, and he could ill afford to let the pivot stone crack or he'd have to order the gate removed and the foundation replaced. He dug the heel of his boot into the mud and made a trench to filter the water away. Come morning he'd have a troop of men dig a more permanent ditch. A little ice on the gatepost timbers he could live with, but he'd not let any water seep into the fissures of the pivot stone and freeze during his watch. There was no excuse for losing the main gate to an unexpected spring freeze.

Setti left his horse and walked along the front of the gate. The pivot stones were greased with fresh oils and the metal plating along the planks was nailed snug. There was nothing out of the ordinary except for the sound of a solitary horse racing up the rampart. The black-coated animal rounded the bend below the gate at full gallop, its metal hooves crushing the stones underfoot like a thresher grinds wheat, and kicking up the loose earth in its wake.

The rider came around, his warm breath pulsing from his mouth in rhythm with the horse's panting. He handled his mount with the skill of a well-trained cavalryman—his long, powerful legs pressed against the animal's side and his heels turned in against the haunches, steadying the horse a good thirty paces down the rampart. Long hair fell from inside his hood, running over his thick shoulders and down past his saddle in ratted thatches.

The full moon silhouetted the outline of his dark image and the bare branches of a Joshua tree growing up beside the road framed him like a portrait. A black raven landed in the branches above the rider and crowed at his coming, but beyond the eerie sound of the fowl's proclamation, there was nothing about the man's flowing black capes that offered any clue to his identity.

Setti slowly unsheathed his sword. There had never been such an odd arrival on his watch and he should have called to the towers for his men to join him, but the man was alone and what danger could there be in approaching the hooded figure and asking him what purpose he had in coming to—

"Setti!"

He spun around and found Nathan calling from tower number four. He said, "Is that you Setti?" He laughed, his voice echoing down over the steep hillside. "Did you lose your way? Your father and mother are already inside the fort."

Setti said, "Bring the ledgers."

"For what?"

"We have an arrival."

Nathan pulled a torch from its post and raised it high enough to cast a yellow glow across the rampart. He said, "What arrival?"

Setti turned back down the rampart. The rider was gone, the full moon filling the emptiness where the horseman once stood. The raven peered down from its barren-branched perch and crowed at the sudden disappearance. The man had vanished into the sagebrush and thistle growing alongside the approach to the fort and Setti ran to the edge. There was no sign of him traversing the steep drop that fell quickly into a narrow ravine below the fort. The road leading back down to the valley was empty and there was no black-robed figure lurking about the rocky hillside above the road.

Nathan marched out the open gate with a leather scroll in one hand and a torch in the other. He offered the ledger, but Setti didn't take it. He removed his helmet and stared down the rampart until the raven flew its perch. What kind of rider vanished into the cold air of evening without a sound?

Setti pushed his hair back off his brow. He said, "Put the ledger away."

What was that? Lehi pulled back the edge of the lambskin blanket and sat up in bed, his head brushing the walnut headboard carved with an intricate pattern of rosebuds. He heard a voice telling him he was blessed because of what he'd done, but there was no one in his bedroom, at least no one awake at this hour. Shemayahu went straight to sleep in the bed on the other side of the guest room and his snoring was as constant as the rise and fall of the blankets covering him. Lehi leaned over the side of his bed to check on the pigeon Mima had sent to Fort Lakhish with him. The bird wasn't cooing or walking about in her small wicker coop and no matter what Mima said about the creature, it certainly didn't know Hebrew well enough to tell him he'd been faithful to the commands of God—and that's exactly what the voice was telling him.

Lehi rubbed his brow, but he couldn't rid his mind of the nightmarish vision of his own bloody body lying on the ground. He'd done what the Lord asked of him and he was to be blessed for his faithfulness for preaching to the people of Jerusalem, but what blessing was there in seeing a vision of his own murder with a warning that Laban and Zadock with the Council of Elders sought to take away his life?

Lehi pulled the edge of the lambskin blanket up under his chin. The bedroom door was built of thick wood slats and the shutters were locked with a metal latch. This was the palace-fort at Lakhish and there was not a safer place to sleep than in the guest room down the hall from Governor Yaush and his wife. Lehi was surrounded by five thousand solders, two impenetrable walls and . . .

What was he to do about this warning? He couldn't flee Beit Zayit. With the help of Ishmael, he'd built the largest olive plantations in all of Judah. It was his livelihood. His father and his great-grandfather before him left it to Lehi. It was to be an inheritance for generations to come and he wasn't about to walk away from it. There were other ways to save himself without abandoning Beit Zayit. He'd hire mercenaries, and he'd arm the menservants at the plantation with swords, and post watches about the estate. Lehi turned on his side and stared at the embers still glowing in the hearth. And if weapons weren't enough, he'd confront the trouble head-on. He was a wealthy man and he could pay Laban not to harm him. They may have their differences on the matter of Uriah, and Laban may dislike Lehi for preaching his Messianic faith in the streets of Jerusalem, but there was no reason for the man to want him dead, was there?

Lehi laid his head on the goose-down pillow and closed his eyes, but the comfort of a well-stuffed head cushion didn't have the power to carry him back to sleep, not with the promise of more dreams waiting in the wings until he dozed, biding the intermission of his sleeplessness before revisiting the stage of his mind and haunting his rest. The pigeon at the foot of his bed cooed and the soft, gentle sound threatened to ease him back into his nightmare. Tomorrow he'd give the bird away.

What good was a messenger pigeon that homed to a dead man?

Jebus fished out the last leather parchment—letter number eighteen—and rolled it open across his writing table. He smeared beeswax over the surface and let the fibers soak in the protective oils before rubbing it clean with a dry cloth. On Commander Yaush's orders, he was to clean and polish the Lakhish Letters, touch-up the faded characters with new black ink and see that they were ready for review first thing in the morning.

A breeze flowed down the stairs and through the open treasury door and Jebus quickly cupped his hand about the flickering flame in his lamp, shielding it from going out. Where did that draft come from? The door at the top of the stairs was shut and Jebus didn't hear it creak open.

"Moriah is that you?"

The boy was to bring him a pot of hot mint tea from the kitchens, but there was no answer and Jebus went back to his work. The Hebrew characters on this last parchment were written in Laban's difficult-to-decipher hand. The man may be captain of the guard, but he would never find employment as a scribe. His pen strokes were cut short. He hardly ever started a new thought with the proper Egyptian phrase, "and it came to pass," and the rigid curls and cues in his letters were far too difficult to read. It would be a much simpler task to search through the copies Moriah made on clay tablets, but he was ordered to clean and wax and touch-up the original letters and leave Moriah's copies locked away in the main vault. No one was to know about them.

Moriah had a flowing hand that was easy to read and much more pleasing to the eye than these chicken-scratched letters. Jebus would never tell the boy such a thing. It would only swell Moriah's head. Better to let him think he was allowed the privilege of copying the most important documents at Lakhish for experience, not because he was the finest scribe to ever grace these basement vaults with his talents. The boy could read and write more languages than Jebus could name. He understood hieroglyphic like a native Egyptian scribe, and there was something unfair about an apprentice having more skill than the master.

Jebus leaned back on his stool and checked the entrance to the treasury. There was no sign of Moriah in the stairwell and no sound of his footsteps descending from the main floor above. Cursed boy! If he didn't return from the kitchens with the mint tea soon, Jebus had a good mind never to graduate him from his apprenticeship. It shouldn't take all night to boil water and when Moriah returned, Jebus was going to tell him what he thought of his laziness.

Jebus finished polishing away the wax. There weren't any faded characters in need of a touch of ink from his pen, except for a phrase near the bottom, along the margin of the parchment. The characters were written in a lighter shade than the others and he was going to have to go over them with black ink. He dipped his pen, placed the tip next to the phrase and slowly inked over the Hebrew characters, careful to follow in Captain Laban's original pen strokes, writing overtop something about a curse against the royal . . .

Another draft of air rushed down the stairs and into the treasury. Jebus threw down his pen and reached for the lamp, but he was too slow to stop the flame from flickering out. The treasury went dark and he felt about his writing table for the flint. It wasn't in the upper corner and he quickly ran his hand across the wood surface to the other side and knocked the ink over the edge, the bottle crashing on the ground at the foot of his stool. Cursed breeze! Why didn't Moriah shut the door when he went for tea?

Jebus found the flint hiding under the leather parchment of letter number eighteen. He lit the lamp and a dim, yellow light filtered across the treasury, its glow falling on the wide-shouldered, thick-armed frame of a tall man. He filled the doorway from post to post and his head reached to just below the crossbeam. He arrived in silence like a spirit from another world and his dark, penetrating eyes made him into a rather unwelcome ghost. He carried a saddlebag over his shoulders like a merchant packing his most valuable goods. He stepped toward Jebus, his black leather boots falling quiet over the rough stone floor and his cape and scarves lifting away from his powerful legs on each stride, revealing a short black kilt that hardly covered his powerful legs. He pulled back his hood and his long hair fell down past his shoulders, the ratted ends dancing over the top of the writing table. He held out a small parchment sealed with Laban's military insignia and authorizing him to carry the captain's most sensitive messages. He said, "I'm the new courier," and his voice rasped like the ends of imported Egyptian papyrus rubbing against a wooden dowel.

He was an odd-looking messenger. He had the stature of a warrior, not a military courier, but who was Jebus to question a delivery sent from Captain Laban? There was no way this man was an imposter. He couldn't get inside Fort Lakhish unless the watchmen let him inside and Setti would never allow a breach of the fort's doubles walls. Lakhish was the safest place in the entire kingdom.

Jebus said, "I'm closed for the day." He fell to his knees and picked the pieces of the broken bottle off the floor, the ink staining his fingers. He said, "Leave your deliveries over there on the table near the door. I'll see to them come morning."

"I'm not making a delivery."

No deliveries? What sort of courier rode all the way to Lakhish without a delivery? Jebus stood from cleaning the floor. He said, "What brings you here?"

"Laban sent me to collect his letters."

"There's no need for that." Jebus stacked the broken pieces of the ink bottle on his writing table and cleaned his hands on his waxing cloth. "Commander Yaush is taking them to Jerusalem."

"Laban wants them now." The courier walked to the front of the writing table. He leaned over, his long hair sweeping over letter number eighteen. He said, "Where are they?"

"You're going to have to speak with Commander Yaush about this in the morning."

"I haven't time to wait till morning." The courier grabbed Jebus by the arm and forced him to sit on his writing stool. It was a powerful grip and it blocked the blood from flowing to his hand. He said, "I make my deliveries by night."

"I'm not going to wake the commander." Jebus pulled free from the man's grip. Didn't he know Jebus bruised easily? If the courier held him any harder he'd not be able to wear his short-sleeved tunic for a month with all the black and blue for everyone to see. "Yaush only just returned from Jerusalem this evening."

"Then let him sleep, but give me the letters."

They were inside the vessel on the edge of the writing table. Jebus really shouldn't give them to the courier, but the man did have authorization from Captain Laban. They had a copy of the letters on clay tablets locked away in the vault and he could let the courier take these originals, couldn't he? Jebus pushed the vessel across the table. "They're in here."

The courier picked through the parchments, his powerful hands quickly going over each letter like an accountant tallying his wealth and when he finished he turned his dark-eyed gaze back onto Jebus. He said, "There's one missing."

"This is it." Jebus rolled letter number eighteen and returned it to the jar with the others.

The courier said, "Did you read it?"

"What kind of question is that?" Jebus laid his hand on the jar of beeswax. "I hardly have time to polish them."

"What about your scribes?"

"What of them?"

The courier fitted the storage vessel into his saddlebag. He said, "Did any of your scribes read these letters?"

"I don't let my scribes read Captain Laban's personal mail."

Well, at least most of his scribes. Moriah's eyes were the only ones that had ever read them from beginning to end and it was a shame the captain would never have the chance to read the boy's skillfully copied letters. They were some of the finest work ever done in this treasury and if Laban liked what he saw—and he was certain to like the clay tablets—there was no telling what sort of promotion the young apprentice Moriah could win for his expert copying.

Jebus stood from his stool, his hands gripping the edge of the writing table. Moriah may be the talent behind the clay tablets locked away in the vault, but as long as he was an apprentice in this treasury Jebus could claim the boy's work his own. If the copies impressed Captain Laban they would win Jebus a promotion. No more drudging about in this drafty basement vault. He could be transferred to Jerusalem and enjoy the sociality of the capital with its fine inns and wonderful feasts, to say nothing of the luxuries afforded military men in the Holy City.

The courier strapped the saddlebag over his shoulder, turned past the writing table and he was beyond the door and into the stairwell when Jebus said, "Wouldn't you rather take finely crafted clay tablet copies to Captain Laban?"

The courier stopped in the door. He was facing the stairs and his words echoed up the stairwell. He said, "You have copies of these?"

"The writing's much better and if you promise to tell Captain Laban that I was—"

"Where are they?" The courier came back to the writing table and leaned in so close that Jebus could feel the force of his breath run over his cheeks. He said, "Get them for me."

Jebus held the solitary lamp ahead of his stride and led the courier from the writing room, under the archway into the repository, down between rows of sealed documents to a vault at the back. He unlocked the door, pulled it open, and let the dim yellow light of his lamp spread over the three clay tablet copies of the Lakhish Letters sitting alone on a small drying table in the corner. They were dry weeks ago, but since no one but Moriah was allowed to handle them, they had yet to be moved onto the top shelf out of sight.

Jebus asked the courier to treat the copies with care. If the man chipped the clay or cracked the letters they'd not impress Captain Laban with enough power to win him a promotion. The courier yanked them off the table and stuffed them into his saddlebags like a wild boar, and Jebus prayed these clay tablets would find their way to Captain Laban unblemished.

The courier said, "Who made these copies?"

"It's my best work." Jebus rubbed his ink-stained hands together. He said, "You'll tell Captain Laban I made them, won't you?"

The courier lunged at Jebus, knocking the lamp to the ground and cloaking the vault in darkness. The pain of cold steel split Jebus through the ribs. He groped for the source of it, his hand running across the hilt of a dagger stabbed deep into his breast and piercing his heart. He collapsed against the drying table, the wooden legs splintering under his weight. He cried for help, but blood filled his lungs. What had he done to deserve this?

His mind went silent.

Sophia closed the shutters on the bedroom window. How did her husband ever expect to get a good night's rest with the cool night air drafting into the room? The hearth was stocked with logs and the flames tempered the chill, but it was a waste of good firewood to heat the outside air. She latched the shutters with a bolt and tied the thick canopy of curtains over the opening. Maybe that would keep Yaush from standing at the window and staring into the darkness. She'd gotten him to change into his sleeping robe, had him sit in his reading chair, removed his slippers, and if she could coax him to lie down in his bed he'd be asleep in no time. A good down pillow and a lambskin blanket would do more to comfort him than hot tea. He needed his rest and she was going to see that nothing upset him, not even the chill of evening.

Sophia turned back to her vanity, rubbed a pomegranate cream over her cheeks, tucked her long, brown hair under the collar of her robe, and told Yaush it was time to stop staring at the fire and go to bed. It was too late to do anything about the letters and he should follow the advice he gave Lehi and Shemayahu—get some sleep and first thing in the morning they could go to the treasury, get the parchments, and read through them. It was the only sane thing to do after arriving from Jerusalem at such a late hour with hardly enough time to eat and retire for the evening. The letters would be waiting for them come morning.

A knock sounded at the door and Sophia said, "Would you get that, dear?"

Yaush didn't get up from his reading chair.

"The door, dear. There's someone knocking." Sophia put away her creams, passed a towel over her face to rid her of the excess, and still her husband didn't move from in front of the hearth. Would she ever get him out of that chair and into bed?

Sophia quickly crossed the room and undid the latch. The door flew open and Setti burst inside on a full march. He passed Sophia without a kiss or even saying, "Good evening, Mother." He went straight to Yaush, leaned over the reading chair, and said, "Did you see anything odd about the palace grounds?"

Yaush didn't look up from staring at the fire.

Setti said, "Papa, did you hear me?"

Yaush spoke softly. He said, "I've seen far too many strange things of late, son."

"You're upset." Sophia left the door open and hurried to Setti's side. She said, "What is it, son?"

"It was an arrival." Setti tapped the hilt of his sword. "A rather odd arrival."

Sophia said, "Did you let him inside the fort?"

"He was gone before I had the chance."

Yaush said, "Where did he go?"

"I don't know. I turned around for a moment and he was gone."

"What did he look like?"

"I didn't get a good look at him." Setti rubbed the back of his neck. "He was a strong man. He wore a kilt that hardly covered his nakedness and he had long hair that reached well past his—"

"Heaven help us." Yaush came out of his chair. "Not him."

Sophia said, "Not who?"

Before Yaush could answer, a terrible wailing sounded in the hallway outside their bedroom. Sophia rushed to the opened door. Moriah stood at the end of the hallway with Jebus in his arms. The white sleeves and neatly pressed cloth of the boy's tunic were covered in bright red blood and the hilt of a dagger rose from the chief scribe's chest. Moriah lowered Jebus to the floor. He reached to remove the dagger, but his hand was shaking and he hadn't the strength to pull the weapon from his master's flesh.

Sophia ran to the boy and knelt beside him. She said, "What happened, dear?"

"I don't know." Moriah touched Jebus with his trembling fingers, the blood-soaked tunic coloring his skin dark red. "I found him like this."

Yaush pushed past Sophia "Did you see anyone?"

"Nothing." Moriah stared at the lifeless body. "No one ever comes to the treasury."

Yaush said, "Where did you find him?"

"He was lying in a pool of blood." Tears streamed off the end of Moriah's nose and fell on the corpse. He said, "He was in the vault."

The door to the guest room at the far end of the hallway pushed open and Lehi and Shemayahu hurried down the wide corridor. The collar of Lehi's loose-fitting sleeping robe fell low around his neck and the untied latches of Shemayahu's sandals slapped against the stone with each step.

"What's going on?" Shemayahu hurried his cane over the floor. "We heard an awful cry and . . ."

Lehi came around in front of Yaush and when he saw the reason for the disturbance he said, "Lord, have mercy on his soul."

Yaush said, "It was Shechem."

"The robber?" Lehi stood next to Yaush. "Are you sure of it?"

"I've never been more certain of anything."

Setti started down the hallway. "I'm going after him and when I catch him I'm going to—"

"No, son. I don't want you going after a man like that. Not alone." Yaush spoke with a commanding voice. "He's too dangerous."

Setti said, "It hasn't been long. I could still catch him."

"It isn't Shechem we're after."

Setti came back down the hall. "Then who?"

"Laban is the cause of this." Yaush took Moriah by the shoulder and lifted him to his feet. He said, "What about the letters, did you secure them?"

"They're gone." Moriah turned from Yaush's penetrating stare. "They're all gone."

"What about the copy?"

"Let him be." Sophia leaned between them. "You're upsetting the poor boy."

"I have to know." Yaush stepped around her. "Tell me about the tablets."

Moriah shook his head. "I'm sorry, sir."

"It's just as well." Shemayahu tapped his cane on the floor. "I never wanted the letters to come to trial."

Yaush said, "You don't understand."

"I understand the letters can hurt my son." Shemayahu pointed his cane at Yaush. "You plotted with Laban to use the letters to convict my son of treason."

Sophia said, "How can you say that?"

"Your husband works for the man."

Sophia took Yaush by the hand. "He risked his commission to try and help you."

Yaush said, "That's enough, dear."

Sophia said, "My husband brought you word of your son's imprisonment."

Shemayahu eyed Yaush down the length of his cane like an archer taking aim. He said, "You didn't deliver the notice."

"He most certainly did."

"Sophia, no more." Yaush reached to take her by the shoulder, but she stepped from his grasp. She said, "My husband studied the letters for months trying to find something that could aid your son in his trial. He didn't eat, he didn't sleep, he did nothing but search for anything that could help set Uriah free and if you can't thank him for

that, you could at least thank him for escorting you to Lehi's plantation to find a good lawyer."

"That was you?" Shemayahu lowered his cane. "You're the masked
rider?"

Yaush said, "Our faith in God and His prophets is greater than
our allegiance to Laban." He pulled Sophia close. "You can't speak a
word of this to anyone. If Laban knew I supported you and your son
he would destroy my family."

"I should thank you for what you've done but it seems divine
providence the letters are gone." Shemayahu leaned over the corpse
on the floor. "They won't cause anyone more suffering. This is the
end of our problems."

Lehi said, "You're wrong about that. We've all been wrong about
Laban." He spoke quietly but his voice was firm. He said, "This is
only the beginning of our troubles."

Yaush said, "What do you mean?"

"Zadock and Laban didn't want the letters to come to trial."

Yaush said, "That's right."

"The letters are a curse to us all." Shemayahu jabbed the tip of his
cane on the stone floor, next to Jebus. "This man is dead because of
them and I don't want my son to suffer the same fate."

"It wasn't the letters that killed Jebus." Lehi slowly removed the
dagger. "He's dead because he was a threat to Laban and it won't stop
here." He pointed the bloody blade at Shemayahu. "Once a man
starts killing, he doesn't stop until he's rid of what threatens him."

Yaush said, "I've read over the letters endlessly and I've not found
anything that could help Uriah."

"That may be the problem." Lehi pushed in next to Yaush. "You
were searching for evidence to free Uriah when you should have been
looking for proof of Laban's guilt."

Yaush said, "What guilt?"

"We'll never know without the letters." Lehi slowly shook his
head. "There have got to be some clues in what Laban wrote. Why
else would he fear them?"

Shemayahu leaned on his cane. "The letters are gone and there's
nothing any of us can do about that."

Moriah said, "There is one thing, sir."

Yaush said, "What is it?"

Sophia touched Moriah on the back of the head. The poor boy had been through so much this evening. She said, "Why don't you go to bed? These men can take care of this."

"I can't, my lady. Not until I show them."

"Show them what?"

Moriah folded Jebus' lifeless arms over his bloody chest. He slowly stood from the corpse, the neatly pressed cloth of his white tunic stained with the blood of his master.

Moriah said, "There's another copy of the letters."

Moriah led Commander Yaush, Setti, and Lehi down the winding back streets of Lakhish. They left Shemayahu and Sophia at the palace to look after the corpse while Moriah sneaked them through the empty side streets and alleyways in the dark of night. They were not to light their torches until they were to the no-man's-land on the other side of the upper wall. Any flames in the secret passageway could kill them, and since Commander Yaush didn't want to go out by the main gates where his men could see what they were doing, they were to follow Moriah's directions without fail. He was the only one who knew another way out of the city. The street narrowed before turning sharp and dead-ending into the east wall, the precipice towering one hundred cubits above them.

"Are you sure we can get through here?" Lehi tapped the butt of his cold, dark torch against the foundation stones in the wall. "I don't see an opening."

Setti said, "There's no secret passage here."

Yaush said, "I designed this fort and I tell you, son, there isn't a secret passage leading to the no-man's-land between the upper and lower walls. We may have to go through the bastion to get in there." He laid his hand on Moriah's shoulder. "We can't get there from here."

Moriah smiled. He said, "Moses crossed the Red Sea, didn't he, sir?"

"That he did, son, but it was water Moses parted." Yaush slapped the thick limestone blocks with his fist. "These stones are ten cubits thick and no scribe from my treasury has the power to part them, no matter how good your penmanship."

"Don't lose faith, sir. Things aren't always as they appear." Moriah inched down along the wall behind a stand of low growing cedars and found the square slab of stone imbedded in the ground and grown over with dead, brown weeds. He rooted them up, found the hand-grip, and lifted away the capstone, releasing the stench of the city's underground sewer, the fumes choking the air. A ladder leaned against the inside wall of the tunnel and Moriah shimmied down into the darkness. He led them along a catwalk built above the level of the water. The sewer ran underground all the way beneath both walls before it emptied into a small streambed in a grove of scrub oak outside the fort, but they weren't escaping the city. Moriah was leading them to the narrow stretch of land surrounding the fort between the upper and lower walls and he paced off the underground distance with his careful stride. Thirty-one, thirty-two, thirty-three . . .

Moriah stopped and felt along the wall until he found the handholds chiseled into the stone. He scaled the tunnel wall, pushed open the capstone and let the fresh night air filter down into the sewer. This was the way into the no-man's-land between the double walls. Moriah helped Setti, Yaush, and Lehi out of the sewer. There were no sheep grazing in this space between the upper and lower walls, no soldiers standing watch, no wild animals making their homes, nothing but rocky soil and stands of weeds and grasses bending to the light breeze that filtered over the lower wall and up the steep incline.

Moriah lit his torch and told them to begin their search over there, below the first parapet where the north wall turned sharp into the east wall. That's where he discarded the potsherds. Setti was the first to find one. It was written in Moriah's flowing pen strokes with something about Laban accusing Uriah of treason, but only a portion of the phrase appeared on the clay fragment and Moriah collected it into his leather satchel.

The largest scattering of potsherds sat along the base of the wall imbedded in the soft earth and faded by the winter rains. The clay pieces were easy to find and they hurried about like children searching for river stones along the shore of a creek, gathering the broken pieces of clay into Moriah's leather pouch. They searched the area twice more, walking side-by-side with torches high, and searching for stray potsherds. When they didn't find anymore among the grasses, Moriah said, "We should take these back to the treasury."

Setti said, "It isn't safe there."

"You could assign a watch."

"No guards." Yaush raised his hand. "I don't want any of my men to know what we're doing." He pointed the end of his torch at Setti. "Do you still have the key to the keep?"

"I'd never lose it." Setti removed a chain from around his neck with a brass key dangling from the end. "I have the only key."

Lehi kept back one of the potsherds he found in the mud and didn't place it in Moriah's satchel. It was the size of his hand, slightly curved like the rounded wall of a large vase. He stabbed the end of his torch into the ground and put out the flame before following Setti, Yaush, and Moriah through the sewer. He was the last to emerge into the moonlit alley of the eastside neighborhood and he helped Moriah replace the sewer capstone before heading to the main city gates.

Lehi stayed a few paces behind the others. He brushed away the clinging soil on the potsherd and held it up to the moonlight that streamed down over the square rooftops of the tall, stone homes lining the street. Why would Laban write such a thing as this? It had nothing to do with Uriah, but then he wasn't searching only for clues to free Uriah. He had to find some bit of evidence that could tell him why Captain Laban feared these letters, and this could be a clue. Lehi stuffed the potsherd under his robe and prayed that once he fitted it into place with the other broken clay fragments it would answer his most baffling question—what were Laban and Zadock hiding?

They reached the main entrance to Lakhish, and Setti ordered the gateman to open it wide enough for them to enter the bastion. Torches hung along the high corridor walls, lighting the yellow brick with flickering flames like the inside of a great stone hall, leading them down the hillside to the lower gate at the far end. The watchmen on the catwalks above came to attention, their swords raised to greet them. Commander Yaush waved them back to their towers reminding them in his powerful voice that they were on watch and there was no reason to make so much of their coming to the main gates in the middle of the night.

A thick, double-plank door was recessed into the bastion wall, twenty paces down from the upper gate. It was reinforced with metal crosspieces angled across the face and bolted from beam to threshold with iron rivets. Setti unlocked the latch and opened the door, stirring the stale air inside. The ceiling was made of tightly placed beams without any mortar showing between the timbers. There were no windows, no back doors, nothing but a small vent cut into the wall just below the ceiling to draw in the outside air. There was also a trapdoor hidden behind a stack of oil vats, and a pile of broken torches discarded from the bastion. The trapdoor was cut into the back wall of the keep. The hinges were recessed into the stone and sealed in place with metal rivets. The door stood no higher than a small child and anyone going out that way had to crawl. It was made of triple-thick timbers, sealed into a metal frame, and locked shut with two latches. Setti stepped around the empty oil vats, jumped over the stack of old torches, and freed the latches. The trapdoor opened onto the no-man's-land between the upper and lower walls, and an evening breeze filtered through the keep and cleared out the musty air.

A stone bench stood against the far wall and Setti pushed a wooden table over in front of it. They gathered around and began sorting through the potsherds, brushing clean the muddied ones and matching the words and edges of one with the other.

The first two potsherd drafts were written on broken pieces of red clay from new wine bottles. The cracked edges fit flush without any gaps between the sections. Lehi let the others search for the matching pieces while he read the lines of the letters as they slowly came together. Uriah was mentioned all through the first two tablets. Laban accused him of treason. He was guilty of delivering Judah into the hands of the Babylonians. He was a saboteur and his preaching of peace with Babylon weakened the resolve of the military. There was a gap where a missing potsherd belonged and Lehi quickly skipped over the emptiness to the next line of writing where Laban accused Uriah of being a liar, a turncoat, of profiteering on the blood of his own people. They were serious claims, but no different than any of the accusations leveled against the other prophets during the war. It had only been a year since the Babylonian armies surrounded Jerusalem, and anyone who claimed the lost war was a punishment from heaven was suspected of treason.

Lehi said, "There isn't anything here we haven't heard before."

"All the prophets were accused of treasonous sayings during the war." Moriah set his elbows on the table. "But why did Laban single Uriah out for punishment?"

"There's something you should know about these letters." Yaush found the missing potsherd that accused Uriah of being an accomplice with the Babylonians and placed it in between the line about Uriah's treason and the one accusing him as a liar. He said, "Laban didn't make any of these accusations until long after the war was over."

Lehi looked up from reading the potsherds. "Why would he do that?"

"It could have something to do with their first meeting." Yaush picked over the stack of potsherds and found another match. "It wasn't until after Laban met Uriah during his inspection tour that the accusations of treason appeared in the captain's letters."

Lehi said, "What happened at their meeting?"

"I didn't think much of it at the time. It was early harvest season last year. Uriah said he had some new wines that would be perfect for entertaining Captain Laban. I met Uriah outside the lower gate on the approach to the fort for the delivery when Captain Laban arrived. I tried to keep Uriah from speaking against the man, but I couldn't stop him from accusing Laban of some sort of dark family secret."

"What secret?"

"He really didn't mention it by name."

"What did he say?"

Yaush scratched the side of his head. "I don't remember exactly."

"You must." Lehi came around the table. "It could help us decipher these letters."

"Well I . . ." Yaush rubbed his brow. "I think it was something about treasures of wickedness profiting a man nothing." He snapped his fingers. "That's what it was. Uriah quoted a proverb. He said Laban's treasures of wickedness would profit a man nothing, while righteousness delivered from death. That's exactly what it was and the moment Uriah said the word *treasures*, I remember that Captain Laban became angry. He was like a wild man. I've never seen him more furious."

Lehi began to pace in front of the table. He said, "Why would an ancient proverb about treasures anger Laban so?"

Moriah said, "Every Jew knows he's heir to the national treasures."

Lehi said, "Of course he is, son, but why would calling them treasures of wickedness rouse such anger in Laban? He's a military man; certainly he's heard cursings much worse than a proverb." He tapped the side of his head with his forefinger. "The sword and brass plates may have something to do with this, but what?"

Lehi fitted the last potsherds in the first two tablets into place and they started on the grayish-yellow potsherds that belonged to the third tablet. The edges were worn. The clay was chipped and the pieces were difficult to match. Moriah told them he scavenged these from the bottom of rubbish bins to find enough to finish the last tablet and they weren't in the finest condition except for the four he'd gotten from Beulah, the daughter of the captain of regiment number seven. The rough clay took the inkwell and it hadn't faded in the rains as much as the others. Setti found the three potsherds that fit along the top, Yaush found two more that fit down the side, and Lehi and Moriah both worked from the center of the tablet, slowly pairing the shapes of the potsherds and connecting the last word of one to the first word of the next.

"This part here." Yaush found three missing pieces that fit three fingers below the top. "This was the letter we saw Hosha Yahu deliver to Uriah at his inn."

Lehi leaned over the table. It was an order for the arrest of Uriah. Commander Yaush was to bring him to Jerusalem to stand trial by order of Laban, captain of the guard.

Yaush said, "I don't blame Uriah for fleeing to Egypt when he read this. If we had arrested him and taken him to Jerusalem, he would have been dead before he ever stood trial. Captain Laban was railing against him something fierce in those days and he'd have found a way to end the poor boy's life in prison. It was a God-blessed thing we didn't capture him."

Lehi raised his gaze from the potsherds. He wasn't at the inn the night Yaush found Uriah intercepting the mail and he had no way of knowing who his *we* included. He said, "Who was with you at the inn?"

"Does it matter?"

"It may help."

"I never would have worked with a man like that if Laban hadn't ordered it."

"A man like what?"

"There was nothing I could do about it." Yaush stepped back from the table. "He had orders from Captain Laban."

Lehi said, "*Who* had orders?"

"He was better at tracking the courier than any of the scouts in the military. We were to wait at the inn disguised as farmers and catch Hosha Yahu delivering the letters to Uriah."

Setti said, "Tell us who it was, Papa."

Yaush lowered his head. He slowly said, "It was Shechem, king of robbers."

Setti said, "You worked with that murderer?"

"I was under orders, son."

Moriah said, "Why would Laban work with a robber?"

"He doesn't work with the man, not anymore. Look at this." Yaush gathered the remaining potsherds and quickly fitted them in place. When he finished placing the last one, there was only one missing potsherd in the last tablet—one about the size of a man's hand near the bottom, down along the margin where there wasn't any writing to be lost.

"This letter was sent after the coronation." Yaush ran his finger over the tablet until he found Laban's words stating that he had made a grave mistake hiring Shechem to track the courier Hosha Yahu. It was a ploy by the robber to get close enough to Laban to understand his military security at the coronation and attempt an assassination of the royal family. And he thanked God in his letter that he and his men were able to thwart the robber's attempt on the lives of the royal family. Lehi leaned closer to read every word. That wasn't entirely accurate. Laban's scribe, a man named Zoram, actually saved the king, but maybe that's what he meant when he wrote that he and his men had saved the royal family.

The letter carried on about Shechem. There were three lines about the insidious nature of robbers, a full phrase of curses against Shechem, and a reiteration of Laban's order to kill robbers on sight without trial, filling nearly five potsherds. The letter concluded with an order for Yaush to increase patrols to find Shechem and his band before they attempted another assassination of the royal family. And then there was an odd addition to the order directing Yaush to concentrate his search for the robber band in the borders of the Empty Quarter, a good hundred and fifty miles south of the hill country where Shechem was known to hide out. Laban wrote that his spies had good information that Shechem escaped into that desolate part of the country to avoid capture and he ordered all future patrols to that part of Judah.

Yaush said, "You see there. Laban has nothing to do with Shechem."

Lehi said, "Did you send patrols as he ordered?"

Setti said, "We doubled them all winter, one patrol to the Empty Quarter every three days."

"Did you find anything?"

Yaush said, "Not a sign of a robber anywhere."

Setti said, "Our men usually find some sign of habitation. Horse droppings, fire pits, some clue that they were about, but they found nothing."

Lehi ran his forefinger over the tablet and stopped near the bottom. He removed a potsherd from the middle of a line of writing. He said, "It was Shechem who tried to kill King Zedekiah, wasn't it?"

Yaush said, "That's right, and if it weren't for Laban's scribe, Zoram, he may well have succeeded."

"What about the princes of Judah?"

Yaush said, "Mulek and his brothers were safe with their mother in the palace."

"Then why did Laban write that Shechem tried to kill the royal family?" Lehi picked up the second-to-last missing potsherd from the table and set it in place.

Yaush said, "I don't know. I assumed Laban meant the king. But you're right, it does say royal family." He read over the letters again and found another reference to the royal family and then another. He pressed his finger against the potsherds. "It's here three times. Laban never says Shechem attempted to assassinate Zedekiah. He always says the robber tried to kill the royal family."

Moriah said, "What does that mean?"

Lehi reached under his robe and brought out the missing potsherd. He fitted it into place along the margin near the bottom of the letter where there were no other writings. He said, "Does it have anything to do with this?"

The four of them gathered around the table and slowly read the words written across the last potsherd . . . *to see the princes of Judah cursed and their father with them.*

Moriah said, "That's it, that's the potsherd I was most concerned over."

Yaush said, "It doesn't mean what you think it does. On the original letters this phrase was near some other blurred writings that were impossible to read, isn't that right Moriah?"

"Yes, sir. I didn't copy it because Laban had rubbed it out."

Yaush said, "Laban could have been writing about the threat Shechem posed to the royal family. There isn't a Jew in the kingdom that doesn't know that the aim of every robber is to murder the king and rule over his kingdom. I'm not excusing the man for writing such a thing. Even if he were simply referring to Shechem and his band of robbers, he should never pen an oath like this. Captain Laban would never murder the king or any member of the royal family."

Setti said, "And why not?"

"The man is sworn to protect them, not curse them to the grave. What does he hope to gain by killing them?"

Lehi sat on the bench and leaned his head back against the wall. There was no reason for Laban to kill the royal family. The man made his living, and a very good one, by protecting the king and his posterity. But if Laban did have something to gain, there was a chance Lehi knew someone who could tell him what it was.

He jumped to his feet. "Moriah, can you get me a small piece of papyrus and a writing pen?"

"I have some in the treasury."

"Get them and meet us in my room."

They left the potsherds on the table and hurried out of the keep. Setti pulled the thick main door shut and it groaned into place against the doorpost, giving up a gust of rancid air and a cloud of dust from the threshold. He latched the double locks and gave orders to the watchmen on the towers that they were to report anyone asking to get into the keep. What Setti didn't know was that by forgetting the most important security measure, he was ensuring the preservation of his life and the life of his family.

Setti left the trapdoor open.

Lehi was the first to enter the palace. The hallway stood empty. Sophia and Shemayahu had taken the body of Jebus, but there was still blood staining the stones. They marched the length of the corridor to the far end and turned into Lehi's bedroom. The fire in the hearth had burned down, but there was enough of a glow spreading across the floor to give light to a small wicker cage with a pigeon hopping about inside.

Moriah came in behind them with a well-inked pen and a full roll of papyrus. Lehi tore away a small scrap from the bottom. There wasn't much room to send a message, but he wrote in small print and explained what he could of the information gleaned from the Lakhish Letters, ending with the most important question: Did Laban have anything to gain by killing the royal family?

Lehi tied the message to the pigeon's leg and walked the bird to the window. He unlatched the shutters and leaned over the sill, but before he could let the pigeon go, Yaush grabbed his arm. He said, "Where's the pigeon taking that note?"

"To Josiah the potter."

"What?"

"There's a chance he's alive." Lehi slowly shook his head. "It isn't a very good chance, but if he is alive, and this bird can take a message to him, then we have to ask for his help."

"Help with what?"

"No one knows Zadock's mind better than Josiah." Lehi cupped the pigeon in his hands. "This may be our only hope to find out why Laban would want the royal family dead."

Yaush tightened his grip around Lehi's arm. "What if this note falls into the wrong hands and Captain Laban finds out I have a copy of the letters?"

Lehi said, "He's going to have to know sooner or later. The letters are the only evidence that can stop him."

"Stop him from doing what?"

"From killing us all."

Lehi threw the pigeon into the air. It circled about the window twice before turning east toward the Dead Sea. There was only one way to know if Mima hadn't gone mad when she told Lehi her bird had the power to deliver this message to Josiah the potter, and that was—a reply from a dead man.

CHAPTER 32

Sparrows blanketed the bluff above Qumran in a sea of brown feathers and Rebekah pushed her way through the bobbing heads and fluttering wings to the pigeon coops on the far side of the cliffs, shooing the wild fowl back with her feet. The sparrows were never this bold on the beachhead, but this was their home and they preened on this rocky summit in the early-morning sunshine, waiting to collect the seeds that dropped to the ground during Samantha and Jeruzabel's feeding. Josiah followed Rebekah to the coop, the sparrows flocking around him, chasing about his feet and jumping to flight above the bag of seed he carried on his shoulders. They pecked at the delicacies hidden beneath the sackcloth—seeds they could never gather on the shores of this barren sea of salt. Rebekah never should have allowed him to bring the full bag of seed from their tent. They only needed a few handfuls to feed Jeruzabel and Samantha, but he insisted on bringing the entire bag and now he had to fend off the pesky sparrows.

The pigeon coop was set atop a small wooden stand on the edge of the cliffs, and sparrows surrounded it like hungry beggars. Rebekah opened the wicker door, pushed Samantha and Jeruzabel back from the bowl and spoke over her shoulder to Josiah, telling him to reach the seeds inside. He didn't do as she directed and she said, "Papa, bring the seeds over and . . ."

Josiah was staring at the sparrows on the ground near the coop, studying the brown-feathered creatures. At least that's what it seemed he was doing until she saw the blue-gray feathered pigeon waddling amid the smaller birds. It was another messenger from Mima with a papyrus tied around its leg. Rebekah quickly picked the fowl from among the sparrows, scattering the other birds with her sudden movement. She unraveled the note. It wasn't in Mima's handwriting. These were educated pen strokes with small letters and a firm hand and they spoke of letters sent from Captain Laban to Fort Lakhish. Rebekah quickly read the note, and when she reached the bottom where the sender asked what Laban had to gain from murdering the royal family, she said, "Papa, this is frightening."

Josiah dropped the sack of seeds and let the sparrows peck at the food. He too read the note and when he finished, his hands began to tremble. He said, "Lord have mercy on us all."

"What does it mean?"

"This explains everything." Josiah rubbed his brow. "Why was I so blind to this until now? I should have understood the private meetings Zadock held in his chambers late at night. And all of Laban's veiled references to Shechem the robber. It all makes perfect sense."

"What makes sense?"

Josiah didn't answer. He took out a writing pen and papyrus he kept in his coin purse and began to write a reply. Rebekah leaned over his shoulder and read about her father's suspicions that Laban and Zadock had formed an alliance with Shechem, and in large, bold letters he wrote the answer to Lehi's question, telling him why he believed Laban would want the king dead. He attached the note to Jeruzabel's leg and threw her to the breeze. She was the only fully sighted homing pigeon left and Josiah didn't want Samantha, the blind pigeon, to carry a message as important as this.

Jeruzabel circled over the bluff twice before heading west toward Jerusalem. She soared beyond the cliffs, leaving the valley of the Dead Sea behind her and flying directly over the hill country.

A small pocket of farmland opened up in a high valley between the mountains with a village of homes clustered at one end. A small wadi stood near the last home. It was filled with winter rains and seeds scattered along the wet shore. Jeruzabel landed on the muddy bank and waddled about, pecking at the seeds. She was in the deepest mud, her legs sinking into the sticky stuff, when a young boy jumped from behind a rock with a net, the corners weighted with rocks. He threw it over her, trapping her under the webbing. He ripped the note from the bird's leg, threw it in the mud and crushed Jeruzabel between his hands. He ran toward the house. He cried, "Papa, I snared a bird for supper."

CHAPTER 33

Ruth balanced the water jar on her shoulder and latched the front door. The houseguests were fed, the dishes cleared away, and no one would miss her while she slipped out for a measure of water. Tonight was the last sunset before the eve of Passover and celebrating the feast required she mix her dough with the coldest water she could find. Warm water caused the flour to ferment and she didn't dare prepare unleavened bread with anything but the most frigid water.

Ruth rarely ventured into the street after dark and never without a lamp to light her way, but there wasn't time to trim the oil if she was to abide by the practice and get the water out of the ground before it was too warm for baking unleavened bread. The city was filled with guests come to celebrate Passover and there were certain to be a good many women carrying lamps to the fetch their water. Tonight she would walk in the borrowed light of other lamps.

Ruth pushed open the gate and stepped into the street, but before heading down the hill toward the Pool of Siloam, she bent over and pressed her hand to the cobblestone. Just at she thought. The ground had gone cold after sundown. It didn't hold any of the warmth of the cloudless day and there wasn't any risk of the earth passing on the heat to the spring water below ground, rendering it too warm. Ruth started down past the darkened gates of her neighbors with the empty water jar tucked beneath her arm. She would draw her water tonight along with every other woman in Jerusalem, no matter how odd it seemed to set it out to cool overnight when she could get perfectly cold water for her baking first thing in the morning.

There was never anyone at the Pool of Siloam this late, but tonight the watering place was alive with the quiet conversations of women queued in lines along the water's edge. Flickering flames from oil lamps dotted the crowded square like stars in the night sky, and the golden points of light reflected over the untroubled surface. The lines were longest where Hezekiah's water tunnel emptied into the main pool, and every woman in Jerusalem swore it was the coldest water anywhere in all of Israel—if not the entire world—for baking unleavened bread. Ruth passed by the long lines and found a place along the far edge of the pool. No one drew water for their baking here, at least no one but Ruth. It was dark on this side without the light of any lamps to light the water's surface. It wasn't the coldest water in the whole world, but it was more than kosher to mix the dough for unleavened bread and she dipped her jar under and let the gurgling water flow into it.

"You forgot your lamp."

A gentle voice carried from along the high walls a little ways down from the pool, and a woman stepped out from behind a stone pilaster, the glow of her lamp lighting her face. What was Sariah doing out of bed? The cold night air turned her pale cheeks red and her long, white robe and blue shawl weren't enough to keep her warm on an early spring night like this. Ruth had left Elizabeth with instructions to see that Sariah was served a cup of warm tea and that her bed had plenty of pillows to prop up her head. Sariah wore a scarf, and since the day Aaron brought her home to board she refused to take it off in Ruth's presence. She said it was an old wound she didn't want Ruth to see; but what sort of injury could be so awful she would hide it? The scarf was the width of a hand. It ran across her brow, above her ears and around the back of her head.

Ruth said, "You should be home in bed."

"Nonsense." Sariah walked the lamp over next to Ruth. "I never miss drawing water before Passover."

"Do you come to Jerusalem every year for this?"

"No dear." Sariah waved her hand. "That's far too long a journey for cold water. We have a large fountain in front of our home where my daughters and I draw water for our bread baking."

Ruth held the water jar close. Why didn't she think to have her own daughters come with her to draw water tonight? Until now she'd thought of this as a chore, not a chance to pass along the traditions of Passover. Ruth said, "That must be nice."

"Nice?" Sariah sat on the edge of the pool. "It's an awful mess with so many children and grandchildren crowded into the kitchen. We manage to cover everyone and everything with wheat flour. You could make twenty loaves from what ends up on the floor alone. Passover is a celebration of deliverance from bondage, but I'm afraid at our home we're enslaved by a mess of flour and . . ."

"And what?"

Sariah lowered her head. "It's nothing, dear."

"It's the child, isn't it?" Ruth took Sariah by the hand. She was a good judge of womanly matters. Sariah had the same small frame, narrow hips and shoulders, and by the way she carried herself, she was a good three months along, no matter how many times she insisted she was not more than two.

"It's not the child I fear most for." Sariah held her hand to her stomach. "It's my husband."

"He'll be back for the trial in the morning."

"That's what worries me."

"There's no reason for that. By this time tomorrow evening you'll be home with your family celebrating a glorious feast."

"We may not celebrate Passover." Sariah shook her head. "Not in the way we're accustomed."

"Don't say that. Of course you will." Ruth sat down next to Sariah and set the water jar between them. "Your daughters will have drawn the water and tomorrow they'll bake unleavened bread; and your sons, they know how to prepare a lamb for roasting don't they? Your home will be filled with the smell of the feast of Passover."

"I wish I could be as cheerful as you." Sariah wrapped her arms around her stomach. "Every night I have the same dream, that this babe will never see Beit Zayit or any of the lands of our family's inheritance."

"Don't talk like that. Of course your child will see your home. Your baby is strong."

"I have no doubt for the baby's health, but . . ." Sariah held her hand to her mouth.

"There now." Ruth used the sleeve of her robe to dry Sariah's tears. "Everything is going to be fine. You're tired and all you need is a good night's rest." She stood from the edge of the pool, took the water jar in one hand, and Sariah by the other. "It's time we set this water out to cool and went to bed."

Sariah didn't stand. She pulled her hand free and slowly untied the scarf from around her head. It fell past her shoulders, revealing a wide swath of skin where her hair had been torn from its place and her scalp scarred with the scabs of a terrible wound. She said, "The man who did this warned me that if my husband ever came to Jerusalem and spoke in favor of Uriah, he'd return with an army to destroy all our vineyards."

Ruth touched the back of Sariah's head, her fingers slowly moving over the uneven scars. She said, "Who would say such an evil thing?"

"Your son, Daniel."

CHAPTER 34

Not a hint of morning sunlight graced the window shutters above the bedpost, but impatience would not stay bridled long, and Jonathan whispered Ruth's name. He had to wake her and tell her today's feast was to be different than other years. He didn't need the added strain of reciting the story behind this evening's feast to their children, not with Uriah's trial set to convene at the palace chambers today and a nobleman from the upper city wanting a set of brass wine glasses polished before sunset. It wasn't the Sabbath, but Hebrew law forbade him to do any work after sundown on the most celebrated feastday of the year; as soon as darkness set in, no labor could be performed.

Jonathan was to buy a lamb without blemish, firstborn, and without any broken bones. He had enough money to hire the animal sellers to see to that, but Jonathan had to take care of his blacksmithing this morning before Uriah's trial. The proceedings at the palace shouldn't take more than two hours, three at best, and he'd have just enough time to deliver the lamb to the temple priests to perform the ritual sacrifice at dusk. He'd even roast the yearling in the hearth for evening meal—a skewering and basting task he usually left to Ruth—but he wasn't going to recite the story of Exodus to the family no matter how long-standing the custom. Today was Uriah's final hearing before King Zedekiah, and it was a bad omen to remember the power of God's deliverance when Uriah had little hope of freedom.

Hag ha-Pesah—the celebration of the birth of a nation the Hebrews called Passover—began tonight at evening meal and tradi-

tion required Jonathan tell his children the story of the day of inde-
pendence when Moses delivered Israel out of bondage; but must he
be the storyteller with so many houseguests celebrating the feast with
them? Ruth was better suited for speaking to an audience and
Jonathan tugged on the linen blanket to stir her from her sleep. He
never should have agreed to let Uriah's wife and children stay on at
the house, and he should have turned Sariah away when Aaron
brought her home and begged lodging for her. It wasn't wise to shelter
these sorts of people, but Ruth convinced him that no one in their
neighborhood would think anything out of the ordinary with so
many guests. The entire city was filled with travelers come to celebrate Passover. Deborah had already paid for her lodging, and he
couldn't turn Sariah away when she was with child. He allowed them
to stay through Passover, but no longer. His home was not an inn.

Jonathan spoke Ruth's name loudly enough to stir a bear from its
winter den, but she still didn't answer and he lay back on the pillow with
his hands tucked beneath his head. Ruth could tell the story of deliverance this year. That was the least she could do for him with so many
concerns begging his attention. Jonathan reached out to shake her from
her sleep, but his hand fell on emptiness. She was up and gone and the
room was silent except for the faint sound of brooms sweeping over the
kitchen floor and the patter of footsteps quietly scurrying about, filling
the house with the sound of the first ritual in preparation for Passover—

The observance of spring cleaning.

Ruth stoked the hearth with a new log and hung a large pot from
the spit. She submerged the dishes, finger bowls and serving plates
and let them cleanse in the boiling heat. If that didn't rid her table-
ware of hamez there was nothing that could. Ridding her home of
leaven was a custom passed down from mother to daughter since the
day of the first Passover. The fleeing Hebrews didn't have time to wait
for grains to ferment or dough to rise, and Ruth hung knives, forks
and spoons on the bricks next to the flames and cleansed them of
leaven. They weren't to eat any hamez during Passover and since all

her cutlery was tainted with a year's worth of the leaven of raising breads, ripening wheat, and all sorts of grains and vegetables, she had no other choice than to boil and bake and heat her crockery until it was ritually clean of any food that had power to ferment. It was Passover and Ruth honored the memory of her fathers' flight from bondage by liberating her home of hamez.

Ruth measured five cups of wheat into the mortar bowl and worked the blunt end of the pestle over the grain. The chaff came to the top and she scooped it away before pouring the flour onto a kneading board and mixing in three cups of cold water drawn from the Pool of Siloam last evening. She sank her fingers into the cold mixture, kneading the dough without any salt or olive oil, her head bent down into her work and her elbows working like the frenzied wings of a chicken. Baking matzoh was a race against time and if she were to prepare her unleavened bread the kosher way she couldn't let the wet flour ferment. She quickly formed the dough into round, flat loaves and set them on a ritually cleaned bread paddle, dropping them onto the hot oven bricks. Finished. The first round of matzoh was baking and she filled the mortar bowl with more grain and started the pestle grinding the kernels. Passover was the only time of year they ate matzoh and the children never let her forget it. It wasn't the finest tasting bread to come out of her oven, but it was a good reminder of the hasty flight of their fathers—the night when Israel was delivered from the destroying angel—though to be honest, they didn't dislike the matzoh nearly as much as they dreaded the preparation for the feast. None of her children enjoyed spring cleaning.

Joshua and Sarah burst from the pantry, their chattering burdened with complaints of too much work and why didn't Aaron and Elizabeth have to help them haul the grain sacks outside to the storehouse? They trailed through the kitchen like one ant following the other, the heavy bags balanced on their shoulders and weighing down their short strides.

Ruth held open the kitchen door for them to pass into the courtyard, reminding them that not a particle of hamez was to be left inside the house during Passover; nothing that could ferment was allowed to remain—no wheat or barley, no rye or oats, and no potatoes or beans. They were to stack all of it in a dry place off the ground and keep the moisture from seeping through the sacks. There was not a worse time to have decaying grains on the property than during Passover. Any leaven to find its way inside was certain to render their home unclean. Joshua told her not to worry; they wouldn't have to burn any of their grain this year. He'd make sure they got every bit of hamez out of the house before nightfall. Last Passover the children left three sacks of wheat in the pantry and they had to burn all of them the next day. Sarah said she was like a Hebrew slave in the days of pharaoh, driven like a beast of burden and begging to be free, but Ruth wasn't about to let the girl go before the work was done. She would appreciate Passover more once she tasted a bit of slavery, though carrying these grain bags to the storehouse was hardly an indentured task.

Sarah stopped in the threshold of the side door, the ends of her reddish brown braids dancing at her shoulders. She turned her freckled cheeks up to Ruth and told her these were the last sacks. There weren't any sacks of grain left inside that could ferment, the house was clean for Passover, and could they please play the searching game now?

Ruth scooted Sarah and Joshua out the door with instructions to stack all the sacks on the wood slats and hurry back to perform the only part of the spring cleaning rite the children enjoyed—the search for hamez.

The last loaf of leavened bread sat on the kitchen table and Ruth was breaking it into ten pieces for the search when the soft brush of reeds sweeping over the floor reached her hearing. She hurried into the main room with the plate of leavened bread in hand. What was Deborah doing? Houseguests weren't allowed to clean her home for Passover, and the only thing she could think to do was take the broom from her and tell her that with so many preparations begging Ruth's attention would she mind hiding the bread. Ruth handed over the plate. Deborah was to be sure and hide the bread where Joshua could find it and if it wasn't too much trouble could she remember where she hid it? There was nothing worse than hiding ten pieces of bread and only finding nine. Ruth stuffed the broom handle under her arm. One overlooked piece of leavened bread could leave the entire house unclean for Passover.

Sariah sat resting in the corner of the room with a linen blanket over her legs, a pillow supporting her back, and a thick cushion softening the hardwood chair. It was the same chair Ruth sat in to relieve the pain of carrying her own children since the day she gave birth to

Daniel. Or did Jonathan build that chair after Aaron was born? It really didn't matter as long as the curved backrest supported the weight of Sariah's unborn. Ruth ordered her to stay there and rest until it was time to leave for the trial. She was not to help with any work in her condition, but when she saw Ruth hand Deborah the plate of leavened bread, she threw back the blankets, got out of her chair and announced she wasn't about to let this tradition go uncelebrated simply because she was miles away from Beit Zayit. This was the same custom Sariah practiced in her home, it wasn't a strain at all, and if Ruth didn't mind could Sariah help with the hiding? Ruth warned her she should rest before they left for the palace, but when Sariah refused to sit any longer, she consented and let her go with Deborah, hurrying through the main floor, hiding the bread where the youngest children were certain to find it—one piece between the wood slats in the stair banisters, another above the mantle, one balanced on the kitchen windowsill, and another on the pantry shelf. They scaled the stairs to the children's rooms to hide the remaining pieces, their laughter filling the house with memories from Passover celebrations in years gone by when they were young and searched for hamez.

Elizabeth knelt in the corner of the kitchen, working a scrub brush over the floor and scouring every tile with fuller's soap down to the cracks between the stones. Her long, black hair was pulled back from her face with a white ribbon and the hem of her outer robe was girded up about her hips, out of the way of her cleaning. She finished the last of the floor, gathered her soaps and oils, hung a new cloth over her shoulder and disappeared out the side door, telling Ruth she was going to go through the property, check every satchel and saddlebag in the manger, clean out every pouch in every item of clothing, and make certain Joshua and Sarah stacked the grain sacks properly and cleaned the water basins, and jars, and anything else that could have possibly touched hamez during the year. She was a godsend of a child and Ruth could never hope to have the house ready for Passover without her.

Aaron finished washing down the kitchen walls with warm water and started on the wood shelves nailed on either side of the windows. He was Ruth's tallest child by a good three hands and she saved the high places for his long arms. They didn't oil the wood but once a year and the sweet perfumed scent of rose petals filled the home with the fragrance of Passover. A clean home wasn't really in memory of deliverance from ancient bondage. The Jews fleeing pharaoh certainly didn't have time for housework, but the cleaning paid homage to the redemption offered by the Messiah, and wasn't that the deeper meaning of Passover—that God would deliver His people from their sins? Ruth took a deep breath and let the smell of the oils fill her. The house of God was an orderly, clean house and hopefully none of her children would ever forget the meaning of spring cleaning—that they should turn to the Messiah with all their hearts, and He would suffer for their sins and make them clean to enter His kingdom.

Ruth told Aaron to reach the perfume-scented oilcloth onto the top shelf and move it slowly over the thirsty wood surface. And as soon as he was done cleaning the top of the windowsills, could he get the cobwebs hanging from the ceiling beams? And there was some dust collected on the timbers above the door in the main room, and after he finished with the wood could he start on the . . . ?

Ruth stepped back and studied Aaron. What was he doing dressed in a long robe? The brown cloth hung from his narrow shoulders with just enough room to let him work the dust cloth over the shelves without limiting his reach. He'd grown a few fingers since Ruth weaved the robe for him last year and the hem fell to the middle of his shins and not a barleycorn farther. His cheeks were red from washing in cold water, his hair was combed, and when he saw Ruth watching him, he finished dusting the last shelf, set the oilcloth on the table and said, "Mama, I haven't time for any more."

"I'd expect an excuse like that from Sarah and Joshua." Ruth set her hands on her hip. "But not from you, son."

"I don't mind the work, Mama, but I have to go by the shop this morning."

"Dressed like that?"

"I have to finish polishing Sariah's bow and have it for her before she leaves for home."

"There's plenty of time for that after we clean the house and search for hamez. Sariah's not leaving until after the trial." Ruth began scouring the end of the kitchen table where the leavened bread sat overnight. "I don't want you missing any of our Passover traditions. What will Joshua and Sarah say if you're not here with them to find the leavened bread?"

Aaron lowered his voice. "Why don't you ask Daniel that question?"

"Don't go speaking ill of the boy. He's your brother and I won't have you . . ."

Ruth turned her gaze to the floor, disappointment catching in her throat. This was the first Passover any of her children would not be home. She'd reminded Daniel for a month that he was to pass the feast with them, but he told her he was at the mercy of Captain Laban and she shouldn't expect him to stop by for the celebration. Ruth steadied her hand on the edge of the table and cleared her throat, but she wasn't able to mask the shaking in her voice. She said, "Daniel didn't say he wasn't coming."

"I know how much you want us together on Passover, but Daniel is never coming back. He doesn't concern himself with traditions of faith anymore." Aaron shook his head slowly. "He follows a different path than us. He—"

"He burned one of Lehi's vineyards to the ground." A tear rolled down Ruth's cheek and off the end of her chin. "Sariah told me last evening."

"I'm sorry I didn't tell you, Mama." Aaron reached his long arm around her and pulled her close. "I didn't want you to suffer with that burden."

"Daniel is going to make things right." Ruth dried her tears. She took a deep breath and smiled up at Aaron. "He'll come back to us, I'm certain of it. And when he does, we'll help him make amends to Sariah and Lehi for their loss and then we'll find a measure of peace in this."

"We may never find any peace in this city."

"Don't say that." Ruth reached up and laid her finger against Aaron's lips. "Everything is going to be fine."

"You don't know that. None of us know what the future will bring."

Ruth lowered her head. "You'll be home for dinner this evening, won't you?"

Aaron kissed Ruth on the brow. "I will, but you must let me go finish the bow."

Ruth sprinkled scented oil onto the cloth and held it out to Aaron to finish the woodwork. "Can't it wait until after the house is clean?"

"Not if I'm going to the trial."

Ruth dropped the oilcloth to the floor. Aaron wasn't going there, not on Passover. This was a feast to celebrate the deliverance of the Jews, and Uriah's trial mocked the very spirit of liberation. Ruth said, "Why don't you leave the trial to your father? It's his business."

Aaron said, "You're attending, aren't you?"

"Sariah needs my care and Deborah has all those children; otherwise I'd not think of it."

"I have my reasons for going as well." Aaron started for the front door, but Ruth took him by the arm and kept him from leaving the kitchen. She searched his face and when she found a fire deep in his blue eyes—a bright burning flame she could never douse—she said, "Why are you so determined to do this?"

Aaron said, "I'm a witness."

Ruth let go of his arm and stepped back. That wasn't true, at least she prayed to heaven it wasn't. She didn't remember any soldier delivering a notice for Aaron to appear at the trial. And if there was a need for him to speak in public, Daniel certainly would have come and delivered word himself. Ruth reached her hand to Aaron's cheek. Her son wasn't going to testify at Uriah's trial; she wouldn't have it. That would only bring him more scrutiny from the very men he should avoid. She said, "None of the lawyers sent for you to testify."

"Uriah's a prophet, Mama." Aaron straightened to his full height, his shoulders back and his chin up. He said, "And I stand as a witness for God in all times and all places."

"Don't talk like that." Ruth patted him on the back of his hand. It was his failed attempt at baptism that made him speak those words, but he'd not been baptized and there was no reason for him to make a public proclamation of his faith. Didn't he understand Uriah's trial was not a religious rite? The Almighty didn't need his public witness as much as she needed him to keep silent about his faith.

Ruth said, "None of us want this trial."

"Papa doesn't seem to mind."

"He doesn't like this any more than we do, but it's his duty, son."

"If he dislikes it so much, he'd put a stop to this madness and see that Uriah went free."

"Your father doesn't decide these matters. He has to follow the law."

Aaron rubbed the back of his neck, ruffling the collar of his robe. "How long must we hide our faith?"

"Aaron, please. Don't make this any harder than it already is."

"I won't hide anymore."

Ruth reached for the cloth of his sleeve and held it between her fingers. "What are you thinking of doing?"

"I won't hesitate to speak out if I'm needed."

"You're not to do any such thing; do you hear me? They don't need you there."

"I'm not afraid to speak my heart."

"This isn't a matter of fear, son. It's a matter of your life and . . ." Ruth glanced about the home. "It's a matter of all our lives."

"Passover is about deliverance from bondage, Mama." Aaron straightened his plain brown robe over his shoulders. He said, "I want to find a measure of that freedom for myself."

"To do what?"

"The freedom to follow my faith."

"This is a different time, and a different sort of bondage." Ruth took him by the sleeve of his robe and pulled him close. She said, "For your own good and the good of this family, you must keep—"

"Passover." Jonathan stood on the landing above the kitchen, peering over the banister. He said, "It's time we got along with keeping the first celebration of the day before I'm gone." He was dressed in his council robes, a pointed black cap pulled over black and white shawls. It was an odd-looking headpiece that didn't protect him from the summer sun nor warm him in winter and he pulled it down far enough to shroud his hearing, but it was impossible to know exactly how much of their words he'd heard until he came down the stairs, walked over to the hearth, and turned his gaze onto the boiling cutlery that Ruth was cleansing for Passover. He didn't look up from the steaming pot, but his words were stern. He said, "You're not going to the trial, son. I won't have it."

"But Papa, I—"

"I won't discuss it with you." Jonathan turned from the hearth, his face reddened by the heat of the fire. "You're to stay and celebrate the Passover with us."

"Passover doesn't begin until sundown."

"It begins right now." Jonathan waved his hand toward Ruth. "Are we ready to start the search?"

"Of course, dear." Ruth pulled her dark-black hair off her ears and tied it back with the ribbon. Every year they ended spring cleaning with the search for hamez. Once the house was cleaned and the bread hidden, the children searched until they found all the leaven-laden morsels and removed them in time for Jonathan to declare their home clean and ready to celebrate Passover. It was an innocent custom, and it brought the sweet taste of Passover to their home. For each piece of bread they found Ruth added a large helping of haroset to their bowl. She shouldn't spoil them with a sweet mix of apples, walnuts, dates, and raisins ground into a pudding and sprinkled with cinnamon. It was to remind them of the mortar their forefathers made to cement the bricks in pharaoh's palaces and pyramids. Though to be honest, her children remembered the size of their portion of haroset more than they ever remembered the struggles of the ancient Hebrews. Ruth nodded to Jonathan. "The bread should be hidden by now."

Aaron stepped over next to Jonathan. "Papa, please let me . . .

The side door flew open and Sarah and Joshua burst inside, drowning Aaron's words with cries for the search to begin. They took their seats at the end of the table with their hands wrapped about their bowls. They ran their gaze around the kitchen, checking the shelves, tabletops, and windowsills for hidden pieces of bread, and they chattered about where they found the hamez last year, and could they please begin now before Sarah burst and Joshua died from the wait?

Elizabeth stepped in from outside, put away her cleaning towels, and informed Ruth all was ready for the offering of a prayer to bless their house and pronounce it clean for the celebration. Sariah slowly made her way down the stairs from the upper rooms. She carried an empty plate under her arm and when she reached the main floor she announced the hamez was hidden in impossible places, and only the most thorough search would uncover it.

Sarah inched to the edge of her chair, ready to run about the house, but Joshua held his head in his hands and mumbled between his fingers something about never finding as much hamez as his sister and if God could hear him, would He please help him find more than

Sarah this year? And if it wasn't meant to be, could he at least get as large a portion of haroset in his bowl? Ruth patted him on the shoulder and assured him there was plenty for all, but he shook his head slowly, quietly complaining he wasn't as good as Sarah and he would end up watching her eat all the haroset on her own.

Deborah ushered her two young sons down the stairs, the boys scurrying about the skirts of her robe. Thank heavens Ruth had made a double portion of haroset or they'd not have enough to fill the bowls of so many celebrating the cleaning of the house.

Aaron said, "Papa, I have to go to the shop to get the bow for Sariah."

Sariah said, "I didn't think you were finished with that."

"I'll have it done before the sun goes down on Passover, but I must leave right now."

"You're not going anywhere, son." Jonathan added a log to the hearth to keep the water boiling under the pot of dishes. "I want you to stay here with the children until the trial is ended."

"But, Papa, I . . ."

"You heard me."

Joshua hurried to Aaron's side. He took him by the hand and had him sit in the chair next to him, telling him he needed his brother's help if he hoped to get any haroset in his bowl, and would he please stay with him during the hunt?

Aaron said, "Well I . . ."

"You see? Joshua needs you here with us." Ruth took the empty plate from Sariah and handed it to Jonathan. She said, "It's time for the search, Papa."

"We begin with a . . ." Jonathan pressed the edge of the plate between his fingers.

Ruth said, "With a prayer."

"That's right." Jonathan set the plate on the table and adjusted the long sleeves on his robe. "A prayer for the . . ."

Ruth said, "The removal of hamez."

"Aaron, why don't you say it?" Jonathan cleared his throat. "You pray better."

Aaron started to stand and protest his father's decree he not go to trial, but Ruth held her hand on his shoulder, kept him in his chair and told him he could pray just fine seated at the table. This may be Passover when they did all their eating standing up, but this wasn't a meal and he could offer the prayer over the search for hamez just fine from there.

Ruth bowed her head with the others, but she didn't close her eyes. She was busy watching her son. He glanced about the room and when he found there was no one with ears to hear his appeal, he folded his hands and thanked God for Passover, for the feast they were to celebrate this evening, and for the ancient deliverance of Israel from Egyptian bondage. He prayed for the house to be clean of hamez and that their hearts, like the unleavened bread they would eat during the feast, would not be aroused to do evil, but to do good continually. His voice softened and he paused before uttering the last words of his prayer. He said, "And Dear Lord, grant us all the power of deliverance."

CHAPTER 35

Mima stayed in the shadows of the giant pillars gracing the front porch palace entrance, away from the view of the soldiers marching along the catwalks and the watchmen at the main gates. The trial was to begin at midday and she had to speak with Lehi before it started, but there was no sign of him arriving with his company from Lakhish. The gates were drawn shut, there were no horses galloping up King Street and the courtyard below the porch stood empty.

Pillars of smoke rose over the city, their dark plumes obscuring the sky and warning of the dangers this Passover could bring. Tradition required the hamez found in the morning search be burned in a midday fire, and with the coming of smoke also came and went the hour for Lehi's arrival. Mima leaned over the porch banister and searched the courtyard one last time, but it was no use. The olive oil merchant was late for the trial and it was best she get back inside the palace chambers before she was missed.

Mima straightened the collar and cuffs on her short-sleeved tunic. They were far too tight to be comfortable, but she wasn't about to wear anything else. This was her most formal shirt and matching green skirt. It was trimmed in gold and her wide hips were accented with a brown leather belt decorated with the sparkling crushed shells of abalone. Her hair was tied into tight curls with cloth ribbons, the longest falling down into her eyes. Baubles hung from her ears on the ends of silver chains, and her lips were colored with a hint of the brightest red pomegranate paste she could purchase from the perfume merchant who whistled every time she passed by his shop and told her that she was—

"The answer to my prayers."

Mima spun around to find Lehi scaling the back steps from the palace stables in company with Commander Yaush and Shemayahu. The hem of Lehi's white robe was covered with red dust from the hill country surrounding Fort Lakhish. The long, hard ride had blown his hair back over his ears, and his face was red from riding under the heat of the sun. He said, "Did you get an answer?"

Mima said, "From whom?"

"The potter."

Mima frowned and she could feel her thick lower lip curl down over itself. "You didn't send him a message."

"It's been nearly two days."

Commander Yaush said, "You never should have trusted her."

Shemayahu came around in front of Lehi. He said, "What if your message falls into the wrong hands."

Mima shook her head and her tight curls waved about like a stand of wheat in a stiff wind. She said, "Something must have gone wrong."

Lehi said, "I was afraid of this."

"Afraid of what?"

Lehi lowered his voice. "That he couldn't answer us."

Mima rubbed her hand across her brow. "I haven't gotten word from him, but that doesn't mean it isn't coming. You must believe he's alive."

"It's time you put the potter's memory to rest." Commander Yaush patted Mima on the arm. "He's dead and he can't help us with this trial."

"He isn't dead." Mima pulled her arm away from his patting. "He's going to bring us the answer we need. You remember that." She pushed her curls back off her brow and pulled her belt higher on her hips. "Josiah will not let us down."

Ezekiel leaned on the sill of the nearest window and peered out at the dirty gray sky. Smoke obscured the sun and filled the air with the declaration that the search for hamez was finished, the homes of

Jerusalem were cleansed. But with Uriah in chains and standing in the center of the royal chamber waiting for a verdict on his bondage, this was like no other Passover Ezekiel had ever celebrated.

Noblemen milled about the main floor, their quiet conversations filling the chamber with their whisperings. The men standing near the windows mumbled something about Uriah's treason, the nobles in the shadows down along the wall argued in favor of beheading for blasphemy, and a large contingent near the front of the chamber whispered that Zedekiah didn't have the courage to kill a prophet, no matter how false he may be. There were few in this gathering with the spirit of Passover on their lips, and they spoke of Uriah's death more than they ever mentioned his deliverance.

The time to call the trial to order was upon him, but without the letters Ezekiel couldn't proceed—King Zedekiah wouldn't allow it. He sat in his throne next to Miriam, his elbow on the armrest and his head in his hands waiting for the letters to arrive. The king and queen made a fine couple, though there was word that their marriage was strained these past weeks by word of the tax revolt and the added troubles of this trial. Miriam didn't engage Zedekiah with her customary conversations. She sat straight in her throne, silent, her gaze turned toward the domed ceiling. And if this trial wasn't enough to burden the royal couple, there were rumors that the Babylonians were planning to return with their armies if the tax wasn't paid, and Ezekiel had only himself to thank for putting the royal family through more anguish. If he could, he'd tell them straight out he was the one who changed the tax from one-quarter to three-quarters of a man's income. There was no reason to cause the royals so much trouble but he couldn't simply tell them, not with Zadock seated at his prosecution table near the front of the chamber. He was watching Ezekiel, his dark eyes focused on him, and he kept staring until Captain Laban marched over with Lieutenant Daniel shadowing his stride. The military men took their seats next to Zadock, the three leaning their heads in to discuss whatever soldiers discussed with the Chief Elder. Daniel was still a boy, but he was a strong lad, and with as much time as he spent in the company of Zadock and Laban, he was sure to gain a certain measure of wisdom. Maybe not wisdom, but he was certainly going to gain a worldly acumen he could never acquire working an anvil in his father's blacksmith shop, though swinging a hammer did have its advantages. These three were always speaking in private and if Ezekiel didn't know better, he'd think them conspirators attempting to confound the outcome of this trial.

Prince Mulek sat with his brothers directly behind the king and queen. He was a good boy, though it wasn't proper for him to throw his ball into the air in a game of catch, and thank heavens Mima quietly entered through the servant's door and took her place beside the child, telling him to hide the ball in the pocket beneath his robe and keep it there until after the proceedings. Ezekiel didn't hear exactly what she said, but whatever she whispered got the boy to hide the red ball from view. The prince was finally learning some public manners.

The Elders of the Jews sat in council chairs set among the marble pillars on either side of the royals. They were the king's advisors in all this, and though Zedekiah was to render the verdict on Uriah's guilt, Ezekiel had it on good word that the king didn't dare proceed without their blessing. Ezekiel leaned on his trial staff to take the weight off his feet. He was the second-highest-ranking Elder on the council, but did he really want this place of honor? He was like King Zedekiah—both of them slaves, beholden to Zadock and without the slightest hope of deliverance on this feast of Passover.

Deborah sat with Sariah and Ruth in the first row of the gallery along the east wall. She leaned over a stone partition, her hand outstretched and her children gathered beside her, peering over at their father and begging to go to him.

Sariah was a little farther down the bench. She was dressed in a white robe with blue trim and the abalone shell sequins shimmered in the lamplight. Her hair was drawn up and tied with a gold band at the back of her head, but it didn't hide the bandages dressing the wound on her skull. She might as well have been alone on a solitary bench at the back of the gallery with her lifeless gaze lost on the chamber door, waiting for Lehi to enter. Her face was pale and it strained her to move her gaze onto Deborah's restless children and back to the chamber door. She was in pain and there was no doubt her injured head and growing womb had something to do with her listlessness.

Ruth held Deborah's babe while she settled her two sons back onto the bench. She cradled the infant in her arms, inched the blanket up around her cheeks and softly sang a song of comfort. Ruth had an abundance of experience raising her five children, but none of them accompanied her to the trial. She was the only member of the blacksmith's family in the gallery—an unusual thing since Ezekiel had never known the woman to attend public meetings without the company of her family.

Ezekiel walked slowly past Zedekiah's throne, careful not to disturb the monarch's pondering. He stood on the steps above the main floor and raised his staff to announce a delay in the trial when the doors at the back of the chamber swung open and Commander Yaush strode inside with Lehi and Shemayahu following him through the crowded chamber.

"Order." Ezekiel tapped the end of his staff, the sound of the wood against the marble echoing about the chamber. "I call this trial to—"

"There's no need for that." Yaush pushed through the last line of nobles at the front of the chamber. He stopped beside Zadock's table, rapped his hand on the wood surface. He said, "This trial is over, sir."

The stir of murmured words rose up from the nobles, and the Elders of the Jews leaned forward in their council chairs.

"What do you mean, over?" Ezekiel lowered his staff. "This trial isn't finished until we see the letters."

"I'm sorry, sir." Yaush removed his riding cloak. He hung the garment over his arm. He said, "The letters were stolen from the vault in my treasury."

Ezekiel said, "Who did this deed?"

"The same man who attempted to kill the king at the coronation."

Zedekiah dropped his scepter at the foot of his throne and it gave up a muted clang. He said, "Shechem?"

Yaush bowed to the king and when his head came up he said, "That's right, sire."

Zedekiah picked his scepter up from the floor. "Why would Shechem have any interest in the letters?

"This is regretful." Zadock came around his prosecution table, his hands cupped in front of his pleated robe and his hem sweeping over the stone floor. "With the letters gone, I must agree with the commander." He nodded to Yaush. "If it pleases this court, it's time to move for judgment in the matter of Uriah the traitor."

"My son's not a traitor." Shemayahu stood beside Uriah, his hand shaking the chains that held him bound and the clang of metal links rising through the chamber like the sound of wild bells. He said,

"Sire, I beg of you a gift of freedom on this eve of Passover. Release my son and free him of the awful slavery of Zadock's accusations."

Zadock said, "Passover has nothing to do with treason."

Shemayahu said, "It has everything to do with deliverance from the lies you've heaped upon my son."

"He brought this bondage on himself and if we had the Lakhish Letters, they would prove, beyond any doubt, that Uriah is a traitor."

"That isn't all they prove." Lehi stepped between Shemayahu and Zadock. "With God as my witness I beg this court the patience to hear me out."

Zadock said, "You'll not preach your faith. This is a trial, not the temple courtyards."

Lehi faced King Zedekiah. He said, "Sire, you asked why Shechem would have interest in the Lakhish Letters and I have the answer."

Zadock said, "What do you know about robbers?"

Lehi began to pace in front of the Chief Elder. "I know that you arranged for the letters to be stolen."

"That's foolishness. There's no reason for me to want such a thing. The letters prove Uriah a traitor." Zadock lifted the hem of his robe off the ground. "All I want is a just resolution to these proceedings."

Lehi said, "I know of your abominations, sir."

Zadock turned his back to Lehi and walked to his chair, but he didn't sit. He took hold of the edge of his table. He said, "My prosecution of Uriah is above reproach."

Lehi spoke in a calm voice, his words filling the chamber with the steadiness of his spirit, and when he spoke his eyes were filled with a certain light. He said, "If you do not repent, your doings will bring about the destruction of Jerusalem and many will perish by the sword and many more will yet be carried away captive into Babylon."

Zadock came around to the front of his prosecution table, his face twisted into a scowl. He said, "How dare you accuse me of scandal."

"I have read of your doings in the *Book of Heaven.*"

Zadock said, "You've gone mad."

Lehi walked to the center of the court. He turned his gaze onto Ezekiel and said, "The words I read were sweet to the taste, but they were bitter food on my stomach and they made me ill because they tell of the evil doings of Zadock and the Council of Elders."

Ezekiel tightened his grip on his trial staff. Lehi was speaking to Zadock, but the words pierced to the center of Ezekiel's soul. How did Lehi know what was written in the *Book of Heaven?* That was the vision Ezekiel was given, the one he'd not mentioned to anyone. The words were sweet to the taste, but they told of the evils of the Council of Elders and Ezekiel hadn't declared it to anyone, not even his closest friends. It was far too bitter a task.

Zadock said, "Where is this *Book of Heaven?* Do you have it with you for this court to read?"

Lehi said, "It was a vision."

"This court can't read a vision."

Lehi said, "It was from God."

Zadock waved his hand in the air. "Until your God delivers this book of yours to this court, there is no evidence that any member of this council has done any evil in this trial."

Lehi slowly shook his head. "You mock God."

"I mock you." Zadock jabbed his finger at Lehi. "You waste this court's time with your convenient dreams and visions from heaven. What will you dream of next—a gold throne for you to sit on with a thousand servants to do your biding? There *is* no *Book of Heaven* with evidence against this court and there *are* no Lakhish Letters." He turned to Zedekiah and said, "It's time we end this charade, sire. I beg you to make your judgment against Uriah."

Lehi walked to Uriah's side. He held the man's chained hand in his. He said, "Is there no one who will stand as a witness of this man's innocence?"

The nobles fell silent. The whisperings ceased and there was not a stir among the crowd except near the back of the chamber where a man pushed toward the front. He said, "I stand with Uriah."

Aaron marched to the front of the royal chamber. He ran his hand through his brown hair and straightened his long brown robe over his shoulders. There was never a reason to dress like this to smelt steel or cut wood for the ovens, but he wouldn't let the formality of this trial keep him from standing as a witness of the prophets of God.

Lehi took Aaron by the arm and pulled him close, his powerful arms encircling him. He softly said, "You shouldn't be here, son."

"I won't let you do this alone. I've already lost Rebekah." Aaron shook his head slowly. "I won't lose another friend."

"Nothing's going to happen to me."

"You don't know that. It could come at anytime and from anyone." Aaron glanced at Zadock and Laban. He lowered his voice to a whisper. He said, "I won't let them harm you."

"There is little you can do to stop these men." Lehi patted Aaron on the shoulder. "Now I want you to go back to your seat and—"

Who are you to question my prosecution of this trial?" Zadock stepped between Aaron and Lehi. He said, "You have no place here, boy."

Aaron said, "I know Uriah is innocent."

"Have you any evidence?"

"I have enough."

"Then I suggest you show us."

Aaron pushed his hair back from his eyes. He said, "I trust Lehi."

"You should be more wise about whom you trust." Zadock motioned to Daniel. "Take your brother from this chamber and see that he doesn't return."

Daniel wrapped his powerful arms around Aaron, but Aaron pulled free and stepped to the center of the chamber. "I'm not leaving until I speak my heart."

"Aaron, no." Ruth stood from the bench seat, her hands outstretched and tears streaming down her checks. "Don't say any more."

Jonathan came out of his council chair and stood on the top step above the main floor. He shook his fist at Aaron. He said, "You'll not speak a word in this chamber."

Daniel leaped up the steps, quieted his father and settled him back into his council chair before coming back to Aaron. He said, "You've ruined our good name by standing with these, these . . ." He raised his fist and shook it at Lehi and Uriah. "These traitors."

Aaron spoke with a firm voice. "When did speaking the truth ever ruin a man's good name? You ruined our good name when you burned Lehi's olive groves."

"Aaron, please!" Ruth called from the gallery, her voice wavering and her body trembling. "Come away from there."

"You're a fool." Daniel swung his fist, landing it on Aaron's lower lip, splitting it open and causing him to reel back a step. Daniel leaned forward, his fist raised to swing again, but Captain Laban ordered him to stand down and let the Chief Elder deal with Aaron.

Zadock said, "Anyone who trusts Lehi trusts a liar."

"That isn't true." Aaron wiped the blood from his chin, staining the sleeve of his brown robe. "Lehi would never lie. He's a . . ."

"I can't hear you, boy." Zadock tapped his long fingers together. "Lehi is what?"

"No, son." Lehi reached for Aaron. "He's only trying to provoke you."

Aaron spoke through the stream of blood dripping from his mouth. He said, "Lehi is a prophet of God."

The noblemen in the chamber erupted in cries against Aaron, cursing him as a Rekhabite and calling for his removal from the court.

Jonathan took the shawls from under his turban and ripped them in half, the savage tearing of the cloth echoing across the chamber. "You have no inheritance."

Ruth lowered her head and Sariah reached over to stroke her hair. Aaron couldn't hear his mother's sobs, but he could see her shoulders rising and falling with sadness. In one brief moment he'd lost any hope of inheriting the smithing business from his father.

Zadock leaned in next to Aaron and lowered his voice to a whisper. "You'll not live long enough to regret what you've done to—"

A pigeon fluttered between them, its wings flapping in Zadock's eyes. He swung at the bird, striking it across the side, breaking its wing and forcing it to the ground. The pigeon retreated beneath the safety of the defense table, dragging its injured limb along the stone floor and peering out from the shadows, turning its left eye to the Chief Elder to study him. No, the bird wasn't studying him, it didn't have power to do that. The pigeon was blind in that eye.

Zadock said, "Would someone get rid of that bird?"

Lehi fell to his knees, his robe spread out over the stone floor. He ducked beneath the defense table and found the bird with a note tied to its leg. An unraveled length of papyrus hung by a cord and he could make out the warning worded very much like what was written in the allegory of the olive tree—that Laban and Zadock were at the root of the decay of the main top of the House of Israel and if they were not cut off and thrown into the fire their unbelief would bring the destruction of this nation.

Lehi inched closer to the note and the bird steadied its foot long enough for him to read that there was good reason for Laban to want the royal family dead. It all made perfect sense, but until reading this note Lehi never considered the implications of Laban's lineage. The captain was the last living descendant of Joseph, viceroy of Egypt, the first monarch of the Hebrews, and the national treasures proved his noble birthright—the brass plates and the sword were his by inheritance. He was the rightful heir to the throne of the Northern Kingdom, and if Zedekiah and his sons were dead, he was the best choice to reunite the Hebrews under one throne. Laban's lineage was the reason behind his madness and the relics were his treasures of wickedness. Lehi quickly scanned down to the last line on the note, warning him to beware of Laban's ambition, but there was no name and Lehi had no way of knowing who sent a message of such . . .

Lehi quickly brought his head up from below the table and turned his gaze to Mima. The queen's handservant was the only one who dealt with pigeons. She was desperate to help Uriah, but how could she fabricate such elaborate schemes to implicate Laban and Zadock? The woman didn't know what he'd uncovered in the Lakhish Letters and there was no way she could know such detail about Captain Laban and his past. It made perfect sense, but maybe this was too perfect. And there was one pressing question about Mima he couldn't answer. Lehi stood from beneath the table and dusted the knees of his robe.

Could he trust what she'd written?

The pigeon skittered out from under the defense table and Zadock followed it across the open chamber to the steps below the throne, calling for the guards to remove the fowl and see that the trial wasn't disrupted like this again. There was no excuse for letting a pigeon ruin these proceedings with its fluttering about and . . .

There was a note hanging from the pigeon's leg. Zadock couldn't read all of it with the bird jumping about, but what he could read chilled him to the bone—beware of Captain Laban's ambitions to the throne of Judah.

Zadock turned to find Mima seated behind the royals. She was his trusted spy, the woman hired to watch the queen, but could she have misled him?

Mima was the keeper of Prince Mulek's pigeons.

Mima leaned forward around the backrest of Mulek's chair to see the pigeon waddling across the center of the chamber, dragging its broken wing. It had a white stripe down its gray back and a blind left eye, but it wasn't Samantha. It couldn't be. She was trained to fly to the fifth-story palace window, not here. Samantha's bad sight may keep her from getting her bearings about the city, but she would never flounder inside this chamber. It had to be a stray from beneath the eves of the palace—a wild bird that had lost its way. At least that's what Mima believed until the bird flapped its good wing and jumped into the air, a strip of papyrus hanging from its leg. The cord securing it came loose and the note slowly fell back to the cold, stone floor.

Mima inched to the edge of her chair. It *was* Samantha and she was carrying a message from the potter. She quickly checked the back of the chamber, near the servant's entrance. Two brown-robed figures hid near the wide pillars. The light from a giant oil lamp silhouetted their forms and cast shadows across their faces. There was no way of telling who they were, until one of them removed his hood and let the lamplight flicker across his face. He had red cheeks and a bald head, and the young woman next to him had dark-black hair falling out of her hood and edging about her collar. The pigeon wasn't a stray. It was Samantha and she wasn't lost. Josiah had let her go inside the chamber and he was trying to communicate with Mima.

She grabbed Mulek's red ball and threw it across the floor toward Samantha. "Go son!" she said, and pushed Mulek out of his chair. "Chase down your ball and bring Samantha's note back with you."

The note came untied from the filthy fowl's leg and landed at Zadock's feet, the damning words written in bold letters. He reached for it, but before his fingers touched the papyrus, a red ball rolled alongside, butting up against the leather of his sandal. It was Mulek's toy, and the prince came sprinting across the chamber toward it, his feet pattering over the stone. Zadock stepped on the note, the edges of the papyrus curling out from under the heel. He snatched the red ball from the ground and wrapped his palm around it, his long fingernails piercing the cloth. Why didn't he recognize the prince as his enemy before now? He could have gotten rid of him months ago instead of focusing his attention on the boy's mother. He held the ball to Mulek's face, the red cloth pressed against the prince's nose. He lowered his rasping voice. He said, "It's you, isn't it?"

Mulek spoke through the cloth. He said, "May I have my toy, sir?"

Zadock spun around, and held the ball up to King Zedekiah. He said, "Do you see this?"

Zedekiah leaned forward in his throne and nodded.

Zadock said, "It belongs to your son."

Ezekiel said, "Why don't you return it to him and we'll get on with this trial?"

Mulek reached for the papyrus note beneath Zadock's foot, but he kicked the boy's hand aside. He said, "You little thief."

"How dare you insult the prince." Queen Miriam stood, the long train of her robe following her to the top of the chamber steps. "Let him have his toy."

Zadock crushed the ball, the red cloth disappearing under the pressure of his grip. He said, "Your son can't be trusted with it, my lady."

"How can you say such a thing?"

"Your son has ties to the Rekhabites."

Miriam said, "You don't know that."

Mima hurried down the steps to Mulek. She took the boy by the hand and started him out of the chamber. "Come with me."

"Leave him here." Zadock stood in front of Mima, blocking her escape from the chamber. He stared at her until she backed away. He said, "I never should have trusted you."

Zedekiah stood from his throne and joined his wife on the top step overlooking the chamber. He reached beneath his robe and brought out a necklace. A single charm hung from the silver brass band, the curves of the snake catching the lamplight and reflecting red and blue and yellow light over the dimness of the chamber. He said, "What does Mulek know about this?"

A stir rose up from the gathering of nobles, the word *Rekhabite* audible above the din. Miriam turned her gaze to Mima. The queen's eyes were filled with a serious light and her voice was a quiet monotone. She said, "Take Mulek out of here and prepare him for the Passover meal."

"He's not going anywhere until he answers my questions." Zadock reached for Mulek's hand. "You're the one we've been searching for, aren't you? You're the palace informant."

Mima took Mulek by the other hand. She said, "Let him go."

"Enough of this." Zedekiah ordered Zadock and Mima to step back from the prince. He held out the charm. He said, "What was this doing in your room, son?"

"It's a . . ." Mulek straightened the purple tunic on his shoulders. He pushed his dark-black hair back off his brow. "It's a symbol of . . .

Miriam said, "It's a symbol of hope."

Zadock said, "Hope in what?"

Lehi came around the defense table. He said, "Hope in the God who led our fathers out of the slavery of Egyptian bondage. The same God who led them to this Promised Land."

Zadock said, "The story of deliverance has nothing to do with this trial."

Lehi said, "Passover begins tonight, doesn't it?"

"This trial is about the traitors among us, not the slaves of ancient

Israel." Zadock kept his foot covering the note. "You Rekhabites and your prophets will destroy this nation with your foolish doctrines of deliverance."

"There's a reason you fear Uriah." Lehi stood next to Uriah. "Why don't you tell us what it is?"

"I fear no one."

"You accused Uriah of being a traitor to silence him."

"I have nothing to hide." Zadock spoke between his teeth.

Lehi said, "You and Captain Laban afflict the Jews at Jerusalem like the poisonous serpents that troubled our fathers in the desert."

"You'll not slander me, sir."

Lehi climbed the steps and reached for the necklace. Zedekiah resisted, but when Lehi touched him on the arm, the king relented and let him raise the brass charm for the assembly of noblemen to see. He said, "Moses fashioned a brass replica of the desert serpents and raised it on the end of his staff and told his people to look upon it and be saved." He turned the brass charm into the light of the oil lamps and let the polished metal reflect its colored light over the gathering. "The only way for you to save yourself from the poison Zadock and Laban have spread among you is to look to Yeshua, the Anointed One and ask His forgiveness and let His atoning blood cleanse you from your sins."

"Pequeah!" Zadock spit, his spittle landing at his feet next to the edges of the note sneaking out from beneath his sandals. He said, "You're nothing but a Rekhabite hiding behind the foolish beliefs in a false God."

Commander Yaush marched across the chamber. He said, "Lehi's not hiding anything, sir."

Laban stood from his seat at the prosecution table. He said, "Commander, that will be enough for now. You're dismissed."

Yaush said, "Uriah isn't the traitor you accuse him to be."

Zadock said, "You know he is. You saw him intercept Captain Laban's letters."

"The Lakhish Letters prove treason against the throne, sir, but it isn't Uriah's treason they uncover."

"I said, that will be all, Commander." Laban slapped his fist across his chest, his breastplates giving up a muted clang. "Be seated and be silent. I'll have a word with you after."

Yaush said, "Not until I tell this court what the letters contain."

Laban spoke slowly, his words resounding in the chamber. "Say anymore and I'll relieve you of your command."

"Sire." Yaush knelt before King Zedekiah. "I am a dog and a most slothful servant if I don't tell you there is another copy of the letters written on potsherds and locked away in the keep at Fort Lakhish."

Captain Laban marched over next to Yaush. "You're dismissed, Commander."

Lehi said, "Why do you silence him when he only uncovers the truth? Tell us what it is you're hiding from this court."

Zadock said, "Laban has only ever tried to punish criminals."

Lehi raised the necklace, the serpent charm dangling in the air. "It's not a crime to wear a symbol of the Messiah in memory of the Son of God who will come to earth to save us from our sins." He returned the charm to the king before crossing the chamber to Uriah. He shook the chains binding the prophet's wrists. "And it isn't a crime for a prophet to speak the word of God, no matter how much Zadock would have us believe otherwise."

Zadock said, "I never said such a thing."

"You fear the words of Uriah and now you will fear my words." Lehi pointed his finger at Zadock and asked, "Isn't it true that you want the royal family dead so you can place Captain Laban on the throne?"

Zadock turned to King Zedekiah. "Sire, certainly you don't believe the lies of this Rekhabite."

Lehi said, "Isn't it true that you conspired with Shechem, king of robbers, to assassinate the king and his sons during the coronation?"

"Never!"

Lehi said, "Zadock and Laban are the traitors in all of this, not Uriah."

Zadock said, "Where did you dream up such falsehoods?"

Lehi pointed to the papyrus sneaking out from under the Chief Elder's foot. He said, "From heaven."

The nobles erupted in a rumble of confusion, and in the din of loud voices Miriam rushed out the side entrance, holding Mulek by the hand and Mima, following close behind with the other princes. Zedekiah shouted above the confusion, ordering the palace guards to clear the royal chamber and take Uriah back to the prison.

Zadock said, "Sire, do you have a verdict?"

"Not now." Zedekiah closed his hand around Mulek's charm and started from the chamber.

"But sire . . . ?"

"I told you, not now. I have matters of Passover to attend to."

Zadock reached the side doors to the chamber ahead of the king. He said, "Have I lost your trust?"

"You were to take care of the tax, but now I have reports the Babylonians are massing their armies near Jericho to ensure we pay it."

"Is that the only matter that troubles you?"

"That would be a good place for you to start."

"Then you don't believe Lehi's accusations?"

"I'm inclined to trust men who risk their lives to establish my throne."

"Am I worthy of such trust?"

Zedekiah lifted the hem of his robe off the floor. "Negotiate a tax settlement with the Babylonians and you'll have earned my good graces, sir."

"May you and your family celebrate Passover well." Zadock opened the door and let Zedekiah into the hall before returning across the chamber to Laban and Daniel. He said, "Meet me in the palace prison." He dropped the prince's red ball on the floor and stamped it beneath his foot until the cloth rent into a hundred torn fibers. He said, "There will be no Passover for our enemies."

CHAPTER 36

Lehi hurried Sariah down a narrow palace corridor. She complained of pain, but they couldn't slow down—someone was following them and their pursuer's footsteps echoed in the shadows behind them. Lehi held Sariah close, his arm around her waist and her body leaning against him. The hallway turned past the palace kitchens and Lehi stopped long enough to look back to find Mima following them. She hurried down through the shadows, her heavy stride slapping her sandals against the stone with a sharp echo that climbed the narrow walls of the corridor. Her arms brushed over her hips with each labored stride. She took a quick breath and fanned herself with her hand. She said, "Thank heaven I found you before they did."

"I should thank you for sending the note. That was very brave of you." Lehi stepped toward Mima with his hand outstretched.

"Don't thank me, sir." Mima shook her head. "Josiah deserves your thanks."

Lehi took back his hand. Must she continue this charade?

Mima glanced back down the hall. "You must leave before Zadock and Laban find you."

Lehi said, "We're going home."

"You can't go there, not until things settle down." Mima took Lehi by the arm. "Do you know the route that heads east from Jerusalem toward Jericho?"

Of course he knew it. He and his sons traveled every byway with their caravans.

Mima wagged her finger as she spoke. "There's an obscure trail that branches off a few miles before you reach Jericho. It leads over some barren wastelands and through some treacherous hill country before it breaks onto the west shores of the Dead Sea."

Lehi slowly shook his head. That wasn't right. The west shores were impassable. You had to travel to Jericho first, then turn south and travel along King's Highway that bordered the eastern shores of the Dead Sea. He said, "No experienced traveler would ever risk going that way."

"That's why you must. It will lead you to the secret city of salt, hidden away from the view of man where no one can find you. You'll be safe at Qumran with Josiah and his people until all this is forgotten."

Why would she persist in this? Josiah's only refuge was in a sepulchre on hills west of Jerusalem. He said, "Please, Mima, let this rest in peace."

"There is no peace, sir. Not until you've escaped Zadock and Laban."

Lehi reached for Sariah's hand. "We'll be safe at Beit Zayit."

Mima said, "Laban is certain to hunt you down there. You heard him. He's not a man you can reason with."

Lehi said, "I won't let him hurt us."

"You can't stop him. No one can."

Lehi said, "What about you? If we're not safe, you certainly aren't. Why don't you go to Qumran?"

"I wish I could. I have to see to Mulek and Miriam. I must see that they're safe before I leave them."

Lehi pulled on Sariah's hand to start her walking down the long corridor. He nodded. "We'd best be going."

Sariah freed her hand. She said, "Dear, listen to Mima."

Lehi said, "We have a good many servants and our sons are strong. They can protect the plantation if need be."

Sariah said, "What about your dream?"

Mima said, "What dream?"

Lehi said, "It's nothing."

Sariah said, "You can't deny it. We must follow your dream."

Before Lehi could answer her, footsteps sounded at the far end of the corridor and a man turned the corner, his long black robes rising and falling with each step, the tip of his turban tilted forward into his stride and obscuring his face. It had to be Zadock. What other member of the council would follow them down these deserted corridors. Lehi started Sariah moving around the corner and down the last stretch of passage toward the door leading into the delivery yard.

Mima followed them, her wide body pressing against Lehi and her voice whispering over his shoulder. She spoke quickly. She said, "Josiah and Rebekah will wait for you in the rock cliffs east of Jerusalem where the trail turns up out of the Kidron Valley and out of sight of the watchmen on the south wall. They'll lead you to Qumran."

Lehi reached the door and pushed it open, the soft light of evening streaming into the dark passage. He said, "I won't trust our lives to a ghost."

"You must do as I say." Mima backed away from the entry and down a side hall leading to the far reaches of the palace, but before she disappeared into the shadows she said, "Josiah will wait until the moon sets over the western hills tonight. If you don't come, he'll leave and you'll never find your way to the safety of Qumran."

Lehi turned out into the delivery yard. The docks were clear of cargo and Lehi steadied Sariah by the hand while she scaled down the ramp. They crossed the courtyard and turned into the archway leading to the livery. The stable boy stood just beyond the stone tunnel, waiting for them in the dusk. They hurried toward him, Lehi keeping hold of Sariah with one hand and balancing his stride with the other.

The stable boy asked three shekels for his work—one for feed, another for watering, and a third for having the horses curried and saddled and ready to ride after the trial—but before Lehi could empty the money from his purse, their black-robed pursuer hurried out from under the archway, the shadows moving off the bearded face of Ezekiel, the Second Elder. He dismissed the stable boy to tend to the animals. He stepped close to Lehi, his voice lowered to a whisper. He said, "It's you, isn't it?"

Lehi helped Sariah onto her horse. He handed her the reins and told her to lead out. They would only travel as fast as she had the strength. He said, "I don't know what you're talking about, sir."

Ezekiel said, "Your children and your children's children will write on a stick for the house of Joseph."

"I'm a Jew, sir. My family has lived in Judah for generations." Lehi untied the leather strap on his stirrup and added a hand's length. That wasn't exactly right. Great-grandfather never told Lehi exactly how the family came to own the land at Beit Zayit and as far as his ancestry, well, great-grandfather left them records of everything but their genealogy. It was an odd thing. He was well versed in the art of letters, and the reading room at Beit Zayit was filled with his writings, but there wasn't a single scroll containing even a solitary generation for Lehi to trace his lineage. He said, "I have no ties to the tribe of Joseph."

"That can't be." Ezekiel removed his black turban, and let the head shawls fall to his shoulders. He held the headpiece with both hands. "I'm certain you're the one I saw."

"You've mistaken me for someone else."

Lehi started pulling himself up into the saddle, but stopped when Ezekiel said, "I've read from the *Book of Heaven.*"

Lehi let himself back down. Ezekiel was repeating Lehi's words from the trial and he was either an imposter or a prophet. He said, "Go on."

"I'm not exactly certain what to tell you." Ezekiel tightened his grip on his turban and the breeze blew his head shawls onto the ground, but he didn't bother to pick them out of the dust. He held still, his body stiff and his gaze riveted on Lehi. He said, "The visions keep returning. They haunt the furthest retreats of my sleep and . . ."

"And what?"

"I haven't slept for weeks." The breeze lifted a swirl of dust over Ezekiel, but he didn't cover his eyes. He said, "My visions begin with the roll of a book, some sort of heavenly scroll written with the same prophecies of mourning and woe you declared in the trial."

"The trial is over."

"Please, sir. I don't know where else to turn. I hear this voice over and over again and it commands me to eat the scroll. The words are like honey for sweetness, but they make me ill because the Jews harden their hearts."

Sariah leaned over the saddle. She said, "He's seen the same vision, dear."

Lehi reached up and touched Sariah on the leg. He said, "It's time we headed home." He started walking the two horses across the livery and Ezekiel picked his shawls out of the dust and stepped into stride next to Lehi. He said, "I remember where I've seen you before."

"We've never met, sir."

Ezekiel came around in front of Lehi and stopped him twenty paces from the gates. He said, "In my dreams, a man gave me a stick to hold, written with the prophecies and history of the Jews since the beginning of time until the last days of the earth."

Lehi pushed Ezekiel aside with a gentle hand. "We really must go."

Sariah said, "Dear, we can at least listen to the man."

Ezekiel said, "In my dream, God raised up another man to preserve the prophecies and history of the house of Joseph—a man whose children were educated in the learning of the Jews and the language of the Egyptians."

Lehi leaned forward to hear the man over the breeze blowing about the yard. His own family was educated in the learning of the Jews, and Lehi hired Egyptian teachers to train all his boys in the language of the Egyptians.

Ezekiel said, "And his children wrote their prophecies and covenants and history on a stick and sealed it up in the ground to come forth in the last days of the earth, and when the man gave it to me, the two sticks became one record in my hand. They grew together to confound false doctrines and lay down contentions and establish peace and bring the people of the latter days to the knowledge of the covenants of God."

Lehi said, "Why are you telling me this?"

Ezekiel reached out and touched Lehi on the arm. He said, "You're the man God raised up to preserve the record of the house of Joseph."

A peace descended over Lehi and he could not deny Ezekiel's words. This Second Elder had the Spirit of God like no other Elder on the council. Lehi said, "You've been blessed with the spirit of prophecy."

"I'm an accountant and a lawyer, not a holy man." Ezekiel placed his head shawls over his hair and fitted the turban back in place. "I have no training for prophethood."

"Trust me, sir. There's no training for this. God chooses you because of your faith, not your schooling." Lehi took Ezekiel by the hand. "And He will make you stronger than flint."

"Who told you that?" Ezekiel spoke quickly, the words rushing out of him. "Who told you that God would make me stronger than flint?"

"Why does it matter?"

Ezekiel said, "Those were the same words I read from the *Book of Heaven*—that God would make me strong as flint—but there's no reason for me to need that strength."

"In heaven's timing there is always a reason." Lehi pulled himself up into the saddle. "The time is coming when God will make you a watchman over Israel."

CHAPTER 37

Daniel covered his mouth to keep the stench from choking him. The air stung tears from his eyes and he wiped them back before scaling down the circular steps to the gate of the lower prison. The jailer stood on the other side and when he saw Daniel, he raised his lamp and let the light filter between the iron bars.

He said, "Did anyone follow you?"

Of course no one followed him. Daniel coughed on the stagnant air. Why would anyone want to come to this rat-infested place? He said, "I'm to meet Captain Laban and Zadock in the—"

"You're late." The jailer's voice whistled between the gaps in his teeth. "They're waiting for you in the back chambers." He rattled the key into the lock, pushed open the gate, and told Daniel to follow him down through the winding catacombs. The stone foundation of the palace arched overhead and made a low ceiling in this underground prison. Daniel leaned forward to keep from hitting his head and stepped over the outstretched legs of prisoners chained to the walls.

The jailer led him down a narrow corridor and inside a circular chamber near the back of the prison. Jeremiah was chained to the wall. His mouth hung open and his parched tongue fell over his lips. He looked up when Daniel entered the room, but he wasn't really looking at him. He gazed past Daniel and mumbled something about the grace of God before dropping his head into his chest.

Uriah knelt in the center of the room, yoked to a stock. His wrists and head were locked in the wooden vice, his face turned to the stone floor with only the back of his scraggly brown-haired head visible. The wooden beam beneath his chest forced the air from his lungs in short, wheezing breaths.

Captain Laban hung back in the shadows, away from the lamplight. His face was dark and impossible to read. Zadock stood beside the captain. He wore a common brown traveling robe without any pleats. The hood came to a point atop his head, hiding the thick thatches of gray hair that hedged about his collar. The robe was too long for his body and the hem dragged on the stone floor and caught beneath the heel of his riding boots.

In answer to Daniel's staring, Zadock said, "I leave for Jericho tonight."

"Why the desert, sir?"

"Someone has to convince the Babylonians to take the life of the traitor who brought this tax revolt upon us." Zadock moved to the center of the room and stood between Jeremiah in chains and Uriah kneeling before the stock. He said, "And there's no better way to convince King Zedekiah we're loyal to him than by taking care of all his problems."

Daniel's gaze flitted between Jeremiah and Uriah. He said, "Which traitor, sir?"

"Not these men." Zadock pulled back the hood of his robe and his graying hair fell to his shoulders. "Ezekiel's the cause of these rumors of revolt. The man altered the Babylonian tax from one-quarter to three-quarters of a man's income and the sooner I tell the Babylonians about his indiscretions, the sooner they'll take him from among us."

Daniel said, "Is there a reason to meet here to discuss the chief accountant's fraud?"

Captain Laban stepped from the shadows, the yellow lamplight revealing the seriousness in his bloodshot eyes. The smell of wine filled the room when he spoke. He said, "Ezekiel isn't the only one who could hurt us."

Daniel said, "We have fifty good soldiers guarding your estate, sir. I won't let anything happen to you."

"Don't be a fool, son." Laban took Daniel by the shoulder. "We can't wait in the bushes to be flushed out and hunted like wild quail."

He leaned on the wooden stock, his hand next to Uriah's head. "We are men of action."

Daniel said, "What sort of action, sir?"

Laban waved his hand at Zadock. "Go on, tell the boy what you're going to tell him."

Zadock lifted the hem of his brown robe and walked around the stock. "You're to keep what we do in the strictest confidence."

"I always do."

Zadock said, "This is a brotherhood. We protect one another and we do for ourselves what our government and our religion could never do." He ordered the jailer to remove Jeremiah from the room. The wrist chains came off with a single skeleton key and Jeremiah limped out of the chamber with the jailer holding him up by the waist. Zadock waited until the doors closed behind them before he leaned his head in close to Daniel. "Our association will bring you more power and wealth than you could ever dream of." He walked a circle around Uriah's kneeling body and when he reached the front of the stock he pulled a short sword from under his robe and pointed it at Daniel. He said, "Tell every scribe and nobleman in the city that Zedekiah, king of Judah, carried out Uriah's punishment in a private ceremony."

Daniel said, "What punishment?"

Zadock jabbed his hand beneath Uriah, forcing the blade into his chest and piercing his heart. Uriah gasped, his wrists jerked against the hold of the wooden stock, and his fingers went straight as nails. He raised his gaze from the floor, his neck arched upward in pain. He cried for God to have mercy on Zadock and Laban and Daniel before falling limp, his head and arms hanging from the stock, and a stream of blood pouring from his chest and pooling on the stone beneath him.

Zadock plucked the short sword from Uriah's lifeless body and held it out. "You'll need this."

Daniel pushed the blade aside and vomited on the stone floor.

Zadock said, "I thought you were a soldier."

Laban said, "Let him be. He's not seen this kind of death before."

Zadock held the blade to Daniel's face. "Bring your brother's steel bow to Laban as an oath of your faithfulness that you'll keep secret what you've seen and heard here."

Daniel wiped his lips clean on the sleeve of his robe. He said, "Aaron won't let me have the bow."

"He won't object." Zadock pressed the warm blade into Daniel's hand. "Not once you kill him."

CHAPTER 38

Mima covered her face with thick white lotions and cleared away the residue from over her eyes. This was her first Passover celebration in the palace and she let the creams soak into her skin. She had to be at her best. Her hair was tied in tight braids and she smoothed the pleats in her evening robe before hurrying down the hall to Mulek's bedroom. The prince sat on the edge of his bed. He was wrapped in a white towel, his hair was still wet from bathing, and he didn't have the sense to put down his collection of arrowheads and dress himself in the clothes she set out for him.

Mima pulled him to his feet, dressed him in a purple tunic with the royal seal sewn across the chest and a leather kilt with silver studs in the pleats. She combed his hair with a porcupine quill brush and straightened his collar before sitting him down on the chair and fitting his sandals over his feet.

The bedroom door flew open and Miriam hurried inside carrying two leather satchels. She set one on the floor next to Mima. She said, "I packed your things in here." She unlatched the other satchel and gathered Mulek's clothes into the leather pouch—three tunics, a linen kilt, a scarf, hand warmers, and a sleeping robe.

Mima wiped the lotions off her face. She said, "My lady, what is it?"

Miriam placed a black cloak over Mulek's tunic and told him not to take it off and show anyone the markings of royalty on his clothing. She forced a cap over his head and pulled it down over his ears. She said, "There isn't going to be a Passover meal tonight for either of you."

Mulek pushed the cap back off his brow. He said, "What's wrong, Mama?"

Miriam said, "You remember Jesse, don't you?"

"The Phoenician prince?" Mima came around the bed and stood next to Miriam. "You're not sending us to Sidon, are you?

"It isn't safe for you here." Miriam tied shut the satchel. "Prince Jesse is a friend to Mulek. He'll welcome you into his palace until this passes."

Mima shook her head. "I'm not afraid of the Chief Elder."

"It's not the Chief Elder I worry about." Miriam leaned out the door and checked the hallway and when she came back inside she said, "It's my husband."

"He wouldn't dare harm the boy." Mima ran her hand over Mulek's cloth-capped head.

"He won't protect him." Miriam began to pace. "I don't know what it is, but Zedekiah has changed. He's not the same man I married, not since Zadock won his trust."

"Your husband's not a fool." Mima took Miriam by the hand and sat her down on the edge of the bed next to Mulek. "You were at the trial. You heard what was said about Zadock and Laban. The king will see them for who they are." She patted Miriam on the hand. "Now go down and celebrate the Passover feast with your husband."

"I can't do that." Miriam handed the satchel to Mima. She said, "There's a chariot waiting for you in the livery. The driver is a friend. He'll see you safely to Sidon. I'll send for you as soon as . . ."

Zedekiah's voice sounded in the hallway outside the bedroom door. He called Mulek's name and said he had to speak with the boy and would he please come into the hallway immediately? Miriam herded them into the dressing closet, told them not to make a sound and left them to hide among the robes hanging from hooks on the wall. She left the door half open and Mima peered through the crack to see Zedekiah march into the bedroom, his voice reaching into the darkness of their hiding place. He demanded to see his son, and Mima could feel Mulek step back among the clothes and cover his ears with the expensive garments to keep from hearing the harsh words.

Miriam said, "He's gone where you can't find him."

"What do you mean, gone?"

"I won't let the Chief Elder accuse our son of treason."

"He didn't call the boy a traitor."

Miriam folded her arms across her breast. "He accused him of being the palace informant?"

"I don't blame the man." Zedekiah held out the brass chain with the serpent charm hanging from the end of it. "Not when he had this among his treasures."

Miriam said, "I told you it was a gift."

"From whom? The same people you and Mulek went to see baptized in the farmer's fields south of the city?"

"Who told you that?"

Zedekiah threw the charm on the floor. "I was there."

Miriam picked the charm off the ground. She said, "What do want from Mulek?"

"I want him to answer for what he's done against Laban and Zadock."

"He's done nothing."

"I want him to tell me that. I want to hear it from his lips. I won't let the boy destroy good men."

Mima reached her hand into the darkness and found Mulek's trembling body hiding among the robes. She pulled him close and held him until he stopped shaking. Miriam was right. They were going to have to leave for Sidon tonight. No, not leave—they were going to have to flee Jerusalem. The prince would not find any protection from his father, and Mima would be his guardian until this passed—a surrogate mother for the heir apparent of Judah—but on this night of Passover she was venturing into something more dangerous than motherhood. She was saving Miriam's firstborn from Zadock and Laban—the very angels of death.

CHAPTER 39

Darkness fell across the shop like an unwelcome guest, but Aaron didn't dare trim the lamps. He couldn't let Papa find him lurking about the shop and he worked in the shadows, the glow of dusk casting enough light for him to dip the bow into the hot oil and let the minerals seep into the steel. The upper and lower arms were curved to just the right arc, the handgrip was nailed over with leather cured from the supple ear of an ox and all that was left was fitting the horsehair drawstring to the right length.

Aaron pulled the bow from the vat and rubbed a chamois over the steel before bending it over his thigh and looping one end of the drawstring around the lower arm and reaching the other end over the notch on the upper . . .

What was that? Footsteps sounded at the door, but Aaron couldn't let go of the bow with the string flexed across his legs. It was too dangerous and he kept it bent in place, his arms shaking against the force of the steel while he checked the shop door.

No one entered from the street and there was no shadow across the entrance. It had to be the creaking of the roof beams, or a rodent scampering about, and he turned back to his work, pulling the end of the drawstring toward the notch at the tip of the upper arm. The bow resisted his pulling and the steel quivered with just the right tension. The arms had more spring than any bow he'd held between his hands, and the steel kept its double-curved shape. It was a powerful weapon with enough deadly force to . . .

The edge of a knife pressed against Aaron's throat and he shivered against the feel of the cold steel. He leaned back to get a glimpse of his attacker, but the unforgiving edge of the blade kept him from turning. The brush of lips passed over Aaron's ear, whispering that there was to be no Passover for him or for any of his friends. It was low and there was no way to know who was telling him there would be no freedom for Uriah, no deliverance for Lehi, and no escape for Aaron. None of them would see the light of morning.

Aaron reached for the knife, but the man pressed it deeper into the flesh of Aaron's neck and warned him not to struggle or he'd make Aaron's death more painful than it need be.

Aaron slowed his breathing, his neck rising and falling against the sharpness. The bow was still flexed across Aaron's thigh and he slowly turned it in his hands, aiming the drawstring toward the sound of the man's voice. He said, "What do you want from me?"

"The bow." The man reached his free hand over Aaron's shoulder. He said, "Give me the bow."

Aaron flicked the looped end of the drawstring out of the notch, shooting the coarse horsehair from the bow like a stone from a catapult and catching the man across the face. He fell back against the forging table with his hands over his eye, cursing Aaron and stumbling toward him. Aaron picked the drawstring off the floor, gathered the metal tipped arrows into a quiver, and stuffed the bow under his arm. He was to the entrance when the man threw himself at Aaron, pinning him against the doorpost. His left eye was a bloody mass of flesh. He turned his head to the side to see with his good eye, and in the twilight Aaron saw the outline of . . .

"Daniel?" Aaron reached for his brother's eye, but Daniel pushed Aaron's hand aside.

He said, "Don't touch me."

"Why are you doing this?"

Daniel raised the knife. "I have my orders."

"Take the bow if you want it." Aaron dropped the steel weapon from under his arm, but Daniel didn't go after it. He pressed the knife against Aaron's chest. He slowly shook his head. He said, "I didn't think it would come to this."

Aaron tried to pull away from the point of the knife, but the unforgiving timbers in the doorpost trapped him there. Aaron said,

"In the name of God, Daniel, don't do this. Please."

Daniel reached the tip of the blade to Aaron's chest. His eyes were wide and filled with a wild light. He said, "I take my orders from Laban, not from God."

Aaron lowered his head. "Not even to spare your brother?"

The shop fell silent and Aaron braced against the doorpost, waiting for the cold metal blade to pierce his chest. He gripped the timbers with one hand and raised the other as a shield from the pain, but there was none to suffer. The metal knife clanged to the ground and Daniel backed away from Aaron. He said, "Get out of here before I forget you're my brother."

Swords and scimitars hung along the front wall of Laban's armory. A shelf of mallets and clubs graced the opposite wall, and a large case of knives and daggers stood beneath an oil lamp in the center of the room. Laban's collection of bows and arrows stood over beyond the pillars. There were three made of polished cedar wood, one of olive, and another of dark wood. Laban pulled on a hook protruding from the wall. It was strong enough to hold the newest addition—the world's only steel bow.

The door to the armory pushed open and Daniel stood in the doorway wearing a black patch over his left eye.

Laban marched around the knife case and stood in front of him. He said, "Where is it?"

Daniel reached his fingers to the patch. He said, "I didn't get it."

"You what?"

"Aaron escaped with the bow."

Laban slammed his fist against the knife case and the blades rattled about inside. "How could you fail like this?"

"I'm sorry, sir."

"Sorry isn't good enough." Laban took Daniel by the tunic. He said, "You let him go, didn't you?"

"I tried but . . ."

"But what? You're stronger than he is." Laban tightened his grip, pulling Daniel close so that he could feel the heat rising up from his powerful body. "Aaron could never escape you."

"He used the drawstring, sir." Daniel lifted the patch and revealed a blood-soaked bandage. When he peeled it away, Laban saw the reason for the boy's empty-handedness. The white flesh of his eyeball was lacerated, the lid swollen, and blood oozed from the wound.

Daniel replaced the bandage and tied the patch into place with a leather cord around his brow. He said, "I can track him down, sir. He's not been gone long."

"Forget him. He's gone and he can't do anything to hurt us now."

"What about the steel bow?"

"I'll use one of my own." Laban took down his most powerful bow from the wall. The curves were angled deeper than the others and the blackwood arms were long enough to send an arrow through a man's chest at a hundred paces. It wasn't nearly as powerful as a steel bow, but he didn't need to shoot over a long distance. He was going to hunt his prey from close up. He strapped the bow over his shoulder, packed his quiver with arrows, and started for the door of the armory, but pulled up beneath the crossbeam. He said, "You have one more chance to prove yourself."

"I'll do anything, sir."

"There's a guard station in the bastion linking the upper and lower gates of Fort Lakhish. Do you know it?"

Daniel stood straight and wiped away a line of blood that dripped from under his patch. "I can find it."

"Copies of my letters are locked inside." Laban set his hand on Daniel's shoulder. "I want them destroyed."

"Commander Yaush won't let me inside the guard station."

"Don't give him a choice." Before Laban went out into the night, he said, "Burn Yaush and his family with the potsherds."

CHAPTER 40

The smell of roasted lamb filtered out through the kitchen window, but it wasn't enough to lure Joshua from his play. He crawled over the courtyard stones and poked the stick into the cracks, digging up a hill of ants. Ruth called from the kitchen window for him to come inside and help. There were chairs to move, the dining table to set for evening meal, and if he didn't come immediately she was going to make him wash again. Joshua hurried through the side door and into the kitchen. Well, maybe he didn't hurry, but he did raise his hands for Ruth to inspect. They were still clean and when she asked if he'd gotten into anything, he promised he hadn't picked up any bugs or thrown any rocks over the back wall. He didn't say anything about his digging, but somehow Mama knew and she ordered him to clean his hands one more time before setting the table for evening meal. Joshua marched to the hot-water pan and washed in perfumed oils. How did Mama always know when his hands were dirty?

Joshua cleared away the chairs and turned them toward the wall. They weren't allowed to sit during Passover meal, no matter how tired his legs went during Papa's retelling of the story of deliverance from Egypt. It was a strange custom to stand and eat, and Joshua asked Ruth why he couldn't have a chair for evening meal. She set aside the unleavened bread to warm on the oven bricks, tied her apron around her waist, and told him only the very young and the very old could sit during Passover, and since he was neither he was going to stand with the rest of the family. And didn't he remember that their fathers had fled from their Egyptian captors on foot and they were going to celebrate Passover the same way—ready to flee at any moment? Joshua removed the last chair from around the table and set it facing the wall. If he were Moses he'd have fled pharaoh, riding on the back of a camel, and then all Israel could eat Passover sitting in a leather saddle. Joshua measured the distance between the table and the kitchen wall with his short arms spanning the space. Maybe Moses was right to flee on foot. Even with the chairs gone there wasn't enough room to fit a camel around the table, and Mama would never celebrate this feast in a stable.

The dinner plates were still warm from *koshering* in boiling water and Joshua hauled them over to the table with the cutlery and the wine glasses. He arranged Papa's place at the head, Mama's next to it, then Elizabeth's and . . .

What about Aaron and Daniel? Not an hour ago he'd heard Papa say Aaron wasn't welcome at the feast, and the last time Daniel came by the house he said not to plan on him for the celebration. Joshua turned to Ruth, the stack of plates balanced under his chin. He said her name and waited for her to answer. She was busy seasoning the pot of boiled potatoes with the bitter herbs she'd powdered last month. He said her name louder, this time telling her that Aaron and Daniel hadn't arrived and it was too much work to set a place if they weren't going to come and celebrate the—

Elizabeth grabbed him by the collar, covered his mouth with her hand, and ushered him back to the dining table. She lowered her voice to a whisper and told him to set out the plates for his brothers, no matter if they came or not. She spoke in a serious voice and told him Mama had suffered enough disappointment today—mentioning Aaron and Daniel would only make things worse.

What did Elizabeth know about making things worse? She hadn't dropped the robin's eggs that he'd found in a nest near the back of the courtyard and cracked them on the stones, and she hadn't lost a game of chase to the boys down the street this morning. If anyone had had a bad day, he had and whatever happened to Daniel and Aaron couldn't be any worse than losing the search for hamez to Sarah. She got twice as much haroset as he did, and if it weren't for Deborah letting him lick the bowl clean, the whole day would have been a loss. Joshua tried to pull his mouth free of Elizabeth's grip, but she wouldn't let go until he nodded he would keep silent.

Joshua set his plate on the corner where the wooden leg supported the thick hardwood tabletop. If he had to stand to eat this meal, this was the best place to do it. He could lean against the table leg and not suffer the pain in his feet like last Passover. Joshua finished setting out the wine glasses with the help of Deborah and her two sons, and Sarah placed the cutlery beside each plate.

It was time to begin and thankfully Mama had forgotten her hairbrush, at least he thought she had until she came after him with a cup of water, the thick bristles of her brush poking out from behind her hand. Why did Mama always comb his hair on feast days? He closed his eyes and let Ruth sprinkle water over his head. The brush stuck on a snarl and he cried loudly for her to stop while he untangled the mess and rubbed away the pain. She didn't usually bother with his hair at the end of the day, but it was his task to ask the first question of the Passover celebration and Ruth insisted he be groomed for the occasion.

Jonathan entered the kitchen from the main room. He was dressed in the clothes of the Passover storyteller—a new white robe Mama had woven for him. He told Ruth he would prefer it if she did the honor of telling the story of Passover, but she quietly reminded him that he couldn't disappoint their guests. He was to tell the story; after all, what would Joshua think if his father didn't preside at his first asking of the Passover questions? Jonathan didn't answer. He slowly walked to the head of the table and waited for Deborah to help Shemayahu to his place and stand him in front of his plate with the help of a cane. Ruth offered to have him sit, but he refused. He wanted the blessings of Passover for his family now more than ever and he lowered his head and mumbled a half-silent prayer that the destroying angel would pass over Uriah this night and he would be freed like the Hebrew slaves of ancient days. An uneasy silence filled the room and Deborah began to cry, her body trembling. Mama tried to comfort her, but she would not stop her crying. She leaned against Shemayahu, telling him that there were two fates for prophets. Joshua leaned over next to Sarah and quietly asked her what a fate was, but she shushed him to be quiet and he set his elbows on the table and listened to the woman say that there were prophets delivered by God to finish their mission on earth, and others delivered to heaven after sealing their work with their lives. Deborah hurried from the kitchen and up the stairs to the loft, her fears spoken between sobs that her husband's mission was finished.

Ruth quickly served the bitter herbs on each plate to break the uneasiness. She set out small bowls of salt water for dipping the potatoes, and passed cakes of warm, unleavened bread about the table before coaxing Joshua it was time for him to begin.

Joshua stood at the head of the table and tipped his head back to look up at Papa. He bit his lower lip between his teeth and quickly went over the question in his mind—the same question the youngest child in every family asked on Passover—and when he was certain he had it right he said,

"Papa, why is this night different from any other?"

A solitary lamp stood in the center of the table, its light flickering onto the domed ceiling arching over the reading room. Nephi pulled his father's chair up to the table and held the scroll with one edge pinned back under his hand and the other pressed under his elbow to keep it from rolling back on itself. The words of the psalm were penned in dark-black ink. It was the verse Lehi recited every Passover and Nephi read through it, the comforting words reminding him of feasts from years past. Nephi was born in this house sixteen years ago tonight, and he'd never celebrated Passover without Papa gathering the family around the kitchen table for the reading of this passage and Mama bustling behind him, humming a Passover hymn while she finished serving the warm, unleavened bread and bitter herbs. Nephi glanced up from the scroll and stared out the open window of the reading room into the darkness of the vineyards beyond the house. Where were his parents now? They said they'd be back from the trial today, but the sun was set and there was still no sign of them. Sariah never allowed anyone to prepare Passover for her—she said she had to feel the *matzoh* kneading between her fingers or it wasn't a proper feast—but when Mama hadn't returned by midday, Nephi's sisters, Rachel and Leah, came by the house to prepare the meal.

The scent of baking bread and roasting lamb filtered into the room, but it didn't replace the peace of Lehi's reading voice or the comfort of Sariah's presence like so many Passovers before. Nephi flattened the scroll against the reading table and turned his gaze into the psalm. "O, give thanks unto the Lord who smote Egypt in their firstborn and divided the Red Sea into parts and made Israel to pass through in the midst of it—for his mercy endureth forever. To him who led his people through the wilderness—for his mercy endureth forever and his . . ."

The reading room door creaked open and Rachel stood in the entryway. The hem of her long robe was girded up and she wore a cooking apron over the expensive light blue cloth. Her hands were white from mixing *matzoh* and when she pushed her long, black hair back off her brow, she left a streak of wheat flour above her eyes. This afternoon, when Mama still hadn't come home, Rachel left her husband, Nathan, with their children at the small home nestled in the trees behind Ishmael's estate and joined her younger sister, Leah, in the kitchen. They told Nephi and his brothers that this Passover meal was going to be as grand as any other. Mama would want it that way if she weren't here to celebrate with them.

Rachel said, "Why don't you come join us in the kitchen? You can read from the scroll while we prepare the meal."

"This is for Papa to read, not me."

Sam stepped in from the hall. He was dressed in a gray tunic that reached well below the belt on his leather kilt. The sleeves were covered with straw from feeding the animals and his sandy brown hair was brushed back off his face. He pulled a stool up to the reading table. "Come celebrate your birthday in the kitchens with us."

Nephi said, "Not right now."

Rachel untied the cords girding up her robe and let the hem fall to the ground. "There's no reason to worry about them."

Sam said, "You're brooding."

"He's the youngest in the family." Rachel crossed to the reading table and patted Nephi on the cheek. "He's allowed to brood."

Nephi pulled back from her hand. "I'm not upset."

Rachel said, "You've been pacing about the house for hours with the look of death on you."

Lemuel turned into the reading room. He leaned his tall, thin body against the doorpost and folded his arms. He said, "I'll die if we don't eat soon."

Rachel shook her head and picked the hem of her robe off the ground. "Is food all you ever think about?"

Laman entered the room with a bottle of new wine in his hand. He waved it in the air. "We might as well start without them. These trials last for weeks."

"Not during Passover they don't." Nephi turned in his chair and peered over the backrest at Sam. "Isn't that right? They never conduct trails during Passover."

Sam raised his hands in the air. "I'm not a lawyer."

Rachel said, "If we start, Papa has a way of showing up at just the right—"

"They're home." Leah stuck her head in from the hallway. "Come quickly."

Nephi pushed past his siblings and ran down the hallway to the anteroom. The front door stood open and the cool evening breeze pushed inside, chilling the entryway with the arrival of Lehi and Sariah. Nephi hurried to his mother's side. Her face was pale and she had trouble standing. He lifted her frail body and started up the stairs to her bedroom. He was to the landing before Sariah said, "No, son, put me down. Your father has something to tell us."

"But Mama, you need to rest."

"There isn't time to rest." Sariah forced a smile and he couldn't resist her pleading brown eyes. He lifted her back down the stairs and sat her on a cushioned chair while Lehi gathered his children in a circle around her. He stood behind Sariah, his hands on the backrest, the wide cuffs on his white robe falling down over the carved wood. He gazed up into the vaulted ceiling of the anteroom and down along the mezzanine before looking back to his family. He said, "I never thought we'd have reason to leave this place."

Laman pushed past his brothers and stood in the center of the circle. He pointed the wine bottle at Sariah. "Mother's in no condition to travel."

Sariah leaned forward in her chair. "If your father says we need to leave our home for a time, then God willing, I'm well enough, son."

The anteroom erupted in chatter, Sam asking if this had anything to do with the trial, Rachel wanting to know how long they'd be gone, and Lemuel reminding everyone he was hungry and could they please talk about this over dinner?

Lehi raised his hands to quiet them. They were going to need enough camels to take all the portions of the family tent, supplies for three months, along with a herd of thirty sheep and goats.

Laman said, "You can't escape with a caravan that size. All the animals will slow you down and they'll leave tracks for any scout to follow."

Lehi let go of the backrest on Sariah's chair and stared at Laman for a long, silent moment before he said, "I don't remember telling you we were escaping."

"Well, it's . . . it's only obvious you fear something." Laman waved his wine bottle in the air. "But there's nothing to fear and there's no need to take this foolish journey."

Sam said, "How long will we be gone?"

Lehi said, "I don't know."

Laman said, "Our lives are here at Beit Zayit. Everything we've worked for generations to build is here—our gold, our land, all our inheritance. Do you really want us to flee like Egyptian slaves?"

Lehi said, "We don't have a choice."

Laman said, "Why don't you let *us* decide that?"

Sariah reached for Lehi's hand. "Tell them what you told me, dear."

Lehi pulled up a second chair and sat beside Sariah. He took her by the hand and said, "It was a dream."

Laman said, "You're asking us to leave our home because of a dream?"

Sariah said, "Hear your father out."

Lehi waited for the room to grow silent before he said, "The Lord commanded me in a dream that I should take you with me and depart into the wilderness."

Laman dropped the wine bottle on the ground at the foot of Lehi's chair, breaking it into pieces. He said, "Who will tend the new growth in the vineyards? Ishmael's sons can't do it alone and none of the menservants are trained in olive culture. And what about the oil stores? Nephi has to stir them twice each week and keep them cool well into summer. He's the only keeper of the oil we have on the plantation. Have you ever thought of that? While we're off traveling the countryside, our oil stores will go bad and then what will we trade with the Egyptians?" He shook his finger at Lehi. "This isn't a good idea, Papa. We should stay and face whatever it is you fear."

"Son, you don't understand." Sariah raised her trembling hand to Laman. She said, "They seek to take your father's life." She turned her gaze onto each of her sons. "And they won't stop with your father."

"Papa . . . ?" Rachel stepped into the circle, her dark brown hair cascading down past her cheeks and hiding her tears. She cupped her hands in front of her and there was a trembling in her voice. "Who wants to kill us?"

"There's no reason for you and Leah to fear." Lehi took her by the hands and pulled her close. She was the eldest child, and in all his years Nephi had never seen her cry. Lehi brushed the tears from her cheeks and said, "You're married into the house of Ishmael. You with your husbands can gather there this evening to celebrate the feast. They won't come looking for you."

"Who won't come looking for us, Papa?" Leah wiped her hands clean on her apron. She said, "Who wants to harm us?"

"That's not for you to worry about." Lehi held both his daughters close. He said, "This will pass over us."

Nephi came around and stood next to Lehi. He was the youngest in the family and it was his duty to ask the questions of Passover. But tonight they were to celebrate as the first Hebrew slaves celebrated—fleeing for their lives—and that didn't merit asking a question.

Nephi said, "This night will be like no other."

CHAPTER 41

Ruth ushered the family out of the kitchen and into the main room. She stood them at the front door, bent at the knees like a frog on the banks of the Nile and told them the story of the first plague to afflict the Egyptians before the Exodus. The children laughed at her posture and to keep them laughing she buzzed a circle around them, waving her arms like locusts to tell of another plague. She told of lice, and hail that burned like fire, and great whirlwinds that toppled buildings, but the Egyptians would not let the Hebrew slaves go—not until the final plague. Ruth unlatched the front door, pushed it open and inched Joshua and Sarah to the threshold along with Deborah's boys. The cool night air lifted Sarah's red hair off her shoulders and chilled Joshua so that he had to rub his arms to warm himself. Ruth lowered her voice and let the story of the final plague fall slowly from her lips. They were to look out into the night and see if they could see what the Hebrews in Egypt saw so many years ago. Passover was a night the destroying angel passed over the firstborn in every house marked with the atoning blood of the Messiah.

Ruth said, "This night is a night of waiting and watching to see if you will be passed over."

Sarah stepped onto the porch and turned around, her gaze set on the doorposts and crossbeam painted with the blood of the lamb Jonathan brought home from the temple this evening. She said, "How will we know if we've been passed over?"

Ruth leaned her head in next to Sarah and told her that if every day she brushed the atoning blood of the Messiah over the doorposts of her life, every night would pass without her fearing.

Sarah said, "Without fear of what?"

Ruth didn't answer immediately. She glanced at Jonathan. He was standing back from the door, his hands folded across his chest and his gaze turned up into the ceiling beams. He wanted nothing to do with these lectures on the doctrines of everlasting life. Ruth held Sarah by the shoulders. How she wanted to tell her that the atoning blood of the Messiah would make her clean in the eyes of heaven, but with Jonathan's impatience this wasn't the time or place to teach the girl of the blessings of atonement.

"Watch the night, dear. Watch and wait for the coming of the destroying angel." Ruth ran her hand over the gnarled wood of the doorpost. "And pray that it passes over you."

The sound of a branch breaking in the grasses beside the trail pierced the cool night air and Aaron pulled up in the middle vineyard. He leaned over the saddle and peered down the trail. There was no white horse like his in the shadows ahead of him and no sound of a rider coming up behind him. The trail was empty, but that didn't keep him from notching an arrow in his steel bow and sighting down the shaft, searching for the source of the sound. Daniel said there would be no Passover for Lehi, and Aaron came to Beit Zayit with a warning for the olive oil merchant—Lehi was to watch the night for Captain Laban like the ancient Hebrews watched the night for the destroying angel.

Aaron slowly moved his sight down through the rows of olives, searching the plowed earth until the tip of his arrow fell in line with a squirrel. The creature skittered up the gnarled trunk of the closest tree and disappeared among the foliage of the main top of the branches. That's all it was—a squirrel—and Aaron put away his arrow, strapped the steel bow back over his shoulder and prodded Beuntahyu forward down the last incline and onto the flatland of the plantation, the light of a full moon flickering between the branches. He kept Beuntahyu striding at full gallop past the gates to the pressing yard, but when the road turned down beyond the entrance to the corrals he pulled up and came around. There were fresh tracks in the soft earth, hundreds of them and they turned out of the main corral and onto the road headed back through the vineyards toward Jerusalem. They couldn't be more than an hour old with the hooves pressed deep into the earth and the moonlight reflecting over the sharp edges of the soil. He inched Beuntahyu up the rise to the corral. Sam never let the camels graze at night, but there were only twenty milling about the pen, less than half the herd. The stable sat on a rise above the corrals. The doors were left open and the stalls stood empty, without a single horse from Lehi's stock boarded for the night. There were enough animals missing from the plantation to stock a small caravan and Aaron quickly reined about and raced down past the burned-out old vineyard and up the rise beyond the main fountains. He slid out of the saddle before Beuntahyu came to a full stop, pushed open the gate to Lehi's estate and marched toward the house.

There was no reason for Aaron to suspect something was wrong, not with the full moon of Passover casting gray shadows on the spring flowers growing up along the path. The hedges were trimmed for a celebration, and the baskets hanging from the columns were laden with the first growth of pink hyacinths. But there were no children racing about the hedges and no festive voices mingling with the cool evening breeze. The windows were shuttered with long timbers and there was no smoke rising from the kitchen chimneys on an evening when the scent of roasting lamb should have lingered about the estate. There was not even a hint of lamb's blood painted across the doorpost and it was certain that Lehi did not plan for his estate to be a safe haven. On this night of watching, the doors should have been opened wide with the family of Lehi peering out into the star-filled sky, waiting for the angel of death to pass them . . .

"Leave this place."

The gruff voice came from behind Aaron and he spun around, notching his steel bow as he turned and aiming a fully drawn arrow at the chest of . . .

Ishmael? The breeze lifted his hair and the shimmering glow of the moon silhouetted his long robe, the light dancing between his feet as he walked and turning his white hair a shade brighter. He said, "You can't be here tonight."

Aaron eased on the bow and lowered it to his side. "I came to warn you."

"We know about Laban." Ishmael pointed at the shuttered windows. "We prepared for him."

"Who told you?"

"There isn't time for talk." Ishmael stopped near the run of hedges and leaned over. "You must go."

"I came to help Lehi."

"He's gone. He fled with his family toward Jericho."

"What about you? Why didn't you go with them?"

"Nothing is going to happen to us." He glanced back toward the thick stand of Cyprus trees where his estate lay hidden among the foliage. He said, "As long as we stay inside with the blood of a lamb on our doorpost, we'll be safe."

"How do you know that?"

"Lehi promised Captain Laban wouldn't come against my house." Ishmael backed away from the hedge. He waved his hand at Aaron. He said, "Now leave quickly before harm descends upon this place."

"I have to find Lehi." Aaron started around the hedge. "Don't you remember? I'm supposed to help him. I was to save his . . ."

A loud crash sounded inside the estate and sent Ishmael back through the Cyprus trees toward his home, begging Aaron to follow. Aaron spun around, his bow drawn, and the arrow aimed at the front door. The sound of his approach was covered by the splintering of wood, crashing of clay and the savage tearing of tapestries from inside the anteroom. The sounds of destruction filled the night air, moving deeper inside the home and a penetrating voice mixed with the breaking of chairs, cursing God, and heaven and earth, and the name of Lehi.

Aaron tried a window, but the shutters were bolted in place with thick iron crossbars. He moved to the next window and tried to pry it back with the tip of his arrow and see inside, but it was no use. It wouldn't come open and he slowly side-stepped down the porch to the front door. He lowered his bow long enough to try the latch. It was unlocked and when the door fell open in his hand the sound of destruction fell silent. The expensive blue Egyptian vases were cracked and their pieces strewn across the entryway. The banister spanning the length of the upper-floor mezzanine was pulled from its moorings and lay broken in a hundred splintered pieces. The lamps were pulled from their perches along the wall, the benches in the hallway leading past the dining room were turned over with their backrests broken, the door to the map room hung on one hinge and teetered from the whirlwind that raged through the estate.

Aaron quickly sighted his arrow about the room, searching for any sign of Captain Laban. The eeriness of the sudden silence begged him to enter, but he would not go inside—his feet wouldn't carry him in. It was better to stay out here and ambush Laban when he tried to—

A flash of white rounded the corner of the estate and Aaron pulled back from looking inside. Captain Laban jumped his horse onto the porch and grabbed the bow from Aaron's grasp before ramming the horse against him and knocking him to the ground, his head snapping against the stone. His vision blurred for a moment and when he rubbed his eyes he found Laban coming around on his mount and hovering over him. The breeze lifted the ends of the captain's cape, the black cloth rising and falling like the wings of a dark angel. He was dressed to ride in the shadows of night with nothing to reflect the moonlight—no studs on his belts, no jewelry around his neck, and no rings on his fingers. He reared his mount, the Arabian kicking at the air and the sharp hooves coming down next to Aaron's head.

Aaron tried to roll away, but Laban leaned over his saddle with the steel bow drawn and told him not to move or he'd not live to take another breath.

"I saw the tracks." Laban squinted down the length of the arrow, sighting it on the center of Aaron's chest. "Why don't you tell me where they've gone and I'll let you go."

"You have my bow, why don't you take it and leave me in peace?"

"It's a very good bow, son." Laban shifted his aim onto Aaron's leg and let go of the string, the arrow bursting across the short distance between them and cutting into the flesh of Aaron's thigh. He cried for Laban to stop and he reached for the shaft with trembling hands, but the captain ordered him to stay down or he'd end his life. Laban prodded closer, the weight-bearing hooves of his horse lifting and falling next to Aaron's head. He said, "Tell me where they went."

Aaron spoke through clenched teeth. "You saw the tracks; why don't you follow them?"

Laban fired another arrow, grazing the flesh of Aaron's upper arm before it broke against the stone porch, the shaft shattering bits of wood over Aaron's bloody wounds. Laban quickly notched another arrow, the bow flexed to its fullest, and took aim at Aaron's chest. He said, "Your brother never should have let you live." His fingers twitched against the pull of the drawstring, but before he released the arrow, Aaron kicked the Arabian's legs. The animal reared back, pulled Laban's aim off its mark and the arrow slashed past Aaron's head, landing in the soft wood of the doorpost behind him.

Aaron jumped from the porch and hobbled through the gardens, the shaft of the arrow slowing his gait. Laban leaped the run of hedges and came alongside. He swung the metal bow like a sling at Aaron's head, but Aaron ducked into the thick bushes growing up beneath the stand of Cyprus trees and crawled on his side, a stand of thorns tearing the skin in his hands, the branches pushing against the shaft of the arrow. The throbbing in his leg begged him to cry out, but he couldn't with Laban circling above him, the muzzle of his horse pushing through the branches, and the rush of hot, damp air snorting from the animal's mouth and bursting past Aaron's neck.

He shimmied deeper into the bush and propped himself against the trunk of a tree. The foliage was an uncertain veil with only a thin covering of leaves to screen him. He leaned his head back against the tree and bit down hard on the end of a branch to keep from gasping in pain while he peered up through the canopy. Laban held still as a mongoose waiting over a snake pit, his nostrils flaring in rhythm to the slow rise and fall of his chest. He leaned over the saddle, sighting the bow back and forth across the bushes like a hunter searching quail, waiting for the slightest sound to direct his aim. He said, "Cursed boy! You'll be dead by morning." He lowered the steel bow. "As dead as Lehi."

Laban spurred around and rode out through the fence. He started down past the fountains, but pulled up when he saw Beuntahyu pawing at the shadows. He took her by the reins and guided her up the road, calling over his shoulder, his gruff voice falling on the deaf branches of Aaron's hiding place. "You'll never get out of here alive."

Aaron waited for the sound of the horse hooves to fade before he took his first full breath—a deep gasp, his chest heaving with the pain. He tore a piece of cloth from his tunic to bandage his grazed arm and tried to stand, but his wounded leg gave out and he fell back against the tree trunk. He couldn't walk out of here, not with an arrow in his leg. He had to stop Laban, but the captain had his bow and his horse and there was not another mount in the stables—all of Lehi's horses were gone. He gripped the blood-stained shaft of the arrow with both hands, the slight pressure numbing his leg with pain. God had healed him before, and now he begged heaven to provide for him once more.

Aaron ripped the arrow from the torn flesh of his upper leg.

CHAPTER 42

The lamb hung from a spit in the hearth, slowly roasting over the embers of a dying fire. It was the main course of the Passover meal and Jonathan was to serve the shank bone on a platter while he told the last story of Passover, and thank heavens they'd reached the end of this celebration. He wasn't given to telling stories and he reached the tongs around the shank bone in the shoulder and pulled. The roast was caught on the spit and refused to come free. He said, "Ruth, would you tell the children the last of this."

"But Jonathan, I—"

"I have to get this lamb off the spit." Jonathan turned back to the hearth. Ruth came around to the front of the table and stood in his place. She folded her hands in front of her and told the children that the lamb they were about to eat was sacrificed on the temple altar at sundown. Jonathan leveraged the blade of a knife between the shank bone and the metal spit. Ruth spoke above the noise of Jonathan's prying and told the children that the Passover lamb was to remind them that the Messiah would die for their sins. Jonathan pulled back on the hilt, bending the blade to near breaking, the knife leveraging against the pull of the roast. Ruth leaned forward and quoted the words of the prophets—that the Son of God would come among them and be a perfect sacrifice for their sins without a single blemish. She said, "And not a bone shall be broken and not a—"

"Cursed lamb!" The shoulder bone snapped and the knife flew from Jonathan's hands, clanging to the floor at Ruth's feet. Look what he'd done—he'd broken the shank bone! He reached for the knife, but before he caught hold of the hilt he glanced up at Ruth. She stood staring at the broken shoulder bone and there was no doubt what she was thinking.

What a loss, this Passover.

The lead camel balked at the top of the trail leading down into the rocky valley surrounding Jerusalem and Sam sidled in next to her. He leaned over the saddle, pulled on her bridle and whispered in her ears not to worry, they'd find some soft ground up ahead, and if not there, then as soon as they got past the Kidron Valley and turned east beyond the city they where were sure to find some better ground to soothe her soft, cloven hooves.

Sam rode behind the family, guiding the caravan down the gentle slope on the west side of the city and then south into the narrow valley, but his prodding didn't keep the lead camel from grunting her displeasure. She jerked against the pull on her bridle, her body bristling under the cargo mounted on her back—a portion of the family tent, three sacks of wheat, and three more of barley and rice. It was hardly kosher cargo on this night of Passover, but since they weren't celebrating, it didn't matter that they were carrying a good supply of grain—a cargo of hamez that was certain to make them unclean to celebrate this feast. Papa didn't say when they were coming back to Beit Zayit, but Sam had to ready the caravan for shipments to Egypt at the end of the month, Nephi had to tend the oil, Laman and Lemuel were needed in the pressing yard for the summer, and there was no doubt they'd be back in time to celebrate the feast of the second Passover next month. Wouldn't they?

The lead camel pulled up on the only soft ground in the Kidron Valley—a wash of sand close to the foundation stones of the mighty south wall. The other twenty camels crowded onto the narrow neck of ground and Sam yanked on the lead camel's bridle. The family was getting so far ahead that he could hardly see them against the darkness, and if he didn't get these animals moving they'd be beyond the city and onto the road to Jericho without him. The lead camel grunted loud enough to draw the attention of the watchmen on the catwalks high above. Thank heaven the south wall towered two hundred cubits high. With the full moon setting over the western hills, there was no way the night watch could see them clearly, but to be sure Sam pushed his horse against the lead camel and got her side stepping beneath the overhanging branches of the willows lining the way. They never should have brought the camels this close to the city. The horses didn't have any trouble traversing the rockiness, but these beasts of burden were certain to break a hoof if they hadn't all ready. They should have gone south, down past Bethlehem, and met up with the trail leading to Jericho without having to traverse the narrow, rocky path of the Kidron Valley, and in the dark no less. Papa didn't say why he wanted to come this way, but with this large of a caravan and his brothers herding the sheep and goats up ahead, they were certain to draw the attention of the very men they meant to avoid.

The lead brayed again, her defiant grunt scaring the crows from the willow branches and bringing Lehi trotting back down the trail with Sariah riding close behind. He said, "Son, what is it?"

"The rocky soil, Papa. They don't like it." Sam reached over and tugged on the camel's bridle, but she wouldn't budge. "We'll have to go back and try running them south of the city and meet up with the road to Jericho over beyond Bethlehem."

"You can't do that." Sariah glanced over her shoulder to the far end of the Kidron Valley where it turned up a rise and onto the plateau east of the city. "We're almost there."

Sam said, "The camels refuse to go any farther, Mama."

Sariah leaned over and reached for the bridle of the lead camel. "We have to go this way."

"Sariah." Lehi took her by the hand. "We tried."

"We can't give up." Sariah slowly shook her head, her hand pressed to her stomach. "They're waiting for us."

Lehi said, "You don't know that."

"Mima promised they'd be there until the moon set."

"She's failed us before." Lehi took a deep breath and glanced into the western sky where the moon hung just above the hills. "It's already too late, my dear."

Sariah let go of the bridle and lowered her head. "They were to guide us to safety."

"We'll find another place to hide our family." Lehi whistled to his sons, and Laman, Lemuel, and Nephi immediately turned the goats and sheep back toward them. Sariah came around on her horse and started down through the herd.

Lehi said, "Sariah, where are you going?"

"I have to be certain." She spurred down through the sheep, the animals jumping out of her way.

Sam started after her, but Lehi said, "No, son, let her go. She'll be back before we get these animals turned out of the Kidron Valley and headed south."

Rebekah climbed the rocky outcrop until she was high enough to see over the hill separating her from a view of the city. The light of the setting moon shone in her eyes and she held her hand over her brow and took one last look over Jerusalem. The square rooftops of homes were nestled safely behind the walls like jewels set against the black midnight sky. The temple rose above the parapets of the west wall, the magnificent stone pillars framing the entrance, and Rebekah sat on a flat stone and pulled her knees up to her chin. Aaron was somewhere beneath this moon celebrating Passover and she prayed he would remember her, though there was no reason to hold such a foolish notion in her heart. She'd been dead these three months and that was more than enough time for Aaron's memory to fade and his heart to pass over her. The life of a nomad was her lot and she would never see Aaron or this city again.

Rebekah closed her eyes to the light of the moon and whispered the wish of her heart—that someday she could return from her desert hideaway and join Aaron in the city of her birth. She kept her eyes closed, waiting for the reassurance of heaven to accompany her prayer, but peace did not come to her soul. She'd prayed the wrong prayer and she was left with nothing but a deep loneliness. She opened her eyes to the city where her beloved Aaron lived and leaned forward over the rocky outcrop to get a better view when a whispering filled her soul, warning her that this mighty fortress-city with its impenetrable walls and thousands of citizens—and dear God, not her Aaron—would be destroyed and all the inhabitants killed unless—

"Run, daughter!" Josiah came over the rise, the last light of the full moon reflecting off his bald head. "Get down the cliffs by the back way."

"We can't leave." Rebekah stood and straightened her robe on her shoulders. "We're to wait until the moon sets."

"We can't wait any longer." Josiah pointed down the steep hillside where the road came around the bend from Jerusalem. A lone rider pulled up, got down out of the saddle and started climbing through the sagebrush and thistle. Josiah said, "We've been followed." He took Rebekah by the hand and started across the outcrops. "We can circle back to our horses once we're down from these hills."

"But Papa, we don't know who it is." Rebekah pulled free.

Josiah hurried over a run of boulders and motioned for Rebekah to follow him. "We can't afford to find out."

Nephi rode point, leading the sheep up the rise from the Kidron Valley while his brothers and father stayed along the flank and rear, keeping the flock from meandering into the high brush and the camels from bolting out of this rocky valley and onto the sandy flats of the plateau above the city. The trail narrowed near the top and turned sharp around a lone Joshua tree. Nephi spurred his mount hard, prodding her up the last of the incline and onto the—

A rider burst across Nephi's path, his black cape swirling on the air behind the powerful strides of a white Arabian. He guided his horse with his legs, prodding her forward with a nudge from his boot and steering her with a turn of his knees. And when he came around Nephi saw the reason he didn't use his hands to rein his mount. It was Captain Laban and he held a fully drawn bow, the outline of it silhouetted by the stars in the night sky. It was the finest bow Nephi had ever seen, with double curves bending away from the handgrip in two half circles. It quivered in Laban's hands with the power of ten bows and when the captain turned in the saddle, the moonlight shimmered over the surface like light reflecting off of . . .

Metal? There had never been a bow made of steel, at least not any Nephi had ever known and he would have stepped closer to admire the workmanship, but he couldn't, not with Laban aiming it at his chest. Nephi reined back, the sheer power of the weapon warning him to find cover. Laban said, "Get down off your horse and get your father."

"What do want with him?"

"Do as I say, boy."

Nephi slowly dismounted and stood beside his horse with the reins in hand. Sam was the first to come up out of the Kidron Valley, and when he saw Laban aiming an arrow at Nephi, he pulled up, raised his hands overhead and said, "We don't have any gold or silver."

Laban turned his bow onto Sam. He said, "I don't want your money."

"We're a wealthy family." Sam got down from the saddle, his hands still raised. He said, "We can give you anything you—"

"I want your father." The captain inched his Arabian forward. "Where is he?"

Laman spurred up the trail and pulled up between Nephi and the captain, his gaze shifting quickly between them. He said, "Why don't you put your weapon down and we can talk about this."

Lemuel reined in beside Laman and leaned his long body over the saddle. He lowered his voice and said, "How did he find us?"

"Fools. I never should have trusted you to keep your father from finding out." The captain brandished the arrow at Laman and Lemuel. "Now get out of my way."

"Find out what?" Nephi stepped from behind the cover of Laman's horse. He said, "What did my brothers promise you?"

Laman said, "I saved your inheritance."

"You haven't saved us anything." Nephi turned to Lemuel. He said, "How did the captain find us?"

Lemuel shook his head. "We didn't tell him we were leaving."

Nephi said, "What did you tell him?"

"They didn't have to tell me anything." Laban smiled through the fletching in his arrow. He glanced at the ground, the glow of moonlight shimmering over the prints in the sand. "You cover your tracks poorly."

"I'm the one he wants." Lehi stepped from the shadows of the Kidron Valley, drawing his horse by the reins and urging the herd before him. He stood in the middle of the sheep like a shepherd watching over his flock. He said, "Let my sons go and you can do with me what you will."

Laban turned the arrow onto Lehi. "You never should have tried to flee."

Nephi shooed the sheep aside and stood beside his father. He said, "We've done nothing to harm you."

"Get back, boy." Laban leveraged his pull on the bowstring. "I'll deal with you once I've finished with your father."

"We're leaving this land." Lehi slowly stepped toward Laban, his hands raised. He spoke in a slow, calm voice. He said, "Let us go in peace and we'll not bother you again."

Laban said, "Is that how you beg for mercy?" He let the bowstring slide to the tip of his fingers, ready to let go. "Not with what you know of your lineage."

Laman leaned over the saddle. "My father knows nothing."

"Silence." Laban kept the arrow aimed at Lehi. "I told you I'd deal with you later."

Lehi peered up at the point of the arrow. "God will deliver us," he said.

Laban said, "Your God has not the power of deliverance."

The rush of an arrow pierced the night air. Nephi jumped in front of his father, shielding him from certain death. The sound of tearing flesh and the snapping of bone echoed across the trail and Lehi reached his arms around Nephi to hold him up. He said, "Dear God, not my youngest son."

Nephi felt for the arrow buried in his chest, but there was no pain. He could find no arrow piercing his body and he glanced up to see the captain falling forward in the saddle, his arms limp, his head down, and the shaft of an arrow rising out of the back of his shoulder like a speared kid-goat—his shank bone was broken.

A lumbering camel appeared out of the shadows across the flat expanse of the plateau and came up behind the captain's lifeless body. The animal reined around past Laban's white Arabian and the light from the torches high on watchtowers flickered across the weary face of Aaron, the son of the blacksmith. He was without a shirt, the collar of his tunic was wrapped around his shooting arm and soaked red with his blood. An old wooden bow hung loose in the hand of his injured limb, the weapon about to fall from his grip. He was bent over, his head reeling from side to side with the rise and fall of the camel's ungainly steps and he listed to the right on the bare back of the animal, his leg covered with blood from his sandal, up past his knees, the leather of his tunic matted against his thigh with blood. The remnants of his tunic were tied in a tight knot around his upper leg. He pulled up next to Laban and slid down from the camel. He steadied himself against the captain's Arabian, the weight of his head and shoulders leaning him forward. He dropped his wooden bow in the sand and reached for the steel weapon still hanging from Laban's grip. Before Aaron swatted Laban's horse and sent the Arabian trotting down the trail into the Kidron Valley where his men were certain to find the half-conscious captain with an arrow sprouting from his shank bone, he said, "This isn't your bow."

Aaron staggered toward Nephi. His head was light, his vision blurred and when he tried to offer a greeting, his tongue caught on parched lips. He lost the most blood at Beit Zayit before he used his tunic to tie off his wounds. He had found an old wooden bow in the stable behind the corrals and he would have caught Laban sooner, but mounting the camel sapped his strength. He didn't remember steering the camel up the trail and down onto the trade route—his mind was too blurred to do anything but let the animal take him where she would and it was pure providence she followed the captain. He didn't even remember taking aim, except that it was the power of heaven that gave him enough strength to shoot an arrow and it was by the very grace of God that he did it before Laban killed anyone.

Aaron raised the bow in the air, the steel glimmering in the starlight. He handed the bow to Nephi and said, "This belongs to you." He smiled like a proud father and then his leg gave out and he fell to the ground.

Nephi carried Aaron off the trail and leaned him against the Joshua tree growing alongside the trail. He said, "This bow isn't mine."

Aaron cradled his injured arm against his belly and held his hand to the throbbing in his right leg. He said, "It's your birthday, isn't it?"

Lehi came around in front of Aaron. "Laban did this to you, didn't he?"

Aaron said, "I found the captain destroying your home."

Laman marched up behind Aaron and gripped a twisted tree trunk with both hands, his powerful arms hovering over Aaron. "What did Laban do to the estate? Is it still standing? Did he take anything?" He cursed the captain's name and spit on the ground.

"Not now son." Lehi waved Laman aside. "We can talk about that later." He pulled Aaron close, the blood from his injured arm smearing over Lehi's traveling robe. "You saved my son's life."

"It wasn't Nephi who was spared tonight, sir." Aaron's hair fell over his brow and he cleared it from in front of his eyes with the back of his hand. He said, "God delivered you the day my feet were healed."

Lehi ordered Laman and Lemuel to get some water to clean Aaron's wounds. He told Sam to unpack the ointments from the fourth camel and asked Nephi to prepare a bed on the back of the camel to carry Aaron into the desert with them.

"You can't go back to the city, not until Laban's gone." Sam hurried over with an open bottle of salve and smeared the thick yellow paste over the wound in Aaron's arm. "He'll hunt you down and next time he'll take better aim."

"It doesn't matter what Laban does to me. Rebekah's gone and my father won't have me anymore." Aaron winced at the stinging salve, but it didn't have power to soothe his abandoned heart. "Nothing matters anymore."

"Stop your brooding, young man." Sariah stepped in around the horses. "Nothing good will come of your self-pity." She walked with her hand on the pain in her womb, but she held her head high. She said, "God healed your feet and now it's time you let him heal your heart."

Lehi said, "Sariah, be gentle with the boy. He's been through a—"

"I don't care what he's been through." She waved her hand in the air. "It's time he got on with his life."

"Mama, don't you see?" Sam covered the salve on Aaron's arm with a clean bandage before slowly picking off the blood-soaked tunic tied around Aaron's thigh. "He's hurt badly."

"I can see that." Sariah's voice grew stronger with each word. She said, "But the wounds in his flesh are nothing compared to the wounds in his heart."

Nephi said, "Mother, he could have died from this."

Aaron pushed his head back against the tree trunk. He said, "I died the day Rebekah died."

Sariah said, "Well then, it's past time you began to live again."

What did Sariah know about Aaron's living? She'd not lost anyone she loved. She had her family with her and all Aaron had was the memory of Rebekah and an order from his father never to return home. Aaron pressed his hand to his thigh to stop the stinging of the salve from growing worse and to keep Sam from tying the bandage too tight. Sariah stared at him, hands on her hips, without saying anything for a long moment. It was a gaze strong enough to unlock the sealed retreats of his heart; but his memory of Rebekah was to remain forever locked away and he wasn't going to let Sariah's kindly smile or her firm resolve change the unchangeable. She had no right to pry. She was meddling in matters that didn't concern her. Aaron didn't wait for Sam to finish tying the knot. He pulled himself up by the trunk with the end of the bandage hanging past his knee, and leaned against the gnarled wood. He said, "You'd all best go before Laban sends his soldiers after you. I'll find a way back to my home and . . ."

Sariah touched her finger to Aaron's lips to stop him from saying more. "We traveled this close to Jerusalem to meet two guides—one to lead us to the safety of a secret city in the desert, and another to mend your heart." She pointed beyond the horses where two figures stood among the herd of sheep. They were dressed in plain brown robes and when they removed their hoods, Aaron recognized the bald head of Josiah the potter and the dark, flowing locks of Rebekah's brown hair. The moonlight bathed her cheeks pale white, like an angel resurrected from a heavenly place, and he rubbed his eyes to make sure the loss of blood wasn't deceiving his mind. It couldn't be Rebekah. She was dead and he wasn't worthy to see a vision as heavenly as this. Sariah took him by the hand to steady him away from leaning against the tree. She said, "For the sake of Moses, boy, say something. Rebekah's alive."

Aaron limped across the dusty road. He couldn't run to her and take her in his arms and shout from the depths of his soul that he'd lived a God-blessed life. He fell at her feet, her hand in his, and his lips pressed against the back of her hand. She was dead, but now she was alive. She was gone from this earth, but somehow God had returned her to him.

"How did you . . . ?" A tear fell from Aaron's cheek and onto Rebekah's hand. He didn't need to ask her how she'd survived the fire. It was enough to know he'd not have to walk this life alone.

"Come with us." Rebekah touched Aaron on the cheek and lifted him to his feet, her grip strong enough to steady his lame leg, and it was like before when Rebekah stood by his side, not caring that he walked like a lame man. And this time he was certain he would be whole. Rebekah would mend his broken heart.

Rebekah spoke softly, her lips graced by the soft light from the night sky. She said, "There's a place in the wilderness where we can find safety from all this for a season. You can heal there."

"You can both heal there." Lehi rummaged about the saddlebags and took out the graft of an olive tree, the end of it wrapped in a cloth. It was the same graft he'd taken from the tree in his burned vineyard, the tree he called the House of Israel. He handed the graft to Aaron and said, "Help us plant this in a new land of promise."

Aaron held the wet burlap between his fingers. How could he leave his father? The day Lehi cut this graft from the ancient olive tree, he said the Council of Elders was like the main top branches and Aaron had to stay and save Jonathan from being cast into the fire with them. He said, "What about my father?"

"It will only be for a short time, just until this passes." Lehi held Aaron by the shoulders. "Then you can return to your father."

Aaron pressed the burlap-wrapped graft from the House of Israel into Rebekah's hand. He would go with her into the wilderness where his heart could heal, and he would help them plant this graft not in a promised land, but in—

A place of refuge.

CHAPTER 43

Three plates sat at Moriah's place on the long oak dining table: one for bitter herbs, another for boiled potatoes, and a third for roasted lamb. Four wine cups surrounded the plates, each one decorated with jewels and glimmering under the light of the oil lamps hanging from the vaulted ceiling of the dining room inside the palace at Fort Lakhish. It was an odd thing for an apprentice scribe to join the commander and his family for Passover, but when Yaush arrived from Jerusalem late this afternoon, he insisted Moriah eat with them. He was the object of the celebration—the reason to hope Uriah would be set free on this night of Passover.

Moriah sat at the foot of the dining table opposite Yaush. The commander wore a cape over his shoulders, and the buttons of his finest military dress flashed in the lamplight. His wife, Sophia, took her seat down one side of the table. She was dressed in a purple evening robe. Her hair was tied back off her neck with a matching ribbon and she was freshly bathed. She nodded to Moriah and said, "We're pleased you could join us for—"

"Where is Setti?" Yaush untied that strap of his cape, smoothed the pleats, and retied it.

It wasn't like the commander to burst out like that and interrupt his wife, but there he sat, rubbing his hands together.

Sophia said, "Dear, you sent him to the main gates."

Yaush glanced at the doors to the dining room. "It shouldn't take him this long."

Moriah said, "Should I go after him, sir?"

"Sit down, boy." Yaush played with the soup spoon. He said, "I should be more patient."

Sophia sipped the wine from her glass. "You're still concerned about the trial, dear."

Yaush said, "Of course I'm not."

"You had that same look in your eye when you arrived from Jerusalem this afternoon." Sophia took another sip. "What happened at the trial today?"

"Isn't it time we were served our food?" Yaush waved to the cook standing beside the door to the kitchens.

"We can wait for Setti." Sophia leaned forward in her chair and motioned for the cook to stay. "Why are you in such a hurry?"

"I'm not in a hurry." Yaush stopped tapping his fingers over the tabletop.

"Then what is it?"

Yaush glanced about the dining room, his gaze never staying long on any object.

Sophia said, "It's Laban, isn't it? Did he threaten you?"

Before Yaush could answer her question, the giant chamber doors on the far side of the hall groaned open and Nathan, Setti's friend and companion on the night watch, marched to the table. He stood beside Commander Yaush, his boots together and his shoulder back. He said, "Setti requests you come to the bastion, sir."

Yaush dropped his wine cup to the table, spilling the cherry-colored ale. "At this hour?"

"Yes, sir." Nathan nodded.

"That's impossible. He was to join us here for dinner."

"All I can tell you, sir, is that an officer arrived from Jerusalem driving a horse-drawn cart and Setti immediately cleared all six towers and sent the night watch away in company with the gatemen. He told us to find a drink at the commissary down the street until he sent for us."

"I told him to secure the bastion, not weaken it." Yaush stood from the table, the legs of his chair grating over the stone floor. He started out of the dining room, tying his cape over his shoulders. "No one was to be allowed inside the fort without my permission."

Sophia said, "I'm going with you."

"You're to stay here with Moriah, do you hear?" Yaush spun around. "Start on the unleavened bread and I'll be back with Setti before they serve the lamb." He pulled the door shut behind him.

Sophia peered across at Moriah, the concern visible in her deep-brown eyes. She said, "I can't let him face this alone."

Moriah said, "Face what?"

"His greatest fear." Sophia hurried around the table and started across the chamber.

Moriah stood when she passed by his chair. It wasn't his place to question the wife of the commander, but he couldn't keep from saying, "What fear is that, my lady?"

Sophia stopped beneath the oil lamp hanging above the door to the dinning hall. "The Lakhish Letters."

Setti would never disobey his father, but when Lieutenant Daniel rounded the bend in the rampart and pulled up outside the lower gates of Lakhish ordering him to send away the watch and let him inside for an inspection, he could do nothing but obey a superior officer.

Daniel drove a horse-drawn cart into the bastion and Setti immediately drew the gate shut and set the bolt. The torchlight fell over the cart stacked with wood from front to back and ten vessels of oil packed beside the stoop. Daniel was dressed in a dark riding cloak without any of the insignias of a proper military man and he issued the most unmilitary of commands—Setti was to unlock the guard station without permission from Commander Yaush.

Setti said, "I can't do that, sir."

"Open it." Daniel tried the latch, but the thick cedar door was sealed with two metal locks. He leaned his head in next to Setti and the stench of strong wine rushed out with his words. "Where's the key for this?"

Setti couldn't let Daniel inside. No one was allowed to see the potsherds. He said, "Why don't you join us inside for Passover? There's plenty of food and you can speak with my father about your inspection."

Daniel balanced himself against the guard station door. He pressed his hand to his brow, rubbing away the haze of his drunkenness, but it wasn't enough to temper his will. He said, "Open this or I'll see you hanged."

The upper gate at Lakhish groaned open and Yaush marched through, adjusting his cape over his shoulders as he came. He slowed in front of Daniel. "What's the meaning of this, Lieutenant?"

A red line of blood leaked out from under a black patch over Daniel's eye. He touched his fingers to his cheek and grimaced before reaching under his cloak for a bottle of strong wine. He took a long drink. "I have orders from Captain Laban to inspect the keep."

Yaush lowered his voice. He said, "What are you looking for?"

Daniel tapped the bottom of the wine bottle to the guard station door. "I think you know, sir."

Setti said, "Why don't we go inside the palace and—"

"Open this and let me in." Daniel stuffed the wine bottle under his cloak like a drunkard protecting his prize.

Commander Yaush nodded to Setti and he slowly pulled the key from around his neck, unlocked the door, and pushed it open. They had started inside when a woman's voice called from the upper gates. Sophia hurried down the open-air corridor, pushed past Daniel's cart, and stepped in next to Yaush. She took him by the arm and said, "What is it? What's all the commotion about?"

Yaush said, "Go back inside and—"

Daniel said, "Do you know what's locked inside, woman?"

Sophia said, "Nothing but some odd documents."

Setti said, "No, Mother. Don't say anymore."

Daniel said, "Who else at Lakhish knows about the copies?"

Moriah was the only one, but Setti shook his head and said, "No one knows anything."

"Get inside, all of you." Daniel unsheathed his sword and forced them into the guard station. He sat them down side-by-side on a stone bench, pointed his sword at Yaush and ordered him to bind his family with strong cords at the wrist and feet before Daniel finished the task, tying Yaush's arms behind his back and binding his legs around the base of the bench.

A table covered with potsherds stood beside the bench, the broken clay pieces lettered with black ink. Daniel picked one up and held it to Commander Yaush's face. "You betrayed Captain Laban for this."

Yaush turned his gaze to the floor and didn't answer.

Daniel pulled the commander's head back by the hair. "How could you let these potsherds destroy the captain?"

Yaush said, "Laban will destroy himself."

Daniel slapped Yaush across the face. "You're a fool."

Setti spit, the spittle landing in Daniel's face. "You're the fool for obeying him."

"Don't talk about your superior officer like that." Daniel swung the butt of his sword at Setti's head, opening a gash on his brow and felling him back on the bench. Blood ran into his eyes and blurred his vision, but he could hear his mother screaming for Daniel to leave him alone.

Daniel said, "Not another word out of you, woman."

Sophia said, "I'll not be silent until you leave my family in peace."

"You don't have a family anymore." Daniel pushed over the wooden table, sending the potsherds crashing to the ground at her feet. "Captain Laban's orders."

Setti shook his head to clear away his lightheadedness. There was no telling how long he laid on the bench with blood streaming from his head. The smell of oil smoke filled the room, and orange flames danced about him. His vision was blurred and he couldn't see his mother. He reached for her hand and asked if she was there, but before an answer sounded, his ears went deaf and the room went black with the darkness that accompanies death.

Scorching heat flared from the wood, and the smoke stung tears from Yaush's eyes. Sophia cried between gasps for breath. She was burning, and Yaush leaned his body in front of her, shielding her from the hottest flames. He called to his son on the end of the bench, but Setti didn't move. He lay closest to the fire, his head rocked back against the wall, his chest still and his body limp. Dear God no! Take me and Sophia, but not Setti. He was too young to die.

Daniel leaned against the outside wall of the guard station, his face singed from the heat of setting the fire. He found the bottle of wine beneath his cloak and guzzled the strong drink. Black smoke swirled from the air vent and curled around Daniel like a noose around a man's neck. He coughed on the foul air and took another swig to clear his throat. A rush of flames burst from the vent in the wall and he stepped back. What was he doing? He wasn't a murderer and no matter how much he wanted to please Captain Laban, he couldn't let Commander Yaush and his family burn to death. He threw down the wine bottle and rushed back inside the guard station. Flames shot up from the wood floor and his cape caught fire. He threw off the burning cloth and staggered forward, his arms raised to protect himself from the searing heat, but it was no use. The fire had spread about the entrance to the guard station, and the smoke chased him back into the bastion. He stood at the door, his face covered with ash and the smell of his singed hair filling the night air with the stench of death. His future with Laban and Zadock was sure—seared with the lives of their enemies. He slowly unhitched the cart, the sound of his undoing masked by the crackling of the fire. He mounted the steed and started her trotting toward the lower gate, down through the smoke that gathered between the high walls of the bastion. He was one of them now, but he'd murdered three innocents to join them and he could never surmount that guilt.

Daniel's deliverance was damned.

Smoke gathered around Yaush, choking him toward unconsciousness. He pressed Sophia's cheek against his and felt her slowly breathing her last. His son's body was sprawled over the bench and he bid him farewell until they would meet again in a better place. Yaush coughed on the thick smoke that sucked away the life of his greatest loves and there was nothing he could do but sink deeper into—

"The sewer, sir." The white cap and curly black hair of Moriah's head rose out the trapdoor. His face was smudged with black soot, but there was never a more glorious sight than this boy. Thank heaven they left the trapdoor open the day they came here to assemble the potsherds, and somehow Moriah had the sense to come looking for them when they didn't return to the Passover meal. He rubbed his eyes to clear the smoke. He said, "We can escape Lakhish by the sewer."

Moriah covered his mouth with the sleeve of his robe, bent over to stay below the worst of the smoke, and dodged the flames. He freed Yaush from his cords and let him carry Sophia out while he lifted Setti's lifeless body through the trapdoor and down the outside wall of the bastion, away from the burning guard station. He spoke quickly, the words falling from his mouth between gasps for breath, telling Yaush the sewer emptied into a small grove outside the lower wall. Moriah had family in Aqabah, an uncle who was a boat builder, and he'd take them in without question. He laid Setti on the ground and let the cool night air revive him. Setti coughed, his lungs heaving the suffocating smoke from his body.

Yaush fell to his knees beside Setti. They were into the no-man's-land between the upper and lower walls, the tall, dew-covered grasses reaching around them. Yaush had lost his command of Lakhish—a post he'd worked all his life to gain—but none of that mattered. Yaush held his son close and drew Sophia and Moriah into his circle with his long arms. They were alive and he had only heaven's promise of Passover to thank for that. Tonight God delivered them, but there was a lingering concern in his soul that the matter of the Lakhish Letters was not over. They would leave this place and follow Moriah to his boat-building uncle in Aqabah, but somehow Yaush couldn't dispel the impression that these letters would not die in the flames of this fire. Yaush turned back toward the guard station. Smoke bellowed from the air vents and a loud crack split the night. The heat of the fire was fierce enough to fracture the pivot stones in the foundation of the upper gate. The Lakhish Letters were gone, the potsherd copies burned into ashes by this great fire, but somehow these letters were not dead. Yaush helped Setti to his feet and they started down through the no-man's-land toward the opening in the sewer. He didn't know how, and he couldn't be certain when, but Lakhish Letters were certain to rise again—

Like a voice from the dust.

EPILOGUE

JANUARY 29, 1935, TEL ED DUWEIR, PALESTINE—

John Starkey left his teacup half full on the rickety plywood table, pushed open the screen door to his tent and spit the foul tasting brew in the sand. He wasn't given to such a fetid habit as public spitting, but afternoon tea in this promised land was nothing like his blessed midday respites in London, and the crumpets in this desert tasted very much like the mortar they excavated last week between the stones in the foundation wall of the double gate leading into the fort.

The tent door banged shut behind him, though there was hardly a reason to have a door on his quarters, given the way the mosquitoes and flies passed through the screens and disturbed his sleep every night. John ran his fingers over the worn wires in the screen door. He would endure the nocturnal insects, along with the scorpions that crawled in the sands by day, the late deliveries of drinking water and supplies from Jerusalem, and the long hours of digging in the trenches high on the summit of Tel ed Duweir as long as this dig provided the shred of the evidence he needed to prove his theory.

John was dressed in khaki, pleated pants, a tan shirt, and a wide-brimmed African hunting hat his wife gave him the day the expedition sailed from Dover. This was no safari and John was no hunter, but Mrs. Starkey believed anywhere her husband went in search of the ancient past was a jungle, and the hat did have power to shield him from the intense Palestinian sun. Even in winter, its rays had a dizzying effect on the mind after hours in the trenches. The hat cast a shadow over his round cheeks and thin English nose he inherited from his great-grandmother, the duchess of Yorkshire. If only he'd inherited one-tenth of her *estate*, he'd have more than enough to continue this dig until he found the evidence he sought. It had to be here somewhere amid these ruins, and he had two years left to find it—the sponsors had signed on for twenty-four additional months and not a fortnight more.

John turned back to the tent, undid his top button to keep the heat from raising a sweat on his brow, chewed on the end of a horned pipe, and read the sign over the door. It was a ritual he observed each day after tea, if it were possible to call it tea. The sign posted over his tent door read: *Wellcome Archaeological Research Expedition to the Near East at Tel ed Duweir*—Tel for mound of buried ancient ruins and Duweir for some Dutch explorer of the sixteenth century who had nothing to do with the real significance of this hilltop. This was the ancient site of Fort Lakhish and John L. Starkey was going to prove it to the world— at least to his colleagues back at the London Museum of Antiquities, who would appropriate more funding if he could come up with solid evidence from beneath the rubble of centuries, certifying that Tel ed Duweir was the legendary Fort Lakhish.

The brash *beep, beep* of a Mercedes sounded in the road that ran alongside camp. It was a new pearl-black roadster with frog-eye head-lights and a chrome bonnet with vents—a thick leather strap holding it shut. It was difficult to tell how new the roadster was with the dust swirling up off Highway 233. It wasn't really a highway; it couldn't even pass for an abandoned country road. There were a hundred washed out gullies in the six-mile stretch from the turn-off at Highway 71 and the wheel ruts swallowed the tires all the way to the hub.

The driver revved the engine, turned the car out of the ruts, and pulled alongside John. He swung open the door, and stepped out and there was no mistaking the short, bespectacled man with bushy eyebrows, dark skin, and a thin, straight nose. It was Dr. Harry Torczyner, the distinguished Bialik professor from the Hebrew University in Jerusalem. He knew more about ancient Hebrew writings than any scholar in the world, and that was no exaggeration.

Dr. Torczyner lifted the skullcap from his balding head and wiped the sweat from his scalp before fitting the yarmulka back in place. He wore a white shirt that buttoned down the side and a matching white tunic that reached to his ankles. He said, "Good afternoon, John. It's good to see you after so long a time." He spoke with a perfect English accent. Dr. Torczyner was a linguist who spoke ten languages better than most natives, and he could read and write the unspoken language of the pharaohs.

Dr. Torczyner stepped past John to survey the dig site. He planted his hands on his hips and set his gaze on the hillside above camp. "So this is the mighty Fort Lakhish."

"It's only logical." John hurried to his side and shook the good doctor's hand. "There are no other ruins in this area as large or as well fortified."

"Have you found any evidence?"

"Some arrowheads and spear tips, and last month we came across a brass implement that could be the blade of a sword."

"You know what I mean, John."

"Well, we thought we had some writings when we excavated the guard station, over there between the gates of the outer and inner walls." John pointed to the top of the hill. "It was a rather large room, probably a locked store room or a keep."

"What sort of find was it, son?"

"There were piles of broken pottery strewn around the room. If you'd like I can show you where we—"

"*Ostraca!*" Dr. Torczyner spun around to face John. "Were there any . . ."

"I'm sorry, Doctor." John shook his head slowly. He knew the answer before Dr. Torczyner finished asking the question. "There weren't any *ostraca* among the *potsherds*."

Potsherds. John had found a good number of the broken pieces of pottery in the guard station, probably a rubbish pile since ancient pottery was always breaking. There was no telling why they were stored there. Soldiers weren't given to keeping a supply of potsherds handy on which to jot down a message, the words becoming the *ostraca* of the ancient past. John scratched the side of his head. If he found any *ostraca* at all, it would be a coup of titanic proportion; but to date they had only found potsherds without any *ostraca* penned over the broken pieces of pottery. John wasn't hoping for a large document. In the ancient world, invading armies destroyed the most important records written on papyrus, clay tablets, and metal plates. But he could pray he would find bits of a scribe's rough draft, a piece of pottery with a portion of a larger document written on the surface, or possibly a letter scrawled onto a single piece of potsherd—any bit of writing he could call *ostraca.*

"That's too bad, John." Dr. Torczyner turned back to study the hillside. "I'd hoped you'd come up with some writings by now."

"Not to worry, sir. It's only been two years." John tapped the sign over his door where the names of the sponsors were painted by his own brush strokes. "We have enough support to keep at it for two more."

"That's nice." Dr. Torczyner offered a weak smile, one that said he'd heard that reasoning before from a hundred other archaeologists who failed to find the evidence they sought. "Show me what you have found. I want to see Lakhish the way General Yaush would have seen it."

"You mean Lord Yaush, sir."

"You can't be certain of that. No one can." Dr. Torczyner raised his thick eyebrows. "All we know from the scant records about this place is that Yaush was a military commander." He rubbed his chin between his fingers. "There's not a shred of evidence that tells us the man was also governor of southern Judah, son. Nothing."

"But if he was, and I believe he was, then wouldn't you at least agree on the wording of the man's title?"

"You used the word *believe,* John—do you actually believe that about Yaush?"

"I meant it as a hypothesis, not some blind faith."

"All good science starts with faith." Dr. Torczyner turned his face into the breeze that swirled up the hillside from the valley floor. "A man who lacks faith, has not the tenacity to endure setbacks."

"I'm simply stating the possibility that Yaush was lord of this region. He'd have to be, by the sheer size of his palace-fort."

"There you go again with your beliefs." The wind had blown Dr. Torczyner's bangs up off his brow and he combed them back into place with his palm.

"What are you talking about, sir?" John removed his safari hat, ran his hand through his hair and replaced the wide-brimmed head covering.

Dr. Torczyner said, "Lakhish was a fort; we're certain of that, but there's nothing that indicates it was also a palace. Not a single written document mentions Lakhish in that context."

"It's possible."

"Don't misunderstand, John. I'm not trying to refute your theories." Dr. Torczyner folded his arms across his chest. "I sincerely support your efforts to prove your faith, but there is no evidence."

"I don't deal in faith." John rolled up the long sleeves on his khaki shirt, and adjusted the collar. "It's just a hunch."

"Very well, we'll call it that and end our speculating for the day." Dr. Torczyner took John by the arm. "Come, show me what you believe to be Fort Lakhish."

"We're going to find some writing that will prove my theories."

"The fort, John. It's time for a tour of your dig." Dr. Torczyner dug his heel into the rocky soil. "Interpret your excavations for me."

John raised his hand toward the ancient road that led from the valley floor to the front gates. It was grown over with brush and much of it washed out from two thousand years of weather, but it was still a road, starting at the base of the hill just below camp, and rising across the west side of the embankment like a great stairway reaching round toward the front gates to the north. John said, "The escarpment is partially destroyed, but the eight-percent grade is normal for ramparts like these." He pointed halfway up the hillside where the remains of the first of two great walls once protected Lakhish. "The trench we dug below the outer wall indicates a thickness of nearly ten cubits, one more than—"

"John!"

"Is there something wrong, Doctor?" John lowered his hand.

"I'm a linguist, not an archaeologist." Dr. Torczyner rubbed his chin between his fingers. "Tell me how Fort Lakhish would have looked if I were Lord Yaush viewing the city from his palace."

"We did find that structure near the center of the hilltop, a very large building with walls as thick as . . ."

Dr. Torczyner left John standing alone, picked his way down from the ridge of camp, through a stand of scrub brush, and up the other side onto the ancient rampart leading up to the double gates.

John said, "Doctor, there's a much easier access around to the north. We built a road for the digging gangs over there."

Dr. Torczyner raised his hands to the sky and let the afternoon breeze blow his gray hair off his brow. "I want to feel what it would have been like to ride a chariot up this hill and into the fort."

"Sir, we don't have any chariots." John followed him down the ravine and up onto the uneven surface they called a road.

"Use your imagination, John. Can you see it? Two great steeds pounding up the approach to the fort with an urgent message from Jerusalem? Doesn't this place inspire intrigue?"

"We're scientists, sir, not movie moguls."

"Fort Lakhish was built by men of great imagination, and if you're to understand what they created so many years ago, my son, you're going to have to use a bit of your own." Dr. Torczyner rested his hand over his chest. "Think with your heart and tell me what Yaush would have seen."

"Well, I . . ." John started up the road ahead of Dr. Torczyner. What kind of a description did the man want from him? He was giving him more than enough data to substantiate their findings. Dr. Torczyner followed him up the hill and around to a line of trenches at the foundation wall of the outer gate. They excavated it down to the base last month. It was a rather large entrance, with enough room for two double-file garrisons of cavalry to pass through in opposite directions; why it was even wide enough for five chariots to ride through side-by-side—the widest gate he'd ever seen—and it could have supported two rather large watchtowers, one on either side of the opening. Immediately after entering the first gate, the riders would have turned sharp to the right, into a bastion—a long corridor with walls rising high above the road, like a protected passage leading from the outer wall up the hillside to the inner wall of the city on the brow of the hill. The bastion must have been a noisy corridor, with the clatter of horses' hooves rising off the cobblestones and reverberating between the walls and mixing with the cry of watchmen from six towers calling to the gatemen below. This was Lakhish, the fort he had hunted for all his life, but for the first time he could feel the pulsing of chariot wheels pulling through the lower gates and trotting up the final approach to the second gate and into the well-guarded city of his studies. It was as if Dr. Torczyner had opened a window to the past and he was just now stepping to the sill to peer through and see what lay beyond the . . .

What was he thinking? He was an archaeologist, not an author of fiction, and he wasn't going to let his objectivity be clouded by imagination. They would never have a firsthand account of the place, no matter how much Dr. Torczyner insisted on this childish reliving of the past. John took out a handkerchief and rubbed the sweat off the back of his neck. If the ghosts that inhabited these haunts didn't leave behind any ostraca recording their doings, John certainly wasn't going to raise the dead and ask them for an accounting. Without any writings he would never know the answers to his ancient questions.

John tipped the brim of his safari hat back off his brow. "If you were riding a chariot . . ."

"Go on." Dr. Torczyner cupped his hand as if he were holding the reins of two high-stepping steeds.

John quickly blurted out his comment. "A chariot driver would have reined up to the outer gate and waited here for the gatemen to open."

"Is that all you can tell me about a fortress you've been searching for all your professional life?"

"Well, it would have been a rather large gate; we know that by the size of the stones we excavated in the foundation wall over by the . . ."

There he went again, reciting facts that didn't interest Dr. Torczyner; he could tell by the way the man uncupped his hands, letting go of his hold on the imaginary reins. John cleared his throat. "You would have had to turn your chariot through this passageway." They turned right and walked between two deep trenches—the foundations of the bastion where high walls once cast a shadow over the corridor—and stopped at what was once the inner gate leading into the city-fort of Lakhish

John said, "This is the only entrance we know about. It appears this area was burned in a great fire." Four large stones, each one with a pivot etched into the top, like a bowl, sat on either side of the gate. They were charred black and the stone was riddled with thermal fractures from intense heat.

Dr. Torczyner ran his hand over one of the stones. "It must have been quite a fire."

A voice carried up from deep inside the trench next to the gate. "Amazing would be a better word."

It came from the wide part of the trench, where the bedouin diggers found a guard station along the west wall of the bastion. The sun-washed blonde hair of Mr. Harding poked above the horizon of excavated stone; then his blue eyes and long face came into view. His head sat perched on the edge of the pit, his open mouth level with the tip of John's boots. He gripped the trench wall with one hand and held the white pages of his notes with the other.

Mr. Harding said, "Afternoon, mate." He was Australian by birth, but had lived most of his adult life two blocks from the London museum where he kept an office on the fifth floor. He'd been with the expedition since day one and it was his humor that had kept them sane for the past two years.

John motioned for Dr. Torczyner to come to the edge of the pit. He began tapping his boot and he shot a stream of dust into Harding's mouth. John said, "Harding manages our digging operation. He can find clues hidden in soil and rock where most archaeologists see nothing but useless dirt."

Harding coughed and waved his hand to clear the cloud of dust around his face. He said, "I'd say fourth-dynasty dust. It was a very dry reign for that particular king."

Immediately John stilled his boot and let the cloud of dust settle into the excavation pit below them. He said, "Harding, we finished with this trench two weeks ago."

Harding wiped the dust from his mouth with the sleeve of his shirt. "I figured a bit more sleuthing was merited."

John said, "They really do need you at the main site. If the diggers find anything they can sell, they'll not let you know about it."

"You've never trusted the bedouins we hired."

"I trust them, just as long as one of us is with them when they're digging." John knelt on one knee beside Harding's head. "Did you leave Miss Tufnell with them?"

"Well . . ."

"Hello, John." Miss Tufnell stepped from the shadows of the pit and smiled up at him from the wide portion of the trench where they had found a number of potsherds—none of them ostraca. They did find an ancient stone bench pushed up against the front of the room closest to the inner gate. John wasn't exactly sure why there was a bench here, and when they hadn't found any more clues among the hundreds of broken pieces of pottery, they moved their digging farther up the hill and into the city.

Miss Tufnell said, "I'm sorry to have left the diggers to themselves, but Harding had this theory and well, I . . ." She was dressed in a white blouse with short sleeves, a pair of dungarees rolled up past her ankles, and white bobby socks that had turned black from the residue left by the ancient gate fire. Her long, brown hair was tied back in a ponytail with a red handkerchief, and her nails bore the only visible signs of female vanity. She insisted on doing her nails every morning, no matter how much the digging and scratching through the soil spoiled the finish. She was holding a piece of blackened rock with a chalky texture, and her nails were filled with the carbon that blackened the excavation nearest the gate. Aged soot had a smell worse than sulfur, but it didn't have the power to keep this woman from working the dig alongside Harding. She said, "We found so many potsherds here last week and Harding thought that—"

"None of them had any writings on them," John said. "We screened every bit of dirt."

"That isn't the point." Harding pulled himself out of the trench and sat on the edge, his legs dangling over the side. "Doesn't it make you wonder why there would be so many potsherds in one place?"

John rested his hands on his hips. "It was a rubbish pile."

"But what use would a soldier have for potsherds? The scribes did their work in the palace treasury." Harding looked up at him. "It's just a thought, John."

Miss Tufnell moved across the excavated pit and stood below them. "It was more than just a thought." She held up a blackened piece of potsherd. "Go on, Harding, tell John what you told me."

"Actually, it was just a hunch." Harding set his palms on the ground beside him and scooted down along the edge of the trench until his legs were dangling over the wall of the guard station, directly next to the inner city gate, the place where the soil and rock was charred black with ancient soot. "This gate area was burned, possibly to the ground by the size of the factures we found in some of the foundation stones."

John nodded. "Go on."

"All the potsherds we found here were the ones that weren't burned in the fire."

"What are you saying?"

"If they were written in ink, all the writings would have been washed away over the years, except for the ones burned in the fire. And if there were ostraca near the fire, the heat would have seared the writings into the clay like a potter's kiln finishes a lacquer."

"That's brilliant." Dr. Torczyner sat down at the edge of the trench next to Harding. "Help me down there, will you?"

John said, "Doctor, we can have the bedouins come back and dig this area again."

"Nonsense." Dr. Torczyner turned onto his belly and shimmied down into the trench with John following him. They lined up along the black trench wall, Miss Tufnell closest to the gate, picking at the dirt with her painted nails, then Harding with his pencil and paper lodged beneath his arm, Dr. Torczyner digging with both hands and John working farthest from the center of the burned ruins.

The dark soil fell in loose bits, like ancient gravel crumbling away from the wall revealing nothing but more burned soil. What were they doing, digging at this wall like children in search of buried treasure? They had already excavated the area, but Harding was a good scientist and John didn't have the courage to end their search just yet. The sun hung low on the western hills beyond Lakhish and soon it would force the end to their digging for the day. Then he could pay the bedouins for their day's work—two shekels and a loaf of bread—and insist they return to camp for the evening meal and forget this nonsense.

The pad of white paper fell from under Harding's arm and black soot marred the first page of his carefully penciled notes. What was Harding doing? He never let his papers get away from him like that. Even though he was a carefree soul, with his note taking he was nothing but careful. John pulled away from the wall and reached over to help him retrieve the pad from the dirty floor when Harding's pencil fell from his shirt pocket. It glanced against the rocky soil, and came to rest over a dark piece of wall that had come loose. It lodged between Harding's feet, next to the white paper. Harding stared at it, his fingers still lodged in the wall where he'd been digging.

It wasn't until John reached for the pencil and paper that he saw the reason for Harding's stillness.

Harding said, "Do you see it?"

"It's carbonized rock."

"Don't move, Harding." Dr. Torczyner knelt beside him. "Get some water."

Miss Tufnell handed over a canteen. "It's mineral water; it won't damage anything."

Dr. Torczyner carefully picked the odd-shaped scrap from between Harding's boots and poured water over it, loosening the ancient soil with his thumb until the lines of flowing Hebrew script came into bold relief. Ostraca! The first writings from Lakhish and all John could think to say was, "Mercy, Harding, do you know what you've found?"

Miss Tufnell let out a small cry and held out two more pieces of broken pottery. They were black with soot, but the writing was impossible to miss. They measured five inches wide and three inches high. The edges were jagged but the writing surface was smooth.

Miss Tufnell handed them to Dr. Torczyner and asked, "What do they say?"

Dr. Torczyner lifted Harding's fragment to the light. "This one is a list of names. Possibly men who lived at the fort, but I can't be certain." He cleaned away the soil from Miss Tufnell's find. He said, "Whoever wrote this was not a wise man."

John stepped next to him. "What is it?"

"In the ancient kingdom a man could be put to death for treason for writing something like this."

Harding said, "Writing what?"

"It's from one of the king's generals, possibly the captain of the guard in Jerusalem."

"And . . ."

"It's a very strongly worded curse against the monarch and his offspring."

"Which king?"

"It doesn't say, but the names in the first ostraca were popular around six hundred B.C. I'd say Zedekiah, the last king of the Jews."

John took potsherds number one and two from Dr. Torczyner and ran his fingers carefully over the surface, touching each Hebrew character that had been seared into the clay by the heat of the ancient fire and preserved for two millennia. He walked to the center of the guard station where he could see over the top toward the center of the fort, over where the bedouins were digging at the foundation walls of what he believed was the treasury of the palace fort, the place where ancient scribes did their work and stored their documents. Why hadn't they found any writings over there? He sat down on the ancient bench that stood against the wall at the front of the guard station, the back of his head propped against the blackened foundation, and the brim of his safari hat pushed down over his eyes. They had their first writings, and he should shout for joy. But instead of answering his questions, the ostraca only posed new ones. What was this bench used for? Was this the workplace of a scribe, or the storehouse for records? Maybe it was a stockade and these ostraca were held under lock and key for a pending trial. The possibilities were endless and if they could find more potsherds, maybe they could find the answers, at least some of them.

Dr. Torczyner stepped beside John. He said, "Is something wrong?"

John pushed the brim of his hat back from his eyes and took a deep breath. "I was just trying to figure out why Commander Yaush would store his records out here, away from his treasury."

"Don't you mean Lord Yaush?" Dr. Torczyner took the two potsherds from John and replaced them with the last one Miss Tufnell had discovered. "You're beginning to think with your heart, son."

John held the jagged-edged piece of pottery with both hands and lifted it to the golden rays of the sunset that angled down over the trench and filled the pit with the last, bright glow of afternoon. The light rested on the Hebrew characters, and written at the top of letter number three was the salutation of an urgent message delivered to the fort by courier. It began: *Hail Lord Yaush, commander of the palace-fort at Lakhish, governor of southern Judah.*

John dusted the sand from the surface of the potsherd and ran his fingers over the carbonized ink letters, tracing the Hebrew characters written two thousand years before. They'd done it! His team of archaeologists was the first to find ancient writings certifying that this hill was the ancient site of Fort Lakhish, and naming Yaush as governor. In fact, they were the first to find any ancient Hebrew writings outside the Old Testament dating back to the days before the fall of Jerusalem. But they didn't really find these writings. Something deep in his soul told him that a power greater than his scholarly ways had guided them to find these letters, and he lifted his gaze to the sunset and watched the last rays of light fall below the western horizon.

God had raised this ancient voice from the dust.

HISTORICAL NOTES

AUTHOR'S NOTE: *Power of Deliverance* is a fictional work based on events recorded in the opening chapters of *The Book of Mormon: Another Testament of Jesus Christ*. The story, settings, and, in some instances, plot lines were developed from historical research of the period. Though it is impossible to review all the sources that contributed to the preparation of this novel, the following notes summarize the basis of historical elements in the story.

CHAPTER 1

Fort Lakhish stood in the hill country about twenty-five miles southwest of Jerusalem, and the description in this chapter is based on evidence from archaeological research at the site (David Ussishkin, "Excavations at Lachish," preliminary report reprinted from Tel Aviv University Institute of Archaeology, 1978, 5:1–2). The double walls surrounding the city-fortress, the large palace structure in the center of the fort complex, and the bastion with high walls and watchtowers have been unearthed and a detailed drawing similar to the one in this book was originally penciled by Dr. Harry Torczyner in his account of the discovery of the Lakhish Letters (Harry Torczyner, "Foreword," in *The Lachish Letters*. Harry Torczyner, ed., Oxford University Press, 1938).

Until archaeologists discovered artwork depicting four-wheeled carriages, it was believed that in Lehi's day only two-wheeled chariots were used for human transport (*Great People of the Bible and How They Lived*, Pleasantville NY: Readers Digest Association, 1974). In this novel, the emergence of four-wheeled carriages is depicted in the arrival of Zadock at Fort Lakhish.

Yaush was a historical character, and in addition to commanding the garrisons at Fort Lakhish, he also governed the southern hill country of Judah. What little we know about him is recorded in the Lakhish Letters—communications with the courier, or outpost lieutenant, Hosha Yahu. Nibley suggested many years ago that both Yaush (spelled Jaush in Nibley's first writings and later Yaush in other papers), along with Hosha Yahu were "cut of the same cloth" as Captain Laban (Hugh W. Nibley, "Portrait of Laban," in *An Approach to the Book of Mormon* [The Collected Works of Hugh Nibley, vol. 6], Salt Lake City: Deseret Book, and Provo: F.A.R.M.S. 1988). However, further study of the Lakhish Letters led Nibley to propose that both men were supportive of the prophets and were very much caught in a crisis of conscience between following their superior officers in Jerusalem, possibly Captain Laban, and following their faith (Nibley, "Dark Days in Jerusalem: The Lakhish letters and the Book of Mormon," in *The Prophetic Book of Mormon* [The Collected Works of Hugh Nibley, vol. 8]. Salt Lake City: Deseret Book, and Provo: F.A.R.M.S. 1989). More of what we do know regarding Commander Yaush's support of the prophets is recorded in the historical notes for Chapter 20.

The first three of eighteen Lakhish Letters written on potsherds—broken pieces of clay pottery—were discovered by Dr. John L. Starkey and other members of the Wellcome Archaeological Research Expedition to the Near East on January 29, 1934 (Starkey, John L., "The Discovery," in *The Lachish Letters,* Harry Torczyner, ed., Oxford University Press, 1938). The letters date to 600 B.C. and are the only writings outside the Old Testament and Book of Mormon from that time period. It is not certain who authored all the Lakhish Letters. Some were most likely penned by the courier Hosha Yahu. The handwriting and language differ between some of the letters, but not enough to arrive at any conclusions as to authorship. Dr. Harry Torczyner suggests that the Lakhish Letters are communications between the mail courier, Hosha Yahu, and Commander Yaush at Fort Lakhish, and the letters mention both of them by name (Torczyner, "Notes on Letter I" in *The Lachish Letters).* The Lakhish Letters make reference to other military communications between officers at Jerusalem—possibly Captain Laban—and Commander Yaush at Fort Lakhish. The letters also name Yaush as governor of southern Judah, and they also mention Captain Elnathan's mission to capture the prophet Uriah, as does the Old Testament (Jer. 26:20–24). In the first novel in this series, *Pillar of Fire*, the mail courier Hosha Yahu was discovered passing Captain Laban's confidential letters to Uriah, and Hosha Yahu killed himself rather than be caught and forced to divulge information about Uriah. In this novel, Captain Laban is depicted as the author of the letters as he was in *Pillar of Fire*. It is unlikely, however, that Laban wrote the letters himself, and it is impossible to authenticate authorship of any of the letters. Laban likely contacted Commander Yaush by letter, and the Lakhish Letters reference such communications. The Lakhish Letters contain military information that would have been similar to Captain Laban's communications. Laban is not mentioned by name and it is unlikely any of these letters came directly from his pen, though they summarize the wishes of the military commanders in Jerusalem with regard to Uriah. The Lakhish Letters are the only source for the names of Commander Yaush and Hosha Yahu. Captain Elnathan, the military officer charged with the mission of capturing Uriah in Egypt and returning him to Jerusalem, and Uriah's father, Shema Yahu (written Shemaiah in the Book of Jeremiah) are named in both the Lakhish Letters and the Old

Testament (Jer. 26:20–24). See also Torczyner, Harry "Notes on Letters II, III, IV," in *The Lachish Letters*. Since it is impossible to determine authorship for all the Lakhish Letters, and in order to develop the story lines in this novel, Laban is named as the author of the letters.

The original Lakhish Letters mention the detrimental effects of the preaching of Uriah and other prophets, claiming that their words weakened the resolve of the military during the war with Babylon—in essence, accusing Uriah of treason. They discuss the inspection of Fort Lakhish by military officers from Jerusalem and they also contain the curse against the king and his offspring. The writings in the original Lakhish Letters are not as detailed as they appear in this chapter; however, all the information fictionalized here is supported by the writings in the Lakhish Letters (Torczyner, "Introduction to the Texts," in *The Lachish Letters*).

***

The cubit had varying standards of length, and in this novel the eighteen-inch Hebrew cubit is the standard measure. The Egyptian cubit measured two inches more than the Hebrew cubit (about twenty inches), because the pharaoh who adopted the use of the cubit for measure had a longer arm and hand than the standard used among the Jews. A short cubit was often used in Hebrew measurements. It was five palms, rather than six (The Church of Jesus Christ of Latter-day Saints, *Old Testament Student Manual: 1 Kings–Malachi*).

CHAPTER 2

The Old Testament records the use of different structures as prisons in Jerusalem (Jer. 37:15). The most frequently mentioned was a complex of prisons in or near the royal palace. In Lehi's day, an upper prison detained thieves, debtors, and others deemed minor criminals or threats to the kingdom. In this prison complex there may have also been a lower prison for traitors and criminals determined to be more of a threat to the kingdom, and it is possible that a pit called the "well of the prison" was located in that part of the prison. Some scholars suggest that the "well of the prison" was in a separate location, though there is no agreement as to the exact location of this detention facility (John Bright, *A History of Israel*, Philadelphia: Westminster Press, 1981). Detainees were lowered into the well by ropes (Jer. 38:6). The well or pit reached far enough below ground that seasonal rains or a rising water table saturated the earth and turned it into mire. It appears that the well of the prison was used as severe punishment for the worst criminals or the most offensive or dangerous detainees, as determined by the king and the princes and nobles of the city. Left long enough, prisoners were believed to face certain death inside the pit (Jer. 38:7–9). The portrayal of Uriah's prison cell is based on descriptions recorded in the book of Jeremiah (Jer. 38:6–13).

***

Seven hundred years before Lehi's day, Moses commanded Israel that, "ye shall not round the corners of your heads, neither shalt thou mar the corners of thy beard" (Lev. 19:27). Orthodox Jews today interpret that injunction as a command for men not to cut their sideburns, and modern Hassidic Jews often wear curling locks of hair that fall from beneath their skull caps and down over their ears. In the days of Moses, however, the prohibition against shaving the head along the side and back of the skull—a practice known as "rounding" among ancient peoples—was part of a greater prohibition against following the customs and practices of Israel's heathen neighbors. The Arabs of Lehi's day, living in the desert wilderness south of Jerusalem along the Arabian Peninsula 1200 years before Mohammed, rounded or cut their hair, leaving a tuft or bowl-cut of hair on the top of their heads in honor of Bacchus, the god of wine. Egyptian styles included shaving the sides of the head and cutting the top short, shaving the entire skull, or allowing for a ponytail in the side of their shaved heads, depending upon the god they honored. The Libyans and Chinese still practice the custom of rounding their hair in honor of idol gods—a practice forbidden to the Israelites (Adam Clark, *The Holy Bible with Commentary and Critical Notes*, New York: Abingdon–Cokesbury Press, n.d., vol. 6). Bible scholars indicate that the hair was used in divination among the ancients, and for religious superstition among the Greeks. At the time of the giving of this law [by Moses], the ancient author *Homer* indicates that it was customary for Greek parents to dedicate the hair of their sons to some god; when they came to manhood, they cut off their hair and consecrated it to deity. If the hair was rounded and dedicated for purposes of this kind, there is a strong possibility that Moses prohibited the rounding of the hair in order to keep the Jews from following after hair styles and fashions that stood in direct conflict with their religious beliefs, similar to the modern-day Latter-day Saint practice of prophets warning against fads and fashions that communicate a rejection of or rebellion against religious belief (*Old Testament Student Manual: Genesis–2 Samuel,* second edition, 186–87). The Old Testament does not indicate that the shaving of the head was an evil practice. In Lehi's day, the prophet Ezekiel shaved his head and beard, burning a third of it as a warning that a portion of the Jews living at Jerusalem would be destroyed. Ezekiel scattered another third of his hair to the wind as a reminder that a portion of the Jews would be spared and scattered about the earth (Ezek. 5:1–4, 12). There is little doubt that the shaven hairstyles popular in Egypt and other countries neighboring Judah during Lehi's day influenced the grooming of Jews at Jerusalem. In this chapter, Laban is shown to loathe the prohibition against rounding the hair. His actions in this chapter are intended to personify the imposition of foreign cultures on Hebrew life as well as to show the growing dislike for holy laws that were originally revealed by ancient prophets in order to set Israel apart from the world—a Jewish cultural rebellion that was gaining popularity among Jews at Jerusalem during Lehi's day.

***

In this chapter, Laban's declaration that there was no afterlife is taken from the writings of Book of Mormon authors who indicate their familiarity with the prevailing sentiments in Jerusalem during Lehi's day, as well as modern religious ideas regarding sin and its effect on eternal rewards. Laban's character includes the belief that it did not matter what a man did in this life, since God would allow for some sin (2 Ne. 28:7–8). In addition, Book of Mormon authors indicate that ancient peoples struggled with the naturalistic idea, still popular today, that life ends at death (Alma 30:18), and Laban's character personifies those powerful irreligious sentiments inherent in Jerusalem society during Lehi's day.

Chapter 3

The Rekhabites were not the only group of religious dissidents in Lehi's day, but their doctrines were similar to many groups (Jer. 35). The prophet Jeremiah and other prophets of his time were not typically associated with any religious faction within Judaism, but they did champion the cause of Rekhabites and others who shunned the popular religious and political fads of their day and called for a return to strict observance of the Law of Moses in anticipation of the coming of the Messiah. The Rekhabites were, in essence, a "Church of Anticipation" (Nibley, "Dark Days in Jerusalem: The Lakhish letters and the Book of Mormon," in *The Prophetic Book of Mormon*, 380–406).

A religious group similar to the Rekhabites called themselves Covenantors. They believed the Jewish religion had gone astray from the true teachings of Judaism and they wanted to worship according to what they called covenants. Among other things, they believed in continuing revelation, the probationary nature of this life, premortal existence and resurrection, and dispensations of the gospel with periods of falling away and restoration. They had a book of covenants called the *Manual of Discipline or Serek Scroll* (Nibley, Hugh W., "Qumran and the Waters of Mormon," in *An Approach to the Book of Mormon)*, and in that manual the authors record that: "Everyone who comes to the united order shall enter into the covenant of God before the eyes of all those who have dedicated themselves, and he shall place himself under solemn obligation by a strong oath to turn [or return] to the Law of Moses even to all he commanded, with all his heart and all his soul insofar as it has been revealed." They believed strongly in prophets, priesthood, eternal marriage, and eternal progeny. A group of these religious dissenters lived at the historic community of Qumran and left us the now-famous Dead Sea Scrolls, dating back as far as 300 B.C. and ending about A.D. 73. Hugh Nibley suggests that the Covenantors' society may have started long before the scrolls were written, possibly as early as seven to eight hundred years before Christ (Nibley, "More Voices From the Dust"). It is possible that the religious refugees of Lehi's day, the Rekhabites, were some of the founders of the group that wrote the Dead Sea Scrolls and who lived on the shores of the Dead Sea.

***

Judah became a true vassal state to Babylon between about 601 B.C. and the final destruction of the city some ten years later. The Babylonian government did not interfere with daily Hebrew life and allowed the noble classes in Jerusalem to govern. The Hebrew army functioned primarily as a police force during the Babylonian occupation, though it is probable they kept watch on the Babylonian army. In this chapter Daniel has returned from a patrol, monitoring the Babylonian troops stationed on Judah's eastern frontier.

***

The beginnings of Nephi's steel bow is unknown and this chapter fictionalizes the origin of that weapon. Nephi refers to his metal bow only once in passing, indicating that it was made of *fine* steel (1 Ne. 16:18). He employs the description "most precious steel" when writing of Laban's sword (1 Ne. 4: 9), and Book of Mormon scholar, John Tvedtnes, suggests that Lehi and his sons were blacksmiths by trade since Nephi described his steel bow in different language than he employs when describing Laban's sword, and only a man familiar with differing grades of steel would make such a distinction (John A Tvedtnes, "Was Lehi a Caravaneer?" in *The Most Correct Book: Insights from a Book of Mormon Scholar,* Salt Lake City: Cornerstone, 1999, 76–98). Hugh Nibley, however, suggests that there is overwhelming evidence in support of Lehi and his sons dealing in international trade with Egypt and, in particular, olive oil. At the turn of the sixth century B.C., selling Israeli olive oil to Egypt was a much more lucrative business than smithing, and in this novel Lehi and his sons are portrayed as having some knowledge of blacksmithing, but hiring Jonathan the blacksmith and his sons to do much of that work for them (Nibley, Hugh W. "Lehi in the Desert," in *Lehi in the Desert/The World of the Jaredites/There Were Jaredites.* ed. John W. Welch [The Collected Works of Hugh Nibley, vol. 5] Salt Lake City: Deseret Book, and Provo: F.A.R.M.S., 1988).

CHAPTER 4

Ornithologists agree that the modern pigeon was bred over many centuries and looks somewhat different than the pigeons of Lehi's day. Modern pigeons are related to the rock dove still common in Middle Eastern countries. The pigeon of Lehi's day would have been slightly smaller in size than the common gray pigeon with a longer, more slender body. However, the physical differences have not changed man's reliance on the pigeon as a carrier of messages. Ancient references indicate that generals in Pharaoh's army used trained pigeons to carry messages from the front lines of battle as early as 2400 years before the days of Lehi. Homing pigeons are known to fly more than a thousand miles in less than forty-eight hours (*World Book*, Field Enterprises Corporation, 1961, 8: 276). Pigeons have been used down through the centuries to carry messages back to their home over thousands of miles. The training of pigeons and their innate guidance system is detailed in the historical notes for Chapter 23.

***

Mima, the Ethiopian handservant, is a fictional character, though it was not uncommon for Ethiopians to live among the Hebrews in ancient times. The most familiar Ethiopian in Lehi's day was Ebed-Melech, a servant in King Zedekiah's court who begged mercy for Jeremiah and was responsible for saving him from starving to death in prison (Jer. 38).

***

The Dead Sea was most likely known in Lehi's day as the Salt Sea, but in this novel it is referred to as the Dead Sea to avoid confusion. It reaches a width of nine miles and its surface is about 1290 feet below the level of the Mediterranean Sea. The Jordan and other streams feed the Dead Sea. There is no outlet except evaporation, which accounts for the high mineral content of the water. There is no record of any marine life living in the waters or along the shores of the Dead Sea—the alkali content is too high for them to survive—hence the name of this body of water. In this chapter, Josiah the potter and his daughter's foiled attempts to find any source of food in the Dead Sea characterizes them as unfamiliar with this territory.

***

Josiah the potter is a fictional character who is intended to represent an ancient character known as the teacher of righteousness who was responsible for some of the writings in the Dead Sea Scrolls (Nibley, "More Voices From the Dust," in *The Old Testament and Related Studies*). Because these writings are dated between 200 B.C. and about A.D. 70, it is impossible for Josiah the potter to actually have written his teachings into those records. In this series of novels, it is suggested that the teacher of righteousness—characterized by Josiah the potter—left a legacy of teachings that are passed orally until they are ultimately written into the Dead Sea Scrolls many hundred years after his passing by those who kept alive his legendary teaching. His teachings are part of the *Manual of Discipline*. The teacher of righteousness in the Dead Sea Scrolls claimed divine guidance for his people, taught them what he knew about the Messiah, required strict observance of the Law of Moses, and introduced the idea of baptism, a sacrament or holy supper, and many other doctrines previously thought to have emerged after the advent of Christ. Some ancient Near Eastern scholars explain that phenomenon by suggesting that Jesus Christ and his cousin, John the Baptist, must have been associated with or educated by the descendants of these people who lived at Qumran up until it was destroyed by the Roman army about A.D. 72. Another possibility, rejected by many, is that the people at Qumran were guided by revelation from God, since their doctrines and organization parallel other dispensations of the gospel as revealed to prophets over the centuries. Among the writings in the Dead Sea Scrolls

are numerous references to a man who either founded the community of
Covenantors at Qumran or who was revered by them enough to be considered their
leader. In this novel he will ultimately become a legendary figure for those who
record his teachings in the Dead Sea Scrolls many hundred years later. As prolific as
the writings are, there is no mention of his name in the Dead Sea scrolls. The only
title given him in the written record is Teacher of Righteousness, and Dr. Hugh
Nibley suggests that may have been a code name to keep him or his descendants
from imprisonment (Nibley, "More Voices From the Dust," in *The Old Testament
and Related Studies*).

The remains of the ancient community of Qumran are located along the
northwest shores of the Dead Sea and are surrounded by rocky outcrops and cliffs.
Archaeologists have found a series of pools fed by a fresh-water spring and
connected by aqueducts and they are attributed to the society called Covenantors
who built the community there about 200 B.C. The first pools were used for ritual
washings and baptisms, the next pools for drinking water and storage, and the
remaining pools were for livestock. There were homes, meeting rooms, and what
appears to be a large communal kitchen and eating area. These structures are dated
to about 300 years after Lehi's day; however, some scholars suggest that the community possibly had its beginnings in Lehi's day or even earlier. In this chapter, the
people at Qumran live in tents and are only beginning to build the structures that
will ultimately be finished many years later by the community responsible for
writing the Dead Sea Scrolls (Nibley, "More Voices From the Dust").

The prophet Isaiah wrote that in the days of restoration and before the coming
of the Messiah, the desert would blossom like a rose (Isa. 25:1). During Lehi's day,
many Jews left Jerusalem seeking to live a purer form of their religion. The
Rekhabites (Jer. 36), among others, went out into the desert in search of a renewal
of their covenants and they hoped to see the desert blossom like a rose. Latter-day
Saints believe that their home in the desert mountains of Utah is a fulfillment of
Isaiah's prophecy that in the days of restoration, the desert will blossom (Nibley,
"More Voices From the Dust").

CHAPTER 5

The greatest threat to fletching on the ends of arrows is mites that eat away and
fray the feathers. Damaged fletching ruins the "trueness" or flight path of an arrow,
and since ancient times archers have protected the feathers on a bow by dipping
them in green tea to repel the insects (Gillelan, Howard G. *Complete Book of the
Bow and Arrow*, New York: Gallahad Books, 1971).

The use of the bow dates to well before the time of our oldest written records,
and by the time of the first Olympic games in 776 B.C., archery had become a
game of skill as well as a means of protection and food gathering (Lawrance, H. Lea
The Archers and Bowhunters of the Bible, New York: Doubleday, 1993). Ancient
bows of the eastern Mediterranean are responsible for the modern design of bows
used today. It was originally believed that the recurved design—the arms curving

away from the shooter in an arching pattern—was an invention of modern times, but Egyptian pictographs and hieroglyphics indicate that the Egyptians adopted the powerful design from their Assyrian enemies. An ancient Egyptian arrow on display at the Egyptian Museum of Ancient History in Cairo was made of reed and has a notch of bone in the end. The ancient pictorial records show Egyptian kings in target practice, and one rendering in particular shows a monarch shooting an arrow through a thick copper target, with the caption: *which had never been done nor even heard of in [history]* (Gillelan, *Complete Book of the Bow and Arrow*). Ancient bows were fashioned using layers of animal horn and sinew to strengthen the arms of the wooden bows. Though there is no record of a bow made of steel, archers were constantly fashioning bows of different materials to improve shooting distance and increase power, and it is not unlikely that they would pursue a bow made of steel if it were possible to smith the metal malleable enough not to break. It is also possible that Nephi was aware of the differing degrees of quality and workmanship when he referred to his bow as made of fine steel (1 Ne. 16:18), compared to the bow he hurriedly assembled from a straight stick as a replacement weapon in order to feed his starving family (1 Ne. 16:23). It is likely that the bow he fashioned from wood did not have the same power, nor could it flight an arrow as far as his steel bow.

***

The number of fifty men assigned to Laban's personal garrison is a common-sized unit for that time period. Nebuchadnezzar, in a letter to his officers, begins his order by writing, "as to the fifties under your command." Scholars of ancient military history also indicate that a typical Babylonian platoon contained fifty men and they were referred to as a "fifty" (Offord, Joseph, "Archaeological Notes on Jewish Antiquities," in *An Approach to the Book of Mormon*). Hugh Nibley indicates that Laban's garrison of fifty was rather small for a city as large as Jerusalem, but it appears that this group of men acted as a police force under Laban's direct orders rather than a larger force of many thousands of soldiers who took their orders indirectly from Laban through intermediary officers of the military (1 Ne. 3:31; 1 Ne. 4:1). It is possible that Laban's fifty were a feared group of soldiers since Laman and Lemuel were more concerned about them than they were the large numbers of soldiers under Laban's command (Nibley, *An Approach to the Book of Mormon*).

CHAPTER 6

Jebus and Moriah are fictional characters, but they are based on what we know about scribes and scribal practices in the ancient Near East. The keeping of records was an art form that required a good deal of education as well as a certain amount of mentoring, and apprenticeship was common among scribes. Prior to the discovery of the Lakhish Letters that date to 600 B.C. and a commemorative plaque left deep underground by the men who dug Hezekiah's water tunnel around 720 B.C., it was believed that Hebrew characters were written without attention to detail or any degree of penmanship. However, the discovery of these records indicates that ancient scribes possessed finely trained skills in the art of calligraphy and letters. Dr Torczyner, after extensive study of the Lakhish Letters, indicates that "the ancient Jews could write quickly and boldly, in an artistic flowing hand, with the loving penmanship of those who enjoy writing. Thus writing was almost common knowledge, and not a secret art known only to a very few; it certainly was practiced by many officials in the king's service." Torczyner also indicates that letter II of the Lakhish Letters is, "the best example of the bold, flowing, and even artistic handwriting of ancient Judah. In the straight lines upon the curved surface, in the energetic features of the God-name, one sees how the "ready scribe" both enjoys and loves to write. This single letter, coming from a place smaller than Lakhish (Qyriat Ye'arim), is in itself sufficient proof of highly developed penmanship in ancient Judah. In this chapter, Moriah is shown to possess these skills in full measure (Torczyner, "Introduction to the Texts," in *The Lachish Letters*).

Ancient records written on papyrus were subject to decomposition in less than a hundred years. Parchment scrolls written on animal hides proved much more resilient than papyrus records. Potsherds, or pieces of broken pottery, were a disposable medium used in notes and letters. More permanent records were imprinted in soft clay that hardened and could be stored—indefinitely if the clay were fired in a kiln. The fired clay tablets could break, but they did not decay like papyrus, parchment, or unfired clay tablets. Metal plates were a recording medium that could withstand the test of time. They were a tedious but purposeful means of preserving in writing the sacred rituals of ancient communities, their laws, religious doctrine of a prophetic nature, and their histories. They were bound together with rings much like pages in a book and were referred to as a codex. Ancient kings, monarchs, and religious leaders used them to record the most sacred or important documents and histories (William J. Hamblin, "Sacred Writings on Bronze Plates in the Ancient Mediterranean").

CHAPTER 7

Hannaniah is a historical figure mentioned in the Old Testament. He was the son of the prophet Azur and he served in the temple as a priest (Jeremiah 28). It is not certain why Hannaniah claimed to be a prophet and told the Jews living at Jerusalem that he had received revelation that the city would be delivered from Babylonian rule. His declaration was in direct conflict with the prophet Jeremiah's prophecy that Jerusalem and all of Judah would be subject to Babylonian rule for a period of seventy years. In this chapter, the motivation behind Hannaniah's false prophecy is money; however, the written history in the Old Testament does not indicate exactly why he acted as he did. More information regarding Hannaniah is included in the historical notes for Chapters 19 and 27.

Bible scholars indicate that there were many corrupt priests and false prophets in Lehi's day. Dr. J. Thompson indicates that the "[corrupt priests and false prophets] had no sense of shame for the loathsome deeds they perpetrated. They neither felt shame nor did they know how to blush." He also indicates that the false prophets were completely insensitive to the evils in which they and their nation were immersed (Thompson, J.A. "The Book of Jeremiah" in *The New International Commentary on the Old Testament,* ed. R. K. Harrison, Grand Rapids, MI: William B. Eerdmans Publishing Company, 1980). In this chapter Hannaniah joins Zadock in the personification of the corrupt practices of their time that Bible scholars indicate were prevalent in Jerusalem (Nibley, "Portrait of Laban," in *An Approach to the Book of Mormon*).

Up until the crucifixion of Christ, God commanded that animal sacrifices be offered in similitude of the sacrifice of the Only Begotten Son of God (Moses 5: 4–8). Prayer and devotion accompanied the sacrifices, and the Law of Moses included a complex set of rules for governing the offering of sacrifices. Originally, the Levite offering the sacrifice presented the animal at the temple and slew the animal with their own hands, but that practice was later replaced by priests who performed the sacrificial act and were given a portion of the meat for their support. The blood of the animal was collected by priests and sprinkled about the altar to signify atonement (Ex. 30:10; Lev. 8:15, 16:18, 17:11). There were a number of different sacrifices, including sin offerings made for crimes where the sin required atonement. Other offerings included trespass or guilt offerings, where the sin offended another as in the case of robbery.

Soothsayers in the Old Testament professed to foretell the future. They claimed to read the future through omens or objects, and their methods included watching the stars (astrology), observing the movements of clouds and animals, tying knots, casting lots, tossing arrows into the air and then reading the pattern of how they fell to determine the future. They were often associated with some sort of payment, similar to payments for astrological and palm readings in the modern world (Hastings, James "Magic, Divination and Sorcery," in *Dictionary of the Bible*, New York: Charles Scribner's Sons, 1909, 566–70).

CHAPTER 8

Nibley suggests that Captain Laban represents the "seamy side of the world of 600 B.C." (Nibley, "Portrait of Laban," in *An Approach to the Book of Mormon*). From the writings of Nephi in the Book of Mormon we learn that Laban met in secret with the Elders of the Jews. We cannot be certain if Captain Laban and Lehi's son Laman had any relationship prior to his return to Jerusalem to obtain the brass plates; however, Nephi associates Laman and Lemuel with the Elders of the Jews by accusing them of the same murderous designs, and it is not impossible that the two eldest sons in Lehi's family had some association with Laban and the Elders prior to their fleeing the capital city (1 Ne. 17: 44).

CHAPTER 9

King David and the prophet Ezekiel both attempted to standardize weights during their lifetime and it is possible that Ezekiel was an accountant or a lawyer in

Jerusalem, charged with the task of dealing with the monetary system in Jerusalem (*Old Testament Student Manual: 1 Kings–Malachi*). His association with the standardization of the monetary system may have raised him fairly high in the accounting hierarchy of the capital city, and in this chapter he is depicted as the chief accountant and chief lawyer in the kingdom.

***

During the final ten years of Babylonian occupation, beginning around 600 B.C., Zedekiah threatened to stop paying tribute to Babylon on three different occasions (John Bright, *A History of Israel*, Philadelphia: Westminster Press, 1981). The first two incidents did not result in any military conflict between the two nations, though the King of Babylon did send troops and threatened to level Jerusalem to the ground if the Jews did not comply with the terms of his rule. The details of why Zedekiah refused to pay the tax are not known and this novel fictionalizes that event (*Great People of the Bible and How They Lived;* see also Nibley, "Dark Days in Jerusalem").

CHAPTER 10

From the rule of King Hezekiah down to King Zedekiah, the Old Testament refers to nobles and princes of the city checking the power of the king at Jerusalem. This "New Aristocracy" was led by a man, or a group of men, referred to only as the "Head of the Palace," and the prophets referred to him as the "wrecker" or the "despoiler" (Nibley, "Portrait of Laban"). The Amarna Letters indicate that the ruling governors and Elders in the ancient cities of Israel, centuries before Lehi's day, were subordinate to men known as the princes of the city (William F. Allbright, "The Seal of Eliakim and the Latest Preexilic History of Judah, With Some Observations on Ezekiel," *The Journal of Biblical Literature*, 1932, 51:148). The Old Testament refers to a similar class of influential and wealthy men in Jerusalem during Lehi's day (Jer. 38). Nibley indicates that their authority was dependent on deception and intrigue. In the Amarna Letters these princes raid each others' caravans, accuse each other of unpaid debts and broken promises, denounce each other as traitors, and, above all else, seek to increase their personal fortunes. From the time of his appointment as king, Zedekiah vacillated between the prophetic call for peace with Babylon and the political pressure from the Elders of the Jews to end Babylonian rule in Judah and normalize relations with Egypt in order to increase trade and ultimately their wealth. We do not know if the Chief Elder of the Jews at Jerusalem at 600 B.C. asserted himself as the "Head of the Palace," but we do know that the prophets accused the elders and the princes of the city of scheming against the king and influencing the affairs of the kingdom, including the perilous decisions regarding payment of tax to Babylon. In this chapter the fictional designs of Zadock and Laban are representative of much of the scheming and deception typical of men of power in Jerusalem and other ancient cities in Israel during Lehi's day (Nibley,. "The Jerusalem Scene," F.A.R.M.S. Reprint, 1980).

CHAPTER 11

Ancient rope makers used methods similar to the pioneers of the American West. They hung threads of hemp or wool from hooks and turned them through hundreds of twists to form a thick rope. Anciently, rope was an expensive commodity and the care of rope was critical. Rope was oiled and stored off the ground, usually on a hook, to keep it from mildew (*Great People of the Bible and How They Lived*).

***

The brass plates were an important family record kept in Laban's treasury and they were considered national treasures (Rolph, Daniel N., "Prophets, Kings, and Swords: The Sword of Laban and its Possible Pre-Laban Origins," *Journal of Book of Mormon Studies,* vol. 2, no.1, 73–79.). They contained records from many centuries before Lehi's day; however, it is likely that a scribe or caretaker of the plates was adding to that record around 600 B.C. since the prophecies of Jeremiah, a contemporary to Lehi, were part of the record (1 Ne. 5:11–13). In this chapter, Elizabeth and Zoram are helping Jeremiah add new plates to the brass record. This story of the brass plates is a major theme in future volumes of this series; however, in this volume, *Power of Deliverance*, they play a more minor role.

Many Bible scholars believe that the ordinance of baptism began in the days of Jesus Christ along with the institution of the breaking of bread and drinking of wine as a sacrament in remembrance of Christ (Hugh Nibley, "More Voices From the Dust"). The book of Moses, however, indicates that baptisms for religious purposes have been practiced whenever the gospel of Jesus Christ has been on the earth. Adam was baptized (Moses 6:64–68) and all the prophets and patriarchs throughout time were also given that ordinance. The Book of Mormon indicates that baptism was practiced long before the advent of Christ upon the earth (2 Ne. 31; Mosiah 18:8–17), and Paul indicates that Moses baptized the Children of Israel in the sea (1 Cor. 10:1–4). Lehi understood the importance of baptism, and his son, Nephi, records that his father saw in vision, many hundred years before that event actually took place, that Christ would be baptized with water (1 Ne. 10: 9–10). The prophet Jeremiah made reference to baptism, and though he does not address the ordinance specifically, he asks the people of Jerusalem to wash their hearts from wickedness in order to be saved (Jer. 4:14), and for that reason, this chapter portrays Jeremiah inviting Ruth and members of her family to submit to baptism.

CHAPTER 12

In this chapter, Sariah reacts to her husband's vision of reading from a book her husband received from an angel. Sariah's response to Lehi's revelation is an attempt to incorporate what scholars refer to as the Heavenly Book motif, and this chapter draws from three sources to describe that motif: Lehi's own account (1 Ne. 1:11–14, 18–19); Ezekiel's account of reading from a heavenly book (Eze. 2:6–10, 3:1–3); and the writings of John the Apostle (Rev.10). The Book of Mormon record indicates that Lehi received two revelations at the time of his call to prophethood. The first seems to be an apparition of a heavenly being and in the first volume in this series, *Pillar of Fire*, it is attributed to the appearance of the premortal Christ (1 Ne. 1:6). The second revelation was an extensive vision where Lehi was given a book in which, among other things, he read of the destruction of Jerusalem (1 Ne. 1:11–14). The prophet Ezekiel, a contemporary of Lehi, had a similar experience in which he was given a roll (book) and commanded to eat it, which was in keeping with the custom and tradition of ancient Israel, signifying that he was eating the bread of life, that he was partaking of the good word of God, that he was feasting upon the words of Christ (Bruce R. McConkie, *Doctrinal New Testament Commentary,* Bookcraft, 1973, 3:507). Ezekiel writes that the words were "in his mouth sweet as honey." Ezekiel also states that the book, after he ate it, made his "belly bitter" (Ezek. 2:6–10, 3:1–3). This feeling of "bitterness" could be a reference to the judgments and plagues promised in the book to those to whom the Lord's word is sent and was cause for Ezekiel to despair and have sorrow of soul. It may also be a reference to the trepidation the prophet felt when he was commanded by God to publicly preach the destruction of Jerusalem he read about in the heavenly book to a people who were capable of killing him for his words. After Lehi publicly testified of what he read from the heavenly book he faced threats of mocking (1 Ne. 1:18) as well as threats of death similar to prophets who had testified before him (1 Ne. 1:19). It is not impossible for Ezekiel to have been aware of the reaction of the Jews at Jerusalem to Lehi's preaching and that may have added to the bitterness he felt in his belly. The Apostle John in the New Testament had a vision similar to those of Lehi and Ezekiel. He was given a book and commanded to eat it (Rev. 10:9–11). John recorded that when he ate the book, "it was in my mouth sweet as honey"; and as soon as he had eaten it, his belly turned bitter. Joseph Smith indicates that the heavenly book given to John dealt with his mission to the tribes of Israel (D&C 77:14), which follows very closely with John's own account in Revelation in which he records that after he read from the book, he was commanded to preach the prophecies he'd read in the book before many peoples, nations, and tongues. It is not unlikely that when John refers to the heavenly book making him sick or bitter in his belly (Rev. 10:10), he was either referring to the destructions written in the book, or the difficulty of his mission and the apprehension it caused. After Lehi read from the heavenly book, he went among the people of Jerusalem and declared to them concerning the prophetic destructions, which he had both seen and heard in vision, and was later told in vision that he had been a faithful servant in the face of danger (1 Ne. 2:1). Despite the prophetic words of destruction, Lehi is joyous to the point of jubilation and praise regarding what he reads in the heavenly book (1 Ne. 1:13–15), a reaction similar to Ezekiel's joy upon reading the word of God, though he does not compare the word to honey, as do Ezekiel and John. Lehi is silent with regard to his personal reaction to the command to go among the people and preach what he had heard and seen, though it is not impossible that he felt similar anxieties to those of Ezekiel the prophet, his contemporary, or John the Apostle. In this chapter, Sariah personifies the apprehension both she and her husband may have felt with regard to Lehi's preaching and prophesying to a wicked people who were not willing to receive him (1 Ne.1:18–19).

***

We do not know when Sariah gave birth to Jacob and Joseph, her two youngest children. The Book of Mormon gives no account as to her pregnancy or the timing of the births except to say that Jacob was born in a *time of tribulation in the wilderness* while Joseph was born during a *time of great suffering in the wilderness,* which may be a reference to two distinct portions of the family's eight-year odyssey in the wilderness (2 Ne. 2:1). The marriage of the sons of Lehi to the daughters of Ishmael, a few years after their departure from Jerusalem, seems to divide the time of tribulation from the time of great suffering. During the first years of Lehi's time in the Arabian wilderness, it appears he and his family camped in the Valley of Lemuel where there was a continually running river of water (1 Nephi 2:9), grain, and conditions that allowed them to set up an encampment with tents for an indefinite period of time. The reference to this time as a time of tribulation may be in regard to the forced departure of the family from Jerusalem and the internal family turmoil that their flight caused. Some of Lehi's greatest words of anguish over his family come from this time period (1 Ne. 2:9–15), as does his well-known dream of the tree of life where he sees in vision his eldest sons rejecting the message of salvation (1 Ne. 8). It is not impossible for Sariah to have been with child prior to her departure, only to give birth to her firstborn in the wilderness in the months following that flight. Nephi writes that the "women" in their company gave birth to children in the wilderness (1 Ne. 17:1–2). This may be a reference to the newlywed women, or it could also include Sariah and Ishmael's wife. Lehi refers to Jacob as his firstborn in the wilderness, and says that he suffered because of the rudeness of his older brothers Laman and Lemuel (2 Ne. 2:1). Jacob would have had to be old enough during the latter portion of Lehi's eight-year journey ending at the shores of Bountiful to be aware of the "rudeness" of his brothers, and that indicates that he may have been born fairly early in the family's flight from Jerusalem. Lehi refers to Joseph as his last-born in the wilderness. The Liahona compass was left at Lehi's tent door immediately after the marriages of his sons to Ishmaels' daughters, possibly the morning after the wedding ceremonies (1 Ne. 16:6–10). The finding of the Liahona ushered in a period of travel through the harshest parts of the Arabian Peninsula, and it is possible that Joseph was born after the family began their journey out of the Valley of Lemuel and traveled toward the land of Bountiful through terrain that would have certainly been the cause of Lehi's *greatest suffering in the wilderness* (2 Ne. 3:1).

CHAPTER 13

Jeremiah was a vineyard owner as well as a prophet, and his writings are filled with metaphors of vineyard keeping (Jer. 12), where he often complains to God that the wicked prosper and have taken root in Jewish society. He preached, as did Lehi and Ezekiel, against increased immorality, selfishness, and their fanatical self-deception and unwillingness to accept that God would allow Jerusalem to be destroyed. He faced opposition from the priests, the mob, from his own townsmen in Anathoth, from the king (Jer. 36:19), and from the army (Jer. 38:4). During Jeremiah's forty-year ministry he was banished from the city numerous times. He was often thrown into prison, only to be released or saved from the dungeons. Many of Jeremiah's visions occurred within prison walls. This chapter depicts the end of one of his banishments from Jerusalem, which began in the previous novel in this series, *Pillar of Fire*.

CHAPTER 15

The first chapter of the book of Ezekiel details a revelation he received after his exile to the northern provinces of Babylon and was living among the captives by the River Chebar. This was about four years after King Jehoiakim was taken by the Babylonians, and his uncle, Zedekiah, was appointed vassal king of Judah (Ezek. 1:1–2). For this reason Ezekiel is considered to be the prophet to exiles. The book of Ezekiel is not a chronological account of visions and revelations and it is not certain if the vision in the opening chapter of the book of Ezekiel was his first. We do not know when Ezekiel was deported from Jerusalem, nor do we know why he was deported to the northern provinces, except that it fulfilled the purpose of God to have a prophet among the captive Jews in that part of the world. It is possible that Ezekiel was still living among the Jews at Jerusalem in the first few years after Zedekiah was made king. In this chapter, Ezekiel is shown receiving his initial inspiration and revelations regarding Israel and his mission among the Jews before his exile from the capital city, and well before he received the vision detailed in the first chapter of the book of Ezekiel in the Old Testament.

Ezekiel recorded his prophecies while living in Babylon and may have been familiar with the practice of Babylonian cuneiform writing when he penned his revelations regarding the sticks of Joseph and Judah. Babylonian scribes pressed a wedge-shaped stylus into moist clay tablets—the most preferred writing medium among ancient Babylonian scribes. Prior to finding another writing medium, archaeologists believed clay tablets were the only writing medium used by Babylonian scribes. San Nicolo theorized that the Babylonians may have also used wooden tablets for their writings, similar to the tablets used by Roman and Greek scribes. The wooden boards were covered with a thick wax coating and the edges raised to allow for the wooden tablets to be placed one atop the other. Archaeologist Max Mallowan made the first discovery supporting this theory of wooden tablets, rather than clay, preserved in a layer of sludge at the bottom of a well in the city of Nimrud in what was ancient Babylon (Keith H. Meservy, "Job: Yet Will I Trust in

Him," in Sydney B. Sperry Symposium, Provo: Brigham Young University, 1978). The cover boards had hinge marks on both sides, making it evident that all the tablets had been joined together, and Mallowan announced his discovery as the oldest known example of a book. The Hebrew word *etz* has been translated in the English King James Version of the Bible as stick or rod, a very strange departure from the basic and more common meaning of wood. Latter-day Saints interpret Ezekiel's prophecy (Ezek. 37:15–20) as the joining of two scriptural records in modern days into one volume of scripture: the Book of Mormon as the stick of Joseph, and the Bible as the stick Judah. It is possible that Ezekiel described his revelation of the stick (wood tablet) of Joseph, based on his Babylonian experience of seeing scribes writing on the wax surface of ancient wooden books called sticks or wood (Meservy, "Job: Yet Will I Trust in Him").

CHAPTER 16

The practice of preparing two identical documents and then sealing one of the two was common practice in the ancient world, and the use of a double, sealed parchment described in this chapter is based on an ancient legal practice common in Israel at 600 B.C. (John W. Welch, "Double, Sealed, Witnessed Documents: From the Ancient World to the Book of Mormon," in *Mormons, Scripture, and the Ancient World,* ed Davis Bitton, Provo: F.A.R.M.S., 1998). The documents had two parts: one was left open, while the other was sealed for later consultation or the use of a judge. When the prophet Jeremiah purchased land near his home in Anathoth (Jer. 32:9–10) he prepared a document, part of it sealed and another part left open. Jeremiah writes that he acted according to the custom and law of his time (Jer. 32: 11), and technical terms of law are part of Jeremiah's description of this document and the transaction of his land purchase (John Bright, "Jeremiah" in *The Anchor Bible,* Garden City, NY: Doubleday, 1965, 237). There are many examples extant today of double, sealed documents. They were typically written on one side of a single sheet of papyrus or parchment with the text copied twice, once at the top and again toward the bottom with a space about 2–3 centimeters wide between the two renderings of the text. In some instances the sealed portion was an exact copy, and in other cases it was an abridgement. The open copy was intended for daily use and the other sealed to prevent fraud and alterations. The open portion allowed for parties to orient themselves with regard to the terms of the contract, while the sealed portion guarded against tampering (Elisabeth Koffmahn, "Die Doppelurkunden aus der Wuste Juda," Lieden: Brill, 1968, 19). A standard sealing procedure included folding the sealed portion, threading bands through holes punched along the middle before affixing a wax or clay impression over the bands. Metal plates were also sealed—similar to the description Joseph Smith gives of the sealed portion of the gold plate record entrusted to him by Moroni (JS–H 1:65). Anciently, holes were cut into metal plate documents and brass wires were used to seal them together. It is possible that the sealed portion of the plates given to Joseph Smith for translation were a second copy or abridgement of the original, rather than additional scripture; however, there is no way to be certain. In this chapter, Miriam prepares a double, sealed document on parchment that was commonly used for legal and otherwise important documents in Lehi's day.

***

In Lehi's day, the only fast ordered by the law was the Day of Atonement. It was regarded as a national day of fast. On that day, the high priest presented two goats at the door of the temple. He cast lots to determine which goat would be sent away into the wilderness and which would become the scapegoat to be sacrificed on the altar. He pronounced a blessing over the head of the first goat, transferring all the sins of the people to the animal, and had a man from the congregation lead it out into the desert for release. The temple was then cleared of everyone but the high priest while he sacrificed the second goat (Lev. 16:21–22). At some point in history, a ribbon or bell was placed about the neck of the goat sent into the wilderness, indicating that this was the goat let free from the temple on the Day of Atonement, and any who should run across the animal should not take it for food and risk the judgments of God. The goat was to roam free, symbolizing repentance and freedom from sin. It was also believed the evil spirit resided in the wilderness and that these people were returning their sins to the devil, carried on the head of this goat. The second goat sacrificed on the altar in honor of the Atonement to be made by the Messiah was called the scapegoat (Lev. 16:23–26). Modern English uses the word scapegoat to identify a person who symbolically suffers some sort of punishment in the stead of another, any person bearing blame for others, or suffering bad luck for another. The modern usage of the word has its roots in this practice from ancient Israel where the freed goat represented the carrying away of sin and the sacrificed "scapegoat" represented the vicarious act of atonement. The Bible record does not specifically name the scapegoat as symbolic of Jesus Christ or the Messiah; however, it does indicate that the high priest offered the sacrifice vicariously in the place of the Messiah who would ultimately offer Himself as a sacrifice for sin.

CHAPTER 17

In this chapter, Rebecca ponders the custom of reciting the Jewish *Shema*, comparing her love for Aaron to the love she has for God and her desire to write that love on her heart, her lips, and the doorpost of the blacksmith shop. Among Jews, the *Shema* is an affirmation of love of God and a commitment to his purposes to love and serve him with all their hearts. The *Shema*—Hebrew for the command to Israel to hear the word of God— is often referred to by Jews as the acceptance of the Yoke of the Kingdom of Heaven (*Encyclopedia Judaica, Jerusalem*: Keter Publishing House, 1972, vol. 14, 1372). Christ may have been quoting the *Shema* from the Old Testament when he taught that loving God was the greatest commandment and adding that a similar, second commandment was to love your neighbor as yourself (Matt. 22:36–37). The entire *Shema* (Deut. 6:4–5) is recited twice daily by devout Jews as part of evening and morning prayer. Jewish martyrs are expected to face death with the *Shema* on their lips and parents are to teach their children to cultivate an attitude of love toward God with the belief that it will change society, guiding men toward righteous living and blessings from heaven (*Encyclopedia Judaica, Jerusalem,* 14:1373). Restoration scriptures contain similar affirmations of love and commitment to God (D&C 101:35–38). The sixth chapter of Deuteronomy where the *Shema* is found includes a figurative command to the faithful to bind the words of this prayer to their foreheads and hands and to put them on the doorposts of their homes (Deut. 6:8–9; 11:18, 20). This decree led to the dual Jewish custom of wearing a *tepillin* around the forehead and upper arm and placing a *mezuzah* on the doorpost of Jewish homes. Jews inscribed scriptural passages on parchment, including the *Shema* but not limited to it, folded them into tiny leather boxes less then two inches square and wore the *tepillin*, Hebrew for phylactery, on the forehead and the left bicep, suggesting that they would fulfill the law with the head and the heart (Samuel Fallows, "The Popular and Critical Bible Encyclopedia and Scriptural Dictionary," 1911, 3:1344). Years after Moses first encouraged Jews to love God and bind his word to their hearts, some Jews, without the guidance of living prophets, viewed the *tepillin* as an amulet or charm with power to ward off evil spirits. At the same time, the use of the *mezuzah*, Hebrew for doorpost, gained popularity. Scriptural passages and the words of the *Shema* were inserted into a tiny, cylindrical box and attached to the door frame. It was customary for Jews to touch or kiss the *mezuzah* each time they left or entered, reminding all who pass to do the will of God as they go out among their fellow man (*Old Testament Student Manual: Genesis–2 Samuel,* second edition (1982), 218).

CHAPTER 18

Isaiah called the land of Israel Beulah, signifying that the Lord delighted in the Jews, as a bridegroom rejoices over his bride (Isa. 62:4–5). Beulah is Hebrew for "married," and in this chapter the character Beulah is named for her desire to wed Moriah.

***

The frequent grammatical use of the phrase "and it came to pass" in the Book of Mormon is similar to its use in the ancient written language of the Egyptians. The original translation of the Book of Mormon contains little or no punctuation, dividing the thoughts by introducing each phrase using the word "and," "behold," and "it came to pass." Ancient Egyptian texts begin each new thought with the same words, "it happened that" or "it came to pass" written as Khpr-n. These points of Egyptian grammar could not be omitted in writing, much the same as punctuation cannot be omitted in English writing. The use of Khpr-n as punctuation is much more common in Egyptian writing than in Hebrew, and since the Book of Mormon was written originally in the language of the Egyptians, it is not unexpected to find that Joseph Smith translated many thousands of sentences and paragraphs that begin with this phrase (Nibley, *Since Cumorah,* second edition, ed. John W. Welch [Collected Works of Hugh Nibley, vol. 7] Salt Lake City: Deseret Book, and Provo: F.A.R.M.S., 1988, 150).

***

Ancient writing was recorded on papyrus made from the reeds of the Nile Delta, on leather parchments made of tanned animal hides, on hardened clay tablets, and on potsherds—broken pieces of pottery. The most expensive writing medium was imported Egyptian papyrus that was not readily available in times of war. The Babylonians preferred the use of clay tablets and though that practice was not common in Israel, the influence of Babylon during Lehi's day may have increased its use among Hebrew scribes. Leather parchment from the hides of animals was the most formal writing surface used in Israel and its use among Hebrew scribes was widespread. Most official documents and records were recorded on parchment. Broken pottery was hoarded in bins and used as a writing medium much the way scratch paper is used today. It was an inexpensive alternative to parchment and it was used in letters as well the work of scribes and may have been used as a practice surface for learning the art of letters. The Lakhish Letters were a collection of eighteen potsherds written with carbonized ink. Dr. Harry Torczyner suggests they were original letters rather than a rough draft, but it is impossible to make a final determination. In this novel the potsherds are employed as a rough-draft medium—and intermediate surface—while the writings from the letters are transferred from parchment to clay tablet (Starkey, "Summary," in *The Lachish Letters).*

CHAPTER 19

The account of Hannaniah the false prophet is taken directly from the Old Testament (Jer. 28). Jeremiah carried a wooden yoke around Jerusalem on his shoulders to remind citizens of the prophesied seventy-year captivity to the Babylonians. Many Bible scholars compare Jeremiah's wooden yoke to the cross Christ would carry six hundred years later. The Old Testament account indicates that Jeremiah welcomed the news from Hannaniah, but challenged its authenticity when so many prophets like Lehi and Uriah were foretelling continued occupation by Babylon and possible destruction of Jerusalem. Hannaniah responded by removing Jeremiah's yoke and breaking it into pieces. It is not apparent whether Jeremiah received a revelation regarding the false nature of Hannaniah's prophecy immediately after the breaking of the yoke, or if he left the temple grounds and returned another day, but the Old Testament is clear that he heard the voice of Lord encouraging him to tell Hannaniah that his false preaching would result in the making of yokes of iron for the Jewish people (Jer. 28:12). Jeremiah declared Hannaniah a false prophet in public, denouncing him for encouraging the Jews to trust in a lie. Then he cursed him to die within the year, in the seventh month (Jer. 28:16–17). Much of the dialogue in this chapter between Hannaniah and Jeremiah is taken directly from the scriptural account (Jer. 28:2, 6–11).

CHAPTER 20

The book of Jeremiah refers to the prophet Uriah as "Urijah," a phonetic preference of the English translators (Jer. 27:20). In the Old Testament account of Uriah's trial his father's name is spelled Shemaiah from the town of Kirjath-jearim while the Lakhish Letters and many bible scholars prefer the spelling Shema Yahu and Qiryat Ye'arim respectively (Nibley, "Dark Days in Jerusalem). The Lakhish Letters indicate that Shema Yahu was accompanied by Yaush to the land of Jerusalem to see to the aid of his son. We do not know what assistance he sought or received, but it is unlikely that Lehi was involved; however, to develop the story in this novel, Shema Yahu is portrayed as seeking help from Lehi.

***

Nephi records that his father kept extensive personal records detailing his visions and prophetic utterances, and that the record he made of his father's history was only an abridgement of a much larger record kept by Lehi (1 Ne. 1:16–17, 6:3). It is possible that some or all of the account Nephi refers to was among the 116 pages of original Book of Mormon manuscript that was lost by Martin Harris. We do know that Joseph Smith referred to those lost pages as the "Book of Lehi," but it is impossible to know if that lost manuscript contained all or only a fraction of Lehi's writings (D&C 3; D&C 10; History of the Church 1:21–23). Joseph Smith shared publicly many intimate details about Lehi and his family that do not appear in the Book of Mormon, and he may have learned much of that information from his translation of the Book of Lehi (Sidney B. Sperry, "Did Lehi Have Daughters Who Married the Sons of Ishmael?" *Improvement Era,* Sept. 1952, 642. A reprint is available through the F.A.R.M.S. Sperry Archive). In this chapter, Aaron reads a portion of Lehi's spiritual history that was abridged by his son Nephi and that appears in the first chapter of the Book of Mormon (1 Ne. 1:11–13).

***

The theme of deliverance is a powerful motif throughout the recorded history of the Jews since the day Moses led the Children of Israel out of Egyptian bondage. Nephi draws on those images to describe his family's spiritual bondage and ultimate flight from Jerusalem (1 Ne. 4:2–3; 5:15). The title for this work of fiction is taken directly from the words of Nephi. His father's preaching of the destruction of Jerusalem angered the Jews to the point of plotting Lehi's murder, and Nephi pauses in his account and reaffirms his faith that God is merciful even unto the *Power of Deliverance* (1 Ne. 1:20).

It is not known whether Lehi struggled in a similar way to Ezekiel, a contemporary prophet, and John of the New Testament (see historical notes for Chapter 12); however, it is possible that Lehi understood the danger of preaching the destruction of Jerusalem by the Babylonians. The political climate in the capital city was polarized between the call for peace by the prophets and the desire of the elders to defy Babylonian occupation (Nibley, "Dark Days in Jerusalem"). It was blasphemous to speak of the destruction of Jerusalem in the heretical times of 600 B.C., and Lehi may have struggled with his decision to appear publicly in Jerusalem and prophesy the coming judgments of God.

CHAPTER 21

Meror, Hebrew for bitter herbs, are eaten during Passover in remembrance of the bitterness of Egyptian bondage. Any plant that is bitter, possesses sap, and has a gray appearance is considered a bitter herb, and lettuce and horseradish are both used. The custom is intended to remind Jews of past bitterness, enable them to distinguish between bitter and sweet in the present, and fortify them for the challenges they are to overcome in the future *(Popular Judaica Library,* "Passover," Philadelphia, PA: Jewish Publication Society of America, 1973, 58).

***

The exact ingredients for haroset differ, but it is generally a paste made of fruit, spices, wine, and matzoh (unleavened bread) meal. Other ingredients include almonds, cinnamon, and red wine. The Yemenite Jews also use chili pepper. It is intended to be a dessert eaten during the celebration of Passover. The word haroset may have derived from the Hebrew word heres (clay), since it is intended to resemble the mortar the Jews made for building pharaoh's palaces and pyramids (Popular Judaica Library "Passover, 58).

CHAPTER 22

The Romans were the first agriculturalists to standardize and write a manual for the growing and production of olives. Olive culture, however, flourished in Israel long before the Roman rise to power and their subsequent fascination for olive production. Ancient Jews were familiar with the olive tree and the tasks associated with its care. The Old Testament and Book of Mormon are replete with references to olive and olive oil production, and most scholars agree that the olive tree had its beginnings in and around the high plateaus of Judah and neighboring countries (John Gee and Daniel C. Peterson, "Graft and Corruption: On Olives and Olive Culture in the Pre-Modern Mediterranean," in *The Allegory of The Olive Tree,* Steven D. Ricks and John W. Welch, eds., Salt Lake City: Deseret Book, and Provo: F.A.R.M.S., 1994, 186–247).

Ancient vineyard keepers began their pruning fifteen days before the vernal equinox and trimmed for the next forty-five days, as recorded in ancient Hebrew texts

(Mishnah, Shebitt 2:2–3). The wood from pruning is hard, crooked, brittle, and knotty and is good only for burning (Mishnah, Shebitt 4:1). The sabbatical year (every seven years) was the season for hewing down the branches and throwing them into the fire.

Grafting was done in the spring in the dark of the moon, and in this chapter Lehi is depicted grafting an olive tree at night. A clean diagonal cut is made across the branch and the end of the graft is sharpened before it is inserted beneath the bark. The seam between the branch and the graft is smeared with a mixture of dung and dirt. Grafting increased the production of olive trees, and it was an important enough practice to the success of Judah's agriculture economy that it was regulated by law. All vineyard keepers were required to graft (Gee and Peterson, "Graft and Corruption: On Olives and Olive Culture in the Pre-Modern Mediterranean," 186–247).

***

In this chapter, the old olive tree in Lehi's vineyard is named House of Israel after the olive tree in the Allegory of the Olive Tree. The central metaphor in the allegory is a tame olive tree that the prophet Zenos compares to the House of Israel (Jacob 5:3). The other metaphors (the wild olive tree referring to non-Israelites; the pruning, digging, and nourishing representing God's care of the House of Israel (Jacob 5:6); the decay in the tame tree representing apostasy from the gospel of Jesus Christ; and the fruit of the tree representing the souls of men as they become good or bitter through their works), are all secondary images to the expression of God's aspirations for the House of Israel. (Hoskisson, Paul Y., "The Allegory of the Olive Tree in Jacob," in *The Allegory of The Olive Tree,* Steven D. Ricks and John W. Welch, eds. Salt Lake City: Deseret Book, and Provo: F.A.R.M.S., 1994, 186-247).

The allegory presents seven identifiable periods of Jewish and world history with Lehi living about the time of the closing of the second period described in the allegory. The most likely era for the first time period in the allegory that correlates with the planting of the tame olive tree, is probably around the times of the patriarchs, about 2100 B.C. By the time this allegory begins, the tame olive tree (the House of Israel) has "waxed old" and about 400 to 600 years could have passed away since it was first cultivated.

The second time period is denoted as the time of the scattering of the House of Israel, and Lehi and his family would have lived in Jerusalem near the end of this period (Jacob 5:4–14). The second time period from the allegory is what Lehi and Ishmael share with Aaron in this chapter, and it details God's attempt to reclaim the House of Israel from apostasy by sending prophets like Moses, Samuel, Elijah, and Isaiah to dig about the tree, prune it, and nourish it. The Lord of the vineyard met with minimal success, with the tree putting forth a few young and tender branches while most of the tree continued to deteriorate (Jacob 5:6). This portion of the allegory (Jacob 5: 4–14) makes clear that the ruling class, the "main top" of the tree was for the most part beyond recovery (Jacob 5:6), and in this chapter Aaron is warned that his father is part of that ruling class and is in danger of the judgments of God.

At some point during this second historical time period described in the allegory, the Lord of the vineyard directs the servant to take three measures to preserve some of the fruit of the tree: cut out those parts of Israel in apostasy (Jacob 5:7); graft other people into the House of Israel (Jacob 5:9); and graft or plant some of the young and tender branches from the House of Israel into other parts of the vineyard (Jacob 5:8).

The first step in this process (Jacob 5:7), may have occurred when the Assyrians destroyed the northern kingdom of Israel in wars beginning around 734 B.C. and culminated with the fall of that kingdom in 721 B.C, when the Assyrians carried away captive many of the inhabitants of that land. The Assyrians carried away citizens of the southern kingdom of Judah as well, though they stopped short of taking the capital at Jerusalem—a miraculous event that may have been the fulfillment of the prophecies of Micah, which are also part of the storyline in this book and are described in greater detail in the historical notes for Chapters 23, 28, and 29. The Babylonians completed this phase of scattering by destroying the southern kingdom in battles between 605 B.C. and 586 B.C. and taking captive the remaining inhabitants of Judah (Hoskisson, "The Allegory of the Olive Tree in Jacob," 186–247).

The second instruction given in this portion of the allegory (Jacob 5:9)—grafting other people into the House of Israel—may have been completed by the Assyrians who, after carrying away captive the ten tribes of the northern kingdom and intermingling them with other nations along the upper Mediterranean, imported people from many nations under their control into northern Israel. This practice led to intermarriage among the Israelites who remained in the land (2 Kgs. 17:24; Ezra 4:2, 10). When the Jews of the southern kingdom returned from Babylon after seventy years in captivity, they had retained their identity as a people, and they looked on their brethren who were the remnants of the ten tribes of the northern kingdom as a bastard nation, having intermarried with gentile nations. The Bible is replete with inferences to Samaritans as racially inferior (Matt. 10:5; Luke 9:52; 10:33, 17:16; John 4:9, 39, 8:48), though the allegory of the olive tree makes it clear that this intermarriage was a step in God's plan to rid the House of Israel of apostasy (Jacob 5:8).

The third instruction given in this portion of the allegory of the olive tree—grafting or planting some of the young and tender branches from the House of Israel into other parts of the vineyard (Jacob 5:8)—involved transporting Israelites faithful to the laws of Moses and their covenants made in the holy temple at Jerusalem to other lands. Lehi and his family qualify as some of the young and tender branches described in the allegory. In this fictional account, Lehi indicates that he and his family will be part of this random scattering in order to preserve some of the good fruit of the House of Israel (Jacob 5: 11-14). The next period of history alluded to in the allegory is the advent of Jesus Christ and it is separated from the history of Lehi's day by a single verse indicating that a long time passed away (Jacob 5:15).

CHAPTER 23

Pigeons employ a dual system of homing. Over short distances of less than about fifteen or twenty miles, the pigeon uses buildings, mountains, bodies of water, and other recognizable features in the local area as a guide. On flights over greater distances, where the route has never been flown and where there are no familiar landmarks, pigeons use a sack of iron at the base of their eyes much like a magnetic compass. The reverse polarity of the earth's crust acts as a magnetic map, guiding the pigeon over many thousands of miles. Once the pigeon approaches its home, the magnetic compass is no longer useful and the bird must recognize familiar geographic landmarks to arrive at its destination. The pigeons in this novel traveled far enough they would have employed both guiding systems to arrive at their final destination. Samantha, the partially blind pigeon in this chapter, Samantha, would not have had difficulty in the initial part of her flight from Qumran; however, once she arrived near the environs of Jerusalem, she would have had more difficulty than other birds finding her final destination.

***

This chapter introduces a collection of scrolls called the Scrolls of the Law. These scrolls are a fictional representation of the ancient texts available to the Elders of the Jews at Jerusalem in Lehi's day, which later became part of the Old Testament record near the beginning of the Christian era. Zadock references the writings of the prophet Micah in this chapter. The book of Micah appears near the end of the Old Testament; however, if it were to be placed in chronological order, it would appear ahead of the book of Jeremiah.

Micah lived at the time of the fall of the northern kingdom and began his preaching about 721 B.C. His prophecies include the foretelling of the fate of both the northern and southern kingdoms, and in this novel the story of Micha and his prophecies are critical to the outcome of Uriah's trial. More detail regarding Micha's prophecies and history are included in the historical notes for Chapter 28. The ancient writings of prophets that eventually became the modern Christian Old Testament were originally written in Hebrew and some Aramaic. There are three ancient, overlapping sources that cover the time period attributed to the Old Testament—the Hebrew massoretic texts, the Greek translations called the Septuagint, and texts preserved by the Samaritans called the Samaritan Pentateuch. Tradition indicates that the Greek Septuagint was translated from Hebrew in 70 days by 72 elders sent from Jerusalem. It was intended for the use of Greek-speaking Jews living in the city of Alexandria about 284 B.C. Many of the Old Testament quotations that appear in the New Testament were taken from this version of the ancient texts rather than the Hebrew massoretic versions that comprise nearly all of the King James Version of the Old Testament. At the time the Septuagint was translated, Greek was the international language; the translations provided the first reading of ancient Jewish doctrines outside of the lands of Israel. At the beginning of the Christian era the Septuagint was the Bible in common use, and it also contained the books we call the apocrypha—sacred books of the Jewish people not included in the King James Version and containing a bridge between the Old and New Testaments. Joseph Smith referred to the Apocrypha as mostly correct but with many interpolations made by men (D&C 91). The Pentateuch is a Greek word meaning the fivefold book. It contains the first five books of the Old Testament written by Moses (1 Nephi 5:10–11; 2 Ne. 3:17; Moses 1:40–41). It is evident that many scribes have added to the text of the Pentateuch. Both the Septuagint and the Pentateuch differ, in some instances, from the Hebrew massoretic texts of the Old Testament. In some cases the Septuagint and the Pentateuch may have preserved older and possibly truer readings of Old Testament passages; however, it is difficult to determine which readings merit preference. After the second destruction of Jerusalem at A. D. 70, many of the ancient texts were lost. Scholars at the Jewish School in Tiberius agreed upon one reading of the many texts and rejected any other versions that surfaced. The King James Version of the Old Testament follows the official Hebrew massoretic text except in a very few passages *(Bible Dictionary,* The Church of Jesus Christ of Latter-day Saints).

In ancient Israel, the punishment for blasphemy served as a prohibition against certain forms of anti-religious speech, usually any utterances considered disdainful, sneering, or contemptuous toward God, or anything related, in a sacred way, to God such as the temple at Jerusalem. The idea of blasphemy also extended to messengers sent by God, like prophets. Christ was accused of blasphemy against the temple, and for claiming to be the Son of God (John 10:22–36). Micah, the prophet referenced in this chapter, was also accused of blasphemy against the temple and against Jerusalem, a city considered holy by the Jews and protected by the laws of blasphemy (Jer. 26:18–19; see also Micah 2–4).

CHAPTER 24

Pella is a fictional character who bears the same name as a small city north of Jerusalem. Jawbone is the English translation for Lehi's name. The Jawbone Inn is a fictitious setting based on what we know about inns in Jerusalem at 600 B.C. Drinking establishments were usually family-owned cooperatives, each with their own clientele which, in Jerusalem, was determined by location. Upper City inns catered primarily to the noble class, while Lower City inns were frequented by commoners. It could have been that some inns catered to specific groups like soldiers or artisans, though there was no law or practice dictating who could or could not patronize a particular inn; it was simply understood where one should go to drink. There could have been as few as twenty inns in Jerusalem during Lehi's day or as many as a hundred such establishments (*Great People of the Bible and How They Lived*).

CHAPTER 26

The account of Uriah's flight to Egypt, Captain Elnathan's mission to capture him, and his subsequent trial are recorded in four short verses in the Old Testament (Jer. 26:20–24). Scholars originally believed that Uriah's trial occurred much earlier than the date attributed to it in this novel, since Jehoiakim is named as the King of Israel, not Zedekiah who later replaced him as king. The Lakhish Letters, however, indicate that Zedekiah was actually on the throne at the time of Uriah's incarceration and trial, and scholars now believe that the ancient scribe, Baruch, or another scribe mistakenly wrote the former king's name in the Old Testament record when the intended king was actually Zedekiah (Nibley, "Dark Days in Jerusalem"). The Old Testament suggests that an initial judgment of death against Uriah was cause for him to flee to Egypt. In *Pillar of Fire*, volume one of this series of historical novels, the Elders of the Jews sentenced Uriah to death in absentia (Jer. 26: 21). The Old Testament records that Uriah was then captured and put to death upon his extradition to Jerusalem (Jer. 26: 22–23). However, the Lakhish Letters indicate that Uriah was not put to death upon his return to the capital city, but rather held in prison for a period of time long enough for his father, Shema Yahu (spelled Shemaiah in the O.T.), to come to his aid (Harry Torczyner, "Notes on Letter III and IV" in *The Lachish Letters*).

The Lakhish Letters record that Uriah's preaching had weakened the hands of the military men and it may have been that Uriah was successful enough in his preaching of peace with Babylon to convince soldiers in the military to not go to war, thereby undermining the desires of the princes and nobles of Jerusalem to rebel against the occupying Babylonians.

Deborah, the wife of Uriah, is a fictional character, but her fear for her husband's life is typical of the concern for ancient prophets. Throughout ancient history up until Lehi's day, prophets were stoned for their testimony of Jesus Christ and their insistence on repentance as a requirement for redemption (1 Ne. 1:19–20). Scripture bears out the dual fate of prophets: some sealed their testimony with their blood, and others lived in order to deliver the people of God either physically or spiritually. In this chapter, Deborah is characterized by her worry for her husband's fate.

CHAPTER 27

The Old Testament records that Hannaniah died as a result of his false prophecies. He prophesied falsely that Judah would break the yoke of Babylonian bondage, and the prophet Jeremiah cursed him to die because he taught the people of Jerusalem to trust in a lie (see historical notes for Chapter 19; Jer. 28:15–16). We do not know the cause of Hannaniah's death, and this chapter fictionalizes that event (Jer. 28:17).

CHAPTERS 28 AND 29

These two chapters are closely related, and the historical notes are considered together. In these two chapters, four major events are juxtaposed just as they are in the Old Testament record—three blasphemy trials of Jeremiah, Micah, and Uriah, and the death of the false prophet Hannaniah. Chapter 26 of the book of Jeremiah places the three blasphemy trials in quick succession. It is possible that the scribes intended to relate these events since the defendants were all prophets accused of the same crime. The blasphemy trials of Jeremiah and Uriah may have taken place about the same time, and in the scriptural account they are related by their chronological occurrence, separated only by the reference to Micah's trial, which took place one hundred and twenty years before. In the opening of Chapter 26, Jeremiah prophesies the destruction of the people of Jerusalem. The Old Testament records that Jehoakim is king, but it is most likely that Zedekiah was actually the king and this is a clerical error on the part of ancient scribes (Nibley, "Dark Days in Jerusalem"; see also historical notes for Chapter 26). Jeremiah is accused of blasphemy by the princes of the city, arraigned, tried, and finally imprisoned (Jer. 26:1–16). The trial sequence in this passage continues with a reference to the trial of the prophet Micah, introduced as a judicial precedence from one hundred and twenty years before (Jer. 26:17–19). A detailed account of Micah's prophecies that resulted in the charge of blasphemy against him are found in his own writings (Micah 2–4). Micah warns of the fall of the northern kingdom that took place during his lifetime; he also foretold the coming destruction of Jerusalem that took place about one hundred and twenty years after his death. He mentions the awful destruction of the northern kingdom in graphic terms (Micah 3:2–3), but the tone of his prophecy changes when he prophesies the fall of Jerusalem, attributing much of the destruction to the appearance of false prophets among the Jews who caused the people to trust in lies. The accounts of Jeremiah and Hannaniah in this novel are intended to show the fulfillment of Micah's prophecies of the coming of false prophets during Lehi's day, more than a century after his death.

The final trial sequence in the twenty-sixth chapter of Jeremiah recounts Uriah's extradition on charges of blasphemy (Jer. 26:20–24). The reference to Uriah coming before King Zedekiah (the Old Testament names Jehoiakim as king; however, scholars agree that it was actually Zedekiah and that scribes mistakenly wrote Jehoiakim) is the only reference to his trial in the Old Testament. There is little information detailing the actual events of the trial, testimony, or verdict. The actual trial scenes in this novel are fictionalized; however, much of the dialogue for Lehi's preaching, as well as Commander Yaush and Shema Yahu are taken directly from the Book of Mormon and the Lakhish Letters respectively. In this chapter and subsequent chapters of this novel, Lehi fulfills his charge to preach to the people of Jerusalem, particularly the ruling class of nobles who were responsible for much of the false prophecy and decline of morality in Jerusalem.

Jeremiah, Chapter 28, details the story of Jeremiah's encounter with the false prophet Hannaniah. It may be coincidence that the three blasphemy trials of Jeremiah, Micah, and Uriah mentioned above are recorded immediately prior to the telling of the story of Jeremiah and Hannaniah; however, it is not impossible that Uriah's and Jeremiah's trials took place about the same time. In this novel the appearance of Hannaniah the false prophet, the trial of Uriah, and the indictment of Jeremiah are shown to occur simultaneously, similar to the timing recorded in the book of Jeremiah (Jer. 26 & 28).

CHAPTER 31

The Book of Mormon indicates that Lehi was warned in a dream to leave Jerusalem (1 Ne. 2:1–2). The dream included two parts: first, a blessing upon Lehi for being faithful to the command to declare the word of God to the people of Jersualem, a task that may have caused Lehi a good deal of concern for himself and his family; and second, a warning that his life was in danger and that he was to take his family and depart into the wilderness. No additional information is given with regard to the instructions of the dream and we do not know if Lehi was told he would not return to the capital; however, later passages indicate that Lehi may not have been aware that he was leading his family to find a safe haven in another land until after he was gone from his home for some time. The dream of blessing and warning is described in the Book of Mormon as a voice, and in this chapter Lehi is shown receiving these instructions in that manner.

***

The Lakhish Letters contain a curse against the royal family. It is uncertain who wrote the curse, but in this novel it is attributed to Captain Laban.

***

Dr. Harry Torczyner ("Notes on Letter I" in *The Lachish Letters*), and Dr. John L. Starkey ("The Discovery," in *The Lachish Letters*) both suggest that the Lakhish Letters may have been stored in the keep along the inside wall of the bastion at Fort Lakhish as important evidence in a trial, especially due to the significance of what is written in the letters. In this chapter the potsherds are returned to the guard station, based on the assumptions made by scholars. The Lakhish Letters most critical to the development of the storyline and plots in this novel are found on letters number one through five.

CHAPTER 33

The central event of the Passover celebrations during the period when the temple was operational in Jerusalem was the Paschal sacrifice. The sacrificing and eating of a lamb commemorated the first Passover meal in Egypt. A lamb or kid goat was slaughtered and eaten as part of a festive meal by every Jewish household on the night of Passover. Individuals brought other sacrifices to the temple, but the Passover sacrifice was brought by groups—a family or a collection of families (Popular Judaica Library "Passover," 26). In this chapter, the family of Uriah the prophet joins the family of Jonathan the blacksmith in celebrating the Passover.

Many customs associated with the Passover have been added since the first celebration of Passover, similar to many customs adopted by Christians over the years as they celebrate Christmas. Some of the customs have grown up around family tradition and others out of compliance with the edict that Jewish parents pass on to their children through story and song a remembrance of the Passover—the day of Hebrew liberation and the birth of their nation. It is impossible to know which Passover customs may have been part of the Passover Lehi and his family celebrated. The formal seder meal celebrated today by Jews with food laid symbolically on specified locations on a ceremonial seder plate accompanied by three cups of wine is an addition to the celebration many centuries after Lehi. It is not known when the customs and traditions of Passover mentioned in this novel were instituted. They were widespread among Jews around the world long before they were recorded *(Popular Judaica Library,* "Passover"). The Passover celebration described in the closing chapters of this novel include references to the basic sacrifice of a lamb, a meal, as well as a number of other customs for which we do not have a date of inception, but are old enough to be included as possible rituals in the days of Lehi. The more modern Passover traditions do not appear in this novel.

When matzoh, Hebrew for unleavened bread, is baked, care is taken to ensure that the entire process from kneading to baking take no longer than eighteen minutes. The flour and water are manipulated, and since hot water accelerates the process of fermentation, it is customary to use "water which has rested overnight" *(Popular Judaica Library* "Passover," 43). It was believed that water in wells became hot as the earth increased its heat during the night, so water was drawn in the evening and then left to rest overnight to cool. The custom of a festive procession of women winding their way to the pool of Siloam on the eve of Passover to draw water for their bread baking still continues today.

CHAPTER 34

Anything that ferments when it decomposes is considered hamez, Hebrew for leaven. The rule regarding leaven applies to five species of grain: wheat, barley, spelt, rye, and oats. Any other fermentation is permitted. Grains that rot but do not ferment, such as rice and millet, are not in this category, and are permitted on Passover. Only food products that have been specially prepared to ensure they contain no hamez are considered Kosher (Hebrew for acceptable), and are permitted during the seven-day celebration of Passover.

The cooking utensils that have been used for hamez during the year are also forbidden for use on Passover, unless they have been cleansed. The cleaning process is called koshering—making acceptable—and requires that utensils and vessels be immersed in a cauldron of boiling water. Utensils can be koshered over a fire, heating them until the metal takes on a red glow. Many people have a complete set of utensils and crockery that are taken out and used on Passover, then put away immediately after the festival until the following year *(Popular Judaica Library* "Passover," 35).

Jewish scripture includes the direction that during the seven days of Passover no one is allowed to possess any leaven. Jews search their homes and remove all hamez and then clean every surface that has come in contact with hamez. Passover occurs in the spring and this coincides with the natural instincts to air out and clean the home after a long winter *(Popular Judaica Library* "Passover," 36).

The searching out and cleansing the home of hamez culminates on the eve of Passover in a ceremony known as bedikat hamez, Hebrew for "the search for hamez." After the master of the house offers a prayer for the removal of hamez, the search begins. Any hamez found is kept back and burned at midday the following afternoon as the last rite to rid the home of leaven. The women of the house usually leave pieces of bread in prearranged hiding places for the children to find. When the ritual search is completed, a declaration is recited that any leaven that has been overlooked "should be like the dust of the earth" *(Popular Judaica Library* "Passover," 36).

CHAPTER 36

Latter-day Saints believe that Ezekiel's vision of the sticks of Joseph and Judah are a representation of the scrolls or wooden tablets where the religious records of two nations—the Jews and the Nephites—were recorded and finally came together as one record (see the historical notes for Chapter 15). The Bible is considered to be the record represented by the stick of Judah, and the Book of Mormon is thought of as the record of Joseph whose descendants, beginning with Lehi, assembled a religious record that spanned over a thousand years on two continents, and which documents the rise of a large nation of Hebrews in the Western Hemisphere. In this chapter, Ezekiel recognizes Lehi as the father of a nation whose prophets and rulers will ultimately be responsible for writing and preserving the ancient record representing the stick of Joseph titled the Book of Mormon. Latter-day Saints view the modern-day coming together of the Bible and the Book of Mormon as companion scriptures as a fulfillment of Ezekiel's ancient prophecy that these sticks would come together and be one in the hand of man (Ezek. 37:16–20).

CHAPTER 38

Nibley suggests that during the fall of Jerusalem, about ten years after Lehi left Jerusalem, a portion of the royal family may have escaped west toward the Mediterranean Sea, seeking refuge among the Phoenicians in Sidon or Tyre. He further indicates that about ten years after this first volume ends, Mulek and his mother may have been saved from death at the hands of the Babylonians by members of the royal family of Phoenicia (Nibley, "Dark Days in Jerusalem"). It is possible that the house of Zedekiah had developed good relations with that nation (Nibley, "The Jerusalem Scene," F.A.R.M.S. Reprint, 1980). In this chapter Miriam sends her son, Mulek, to find refuge with Jesse, Prince of Sidon, to protect her son from any repercussions after Uriah's trial and the revelation that he was the palace informant.

It was common for young boys to carry secret messages into closely guarded areas, past soldiers, and in and out of city walls. They were not perceived as a threat and could pass unnoticed by soldiers. The Lakhish Letters indicate that the captain of the guard at Jerusalem and Commander Yaush at Fort Lakhish suspected a boy by the name of Mulek of carrying messages for the prophets (See Nibley, "Dark Days in Jerusalem").

CHAPTER 40

Central to the celebration of Passover is the telling of the story of the Hebrews' escape from Egypt. The storyteller is usually the master of the house, but anyone is allowed to act in that capacity. Modern-day recounting of the story has been proscribed by Jewish rabbis; however, the family gathering of ancient Jews included a recounting of the ten plagues sent against Pharaoh. It also included the brushing of lamb's blood over the doorpost as a sign of the protection gained from the Atonement of the Messiah and to protect from the coming of the destroying angel—hence the name Passover *(Popular Judaica Library* "Passover," 68).

During the telling of the Passover story or at some point during the meal a child, usually the youngest in the family, is expected to inquire about the history of the event. Over the centuries four questions have been formalized; however, the inital question that seems to have been required of children for many centuries at the beginning of the telling of the Passover story is the question, "Why is this night different from any other night?" In this chapter, Joshua is assigned the task of asking that question, which begins the telling of the Passover story by his mother.

***

There is little detail in the Book of Mormon surrounding Lehi's escape into the wilderness (1 Ne. 2:4). The first books in the Book of Mormon are primarily a family history and do not mention others who may have been associated with Lehi and his family. Later books in the Book of Mormon follow this pattern, detailing the religious and political life of a growing nation living somewhere in the Americas, while avoiding mention of other nations thriving on the same continent and with whom they may have had contact or even trade relations. Book of Mormon authors follow what scholars call a patriarchal record, omitting mention of other non-familial members of their group as well as neighboring nations (John L. Sorenson, *An Ancient American Setting for the Book of Mormon,* Salt Lake City: Deseret Book, 1996, 49–62). It is not certain if that practice was because of petty jealousy, or if it was the proscribed method for preparing and keeping family and national records. We do know that Lehi left Jerusalem with his family. We do not know how long he was in the wilderness before he began a three-day, forced march down the coast of the Gulf of Aqaba (Nephi calls it the fountain of the Red Sea), ultimately taking refuge in the Valley of Lemuel along the banks of the river Laman (1 Ne. 2:5–6). Nephi gives an accounting of who actually accompanied Lehi on this portion of they journey, again omitting reference to anyone who may have assisted them or traveled with them up until that time. It is not impossible that others were involved with Lehi's initial departure. In this chapter, Aaron accompanies Lehi and his family out of the land of Jerusalem.

CHAPTER 41

It was not until Lehi was warned in a dream that he understood his life was in danger (1 Ne. 2:1–2). Nephi indicates that Lehi was aware of the fate of ancient prophets before him who were publicly stoned or driven off; however, Lehi was a wealthy businessman, possibly a caravaneer and trader of olive oil, and it was highly unlikely that the Elders of the city would carry out a public execution of a man considered to be one of their peers. It may be that the plan against Lehi was more of a secret assassination attempt rather than a public humiliation. In this novel, the plot against Lehi is a secret plan, rather than a public one.

***

Angels are usually messengers of God; however, the scriptures record that the devil has angels—those spirits who followed him in the premortal war in heaven and were thrust down to the earth. Restoration scriptures reveal that there are two classes of heavenly beings who minister for the Lord: those who are spirits, and those who have bodies of flesh and bone. Spirits are those beings who either have not yet obtained a body of flesh and bone (unembodied), or who have once had a mortal body and have died, and are awaiting the resurrection (disembodied). Usually the word angel means those ministering persons who have a body of flesh and bone, being either resurrected from the dead (re-embodied), or else translated, as were Enoch and Elijah (D&C 129). The angel of death spoken of with regard to the Passover was the final plague sent against Egypt. It is not known if that was a figurative passage representing a curse of death against the firstborn child of every household that did not profess faith in the Messiah by painting lamb's blood across the doorpost of the home, or if there was an actual heavenly being sent to minister that penalty. In this chapter, Laban is compared to the angel of death because of his intent to carry out murder.

CHAPTER 42

The shank bone of the lamb—zeroaʿ in Hebrew—is placed on the plate in memory of the Paschal sacrifice. Zeroaʿ literally means forearm and is symbolic of how God brought Israel out of Egypt with an outstretched arm. In this chapter Jonathan breaks the shank bone of the Paschal lamb his family is about to eat. With an arrow, Aaron breaks the shank bone of Laban, symbolizing Laban as the antithesis of good and marking him unfit to stand in the place of the Messiah with his arm stretched out with salvation. In essence, marking him as the opposite of Christ.

CHAPTER 43

We do not know why the Lakhish Letters were stored in the guard station between the upper and lower gates of Fort Lakhish. History suggests that the guard station may have been a receiving area for incoming mail, or that the guard station was the post of the senior military officer on duty at the gates. In this novel, Setti, son of Yaush, is portrayed in that senior officer role. The Lakhish Letters may have been kept with other official papyrus and parchment records, and they were the only records able to withstand the great fire that took place at the gate entrance. History suggests that the Lakhish Letters were kept in the guard station for a pending trial. Dr. Torczyner suggests that the letters were exculpating evidence against the courier or military officer Hosha Yahu. We do not know the fate of Hosha Yahu, except that he appeared to be somewhat supportive of the prophet Uriah, and in a fictionalized account in *Pillar of Fire*, he killed himself. It is uncertain what caused the fire that burned the guard station, and Dr. Torczyner suggests that the records were burned in the final Babylonian incursions that leveled Jerusalem to the ground and destroyed Fort Lakhish by fire about eight years after Lehi left Jerusalem (Torczyner, "Introduction to The Texts," in *The Lachish Letters*). In this novel, however, Daniel is shown burning the guard station to cover exculpating evidence against Captain Laban. Whatever the reason for the storing of the Lakhish Letters in the guard station at Fort Lakhish and the subsequent cause behind their destruction by fire, some of the potsherd records survived to provide modern readers of the Book of Mormon and Old Testament another voice from the dust.

EPILOGUE

Scholars of ancient scripture suggest that the abundance of records from antiquity unearthed during the past fifty years are a fulfillment of Book of Mormon prophecies declaring that the word of God and his prophets would come forth out of the dust (Nibley, "More Voices From the Dust"). The Book of Mormon declares that the words of the ancients would cry from the dust (2 Ne. 33:13; Moroni 10:27). This epilogue depicts one of several archaeological discoveries that support those ancient declarations.

***

It was common practice among scribes and anyone educated in the art of writing to collect broken pieces of pottery from dishes and pots and use them as writing materials. Papyrus imported from Egypt was a very expensive writing medium, as were the preparation of metal, leather, and clay tablets. Potsherds were an economical use of the flat clay pieces and they required little or no preparation. Scholars refer to the broken pieces that contain no writing as potsherds. Clay pieces with written words from ancient times are refereed to as ostraca. It is unlikely that ancient Hebrews had more than one name to describe the pieces of broken clay they used in their writing and in this novel the ancient historical characters refer to them as potsherds, regardless of whether they contain writings, while the modern characters in this epilogue refer to them as either potsherds (broken clay pieces without writing) or ostraca (broken clay pieces with writing).

***

The Lakhish Letters are the only written Hebrew record outside the Book of Mormon and the Old Testament that date to about 600 B.C. when Lehi and his family lived at Jerusalem. They are a critical element in the development of the stories and plot lines in this novel, and the epilogue is an account of their finding. The epilogue follows archaeologist John L. Starkey's personal account of his discovery of letters written on clay potsherds and dating to the time of Lehi and his family (Starkey, "The Discovery," in *The Lachish Letters*). Mr. Starkey was the director of the Wellcome Archaeological Research Expedition to the Near East and, with the help of assistant archaeologists Mr. L. Harding and Miss Tuffnell, he found the first writings that ultimately proved Tel ed Duwier to be the site of the ancient Fort Lakhish. Three ostraca were discovered on January 29, 1935, while fifteen more were unearthed in the following weeks.

It is not clear from Mr. Starkey's account whether Dr. Torczyner was present when the first ostraca were discovered, or if he was called in to evaluate the find immediately after. The description of his car is based on a photograph taken at the base of the dig site prior to the beginning of excavations on March 10, 1933 (David Ussishkin, "Excavations at Lachish," preliminary report reprinted from Tel Aviv University Insititue of Archaeology, 1978, vol. 5, 1–2). Dr. Torczyner did accompany the letters back to London where he spent June and July of that same year carefully studying and translating the letters from ancient Hebrew into English (Torczyner, "Foreword," in *The Lachish Letters*). Based on the popularity of the names listed on the first letter, Dr. Torczyner concludes that these letters date to 600 B.C. (Torczyner, "Notes on Letter I" in *The Lachish Letters*). Dr. Torczyner wrote that these letters were the most valuable discovery yet made in the Biblical archaeology of Palestine. They were the first authentic and intimate contemporary reports from Jews faithfully following their God. They shed light on their inner political and religious struggles, and they add valuable information to the accounts given in the book of Jeremiah, particularly with reference to the account of Captain Elnathan capturing Uriah in Egypt and returning him to Jerusalem to stand trial (Torczyner, "Introduction to The Texts," in *The Lachish Letters*).

LIST OF REFERENCES

Allbright, William F. "The Seal of Eliakim and the Latest Preexilic History of Judah, With Some Observations on Ezekiel," *The Journal of Biblical Literature*, 1932, vol. 51, 148.

Bright, John. *A History of Israel* (Philadelphia: Westminster Press, 1981).

———. "Jeremiah" in *The Anchor Bible*. (Garden City, NY. Doubleday, 1965), 237.

Church Educational System (The Church of Jesus Christ of Latter-Day Saints), *Old Testament Student Manual: Genesis–2 Samuel,* 1982.

Church Educational System (The Church of Jesus Christ of Latter-day Saints), *Old Testament Student Manual: 1 Kings–Malachi,* 1982, 33–34.

Clark, Adam. *The Holy Bible with Commentary and Critical Notes.* vol 6, (New York: Abingdon-Cokesbury Press, n.d.).

Encyclopedia Judaica, Jerusalem: vol. 14 (Keter Publishing House, 1972), 1372.

Gee, John, and Peterson, Daniel C. "Graft and Corruption: On Olives and Olive Culture in the Pre-Modern Mediterranean," in *The Allegory of the Olive Tree,* eds. Steven D. Ricks and John W. Welch (Salt Lake City: Deseret Book, and Provo: F.A.R.M.S., 1994), 186–247.

Gillelan, Howard G. *"Complete Book of the Bow and Arrow"* (New York: Gallahad Books, 1971).

Great People of the Bible and How They Lived (Pleasantville NY: Readers Digest Association, 1974).

Hamblin, William J. "Sacred Writings on Bronze Plates in the Ancient Mediterranean" (F.A.R.M.S. preliminary report, 1994).

Hastings, James "Magic, Divination and Sorcery," in *Dictionary of the Bible* (New York: Charles Scribner's Sons, 1909), 566–570.

Holbrook, Brett L. "The Sword of Laban as a Symbol of Divine Authority and Kingship," *Journal of Book of Mormon Studies,* vol. 2, no. 1, 39–72.

Hoskisson, Paul Y. "The Allegory of the Olive Tree in Jacob," in *The Allegory of The Olive Tree*, eds. Steven D. Ricks and John W. Welch (Salt Lake City: Deseret Book, and Provo: F.A.R.M.S., 1994), 186–247.

Hunt, Wallace E. Jr. "Moses' Brazen Serpent as it Relates to Serpent Worship in Mesoamerica," *Journal of Book of Mormon Studies,* vol. 2, no. 2, 121–31.

Koffmahn, Elisabeth. "Die Doppelurkunden aus der Wuste Juda" (Lieden: Brill, 1968), 19.

Lawrance, H. Lea *The Archers and Bowhunters of the Bible* (Doubleday, New York, 1993).

Meservy, Keith H. "Job: Yet Will I Trust in Him," in Sydney B. Sperry Symposium, Provo: Brigham Young University, 1978.

McConkie, Bruce R. *Doctrinal New Testament Commentary* (Bookcraft, 1973), 3:507.

Nibley, Hugh W. "Dark Days in Jerusalem: The Lakhish letters and the Book of Mormon," in *The Prophetic Book of Mormon* [The Collected Works of Hugh Nibley, vol. 8] (Salt Lake City: Deseret Book, and Provo: F.A.R.M.S., 1989).

_____. "Qumran and the Waters of Mormon," in *An Approach to the Book of Mormon* [The Collected Works of Hugh Nibley, vol. 6] (Salt Lake City: Deseret Book, and Provo: F.A.R.M.S.).

_____. "Portrait of Laban," in *An Approach to the Book of Mormon* [The Collected Works of Hugh Nibley, vol. 6] (Salt Lake City: Deseret Book, and Provo: F.A.R.M.S. 1988).

_____. "Israel's Neighbors," F.A.R.M.S. Reprint, 1984.

_____ "Lakhish letters," eds. Noel B. Reynolds and Charles D. Tate. *Book of Mormon Authorship: New Light on Ancient Origins* (Provo: Brigham Young University Department of Religious Studies, 1982).

_____ "Lehi in the Desert," in *Lehi in the Desert/The World of the Jaredites/There Were Jaredites.* ed. John W. Welch [The Collected Works of Hugh Nibley, vol. 5], (Salt Lake City: Deseret Book and Provo: F.A.R.M.S., 1988).

_____. "More Voices From the Dust," in *The Old Testament and Related Studies.* [The Collected Works of Hugh Nibley, vol. 1] (Salt Lake City: Deseret Book and Provo: F.A.R.M.S., 1986).

_____ "The Jerusalem Scene" (F.A.R.M.S. Reprint, 1980).

_____ "The Lesson of the Sixth Century B. C." (F.A.R.M.S. Reprint, 1984).

_____ *Since Cumorah,* second edition, ed. John W. Welch [Collected Works of Hugh Nibley, vol. 7], (Salt Lake City: Deseret Book, and Provo: F.A.R.M.S., 1988).

Offord, Joseph. "Archaeological Notes on Jewish Antiquities," in *An Approach to the Book of Mormon*, [The Collected Works of Hugh Nibley, vol. 6], (Salt Lake City: Deseret Book, and Provo: F.A.R.M.S., 1986).

Popular Judaica Library, "Passover" (Philadelphia, PA: Jewish Publication Society of America, 1973).

Ricks, Stephen D. and Sroka, John J. "King, Coronation, and Temple: Enthronement Ceremonies in History," in *Temples of the Ancient World.* ed. Donald W. Parry (Salt Lake City: Deseret Book, and Provo: F.A.R.M.S., 1994).

Rolph, Daniel N. "Prophets, Kings, and Swords: The Sword of Laban and its Possible Pre-Laban Origins," *Journal of Book of Mormon Studies,* vol. 2, no. 1, 73–79.

Sorenson, John L. *An Ancient American Setting for the Book of Mormon* (Salt Lake City: Deseret Book, 1996), 49–62.

Sperry, Sidney B. "Did Lehi Have Daughters Who Married the Sons of Ishmael?" *Improvement Era 55* (Sept. 1952) 642. (A reprint is available through the F.A.R.M.S. Sperry Archive.)

Starkey, John L. "The Discovery," in *The Lachish Letters,* ed. Harry Torczyner (Oxford University Press, 1938).

_____. "Summary," in *The Lachish Letters,* ed. Harry Torczyner (Oxford University Press, 1938).

Thompson, J.A. "The Book of Jeremiah" in *The New International Commentary on the Old Testament,* ed. R. K. Harrison (Grand Rapids, MI: William B. Eerdmans Publishing Company, 1980).

Torczyner, Harry. "Notes on Letter I" in *The Lachish Letters,* ed. Harry Torczyner (Oxford Press, 1983).

_____ "Notes on Letter II, III, IV," in *The Lachish Letters,* ed. Harry Torczyner (Oxford Press, 1983).

_____. "Introduction to the Texts," in *The Lachish Letters,* ed. Harry Torczyner (Oxford University Press, 1938).

Tvedtnes, John A. "Was Lehi a Caravaneer?" in *The Most Correct Book: Insights from a Book of Mormon Scholar* (Salt Lake City: Cornerstone, 1999), 76–98.

Ussishkin, David. "Excavations at Lachish," preliminary report reprinted from Tel Aviv University Institute of Archaeology, 1978, 5:1–2.

U.S. Army Map Service, "Jerusalem Southwest Asia," (AMS K502, Sheet NH 36–4, 1958).

Welch, John W. "Lehi: The Calling of a Prophet," in *The Book of Mormon: First Nephi, The Doctrinal Foundation, papers from the second annual Book of Mormon Symposium,* Monte S. Nyman and Charles D. Tate, eds. (Provo: Brigham Young University, 1986).

_____ "Theft and Robbery in the Book of Mormon and Near Eastern Law," (F.A.R.M.S. Reprint, 1992).

_____ "Double, Sealed, Witnessed Documents: From the Ancient World to the Book of Mormon," in *Mormons, Scripture, and the Ancient World,* ed Davis Bitton (Provo: Foundation for Ancient Research and Mormon Studies, 1998).

World Book, "Homing Pigeons," vol. 8 (Field Enterprises Corporation, 1961), 276.

NORTH
E
S
W
ASSYRIA
ISRAEL
SIDON
MOUNT CARMEL
FORT MEGIDDO
SAMARIA
ANATHOTH
QUMRAN
QIRYAT YE'ARIM
JERUSALEM
HEBRON
FORT LAKHISH
Besor River
JUDAH
AQABA
RAPHIA
GREAT SEA
SINAI DESER
PELUSIUM
TANIS
NILE DELTA
MEMPHIS
NILE RIVER